David Clement-Davis lives in ⟨...⟩ and travel journalist. His work ⟨...⟩ strange and exciting things – he has ridden a horse across the Namib desert, been dolphin-watching in Costa Rica, scuba-diving in Africa and thrown himself from an aeroplane at 3,000 metres (with a parachute) over Kent. In his spare time, he likes to go riding, often through Richmond Park where he loves to watch the fallow and red deer wandering through the bracken.

FIRE BRINGER is his first novel. His second novel, THE SIGHT, is also published by Macmillan Children's Books.

'Epic stuff, complete with bloodcurdling action and a dramatic finish!'
Time Out Kids Out

'A moving, engrossing tale of love, loyalty, bravery, treachery and, ultimately, sacrifice from an exciting new talent.'
London Parents' Guide

'Few first novels can be quite as gripping as this . . . thought-provoking, emotion stirring . . . it is an epic animal adventure. A racy volume full of courage, loyalty, love, and hatred.'
Oxford Times Weekend

'Powerful themes of nature, belief, loyalty and destiny together with first-rate writing and strong characters, make this a totally absorbing story.'
Shelf Life

'This ambitious and imaginative first novel promises well for the future.'
Books for Keeps

Fire Bringer

David Clement-Davies

MACMILLAN
CHILDREN'S BOOKS

First published 1999 by Macmillan Children's Books

This edition published 2000 by Macmillan Children's Books
a division of Macmillan Publishers Limited
20 New Wharf Road, London N1 9RR
Basingstoke and Oxford
www.panmacmillan.com

Associated companies throughout the world

ISBN 0 330 39010 4

13 15 17 19 18 16 14

A CIP catalogue record for this book is available from
the British Library.

Phototypeset by Intype London Ltd
Printed and bound in Great Britain by
Mackays of Chatham plc, Chatham, Kent

For my parents and for Naia

And for Tor and Daisy too,
remembering Richmond Park

I'd like to recommend Norma Chapman's invaluable
little guide to deer and thank Yolande at Roehampton Stables for letting
me ride in Richmond Park; Tim Booth for endless encouragements,
my agent Caroline Walsh for saying 'it'll happen' and then
making those words come true and Rebecca McNally for doing
such inspiring yet firm editing; finally, though sadly she will
never see it, my friend Helen Boyd, a sometimes overfond animal
lover and very warm human being, for all her kindnesses and for
lending me the cottage that gave her so much pleasure.

Acknowledgements

The author wishes to thank the following for permission to reproduce copyright material. All possible care has been taken to trace the ownership of all quotations included and to make full acknowledgement for their use. If any errors have accidentally occurred they will be corrected in subsequent editions provided notification is sent to the publisher.

Extract from 'Rannoch, by Glencoe' in 'Landscapes' by T.S. Eliot, by permission of Faber & Faber Limited.

Extract from 'And now the leaves suddenly lose strength' by Philip Larkin, by permission of Faber & Faber Limited, and in the USA by permission of Farrar, Straus & Giroux.

Extract from 'The Stone Man' by Geoffrey Hill, by permission of Penguin Books Limited.

Extract from 'Under Ben Bulben' by W.B. Yeats, by permission of A.P. Watt Limited on behalf of Michael B. Yeats, and in the USA by permission of Simon & Schuster.

Dedication from 'Mother o' Mine' by Rudyard Kipling, by permission of A.P. Watt Limited on behalf of The National Trust for Places of Historic Interest or Natural Beauty.

Extract from 'Another Weeping Woman' from Collected Poems by Wallace Stevens, by permission of Faber & Faber Limited, and in Canada and the USA by permission of Alfred A. Knopf Inc.

Contents

Part Three

Part One

1

Birth and Prophecy

When the Lore is bruised and broken,
Shattered like a blasted tree,
Then shall Herne be justly woken,
Born to set the Herla free.
Herla Prophecy

A lone red deer was grazing across the glen, swaying through the deep tangle of heather which covered the hillside. The stag's coat glinted russet and gold in the dying sunlight slanting down the valley and on its head a pair of ragged antlers reared into the sky, like coral or the branches of a winter oak. The stag was a royal with twelve spikes, or tines, on its proud head and its antlers marked it out instantly as an animal of power and distinction. The antlers' beams were covered in summer velvet, the downy grey coating that lines new antlers as they grow. From their base, the two sharp brow tines flayed out like curved daggers. Above them the bez tines were slightly smaller and, further up the beams, the trez tines rose larger again, before the antlers flowered into their high cups.

The stag's fur was already thick but this could not hide a series of cuts and wounds on its sides and haunches, the marks of innumerable battles, and a livid scar that ran from the bottom of its neck clear to the base of its spine. The deer was not an unusual sight in the glen, for although this was long ago, in the days when the Great Land was still known to many men as Scotia, red deer were as plentiful then as they are in our own time. But it was unusual to see such a magnificent animal and such a splendid head of antlers.

Suddenly the stag flinched and swung its head towards the beech wood on the edge of the western slope. Its ears pressed forward, its muscles tensed and its nostrils began to flare, sending out wreaths of vapour that hung in the air. The stag's huge eyes pierced the thickening twilight, casting restlessly along the shadow of the trees. But the scent it had caught on the breeze was lost and the deer's head returned to its mossy pasture, nosing through the undergrowth, rooting out the juiciest of the summer stems.

As it went the deer's legs carried it gently back and forth like rushes on a pond. Now and then its hoofs would slip into a crevice, hidden below the deepening covering of vegetation, but the stag never once lost its footing. Its great body would compensate instinctively, like some huge yet graceful cat, so that it seemed almost to be a part of the landscape around it, inseparable from the contours which made up its home.

All around the silence was deepening with the evening. The stillness was broken only by the distant cry of a goshawk glorying in the hunt, the lonely hallooing of a night owl or the cracking flurry of a pheasant as it broke cover and exploded into the gloom. But everyday sounds like these did not frighten such an experienced animal. The stag's body might brace to deflect the sudden violence of the noise, but it went on feeding. A hind or a young buck might have been unnerved by these sounds. But not a beast that had spent so many years in the Corps. Not the veteran of countless battles.

Not a deer whose sight, smell and sense had taken him so quickly up the ranks of the herd. Not Brechin, Captain of the Outriders.

Brechin had reached a rocky hillock, purple with vegetation, and he was just settling in to enjoy a thick sprig of gorse when he suddenly threw up his head again. Now his eyes shone with recognition at the scent he had just caught again. But this time Brechin snorted and stamped the ground angrily. He dropped his antlers, then, aiming his head towards the north-west corner of the wood, he raced off along the edge of the valley, tossing his head as he ran. As he neared the wood he began to swing his antlers right and left in a great arc and then, abruptly, no more than three branches' length from the trees, he crashed to a halt and stamped the earth.

'So,' he shouted furiously. 'Now Herla spy on Herla?'

Brechin had used the deer's name for their own kind, but it brought no response. From far away the cry of an eagle haunted the breeze but nothing stirred in the wood.

'Come, I'm no green hind to be stalked like a rabbit,' continued Brechin. 'Show yourself. I nosed you on the other side of the valley.'

At this the trees started to rustle and the antlers and head of a young stag pushed through the leaves. A red deer stepped into the open. There was a splash of black on its muzzle and its antlers were in their fourth growth, with eight spikes, two tines at the top of each beam and its bez and brow tines below. It was also in thick velvet. Brechin's eyes softened a little as he recognized a youngster from the Corps.

'Well, Bandach,' said the captain coldly, 'I never thought I'd find you creeping about the wood like a lost brailah.'

The young deer's antlers lifted immediately. For a deer to

be called a brailah, or hedgehog, is a great insult and there
was a challenge in his reply.

'I'm no brailah, Captain Brechin,' answered the newcomer
slowly, 'and I'll fight any deer that says so.'

'Bravely spoken, Bandach.' Brechin smiled. 'Then perhaps
you'll tell me why you've been watching me since I topped
the hill.'

Bandach's eyes flickered but still he held the captain's
gaze.

'I bring a message from Drail.'

Brechin nodded calmly.

'So, now even you spy for Drail,' he said sadly.

Drail and Sgorr had spies everywhere nowadays.

'I was watching you, Captain Brechin. But not spying.
Bandach spies for nobody. Not even the Lord of Herds.'

'The Lord of Herds,' snorted Brechin contemptuously. 'I'd
never have used such a title when I was your age. Isn't
"Lord of the Herd" enough without Drail wanting to rule
throughout the Low Lands?'

Bandach didn't answer.

'Very well, then,' said Brechin, pretending to graze but
listening closely, 'deliver your message.'

'Drail has summoned the council,' said Bandach. 'At
Larn.'

'Summons, meetings. Can that soft-foot think of nothing
else? Well then, tell Drail I'm busy.'

'But, Captain Brechin—'

'Enough. Drail knows that one of my does is near her
time. I must see to her.'

Bandach stirred back and forth nervously. Brechin was
famous for his shows of disrespect towards Drail and
admired by many for it, including Bandach himself, but such
open disregard for his orders could mean serious trouble.

Drail would not flinch at punishing the messenger for the message.

'Captain Brechin,' he continued more courteously, 'when may I say you will come?'

Brechin looked out across the valley. The light was fading quickly now and in the creeping haze clouds of gadflies were billowing into the air. A deep stillness was settling in over the glen and as the deer looked up he saw the evening star specking through the darkening blue. Larn, the time when the great star brings together the Herla to ruminate and discuss the day, was close at hand.

'When I can, Bandach,' Brechin snorted and with a toss of his head the captain turned and ran along the edge of the wood. But before he had reached the end of the trees the deer stopped and looked back.

'And Bandach,' he called, his strong voice echoing across the valley, 'if you must, you can give Drail my apologies. Herne be with you.'

With that Brechin was gone.

The young deer stood motionless. He was shaking but he was deeply relieved that Brechin had tempered his reply to Drail. Drail had grown increasingly unpredictable. As the sun finally vanished beyond the horizon Bandach nodded his head with a new resolution.

'And Herne be with you too,' he whispered, and disappeared into the trees.

The evening star was already bright by the time Brechin reached the home valley. He paused on the brow of the hill and looked down at the herd grazing across the grass below. In front of him there must have been two hundred red deer, feeding quietly in the twilight. Some were sitting down to ruminate, bringing back into their mouths the grass, bark and berries they had collected during the day and stored in their bellies; chewing steadily on the rich pellets to release the nourishing juices.

In the meadow that opened out at the bottom of the valley the deer were made up mostly of hinds, the females, with their young fawns suckling greedily or nestling under their legs. Much further up the valley the stags were set well apart in stag parties or grazing alone in the glen, the older stags higher up the hill. Except at the time of the rut, when the stags fight to establish their harems and wrestle for control of a group of hinds, males and females in a wild red deer herd live apart, often at some distance. It was unusual for them to be so close now, for it was July and nearly all the hinds had calved weeks ago. The youngsters were already venturing out to make friends or testing the strength of their young legs.

As Brechin watched he spotted a hind who had been in his harem two seasons before and a yearling grazing nearby. Brechin's bloodline ran strong in the herd and he recognized one of his own calves. Its first head of antlers was coming, but Brechin smiled as he realized that he didn't even know the youngster's name. No matter, he thought to himself. It was only right for them to be distant while the calf was still with the hind. When he carried his second or third head Brechin would get to know him properly and start to teach him the ways of the Outrider.

As Brechin looked on he felt the powerful protective instinct that is the bloodright of the Outrider rise in his belly and was relieved to see the silhouettes of his fellow Outriders crowning the neighbouring hills. Their antlers rose and fell as they fed and watched in the calm evening. He could make out the thick, shaggy form of Greyneck, the quick, youthful movements of Tarn, and the single, ragged antler of Crinnan.

Brechin walked on slowly until a snort came from his left. Two stags were racing across the ground to meet him.

'Who goes? Hernling or Lera?' one of them called.

Lera is the deer's word for all animals, except of course man, but the deer see themselves as different; they are Hernling, creatures that enjoy the special protection of the forest god Herne.

'Hernling,' replied Brechin. 'Friend of the forest.'

'Come then and tread lightly,' came the formal greeting and two deer were at Brechin's side. It was Spey and Captain Straloch. Both were royals, with twelve tines fanning above their brows.

'Brechin,' said Straloch breathlessly, 'we hardly heard you.'

'No, Straloch,' replied Brechin with a smile. 'How is the herd?'

'The evening goes well. Tarn nosed fox beyond the stream just before Larn, but the scent has gone. We have warned the hinds to be careful.'

'Good.' Brechin nodded. 'But see they keep a keen eye.'

A deer herd is at its most vulnerable just after fawning. The herd lives in constant threat of attack and a fox is fully capable of taking a young fawn. But with their newborn calves the female deer are easily frightened and, as much as the loss of a young fawn, the Outriders now feared a stampede. Deer are flight animals but when the herd is with very young calves their habits change dramatically. Flight can be disastrous for the fawns and so the herd tend to bunker down, usually in a shaded valley like this one, and rely on the Outriders to scare off predators and fight if necessary.

'What news of the council meeting?' asked Brechin.

'Council meeting?' said Spey with surprise. 'We've heard nothing of a council meeting.'

'I thought not.' Brechin nodded gravely.

'Is anything wrong, Captain?' asked Straloch.

'Perhaps. Drail sent a message that he has summoned the council. But all the Outriders are here. He knows that the council cannot meet without the captains of the Outriders present.'

'Shall I call them?'

'No, Spey. Stay here and keep watch. The fawns are more important.'

With that Brechin ran on down the hill. As he dipped into the meadow he saw a group of Corps members trotting up the opposite hill towards the Home Oak. So a meeting *was* to take place. A full moon was climbing the sky now and in its strong, blue light Brechin made out Drail's massive form moving slowly up and down the lines of assembling stags. He snorted in disgust as he spotted an antlerless deer behind him. It was Sgorr, Drail's second in command.

'Hatred and fear,' said Brechin sadly to himself, 'that's all they are breeding in the herd. And cruelty.'

Brechin turned west towards the little stream that bubbled along the meadow at the bottom of the valley. Nearby, in the sludgy ground by the water, a hind had made a wallow and was rolling around in the delicious, cooling mud. Brechin plashed over onto to a strip of green that edged the trees, where six or seven hinds were feeding, chewing steadily on the cud, and raced forward as he caught sight of the single rowan tree.

Beneath it Eloin, the hind Brechin had mentioned earlier, was lying on her side in the long grass. Her belly was swollen and as she slept her flanks rose and fell noiselessly and every now and then her smooth body twitched with pain. Hinds can mate as early as two, especially woodland deer which tend to mature quicker than deer that live in the open, but there is some variety in their breeding habits. Eloin was a five-year-old now and had mated with Brechin late the previous winter. At four she was not exactly old to mate for the first time, but some in the herd whispered that the beautiful hind had been holding herself back. The pregnancy had been an unusually long one too and Eloin was one of the last to drop her fawn. Brechin knew that it meant danger for both calf and hind.

He padded up to her side and as he looked down his eyes grew dark with worry and love. The thought of losing Eloin filled him with an aching confusion.

When red deer have mated they separate and do not show much concern for one another, especially during calving. But although Brechin's strength and prowess had won him seven hinds the previous autumn, he was unusually fond of Eloin. Knowing that she was having difficulties calving, he had spent the last eight suns checking up on her.

The most unusual part of their coupling, though, was that last season Brechin had not even had to win Eloin in the rut. When the stags fight for their hinds the home valleys echo with the clatter and scrape of clashing antlers. After the victorious deer have chosen their mates one or two of the younger deer may step in to claim the remaining hinds. But very occasionally a brave hind will come forward and attempt to choose a mate for herself. She risks being gored in the process but when Eloin had padded up to Brechin and, without even lowering her head as was expected of her, had touched the base of both his antlers with her muzzle, Brechin had simply muzzled her in return and together they had walked away. All agreed that their mating was made by Herne.

All but Drail. He had wanted Eloin for himself and when she had stood with a captain of the Outriders he had been consumed with jealousy. Perhaps that was part of the reason for the change in him, thought Brechin now, as he looked down at his beautiful hind. He lowered his head and licked Eloin's face.

'Eloin,' he whispered softly. 'Eloin. Wake up.'

The hind opened her eyes and tried to lift her head.

'Brechin. I was sleeping.'

'Lie still, Eloin. You must rest and be strong.'

'Forgive me,' said the hind, sinking back into the grass. 'I'm too weak.'

'When is your time, Eloin?'

'Soon. Very soon now. He kicks like Herne.'

'Will you be the last?'

'Yes,' she said. 'Bracken dropped her fawn this morning.'

Brechin knew the name. Bracken was a doe who had stood with one of Brechin's Outriders last autumn, an ageing stag of about ten years named Salen. She was a slow hind and rather timid but was still quite a catch for Salen. He had had a bad fall the previous summer and this would be his last season as an Outrider. He had been lucky to have any hinds at all, let alone a newborn calf.

'Salen will be very proud,' said Brechin delightedly. 'Is it a buck or a doe?'

Eloin looked back sadly at her mate.

'Neither, Brechin,' she said. 'The calf was stillborn.'

Eloin looked towards the trees and in the shadow of an oak Brechin saw Bracken. She was standing quite still in the grass. Her head was tilted slightly to one side. Every now and then her haunches would flinch and her muzzle drop to nudge the little body lying motionless at her feet. It was a dead calf.

Eloin laid her head on the earth again. One of the most painful sights in the forest is a mother deer and her dead fawn. The hinds will stay by their fawns for days, waiting for them to move or nuzzling them to feed, until at last, filled with endless confusion, they simply walk away.

'Don't worry,' said Eloin, sensing Brechin's concern. 'Bracken was weak but I'll bear you a fine little Outrider.'

'Eloin,' Brechin whispered, 'I must leave you for a while. Drail has summoned the council to the Home Oak.'

'And the Outriders?'

'Bandach says we are called but when I got back to the home valley none of them knew anything about it.'

Eloin stirred and tried to raise her head again. A deer's instinct for danger is its chief weapon in the world.

'Be careful, Brechin,' she said. 'You know how jealous Drail is.'

Brechin snorted.

'If Drail wants you he must fight for you at Anlach,' he said. 'That is the law. And if he fights I could take the old soft-foot with one antler. And a broken one at that.'

'Yes. But there's Sgorr and the younger stags. They have no duty to sprig nor thorn. Be careful, that's all.'

'I'll be careful and when I return I won't leave you till you have calved.'

Brechin pressed his muzzle gently between Eloin's ears and turned away. Across the stream he spotted an old hind named Bhreac grazing on the bank and he ran straight up to her.

'Bhreac,' he said, 'Eloin is near her time and I'm worried. Will you watch her for me?'

Bhreac looked irritably at Brechin for with the years she had come to be no lover of stags, even an Outrider captain like Brechin. But nonetheless she lowered her head deferentially. Reassured a little, Brechin cantered off towards the meeting place. The moon was midway up the sky now and

in the distance the Home Oak was surrounded with stags.
As Brechin rose up the hill Eloin stirred restlessly by the
rowan tree. Her eyes were beginning to mist over with pain
and with great difficulty the hind got to her feet. Eloin's time
had come.

What Brechin had said about being able to take Drail with
one antler was true. Drail was old – nearly eleven – and
virtually lame now, and although he could still hold his own
against many a young stag he was no match for Brechin, the
greatest fighter in the herd. Indeed Brechin could have beaten
Drail even in his prime, though it would have been a bloody
business. Brechin had never had any ambitions towards the
lordship of the herd but recently he had been pushed further
and further towards challenging Drail's authority.

The organization of a deer herd is not especially complex.
There may be up to two or three hundred deer in a large
herd like this one, grouped together in loose associations
through family ties and friendships. The binding principle
among the stags is the Corps, which every male deer must
enter, paying allegiance to the Lord of the Herd. Alongside
the Corps come the Outriders, elite stags chosen for their
strength and courage and usually natural loners. The Outriders are scouts and fighters, who look for new pastures and
patrol for predators. The most important of the Outriders are
styled Captain, like Brechin.

These simple structures give the herd a strong unity,
except in late spring when the deer's antlers fall and the
herd's hierarchy is disrupted, and at Anlach, at the beginning
of autumn, when the deer rut. The rut is the most important
event in the deer's year, when the males fight for mates and
settle scores. It is at this time and this time only that a stag
may challenge for lordship, which normally happens once

every four or five years. But Drail's lordship had not been challenged for over six years now.

This was not because there was no stag strong enough to defeat him but because a new system had been introduced into the herd. Through a network of invented titles and privileges Drail had gathered together a close and loyal group of males from within the ranks of the Corps. It acted both as bodyguard to Drail and as a kind of secret police, spying on the Corps and the hinds and reporting any signs of discontent. It had been called the Draila and was both resented and feared. But the most feared of all was its leader Sgorr, the hornless deer, or hummel as they are also called, who Brechin had spied with Drail earlier.

Sgorr was not a birth-member of the herd but had appeared just three summers before from over the northern hills. When he arrived, asking for pasture, the young stag had been wounded in one eye and had claimed to have lost touch with his home herd after an attack by a wolf. But many dark rumours had already grown up around him. Some said he had a terrible secret. Others that he had made a pact with the forest god and had been driven out of his own herd for treachery. Some even said that he had broken the oldest law of all and had spent time in the company of men.

Whatever the truth, Sgorr had rapidly won Drail's confidence and had now been promoted far beyond his seven years. Drail was ageing fast and as he became more and more lame Sgorr played on his fears of being ousted. It was Sgorr who had come up with the notion of the Draila two seasons before and he had personally masterminded its creation, choosing and grooming young stags himself, cleverly spying out the most discontented members of the Corps and promoting them rapidly.

Brechin had mistrusted Sgorr from the outset, though he

could see the young stag was very clever, and he had immediately opposed Sgorr's entry into the herd. Subsequently he
had watched Sgorr's activities with quiet disgust. But if
Brechin had a weakness it was that he was a soldier and
Outrider first and preferred not to get involved in the politics
of the home herd.

It was not until Sgorr had sought control of the Outriders
too that Brechin had shown open opposition. With the other
captains he had fought hoof and antler to stop Drail forcing
members of the Draila on the Outriders. Drail had responded
by sending the Outriders to roam further and further afield,
on increasingly dangerous and unnecessary scouting ex-
peditions. The Outriders had lost six members since the
spring. One had been taken by wolves. Three killed by men.
Two had vanished without trace, including Brechin's own
brother, Whitefoot.

Meanwhile Drail's ambitions had grown with his power.
His power base now stretched far beyond the herd itself;
hence the newly invented title, 'Lord of Herds', which
Brechin had so scoffed at in the glen. But the title represented
far more than a name, or the simple reflection of Drail's
vanity, for many of the red deer across the Low Lands now
recognized his authority and, before Anlach, would come to
pay him homage. The home herd was the largest red deer
herd in the Great Land, and the Draila had won support
from other lords by offering help against their own enemies.
Drail's methods had begun to spread like a virus and his writ
now ran as far north as the Great Mountain and even to the
edges of the High Land.

Yet to Brechin the greatest threat posed by the Draila was
within the herd itself, for the Draila stags were becoming
increasingly aggressive. Apart from predators, starvation and
disease the main causes of harm to a deer herd are wounds

inflicted during the rut. But although stags will fight often, especially during the rut, their battles are mostly for show and their encounters rarely result in any serious damage. A directly fatal injury is virtually unheard of. But that was beginning to change. The encounters were proving more and more ferocious and Sgorr had even begun to train the young stags to use their antlers in an entirely new way; to sharpen them on rocks and stones and cut and jab with the points and to aim for vulnerable parts of the body. It meant that last autumn there had been far more injuries than normal and one stag, who had been caught in a fight over a hind with two Draila, had even been killed.

The habits of the hinds had also changed under Drail's lordship. His consuming desire for control had meant that the Draila had forced the females to live much closer to the stags. The herd had become much less mobile and for three seasons now they had used the same Home Oak. Brechin did not approve of this, though he was strangely glad to be so close to Eloin.

As Brechin climbed the hill he heard a familiar voice in the darkness. It distracted him from his dark thoughts. Ahead of him a group of yearlings were sitting in a circle in the grass, their spindly legs folded under them, and listening, wide-eyed, to the old deer addressing them. Most of them were around nine months old and had stopped suckling. But they were not too old to listen to a good story.

'And so, when the forest was young,' the old stag was saying, 'Starbuck stole the magic antlers from Herne and won a promise that for evermore the deer would roam as free as the wind.'

It was Blindweed, the storyteller.

'Spinning more of those old tales,' Brechin chuckled to himself. He remembered many cold winter nights sitting at old Blindweed's feet lapping up the stories of magic antlers, enchanted forests and of Herne himself. The ancient stag seemed to have been no younger then.

No one in the herd knew how old Blindweed really was. Some said he was fifteen, others even older. Eight is a good age for a red deer and thirteen about their natural span, but in exceptional circumstances they can live to as old as twenty and even older. You cannot, except in young deer, tell the precise age of a stag from his antlers, though the number of tines and their size is a good indication, for you find few royals below the age of five or six. Blindweed had a fine head, with nobbly, pearled antlers that rose to fourteen points on his brow. But it was clear that they had gone back, as it is called when they weaken, and would never be as strong as they had been in his prime.

'Well, that's quite enough for one moon,' said Blindweed suddenly. 'Your mothers will be scolding me with the morning.'

'But what happened to Starbuck?' shouted an eager voice from the back.

The fawns took up the cry.

'Yes, yes, how did he steal the antlers? Come on, Blindweed. Tell us.'

The old deer chuckled to himself.

'Very well, but then to your mothers. Promise, now.'

'We promise,' came the cry, except from the young fawn who had shouted out first.

Blindweed gathered himself and began, as Brechin padded up behind them.

'Well then, let me see. Yes. For days and days Starbuck travelled through the forests, driven by wind and snow, hunted by fox and wolf, but he was always too quick for them. Then, at last, he passed through the Great Glen and entered Herne's Wood. He travelled on until he reached the clearing and saw Herne himself lying by a brier, fast asleep. Above, hanging from the bow of an oak, were Herne's antlers, which he always takes off when he rests.'

The young deer shuffled excitedly in the grass.

'Well, as you know, only Starbuck could tread lightly enough in the wood not to wake Herne and so, very slowly, he crept past the sleeping deer god, stood on the tips of his hoofs and, with his muzzle, plucked the antlers from the tree and put them on his own head.'

Blindweed paused portentously.

'Yes, yes, and what happened then?' shouted an eager fawn from the front.

'Then there was a sudden thunderclap that shook the roots of the forest and Herne awoke.'

The fawn nuzzled closer to the others.

'When Herne saw that his antlers were gone he sprang to his feet and stamped his hoofs and snorted, and his red eyes flamed and he cried out in a great booming voice that made the branches shake. "Who wakes the spirit of the forest? Who dares to steal Herne's antlers?" As you can imagine, even Starbuck was frightened by Herne's anger, but he held his courage and answered coolly:

' "It is I, Starbuck the deer. I wear the antlers."

' "Give them back," cried Herne furiously, and with that he leapt on Starbuck. But Starbuck was wearing the magic antlers and so, with a single spring, he jumped high over Herne's head and landed far off at the edge of the clearing. Herne turned but he knew that as long as Starbuck had the antlers he could never catch him. Then Herne realized he was beaten.

' "What is it you seek?" said Herne in a gentler voice.

' "No more than you," answered brave Starbuck. "I seek

antlers for the deer, to protect them from Lera. It is not much to ask, Lord Herne, for we are Hernling yet we wander in the world with nothing to protect us but our senses and our speed."

'Well, Herne thought for a time and then he answered, "Very well, Starbuck, if you are sure that is what you want."

' "I am sure," said Starbuck, and with that he took the antlers off and gave them back to the god.

'When Herne had his horns back he seemed terrible indeed and he looked at Starbuck closely and said in a strange voice, "Starbuck, you are a brave and bold Hernling, so I will grant your wish though I could drive you from here like an autumn leaf tossed by the wind. But what you seek I will give only to such as you, foolish young stags who wish to fight. The hinds shall not be touched. Also, because you stole this prize from me, you shall have antlers with every season only and each year they shall fall from your heads when the spring rains shower the earth and leave you bald and naked, to be laughed at by every Lera. Until, when the spring flowers have blossomed and summer is beginning to ripen, they will grow again like the branches on the trees. And I will tell you this: what you seek is full of danger, so be certain."

'Starbuck was so flushed with his victory that he hardly heard Herne's warning and assured the god that he was indeed certain.

' "Very well then, Starbuck," said Herne. "Go over to that oak. At its bottom, though the oak is barren with winter, you will see a single leaf. It grows all year round, for it is filled with Herne's spirit. Eat it, Starbuck, and your wish shall be granted." So Starbuck approached the oak and there he saw a single withered leaf which looked dried and dead, though it was still on its stem. Gingerly, he pulled at it and it came away and he stood there in Herne's Wood munching on the stem. It tasted bitter and earthy, like peat moss and burnt bracken, and when Starbuck had finished he stood around blinking and waiting for something to happen. As he did so he realized that Herne had vanished.

' "Tricked," said Starbuck angrily, for nothing was happening. But suddenly, like the sound when the earth shakes, Herne was speaking again and his voice was all around. "Starbuck," he was saying, "your wish is granted. But because you stole this gift, the things you seek shall be both blessing and curse to Herla. So tremble, Starbuck, and run." Starbuck felt a terrible pain in his head and saw a blinding light and he turned and bolted in terror. He hurtled back through the wood, the branches of the trees tearing at his sides and haunches, his face scratched and bruised, and all along he was driven by the agonizing pain, as though his head would burst open.

'He thought he must run on for ever as the trees lashed passed him. But at last the pain began to subside and Starbuck broke clear of Herne's Wood and came to a stop in the sunlight by a clear pool. There the exhausted Starbuck reached down to drink and as he did so he saw his reflection in the water. His face was scratched and bruised by his flight, his clear eyes blinking in the day, and on his head were a pair of mighty antlers, vaster than any deer has known. And that is how the brave Starbuck won horns for the Herla.'

The assembled fawns were silent, their young mouths hanging open with amazement.

'So,' said Blindweed in a cheerful voice that broke the spell, 'which young fawn can tell why Herne's gift was both blessing and curse?'

The young deer looked back and forth to each other wonderingly.

'Come now, there must be one of you. What ever do they teach you nowadays?'

Suddenly the calves turned their heads, startled by a voice that sang out from the back.

'The antlers of Hernling are blessing and curse,
For they mean we must fight for the chance to be first.
Though they help us protect both the herd and each other,
At the time of Anlach, we must fight one another.'

'Captain Brechin,' said the startled storyteller. 'I didn't see you there'.

'Forgive me, Blindweed,' replied Brechin as he entered the circle, 'but I couldn't help listening. You still tell a fine tale.'

Blindweed was delighted.

'Fawns,' said the old deer, remembering himself, 'have you forgotten your manners? Welcome Captain Brechin, the bravest of the Outriders.'

Most of the fawns were too overawed to do anything at all.

'Sit still, little ones. And don't let me disturb you further, Blindweed,' said Brechin. 'I have stayed too long already. Continue your story.'

'No, Captain,' replied Blindweed with a mixture of embarrassment and pride. 'It's very late and if we sit here talking how will they ever grow up to be brave Outriders? Come now, be off with you.'

At this, some of the calves began to grumble and the young fawn at the back shouted out, 'Tell us another story, Blindweed. Tell us about the First Stone.'

'Yes,' said another.

'Now, now. I'll tell you tomorrow. I promise.'

'Tell us about Willow, the Mother of Hinds.'

'Tell us the Prophecy, Blindweed,' said the fawn that had spoken first. His name was Lychen. The fawns took up his cry.

'Yes, the Prophecy. Tell us the Prophecy.'

'Silence,' snapped Blindweed angrily. 'The Prophecy is no mere fable to be fed to young fawns. It is part of the Lore. Now stop being foolish.'

'I bet Captain Brechin wants to hear it,' said Lychen boldly. 'Go on, Blindweed.'

'I'll muzzle you if you don't be quiet,' said Blindweed furiously. 'Captain Brechin has much more important things to do than listen to a lot of little soft-foots and an old storyteller.'

But the calves weren't listening to Blindweed. They were looking up at Brechin.

'Please, Captain Brechin, sir,' said Lychen in a bold voice, 'you want to hear it, don't you?'

Brechin looked down at the calf and his heart was suddenly pierced with worry for Eloin. But he smiled.

'If Blindweed will tell it,' he said, 'I would be honoured.'

'Hooray,' shouted the fawns delightedly. 'Go on, Blindweed, tell it. The Prophecy. The Prophecy.'

'Very well,' said Blindweed irritably. 'If the captain insists. But silence, all of you. This is not for fooling.'

The fawns had already fallen silent as Blindweed readied himself. Even Brechin felt a thrill as the ancient stag swayed his gnarled antlers back and forth, closed his eyes, and as though talking to the moon, began to recite:

'When the Lore is bruised and broken,
Shattered like a blasted tree,
Then shall Herne be justly woken,
Born to set the Herla free.

On his brow a leaf of oaken,
Changeling child shall be his fate.
Understanding words strange spoken,
Chased by anger, fear and hate.

He shall flee o'er hill and heather,
And shall go where no deer can,
Knowing secrets dark to Lera,
Till his need shall summon man.

Air and water, earth and fire,
All shall ease his bitter pain,
Till the elements conspire
To restore the Island Chain.

First the High Land grass shall flower,
As he quests through wind and snow,
Then he breaks an ancient power,
And returns to face his woe.

When the lord of lies upbraids him,
Then his wrath shall cloak the sun,
And the Herla's foe shall aid him
To confront the evil one.

Sacrifice shall be his meaning,
He the darkest secret learn,
Truths of beast and man revealing,
Touching on the heart of Herne.

Fawn of moonlight ever after,
So shall all the Herla sing.
For his days shall herald laughter,
Born a healer and a king.'

Blindweed finished and opened his eyes. A slight breeze had come up as if from nowhere, rustling the grass. Brechin shivered. His old scar suddenly pained him. The deer looked at each other in silence and Blindweed shook his tired head.

'Right,' he said at last. 'It's time.'

Without any further protest the young fawns got to their feet. They thanked Blindweed as they went and began to run down the hill together, back to the safety of their mothers. Soon only one was left by Blindweed's side. It was Lychen.

'What does it mean?' asked Lychen in a little voice. 'The Prophecy. Is it true?'

'What does it mean?' said Blindweed. 'Well, Lychen, why don't we ask Captain Brechin?'

Brechin was standing, gazing back towards the Home Oak.

'Excuse me, sir,' said Lychen nervously, 'but do you know what the Prophecy means? Is it true?'

'No, little one,' said Brechin, looking down, 'I don't. But as for it being true I will say only this. There is more truth in Blindweed's stories, though they are only stories, than there is in the heart of many a stag. So listen to them well. Now off with you, I have business to attend to.'

'Thank you, sir,' said Lychen and, caught between fear and pride, with a skip the fawn turned and shot off down the hill. When he had gone Blindweed walked slowly up to the captain. He had heard something serious in Brechin's tone and he sensed something was wrong.

'Captain Brechin,' he said gravely, 'it is very good to see you again and to know that at least some of the Hernling remember the old tales. Nowadays everything has changed. No one listens any more. And what with Sgorr and the Draila, they would drive away the spirit of Herne.'

'Yes, Blindweed, there is much trouble in the Low Lands.

But if I remember the old tales it is because you taught us them so well. You taught us that in those tales lies the secret of the Lore.'

'Ah, yes,' said Blindweed, shaking his antlers. 'The Lore. It is too much abused.'

'Well, Blindweed,' said Brechin, suddenly flexing his haunches and snorting, 'I'm glad I've seen you, for tonight it is the Lore that I shall need.'

With that the captain raced away, up the steep gully towards the Home Oak. The full moon hung in the sky, bathing the valley in a luminous, eerie light as Brechin approached the meeting place. The wind had strengthened, sending great shoals of cloud scurrying across its haunted face. On the exposed plateau, that is such a common feature of the southern glens, twenty Corps members were assembled and around them stood the closed ranks of another fifteen Draila. As Brechin crested the plateau four of these stags broke away and ran up to meet him. They were lead by Narl, a young buck who only that spring Brechin had nearly come to blows with when he blocked his admission to the Outriders.

'Herne be with you,' called Brechin loudly and with little warmth.

'Brechin, you're late,' said Narl, ignoring the traditional greeting. 'Drail is growing impatient—'

'Captain Brechin to you,' Brechin bellowed. He had halted and already his front haunches were set forward. The three other stags stopped behind Narl and as Brechin pointed his brow tines and stamped, they edged in behind their leader.

'Forgive me, Captain Brechin,' said Narl sarcastically, but clearly intimidated by the huge antlers, 'I forgot how keen the Outriders are on their titles. But if you'd be so good as to join us, *Lord* Drail has something to tell you.'

Under any other circumstance Brechin would have charged Narl. But now he was keen to know what was happening at the meeting place. He had delayed too long.

'Surely you mean *Lord* Sgorr?' said Brechin contemptuously, and he pushed straight through the four deer. 'Well then, what are you waiting for?'

Brechin surged on across the heather as the four Draila brought up the rear.

Blindweed was deeply troubled when Brechin left him to go to the meeting place. For two seasons now he had watched the plots of the Draila with mounting disgust. He hated what Sgorr was doing to the herd and though he understood little of politics, he knew that it would bring nothing but harm. Sgorr had even tried to ban the old stories, though too many Corps members had opposed it. But tonight there was something else. He couldn't quite scent it out but Blindweed had spent too long immersed in the legends of the Herla not to carry something of their magic and not to trust his instincts. Tonight his scars ached and the pain in his left foot had returned. He knew in his bones that something was happening.

He was pondering these things as he walked slowly towards the bottom of the home valley when suddenly he saw a group of thirty Draila moving rapidly up to the meeting place. They were packed tightly and running along a slight gully, out of moonlight, as though trying to avoid being seen. He stopped dead in his tracks but as soon as he did so he realized he was upwind of them. Two Draila nosed him immediately, broke from the group and raced towards him.

'Hey, you!' shouted one as they neared the storyteller. 'What are you doing lurking so close to the Home Oak?'

'Nothing, Captain,' said Blindweed. 'I was just telling some stories to the fawns. They like to sit out on the hillside.'

'Why, it's only old Blindweed,' said one of the others. 'We don't have to worry about him.'

'Worry about me?' said Blindweed. 'Why, Captain, is there trouble in the herd?'

'Never you mind,' said the captain. He looked a little guiltily at his companion and then added in a softer voice, 'The Outriders have nosed fox. You'd better get back to the home valley.'

'Certainly, Captain. Thank you for your concern.'

The stags raced off again and Blindweed continued on his way, a good deal more troubled than before. In the meadow at the bottom of the valley the herd seemed quiet enough, though Blindweed noticed other Draila moving about amongst the hinds. Every now and then they would stop to talk to them and seemed to be trying to reassure them. Then they would move off to their captains and report. There was much nodding of antlers. Blindweed pretended to graze and as he did so he swayed closer and closer to three stags who were standing by a small thicket. He managed to edge to the far side of the thicket, just out of sight but near enough to overhear their conversation.

'When is it to be?' one was saying in a voice that shook with emotion.

'Soon, Brach, very soon,' whispered another. 'You must be patient. Everything is set.'

'It's this damned waiting I can't stand,' said the first.

'Silence,' said a third voice, older than the other two. 'We need you to be calm when it comes. It's your job to reassure the hinds.'

'Yes,' agreed the first, 'and it won't be easy. What if they bolt?'

'They won't leave the fawns,' said the older voice calmly. 'And if they try, there are enough Draila to hold them. But we must be certain of the lead hind, Fourleaf. Now, I've got to get going. I have the Outriders to attend to.'

The stag who had just been speaking turned on his haunches and set off into the darkness. Blindweed was dumbstruck. Very softly the old deer backed away from the thicket and padded back towards the stream. He stopped to drink, his old, calloused lips sucking at the cool water. Then he set off along the bank again, his head buzzing with the talk of plots. At last he reached a clear stretch of open ground and he froze as he heard a snort of pain. It was a hind straining with her unborn calf.

'Stand off there, in the name of Herne,' cried an angry voice from the darkness. It was Bhreac, the old doe that Brechin had asked to watch over Eloin. She had nosed Blindweed coming down the stream and now her instincts were roused.

'I mean no harm, old one,' said Blindweed softly, realizing what was happening. 'Who is it that's calving?'

'Blindweed, it's you,' said Bhreac less harshly, 'I didn't realize. It's Eloin. One of Captain Brechin's hinds. He asked me to watch her.'

'I just saw the captain on the hill,' said Blindweed. 'He was going towards the Home Oak. Bhreac, there is trouble in the herd tonight. The Draila are out.'

'Stags,' snorted Bhreac in disgust. 'They always mean trouble. But we hinds have more serious things to think of. Blindweed, I fear this will be a hard one. I have never known a hind to be so late.'

The old deer nodded gravely.

'Don't fret,' he said. 'Eloin is strong and the calf of Captain Brechin has a better chance than most.'

'Still,' said Bhreac, 'I wish there were something we could do.'

But the two old deer were silent now. They were listening to Eloin's breathing. It was shallow and painful. They wanted to help her but they knew she had to do this alone.

When Brechin arrived at the meeting place the Lord of the Herd was addressing the stags from under the spreading branches of the Home Oak. Drail had twelve points to his antlers but from their size and thickness it was clear that they had already gone back.

His voice was fighting the wind as his great, shaggy form limped back and forth. The ranks of Draila around him were nodding enthusiastically. Brechin smiled as he recognized some of Drail's own sons among his bodyguard. It was typical of Drail to grant special privileges to his own.

Drail was not an unattractive deer but his eyes had a wary, cruel look. To the left of Drail Brechin caught the glint of Sgorr's single eye in the moonlight and the flash of his long front teeth. A deer with no antlers can sometimes grow fierce teeth which, when used skillfully, can prove nearly as dangerous. On Sgorr's head were the stumps of bone where the antlers had failed yet again. His left eye, now just an empty socket, was closed up by a deep scar that ran straight across his left scent gland.

'And these rumours and lies must cease,' Drail was saying. 'If any deer has a genuine complaint he can bring it to me or to Sgorr. The Draila will be happy to investigate . . .'

As Brechin drew nearer and trotted up the line towards the tree, some of the Corps members stamped appreciatively. Drail broke off at once to address the captain.

'Brechin. So good of you to join us,' he said sarcastically. 'We thought you had got lost. Bandach gave me your heartfelt apologies but still, perhaps you can tell the young Corps members why a captain of the Outriders chooses to come so late to a meeting of the council?'

'Lord Drail,' replied Brechin coolly, 'perhaps you are mistaken. The Herla may only stand in council when all the captains of the Outriders are present. I see here only young bucks. But no captains. Where are Straloch and the others?'

At this one or two of the members of the Corps nodded their antlers in agreement, but others of the Draila stamped and moved forward.

'But you are present, Captain Brechin,' said a thin, hard voice. It was Sgorr. 'Don't the Outriders see you as their lord? You can represent them.'

'Sgorr. You know full well that the captains of the Outriders meet as equals. Equally they must be present if the council is to be called.'

'That may be,' said Sgorr, smiling, 'but isn't it strange that such a respected Outrider cannot come when the Lord of Herds asks? Is nothing sacred any more?'

Sgorr's tone was sly and sneering.

'Lord Drail,' said Brechin. 'All the herd knows that one of my hinds, Eloin, is very close to her time. The pregnancy is proving difficult and I had to attend to her first. Perhaps even the captain of the Draila can understand that?'

'I only understand,' said Sgorr coldly, 'that Captain Brechin shows little respect. Perhaps he forgets that the council comes before any other matter in the herd. Besides, isn't it strange that he spends so much time with a hind?'

As though on cue the Draila nodded and snorted.

'As I've said,' continued Brechin calmly, 'this is no council, so I cannot see—'

'Silence, Brechin,' cried Drail suddenly. 'You forget yourself. Now I have something to say to you, all of you. Captain

Brechin, you are an example of just how little respect is shown in the herd. It is time that stopped, time some changes were made. First and most importantly Anlach will be with us soon enough, so the members of the Corps should know that I, in consultation with Sgorr and the Draila, believe that it is dangerous and wasteful to the strength of the herd that there should be such regular challenges for the lordship. And as for the choosing of hinds . . .'

The wind had dropped now and Drail's voice sang in the moonlight. If the members of the Corps had not been rooted to the spot by the sheer enormity of what they where hearing they might have noticed a group of thirty or so Draila moving silently through the heather behind them.

'Therefore,' bellowed Drail, 'the members of the Draila have voted that I should continue to guide you for three more summers at least.'

Drail paused to listen for the effect of his words as the Draila began to close in around him. They had already heard the news. Brechin stood quite motionless. He didn't know whether to laugh or shout. Indeed he could hardly understand what Drail was saying. Not even he had suspected that Drail would try this. To hold himself in place without even a challenge! It was unthinkable. It meant – Brechin tried to weigh up the idea – it meant abolishing Anlach. It was like abolishing the forest itself.

Across the home valley a hind, heavy with her fawn, winced in pain. Nearby an old doe came forward but Eloin stamped and told her to stand off. Eloin lifted her head and sucked at the air. Her muscles tightened and she started to shake. Around her the forest and the stars and the great moon began to swim before her eyes.

*

'No. It is unthinkable. You cannot. It is against all the laws of Herne.'

Brechin was speaking now, in a clear, strong voice. The thunder of his words made even the assembled Draila stir uneasily.

'It is already done, Brechin,' said Sgorr, stepping forward and baring his teeth, 'and many of the herds in the Low Lands have accepted Drail's command.'

'You're a fool, Sgorr,' shouted Brechin. 'The Corps will never allow it. And you,' he continued, turning suddenly to address the younger stags, 'listen to me. Drail has gone mad.'

But as he said it Brechin started. From the darkness antlers were emerging on all sides. Lines of Draila were flanking them everywhere. Their heads were lowered and their antlers prone. The trap had been sprung; they were completely surrounded. For a moment irresolution wavered up and down the Corps.

'You were saying, Captain Brechin?' sneered Sgorr.

'No,' shouted Brechin. 'If the Corps accepts this, the Outriders never will.'

'Ah, yes,' said Sgorr coolly, and as he did so five Draila stepped towards Brechin. 'The Outriders. I believe Lord Drail was coming on to that.'

Suddenly the assembled stags were transfixed by a great, bellowing bark that shook the air from across the valley and, as they looked on, they saw the silhouette of a deer on the far hillside. He was surrounded by four stags and their antlers were burying themselves deep into the deer's sides, slashing and goring at his flanks. It was Captain Straloch. The cry was taken up from another hilltop and then another, until it seemed that the whole glen echoed with the cries of pain.

*

'Oh, Herne. What is happening?' shouted Eloin as she stood shaking by the rowan tree. 'The pain. It's terrible.'

The two old deer standing nearby were motionless but their bodies too were trembling. Yet their worry was no longer for Eloin and her calf. They had heard the cries of the Outriders on the hills and fear was moving through the herd like a wind.

'Who fights with me?' cried Brechin. 'Who fights for the Outriders?'

Brechin lowered his head and charged straight at Sgorr and the Home Oak. But his way was suddenly blocked by a forest of bone as a line of Draila lowered their antlers and closed ranks to block the path to the Lord of the Herd. He pulled up on his haunches and pawed the earth violently.

He had to think quickly. All around him stags were locking antlers. Brechin swung round as a young Corps member cried in pain. A Draila had charged him and gored him in the side with his brow tines. Other members of the Corps were standing down, intimidated by the surrounding stags. But a few were fighting, bucking with their antlers or rising up on their hind legs to box in the manner of hinds and of stags in velvet.

Suddenly Brechin noticed that to his right the way was momentarily open, leading up to a patch of higher ground. Brechin dashed for the opening, bucking and tossing as he ran. In an instant he was clear, rising up above the mêlée. He felt the wind on his face and his head began to clear. But, as he stopped on the hillock and wheeled round to survey the scene, he saw another stag racing towards him. Brechin dug in his hoofs and prepared to fight. The stag came nearer and nearer and suddenly Brechin heard a familiar voice. It was Bandach, the young stag who had brought him Drail's message earlier in the day.

'Bandach,' cried Brechin delightedly. 'At least some stags have sense and courage.'

He had noticed that Bandach's face was torn open at the cheek.

'But I doubt the others will fight,' panted Bandach. 'There are too many of them and we're still in velvet. Have you noticed? The stags whose antlers came out of velvet first are leading the attack. Sgorr must have picked them out specially. But many of the Corps members' antlers are still too soft to be much use. We never even nosed them creeping up on us.'

'Brave Bandach,' said Brechin. 'You'll make a fine Outrider.'

As he said it Brechin and Bandach looked at each other and there was the full horror of recognition in their eyes. But they did not have long to share it for in that instant they heard a bellow from below. A Draila had spied them on the hill and now ten or twelve stags were racing towards them.

'Well, Captain. Do you think me a spy now?' said Bandach, his eyes gleaming with pride. 'Come then, let me show a captain of the Outriders how a young stag can fight, for they mean to kill you, Brechin.'

'No, Bandach,' said Brechin quietly. 'Eloin. You must warn Eloin. Sgorr hates me and I fear what he will do to my calf if anything happens to me. And Eloin – when I am gone Drail will try to take her. You must save them, Bandach.'

'But Captain—'

'Please, Bandach, do as I ask. Quickly.'

The young stag stared into the captain's eyes. At last he nodded.

'Herne be with you always, Captain Brechin,' he said as he turned.

'And with you too, Bandach. Run freely.'

As the Draila reached the bottom of the hillock Bandach slipped back down the side of the hill and made for the rowan tree by the stream. But at the bottom of the slope he turned to watch the ghostly scene above him. On the hill Brechin was encircled by eleven stags. They came slowly, warily, with one stag slightly to the front. It was Narl. Brechin lowered his antlers and readied himself. Below, most of the fighting had died down and the red deer looked up. Even Drail shuddered at that unnatural sight. On a hillock above the Home Oak, silhouetted by the full moon, Brechin, Captain of the Outriders, was fighting for his life.

He swayed right and left like a dancing Lera, filled with the spirit of Herne. Five times the circle closed in on the deer. And five times he emerged again, bucking his great antlered head. But on the sixth charge a Draila caught Brechin in the haunches and another straight in the flanks. Brechin lifted his head and let out a cry that rent the sky. The deer's front legs buckled before him and he crashed to the ground. Even the Draila paused as the captain tried to stagger to his feet again, his bloodied mouth crying out and scything back and forth. But at last Brechin's head dropped and the stags moved in. There was one last bellow of pain that seemed to tear open the heart of the world and then a terrible silence descended on the glen. It was finished.

At the bottom of the valley, by the rowan tree near the stream, a hind was lying motionless, her long neck limp in the grass. Eloin's eyes were closed but her sides rose steadily up and down as she panted with exhaustion. At her side something was stirring in the wet grass; a newborn fawn that had nearly cost Eloin her life. The little creature's thick, woolly coat was wet and sticky and it was kicking its legs and blinking as it tried to stand up, its sleek little ears twitching helplessly in the darkness.

2

Changeling

O soul, be chang'd into little water drops
And fall into the ocean, ne'er be found.
Christopher Marlowe, 'Doctor Faustus'

'No, you old fool, stay here. What could you do to help at your age?'

'I can still fight, can't I?' mumbled Blindweed. 'My antlers may have gone back but they can still strike a blow or two.'

'You couldn't take a fawn, Blindweed,' snorted Bhreac irritably. 'Be sensible. If they are fighting in the herd, so be it. Let the old look to the young.'

As Bhreac spoke Eloin lifted her head and strained her neck back over her shoulder to lick her little fawn's muzzle. She sank back again, exhausted by even this tiny effort.

'Come on, Blindweed,' said Bhreac. 'Let's see if we can do anything for Eloin.' Blindweed nodded resignedly as Bhreac wandered over to the hind.

'Well, my dear, that was a close thing,' said the old hind kindly. 'But my it was worth it. He's a fine one. I've never seen such bold eyes and so many freckles on a back. They're like snow leaves dropped from the clouds.'

Eloin opened her eyes and smiled faintly.

'Yes,' she said. 'It was worth it.'

But then Eloin's eyes clouded again.

'But it was terrible too. I thought the whole herd was crying out.'

Bhreac and Blindweed looked at each other gravely as the little fawn nuzzled closer to its mother's side.

'What will you name him, my dear?'

Eloin looked back at her fawn. His tail was flicking back and forth as he tried to get to her milk.

'If it had been a doe I would certainly have called her Bhreac,' said Eloin. 'But as it is, why not Rannoch?'

The name was well known to the Herla for Rannoch had been one of Starbuck's calves.

'Rannoch. It's a good name,' said Blindweed in the background, nodding his old antlers approvingly. 'Herne himself would be pleased.'

'Thank you, Blindweed. What do you think of it, my little Rannoch?'

Rannoch wagged his tail furiously but his evident pleasure was from the milk that he was suckling at his mother's side, not because he understood a word of what the grown-ups were saying.

'Ouch. Don't bite so hard. You've plenty of time to grow up like Brechin.'

Bhreac cast Blindweed an urgent look but the old deer shook his head.

'Eloin, may I see your little one?' he asked, stepping forward.

'Certainly, Blindweed. May the teller of tales be the first stag to welcome him to the herd.'

'Come then, Rannoch,' said Blindweed softly, nudging the young fawn with his muzzle. Blindweed's gentle buffet swung the calf round and he stood there blinking up at the old storyteller, his front feet splayed slightly out in front of him

and his tail twitching furiously. Blindweed stretched forward
to give him a lick on his nose but as he did so he suddenly
stopped and pulled back.

'In the name of Herne,' he gasped, drawing in his breath
sharply.

'What is it?' said Bhreac.

Blindweed was muttering something under his breath.

'*On his brow a leaf of oaken*,' he mumbled.

'Blindweed, what on earth's the matter?'

'Look,' replied Blindweed as he gazed at the patch of
white fur in the centre of Rannoch's forehead.

'Why, it's only a fawn mark,' said Bhreac. 'I thought
something was wrong'

'Yes, but look at the shape,' Blindweed whispered.

In the centre of Rannoch's forehead, formed by a slightly
raised tuft of white fur like a plash of snow, the little stag's
fawn mark was in the shape of a perfect oak leaf.

At the Home Oak Drail was counting the cost of the night's
work while the Draila moved about the meeting place
making sure of the Corps members.

'Well, Sgorr,' said Drail as the captain of the Draila
marched up to him, 'what's the count?'

'One of the Corps killed and several injured, Lord Drail,'
answered Sgorr. 'The rest have come over.'

Drail nodded contentedly.

'Bandach escaped,' added Sgorr a little nervously. 'But
we'll catch him before the sun's up.'

'Do so. And the Outriders?'

'Two evaded us. Salen, though he was badly wounded,
and Captain Spey. But otherwise it is done. They are dead.'

The two were silent for a moment. Even they felt the
enormity of what they had done.

'It's bad that Spey got away,' said Drail. 'He's a fast one. Still, what of the Draila?'

'A few have damaged their antlers for they are still softer than I would have liked.'

But Sgorr bared his teeth; it was the only way he knew how to smile. He was pleased that his trap had gone so smoothly and though Brechin's stand had been impressive, there was at least a compensation. He could see that Drail was deeply displeased that Brechin had fought so bravely and it always gratified Sgorr when Drail was displeased. It made him all the more malleable.

'Where is he?' asked Drail.

'Brechin? Still on the hillock, Lord.'

'Well then, let us pay our respects.'

The two stags ran up to the hillock but before they passed beyond the Home Oak Sgorr stopped and muttered something to a stag. He nodded and set off back down the hill towards the bottom of the valley. Then Sgorr continued on his way, careful to keep slightly behind Drail's limping gait. As they went, the lines of Draila dipped their antlers. Brechin was lying in the centre of the hillock. His great body was badly broken and his tongue lolled from his mouth. His eyes were closed and his sides and haunches were still bleeding. Sgorr hung back as Drail circled the corpse.

At last the Lord of the Herd stopped and bowed his antlers. He hooked them into Brechin's and with a great effort lifted the bloodied head from the ground. Then he bucked the skull up and down twice, before letting it drop limply to the earth. Drail was about to walk back to Sgorr when he suddenly stopped and turned round again. He walked back to the body and then did something that even the assembled Draila winced to see. He swung round, pawed the earth with his hind hoofs and kicked out at

Brechin's head. The blow caught Brechin full on the right antler and with a great crack snapped the horn clean in two. Gratified, Drail walked back to Sgorr's side.

'A fine blow, my lord,' said Sgorr fawningly. 'That one would please many a young hind.'

'Herne's teeth!' said Drail. 'Eloin. I had quite forgotten. Go, Sgorr.'

'And if the calf has come?'

'By Herne,' snorted Drail, rounding on Sgorr. 'Must I tell you everything? You haven't done so much fighting this night that those teeth can't deal with a newborn fawn.'

Sgorr bowed his head and backed away. Turning on his haunches he called four Draila to his side and led them away down the hill.

When Bandach saw Brechin fall on the hillock he made straight for where the hinds were gathered by the stream, running as fast as his legs could carry him. But as he neared the meadow he saw that the whole place was swarming with Draila. He smelt the fear on the air as the hinds blinked and looked about them nervously. A stampede had indeed only just been avoided when the cry had gone up from the Outriders and now the Draila were moving among them, trying to calm them. The lying words of the Draila had begun to reassure the hinds, for they wanted to believe what the Draila were telling them about a minor rebellion in the herd that had soon been put down.

Those hinds who asked difficult questions were being separated from the rest. Bandach could see twenty hinds being rounded up quietly and led away to the Home Oak with their fawns in tow. Every now and then a hind, followed closely by her calf, would try and break from the group but the Draila would pounce on them and herd them back, not flinching to use their antlers to do it.

As Bandach watched the group passing now, from the safety of a yew tree, he saw a hind slip away and make towards him. Bandach recognized Fourleaf, the lead hind. He backed away slightly and tried to press into the trees behind him but as he did so he stepped on some dry wood and the snap alerted her to his presence. Fourleaf stopped in her tracks, her senses on full alert, her eyes blinking nervously and her sleek muzzle sniffing the air.

'Who's there?' she called under his breath.

'Fourleaf. It's me. Bandach. In here, quickly.'

The doc pushed forward into the trees and for a moment stood there shaking as she looked into Bandach's eyes.

'Bandach, did you hear it? The terrible noise. And now the Draila—'

'I know,' said Bandach. 'They've taken the herd.'

'It can't be true, Bandach. Have they killed the Outriders?'

Bandach looked back at her. His eyes told the full horror of what had happened.

'Fourleaf, we can't stay here, it isn't safe. Besides, I have a duty to perform. Brechin asked me to warn Eloin. You know she is near her time. It was his last wish.'

Fourleaf had hardly been listening but this news brought her back to her senses.

'Brechin is dead?'

'Yes.'

'Then we must hurry, Bandach. There's no time to lose.'

But with that the two deer heard a noise along the edge of the wood. The Draila guarding the hinds had noticed that Fourleaf was missing and now five of them were coming back to find her. They had already nosed her on the breeze and were moving quickly along the thicket.

'What are we to do?' said Fourleaf desperately. 'I've led them to you.'

Bandach stamped back and forth in the leaves as he tried to think.

'There is no way back through the thicket,' he said. 'We must try our luck in the open. If we run hard enough we can make the far trees and the slope. There's a trail there I know well. It leads back through the glen to the stream.'

Bandach knew it was desperate: there are few hinds that can outpace a stag. But it was their only chance. Then, suddenly, Fourleaf did something extraordinary. She stepped backwards out of the thicket into full view.

'Goodbye, Bandach,' she called softly. 'Herne be with you.'

Before Bandach even realized what was happening the Draila had surrounded the hind and were escorting her back to the group.

When they had gone he slipped out of cover and ran across the valley. The path through the wood that Bandach had talked of was a long way round to the stream and Bandach knew instinctively that he hadn't much time. He ran desperately, hurtling through branch and thorn. Every now and then the trees below him would thin out and he could see the Draila and at one point the wood opened completely and Bandach caught a view clean across the glen towards the Home Oak. He fancied he saw Drail and Sgorr on the hillock where Brechin had died, but on he ran, not daring to stop or look back.

The path began to drop again and Bandach followed it down. He was rounding a bend where the track swung sharply south when he suddenly lurched off the path to avoid two Draila who were blocking the way ahead. Bandach nearly tumbled down the hill, but he held his balance. The

Draila heard him though and in an instant were on him. His attempt to avoid them had been a mistake, for now they had the advantage of height.

'Bandach, we had heard you'd escaped,' cried one Draila, as both deer lowered their antlers and advanced slowly towards him. 'But where are you going now? Perhaps to warn Eloin that Sgorr wants Brechin's fawn?'

Bandach backed away but his haunches were against a tree now. He dug in and prepared for the charge. The first deer threw himself forwards and Bandach rose to meet him. They collided heavily and their antlers knocked together with a loud crack, tearing some of the velvet from the Draila's horns. The Draila had had the momentum of the slope and Bandach was dazed. But the Draila was winded too. He recovered himself and charged again as Bandach rose to the attack.

A thundering crack split the air as the deer's heads collided. Bandach was holding his ground but on the next charge the second Draila came in too and, as he locked with Bandach, the first Draila dropped his head and aimed his brow tines straight at Bandach's throat. Luckily, he slipped on the verge and his antler caught Bandach's side instead, tearing through the fur to leave a deep gash. The two Draila regained their footing as Bandach looked down at the open wound. He was bleeding badly. The slope had given the Draila an impossible advantage. Bandach braced for the next charge.

Suddenly there was the sound of splintering branches and churning leaves. From above a shape was hurtling towards them. There was no time to get out of the way as the charging stag reached them. His trez tines caught the Draila who had wounded Bandach, full in his side. The startled animal bellowed in terror and tried to swing right with his antlers

but the impact of the blow knocked him clean off his feet
and threw him sideways. The charging deer crashed on top
of him, lost its balance and together they tumbled down the
slope.

Bandach didn't waste a moment. Almost as soon as the
unknown deer collided with the first Draila Bandach dipped
his head, turned it slightly to one side and lunged. The prone
brow tine was aimed straight at the second Draila's chest, at
the soft flesh where the haunches meet, and Bandach's aim
was true. Being below the attacking deer now gave Bandach
the advantage, for the tine passed in and up. The deer bucked
free and, bleeding badly, he turned and fled. Bandach shook
himself and looked round.

Below he could see that the other Draila had got up and
was also running. Nearby, the unknown stag was pulling
himself to his feet. His right antler had snapped in two and
part of it was hanging off the beam, covered in blood
and torn velvet. Then Bandach blinked in recognition. It was
Salen whose hind, Bracken, had given birth to the stillborn
calf. The old stag came towards him up the slope. But as he
walked his front legs suddenly gave way and he stumbled. It
was only then that Bandach noticed the deep gash on his
flank.

'Salen, Salen! You're wounded,' cried Bandach as he
rushed forward.

'Yes,' panted Salen desperately. 'They came on us downwind. We thought they were Outriders at first and by the
time I realized what was happening it was too late. The
cowards attacked us in groups. There were too many of
them, Bandach, too many'.

'Hush, Salen,' said Bandach. 'Don't speak.'

'I saw you from above the path,' Salen went on, struggling
with his breath. 'I was resting up there in the bracken. When

I saw you pinned against that tree I realized you hadn't a hope. I knew with this wound there was little chance of helping you on flat ground, but with that slope there was a slim one.'

'You saved my life, Salen.'

'At least I did some good then.' Salen nodded, his breathing shallow now and his eyes glassy. 'Those damned Draila. They've taken Tarn, Straloch and Crinnan. I passed their bodies by the old cairn. I saw them catch Spey on the east hill. We've all gone, Bandach, all of us. The Outriders have been destroyed.'

'Hush, Salen. Try not to move.'

Salen's head was swaying back and forward now. But suddenly his dazed eyes seemed to clear.

'Bandach, tell me. What of Captain Brechin?'

Bandach hesitated. 'Salen, you're wrong,' he said suddenly. 'You're not the last of the Outriders. I saw Captain Brechin escape over the western hills.'

'I knew it,' sighed Salen. 'They'd never take Brechin. Then at least there is some hope.'

Salen's body began to shudder violently. His legs shook and with a great sigh he laid his head on the forest floor. In the valley bottom the Draila had finally settled the hinds and the nervous mothers were beginning to graze again. But suddenly, as though of one body, the hinds and their fawns flinched and pricked up their ears to listen. From the hillside they heard, for the last time on that terrible day, one more bellow of pain. It was Bandach, mourning for Salen.

'Enough of your silly stories, Blindweed,' snorted Bhreac by the rowan tree. 'Can't you see you're frightening Eloin?'

Eloin's little calf had started to feed again.

'They're more than just stories,' grumbled Blindweed.

'Nonsense. Besides we've more important things to worry about than a fawn mark.'

Eloin, who had been deep in thought, pricked up her ears. 'What do you mean, Bhreac?' she said. 'What's wrong?'

Bhreac was silent. She looked nervously at Blindweed.

'What's happened?' said Eloin, struggling to get up.

'My dear,' answered Blindweed quietly, 'there has been fighting in the herd. The Draila are up to something.'

'Brechin?' cried Eloin. She was up now and pawing the ground as Rannoch tried to nudge between her legs.

'I don't know. I last saw him going to the meeting place'.

'Then I didn't dream it. The cries from the hillside?'

'No, you didn't dream it,' said Blindweed. 'The Outriders have been attacked.'

Rannoch seemed to sense his mother's fear for he nestled in beside her, looking up nervously at the two old deer.

'I must try to find Brechin,' said Eloin, glancing about her desperately. Nearby she saw Bracken, her dead newborn fawn lying motionless at her feet, as she grazed listlessly by the trees.

'No, my dear, it is better that you stay here with the little one,' said Bhreac. 'Blindweed says the herd is swarming with Draila. Blindweed? What are you doing now, you old fool?'

The storyteller had wandered off to the edge of the stream and was pushing his muzzle into the side of the bank, as though trying to pick up a scent.

'This is no time to graze Blindweed,' snapped Bhreac. 'Have you gone mad?'

But when Blindweed lifted his head it was stained with mud from the wet ground. He trotted back towards them.

'Blindweed. Stop fooling,' said Bhreac.

'Silence, hind,' snapped Blindweed suddenly. 'Eloin, I am

old and have strange ways and there is much trouble in the herd. I do not understand politics. But I know this: that fawn mark of little Rannoch's will bring him nothing but trouble. Will you trust me, Eloin?'

Eloin didn't understand but as she gazed back into the old storyteller's grave eyes she realized he was deadly serious. She nodded.

'Come here, Rannoch,' said Blindweed. He nudged the fawn and Rannoch swung round, startled. The old deer reached down and, with one swing, rubbed his nose across the little fawn's forehead. The smear of mud stained Rannoch's fur, almost completely masking the white leaf.

'That's better,' said Blindweed. 'We can't have you wandering around with a fawn mark like that and making the other deer jealous, can we now?'

Rannoch blinked up at Blindweed, then, suddenly frightened of the huge mouth and great tongue, he turned back to his mother. Eloin let him come and stood gazing out across the home valley. She hardly knew why, but she felt better for what Blindweed had done.

'Oh, Brechin,' she whispered. 'I wish you would hurry'.

As Sgorr ran, his Draila behind him, he let the wind score his face and his lungs swelled with pleasure. The night's success had surpassed even his wildest expectations. The Outriders, who he had tried to outmanoeuvre for so long, were crushed. Brechin was dead and now a new time was beginning in the Low Lands. Drail would not be challenged for three summers at least and thus Sgorr's own position was secure.

Drail. He's an old fool, thought Sgorr to himself. But he won't last. He's lame and tired. But I must bide my time.

Then they'll see. Then let them talk, when a hornless stag is the Lord of Herds.

Bitterness welled up in Sgorr's stomach. He remembered the days of terrible humiliation when his antlers had first failed. Then the contempt with which he had been treated by stags so much stupider than himself. That was before he had been driven out and forced to wander the forests alone. Ah, but it had been fate that he had stumbled on this bunch of brailah. If it hadn't been for the gullible, lame Drail, Sgorr thought, where would he be now?

His thoughts turned to Brechin and he bared his teeth with satisfaction. Brechin had fought hardest to prevent him entering the herd; now Brechin was dead and he was on his way to fetch Eloin. The beautiful Eloin. Drail would have her. For now at least.

As Sgorr pictured Eloin he felt a strange confusion enter him. It was the closest he had ever come to loving anything in his life. He thought of her sleek fur and her proud muzzle. Of her huge eyes and her bold temper. But as he thought and he tried to picture the two of them together, the vision failed. 'How could she ever want to stand with me?' he said to himself bitterly. With one eye. With no brave antlers to fight his place. But he must have her somehow. Then he hit on it. Eloin's calf. Soon, Eloin, soon. Then he would have revenge for his own ugliness.

Sgorr was shaken from his thoughts by a stag running towards them from across the valley. It was the Draila that Sgorr had sent off from the meeting place.

'Well?' he said as the stag came up to him and bowed. 'Have you found her?'

'No, Captain Sgorr. But a hind over there says she thinks she's beyond the stream.'

'Good. Then let us see.'

Sgorr wheeled round and ran straight for the pasture towards Eloin and Rannoch.

Blindweed was moving restlessly up and down the edge of the stream, trying to scan the valley for signs of movement or for any approaching Draila as Bhreac tried to reassure Eloin.

'Brechin will be all right, my dear,' the kindly old doe was saying, 'you'll see. He hasn't ever been beaten.'

'No,' agreed Eloin nervously. 'I'm sure you're right.'

From the corner of her eye Eloin saw Bracken flinch and the two deer heard the trees on the mountainside rustle.

'A stag,' whispered Eloin. 'Coming down the hill.'

Blindweed had heard it too and was with them again.

'Brechin?' said Bhreac.

The branches parted and, as the deer emerged, Eloin shook her head.

'No,' she sighed sadly as she spied Bandach running towards her. He raced straight over to the group. He was panting heavily and drenched in blood and sweat.

'Forgive me stealing up on you,' said the young stag as he reached them. 'Captain Brechin sent me.'

'Brechin? He's all right?'

Bandach lowered his head.

'No, Eloin, I'm sorry,' he answered. 'The Outriders are gone.'

Eloin began to shake. Her haunches flinched and she walked backwards as Rannoch tried to stay under her soft belly.

'What have they done?' cried Blindweed. 'Stags do not kill each other.'

'Drail has gone mad,' said Bandach. 'He has forbidden Anlach.'

'But he can't.'

'The Draila are everywhere. And Eloin, I have come to warn you. They are coming to take you to Drail.'

'Drail?' cried Eloin. 'Never.'

'It is worse than that,' whispered Bandach, looking down at Rannoch. 'Sgorr. He is coming to kill your calf. I must get you all away.'

Suddenly the terrible sadness that was filling Eloin's heart was swept away. Now all she could think of was saving her fawn. She would gladly die if she had to, but she must protect her little one.

'We will go west over the valley to the next glen,' said Bandach. 'From there into the high mountains. Perhaps even into the High Land itself.'

Bhreac looked fearfully at the hind. To the Low Land deer the High Land was a distant, sinister place, surrounded by legend and fable and cloaked in mystery.

'But the little one,' said Bhreac, 'he'll never survive the journey.'

'We must try. It's his only hope.'

'Yes,' agreed Eloin, 'we must try.'

'It's too late,' cried Blindweed.

Blindweed was looking across the stream. In the distance, no more than thirty trees away, Sgorr and five Draila were hurrying towards them.

'We're lost,' said Bhreac.

'Hush,' snapped Blindweed. 'I've an idea. If only we had more time.'

'If time is all you need,' cried Bandach, 'you shall have it. But hurry with your plan, for Herne's sake.'

Bandach leapt forward on his front haunches and, tossing back his antlers, he splashed through the stream. Up the facing bank he ran and then, bucking and kicking, he shot forward diagonally across Sgorr's path. He was out in the middle of the valley when the Draila spied him and, as he had gambled, the whole group swung away to follow him. Bandach had guessed that Sgorr would not risk depleting his own bodyguard, nor deprive himself of such a prize.

On Bandach sped, with the wind in his ears and anger pumping his heart. He was fast and young and for a while he held them off. But at last the day's terrible exertions and the fight on the hillside began to catch up with him. He slowed and the Draila drew nearer. Then they caught him. He kicked out behind him but an antler caught him in the leg and he tripped. Bandach would never get up again.

Sgorr led the Draila slowly back across the stream. He wanted to savour this moment. As they reached the far verge, he saw Eloin ahead of him, along with the fool of a storyteller Blindweed and an old doe he didn't recognize. From Eloin's shape he knew instantly that she had already calved.

'Eloin,' he said in a silken voice as he ran up. 'I hope you are well.'

'Don't bring your foul, lying tongue here, Sgorr,' spat Eloin, backing away.

'My dear, such manners hardly befit a captain's hind.'

'You'll pay dearly for what you have done, Sgorr.'

'What I have done? Ah, but of course. You've been consorting with traitors and spies. Then you know everything?'

'I know that you have poisoned the herd. I know that you have killed Brechin and the others. I know that you have broken the Lore.'

'That *is* a pity. I had hoped to bring you the news myself.'

'If I had an antler, Sgorr, I would poke out that patch of pondweed you call an eye.'

'Yes. It's understandable you're upset,' said Sgorr softly.

'Perhaps you should be thinking of more pleasant things. Well then, I've a surprise. Drail wants to see you.'

'Drail,' snorted Eloin. 'I'd rather die than stand with that lamehorn.'

Sgorr was mightily pleased, for in his twisted mind he had thought it impossible that Eloin should not be drawn to the Lord of Herds.

'Well,' he said, 'it may only be for a time. There are others who would protect you, and I am young.'

Eloin stared back at Sgorr in disbelief.

'You, Sgorr?' she said. 'You? I'd rather Drail than you in ten thousand years. You'll have to find some other doe to bathe your eye and lick you between the ears.'

The insult was aimed well and Sgorr winced.

'Very well, Eloin. Drail shall have you. But now,' he continued, his voice dropping, 'perhaps you'll introduce me to your new fawn. I bet he's a bold one, if his mother's anything to go by.'

Bhreac cast a terrified glance at Blindweed.

'What do you want with a fawn, Sgorr?' said Eloin. The three deer were trying to move together to shield the fawn behind them.

'Can't a stag show an innocent interest in a new life?'

'No doubt Drail also has an interest in Brechin's buck.'

'So, Eloin, it's a buck. How gratifying. Ah, my dear, but you're wrong. Drail has no interest whatsoever in Brechin's fawn. Now stand aside.'

Sgorr bared his teeth and the Draila around him advanced.

'Very well,' said Eloin coldly, 'you shall meet Brechin's fawn. There . . .'

As Eloin stepped aside Sgorr stopped in his tracks. He was bitterly disappointed.

'Stillborn,' snorted Sgorr with disgust. On the grass by

Eloin's feet was a dead calf, lying limp on the ground. 'A great pity. But we must not let it spoil Drail's triumph. He is waiting for you.'

'I've told you, Sgorr,' whispered Eloin between her teeth, 'I would rather die than run with Drail.'

'Come now. There's no need for histrionics. The Draila will escort you in honour to the Home Oak.'

Sgorr cast a glance at the Draila who immediately moved closer.

Bhreac suddenly stepped between them.

'Don't you lay an antler on her,' cried the old hind. 'What do you want with her anyway? It's not the season.'

'Much has changed in the herd,' said Sgorr, smiling. 'But as for hurting her, they wouldn't dream of it. Shall we go?'

'Never,' cried Eloin. 'And if you refuse to fight me, Sgorr, remember, there are plenty of poisonous plants in the forest. But before I die, Sgorr, I will tell Drail that I have done it because of you. That you wanted me and I couldn't bear to live.'

Sgorr hesitated. Then he smiled cruelly.

'Very well, Eloin. We may not be able to force *you*. But perhaps there are others who you care about.'

'What are you doing? Get off, you brutes,' shouted Bhreac, as two Draila started prodding the old deer with their antlers.

Blindweed tried to come to her aid but two others were on him, forcing him back.

'So you see, Eloin,' continued Sgorr coldly, 'you have a choice.'

'Don't listen, Eloin,' cried Bhreac, bucking at one of the Draila. 'I'm old. I don't care what they do to me.'

Eloin still hesitated and Sgorr spoke again.

'Most touching. But there are others still who can suffer

if you refuse. You there,' said Sgorr turning to the Draila, 'fetch me that hind over there, and her calf.'

Sgorr had spotted the hind called Bracken and the newborn fawn with the snowy back, standing silently at the edge of the forest.

'All right, Sgorr,' said Eloin. 'All right. Leave them alone. They've done you no harm.'

Sgorr looked closely at the beautiful hind.

'And no poison?'

'And no poison.'

'Very well, then.'

'But, Sgorr,' said Eloin, 'you must promise me not to harm Bhreac or Blindweed. They're old. They can do nothing to you.'

Sgorr peered back into Eloin's huge, proud eyes. Again he felt that strange confusion.

'Such tenderness,' he said. 'Perhaps one day I too may hope to receive a little of it myself?'

Eloin's eyes flickered.

'Perhaps,' she nodded bitterly.

'Very well, then. Release them. It is time we were at the Home Oak'.

With that the Draila surrounded Eloin and, with Sgorr at her side, they led her away. As Eloin ran she felt as though her heart was being torn out. To leave little Rannoch with another doe was almost more than she could bear. But then she thought of Brechin and the sadness overwhelmed her.

'There's one thing I swear,' she whispered between her teeth, 'by Herne and by the ancient Lore. I shall never have a calf again.'

As the group were crossing the valley they passed Bandach's body lying still on the bloodied ground. Bandach, who had won them time to take Rannoch over to Bracken.

Time to explain a little of what was happening. Time for Blindweed to drag Bracken's dead fawn to Eloin's side.

'Thank you,' whispered Eloin.

On the meadow two old deer were standing stock-still and a newborn fawn was nuzzling up to a bewildered hind. Bracken shook her head sadly as she watched Eloin being taken away. She had only just learnt the terrible pain of loss that a hind can feel for her young. She looked down at her own dead calf in the grass and quickly looked away.

'I don't understand any of this,' she said softly, but with that she felt a strong, new life tugging at her belly and, though she knew that this little fawn at her milk wasn't her own, she felt the powerful forces of maternal love rising inside her.

'Eloin will be all right, Bracken,' whispered Bhreac.

The old deer turned to Blindweed.

'Come, you old fool,' she said. 'Let's get Bracken and Rannoch away from here. Blindweed. Blindweed?'

But Blindweed wasn't listening.

He was looking at Bracken and the tiny fawn with a smear of mud across his forehead.

'What? What's that you say?' said Bhreac.

'*Changeling child shall be his fate*,' muttered Blindweed. 'It's the Prophecy. The Prophecy.'

3

The Edge of the Trees

Give it an understanding, but no tongue.
William Shakespeare, 'Hamlet'

So autumn came. The bees broke their honeycombs with sweetness and the apple began to drip on the stem, fattening with burrowing grubs that bruised its skin to ochre. Petals fell and, on the stirring earth, turned sickly with their scent until every Lera that understood the seasons caught a warning breath on the breeze.

In a meadow on the edge of the home valley two fawns, little more than four months old, were running through the grass. They had both lost their white spots and their coats were no longer woolly. They tossed their heads gleefully as they ran, full of excitement at being allowed to wander so far from their mothers' sides. But as they came to the bottom of the meadow a third fawn called to them. He too had lost the snow leaves on his back.

'Hey. Wait for me,' he shouted and was preparing to launch himself after them when a grown-up voice called him back.

'Rannoch. Rannoch. Where are you going?' called the hind sternly. It was Bracken.

The calf's ears dropped and he hesitated. Then, dejectedly,

he turned and walked slowly back to his mother who was grazing by some ferns.

'Tain and Thistle are going to the tree stump, Mamma,' said Rannoch, wagging his tail enthusiastically, 'and I want to show them . . .'

The little deer raised his head expectantly.

'Not today, Rannoch,' said Bracken. The hind looked about her nervously.

'The tree stump's a long way off for such little legs and evening isn't so far away. You know I don't like you wandering off.'

'But, Mamma, the other fawns are allowed to play on their own. Why must I always stay so close? It's not fair. Besides, I can look after myself better than most.'

'I'm sure you can, Rannoch. But not today. Do as I ask, my little one, and if you are good I will come down to the tree stump with you tomorrow. Now, why don't you come and suckle?'

'But, Mamma,' protested Rannoch.

But the young deer could see that his mother had made up her mind. He sat down sulkily by her side, thinking all the time of Tain and Thistle playing in the meadow.

A calf will stop suckling between four and nine months old and Rannoch still drank from his mother's milk. He looked at her side now and suddenly felt hungry. But Rannoch was cross and instead of nuzzling in to feed, he laid his head on the ground. After a while Rannoch looked so miserable that Bracken licked his nose.

'Rannoch,' said Bracken, 'you know it's only because I love you.'

'I know, Mother,' answered Rannoch, 'but it's not fair. All the fawns laugh at me because I have to stay at home when they go out to play.'

Bracken gazed down lovingly into Rannoch's eyes and her heart melted.

'Laugh at you, do they? We can't have that, can we? Go on then, but be back before Larn.'

'Oh yes, yes. Thank you. I promise I will,' cried Rannoch and he was about to race away when his mother stopped him again.

'What, Mamma?'

'Before you go, let me look at you.'

Rannoch knew what was coming. He raised his head obediently.

'I thought so,' said Bracken. 'Come over here.'

'Oh, Mother, do I have to?' grumbled Rannoch as he followed her to the trees.

He watched Bracken warily as she plucked some black-berries from a branch in her lips and dropped them onto a small pile of leaves on the ground. Then she squashed them in the cleft of her foot until the berries and the moist leaves had turned to a ruddy brown dye.

'Come here, Rannoch,' said Bracken, scooping some of the mixture onto her tongue.

'But why do you always do this?' said Rannoch as Bracken rubbed the mixture on his forehead, making the fur darker again.

'It's good for you, my little one. It will make you all the more handsome.'

Rannoch shook himself.

'I don't care. I don't like it.'

'You will learn in life, my little one,' said Bracken, 'that grown-ups do things you sometimes may not like. But more often than not it's for your own good. Now run along. Be back before Larn, mind,' she cried as Rannoch tossed his head and raced away.

Rannoch was delighted that his mother had let him go. But he was still furious that he among all the fawns had to put up with the ritual of the berries and so much trouble when he wanted to play. By the time he got halfway down the meadow, though, he had forgotten all his resentment and was so excited he felt his heart would burst. The sun was glittering in the field and in the distance Tain and Thistle were playing by the old tree stump, taking turns to run at it and throw themselves into the air.

'Look out there,' shouted Rannoch as he launched himself across the log and landed right next to the two young friends.

'Rannoch!' cried Tain delightedly. 'We thought you weren't coming.'

'Your mother let you go then,' said Thistle a little unkindly. Thistle was jealous of Rannoch's friendship with Tain. But before long the three fawns were running and skipping across the log and playing happily in the meadow as they felt the wind on their faces and the strength growing in their young legs. It was a good while before Rannoch began to tire of the game and wandered away from the log in the direction of the trees. He stood there gazing into the distance and was soon lost in thought.

'Rannoch,' called Tain, who had just executed what seemed to him a particularly spectacular leap, 'aren't you playing any more? What's wrong?'

'Oh, leave him. He's always dreaming,' said Thistle as he too launched himself over the stump. But Tain was already padding off towards his friend.

'I'm tired of that game,' said Rannoch as the fawns reached him. 'I want to do something else.'

'What?' said Thistle, aimlessly nosing a beetle that he had just seen lumbering through the grass. He turned it over with his muzzle and watched it kick its legs helplessly in the air.

'Don't really know.' Rannoch shrugged. 'Something more adventurous.'

'We could go down to the stream,' suggested Tain.

'And tease the fishes,' added Thistle more enthusiastically. He had just upended the beetle again.

'Boring,' said Rannoch.

'I could make up a story,' suggested Tain.

'No,' said Rannoch. 'I want to do something really fun, like . . . like . . .' Rannoch lowered his voice and looked hard at his two friends. 'Like going into the forest.'

'Rannoch!' said Thistle disapprovingly, losing interest in the beetle which, much relieved, scuttled away under a branch. 'You know we're not allowed into the forest alone. We're still too young.'

'I know, I know. But just think what an adventure it would be.'

Thistle looked nervously at Tain.

'What do you say, Tain?' asked Rannoch, his bright eyes twinkling. The thought of the forest and all its dark places made Tain shudder.

'Oh, I don't know, Rannoch,' he said quietly. 'We really shouldn't. My mother told be never to . . .'

'And mine,' agreed Thistle.

'Yes. Yes. But we could just go into the edge of the trees. Down at the stream by that big oak. I was listening to some bucks the other day and one said he had seen an owl's nest.'

Tain's eyes opened wide.

'Well,' said Rannoch, who had already made up his mind, 'are you coming?'

'But we'll get into trouble,' said Thistle.

But Rannoch was already gone, running back up the hill. Tain and Thistle looked at each other doubtfully.

'Come on then.' Tain shrugged. 'Just to the edge of the trees.'

The three fawns ran as fast as their legs could carry them with Rannoch leading the way, skirting the home valley and the grazing herd. When they came to the edge of the western hill they paused and looked down. Below them was the stream and beyond it the big oak that marked the edge of the forest. They stopped and then raced down towards it. But before they had even reached the stream Rannoch pulled up suddenly and looked around him, startled, his ears standing up and his tail twitching.

'What's wrong?' asked Tain, coming up to his side.

'I don't know,' said Rannoch. 'I feel funny.'

'What you mean,' said Thistle, 'is you've changed your mind.'

'No. I just . . . I don't know what it is. I've never felt like this before.'

'Felt like what?' said Thistle irritably.

'It's a sort of tingling feeling. I can't describe it. It's as though it's inside me and yet it isn't. But I feel, I feel . . .'

'What?' asked Tain, more kindly.

'I feel as if something bad is happening. Something wrong.'

'You're just frightened.' Thistle's thin face looked rather unkind.

With that they heard a sound from beyond the trees to the right, where the stream curled round out of sight. The three fawns walked slowly forward until they caught sight of three more deer by the edge of the water. One of them had his back to the stream. It was a fat little fawn named Bankfoot, who everyone laughed at in the herd because he was so slow and had a stutter. The other two were prickets, young deer with their first heads; single spiked antlers that rose straight above them.

'Oh, it's only Bankfoot,' said Thistle. 'They're just teasing him.'

'Hush,' said Rannoch. 'Listen.'

The two youngsters facing Bankfoot were a year older and considerably bigger. They were pushing forward, nudging Bankfoot with their noses.

'L-l-l-leave me alone,' stammered the terrified little fawn, digging in with his feet and trying to stop them edging him into the water.

'Don't you want to go for a swim?' sneered the oldest. His name was Braggle and he had a reputation for picking on the younger, weaker deer. His friend, whose name was Raggling, grinned stupidly at him.

'N-n-n-no,' said Bankfoot, 'I don't. Go away.'

'N-n-n-no?' mocked Braggle, imitating his stutter. 'But we want to see you float.'

Braggle gave Bankfoot another shove.

'Ow. Stop it, you bully.'

'Bully, eh?'

Braggle pushed Bankfoot again. His hind hoofs were almost in the water now.

'I'll teach you to wander away from your mother,' Braggle continued. 'You're lucky a Draila hasn't caught you. But now I want to see a little ball of fur go bobbing down the stream.'

Braggle was about to bash Bankfoot again when he got the shock of his life. He felt the breath leave his lungs and he found himself sailing through the air. He landed with a great splash right in the middle of the stream and a draught of water went straight up his nose. The stream wasn't deep so he could stand easily, but when Braggle picked himself up, coughing and spluttering, he was drenched and very startled. Raggling watched nervously from the bank. Without his friend he wasn't very brave.

'Pick on someone your own size,' cried Rannoch furiously.

Bankfoot was also startled but Rannoch's eyes were blazing with anger. When Braggle saw the fawn who had just knocked him into the water, he was as furious as he was amazed. Rannoch was nearly half Braggle's size, antlerless and considerably weaker. Braggle walked slowly towards him through the water, trying to look as menacing as possible. But although Rannoch hated fighting, he held his ground.

'Very brave,' said Braggle, 'sneaking up behind me like that. Well, if you don't like me picking on fatty here, perhaps you'd like to go for a swim instead?'

'No, thank you,' answered Rannoch coldly.

'It's Rannoch, isn't it?'

'What's it to you?'

'Nothing. Just that I'd expect a selach to run with a weakling like Bankfoot.'

'And I'd expect a bully like you to pick on a smaller fawn,' said Rannoch, furious and deeply stung by the insult. Selach is the name deer give both to fawns who have no known father and to hinds with no living mate. Even though stags and hinds usually live apart and the hinds have the sole responsibility for rearing the calves, for a fawn not to have a father is a great misfortune and the other fawns were always joking about it. Tain and Thistle were in the same boat in this regard for their fathers had also died that night on the hills. Though Rannoch knew nothing of what had really befallen Brechin, he felt the lack of a father deeply.

'Don't worry,' sneered Braggle, 'I wouldn't dream of bullying Bankfoot now you're here.'

Rannoch gulped. Braggle really was much bigger than

him. But suddenly Braggle hesitated. Then he snorted and turned away.

'Oh come on, Raggling,' he said, 'let's get back. I'm bored with all these selach. Let's leave them to talk about their mothers.'

Rannoch looked round and was relieved to see that Tain and Thistle had come up behind him. Braggle and Raggling could probably have beaten all four of them in a fight but the new arrivals had tipped the odds uncomfortably. Besides, apart from being cold and wet, Braggle really was a coward at heart.

'See you again,' called Braggle in the distance. 'Count on it.'

'C-c-c-coward,' piped Bankfoot after him, but the older deer were gone.

The four fawns stood on the bank for a while, deeply shaken. At last Bankfoot trotted up to Rannoch.

'Th-th-thank you, Rannoch,' he said.

'It's nothing,' answered Rannoch a little coldly. 'But you shouldn't wander off on your own like that. Come on, you two.'

'Rannoch, I don't think we should,' said Tain sheepishly. 'Not today. It's getting late and your mother will be angry. So will mine, for that matter.'

'Yes,' agreed Thistle, 'I should get back too.'

'Fine,' said Rannoch angrily. 'If you're frightened I'll go myself.'

Rannoch turned and trotted off in the direction of the wood.

'I'll g-g-g-go with you, Rannoch,' called Bankfoot.

'You? You should get back to your mother's milk.'

As Rannoch ran he was sorry he had snapped at Bankfoot and he could have done with the company. But he was disappointed with Tain and Thistle, and the business of the berries and Braggle's insult had suddenly made him smart with shame. He was an adventurous little deer but his instincts were always being held in check by Bracken.

At least now I can go exploring, Rannoch thought to himself, and his spirits perked up a little as he stopped by a big oak. The great twisted tree stood just in front of the main line of the forest and its bowl was heavily furred with moss. It branches stretched wide above him and were thickly decked with yellowing oak leaves with their distinctive florid shape. Rannoch looked about him. Behind him the meadow was emptying of deer as the animals returned to the home herd to feed again before Larn. The sunlight was just beginning to fade and Rannoch could smell the evening on the breeze. He looked back past the oak tree and gulped.

The line of the forest stretched right and left as far as Rannoch could see; a wall of mystery. But here the trees were set forward a little and, being mainly oak and elm, they were spaced wider than elsewhere, so that Rannoch could see quite a way back into the gloom. Through the dark webbing of wood and brier the great trunks glinted here and there in the streams of sunlight breaking through the canopy and the pools of colour on the forest floor made the darkness around seem all the more mysterious.

The forest is a place that all young fawns dream about, especially when their herd, like this one, is a not a woodland herd and is used to grazing in the open. Rannoch was powerfully drawn to it as a place of enchantment, of danger and of wonder. The forest is said to be Herne's home. With small fawns like Rannoch the hinds are careful not to let them wander in the forest on their own, for they know the dangers to a very young fawn if he should get lost in the treacherous shadows of the trees.

But Rannoch was thinking of none of this now as he edged closer to a trail of trodden leaves that cut through a blackberry bush and swung into the wood. He had forgotten his mother's strict prohibition and was thinking only of finding an owl's nest. As his nose edged into shadow he paused again. His legs were trembling violently. Plucking up his courage, the little fawn disappeared into the gloom.

Rannoch would remember that moment for ever. He had been into the trees before, but that was with Bracken. Now, all alone, he felt like he was stepping to the edge of the adult world. Suddenly the air was thick around him and the great tree trunks reared up like giant antlers. The fawn's senses came alive as he drank in the strange scents of decaying wood, leaves and moist earth. He felt the ground damp and springy under his hoofs and the air rich and warm around him.

He walked very slowly, knowing instinctively that he had to stay on the path and peering about him as his eyes adjusted to the dappled light. Around him he heard new and wonderful sounds and flinched nervously as a bird fluttered in its nest or a squirrel that had been watching him from under a branch shot round the top of it and darted up a trunk. It seemed as if the leaves on the forest floor were alive as the ground rustled and crackled with insects and animals.

Then Rannoch froze as he heard it for the first time. The hollow, melancholy hoot of an owl high up in the branches ahead. The other fawns would be green with envy, thought Rannoch eagerly to himself as he pressed on down the path. He kept looking down as he went, to make sure that he stayed on the trail. Luckily the owl's call was taking the fawn in the right direction.

It got darker as he padded along, for the canopy was getting heavier now and the dying sunlight could no longer penetrate the tangle of leaves that festooned the boughs. Rannoch blinked in the gathering gloom but he was too caught up in his quest to notice that the ground under him was beginning to change as the trail veered away to the left. His eyes were locked on the tree trunks above as he was drawn on by the sound of the owl, hooting loudly to welcome in the evening.

Rannoch's heart jumped as he spotted a shape on a branch above. It was a young tawny owl perched far out on the end of a branch, hallooing to himself as his huge, imperial eyes guarded his secret bower. 'Hoo Hoo, what's this?' said the owl to himself as he spied Rannoch below. But even if the owl had been able to speak Rannoch's language, the tawny was hungry and in no mood to talk, so instead he opened his wings and lifted himself off his branch. He swooped down right over Rannoch's head and circled him three times before disappearing into the trees beyond.

'Hello there,' shouted Rannoch delightedly as he ducked and span round. 'Come back.'

But the owl was gone. Rannoch shrugged. Although they'd probably never believe him, at least he'd be able to tell the others he had seen a real owl. And in the middle of the forest too. Rannoch suddenly realized that it must be close to Larn. He should have been home long ago. He turned to retrace his steps but when he looked down, the track had vanished. Instead he was surrounded by trees, tall and dark and all looking very much the same.

Rannoch was filled with the desire to run, run as fast as his legs could carry him, back to Bracken and the home herd. He felt fear bubbling up inside his stomach and his tail quivered as he peered around him.

'I recognize that branch,' said Rannoch out loud, and he started as his voice echoed round the trees. He looked around him and then, convincing himself that he did indeed recognize a tree, he set off in the wrong direction.

As Rannoch walked the trees seemed to get thicker. He was scratched by thorns and very soon he wanted to give up. But he kept going. At one point he came to a tiny clearing in the canopy above and his spirits fell even further as he looked up to see that the blue was turning inky and the stars were pricking through the sky. Later on he started and bolted when he stumbled on a grass snake uncurling its smooth body in the brown undergrowth.

Eventually Rannoch came to a second and larger clearing and here he paused to collect himself and beat down the fear that kept threatening to overwhelm him. The little calf sat down in the soft leaves and looked around him. In the sky above, the moon had come up and its ghostly light cast long, quivering shadows through the trees. Rannoch lowered his head dejectedly, laid his muzzle on the ground and closed his eyes. But as he did so he scented the earth and he was up again, wide awake, alert and quivering. Rannoch sniffed the earth again and then he was sure. The thick, cloying animal scent lay freshly on the ground, a mixture of deer and cat. Rannoch had scented a fox.

The fawn had never actually seen fox but he and Bracken had been coming back to the home valley one day, after a short excursion away from the herd, when his mother had picked up a scent at the bottom of the meadow. It was an old spore and faint but Bracken had made sure that Rannoch remembered it. Now, here in the wood, the odour was ten times more powerful. Rannoch looked around and he could see immediately that the leaves had been disturbed where the animal, only a little while before, had been scuffling for food. The fawn's eyes cast fearfully around him.

He was trying to spy any movement in the trees, but he

could see nothing beyond the pool of moonlight that encircled him. Yet, in his mind's eye, he could already see the face of some terrible beast, snarling in the darkness, its teeth and red eyes glinting, as it advanced on him.

Rannoch froze as he heard it. Not five antlers away. A rustle from a clump of bushes right in front of him and the sound of an animal moving slowly towards him. Rannoch began to shake uncontrollably and his legs nearly gave way. He backed away in the clearing till his haunches where pressed against an old log, and there the fawn waited, his ears lowered helplessly, his body quaking. The fox was closing in.

Rannoch's terrified eyes opened wide with horror as he saw the bush ahead of him quiver and part and then the animal step clean into the middle of the clearing.

'Bankfoot!' cried Rannoch joyfully, as the fat little fawn nearly tripped over a branch in front of him.

'Bankfoot. What on earth are you doing here?'

Bankfoot stood blinking in the moonlight as Rannoch ran up to him. He was obviously just as terrified as Rannoch.

'R-r-rannoch,' he said, hardly able to contain his relief. 'I've found you. I've been l-l-looking for ages and ages.'

'Bankfoot. You gave me the fright of my life. I thought you were a fox.'

'F-f-fox?' stammered the petrified fawn, and he started trembling all over again. The sight of a fawn more frightened than himself made Rannoch feel stronger and he was mighty glad to see the little deer. But Rannoch realized they were still in danger.

'A fox has been in this clearing,' he said in a very grown-up voice, 'so we'd better get moving.'

'Y-y-yes,' said Bankfoot, amazed at how Rannoch knew a fox had been by.

'Well then, what are you waiting for?'

Rannoch led Bankfoot out of the moonlight back into the trees. If he had only known what was best he would have stayed in the clearing. They could see better there, there were lots of warm leaves to snuggle up in and the fox, who had indeed been rooting there for food, would not return that night. He had nosed a brailah and was now hunting it down a shallow gully nearly quarter of a mile away. Soon Rannoch and Bankfoot were completely bewildered again, lost in the wood as the night came in and the branches echoed with strange and threatening sounds.

The two fawns were quickly exhausted and at last, by the edge of an elm where the whispering breezes that made it this far into the forest to sift and stir the earth had heaped a pile of soft leaves against the bowl, Rannoch and Bankfoot stopped. They were too tired and frightened to go on but at least they had left the scent of the fox behind. So they lay down on the bed of leaves and curled up, their necks resting on each other's warm sides. They closed their frightened eyes and drifted into a darkness that was hardly less menacing than the world around them.

Rannoch had a strange dream that night. He was again in a clearing, but a clearing three times the size of the place where he had smelt the fox. All around were huge oak trees, knotted and twisted with age, and a breeze was blowing, making the dry leaves rustle and sigh like water. Rannoch knew, as dreamers know, that it was night-time and yet the forest was lit by a strange light. Then something was coming towards the fawn.

But Rannoch wasn't frightened. Instead he felt a deep calm as a huge deer stepped into the clearing towards him. He was larger than any deer that Rannoch had ever seen and his antlers rose proud and terrible above him. As the fawn stood there the stag began to talk to him. His voice

was deep and thunderous but Rannoch couldn't understand
him. Then the wind began to rise in the trees and the leaves
swirled and flurried across the forest floor so that the whole
wood seemed to be talking to Rannoch and saying just one
thing: 'Listen.'

Rannoch woke with a start. Bankfoot was still asleep,
stirring restlessly beside him. His tail twitched nervously in
his dream and Rannoch could sense the fear that was still
with him. It was dark in the forest but as Rannoch sniffed
the air he realized that he could smell the morning not far
off and the small patches of sky he glimpsed through the
canopy above him were paling. The fawn got up and shook
himself.

'Bankfoot. Bankfoot,' he said softly, 'wake up.'

The fat little fawn stirred and opened his eyes.

'R-r-rannoch. It's you. I thought Mamma . . .'

'No,' said Rannoch kindly, 'but come on. We should get
moving.'

The two fawns set off again and soon felt in better spirits,
for their sleep had refreshed them and, as the morning came
on, the forest grew lighter. After a time they even started to
play where the trees opened. They invented a new game that
involved running as fast as they could at the leaves heaped
on the forest floor and bowling round and round in the
scattering foliage. They even played hide and seek, until they
lost each other for longer than either of them liked.

By midday though, the forest was a much more welcoming
place. The canopy above them had thinned again and in the
bright sun the trees began to glow gold and red about them.
As they went they saw many wonderful things. Rannoch
stumbled on a family of red squirrels collecting acorns for
the winter, some of which they dropped on his head furiously
as they scuttled up a tree. Bankfoot discovered how many

secrets lie on the forest floor and his nose soon became skilled at overturning logs and branches where the startled woodlice and beetles, busy at autumn burrowing, would duck away into deeper crevices to hide themselves from the light.

They came on a stream which gargled sulkily as it pressed through the trees, its muddy course nearly choked with leaves and earth. Here they spotted a stoat dipping its sleek black nose to drink. Its tongue, that seemed nearly as long as its snout, slipped out to lap the brackish water and its whiskers twitched in the dry air. When the stoat spotted them on the other bank and bared its bright, white teeth and pink gums, fear took them both by the throat, making their stomachs churn and their legs shake and freezing them to the spot. But the stoat had little ones to feed and two fawns were too much for her, so she darted away into the undergrowth.

By the afternoon Rannoch and Bankfoot were less happy again. Bankfoot had a stomach-ache from drinking from the stream and both fawns were desperately hungry. They were walking dejectedly through an avenue of silver birch trees when Bankfoot stopped, horrified.

'Look,' he said, staring blankly at a mossy tree stump.

Rannoch peered down at the stump and his heart sank too. He recognized the speckled red mushroom in its middle. They had passed this very same spot before.

'We're going in circles,' cried Rannoch.

The fawns pressed on in a new direction but by the time twilight came to the wood and the darkness crept out again from behind the trees, the fawns' spirits were failing. Bankfoot kept talking and telling jokes, for the little fawn was naturally cheerful, but Rannoch was deeply worried at the prospect of spending another night in the forest.

Rannoch was leading Bankfoot through a dense tangle of trees when he suddenly stopped and his ears came up.

'W-w-what is it?' said Bankfoot.

'Hush,' whispered Rannoch. 'Look.'

The two deer peered through the thicket. Ahead of them, below a great sycamore, they saw a very rare sight in the wood. It was a family of badgers venturing out of their set for the evening. The father badger was snuffling out of his hole. He stopped as his great black and white head emerged and sniffed the air. Then his podgy body came out. He shuffled around the tree and when he thought that the coast was clear, he returned to the hole and called to his wife. A pretty female badger popped out and then two cubs, no bigger than large hedgehogs. They sniffed and snorted round the tree, then the parents stopped and started talking to each other urgently. They seemed to be arguing.

'I w-w-w-wish we could speak their language,' said Bankfoot in Rannoch's ear. 'Then we might have asked them the way.'

'Ssssh,' whispered Rannoch. 'They'll hear you.'

Badgers are famously shy and the presence of another animal would surely have sent them lumbering back into their set. But then something very strange happened. As Rannoch and Bankfoot strained to understand what the badgers were saying, Rannoch felt a tingling in his body. It was just like the feeling he had had on the hill, only this time he didn't sense that anything was wrong. A breeze had come up and the high canopy above rustled and quivered and seemed to be talking with a voice from Rannoch's dream. As the fawn listened to the badgers, his eyes opened in amazement for, though their tongue was different, he realized he could understand what they were saying.

'No, no, no, my dear,' the father badger scolded. 'That fox may be about.'

'But we promised the little ones we'd show them the meadow,' said the mother badger.

'Oh yes, Papa,' cried one of the baby badgers, 'please do take us.'

'Well, really, I don't know,' continued the father badger. 'Besides we should be collecting food. The larder's low and winter isn't far off.'

'But we could just go for a little while,' said his wife. 'We can pick up the trail over there, behind the big log. It runs straight to the edge of the trees. We can just go and have a peek and be back well before morning.'

'Well, maybe,' muttered her husband.

But suddenly the badgers turned and looked behind them.

Bankfoot had sneezed.

When the father badger spoke again it was to hurry his wife and little ones back to the set. He snarled like a cat as he backed down the hole but Rannoch found he could no longer understand him.

'I'm v-v-v-very sorry, Rannoch,' said Bankfoot when they had gone.

But Rannoch wasn't really listening. He was still wondering at what had just happened.

'Rannoch, are you all right?'

Rannoch shook himself and nodded.

'Yes. I'm fine. Now, we should get on.'

'It's all very w-w-well for you to say, but where shall we go? We're l-l-lost, remember.'

'Over there,' said Rannoch, pushing into the open, 'behind that tree stump. There's a trail.'

'Don't be s-s-silly,' said Bankfoot. 'How do you know?'

Rannoch looked at him but for some reason thought

better of telling Bankfoot what had just happened. He didn't understand it himself.

'I just feel it, that's all,' he said and trotted past the badger's set to the log. But when the fawns reached it Bankfoot was amazed to see a narrow track, largely obscured by leaves, stretching right and left through the forest.

'But h-h-h-how?' stammered Bankfoot.

'Luck. Come on.'

'Which way?'

Rannoch hesitated.

'Down here,' he said at last, turning left.

This was a guess, for the badgers had said nothing about the direction of the trail. But this time Rannoch had chosen right and soon the fawns found themselves running through the wood as fast as their legs could carry them. The trees began to thin, the canopy opened and at last they passed the edge of the trees and found themselves at the bottom of the meadow where the stream turned west under a bright sky flecked with stars.

'Hooray for Rannoch,' cried Bankfoot, jumping high in the grass.

'Stop fooling, Bankfoot. We'd better hurry. You know what they'll say.'

As the two friends reached the edge of the valley where the home herd were settling in to ruminate again in the evening, they saw two hinds racing towards them. It was Bracken and Canisp, Bankfoot's mother, a pretty hind with large dappled ears. The anger on their faces as they approached made the two fawns stop in their tracks and lower their tails.

'You bad fawn. Where have you been?' cried Canisp as she ran up, but she could hardly disguise the relief on her face.

'Oh M-m-mother, Mother, Rannoch pushed Br-Br-Braggle into a stream because he was bullying me,' cried Bankfoot, releasing all the tension that had built up inside him in one go, 'and I followed him into the forest as the others didn't want to go and he thought I was a f-f-fox and we got lost and slept in some leaves and we saw squirrels and a stoat and badgers and then Rannoch knew where the trail was, though he couldn't have known and . . . and here we are.'

'The forest,' said Canisp sternly as Bankfoot tried to nuzzle under her belly to suckle. 'Well, my young fawn, I shall have something to say about that. Now, run along with you, it's way past your bedtime.' She gave Bankfoot a buffet with her muzzle and drove him off across the valley.

'Goodbye, R-r-rannoch,' called Bankfoot as he ran, 'I know we'll be friends.'

Rannoch stood silently waiting for his mother to speak as the hind glared down at him.

'Well?' she said at last.

'I'm sorry, Mamma,' said Rannoch, lowering his head. 'I didn't mean any harm. It's just that . . . I've never had an adventure before.'

Bracken shook her muzzle and licked the little fawn lovingly on the nose.

'Well, you certainly seem to have had one now,' she said. But then Bracken's eyes grew worried again.

'You could have been killed. You know that, don't you? You must promise me never, ever to do anything like that again.'

'I promise, Mother.'

'Very well, then. Now it's high time we were back.'

The two deer set off, trotting slowly across the meadow. But as they went Rannoch turned to Bracken.

'Mamma,' he whispered, 'can I play with Bankfoot tomorrow?'

Bracken looked down at the little fawn. Again she meant to be angry, but his eyes were too bright to resist.

'We'll see,' she said softly. 'We'll see.'

4

Flight

The wolf that follows, the fawn that flies.
A.C. Swinburne, 'Atalanta in Calydon'

Rannoch's punishment was to stay within Bracken's sight for nearly a quarter of a moon's cycle. It felt like an eternity to the little deer. After that he was under strict orders to return to her side well before Larn every evening. In fact, this now applied to all the calves, for there was trouble in the herd, and two suns after Rannoch's adventure Drail imposed a curfew on the Herla. It was near Anlach and the stags were restless. The blood was rising in the stags and with no natural outlet and no potential challenge to the Lord of the Herd, they were on edge.

The hinds felt it too and became very agitated. That autumn, when the hills should have been resounding with the warning bark of rutting stags and the crack and scrape of antlers, the home valley was eerily quiet. The stags were still beginning to establish their harems and make their stands with their mates, but when the strongest deer with the finest antlers would normally have won out, now the Draila would gang up with one another to win and hold mates. Sgorr himself, who, without antlers, probably would have won no mate, had chosen seven hinds. They were forced to stay near him at the Home Oak.

Sensing the unrest, the Draila, whose ranks had swollen considerably and now comprised nearly a third of the herd, also became more officious in their duties. They patrolled everywhere and any sign of dissent was dealt with ruthlessly. Sgorr took a keen interest in the punishments and his horn-less presence became more and more feared as his authority grew and grew. Meanwhile Drail's personal power was spreading even further afield. That autumn over seven herd lords had come to pay him homage and now wherever he went he insisted on being styled Lord of Herds.

Yet the most horrible aspect of the new regime was the new schools for the fawns. Normally young deer learn on the hoof with their mothers or when they gather after Larn to listen to the old tales and the Lore. But Blindweed's stories had finally been banned and there was no talk of Herne in the herd now. Instead the young deer were forced to gather in the mornings and members of the Draila would address them. They would teach the need for discipline in all things and for respect for the Draila, and tell them stories of the strength, prowess and goodness of Lord Drail, 'Protector of Herla'. And every story was sure to include some stirring reference to Sgorr.

At these 'schools' the fawns were also taught to show absolute loyalty to the Draila, even above their parents. Indeed they were encouraged to spy on their parents 'for the good of the herd' and report suspect conversations to Sgorr's agents. This meant mostly spying on their mothers who looked after them. But, although stags and hinds separate, hinds will show a keen interest in the affairs of their mates for a long while after Anlach and so news of the stags too was quickly relayed back to the Draila. A new group was

formed for the older male prickets which was styled the
Drailing, and every day they would march up and down
the meadow in neat lines singing a special song. It went like
this:

> *Deer are we, we cannot fail,*
> *Born to serve the herd and Drail,*
> *Fearing neither cold nor thaw,*
> *We follow in the slots of Sgorr.*
>
> *Bowing to the Draila's call,*
> *Deer that never trip or fall,*
> *Discipline will set us free,*
> *We swear eternal loyalty.*

Mistrust was rife for the spying of fawn on hind and buck
was working on the herd like a poison. Soon no deer trusted
another and hinds were so frightened of saying anything in
front of their children that even the young calves began to
run riot. If a hind dared to scold or discipline a pricket she
faced the threat of being reported for criticizing the Drailing.

The only exceptions to this general atmosphere of hatred
and mistrust were among the selach, the single hinds with
young fawns and no living mate in the herd. This group
included Bracken and Canisp, as well as Tain and Thistle's
mothers, Shira and Alyth. There were about twenty such
hinds in all and they usually kept together. Not all their stags
had died in the battle that terrible night. Bankfoot's father
for instance had been lost to a wolf that spring, but most of
the hinds' stags had been among the Outriders. Although it
was forbidden to speak that name in the herd now, the other
stags knew it and it made them reluctant to look among the
selach for a mate.

But the selach generally had a better time of it than the

other deer, although Bracken was in constant fear for Rannoch. The timid hind had told him nothing of his real mother nor of the strange fawn mark on his brow, which she went on concealing with the mixture of leaves and berries. She hardly knew why she did it, for she understood little of Blindweed's strange mumblings. But she did realize that it was better if the little fawn didn't stand out in any way.

Blindweed had shown her how to make the dye and, every now and then, the old deer would visit the hind and her fawn and nod gravely as he watched Rannoch grow. Rannoch and the others were too young to enter the Drailing and, although it was very dangerous, Blindweed made sure that Rannoch and the other selach heard some of the old tales. He was especially interested to hear of Rannoch's adventure in the forest and kept asking the calf questions he didn't understand until Bhreac told him to shut up. Old Bhreac was a favourite among the selach and she often acted as nursemaid to the fawns. Blindweed and Bhreac were often seen arguing together but the two old Herla had grown very fond of one another and spent many hours grazing in the meadow.

Then there was Eloin. The night she had gone away with Sgorr, Eloin had pined for Brechin and Rannoch and grown so sick at heart that Drail thought she would die. But then something stirred in the doe's heart and she grew well again, as well as any hind could, that is, who longs for her little calf. When normally she would have mated again and then returned to the hinds, the Draila made sure that she stayed close to the Home Oak. That Anlach Drail had tried to mate with her without success. But whereas the other hinds in his harem had all been dismissed, Eloin alone was kept constantly at Drail's side. The hinds in the herd thought this very strange and Eloin could often be seen pacing the hillside and running up to the hillock where Brechin had died, to look out eagerly across the Herla, scouring the valley in the hope of spying Rannoch.

So, in the home herd, autumn grew old. The deer smelt the scent of winter on the wind and huddled together for warmth. The branches in the forest thinned and the meadow was covered in brittle leaves that drifted and churned across the ground, stirred by the winds that came down from the north. When the deer went down to the stream to drink and dipped their tongues in the water, they tasted ice on their lips and muttered together gravely, for they realized that the winter hurrying down from the mountains would be harsh and cruel.

It was late autumn when Bracken finally relented and allowed Rannoch greater rein to wander further from her side. It was one of those bright, cold days when the sunshine seems to turn the sky to liquid light and everything is filled with a restless expectation that Rannoch, Tain and Bankfoot set off to play by the top of the stream.

'W-w-w-wait for me,' panted Bankfoot, trying to keep up with the two fawns as they ran across the meadow. They had become firm friends and now spent most of their time together.

'Come on, then,' laughed Rannoch as the calf padded up to them.

'Well then, what shall we do?' asked Rannoch.

'Let's go to the lake,' said Tain.

They all agreed this was a fine idea and set off up the meadow to the lake. It wasn't really a lake but a place where the stream was widest as it entered the valley and hit a patch of soft gravel below a high, flat rock. A pool had formed where the ground fell away to the right and here the fawns loved to stand and watch the little fishes as they darted and shimmered back and forth among the long reeds.

When the three friends arrived they were delighted to see that the pool was swollen with rain from the hills and the stream was dancing and gurgling over the stones. The fawns skipped around the side of the pool in the sunlight, crying out as they spotted a fish or tiptoeing as close to the water as they could without falling in. They had been at this game for a while when Tain stopped them. He had heard something.

A group of deer were coming down the valley, singing as they went. Their song ended with the Drailing's familiar chant, 'We *swear eternal loyalty*'. Suddenly a group of ten prickets came into view and marched straight up to the youngsters at the pond.

'H-ALT,' cried the fawn at their head and the deer came to a stop. Rannoch shivered when he saw who it was. Braggle had just been promoted into the Drailing.

'I told you we'd meet again,' said Braggle as he saw Rannoch. 'I see fatty still expects you to protect him.'

'You just sh-sh-shut up,' stammered Bankfoot.

'Oh dear,' sneered Braggle, 'we w-w-will have to teach you all some manners, w-w-won't we?'

He turned to the assembled prickets.

'Drailing!' he shouted.

The battle was a brief one. Rannoch, Tain and Bankfoot fought hard but these prickets were much bigger and they were outnumbered by more than three to one. They kicked and buffeted the Drailing and many of them went home that day with black eyes and bruised ribs. But at the end of it Tain and Bankfoot had been subdued, while Rannoch was surrounded by five prickets. He was badly shaken.

'Not so bold now, eh?' said Braggle. 'And now I owe you.'

With that Braggle and the Drailing began to push the fawn towards the pool. The lip of the pool on this side was raised about three antlers above the water and Rannoch gulped as he looked down. But rather than allowing himself to be pushed in, Rannoch suddenly turned and, lashing out with his hind hoofs, one of which caught a Drailing on the muzzle, the little fawn dived head first into the pool. He hit the cold water with a splash and went down. His little legs kicked as he sank and his body span round and round as the startled fish shot away to hide in the reeds.

Down he went and the icy water rushed in around him, filling his nostrils and stinging his eyes. Rannoch hit the bottom but instinctively he pushed upwards with his legs and rose again towards the sunlight. His head broke the surface and he gasped desperately for air. But the life-giving breath was quickly swamped by water that made him choke as he went down again. Fawns do not naturally like water and Rannoch had no idea how to swim. He kicked again with his legs and this time the rhythm became more even and he started to paddle. Rannoch's head broke the surface again and he managed to stay up, coughing and spluttering violently. Braggle waited just long enough to see him emerge a second time.

'Now that's a real soaking,' he called delightedly. 'Don't you forget it.'

Highly pleased with himself, Braggle marched the prickets off down the meadow, singing as they went.

When they had gone Tain and Bankfoot ran over to the pool where Rannoch had managed to swim to the edge. Now he was climbing the bank where the ground shelved upwards, sneezing and shaking himself furiously.

'Rannoch. Rannoch. Are you all right?' shouted Tain. 'We thought you would drown.'

'I'm fine,' spluttered Rannoch. In truth he was furious, but it was only his pride that had really been hurt.

'But that Braggle,' snorted the bedraggled calf as he dripped onto firm ground. 'Just you wait. Tain, Bankfoot, what's the matter?'

Tain and Bankfoot were staring at Rannoch in amazement. The little fawns looked at each other wonderingly, their eyes as big as dandelions.

'R-r-rannoch,' stammered Bankfoot, 'your forehead.'

'What's wrong with my forehead?' said Rannoch irritably. 'It's wet, that's all.'

'No,' said Tain. 'There.'

'What are you talking about?' said Rannoch and he turned back to the pond.

The fawn looked down and tried to see his reflection in the surface. The image was broken at first but then, in the sunlight, the water grew still again and Rannoch's eyes opened wide with confusion. In the middle of his forehead, where the drenching he had just received had washed away Bracken's dye of berries and leaves, there was a patch of pure white felt in the shape of a leaf.

'It's like an oak leaf,' whispered Tain.

'W-w-what does it mean?' stammered Bankfoot, also gazing down into the water.

'I don't know,' said Rannoch quietly, but he felt strange all over and his body was tingling. Rannoch was afraid.

But Tain came to the rescue.

'Come on,' he said sensibly, 'Bracken will tell us what it is.'

Rannoch nodded and together the three fawns set off back to the home herd.

As they left a shadow fell across the surface of the pool and the head and antlers of a young stag shivered on the water. On the flat stone above, from the hiding place where he had seen everything, a Draila's steady gaze followed the young fawns across the meadow. Then, turning away and trotting down the hill, the deer suddenly surged forward and raced towards Sgorr and the Home Oak.

Bracken was petrified when she saw Rannoch returning between Tain and Bankfoot with his strange fawn mark open to the world. She shepherded them straight over to a thicket, away from the herd, scolding and cajoling them all the while. Luckily, so close to winter, the herd were too busy feeding to have noticed the three fawns coming up the valley, let alone pay any attention to a fawn with a white fawn mark on his forehead. Bracken had secreted a store of leaves and berries ready for the winter and, as the three fawns watched, she began pawing the ground, preparing the mixture.

'There,' she said at last when she had rubbed it onto Rannoch's forehead. 'That's better. You gave me such a fright.'

Rannoch suddenly realized why his mother had put him through the ritual of the berries, but he was too bewildered to speak. Bankfoot was the first to pluck up his courage.

'B-b-bracken. W-w-w-why must he cover it up?'

Bracken looked down at Bankfoot and tried to smile.

'Because, my dear, times are bad in the herd right now. So it's best, that's all. It's a special mark and some deer might not like it. They might be jealous.'

'Do you mean the Draila?' whispered Tain.

'Yes.' Bracken nodded. 'And others. It's better that Rannoch looks just like you and me.'

At the mention of a special mark Bankfoot looked at his friend with a new wonder.

'But I think it's very f-f-f-fine,' he said.

'Yes,' said Bracken, 'it's very fine. But it doesn't mean that Rannoch is different in any way. You must listen to what I say and you must promise me that you won't breathe a word of this to another Herla. It'll be our secret.'

The fawns stared back at Bracken nervously, but they understood the seriousness in the hind's voice.

'We promise,' they said.

'Good. Now run along the both of you. It'll be Larn soon and your mothers will be wondering where you are.'

Bracken led Rannoch up the valley to a patch of mossy heather near the other grazing selach and the hind lay down. Rannoch lay next to her, rested his little head on her flank and closed his eyes. Bracken began to ruminate, chewing steadily as she gazed ahead. As she munched, her eyes were thoughtful and very grave.

'My poor Rannoch,' whispered Bracken softly, 'you don't understand any of this, do you?'

Bracken looked down at Eloin's fawn. In truth neither did she. But Bracken had been right to waste no time in covering the fawn mark. As soon as Sgorr heard the news of a Herla with a white oak leaf on his forehead, he sent orders that the fawn be found and brought to him immediately. Members of the Draila were already moving through the valley, searching for the strange deer. The hinds shook their heads in bewilderment as the stags moved among them, prodding their frightened calves and glaring down into their faces.

Deer are naturally superstitious, so the news of an oak leaf was soon moving through the valley like wildfire. But nowhere they went could the Draila find evidence of the calf, and after a while the young captain who had reported it

himself began to worry he had been mistaken. Two Draila
reached Bracken and Rannoch at Larn. But Bracken shook
her head and, seeing nothing out of the ordinary about the
fawn at her side, the Draila moved on. The hind got up
immediately and led Rannoch through the grazing selach to
an old deer standing on her own.

'I've heard,' whispered the kindly old doe as the two came
up. 'How is the little one?'

'He's fine. For the moment,' said Bracken. 'But Bhreac.
We must do something. It won't be long before the secret's
out.'

Bhreac nodded.

'Perhaps we should go,' she said. 'Blindweed is always
saying that if Rannoch's secret is known we should get away
from here. With what has been happening in the herd he
may be right. I don't understand anything of this prophecy
but I know that Drail and Sgorr wouldn't hesitate to harm
a fawn. But where can we go? Winter is here already and
the stags will be faster than a hind, a fawn and an old doe.'

Bracken was touched that Bhreac was so ready to go with
them.

'We must go into the mountains,' she said half-heartedly.
'Into the High Land, as Bandach said. It's the only place
where Drail won't be able to find us. But whatever we do,
we must do it soon.'

'Three deer travelling alone in winter will be easy prey,'
said Bhreac gravely.

Bracken shivered.

'What's wrong, Mamma?' asked Rannoch. 'Why do we
have to go?'

'Hush, my dear,' whispered Bhreac. 'Your mother and I
are trying to think.'

'Perhaps some of the others might come with us,' said

Bracken hopefully. 'There's Canisp and Shira. They've talked about leaving the herd.'

Rannoch's ears perked up, for that meant Tain and Bankfoot too.

'No, my dear,' said Bhreac gently, 'we cannot endanger any of the others. Besides, seven deer would be easier to follow than three. No, we must go alone.'

Bracken nodded, though she was disappointed and terrified of the journey that now faced her and the calf.

'Don't worry, Mamma,' said Rannoch, shaking his tail, 'I'll be with you.'

'Bravely spoken, little one,' said Bhreac. 'And so you shall.'

Bhreac lowered her head and licked Rannoch on the ears but when she looked at Bracken her old eyes were grave.

'I wish I knew where Blindweed was,' she sighed. 'He may be an old fool, but he would tell us what to do.'

At that very moment Blindweed was being escorted towards the Home Oak. Five Draila had been sent to fetch the storyteller and bring him before the Lord of Herds. The old stag tossed his head and snorted angrily as the Draila pushed and prodded him up the hill and kept grumbling that he had never been treated so badly in his life. By the time they reached the Home Oak Blindweed was seething with indignation. Sgorr was at the tree, standing beside Drail and ten stags who formed Drail's inner bodyguard. Eloin was there too and she flashed the old deer a terrified look as he approached. He knew immediately that something was wrong.

'Blindweed. It is good of you to come,' said Drail benevolently. 'It is so long since we have seen you at the Home Oak.'

Blindweed lowered his antlers.

'The lord is kind,' he answered coldly, 'but I fear you have little need of my services.'

'Not at all,' said Sgorr. 'But we have been busy and you know how it is.'

Blindweed nodded slowly.

'I know how it is. How may I be of service to the lord?'

'Blindweed, Lord Drail finds he misses your stories and your wisdom,' said Sgorr slyly, 'and this evening we would listen to the Lore again.'

'You surprise me,' said Blindweed, looking nervously at Eloin. 'In the herd it is dangerous to speak of such things.'

Eloin's eyes were fixed on Blindweed's now.

'My dear Blindweed. You must understand that for some of the deer it is better not to fill their heads with strange stories that frighten and confuse them. They just wouldn't understand. But among deer like ourselves, it's different. Now Drail would be entertained.'

'Very well. A story of Starbuck, or of Herne, perhaps?'

'Later. I myself am very fond of the fawn's tales. But first we would hear the Prophecy.'

Eloin's body flinched and she almost started, but Blindweed showed no emotion.

'The Prophecy,' he said blankly. 'Why should Lord Drail want to hear that old thing? There are far better tales to while away an evening and much less silly ones at that. The first stone for instance, when Herne came down—'

'Blindweed,' said Sgorr less gently. 'The Prophecy, if you please.'

Blindweed was desperately trying to think of some way out but it was obvious that he could not avoid reciting. So he began slowly, falteringly and as he spoke on the hill even

Sgorr shivered. But when he had finished Sgorr came forward and peered at him coldly.

'My dear Blindweed. It was well spoken. But haven't you missed some of it out?'

'I may have done. It is very old and there are many verses.'

'Indeed,' said Sgorr. 'But I distinctly remember a part about a fawn mark.'

Blindweed had indeed left out this verse but now he feared it would give too much away to hold back any longer. All he wanted to do was find out whether they had captured Rannoch already.

'Oh yes,' he said, 'there is. But that is not usually considered a part of the proper poem. But if the Lord of Herds—'

'The Lord of Herds wishes it,' said Sgorr.

'Very well. Now, let me see, how does it go?

> 'On his brow a leaf of oaken,
> Changeling child shall be his fate.
> Understanding words strange spoken,
> Chased by anger, fear and hate.'

As he finished Blindweed could see that Eloin was shivering. Afraid that she would betray herself, he snorted loudly and addressed Sgorr again.

'There. Just a bit of old nonsense. I much prefer the story about Herne's golden hoofs. When I was a young deer I used—'

'Silence!' cried Sgorr suddenly. 'Blindweed, tell me what you know of a fawn in the herd with an oaken mark on his forehead.'

Blindweed blinked, but it was clear to him now that Sgorr was only probing and that Rannoch was still safe. How it had been discovered, Blindweed could not guess.

'A white leaf?' said the old stag, feigning surprise. 'Impossible. I would have heard about it.'

Sgorr looked hard at Blindweed. He felt sure that if any deer knew of the whereabouts of the fawn it would be the storyteller. Sgorr knew that the deer couldn't be one of the older fawns, for all the fawns over a year old had to enter the Drailing where such a thing was bound to be discovered. So if his captain had spoken true, and Sgorr believed he had, he must be among the yearlings. How he had been hidden away Sgorr didn't know, but he guessed that Blindweed had something to do with it.

'My lord,' said Blindweed, turning to Drail suddenly, 'if it is true I would like to see this fawn.'

'The Draila have been looking for him all evening but have found nothing,' said Drail absently.

'Then the story must be false,' said Blindweed, greatly relieved. 'You know how the herd talks.'

'Perhaps,' snorted Sgorr. 'It is strange how such a thing could have been concealed for so long.'

Again Sgorr's single eye bored into Blindweed's thoughts.

'Strange indeed,' said Blindweed rather too casually, and then the old stag overstepped himself.

'But what matter if it is true? The Lord of Herds hardly believes such tales.'

As soon as he said it Sgorr knew that Blindweed was covering up. But he was determined to wait, for he had already decided that he would get nothing from Blindweed with threats. He remembered well Blindweed's courage that night with Eloin at the stream.

'You surprise me,' he said. 'A teller of tales who doesn't believe his own words. But you are right. They are only tales. The Lord of Herds is simply concerned that something so strange should be valued and honoured. Now, we thank you for your time, Blindweed. It is late and I am sure you have better things to do.'

Blindweed bowed and turned to leave.

'But Blindweed. You will be sure to tell us if you hear anything?'

Blindweed looked back and, with a last glance at Eloin, he nodded again as he set off slowly down the hill. When he was almost out of sight Sgorr turned to two of the Draila next to him and flicked his head. The stags bowed and set off after him.

'Well, Sgorr?' snorted Drail when they had gone.

'Well, my lord?'

'Tell me, then,' said Drail, gazing out across the valley at the dark outlines of deer grazing on the heather below. 'Do you believe it?'

Sgorr looked carefully at Drail and he smiled inwardly.

'I trust my captain's eyes, my lord.'

'No, Sgorr. I mean the Prophecy. Do you believe it?'

Sgorr hesitated.

'No, my lord, I do not believe it,' he said at last. 'But I believe this, my lord. I believe that the herd may believe it and that a stag with a white leaf on his head could become the focus for every foolish dreamer and malcontent in the valley. I believe that such a one could become a danger to you.'

Drail was quiet for a time. He began to pace up and down restlessly and then, turning to Sgorr again, he stamped the ground.

'Very well. Find him, Sgorr, and bring him to me.'

'Given time, my lord, I will find him. But tonight it is too dark. Besides, some means is being used to hide him. Tomorrow we will—'

'Tomorrow! Must I always wait for my will to be done?

And what if when tomorrow comes you still cannot find him?'

'Indeed, my lord. That is a possibility I had considered. He must be among the yearlings and there cannot be that many young, male fawns of under a year old. It would not harm the stock to remove them all.'

Drail looked hard at Sgorr as Eloin shivered beside him. Cruelty was in his blood now.

'Very well, then,' he agreed at last. 'We will wait till tomorrow, after Larn. Then, if there is still no news, put the Draila to work.'

Sgorr smiled. As soon as his captain had brought him the news of Rannoch, Sgorr had set to work trying to see a way in which he could turn it to his advantage. If Drail acted against the yearlings so blindly, Sgorr would have the perfect opportunity to spark a revolt and to place himself at the head of the herd.

The deer stood together and stared out over the hills. They did not notice Eloin slipping quietly away. Most of the guards had been dispatched to look for Rannoch and in the excitement no one was watching her, so she found it comparatively easy to drop down behind the Home Oak and run, as fast as she was able, to find Bracken and her fawn.

'Listen to me, all of you,' Bhreac was saying urgently in the darkness on the edge of the meadow. 'We must go, as quickly as possible.'

Behind the old deer stood Eloin and Bracken. Around them were about twenty of the selach. Canisp was there. Shira and Alyth too. The hinds, those that Bhreac had managed to muster without alerting the herd, were standing blinking nervously, trying to understand what Bhreac was telling them.

'Your fawns are in danger,' Bhreac went on gravely. 'You must get them away from here. The yearlings anyway.'

'But where shall we go?' said a hind called Linden. 'With no stags to protect us we won't have a chance travelling in winter.'

'Your fawns won't have a chance if you stay here. We can go west through the woods and then set out north beyond the valley.'

'But why must we go?' said another hind called Shian. 'I don't believe that Drail would do anything to harm the little ones.'

'Don't be foolish, Shian,' said Canisp from the back. 'Haven't you heard what Eloin has been saying? Can't you see what's happening in the herd?'

'I know, I know,' said Shian a little guiltily, 'but my fawn has done nothing. Why should they harm him?'

Again Bhreac tried to explain about Bracken's fawn but half the hinds looked at her uncomprehendingly.

'Why don't you give them Rannoch then?' said a deer suddenly. She was called Brora and had once been one of Captain Straloch's hinds. 'It isn't right that we should all suffer for the sake of a single fawn. Besides, if there is anything in the Prophecy, perhaps the lord should know it.'

At this the hinds began to murmur and Bhreac fell silent, for she knew well what they were asking of their friends. But Alyth stepped in.

'Shame on you, Brora,' she snorted. 'You would have a little one given up to the Draila to be killed? What if it were your fawn?'

'It's only Bracken and Bhreac who say he will be harmed,' replied Brora rather shamefacedly. 'How do we know what Drail wants with him?'

'Eloin knows all right,' said Bhreac, suddenly roused

again. 'And if you can give him up to Sgorr and the Draila
so easily you make me ashamed to bear the name of Herla.
Have you forgotten Captain Straloch?'

Brora fell silent but Shian began to speak again.

'I would not give Rannoch up,' she said loudly, 'and this
sun I have seen the Draila searching for him and I am no
lover of theirs. But I cannot believe what you say about the
danger to the yearlings. Not even Drail would do such a
thing. You are frightened and that I understand. Well then,
go if you must and I wish you luck and Herne's speed. But
what you ask of us is too much.'

'Shian. We ask nothing of you,' said Bracken, stepping
nervously into the group. 'We warn you, that is all. If Eloin
had not come with news of Drail's plan we would be gone
long before now.'

At the mention of Eloin another hind spoke out. Her
name was Dorain and she had once stood with Brechin too
and, although hinds are not generally competitive once they
share a mate, somewhere she felt a deep jealousy of Eloin. In
truth some of the hinds had always resented her for stepping
forward at Anlach.

'What has Eloin to do with this?' she said. 'She stands
with Drail. For all we know she is setting a trap for us.'

This had a powerful effect on the assembled hinds for
many believed, knowing nothing of that night by the stream,
that Eloin had betrayed Brechin. At last Eloin herself spoke.

'Why should I wish to trap you?' she said proudly.

Her heart was full of anger and bitterness at the stupidity
of the deer.

'I don't know,' answered Dorain. 'But there are many who
would see the Outriders' hinds driven from the herd. Besides,
you have no fawn yourself. Maybe you're jealous.'

Bracken threw a pained look at Eloin.

'You're wrong,' said Eloin, her huge eyes flashing. 'I hate Drail as much as any here. As for Sgorr I shudder to speak of him. But it is because I *stand* with him – as you call it, though he can hardly limp – that I know the danger that your fawns are in.'

The dignity with which Eloin spoke seemed to stir the hinds, but Dorain broke the spell.

'All I know,' she said, 'is that I would rather eat poison berries than answer to Drail.'

'Dorain is right,' agreed Shian. 'We cannot trust Eloin and I would rather take my chance here than take my fawn out into the hills in winter to Herne knows where.'

Some of the hinds muttered in agreement and when Bhreac spoke again there was anger in the old doe's heart.

'You are fools. But be that as it may, we have done what we can. Now we must hurry. Any hind and her fawn who wishes to join us is welcome. Let the others go back to their grazing.'

The hinds stirred and looked nervously at one another. But Linden, Dorain, Shian and Brora turned and started to walk away. Other hinds followed their lead. Finally there were only five left. Canisp, Shira and Alyth stayed. The other two were called Morar and Fern. Morar was a six-year-old with a yearling buck called Quaich. The young hind named Fern was unusual in that she had two fawns. They were twin does called Peppa and Willow.

'Well then,' said Bhreac, trying to sound as cheerful as possible, 'so few. Never mind. We will travel faster. Go and wake your little ones. We must leave right away. We will meet at the pool. But make sure to go by different paths so as not to arouse the suspicions of the Draila. The curfew still holds but, thank Herne, the night is overcast so we have a chance.'

The hinds nodded and padded away to wake their fawns.

'Well, my dear. We have done what we can,' said Bhreac, turning to Eloin. 'You must not blame yourself if the hinds are fools. Now, what will you do?'

'You are coming with us, surely?' said Bracken genuinely, although the thought of losing Rannoch pained her deeply.

Eloin was silent for a while. When she spoke she was shaking.

'No. I am staying here.'

'But Eloin,' whispered Bracken.

'I've made up my mind. If Drail really plans to harm the yearlings I may have some influence yet to stay his will. Besides, if he finds I have gone with you he will never stop hunting you.'

'You may be right, my dear,' said Bhreac sadly. Eloin could see that the old hind was deeply affected and her tone suddenly changed.

'Well then, it's settled,' she said cheerfully. 'Now, you must get away from here. But Bracken, may I say goodbye to Rannoch?'

Rannoch was standing with Tain and Shira when the hinds arrived. The little fawns were sleepy and bewildered for it was very late by now and they hardly understood what was happening. While their mothers had been at the meeting they had been allowed to play together, watched by one of the younger hinds.

'Rannoch,' said Bracken softly, calling the fawn to her side. 'We are going on a journey.'

'Yes, Mamma,' answered the little fawn gravely, blinking up at her.

'But before we leave I want you to meet a deer who has been very kind to us,' said Bracken quietly as Eloin walked up to Rannoch.

Eloin's eyes were full of love. 'Hello,' she said softly. 'Your name is Rannoch, isn't it?'

'Yes. Who are you?'

'My name is Eloin, little one. I am . . .' Eloin faltered. 'I am . . . a friend of your father's.'

'Of my father's?' said Rannoch, his eyes opening wide. 'I never knew my father but Mamma says he was brave and strong.'

'Yes, Rannoch, Brechin was brave and strong and he would be proud to see how you have grown into a fine little fawn.'

Rannoch was embarrassed, but as he looked at Eloin he felt something strange stir inside.

'And now you must be brave and strong like him,' Eloin went on, 'for on your journey there will be no bucks to guard your mother, so you and your friends must be the stags.'

'Yes,' said Rannoch wonderingly. 'We'll try.'

'Now. Let me say goodbye to you properly,' said Eloin.

Rannoch wanted to run back to Bracken as Eloin came closer and licked him gently on the muzzle, but something told him not to resist. He just stood there with his tail quivering until Eloin's loving gaze released him and he ran back to Bracken's side.

Shira and Tain were ready now, their breath turning to steam in the frosty darkness. Bracken and Bhreac took their farewell of Eloin, which would have been almost too painful for the old deer if Eloin hadn't been so strong, urging them all to hurry and wishing them luck. Finally they were set.

Rannoch looked back as they padded into the darkness and he saw Eloin watching him, then he turned away and trotted up close to Bracken's side. As the deer vanished into the night Eloin shook herself. It would have been impossible

to lose her little one a second time if she hadn't known that
this was the only way to save him and that she herself had
much to do. She set off too, skirting west towards the pool.

As they had been told, the hinds took different paths to
the stream. The night was black and the Draila were tired
after their search for Rannoch. Besides, the word had gone
out that they would have hard work the following sun, so
they were mostly off guard. But as Bhreac, Bracken,
Rannoch, Shira and Tain made their way through the night
they might have been caught by two Draila who grew suspicious when they saw the deer moving quietly through the
blackness, if a hind had not suddenly emerged behind them
and ordered them to escort her to the Home Oak. It was
Eloin.

So they reached the pool without incident. Alyth, Morar
and Fern were there already with their four calves but
Canisp and Bankfoot were nowhere to be seen. Tain was full
of the adventure and kept conjuring up stories of the woods
and the mountains, but Rannoch was subdued for he knew
that the deer had to leave because of him and he didn't
understand why. Thistle kept close to Alyth. He was upset
at leaving his friends and he was already thinking of spring
when he was due to go into the Drailing.

They waited and waited and Bhreac began to get very
nervous, for she could scent the morning on the breeze and
still Canisp had not arrived. At last the old deer made a
decision.

'We'll have to go,' she said gravely. 'They know the path
we are taking.'

Rannoch's ears pricked up.

'But Mamma,' he whispered to Bracken, 'we can't leave
without Bankfoot.'

'There is nothing we can do,' said Bhreac. 'Don't worry, my little one, he'll be all right.'

So the hinds and their fawns began to climb the hill behind the flat rock where the Draila had spied Rannoch's fawn mark. The hinds went in single file, the fawns at their side and Bhreac in front, snaking up the mountain through the thin covering of trees on this side of the valley. By the time they reached the top of the western hill and stopped to look back, the darkness had lifted and dawn was beginning to come up, streaking the mist with bands of pallid gold. But the skies were still heavy with cloud and the light was slow to come. In the valley below they could see the herd, mostly lying down or beginning to wake and stir, rising to graze or to feed their young. The stags too were stirring and members of the Draila were already gathering at the Home Oak. The hinds shuddered as they watched their antlers cutting through the chill air.

In the half light the hinds never spied the old stag who was watching them from the meadow. It was Blindweed. His eyes were moist and his limbs tired.

'*Chased by anger, fear and hate,*' he muttered to himself sadly and, shaking his head, the storyteller turned away.

'Come,' said Bhreac quietly on the top of the hill but, before she led the hinds away, she called Rannoch to her side.

'You don't need to hide that any more,' she whispered.

Bhreac began to lick Rannoch's forehead until the leaf stood out clear on his brow. Then the hinds, five of them accompanied by an old doe, led their little deer out of the home valley. As Eloin's fawn went he felt something fall on his face. It was cold and tingly as it melted on his nose.

It had started to snow.

5

The Bridge

Quoth the Raven, 'Nevermore'.
Edgar Allan Poe, 'The Raven'

Though this was the first snow of winter it fell thick and fast, as it will in Scotia, in great wet flakes that flurried and swirled in the air. Soon the hinds could hardly see where they were going and the pace became desperately slow. But the blizzard also brought a blessing, for it meant that when news reached Drail of a group of deer who had taken their calves and abandoned the herd, the Draila could not act for a full day. Scouts were sent to the brow of each hill but they could see nothing in this weather and they soon returned to wait until the skies cleared. When they were finally able to travel, a full sun later, Drail had no idea where the hinds had left from or where they were going. He sent out four parties of deer to scour the hills and others to warn the neighbouring herds to look for a calf with a white leaf on its brow.

The hinds spent the first morning out of the valley resting on the edge of a small copse, huddled together and shivering in the bitter cold. The fawns were the worst hit for their little hoofs were soon frozen as they sank into the white, but they also found delight in the snow and the adventure. Bhreac in particular was keen to move them on, realizing that the weather would mask their escape. It had stopped snowing for a while during the morning but by noon it started again, as thick as before. From the edge of the home valley the landscape began to flatten out and form the more regular contours of the Low Lands. The deer found themselves travelling across a patch of down where the undulating ground proved difficult to cross for in its folds the snow heaped thick and left snowdrifts which the fawns sank into up to their haunches.

At one point Tain disappeared altogether and if Rannoch hadn't been watching him and marked the place where Alyth and Shira could dig him out with their hoofs, Tain might have frozen to death. But the little fawn was unhurt, though his nose was throbbing with cold, and the deer pushed on again into the winter.

By the afternoon of the next sun the snow began to get finer until it eventually stopped altogether and the sky began to clear, giving way to great patches of blue that looked as icy as the ground below. The deer's spirits lifted with the weather and they made better progress. Rannoch, Tain and Thistle trotted along together, though the other calves stayed with their mothers. Thistle had cheered up a little and they laughed and joked and even found time to play, rolling around in the blanket of white. But at last, as Larn approached again and the evening star began to pierce the sky, a new fear entered the hinds' thoughts.

As they came to a wood and looked back across the downs they realized that their hoofs had laid a clear trail in the snow. It was with sinking hearts that the hinds entered the trees where the ground began to rise. A deer's mood is infectious and soon the fawns were nervous, their fear compounded by their unfamiliar surroundings. Among the calves only Rannoch felt more confident, for he had been into a wood before, and now he came into his own, trotting up and down and reassuring the others. He was running back towards Bracken when he overheard the twins, Peppa and Willow, talking under their breath as they padded along behind their mother.

'I'm frightened, Willow,' Peppa was saying, as darkness closed around them. 'The trees look like huge Draila.'

'Don't worry,' said her sister quietly. 'I'll look after you, Peppa.'

'But there are things in the forest,' Peppa went on nervously. 'I wish I was at home.'

Rannoch fell into step with the little does.

'Your sister's right,' he said cheerfully. 'There's nothing to worry about. I've been in a wood alone before and I've seen an owl and badgers and I was even lost for two nights but nothing happened.'

Peppa was very impressed but Willow said nothing. She turned her head away disdainfully.

'My name's Rannoch. You're Peppa and Willow?'

'That's right,' answered Peppa, no longer thinking of the big trees. 'We're twins.'

'I can see that,' laughed Rannoch. 'Are you Willow or Peppa?'

'Peppa.'

'So you must be Willow?' said Rannoch.

Willow didn't answer.

'Willow it is then. It's very nice to meet you.'

'And you,' said Peppa. 'Willow, what's wrong? Why don't you say anything?'

Willow still refused to speak and the three fawns walked on for a while without talking. Rannoch finally broke the silence.

'This is fun, isn't it? I mean, how many other fawns would get to visit the forest?'

'How many other fawns would want to?' said Willow suddenly.

'I didn't mean . . . I was just trying . . .'

'Well don't. We're fine on our own, thank you.'

'Willow,' scolded Peppa. 'Why are you being so unfriendly?'

'Because it's his fault that we're here at all.'

Rannoch was hurt but he tossed up his head proudly.

'Well, I'm very sorry, I'm sure,' he said.

With that he ran on along the trail of deer, winding through the wood. He was angry and by the time he reached Bracken he felt miserable again. Bracken was with Bhreac and they were talking seriously.

'Not now, dear,' said Bracken when her fawn arrived.

Rannoch ran over to Tain who was telling Thistle a story he had just made up. He fell in with them and listened for a while, but his heart wasn't in it and he was soon lost in his own thoughts.

The deer went on and at last they came to a wide clearing where the ground evened out. Bracken and Bhreac stopped to wait for the other hinds.

'We'll rest here tonight,' said Bhreac when the others had all arrived. 'The fawns are tired and it's too dark to go on. If anyone's following they'll have to stop too.'

The hinds nodded in agreement but now Shira stepped forward.

'Bhreac,' she said quietly. 'Do you know where we're going?'

The hinds pricked up their ears, for they had been wondering this all day.

'Not really, my dear. If we are to escape Drail we must

get as far away as possible, even to the High Land if we can.'

There was not one among the hinds who really knew where the High Land was and they feared its name, but at least the sense of purpose and the thought of getting as far away as possible seemed to reassure them and they began to move about the clearing, smoothing the ground with their muzzles, clearing away the covering of settled snow and finding places where they could lie down with their little ones. But just as they were settling down they heard a noise that made them start and blink in terror.

'What's that?' whispered Tain to Rannoch.

The two fawns were shivering in the frosty air as they listened. In the darkness, through the trees, came a sound that haunts all Herla. A low, quivering howl that seemed to rise from the depths of some wounded beast and echo through the night before it was lost again on the wind. The terrified deer shivered and the hinds, lost suddenly in their desire to run but held fast by their fear for their fawns, moved back and forth about the clearing like fish wiggling on a hook. Shira's eyes darted back and forth looking for a thicket or a patch of bramble where she could hide Tain for a while if it came to flight.

The howl came again and was then picked up by another and another.

'Wolves.' Bracken shuddered.

The other hinds had heard her and though they knew the sound well, the word had its own power to add to their terror.

'Yes,' said Bhreac loudly so that the others could hear her, 'but listen. They're far away. Probably in the mountains. They won't trouble us tonight.'

Bhreac's words calmed the deer but she could see that

they were all deeply disturbed, especially the little fawns. Peppa was nudging up to Willow while Quaich was nestling under his mother's belly, hiding his head from the awful noise and trying to suckle at the same time. To add to the misery, in the clearing the temperature had fallen again and a wind had come up, shaking the forest around them and howling through the dark branches so that the fawns thought that the wolves, who they were hearing for the very first time, were coming closer.

'This is no good at all,' whispered Bhreac, but then the old deer had an idea.

'Come on, form a circle,' she said. 'I'm going to tell you a story.'

The hinds were pleased and they shepherded the fawns into a ring. There they sat; Rannoch, Tain and Thistle together, Quaich, Peppa and Willow; their mothers circling them to shield them from the night and old Bhreac thinking desperately of a tale to lift their spirits.

'I'm no Blindweed,' she said at last, looking about her rather sadly, 'but I'm going to tell you the story of Starbuck and the wolf.'

As she said it there was another howl from the mountains and the fawns shuddered.

'Yes . . . well,' she began. 'It was a long time ago when Starbuck had crossed the Great Mountain and had come to the High Land. No deer had ever been so far north except the reindeer who have always lived in the snow. Starbuck ran free across the heather and drank from the great lochs and was happy. But one day when he was walking along the foothills of the Great Mountain he saw footprints that made him shudder. They were the marks of a wolf that had come down alone from the hills to hunt.

'Now Starbuck knew that he was in danger, for the pad

marks were fresh and he had no chance against a wolf, even a wolf on its own. So he began to look around him for a place to hide. Ahead, he saw a thicket and he backed inside it so that only his antlers were showing and they looked very much like branches. There Starbuck waited. He didn't have to wait long for the wolf had scented him on the wind and was now retracing his steps, sniffing and slobbering as he went. Starbuck could see the wolf's shaggy sides shaking with excitement as he padded along, and the lines of shiny white teeth glinting in his muzzle.

'But Starbuck wasn't afraid,' Bhreac added quickly, for she could see she was frightening the fawns. 'Oh no, he was far too clever to be afraid. Instead he waited as the wolf came right up to the thicket. He could hear him muttering and cursing to himself that he had lost his lunch. Well, when the wolf was right next to him, Starbuck shook his antlers gently and said in a deep voice:

' "Why are you complaining, old wolf?"

'The wolf nearly jumped out of his skin, for he thought he was being addressed by a tree. "Who's there?" he snarled.

' "Just a tree," answered Starbuck. "But why do you disturb my sleep with your mutterings?"

'The wolf, who was old, nearly blind and rather stupid, was too amazed to do anything but answer the tree. "I smelt a deer," he said, "and now I've lost it and I'm hungry."

' "Well, well," said Starbuck, smiling, "I don't know anything about a deer but I do know this. Herne wouldn't be pleased to see you roaming about trying to harm his favourite Lera. Did you know that Herne especially loves the deer?"

'At the mention of Herne,' whispered Bhreac, 'the wolf was very afraid, for he had begun to think that he was bewitched and perhaps it was Herne himself who was addressing him.

' "No I didn't," he said respectfully, "but I must eat, mustn't I?"

' "Well, yes," said Starbuck, "I suppose you must. But the grass and the trees and the glens have much tastier things than the hide of some old Herla."

' "Oh," said the wolf. "What?"

' "Berries for a start," said the cunning Starbuck. "And if you reach up to my branches you will find some especially juicy berries to fill your tired old stomach."

' "Thank you," answered the wolf.

'He wasn't at all pleased by the idea of berries but was too afraid to be rude to the talking tree. With that the wolf lifted himself on his back legs and tried to reach the berries that he thought were growing on Starbuck's antlers. Starbuck didn't waste a moment, for as soon as the wolf's muzzle came close he tossed his head forward and caught him such a blow in the face with his antlers that his front teeth were knocked out and he was sent flying backwards, over and over. He picked himself up and with a yelp of terror went hurtling away, his tail between his legs. And from that day on, whenever he scented deer, he would remember the talking tree that had knocked out his teeth and would go off to hunt some smaller Lera.'

The fawns were delighted by this story and felt much better about the howls that were really a good many miles away. All except Thistle, who was grumbling to himself.

'I think it's a silly story,' he muttered. 'Who ever heard of a talking tree? Besides, how could Starbuck understand a wolf anyway?'

'Because Starbuck is a special deer,' said his mother kindly. 'And besides, it's only a story.'

'I loved it,' said Tain, 'especially because Starbuck *can* talk to the Lera.'

'Now, now,' said Bhreac, 'enough chatter. If we don't all get some sleep how will we ever travel anywhere?'

The fawns began to calm down again and soon most of them were fast asleep.

'I've never heard that story before,' whispered Bracken to Bhreac as she watched Rannoch drift into dreams beside her. 'Who told it to you?'

'No one,' chuckled Bhreac. 'I made it up.'

Rannoch woke with a start. He had had dark dreams that night. First he had dreamt he was being chased by a strange hornless deer with sharp teeth. Then he had dreamt of wolves and wind and high, lonely places. As he looked around him now he was shivering. It was still dark and the others were fast asleep. Bhreac was muttering to herself in her own dreams and Peppa, Willow and Quaich were curled up snugly by their mothers. Tain and Thistle, who already thought themselves too old to rest at their mothers' sides, where further off on their own. Rannoch got up and shook himself but he felt wobbly on his feet and his ears were ringing. Something in him was unsettled and he felt strange. Around him the forest was quite still, for the wind had died and nothing was stirring in the darkness.

Rannoch wandered to the edge of the clearing, ate a few desultory leaves and peered into the wood. Then, quite unafraid, he stepped into the trees. It began to grow light as he walked and slowly the trees became discernible, so Rannoch felt confident that he could easily find his way back to the hinds. He was just beginning to enjoy himself when he suddenly stopped. From up ahead he heard a noise.

It was a furious flapping and cawing. Rannoch pressed slowly forward until he saw a sight that nearly made him laugh out loud. It was a big black crow, bigger than any bird

Rannoch had ever seen. It was flapping its wings and cawing furiously as it tried to lift itself from the log it was standing on. But each time it flapped and tried to take off the effort ended in a flurry of irritable squawks. Rannoch tingled as he realized he could understand what the bird was saying.

'Quite absurd,' cried the bird in a sharp, snapping voice as he flapped and strained. 'Quite absurd. Never land in a wood again. Nevermore. Nevermore. Crak, Crak. Now what am I to do? To do? Oh I wish I'd never got up.'

As Rannoch came closer the bird stopped flapping and eyed him carefully, his long pointed beak tilting left and right as he did so and his little eyes sparkling.

'Well, what are you looking at? Looking at? Crak, Crak,' said the bird, clicking his beak together.

'I'm sorry,' said Rannoch. 'I was just wondering if you were all right.'

'Do I look all right? Crak, Crak. Look all right?'

'Well, no,' said Rannoch politely, 'you don't.'

'Well, don't just stand there. Stand there. Crak, Crak. Do something. Do,' said the bird irritably.

Rannoch walked up to the log and now he realized that there wasn't just one log but two and that one of the bird's feet was wedged in between them, where the log had rolled as the bird had landed on it to get at a particularly juicy looking woodlouse.

'Shan't walk again. Crak, Crak,' cried the bird. 'Nevermore. Nevermore. Oh do hurry up.'

Rannoch lowered his head and began to push at one of the logs. After a lot of straining and butting it started to wobble, just enough for the bird to pull his leg free and lift himself into the air in a shower of feathers. He landed just next to Rannoch and began to hop around painfully, cawing and screeching and snapping his beak. Finally he seemed to calm down and then he suddenly wheeled on Rannoch and fixed him with a beady and very suspicious eye.

'What did you say? Did you say?' cried the bird.

'Me? What do you mean? I didn't say—'

'I thought so,' cried the bird, nearly taking off again. 'You spoke to me. Quite remarkable. Crak, Crak. Where did you learn it?'

'Oh. I didn't. It just sort of happened,' answered Rannoch.

'Nonsense,' said the bird. 'Don't be silly. Anyway. What are you doing here? Crak.'

'I'm here with my friends,' said Rannoch. 'We're running away.'

'Running away. Crak, Crak. Running away. So you're with that lot heading north? What do you want to run away for?'

'Well, the Draila . . .' Rannoch began, and he was about to tell him something of his adventure when the bird suddenly lost interest and flew up onto the branch of a tree. He fluffed his feathers on the bough and then looked down coldly on the little fawn.

'What's your name?'

'Rannoch. What's yours?'

'What's mine? Crak. Crak, Crak, answered the bird, whose name really was Crak and who always had great difficulty explaining the fact.

'Pleased to meet you,' said Rannoch. 'I've never met a crow before.'

The bird took off again and landed right next to Rannoch.

'What did you call me?' he screeched. 'A crow? A filthy, greedy, tricksy crow? How dare you?'

'But aren't you a crow?'

'No I'm not and I'll thank you not to be so impertinent.'

'I'm sorry,' said Rannoch, who had decided that this bird was really very rude. 'What *are* you then?'

'What am I? Am I? Crak, Crak,' said the bird, strutting around proudly. 'I'm a raven of course.'

'Oh,' said Rannoch, who had never seen a raven before and wasn't at all sure he wanted to again.

'And you are a fawn,' said Crak, walking straight up to him and sticking his beak in Rannoch's face, 'but a strange one to be sure. To be sure. Crak, Crak. Well, if you think I've got time to stand around in a wood all day, you're wrong.' And the bird lifted into the air again and flew straight upwards. He landed on a branch high in the canopy.

'But if you're running away,' he called down to the fawn, 'you're going in the wrong direction. You won't get through up ahead. Crak, Crak.'

With that the raven lifted into the air and was lost in the trees, cracking and cawing as he went.

'Wait. Come back,' cried Rannoch. 'What do you mean?'

But the raven was gone. Rannoch was left alone thinking to himself that he had never met such an insulting creature in all his life. The bird hadn't even said thank you.

By the time Rannoch made his way back to the clearing the others were awake and preparing to leave. The hinds had breakfasted on some acorns and a small juniper tree nearby. Bracken scolded Rannoch for wandering off again but she was too full of thoughts of the journey to be really angry. Bhreac was readying the others, talking to the hinds and encouraging the calves.

'Well,' said Shira, 'which way now?'

'We'll keep going straight ahead,' answered Bhreac. 'Come on, we better get moving.'

At this Rannoch stepped forward.

'I don't think we should go north,' he said as importantly

as he could, then imitating the bird, 'We can't get through that way.'

The calves, all except Willow, were very impressed by this but Bracken just nudged Rannoch gently.

'How do you know, my dear?' she said, smiling.

'A raven told me,' answered Rannoch brightly.

Some of the fawns giggled and Bracken licked the little deer.

'Of course a raven told you,' she said gently, for she assumed that Rannoch had had another of his dreams. 'Now don't you worry. Bhreac knows best.'

'But Mamma. A raven really did tell me.'

The hinds had no time for Rannoch's story and, with Bhreac and Bracken taking the lead, they pressed on through the trees. The forest began to open out and they made good progress. The trees were thinning and the ground was rising, so that the deer could see a long way back over the path they had taken. Ahead there was a break in the forest over a wide stretch of ground and then the trees began again, banking very steeply upwards. Bhreac was leading the deer out into the open when Fern called from the back.

'Quick,' she cried, 'down there. There's something moving through the trees.'

Bhreac and Bracken ran back to take a look and Bhreac nodded gravely. She had seen a flash of movement through the branches. A deer was coming towards them and, though it was still quite a way off, they could clearly see it was running fast.

'Hurry,' whispered Bhreac, 'across there. It will be easier to tell who it is if we get some height.'

So the hinds began to run across the open ground, the fawns going as fast as they could. The group disappeared again into the far trees and paused to look back. The deer was coming on. They were going to move off again when Bracken suddenly stopped them.

'Wait,' she said, 'I think it's a hind.'

'You're right my dear,' said Bhreac, 'and she's not alone. There's a fawn with her.'

'Bankfoot,' shouted Rannoch delightedly. 'It's Bankfoot and Canisp.'

By the time Canisp and Bankfoot reached the open ground the others had made their way back to the edge of the far trees. Rannoch and Tain hopped up and down as Bankfoot puffed up to them.

'My dear, how did you get away?' cried Bhreac. 'We thought we had lost you.'

'No time,' panted Canisp, 'they're coming. Up through the wood. Bankfoot and I found it easy to track you through the snow. So did the Draila. I saw them in the distance when we entered the trees. They can't be far off. What shall we do?'

'That's obvious, my dear,' cried Bhreac. 'Run. For your lives.'

The hinds and fawns turned as one and dashed up the slope into the trees. They rose quickly, stumbling and tripping as they went, but pushing on regardless. At a snowy outcrop of rock that broke a hole in the sparse webbing of forest, they paused and looked down. The calves began to tremble. On the open ground below, three stags were standing, looking round them and scenting the breeze. Bhreac recognized them as captains from the Draila. Then, coming from the lower forest, another stag appeared, and another, until, on the grass beneath them, there were at least twelve stags, their antlers lifting and nodding as they pawed the ground and scented their quarry.

The hinds ran on almost blindly, darting and weaving in

and out of the trees, pausing only to help up their calves. Peppa was desperate as she ran and Bankfoot, though he kept up with Rannoch, was puffing badly. The ground was rocky and the loose earth slid under their hoofs and slowed them down. Again the trees began to thin, which would have been a help to their flight if the snow hadn't fallen thicker here, so much higher up, and turned icy, making the deer slip and slide as they went. They were beginning to tire when Rannoch suddenly stopped.

'What's that?' he whispered.

The hinds had heard it too and now the deer were bunching together and listening in the approaching twilight. Through the trees, from somewhere up ahead, they heard a great rushing sound. It sang like a wind.

Rannoch and Tain ran forward with the hinds and the deer gasped as they reached the edge of the trees. In front of them they saw a sight that stole their hopes away. They were on the edge of a ridge where the ground suddenly plunged away, disappearing into a sheer gulf. The chasm was at least three trees wide and the deer backed away fearfully as they looked over the beetling ravine. The walls were of smooth rock and in the gorge below a river ran fast and angry, bubbling over the huge boulders that dotted its path. The deer were completely cut off.

'What now?' panted Shira, looking out desperately across the void.

Even Bhreac was at a loss.

'They'll be on us soon enough,' said Bracken.

'My little ones,' cried Fern, as Peppa and Willow peered over the edge.

The hinds shuffled about nervously on the ridge until Bhreac spoke again.

'Bracken, you take Rannoch and try and skirt back down

behind them,' she said. Then she lowered her voice. 'We'll go back and give ourselves up.'

'No!' cried Bracken.

'My dear, it's the only way. We're lost. Look.'

In the trees below, a trail of antlers was weaving upwards.

'Go quickly,' said Bhreac. 'Get Rannoch away. Rannoch? Where is he now?'

Bhreac looked around and saw the little calf further off, near the edge of the ravine. He was rigid and shaking, his head lifted in the air.

The hinds looked up as they suddenly heard a squawking and cawing high above Rannoch's head. In the cold blue a large black raven was wheeling high above them.

'Rannoch. What are you doing?' snapped Bhreac. 'Come here. You must hurry.'

'Wait. Wait,' said Rannoch as he nodded at the bird.

'Quickly,' he cried suddenly. 'There's a way over. Along here.'

'What do you mean a way over?' said Bracken. 'How do you know?'

'There's a bridge,' said Rannoch, though the raven had hardly had time to tell him what a bridge was. 'Please trust me.'

The calves looked wonderingly at Rannoch, but Bankfoot suddenly piped up.

'P-p-p-please, do as he says. If he says he knows the way, he does.'

'Well, he did know the way would be blocked,' said Shira, who was desperate to run anywhere.

'There,' shouted Fern.

The hinds turned to look back down the hill and shuddered as they saw the antlers not ten trees' length below.

'All right, Rannoch,' said Bhreac, 'lead the way.'

Rannoch turned and ran west through the trees, with the hinds and the fawns following him as fast as they could. He kept to the edge of the ravine. The path of the river that had gouged its way through the soft stone hundreds of centuries before, was a twisting one and the deer wound left and right, following its rough contours. At last, though, they came to a bulge in the ridge where the gorge narrowed very slightly and here, amidst a crop of thick and snowy bracken, Rannoch stopped and looked ahead proudly.

In front of him, strung high across the ravine, was an old rope bridge. It was pinned into the earth by four wooden stakes at each end and it sagged badly in the centre. But though it had been put there and forgotten nearly fifty years earlier, its planks were still in place, covered now with a thin layer of snow.

'There,' cried Rannoch. 'I told you so.'

The other fawns were talking excitedly as Bracken and Bhreac came up beside him.

'So you did, my dear, so you did,' said Bhreac gravely, 'though for the life of me I don't know how. But we'll leave that till later. Now we must take them across.'

'Who will go first?' said Bracken nervously.

As she stood there, she smelt a scent that made her shake. It was old and faint but it was a smell that she had been taught to fear from as early as she could remember. The smell of man.

'Let me,' cried Rannoch, filled with pride at the thought of leading the deer out of danger.

Before Bhreac or Bracken could stop him Rannoch had run forward and was standing on the edge of the bridge. The fawn paused as he looked down into the plunging ravine but then, very gingerly, he stepped out onto the first plank. The bridge shook under his weight and the planks quivered, dislodging their powdery covering.

Rannoch waited until the bridge was still and then he took another step and another. His legs were shaking badly and as he looked down he felt his stomach fall into the gulf. The air around him was cold and there was a great updraught of wind that filled his ears with thunder and made him dizzy and sick.

Rannoch looked straight ahead and kept going. Step after step he took, until he was right out above the centre of the ravine. The bridge had originally had two ropes on either side, one at about the head height of a hind and the lower rope level now with Rannoch's eyes. From these lower ropes thin lines of cord held the planks in place, but the lower rope on the left-hand side of the bridge had worn through and broken and its trailing tendrils hung down into the abyss. Here new bits of cord had been attached to the higher rope to hold the planks in place, but they were few and far between. There was little to stop Rannoch plunging over and as the fawn went he kept well to the right, with only the thin lower rope to hold his course.

Bracken and the others watched him from the near bank, their hearts in their mouths. But by the time Rannoch was beyond the middle of the bridge he felt calmer and the ringing in his ears had stopped. He was even exhilarated and his senses began to open as he mastered his fear. The fawn started to walk more quickly, till at last he was nearly running. But just as he neared the far side there was a great crack.

The whole bridge shook and Bhreac and Bracken started as Rannoch slipped. One of the planks near the end of the bridge was rotten and Rannoch's back legs had gone straight through. The fawn's front body slammed onto the bridge and he rocked sideways, only prevented by the thin rope and the bits of cord from falling to the rocks below. Rannoch scrambled forward desperately with his front hoofs scratching and scraping at the wood.

Slowly he pulled himself up again and clambered on. As his body pressed on the ropes he saw the wooden posts in front of him shudder. But at last he was safe. He had made it to the other side.

'Well done, Rannoch,' shouted Bankfoot.

'Come on,' called Rannoch breezily. 'It's easy.'

Bankfoot was the next to try the bridge, followed closely by Canisp. When the fat little fawn reached the break in the bridge he started to tremble terribly but Rannoch shouted encouragement from the bank and eventually Bankfoot leapt over it and ran to join his friend. Then came Fern, with Peppa and Willow. Morar and Quaich came next, then Shira and Tain, Alyth and Thistle and finally Bracken and Bhreac. It was a strange sight to see the hinds and their fawns crossing the terrible void and when old Bhreac reached the other side she snorted with relief.

'I'm far too old for this sort of thing,' she panted. 'I've never been so frightened in all my life. But I made it.'

'Maybe for nothing,' said Morar. 'Look.'

Bhreac swung round to see the Draila standing on the far side of the ravine. They were gathering at the verge and the leading stag had dropped his antlers and was edging out into the gulf after him.

'What do we do now?' said Canisp.

'I know,' cried Rannoch.

The fawn ran up to one of the posts that was holding the lower rope in place. He started butting and bashing the post with his head.

'What's he doing?' said Bracken.

'Come on,' cried Bhreac, 'follow Rannoch.'

The hinds started to kick and bash at the posts themselves and they began to ease loose. Three Draila were nearly in the middle of the bridge by now but they stopped, for the bridge was quivering badly, and slowly, trying to keep their balance, they began to retreat. Suddenly they lurched and nearly tipped into the ravine. There was a singing sound and the bottom right-hand post came free. With it the lower rope snapped and then they all began to snap, whipping round and lashing through the air. The last Draila just made it to the bank as, with a terrible crack, the rope bridge broke completely and clattered into the ravine below.

The fawns cheered as the stags snorted and stamped the ground angrily.

'Hinds, you've escaped us for now,' cried the lead Draila furiously over the gulf. 'Make the best of it. We'll find a way round and we'll never be far behind.'

With that he turned angrily and led the stags back down the hill.

On the far side of the ravine the hinds were overjoyed. The fawns had gathered round Rannoch and were cheering and complimenting him. Even Willow smiled when he looked at her. The little fawn smiled back happily. For some reason he felt a new pride in the fawn mark on his head.

6

Man

Here the crow starves, here the patient stag
Breeds for the rifle.
T.S. Eliot, 'Rannoch, by Glencoe'

The hinds and their fawns spent their first night of real freedom in a gully near the bridge. It was still bitterly cold but they had some shelter from the wind and a fresh, clean stream gave them all the water they needed. The calves were elated. The tension that had existed between them before had snapped like the ropes on the bridge and now they talked and played happily together. They began asking questions about one another and Rannoch, Tain and Bankfoot did a lot of showing off.

Peppa kept quizzing Rannoch about the mark on his head, which she thought was splendid and, though Rannoch had little to say on this subject, Bankfoot wouldn't stop regaling them all with the story of how Rannoch had helped him by the stream and had found the path back to the meadow. But talk of the home valley made Quaich miserable and after a while the fawns became subdued again and sleep wasn't far to follow.

The hinds grazed in a group close by. They were all exhausted, as much by fear and its release as by the journey itself. Canisp's front hoof was hurting and Morar was a nervous wreck but, for the first time in three suns, at least the hinds felt safe. They would have slept too but their minds were still buzzing with the events at the bridge and Rannoch's part in them. It was Alyth who broached the subject first.

'You know, I believe he really was talking to that raven,' she whispered as she chewed thoughtfully on the cud.

'The Prophecy?' said Shira.

'Nonsense,' said Bhreac immediately.

'Well there's something special about him, prophecy or no prophecy,' said Fern.

'Yes, and you must admit that the mark is very strange,' added Morar fearfully.

Bracken looked nervously at the other deer for, since that night when she had lost her own fawn, her only wish had been to protect Rannoch and to hide him away. Canisp saw the fear in her eyes.

'Well, I don't really believe in prophecies,' she said quietly, 'but if a fawn mark in the shape of a leaf means that in some way he is protected by Herne, then it is a blessing.'

A gust of wind licked round the edge of the gully and suddenly made the place howl so that, with the mention of Herne, the hinds shuddered.

'Stuff and nonsense,' said Bhreac suddenly. 'These are tales for young fawns, not sensible deer. Anyway, the Prophecy plainly talks of a changeling. Rannoch is no changeling.'

She looked nervously at Bracken. Bhreac had already decided that revealing anything of what she knew about that terrible night would only make the hinds more frightened.

'Besides, what good will it do us? With talk of prophecies who is likely to take us in? We mustn't speak of it again.'

The hinds nodded and looked back towards their sleeping calves.

'But there's something else,' whispered Bracken fearfully. 'That bridge. Did you smell it?'

Bhreac looked back gravely.

'Yes, my dear. We are close to man.'

With that the hinds fell silent and soon they too settled down to sleep until the morning broke bright and brittle around them. They travelled north-west, leaving the ravine behind them. The ground dropped away steadily, the trees disappeared and they soon found themselves in a narrow valley in a region of low-lying hills. The snow was less thick here and their pace would have been good if they hadn't now been confronted with the problem of food. Only Quaich and Peppa were still suckling and the other fawns were growing and needed as much nourishment as possible. But as they had come through the trees they had had little chance to browse or look for berries and now they spent much of their time scraping and digging in the snow to get to the grass beneath. When they did so they found it meagre and tasteless, with very little goodness in it.

At Bhreac's suggestion two of the hinds scouted ahead, returning regularly to report what they had seen. It was a strange feeling for the hinds to be acting like Outriders. The calves travelled in a group, flanked by their mothers, except for Quaich who always kept to Morar's side. It was close to Larn and the deer were nearing the end of the valley when Bhreac pulled them up. Fern and Shira, who had been sent up ahead, were racing towards them. The fawns immediately saw the fear in their eyes.

'What is it? What's wrong?' asked Bhreac.

Shira was the first to speak, fighting back the breaths that came to her harsh and shallow.

'Up ahead. Fern smelt them first and then I saw one. There are men up there.'

The news drew the deer together. Fern was all for turning round but Bhreac was afraid that the Draila might have found a way round the ravine. One thing was for sure, they couldn't stay where they were for very long. Bhreac's plan was to wait until dark and then to try and skirt around the humans. So, when night had wrapped them in secrecy, the deer turned east, climbing out of the shallow valley, going slowly and listening all the time.

Bhreac had miscalculated though, for although Shira had indeed seen a human at the end of the gully – not a man as it happens but a young boy throwing stones at a cairn – their dwellings were eastwards too, where the hills opened out around a shallow loch. The deer didn't scent them until it was too late, for the wind was from the west, carrying the smell of their fires and their lives away from the hinds' sensitive nostrils. Alyth was the first to stop and start fearfully, as she tipped the brow of the gentle hill they had been travelling across. The deer came up behind her and they all froze as they looked down.

They blinked nervously as they took in the scene below. What they saw was a number of huts, not more than fifteen, spread out sparsely near the water. A track ran off down the valley, vaguely connecting the dwellings, and thin plumes of smoke rose from their peat-covered roofs as the strange glow of orange firelight shone out from their windows into the darkness. The brightest glow came from a hut near the water where a fire had been built outside. A group of humans were laughing and joking as they gathered round it. The deer did not have names for what they were seeing and they stirred fearfully as the strange sounds and smells drifted up towards them.

They did not know it, but the deer had come on a community of crofters that had worked and lived and died in this spot for over four hundred years with little change coming to affect their ways. It had been they who had built the bridge over the ravine but they had never found any real use for it and had let it fade again out of memory. They were simple people who had little knowledge themselves of the great encampments that people were beginning to build in Edwinburgh to the east or Inverness to the north.

For this was a time long before the days when man's success took him to every corner of the wild and drove the wolf from its home. He still had no knowledge of the machines that would lay everything open and drive out the spirit of Herne. It was two hundred years after the four tribes of Caledonia – the Scots, the Picts, the Britons and the Angles – came together to form the kingdom of Scotia and over a thousand years after the Roman emperor Hadrian had built his great wall. It was two generations before the civil wars that led the English King Edward, the Longshanks, to invade the northern lands, and before the rising of Wallace that raised the heart of a people and inspired the Bruce to free his countrymen at the battle of the Bannockburn. It was, for men who believed in such things, a golden age which had begun with William the Lion and now saw peace in the Great Land under the rule of the third Alexander, free from the rivalries that inflamed the clans and brought misery both to man and to Lera.

Free that is except in the north-west, for the Norsemen still reigned in the islands of the Shetlands and the Hebrides – the Western Isles – and from time to time one of these crofters, gripped with the urge to travel and fight, might venture forth and perhaps return to tell tales of the terrible Vikings to warm a winter evening, happy now to grow old and die where he had been born. But tonight they had no thought of such things, for two among them were to be married and now they were feasting by the fire, full of ale and whisky. Happily for the deer, they were drunk and quite oblivious to the animals that were watching them.

Besides, they had already hunted that day. Rannoch saw it first and asked Bracken what it was. There, over the fire, the boy whom Fern had spotted earlier was standing turning a spit. Pinned on its wooden shaft, crackling merrily in the sparking glow, was the whole carcass of a young fallow deer.

'Nothing, Rannoch.' Bracken shuddered but the smell of the meat came to the deer's noses and so sickened and frightened them that Bhreac hurried them away across the snow. As they went the spit boy looked up and nudged his father, but the old man was already asleep.

'Try to get some sleep, Rannoch,' said Bracken softly in the night. The deer had settled at the bottom of a meadow, well away from the crofters.

'Mamma,' whispered Rannoch as he nestled by her side, 'what is man?'

Bracken looked into her calf's eyes.

'Man? Man is something you must always fear.'

'But why must I fear him?' asked Rannoch.

'Because, my little one,' she said, remembering the Lore taught to her when she was a young fawn, 'man is cruel and cold. He eats up everything he touches. He enslaves Lera and breaks the laws of the forest. Because, Rannoch, he is the only creature that hunts without need.'

'Why?'

'That, my dear, I don't know. Perhaps because he can.'

'Well, I don't like his smells,' said Rannoch.

'No, my dear. Nor do I,' whispered Bracken, shivering as

she remembered the fire. 'Now get some sleep. You'll need all your strength for tomorrow.'

Bracken thought that the fawn was drifting towards dreams when he stirred again and opened his eyes.

'Mamma?' he whispered again.

'What is it, Rannoch?'

'Why are the Herla so full of fear?'

Bracken looked down sadly and licked Rannoch on the forehead, but she said nothing.

The next day brought more bad weather. A blistering wind swept across the hills and though it wasn't actually snowing it might as well have been for the gusts tore across the ground and swept up the surface snow, scurrying around the deer's faces as they tried to make headway. Canisp was beginning to limp and Quaich was sickening. Indeed all the calves were hungry and miserable and, though she kept it to herself, soon Bhreac began to worry about food.

Rannoch, Bankfoot, Tain, Thistle and the twins travelled together and Tain kept them all amused for a time and made them forget some of their woes with a story that he had made up about Rannoch. The fawn was embarrassed, especially in front of Willow, and he kept telling Tain to be quiet.

By late afternoon the fawns were thinking of summer pastures and rich grasses; anything they could to take their minds off the cold and wet. All around them was nothing but high, flat hills which kept rising all the time, treeless and windswept. There was no cloud cover at all and as evening approached the temperature began to drop still further, so that the hinds became really fearful.

'We must find some shelter,' Bhreac whispered to Bracken as the deer began to climb a hill that was steeper than the downs they had already crossed, 'or we'll all be dead by morning. Look at Quaich; he can hardly walk.'

'I know,' said Bracken. 'There may be some trees beyond this hill. It's our best hope'.

But when the deer reached the top their hearts sank, for ahead the landscape was the same as before with more treeless hills, blanketed in white. They were more exposed than ever. The calves huddled together for warmth and the wind howled and screeched off the hilltop.

'Quaich can't go on,' said Morar desperately. 'I must find him somewhere to sleep.'

'Yes, Morar,' answered Bhreac kindly, looking back to the fawn who was standing by Peppa and Willow. His little legs were shaking uncontrollably.

'We'll go back down and shelter in the lee of the hill.'

The path they had taken up the hill had not provided the deer with any cover, so Bhreac decided to lead them on a little, along the escarpment they now found themselves on, in the hope of dropping down into some more sheltered spot. But as they walked in the biting wind Tain suddenly came on something hard under his hoofs and called to his mother. It was a flat, stone rectangle, badly weathered and half covered in snow, but too regular to be natural.

'Man?' asked Bracken nervously.

Bhreac nodded.

Ahead, Tain found another stone and another and then he shouted as he saw a whole pile of stones. The deer came over and there, cut into the hill, was a wide rectangular pit, walled with heavy rocks. The hinds began to back away nervously.

'We must get out of here,' said Bhreac.

'Wait,' said Bracken. 'Can you smell it?'

'What?' asked Bhreac, sniffing the air.

'That's exactly it. Nothing. There's no scent. None at all.'

The hinds began to smell the stones and they soon realized that Bracken was right. If man had made this, he had not been here in years. Bracken looked at Bhreac who had had the same idea.

'Shelter,' she whispered.

The hinds and their fawns crept off the stone paving they had stumbled on, down into the wide recess. The place offered perfect shelter from the bitter wind which whistled over their heads now, and though there was snow on the ground, for the roof was open, the deer soon felt much warmer. They lay down, side by side, and listened to the storm outside, taking comfort in the stones and earth and the strange setting. The wind died and the place became perfectly silent; chill and eerie under a huge black sky spattered with stars that made the fawns dizzy as they gazed up into the vastness.

'Mamma,' whispered Peppa, her breath turning to ice, 'where do stars come from?'

'The stars, my little one?' said Fern, lifting her sleek muzzle to the heavens. 'The stars are the souls of Herla. For when deer die Herne takes them and with his antlers he tosses them into the night and there they stay, shining on the lives of all Lera.'

'And is Starbuck up there?' said Tain, stirring from Canisp's side.

'Oh yes, Tain,' said Fern. 'You see that great band across the sky where the stars are like a thicket?'

The fawns were all looking up intently now and they nodded, all except Quaich who was sleeping against Morar's flank.

'Well, that is Starbuck's herd,' said Fern. 'And if you look over there, where those great stars are grouped together, you can make out the body and antlers of the mighty stag who guards them.'

Fern was staring up at the constellation that men call Sagittarius and as the fawns followed her gaze towards the twinkling canopy they could indeed see the outline of a giant deer.

Fern nodded. 'Yes, that is Starbuck. He runs across the heavens for ever, unafraid.'

Bhreac looked at Bracken and smiled knowingly, but the fawns were lost in wonder as they peered out into the inky night. They felt warmed and comforted, as though a great father were looking down to protect them.

'Bhreac?' whispered Bracken as the hinds and their fawns began to slumber. 'Why do you think there is no scent of man here?'

'I don't know,' answered the old deer, roused from her thoughts. 'For man surely made this place. But I can scent nothing. Nothing at all. It's as though he was never here. But it's a piece of luck for us, for I think if we hadn't stumbled on it when we did it would have been disastrous. Especially for Quaich,' she whispered. 'Look at the poor little thing.'

Quaich's thin flank was rising up and down rapidly as he shook with cold.

'Well then, I suppose we have man to thank,' sighed Bracken as she closed her eyes, 'wherever he went.'

The hinds too fell asleep in the stony hollow which had been built and abandoned over a thousand years before. For the deer had come upon the remains of an old Roman hill fort. It was the furthest northern outpost of the legions sent to civilize Britain by the Emperor Hadrian and was nearly one hundred miles north of the great wall that closes the mouth of Scotia from Tynemouth to the Solway Firth. But this place had never found its way into any human history, except among the stories of the young men stationed here for but two brief winters. It had been raised as a sentry point but in its time had attracted violence and death when it became a focus for the tribesmen that had lived close by.

A terrible battle had been fought on its northern slopes before the soldiers had gratefully received the order to abandon it. But for a time there had been peace on the hilltop too and the young men far from home had gazed up at the stars and told stories of *their* gods, of Mercury and Apollo, of Bacchus and Athena, and longing for the hot, warm scents of the south, for their mothers and loved ones, had cursed the wind and wondered what strange force had brought them so far from home, or if their lives would ever be free from fear.

So the soldiers had left – those that survived – and marched south again and the fort had fallen in on itself. The wind came, and the snow and the hard, grey drizzle that hangs like a fog over Scotia. The sun had burned down too and with the passing of time the stones had been bleached and washed clean of the scent of man. The fort, or the hollow as it now was, had passed back into the hands of the earth. So it seemed to Lera and the deer that were now protected by its walls that man had never been here at all.

Rannoch stirred restlessly in the darkness and tried to turn over. He opened his eyes and blinked up at the sparkling canvas of stars. He felt cold suddenly and, though he was at Bracken's side, terribly alone, for he had just had a strange dream. A man, or what he thought was a man, had been standing above him just on the edge of the hollow. Draped around his shoulders he was wearing the skin of a red deer and on his head was a pair of antlers. The man's arms were cut and bleeding, but as he stood there he smiled and held up a handful of leaves and began to rub them into his wounds.

At first Rannoch had wanted to move and run, run anywhere, but he had only been able to lie there, helpless and
afraid. But, as he watched, he grew strangely calm again
and he closed his eyes in his dream as he opened them on
the hill. Although Rannoch felt alone there on the hill, there
was also a strength stirring in that inner sense that was
awakening in him. Rannoch shivered as he heard the wind
moan gently above him. The scent of the earth was heavy
around him, and then suddenly he felt that tingling and
shaking all over his body. As though drawn by a force he
didn't understand Rannoch got up and looked over to
Quaich. His head was resting on Morar's warm stomach,
rising up and down with her steady breath. But the fawn's
own breath was shallow and painful and his legs twitched
as he shivered bitterly.

Quietly, without waking Bracken or the other deer,
Rannoch picked his way over to where Morar and Quaich
were lying. He looked down for a while at the helpless little
deer and then, quite suddenly, he lay down next to him,
curling his legs up and resting his own body against Quaich's.
The little deer stirred but didn't wake and after a while he
seemed to relax, warmed between his mother and the fawn.
That night, Quaich dreamt of his father and as he did so his
breathing became gentler and more regular.

By morning Quaich had recovered a little, though
Rannoch had left his side by the time he awoke. He sat in
the hollow as his mother licked and groomed him. But it
was clear to the hinds that he was too weak to travel. He
suckled greedily at Morar's side that day while the others
brought her food and, towards Larn, he was even up and
walking around. The deer decided to stay where they were
for another night though, and so they settled down again
under the stars. Again Quaich dreamt that his father had

come to him in the night and warmed him and the next morning he felt very refreshed and well enough to travel.

The weather had also grown a little warmer, and the deer set off again through the snow, heading north-west. They came on a shallow burn at midday and drank from its waters and even found a clump of blackberries with a few shrivelled fruits on its bushes. It was hardly enough for a full-grown deer but at least it was something and the hinds insisted that the fawns have what there was. Beyond the burn they came to a peat moor and crossed its soft flanks, slipping through the slushy snow into pools and bogs where man had cut away the turf to feed his fires. Rannoch's fawn mark was soon obscured from falling again and again into the brackish puddles.

So on they travelled, uncertain of where they were going or what they were looking for, feeding as best they could and turning away to the west or east to avoid the few signs of man they came across. They travelled like this for three suns, crossing hill after hill, rising higher as they did so yet seeing no sign of other deer. At last the slopes dropped away into a wide valley and below they saw a great river and a forest beyond.

Bhreac grew anxious as they came down the slopes to the river's edge, for it was wide and swollen and its fast current bubbled east and west as far as the old deer could see. But the deer's hearts had lifted at the sight of the forest stretching away to the west, as it promised food and shelter, and now they were determined to cross.

Alyth ventured into the water first but the river was soon up to her haunches and the swift stream tugged so hard at her legs that she was nearly knocked over. So she backed out again and the deer turned west, running along the river bank.

Rannoch and Tain rushed on eagerly ahead and, after a

time, the two fawns shouted back that they had found something. They had come upon a narrow section of water where
a length of thick hemp cord had been strung right across its
width. Though there was no raft in sight, for it had been
tied carelessly one day and had been washed away in an
autumn torrent, this was a ferry point where man had used
his ingenuity and learnt to keep dry and safe by pulling
himself from one bank to the other on planks of wood. The
deer had no notion of what the cord was for but it gave
Rannoch an idea and, remembering how the rope at the
bridge had stopped him tipping into the ravine, he suggested
that the deer could use it to stop themselves being swept
away by the river.

Bhreac wasn't at all happy with the idea for she hated
water but the others thought it a good plan and Alyth ventured out first, going slowly and letting the rope steady her
in the middle of the river where the current was fastest. In
fact this was the shallowest part of the river, the only place
where the deer could have crossed in safety, for at its deepest
point the water only came up to her haunches.

Though the river was bitterly cold Alyth was on the other
bank in no time and calling to the others to follow. The
hinds led their fawns into the water, making sure that there
was always a fawn between two adults, although the twins
insisted on crossing together. Canisp went first, followed by
Bankfoot, then Bracken and Rannoch and the rest. Bhreac
grumbled sourly as she brought up the rear.

The fawns were soon soaked as the river rushed cold and
furious over their fur and made their legs quiver. But all of
them kept their heads well above the surface and, steadied
by the rope, picked their way over the stones. Rannoch,
Bankfoot and the twins had all reached the further bank and

were shaking themselves dry, when Willow suddenly cried out.

A heavy branch that had broken off a tree high in the hills and fallen into the plunging waters, was rushing downstream straight towards Quaich. Quaich, whose legs were weak and who was making slow progress, froze and began to shake uncontrollably. The little fawn would have been hit full on if Bhreac, roused by Willow's shout, hadn't thrown her body in front of him.

The log struck the deer full in the side, spinning off her flank and only narrowly missing Quaich. The old deer was badly winded and far away from the rope. The river bed dropped away suddenly and Bhreac slipped, plunging forwards and disappearing into the water. Her head came up again, spluttering and wheezing, but the current had her now and hurled her against the cord.

Her neck caught on it and for a moment she was held. But suddenly, as the blocked waters gained power, Bhreac was swept under and away. Morar and Quaich managed to gain the bank but, although she kicked and struggled desperately, Bhreac was carried further and further downstream.

The hinds and the fawns ran after her, shouting frantically as they watched their friend fighting to keep afloat. But the strength was gone from her and her head kept plunging down into the icy depths. On the deer ran along the bank, watching the ghastly spectacle helplessly. Suddenly they all cried out in horror. Ahead lay a great rock. The river was bubbling and foaming around its granite sides and Bhreac was hurtling straight towards it.

Bhreac hit the rock full on and her body went limp. To the right of the rock the river gave onto a small tributary and now Bhreac's body was carried into it and away from the torrent, so that in the foamy swell she was lifted right onto the sloping bank where she lay motionless.

The hinds feared the worst but as they approached, the fawns let out a joyful shout. Bhreac had raised her head. She staggered to her feet and looked around her. Then her legs suddenly buckled again and she sunk back down onto the bank. By the time the deer got to her Bhreac was quite still, her eyes open but not a spark of life coming from the dark orbs. Bhreac's great, kind heart had given out.

The fawns stood watching in horror as the hinds licked and nudged her. But it was no good. They all stood there, staring down blankly at their old friend. It started to snow again, the flakes dying on the foaming water.

Very quietly, Shira came up to Bracken.

'Come, my dear,' she said gravely. 'The little ones are cold and Bhreac would have wanted us to think of them first.'

Bracken was too stunned to speak. Walking slowly and looking back as they went, Shira led the deer over to the shelter of the trees.

That night they were too dazed to know what to do. They kept to the edge of the forest, near the river and looked out mournfully as the swirls of snow shawled the land with a cold beauty. They talked very little and spent most of their time foraging half-heartedly for food. The fawns settled down to sleep as best they could beneath the trees while their mothers talked quietly together.

With Bhreac gone they felt leaderless and desperately alone, but worst hit was poor Bracken. She knew that without Bhreac she might have given up long ago.

'Oh, Herne,' she muttered to herself as she watched Rannoch and the others sleeping, 'let me be strong enough to protect him.'

The next day the hinds agreed that they should keep to

Bhreac's plan to head on towards the High Land and press north-west, using the forest for cover as long as they could, but also keeping on the edge of the open. This way they could have a better command of the country and watch for any signs of the Draila.

The deer set off late that morning. It had stopped snowing and the day was clean and clear. It was about midday when Canisp pulled them up. She had noticed tracks on the edge of the trees. They were slot marks and all around them lay deer droppings, scattered about like little blackened acorns.

'Herla?' whispered Bracken.

'Yes,' said Canisp, sniffing the ground and twitching her nose, 'and the slots are quite fresh too. But not red deer. Look at their size – they're much smaller than ours. And you notice the way they point at the end?'

Now, on the lower branches of the trees and the bushes, the deer began to scent the musk that the unknown Herla had rubbed off from the glands on their own bodies to mark their territory.

'We'd better be careful,' said Fern, 'until we know if Drail has sent word. Not many of the Clovar acknowledge Drail but some came to pay their respects to him at Anlach.'

Bracken nodded. Though all deer are called Herla, Clovar is the special term red deer use for other species in the Great Land, including roe and fallow deer.

'I'll go ahead with Canisp,' said Fern. 'You stay here with the fawns.'

The two hinds set off straight away and the others waited nervously as the sun rose high into the blue, its weak yellow light softening the snow. Afternoon was approaching when they sighted the hinds again. In the distance, further up the valley and clear of the forest, Fern and Canisp were running back towards them. They were flanked by four stags. The fawns were amazed, for their antlers rose like palms from their heads and they were small, hardly bigger than the hinds at their sides. The friends stirred fearfully, but Canisp called out to them as she ran.

'It's all right,' she shouted happily. 'They're friendly. They've never even heard of Drail. And it's wonderful. There's so much food.'

The stags were fallow deer and they bowed their strange antlers to the hinds as they reached the trees. The most senior deer was called Scarp. He was rather a handsome, dappled deer with splendid fanning antlers, but he had a strange, lost look and a tendency to stare. He bowed especially low as he came up to them.

'Welcome,' he said. 'Canisp has told us all about your journey. Very terrible, I'm sure. Well, never mind, you're safe now. That's all that matters.'

The other stags were soon inspecting the fawns and welcoming the hinds. They seemed particularly interested in the bucks. The hinds were all rather bewildered by the warmth of the stag's welcome, for although it is not that unusual to see different species of deer together in the wild, it usually takes time for them to learn each other's scents and habits. The fallow deer showed no such reserve.

'You must all be very tired,' Scarp went on, 'and hungry, I'll bet. We'll soon see to that. Come along, come along.'

Scarp turned and, as though it were the most natural thing in the world, made to lead them back in the direction they had come.

'Wait,' said Shira, stepping forward suddenly. 'This is all very well but we don't know anything about you. I mean, how many of you are there? How far is your herd? Where's the Home Oak?'

Scarp looked rather expressionless.

'The Home Oak?' he said. 'I don't know what you mean,
I'm sure. But as for how many we are and where the herd
is, you'll see soon enough.'

Canisp had already called Bankfoot to her side and was
getting ready to set off but Shira looked doubtfully at
Bracken and Scarp saw it.

'Please don't worry,' he said immediately. 'You're among
friends now, I assure you. Please come along.'

'Come on,' said Alyth. 'What are we waiting for?'

'I suppose it's worth taking a look,' said Shira.

As the others set off with the stags, Bracken turned to
Rannoch.

'Rannoch?' she whispered softly, for she could see he was
holding back. The little fawn was standing in the shadow of
the trees, shaking.

'What is it, my little one?' said Bracken. 'Is anything
wrong?'

'Oh, Mamma,' said Rannoch, 'I don't know. I don't think
they really mean us harm. But . . . but I don't like their eyes.'

Bracken nuzzled the fawn.

'Well, let's follow them at least. But stay close to me,' said
Bracken as confidently as she could. 'I promise, whatever
happens, no harm will come to you.'

Bracken and Rannoch set off too. The trees swung west
in a great arc and after a time the hinds and the fawns
spotted a large herd of fallow deer, grouped over a wide
stretch of open ground and mostly sitting down. They
noticed immediately how close the hinds and the stags were
to one another, even intermingling in places. They were ruminating in the snow but as the deer approached they hardly
stirred or looked up. There wasn't much pasture uncovered
but Bracken noticed how extraordinarily well fed they all
looked. Even fat. Scarp led the group through the herd to

the edge of the forest where eight more stags were waiting in a semicircle.

'We would like to thank you for your welcome,' said Alyth as they arrived. 'Where is the Lord of the Herd?'

The stags looked at each other in bewilderment, before a deer called Dearg stepped forward. Like Scarp his eyes had a strange, faraway look.

'We have no need of a Lord of the Herd here,' he answered quietly.

'No lord?' said Alyth with surprise. 'Who's in charge? Perhaps a captain of the Corps, or an Outrider?'

'We have no Corps or Outriders,' answered Dearg simply. 'These things are not necessary.'

'Not necessary? But who guards you from Lera? Who makes your decisions?'

Dearg smiled.

'We all make decisions in the park,' he said. 'Communally. But you don't need to trouble yourself with such things. You look tired and I'm sure your fawns want to eat.'

Although Bracken and Shira held back a little, the thought of food was too much for the hinds to resist.

'What's a park?' asked Quaich as they went, but Morar shook her head.

Scarp led them over to a patch of low ground, almost completely clear of snow. Here the deer were astounded to see a huge pile of dried grass.

'Help yourself,' said Scarp cheerfully. 'There's plenty for all.'

'But where does it come from?' asked Bracken.

'We collect it in the summer,' answered Scarp, looking rather distracted, 'ready for the cold times.'

As Rannoch and the others approached, they sniffed the fodder nervously and were surprised to find that it smelt strongly, not of grass but of herbs, rosemary mostly and thyme and other plants that they didn't recognize. Indeed they could see now that herbs were mixed in with the dried grass. Their lips began to water as the thick scent came to their nostrils, for they were all desperately hungry. Rannoch held back though, for he was still very nervous and he fancied that underneath the pungent, almost cloying smell, he had caught the faint breath of some other odour. The fawn couldn't fathom what it was but it made him feel vaguely sick.

The sight of the food was so good, though, that the other fawns and their mothers dived in, munching happily at the delicious feed. Not even Shira could resist, although she ate nervously and kept looking around her.

When they had had their fill Scarp led them back again towards Dearg and the other stags but as they were running through the fallow herd Fern suddenly cried out in amazement. Among the strange palmed antlers, she had spotted a single red deer. The great spiked tines on his head, twelve in all, and his heavy, dull-brown winter coat looked oddly out of place among these Herla, but the stag seemed perfectly at home.

'Look at his feet, Bracken,' said Fern. 'It's Whitefoot.'

Fern had recognized Brechin's brother, the Outrider who had gone missing two seasons before.

'It can't be,' whispered Bracken, looking suddenly at Rannoch. 'What's he doing here?'

'Let's find out,' said Alyth.

Scarp tried to dissuade them but the hinds swung away towards Whitefoot. Bracken's heart was pumping but, as the hinds and the fawns approached, Whitefoot hardly raised his head.

'Whitefoot. Whitefoot. It *is* you,' cried Fern, as the hinds gathered round him.

Brechin's brother lifted his antlers. He had a good face, strong and clear as Brechin's had been, with large scent glands and a wide muzzle. But when he looked at the hinds his eyes were glassy and he hardly seemed to register the red deer's arrival.

'It's me, Whitefoot. Fern. What are you doing here?'

The stag didn't say anything. He went on munching on the dried grass in his mouth.

'Whitefoot, don't you recognize me? We've run away from the home valley, Whitefoot. Drail and Sgorr have taken the herd and destroyed the Outriders. Whitefoot?'

There seemed to be a flicker of recognition in the stag's eyes but when he spoke his voice had a distant, melancholy sound, as though he was trying to remember an old dream.

'Well, you'll be safe here.' He nodded slowly. 'Hinds are always safe in the park.'

'But, Whitefoot,' said Shira desperately. 'What's wrong with you?'

'Come,' said Scarp, suddenly stepping up. 'We should get back to Dearg.'

'But, Whitefoot . . .' pleaded Fern.

Whitefoot had turned away and was gazing out towards the trees.

The hinds were considerably unnerved as they followed Scarp back to the other fallow stags and Rannoch kept looking over his shoulder towards Whitefoot.

'Now, that's better, isn't it?' said Dearg as Scarp and the hinds returned. 'And I see you've met an old friend. I am glad. We'll all rather fond of Whitefoot here, aren't we, Scarp? He's quite a novelty in the park and very swift. Now listen to me. I have some splendid news. We have been discussing you while you ate and have decided that you are very welcome to stay with us. We need hinds in the herd and fawns are always welcome in the park.'

Canisp and Morar greeted the news more enthusiastically than the others, who were now on edge, but it was nearing Larn and too late to move on. So the hinds agreed they should stay with the fallow deer for one night at least. Fern, for one, wanted to learn more about what had happened to Whitefoot.

Dearg told the deer they were welcome to wander among the fallow deer as they liked and to help themselves to as much food as they could eat. By morning the hinds were certainly impressed with the state of the herd and some of their initial fears had been allayed. The deer were so well fed that it could have been high summer. The reason was obviously their method of storing up food, unknown in any other deer herd, and the hinds soon discovered that there were several piles of dried grass and herbs around the edges of the park.

That second evening the hinds and their fawns drifted among the herd trying to make friends and resting from the journey and the shock of Bhreac's death. For three suns they continued like this and soon they all felt refreshed and stronger again. Quaich recovered considerably and, as Morar fed, her milk became richer and nourished the calf greatly as he suckled on her flanks. Thistle seemed to have cheered up too and now something happened that made the calf very proud. Two little furry bumps appeared on his head. They were the pedicles that would, next season, form the base of his first antlers.

The deer got nothing more from Whitefoot though and Bracken kept a keen eye on Rannoch. The fawn wouldn't touch the strange fodder and he was scratching for pasture late one morning when he saw Bankfoot, Thistle and Tain wandering over to him.

'Hello, Rannoch,' said Tain. 'You seem unsettled. What's wrong?'

'Oh, nothing,' answered Rannoch, scraping the snow.

'Well, you've hardly said anything for three suns,' said Thistle irritably.

'I've been thinking,' said Rannoch, 'and I don't like it here.'

'Why not? It seems nice enough to me'

'Yes,' agreed Bankfoot. 'At least there's l-l-lots to eat.'

Bankfoot was growing quite fat again.

'I can't explain it. It's just a feeling, that's all,' said Rannoch.

'Not one of your feelings,' said Thistle coldly.

'Yes. One of my feelings. What do you think, Tain?'

'Oh, I don't know. It's all right, I suppose. There is lots to eat. There's just one thing, though.'

'What?' asked Rannoch keenly.

'Well. It seems rather boring to me, that's all. I mean, have you seen the fawns? They never do anything. They never have any fun. Bankfoot and I tried to get some of them to play yesterday by the trees but they just stared at us blankly. I don't think they know what it is to play.'

'I know what you mean,' agreed Rannoch. 'But they're all like that. So calm. Even the stags. And that's another thing. Have you noticed how few stags there are?'

'And their eyes,' whispered Tain. 'They frighten me.'

'Stop it,' snapped Thistle, suddenly rounding on Rannoch. 'It's you. You're always causing trouble, Rannoch. You and that mark. We had to leave the herd because of you and now I suppose you want to leave here too. Well, it's wrong. I like it here and you're only saying this because you want to be the centre of attention all the time. You want to be special. Well, I'm not going to listen.'

Thistle turned and ran back towards his mother.

'Well, perhaps we should keep an eye out,' said Rannoch, as he watched Thistle go. 'What do the other fawns think?'

Neither Tain nor Bankfoot had seen much of the others, so they agreed to talk to the fawns and meet at Larn near a young birch tree. Tain and Bankfoot set off together and Rannoch wandered over to the forest. He felt drawn suddenly to enter the wood but instead he trotted along its northern edge looking for the twins, lost in his own thoughts but relieved that he had at least had a chance to share some of his worries with his friends.

He was coming around a spur of trees when he saw Peppa and Willow near a group of the fallow deer. The hinds and fawns were lying down in the snow. Fern was nowhere in sight for there were two stags with the group and she had felt confident enough to wander away from her fawns to feed at the dry grass.

'Hello,' Rannoch called. 'I was looking for you.'

The twins greeted him warmly and Rannoch explained about the meeting and some of his fears.

'I'm sure there's nothing to worry about,' he said as cheerfully as he could. 'Let's walk up here though, where we can talk properly.'

The three of them were wandering away from the fallow deer when Rannoch stopped dead. He began to blink and look around him.

'What is it, Rannoch?' said Willow.

'Danger,' answered Rannoch immediately. He had smelt something strange on the air.

The twins glanced round nervously but the fallow deer

seemed unmoved and the stags appeared to have scented nothing. Rannoch turned and looked towards the trees. The three fawns froze. The trees rustled and suddenly a fox poked his head through the leaves. It was only about a tree's length from where the fallow deer were sitting.

The fawns' first instinct was to bolt, but the fox was quite a way from where they were standing. Instead they stood mesmerized as the animal emerged into the snowy daylight. It was a large vixen, long and sleek, with a great bushy tail.

'They'll see it in a minute,' whispered Rannoch.

The fox trotted forward across the snow and looked about unafraid.

'There,' whispered Willow. 'The stags, they've seen it.'

The two stags had indeed seen the fox and turned their antlers towards it. But then, to the fawns' horror, they simply turned away again. The fox was approaching the fallow hinds and their fawns.

'Why don't they do anything?' said Peppa desperately.

'I don't know,' whispered Rannoch.

The fox was now only a branch's length away and it stopped and sniffed the air. Then, making up its mind, it swung right, towards a hind and a very young fawn who were standing a little off from the main group. Although some of the hinds were now looking towards the fox, they seemed completely unmoved.

'Do something,' cried Willow.

'Look out!' shouted Rannoch, beginning to stamp the ground.

Some of the hinds turned their heads towards Rannoch but they still didn't stir and the three fawns began to shout frantically. But the fox trotted forward quite calmly, licking its lips. The horrified fawns watched as it approached the mother and her little one.

'At last,' shouted Rannoch, for now some of the hinds had got up.

But rather than bolting, they simply walked calmly away.

'The mother must do something,' gasped Willow.

'Yes,' shouted Peppa. 'Look.'

The hind had seen the fox. She began to stir fearfully and to bleat, but rather than run over to her fawn, who was still unaware of the vixen's approach, she turned her back on the fox and started to kick at the ground with her back hoofs. The fox stopped again, its body quivering. Suddenly it sprang forwards, leaping through the snow. The fawn had seen it and, seized with terror, she bolted towards her mother. But the fox was now between the fawn and the hind and the little creature froze. The fox was on her in an instant. Its jaws caught the fawn straight in the throat and the vixen bit deep, pulling her to the ground and shaking her little head to and fro. It was over.

Very slowly the fox started to pull the fawn's body back towards the trees. The fawn's mother stood blinking in bewilderment and then she simply turned away and trotted back to the other deer, who had already begun to settle down again. There was a rustling by the trees and the fox was gone.

'I don't understand,' said Peppa, her voice trembling with shock. 'They didn't do anything. They didn't even run.'

'No. Nor do I,' whispered Rannoch. 'But I know one thing. We must get away from here.'

At Larn both the fawns and the hinds had gathered together. When Rannoch told Bracken what they had seen she immediately summoned the others. Bracken felt a new strength rising within her now as she nuzzled the calves into the centre of the group and quizzed them carefully about the vixen. Only Thistle was missing and when Alyth heard the fawn's story she was frantic with worry for her calf. But all the hinds soon agreed that something was wrong in the herd and, now they thought of it, each had a story of some strange incident among the fallow deer.

Fern told how she had seen the hinds ignore a young fawn who was caught in a thicket and Alyth said she had overheard Scarp and Dearg talking strangely about the fawns, saying how good it was to have some new males in the herd. She had also noticed that whenever the hinds took their fawns to feed, the males would be allowed to eat first and if a doe tried to help herself the hinds would kick her and bash her with their muzzles. Only poor Morar was reluctant to listen, for her nerves were shattered and she feared for Quaich if the hinds decided to leave. The hinds were engaged in their discussion when they saw a group of the fallow stags running towards them. Scarp and Dearg were with them and they bowed to the hinds as they approached.

'Dear, dear,' said Scarp immediately. 'The hinds tell me you are not happy. Is there anything we can do?'

'Yes,' said Bracken angrily, surprised at her own courage. 'You can tell us why a fawn was taken by a fox today and the stags did nothing.'

'Yes, I heard about that.' Scarp nodded seriously. 'Most unpleasant. But such things happen, I'm afraid.'

'But one of you could have stopped it,' cried Bracken.

Scarp and Dearg looked at each other quizzically.

'I suppose so,' said Dearg, 'but the stags didn't see why it was necessary. After all, it was only a young doe.'

'Only a young doe!' shouted Bracken.

The stags looked back at her blankly.

'Yes. There are plenty of does in the herd. The fox had to eat and, well, the fawn was there. Now if it had been Rannoch here, or even Bankfoot, then of course it would have been different, I assure you. I really don't see why you're getting so upset.'

Rannoch glared up at Scarp.

'In Herne's name, what are you saying?' Bracken cried, stamping the ground. 'Don't you even care about the fawn?'

'Now, now, my dear,' said Dearg softly. 'Of course we care. But the stags didn't see the point of risking an injury for a doe, that's all. You shouldn't trouble yourselves about it, really. It's sad, but then a Herla's life is full of sadness. That's Herne's way.'

'Well, I think it's horrid,' said Alyth.

'It *is* horrid,' said Scarp, 'but you'll have forgotten about it in the morning, I promise you. Why don't you all go up to the feeding place and have an extra graze.'

'That's another thing,' said Bracken. 'There's always food at the feeding places, yet I've never seen a deer taking it there. And where do you keep it?'

Scarp gave Dearg a sharp look.

'I've told you,' he said. 'We collect it in the autumn. The stags store it in the woods and put it out at night, when you're sleeping.'

'No! It isn't true!'

The voice came from beyond the group.

'Thistle,' cried Alyth delightedly, rushing up to her calf. She tried to lick him.

'No, Mamma. I must say something,' said Thistle, nudging her away. 'Rannoch was right. I was walking up by a feeding place when I saw them. Putting out the dry feed.' Thistle lowered his voice to a whisper and a hush fell on the listeners as he spoke.

'Men,' he said.

The hinds looked aghast.

'They add those herbs to the grass,' Thistle went on. 'That's why we couldn't smell them.'

'That's it,' cried Rannoch. 'That's what I scented.'

Dearg suddenly nodded to Scarp.

'It's all right,' he said calmly, 'there's nothing to worry about.'

'Why didn't you tell us this before?' cried Bracken furiously.

'We would have done, all in good time. But we didn't want to frighten you, before you came to understand.'

'Understand what?'

'About the feed. Some Herla are naturally nervous, aren't they?'

'We must get out of here,' said Bracken suddenly. 'If there are men about, we're all in danger.'

'No, no,' soothed Scarp. 'They won't come into the park, not at this time of year. It's unheard of, really. Besides, a hind has little to worry about.'

'Quite,' said Dearg calmly. 'And your bucks are hardly old enough, are they now? I mean, not an antler among them.'

'What do you mean?' stammered Bracken.

'Well, I don't want to be rude,' said Dearg, 'and I'm sure one day they'll all grow up to serve the herd proudly in the Hunt—'

'The Hunt?' gasped Bracken.

The hinds stared at the stags in disbelief but the full horror of understanding was beginning to dawn on them.

'Oh dear,' said Dearg mournfully, 'I've said too much, haven't I? But they'll get used to the idea. We all do. White-foot did. I mean, what else is a stag for but to die bravely in the Hunt?'

Dearg's eyes looked glassy, with a distant, desperate gleam.

'We shouldn't really be talking about this in front of the fawns,' said Scarp. 'They're too young to understand such a difficult idea as the Hunt.'

'Tell us,' said Shira coldly.

'Very well.' Scarp nodded. 'You had to know eventually. That is what we're here for. The Hunt. Then a stag may serve the herd by running well and dying bravely. They come about fifteen or twenty times a year. That's all. And never when the hinds are fawning or during the rut. In return they bring us the feed when the snows are very deep and sometimes even bracken from the hills. So you see, the herd always has enough to eat.'

'They?' whispered Bracken, feeling sick. 'Who are they?'

'The men,' said Scarp blankly, 'from the other side of the forest, to the east, where the great stone walls are. They bring the horses and the dogs and the stalk begins in the park. Then we must all run and every stag must do his duty.'

'But it's terrible,' whispered Bracken, shaking furiously.

'Terrible? It is life, that's all. In the park it's always been that way.'

'But why don't you do something?' cried Alyth. 'Why don't you run away?'

Scarp and Dearg stared at her but they didn't seem to understand what she was saying.

'You could go into the mountains,' said Alyth. 'Anywhere but here. You could come with us.'

'But I don't understand,' said Scarp quietly. 'Why should we want to? In the mountains some of us would be taken by wolves or dogs. The dangers in the wild are far greater than in the park. Here the herd is always stable. The men never take too many of us, although I can't say we wouldn't be happy to have your bucks for too many does were born in the herd this year. In return we have all we can to eat and we are happy.'

'Happy!' snorted Alyth. 'I've never seen such a bunch of soft-foots. You're all mad.'

'No, my dear,' said Scarp quietly, his large eyes smiling back at her. 'It's better in the park.'

'We're getting out of here,' cried Bracken, 'and if any one of you tries to stop us, they'll feel my hoof, stag or no stag.'

'We wouldn't dream of stopping you,' said Dearg. 'We hate violence. We are just sad that you can't see the truth.'

'That's right,' said Scarp. 'Of course you're free to go, if you must. It is a great pity though.'

Scarp and Dearg turned without another word and, with a last sad look at the bucks, led the stags off into the darkness. The hinds stared at each other, stunned. Alyth was all for leaving there and then but Bracken persuaded them to wait until morning. She wasn't frightened of the men any more and she was convinced that Dearg and Scarp would do nothing to stop them.

So, as dawn came, stretching its blood-red fingers across the snowy park, the hinds and the fawns got ready. But just as they were setting off, Morar came up to Bracken and Alyth.

'I'm sorry, but we're not coming,' she said guiltily.

'What do you mean, not coming?' cried Alyth. 'You've got to.'

'I've made up my mind, Alyth. Quaich can't travel any more.'

'But Morar,' said Bracken, 'you heard what Scarp said.'

'I know. And it's clear that he won't be in danger, not now anyway. When he grows up he can make his own choice about the park.'

Morar looked back lovingly at the little deer who was standing further off in the snow.

'He won't survive the winter, Bracken,' she whispered sadly, 'not without this food to thicken my milk.'

They did everything they could to dissuade Morar but she was adamant and so, reluctantly, the hinds and their fawns set off towards the trees. As they went Fern looked out across the fallow deer herd, to the single red stag grazing in the distance. Whitefoot lifted his head slightly and, as though he had heard some distant echo, he half looked round. But he never saw the hinds and his antlers dropped again towards the snow.

Morar and Quaich watched the hinds quietly, side by side. But suddenly, when they were quite a long way off, Rannoch turned and ran back to his friend.

'Goodbye, Quaich,' he called. 'I shall miss you.'

The little fawn blinked back at him. He didn't know why, but he felt a strange gratitude for the fawn with the white birth mark and he came forward and licked his muzzle.

'Goodbye, Rannoch,' called Morar, as Rannoch ran back to the hinds again. 'Herne be with you.'

The red deer wound up along the edge of the forest. A few of the fallow deer looked up as they went, but most of them hardly noticed their passing. To the north the forest swung east and, remembering what Scarp had said about the men and their stone walls, the hinds led their fawns away to the west and the bottom of a low hill. They looked back one more time as they began to climb out of the park but could see nothing of Morar and Quaich, so they turned away again. The deer and their fawns had begun their journey once more.

7

Lord Above the Loch

The first of earthly blessings, independence.
Edward Gibbon, 'Autobiography'

For seven suns the hinds led their fawns north-west. They crossed hills and small glens. They followed the path of a burn for a day until its course was lost among the tumbled rocks and they turned away through a forest dappled with winter sunlight where they saw the tracks of other Herla and hurried on. On the second sun another snowfall hit and what grass was showing was lost under its covering so that Bankfoot even began to dream of the dried grass they had been given by the fallow deer. That night they heard wolves from the north-east where the mountains were growing steadily in the distance. But again the wolves were far off and though the hinds and the calves sorely missed Bhreac, they managed to keep cheerful enough. Bracken had come into her own now, somehow released by the anger she had shown in the park, and she was often seen running on ahead with Rannoch at her side.

Of man they saw and smelt nothing more and they were glad of it. Their spirits were rising now and the calves seemed to be coping well enough, although the winter that was settling in around them was a bitter one. Rannoch and

Willow were striking up a strong friendship, for the little doe had come to trust the fawn. She thought him kind and handsome and she wondered about the fawn mark on his forehead. If she dared to mention it, though, Rannoch would grow shy and sullen, so she learnt not to talk of it.

After several more suns they came to a patch of wide moorland that lay cold and white before them and crossed it in a biting westerly wind. The fawns shivered as it started to snow again for, though they all had thick winter coats, when the soft, white flakes had settled on their fur and melted through to the skin, the icy water chilled them to the bone and, with the cutting wind, they felt they had little real protection. They pressed on and once more the hinds began to ask themselves if their journey would ever end. The moor ran northerly and when the deer reached its edge they stopped and gasped as they looked down.

In front of them was a wide glen, vaster than any they had ever seen. It seemed to stretch on for ever, cutting deep into the hills to their right. Its near slopes were rocky and its far slopes were banked with tall trees that glistened and smoked under the powdery snow. But what made the fawns catch their breath was the great loch that stretched out before them in the bowl of the valley. Its waters seemed as smooth and cold as winter itself.

Rannoch went first. He started to run suddenly, tossing his head and kicking out his back legs behind him. Tain followed. The fawns started to race and Bankfoot came too. He was stammering and stuttering for Rannoch to wait for him, but the fawns couldn't hear him. Peppa and Willow soon picked up the chase and then Thistle, who looked on coldly at first but found the sight irresistible. Soon they were charging delightedly down the slope. Bankfoot slipped and his fat little body went rolling through the snow but he picked himself up, unhurt, and charged on.

At the top of the valley, Fern looked at Bracken and smiled, and the hinds ran too, following their calves only a little more carefully down the slope. But as she ran and felt the wind on her face, Bracken also began to race. All that had happened in the home herd and since had somehow worked to age her, to make her forget the joy of being a deer. But as she saw the little ones running and knew that Rannoch was safe, she felt a weight lift from her heart, so that when she reached the bottom of the valley and came to a stop in front of the lake, it wasn't just the wind that had brought tears to her eyes.

At the bottom of the hill the fawns were already by the loch as the hinds ran up behind them. It had stopped snowing and Bankfoot was lapping at the waters while the others were beginning to graze, for the snow here had melted to reveal thin tufts of grass, scorched by the cold. Bracken ran up to Rannoch and began to groom him tenderly as the others milled around the lake, until Canisp, who had wandered further off round its western edge, suddenly called them over. She had found a great number of hoof marks in the mud.

The hinds scented the place and they agreed that the marks belonged to red deer. They must have been here no more than a sun before. Then Shira noticed the trees. Here and there, on the edge of the wood that banked the slope, the trunks were pale where bark had been rubbed away and the hinds saw a clear browse line where the leaves and branches had been eaten, leaving a visible line across the forest wall. As they scented the place they smelt a strong musk boundary too.

From the extent of the damage the hinds realized that

quite a large population of red deer must be nearby. They huddled together to discuss what they should do and eventually decided to follow the northern edge of the loch, going east up the valley to try and avoid them.

But suddenly Bracken spotted them, high up on the western slopes where the trees cleared: three stags. Their antlers were well developed and they looked well fed and strong. It was too late to run. When the first stag caught sight of them he raised his head and let out a deep bellow. It alerted the other two and then two more stags appeared from the trees. The deer came together and then one set off swiftly up the valley, trotting forward briskly with his head held high, as the other four turned and ran down towards the water. By the time the stags reached them the hinds had formed up in front of the calves and were waiting nervously with their ears raised. The stag who had bellowed, a ten-pointer with a suprisingly small body for such a heavy head, was the first to speak, and when he did so his tone was hardly welcoming.

'I am Birch,' he said gruffly. 'We've been expecting you. Drail has sent scouts across the Low Lands.'

The hinds started at the mention of Drail.

'Where is the one with the mark?' asked Birch.

'Over here, Captain,' cried a larger stag named Braan, who was a four-year-old. He was standing over Rannoch and peering down at the leaf on his head.

'And I'm his mother,' said Bracken, stepping forward angrily. 'And if any stag wishes him harm—'

'His mother?' said Birch, his tone softening a little. 'It is as we had heard. But come, the Outriders will take you to the Home Oak.'

There was little they could do, so with Birch and the stags flanking them, the deer were led along the loch towards the home herd. As they walked Alyth talked to Braan and, though he ventured little, she did manage to discover that they were all Outriders. It seemed that the organization of the herd was very much the same as it had been in the hinds' own herd in the days before Sgorr.

When they reached the main herd the deer were spread out above the loch by the edge of a large forest, the hinds already well apart from the stags for it was past Anlach, the rut was long over and the harems had broken down. The stags were sprinkled loosely on the hillside above them, some in the trees and others on the open slopes. They were mostly apart from one another too, for though it would soon pass, the enmity they had felt for each other during Anlach was still flowing strongly through their veins. Some, however, had begun to form into stag parties and now and then the hinds would hear the reassuring click of antlers as they welcomed each other.

Everywhere the hinds saw signs of the past rut though, for in the ground near the loch were the drying remnants of muddy wallows which rutting stags so love to bask in before Anlach, rolling around in the sloshing earth and showing off in front of the hinds. On the hills and among the trees there were also the tell-tale scrapes made to mark out territory as the stags move in on the females and prepare to make their stands. The sight pleased the hinds greatly, for they hardly dared remember what it was like to be normal deer.

The Home Oak was set back to the west, within the forest itself, for this was essentially a woodland herd which explained why the majority of the deer were so large. With an abundance of acorns and rich browsing, woodland deer will grow bigger than deer that live mostly in the open.

In a clearing by the Home Oak the hinds could see a group of stags surrounding the lord. The deer who had set off from Birch earlier was here too and it was evident as they approached that he had brought news of their arrival in the valley, for the guard stags immediately nodded them through without a challenge. As they trotted through the trees they began to see deer all around them, some browsing on lichen and moss, others on bark, and as they approached the oak they saw the lord sitting down quietly, his breath smoking in the winter air.

His coat was a rich winter brown, with the last gleams of russet on the back. He was very shaggy and he had a magnificent throat sack and, as a twelve-pointer, a splendid pair of antlers that rose proudly above him. They were easily as impressive as Brechin's had been, with beautiful pointed cups. He was understandably proud of these antlers, which at Anlach had won him lordship yet again, but though he was a royal he had already reached his eleventh year and he knew that it would not be long before he faced a real challenge to his authority.

But now he had secured his place once more and he continued to rule the herd as he had done for five summers, benevolently and with wisdom. He did not get up as the hinds and fawns neared and sniffed the air. Birch approached him respectfully and talked to him for a while before he rose slowly and stepped forward to survey the newcomers. He seemed to be looking for something and when he saw Rannoch, who was standing behind Bracken, he nodded to himself and began to address the group.

'I am Tharn, Lord above the Loch,' he said in a quiet, steady voice, 'We've been expecting you. Members of the Draila came looking for you not six suns since.'

Tharn watched with interest as fear flickered across the hinds' faces.

'Do not worry,' said Tharn almost angrily, 'I sent them packing. Tharn does not bow to a "Lord of Herds".'

Bracken looked at the others with relief.

'You are very lucky though,' said Tharn, 'that you didn't stray to the west or the east. For everywhere in the Low Lands nowadays the Herla have become soft-foots, even the woodland deer. There are other herds that would have handed you over without another thought. Well now, let the little one step forward.'

The hinds were silent as Rannoch stepped gingerly into the open. The stags around Tharn came in closer to have a look and soon they were muttering and nodding to themselves gravely.

'Well,' said Tharn, when he had finished scrutinizing Rannoch, 'this is a rare thing. Very rare. We shall have to see. I do not know what you plan, but if you wish to stay with us for a while the herd must sit in council. Tonight you are safe though. I give you my word.'

The hinds and their calves were led back out of the forest, down the slope and across the valley to another part of the wood where the does were wintering. The lead hind was a doe called Selta and she welcomed them warmly, as did the others, asking them questions about their journey and admiring the little ones. But when they saw Rannoch many of the hinds fell silent and moved away.

The others, especially Bankfoot and Willow, felt bitterly sorry for their friend, but they too were soon caught up in the warmth of the welcome. The loch seemed to have a strangely calming effect on the herd, which was clearly a happy one. There were no Draila here and no Drailing and the forest gave excellent browsing. It was rich in oak, beech, ash and hawthorn, with plenty of bramble and even a good crop of ivy. The loch also gave the herd a natural protection from the south and, of course, as much water as they could ever care to drink. Bracken and Rannoch were sipping at its edge the next day, when Birch ran up to them.

'Herne be with you,' he called politely. 'Forgive me for disturbing you, Bracken, but Tharn would like to see you and the little one.'

The three of them ran up to the forest and the Home Oak and as they approached they saw that Alyth was already there. Tharn greeted them and looked at Rannoch for a long time before he spoke.

'The council has met,' he said at last, 'and we have decided to ask you to stay with us, if you will. All of you.'

There was something particular in the way Tharn said 'all of you', and Bracken looked at him keenly.

'Yes, Bracken.' Tharn nodded gravely. 'There was doubt about the little one. Some of the stags believe a mark like his to be an evil omen and there is much superstition among the Herla here. One stag in particular, a hart named Colquhar, was against him staying. But don't worry,' added Tharn, seeing the distress on Bracken's face, 'that is done with now.'

Tharn tossed his antlers back and stamped the ground. He had had to fight Colquhar himself, only that morning. Alyth and Bracken thanked the Lord of the Herd but as they were setting off from the oak, Tharn called Bracken back.

'Bracken, I wanted to speak with you alone,' said the deer. 'Walk with me a while.'

Bracken nodded and told Rannoch to go back with Alyth. Then the hind and stag set off through the trees, the sun spangling their backs as it filtered through the leaves.

'Tell me, Bracken,' said Tharn when they were well away from any other deer, 'what do you know of the Prophecy?'

'Prophecy?' said Bracken, without a flicker of emotion.

'Yes.' Tharn smiled. 'When the Draila came to us with news of a fawn who had been stolen from the herd, they also tried to hide it. Don't they think we know the old stories? I knew immediately that a fawn with an oaken mark was of more importance than the Draila were trying to make out. Not that that matters, for I am lord here and I will not be ordered around by Drail or Sgorr or any of his brailah. But tell me,' he added, dropping his voice, 'do you think he is the one?'

Bracken kept perfectly calm.

'Lord Tharn,' she said quietly, after a while, 'a white fawn mark like Rannoch's may be strange. But the prophecy — there are many other things in it.'

'Ah yes,' agreed Tharn, 'that's what I told the others. Your fawn is no changeling, so you yourself are proof perhaps that this is just one of Drail's twisted fantasies.'

Bracken was silent as she struggled to hide her emotions.

'But Bracken,' Tharn went on, 'have you noticed any-thing . . . anything different about your little one?'

Bracken shook her head.

'No matter,' said Tharn wistfully. 'No matter. It's just that if there were anything in it, I believe such a one should be treasured. Yes, treasured indeed.'

They had come to the edge of the forest and Tharn was looking down across the loch now with a sadness in his eyes. Bracken was about to speak when Tharn suddenly shook himself.

'Just listen to me. I'm getting old and foolish,' he snorted, 'and that, Bracken, is what I really wanted to talk to you about. For my time above the loch is coming to an end and when it comes I cannot guarantee your fawn's safety. Whether there is any truth in this prophecy or not, these are bad times in the Low Lands and there are many, even in this herd, who would look with a cold eye on Rannoch. There are others still who seek Drail's favours. Colquhar for one. I will do everything in my power, but you must be ready, Bracken. If anything happens to me you must be prepared to fly again.'

When Bracken reached the hinds again, Alyth, Canisp and the others were eagerly discussing the news. There was little hesitation that they should stay, for a while at least, for they had already made friends and the winter was getting worse. So the hinds decided to settle with the deer above the loch and try to make a new life for themselves.

Winter tightened its grip. The snow came in waves of white and on the edges of the loch the waters froze, stretching out sheeted ice fingers. The wolves called from the mountains and the air in the valley was like steel. Nature spread out her arms across Scotia and blew her icy breath across the mountainsides until the flakes of white piling against them trembled and turned to stone.

But as surely as calf follows hind, so spring came again to the Great Land. The earth span and the sunlight warmed Nature's hands and she turned her breath softly on the rivers again, melting the ice sheets where the otter had skated, and sending streams of cool water rushing down the valleys from the mountain eyries to greet the sea. The forest bloomed and the crocuses pushed their heads through the heather as the shoots of young grass stretched themselves and sang. Everywhere the Lera opened their eyes, throwing off winter's sleep, and raced out to meet the season's day.

Among the deer, under the calm eye of Tharn, there had been peace. Rannoch and Bracken had stayed close to each other during the cold time, for although Tharn had given instructions that the fawn was to be treated like any of the other deer, there were still many who were suspicious of him.

They soon got used to browsing in the trees and nestling in the thick undergrowth to sleep, and in truth they found it much warmer in the wood.

Time and again Rannoch had asked his mother why the deer treated him so strangely and if he really was different, but Bracken had always nuzzled him and told him it was only because they were jealous. With time, though, the Herla forgot some of their fear of the mark and by the time the snows began to thaw and the deer started to scent the spring, the hinds and their fawns felt that perhaps they had found a new home.

It was a bold spring morning, still cold but with the distant sun bringing the promise of new life. Across the loch a blue mist hung low with the dawn, in thin bands that stretched across the forest like tree lines browsed by deer. The mist hung in the air, dissolving in places and curling in wisps from the ground, so it looked as though the frost that glinted like crushed diamonds on the earth was lifting upwards. The light that slanted through the trees above the loch shone and faded into bands of silver and black that made the shadows glow. Along the edge of the forest the branches hovered in this half light as though floating on the breeze that whispered down the valley.

Suddenly a branch moved in the forest and began to sway through the trees. A stag was making his way along the edge of the wood, stopping every now and then to browse noisily on the young shoots already budding, tearing at the juicy twigs and munching heavily with his strong jaw. He was about six years old and a ten-pointer. He had a keen look and at every sound he would swing his antlers left and right to challenge the distant noise. His winter coat was thinning but his throat was still shaggy. His name was Colquhar.

As Colquhar came to the end of one portion of the trees

he suddenly stopped and, lifting his head, he pushed out his chest. His front right hoof began to paw the ground and his head moved slowly left as he peered down over the loch. He was looking towards a stony outcrop now, about halfway down the hill, and as he watched, his eyes narrowed into a hard, unfriendly stare. If those eyes had been arrows they could have carried his anger as swift as starlings across the valley to where two fawns were walking through the sunlight.

'But why, Rannoch?' Willow was saying, as the young deer reached the group of stones. 'The others want you to play.'

'No they don't,' said Rannoch. 'Besides, that's all they ever think about. Play.' Rannoch had grown and the two furry pedicles above his head were already quite pronounced.

'But I don't understand,' said Willow. 'You said before that they won't play with you and now you say you don't want to play at all.'

'I know,' said Rannoch, 'but the truth is they only play with me because they've been told to, not because they want to. They're frightened of me.'

'I'm not frightened of you.'

'You haven't heard what they're saying. About this prophecy. Thistle recited it again the other day in front of the others and I asked Tain to teach it to me. Tain's changed towards me. Even Bankfoot has changed.'

'No they haven't. Anyway, why listen?'

'It talks about an oak leaf, Willow. That's why we had to leave the home herd.'

'It's just a silly story, that's all. Fern says there's lots more in the Prophecy than a fawn mark. About a changeling and other things. It's got nothing to do with you.'

They were beginning to climb up out of the valley now

and Willow was silent for a while. She was thinking of some way to console her friend.

'Come on,' she said at last. 'Lets go back to the loch and find Peppa.'

'No. I want to be on my own.'

'You don't want me to be with you?' said Willow.

'No. Yes. Oh, I don't know,' cried Rannoch suddenly, setting off at a run. Willow hung back and watched him and then ran after him towards the top of the hill.

'I'm sorry, Willow,' said Rannoch as she caught up with him. 'It's just that I don't understand.'

Rannoch turned and looked at her, then said in a whisper, 'Tell me, Willow, do you think I'm different?'

Willow's large, bright eyes looked back at him calmly. She looked at his fine young face with its high forehead and the strange fawn mark in the middle of his temple.

'Of course I think you're different,' she said and touched his nose with hers.

'No, not like that,' said Rannoch. 'I mean, do you think I'm strange?'

'No, I don't,' answered Willow. 'I think you're . . .'

'But this mark,' said Rannoch, 'and the forest and the raven and my dreams and I feel strange sometimes.'

'Its only because you're sensitive and intelligent,' said Willow kindly.

'But I see some of the others watching me and I know they're frightened of me. Perhaps I should go away,' Rannoch added, dropping his head.

'Don't talk like that. You have lots of good friends and besides, if you went away I would have to come with you and I don't think I want to go out there again, not just yet.'

The fawns had stopped at the top of the valley and were looking north across the hills. In the distance they could see the tips of great white mountains that rose much higher than the surrounding peaks. The tree line hardly rose to their foothills and their tops were furled in huge swirls of cloud.

'Willow,' said Rannoch almost to himself, 'do you think Tain's right?'

'About the Prophecy?'

'No. He says the Great Mountain is over there, where Starbuck first met Herne, and that beyond is the High Land where Starbuck still lives. I don't believe it, but it's a good story, isn't it?'

'Yes,' said Willow, gazing out at the high peaks that looked so distant and forbidding.

'You know,' said Rannoch, 'I think that I would like to climb the Great Mountain one day.'

'Well, I shouldn't,' said Willow. 'I think it's probably cold and dangerous and I much prefer it here.'

The two calves were walking along the ridge now, where the hill sloped away into downs covered in lush young bracken. This was further than they had ever strayed but as they looked they saw a stag party feeding nearby and, reassured, they wandered on. They started to graze in the warm sunlight and talked as they did so, but moving all the time, so after a while they found that they were quite a long way from home. Willow eventually suggested they turn back but as she did so she saw that Rannoch was standing stock-still, his ears pricked forward.

'What is it?' she said.

'Can't you feel it?' whispered Rannoch.

'It's you who has those feelings,' said Willow half teasingly, but as she said it she felt it too, a kind of shaking in her legs. Willow began to tremble.

'Listen,' said Rannoch.

The stags nearby had raised their antlers and their heads

were cocked. Then, on the breeze, they caught it; a sound that sent fear flowing through them. In the distance came a low, hollow barking that made the air shake.

'Wolves?' whispered Willow.

'No,' said Rannoch, 'look.'

The fawns saw something they barely understood. In the distance, along the valley ridge, a group of men were racing towards them. It seemed at first as though they were floating on air, but as they rose up the hill the fawns saw that they were carried along on great antlerless stags. Although the others knew instantly what they were, the fawns had never seen horses before and the pounding of their hoofs filled them with terror. All they had seen of man on their journey had made them fear and mistrust that creature, but as they watched these animals, so like themselves, tamed to man's will and carrying the humans towards them, a new horror awoke in their young minds.

Worse even than this though were the creatures that ran before them, snapping and barking as they went. The pack of deer hounds had found their scent and were baying for blood. Suddenly, the air was rent with a deafening noise that spoke neither of man nor beast. A high, lingering note that changed again to a hollow call. It was the sound of a hunting horn.

'Run. Run for your lives,' cried a stag nearby and in a sudden, darting movement the whole stag party swung round on their haunches and bolted like a flock of birds. Rannoch and Willow went with them, hurtling blindly east along the ridge. The stags moved like lightning, for a frightened deer is one of the fastest creatures in the wild. But the fawns somehow managed to keep up with them, for a time anyway, until the deer swung into a small gully at the very end of the valley's escarpment where the hills reared up again. Now the stags began to pull away. The barking and baying and pounding and the strange wail of the hunting horn came nearer and nearer. The fawns ran on blindly but suddenly, out of sheer instinct, Rannoch dived to the right into a stretch of ground where the bracken was thickest.

'Quick. Follow me,' he cried and Willow went with him.

They vanished into the undergrowth just in time, for the hounds were on them. The dogs swept past like a wind, straight up the gully, and the horses followed, churning up the ground with their hoofs.

'Are you all right?' whispered Rannoch when the thunder had passed.

'Yes,' gasped Willow, 'I think so.'

'Look,' said Rannoch, raising his head above the bracken. Willow lifted her head too. In front of them the stags had reached the end of the gully and were trying to climb up its closed face. But the slope was steep and the hounds were already on them, snapping and biting at their haunches. Five of the dogs had cornered the stag who had cried out first and now he had swung round and was scything right and left with his antlers. One of the dogs yelped bitterly as a tine caught its side but it looked as if the stag would be pulled down, when suddenly the air was rent with a final blast of the strange horn.

The dogs looked back fearfully to where the men, who had climbed down from their horses, were advancing towards them and shouting angrily. The dogs became confused and some of them began to whimper as the humans waded in and pulled them off, kicking and hitting them. The stags' hopes lifted for an instant. But then one of the men raised something that looked like a branch to his eyes and pointed it at a single deer climbing the verge to the right. There was a swishing noise and Rannoch and Willow watched amazed as the stag simply crashed to his knees and rolled down the slope. From his side, where a thin wooden shaft had entered his flesh, the stag's hot blood was already staining the grass. To the left another deer fell and then another, until the only stags left standing were those at the bottom of the gully with their backs against the hill.

Then the men, who had formed up in a line, began to shout and whistle. One by one they lifted their hands to their backs and pulled out the strange objects that had been slung across their shoulders and which now glinted and flashed in the sunlight. Some of these objects were long and thin, with sharp pointed ends. Others branched at the bottom like the antlers of the fallow deer. The fawns had no notion of what a sword was for, but they soon understood as the humans began to swing them in front of them, advancing on foot towards the waiting deer. Rannoch and Willow blinked in horror at that slaughter. But when it was over every stag that had entered that gully, fifteen in all, lay dead on the earth. The fresh young grass had turned from a spring green to a deep, bruised crimson. Then one of the men bent down. He was tall, with hair the colour of a red deer and a long, thick beard. When he raised himself up again and turned to the others with a great shout, he was holding aloft a single five-pointed antler.

'Come away,' Rannoch whispered in horror, backing off through the bracken. 'Willow?'

Willow shook herself from her trance and turned to follow Rannoch. But suddenly there was a howl from in front of them. One of the hounds that had been pulled off the stags had made its way back to where the fawns had hidden in the bracken. It had spotted them.

'Run, Willow, run,' shouted Rannoch desperately, as the hound leapt forward, its teeth and snarling gums keen to avenge themselves for the kill that had just been denied them. Willow didn't need to be told twice. She sprang forward, lifted on a wave of terror. Rannoch followed and the fawns dashed for their lives. But the dog was hungry and was soon gaining on them. The hound was almost at their heels when Rannoch suddenly veered away to the left to try and draw it off Willow.

The hound swung after him, barking and snapping at his legs. Rannoch could almost feel its hot breath on his haunches as he ran, the tears blinding his eyes. It was hopeless, the dog was on him.

The ground dipped suddenly and as the dog's teeth closed Rannoch threw himself forwards and kicked as he did so. A deer can jump much further than a dog and as the fawn took off, the dog's teeth snapped shut on empty air. It pulled up for an instant at the ditch, startled by Rannoch's leap and looking around stupidly as Rannoch found himself on level ground again and hurtled on. With a howl, the hound took up the chase once more. On Rannoch sped, with the dog following him. It began to close again and suddenly Rannoch broke clear of the bracken and looked ahead in terror. He had been running back up the gully and now, in front of him, he saw a forest of horses and men and his nostrils were swamped by their scent.

Rannoch swung away to the right. But the other hounds had seen him and the air behind was shattered with their cries as they too took up the chase. Rannoch felt as if his heart would burst. His head was pounding with the noise of the dogs and as he looked ahead he felt his spirits fail. To the right of where the stags had fled, the gully had opened out a little but now Rannoch was nearing its end and its sides were steeper than the fawn could manage. He was lost.

'So this is where it ends,' he said to himself bitterly as he ran, 'fleeing from the herd to be torn to shreds.'

With that the fawn's senses began to swim and Rannoch felt as though he were falling. He touched ferns and smelt dry earth.

'They're on me,' he cried as a terrible pain gripped his back leg and everything went black.

Part Two

8

Sgorr

Cruel he looks, but calm and strong,
Like one who does, not suffers wrong.
Percy Bysshe Shelley, 'Prometheus Unbound'

A hind was grazing on the hill in the weak spring sunshine.
She had a smooth red coat and her huge eyes looked proud
and defiant. But there was a sadness in them too as she gazed
out across the valley. She was still fairly young, seven years
old, but in the lines around her scent glands there was the
sign of some tragedy that had aged her more than her natural
span. A stag, old and limping, wandered past the Home Oak
towards her and called softly, but the hind took no notice
and it was only when he had nearly reached her and he
called again that she turned her head.

'Blindweed,' said Eloin, surprised to see the storyteller so
close to the Home Oak. 'Blindweed, I'm sorry, I must have
been daydreaming.'

'That's all right,' said the storyteller, coming up to her
slowly. 'It's all I'm good for myself nowadays. But what were
you thinking of so sadly?'

The hind smiled at her friend. Blindweed looked very old.
His antlers were deeply rutted, like the arms of a weathered
oak.

'I was wondering about Rannoch.'

'He's all right, Eloin. I'm sure of it.'

'But they haven't given up searching.'

'No. But they've found nothing either.'

'He'll be nearly two by now,' said Eloin wistfully, gazing out across the grazing herd. 'I wonder if he is growing up to look like Brechin.'

'A fine little Outrider.'

'I miss them, Blindweed, but at least I can believe that Rannoch is still alive. Brechin will never come back. Never.'

Eloin lowered her head.

'Brechin's with Starbuck,' whispered Blindweed kindly, 'and Herne.'

'I suppose so, but I still miss him, Blindweed.'

'And I miss Bhreac,' said Blindweed, shaking his head, 'but we must be strong. I am glad at least that she is with your fawn. I know she will do everything she can to protect him.'

'You're right, I mustn't be gloomy. It's just that some days it's so hard. I remember when the Outriders crowned the hills and roamed free. Now the Draila have destroyed everything and the Drailing are so powerful that the hinds even fear to bear fawns.'

'I know.' Blindweed nodded gravely. 'But perhaps . . .'

The old storyteller paused.

'Perhaps?'

'The Prophecy.'

'Do you really believe it, Blindweed?' said Eloin, looking hard at her old friend. 'Can Rannoch really be the one?'

'It's the only thing that has kept my heart from breaking these past years.'

The two friends were silent now as the thin sun shone down on them. It gave them little warmth.

'But have you ever thought what it says, Blindweed?' said Eloin suddenly, looking deeply into her old friend's eyes. 'I've been thinking about it a lot lately. *Sacrifice shall be his meaning*. That's what it says. Sacrifice, Blindweed. What did I give birth to him for?'

'That none of us may know,' said Blindweed gravely, 'until the Prophecy is fulfilled. And if it is to be fulfilled Drail and Sgorr must never find out that he is a changeling. Or they will not stop hunting him until they have uprooted the Great Land.'

As the old friends were talking, three stags were walking through the spring grass on the western hill above the home herd. The youngest had a fine head of antlers while the oldest, who was leading, walked with a limp and his antlers had already gone back. The stag next to them, who was talking to them now, kept dipping his head to the leader and, though the herd had not yet shed, he had no antlers at all.

'Did the inspection please you, Lord?' said Sgorr syco-phantically, blinking with his single eye.

'Yes, well enough,' said Drail. 'You've trained them well.'

'The scouts have returned from the north once more,' said Sgorr.

'What news?'

'All the Low Land herds now pay you homage.'

'All except Tharn,' said Drail angrily. 'Why does he still resist me?'

'He's proud,' answered Sgorr, 'and he's too fond of his Outriders to give them up without a fight.'

'Outriders,' snorted Drail. 'Will I never be rid of them?'

'They are loyal to him, Lord. I even believe they love him.'

'One day they will be loyal to me,' said Drail bitterly.

'And love you too,' Sgorr added quickly. His tone was simpering and sarcastic.

'No, Sgorr, not even I am vain enough to believe that. But there are two ways to command loyalty. Love and fear.'

'Indeed,' said Sgorr, 'and Tharn is a fool. His rule carries the seeds of its own destruction. By maintaining Anlach he ensures that one day soon he will be overthrown.'

'True. But how do we know that the Outriders will come over even then? They're woodlanders and nothing we have tried has enabled us to infiltrate his herd.'

'That is not quite true,' answered Sgorr quietly, gazing out into the day. 'There's one who might yet be persuaded.'

'Then we shall have to bide our time,' said Drail, 'before all the Low Lands are mine.'

Sgorr cast Drail a sly and contemptuous look.

'There is still no sign of the runaways,' he said, and he was gratified to see fear flicker across Drail's face. Drail pulled up in the grass and shook his head.

'I don't understand it,' he muttered to himself. 'Where can they be hiding?'

Yes, you old fool, thought Sgorr, chuckling inwardly. You're still terrified of the Prophecy.

'Who knows?' he said out loud. 'When the Draila arrived at the loch, Tharn had seen nothing of them. They were certain he wasn't lying to them. Yet Tharn's is the only herd that would shield them. It's a mystery.'

'We must find them, Sgorr,' said Drail, and then he added, 'Not because of that calf, you understand. As you said, he is no changeling.'

Sgorr smiled to himself again.

'But because all the Herla must know that none can escape me,' Drail went on. 'They must be made to suffer. All of them.'

'And they will,' agreed Sgorr, 'when we find them.'

'So,' said Drail with sudden irritation, 'instead of talking to me all day, why don't you send out some more of the Draila? Right away. Now I'm tired and I want to see Eloin.'

Drail suddenly ran forward in the grass, leaving Sgorr and the younger stag alone together on the hill.

'Well?' said the second stag quietly, when Drail was out of earshot.

'Soon, Narl,' muttered Sgorr, 'very soon.'

The two of them walked on and Sgorr was smiling again as he watched Drail limping back to the Home Oak. When they had reached the bottom of the hill Sgorr pulled up once more.

'Narl,' he said quietly, 'what news from the inner spies? Anything suspicious? We must have absolute control when the time comes. They must report to me if they notice anything. Anything at all. Do you understand me?'

'Yes,' said Narl. He paused and a thoughtful look entered his face. Sgorr saw it.

'What is it?'

'It's probably nothing,' said Narl, shaking his head. 'It's just that Reen was coming home the other day when he saw Blindweed by the stream.'

'The storyteller?' said Sgorr with surprise. 'I didn't think he was still alive.'

'Yes, although they say he's gone a little mad. When Reen approached him he didn't see him for a while. He's practically blind now.'

'And?'

'And he was talking to himself. Mumbling something about the Prophecy.'

'The Prophecy?' said Sgorr with sudden interest. 'What was he saying?'

'First, Reen says, he recited part of it. Then he started chuckling to himself.'

'Go on,' said Sgorr, who was listening closely now.

'Well, this is the really odd part,' said Narl. 'He suddenly said, "If they only knew about Bracken's dead fawn, poor little thing," and then he started chuckling again.'

Sgorr stopped in his tracks. He was thinking back. He was summoning back that night by the stream. He could see Eloin in his mind now, standing in front of him, moving slowly aside to reveal the dead fawn. Sgorr had always thought there had been something slightly strange about that. About the triumph in her eyes. Something subtly wrong. Then her sudden, passionate desire to protect Bracken and the calf by the trees.

'Quickly,' cried Sgorr, his mind flaming. 'Bring Blindweed to me and fetch some of the Draila. I'll meet you by the rock. And tell the Draila to sharpen their antlers.'

'What are you going to do?'

'Question Blindweed, of course,' cried Sgorr, as he set off at a run, 'and find out what he means about the dead fawn.'

But as Sgorr ran he had already guessed.

As Larn came in over the home herd a calf with his first head was walking by the river towards the big rock where he so liked to go and play when he could escape the all-consuming duties of the Drailing. He knew he should never have been out so late and the thought of one of the Drailing's endless punishments made him especially wary. He was just nearing the rock when he stopped and looked ahead of him in horror.

He saw a group of stags in front of him, surrounding an old deer. The deer was on the ground and one of his antlers was snapped off. His muzzle was covered in blood and his eyes were so swollen he could hardly see the Draila around him. As the terrified fawn looked on, one of the stags turned again and kicked him straight in the face.

'Why don't you just tell us, Blindweed?' whispered Sgorr coldly in the darkness, turning his back on the stag on the ground. 'And we'll make it an easy death.'

'I don't know anything,' answered Blindweed bitterly. He tried to lift his head from the grass but sank back helplessly.

'Of course you do.' Sgorr smiled. 'I already know anyway. I just wanted you to confirm it.'

'Never,' spat Blindweed.

Sgorr walked straight up to the injured stag and stood over him.

'Let's go through it one more time,' he said angrily. 'That night, by the stream. When Eloin showed me her dead fawn. It wasn't her fawn, was it? It was Bracken's. So that makes the fawn with the mark Eloin's fawn, and consequently Brechin's. Not only does the blood of a most hated Outrider flow in his veins but he is what you might call ... a changeling.'

'I don't know anything,' mumbled Blindweed, trying to choke back the blood in his mouth.

'Yes you do,' sneered Sgorr. 'That prophecy of yours. It talks of a fawn mark and a changeling.'

Blindweed was silent now and Sgorr threw Narl a glance. The stag kicked Blindweed again.

'Don't think I care,' Sgorr went on casually, as Blindweed bellowed in pain. 'I'm not foolish enough to believe it. But I've devoted my life to knowing everything I can in the home herd. It's more a matter of pride.'

'And pride will destroy you,' cried Blindweed suddenly, spitting blood from his swollen lips, 'when He comes.'

'Ah, so now we come to it. So it's true about Eloin?'

'Yes, it's true. And you'll rue the day you let him escape.'

Some of the surrounding Draila looked at each other nervously for, though it was forbidden to talk of Herne and the Prophecy, rumours and murmurings still survived in the herd.

'Dear, dear,' said Sgorr, 'we are getting carried away. I shall do nothing of the sort. I'm not a stupid, superstitious Herla to believe some made-up legend about Herne. Look at me, Blindweed, if you still can. I am Sgorr and I fear nothing.'

'Until Rannoch returns,' said the storyteller, blinking up at his torturers.

'So,' cried Sgorr, swinging round. 'Thank you, Blindweed. His name is Rannoch.'

'It does not matter what he is called,' sobbed Blindweed, racked with anguish that he had betrayed the fawn. 'Rannoch. Herne. He is the one.'

'Really!' snorted Sgorr suddenly. 'I'm weary of this. Goodbye, Blindweed. Be assured that with you shall die the last of the old tales and the lies of Herne and the Herla.'

Sgorr turned away with distaste and, with Narl following him, he ran back towards the Home Oak. As they went there was a final, exhausted bark of pain from the old storyteller.

'I don't understand it,' said Narl as the stags ran up the valley in the darkness. 'If the Marked One is a changeling then maybe there is some truth—'

'Narl,' snapped Sgorr, 'if you wish to serve me then try and hide your stupidity. There's no truth in it.'

'Then why were you so keen to know about the calf?' said Narl.

'Simple,' answered Sgorr. 'Because it serves our purpose. When Drail hears of it he will be even more terrified than he already is. And his fear makes him weak.'

'Besides,' said Sgorr to himself with pleasure as they ran through the night, 'when Drail learns of Eloin's part in this, it will drive them even further apart.'

Sgorr waited a full ten suns to tell Drail what he had discovered. He was looking for the moment the news would have the most startling effect. It came by the Home Oak where Sgorr had gone as usual to report on the activities of the herd. When he approached in the bright sunlight he smiled as he found Eloin and Drail arguing, as they so often did.

'Can't you forget him?' Drail was saying to the hind.

'Never.'

'I thought with time you would grow to care for me,' said Drail quietly. 'Is it not fine to be favoured by the Lord of Herds?'

Eloin looked coldly at Drail. For two seasons she had been held in Drail's harem by force, but they had still not mated, for Eloin had used every wile to reject him and keep her oath. The autumn before last she had managed this by stirring up jealousies among his other hinds and making them fight for Drail's favours. The previous Anlach it was only by pretending to be sick that she had kept him away. But Eloin knew it could not be long before she would have to give in, and she hated him now more than ever.

Drail was very old to mate, for as a stag loses his strength and can no longer fight for hinds he will rarely mate after the age of eleven in the normal life of a herd. But two of Drail's hinds had born calves last summer, though they were both weaklings. Drail was displeased with them and it was Eloin's calves that he really longed for.

'When summer comes,' said Drail, 'you will bear me a fine stag to further my bloodline.'

As Sgorr stood behind them he winced. None of his own hinds had ever calved.

'No, Drail,' answered Eloin coldly, 'I will never give you a calf, stag or hind.'

There was something in the way she said it that made Drail pause. The stag turned his head and looked at her closely.

'What do you mean?'

'I'll never give you calves because, my dear, you have wasted much time on the wrong hind,' Eloin lied. 'All my fawns will be stillborn. That is Herne's curse to me.'

'No,' came a voice suddenly from behind them, and Drail swung round furiously to see Sgorr standing there watching them.

'Sgorr,' he snorted, 'how dare you interrupt us?'

'Forgive me, Lord,' answered the stag, bowing his head, 'but I thought it right to speak. Especially since Eloin is lying.'

'What do you mean, *lying*?'

There was something in Sgorr's voice, something threatening and knowing, that suddenly chilled Eloin's blood. The hind glared at him.

'Because she has already given birth to a fawn that lived. Brechin's fawn.'

'Brechin's fawn?' said Drail in amazement. 'But it died. You saw the body.'

Eloin was silent, staring at Sgorr. She was trembling.

'I saw *a* body,' said Sgorr slowly. 'But it wasn't Eloin's fawn. It belonged to a hind called Bracken.'

'How do you know this?'

'The storyteller told me,' answered Sgorr, smiling at Eloin, 'before he died.'

'Blindweed!' cried Eloin. 'What have you done?'

'Silence!' shouted Drail and the hind dropped her head. Drail paused. He was trying to remember where he had heard the name before.

'Bracken?' he said at last. 'But isn't that one of the hinds that we are looking for?'

'Yes,' answered Sgorr, 'and she is looking after the fawn with the oaken mark. Eloin's fawn. His name is Rannoch.'

'Eloin's?'

'They were changed,' said Sgorr portentously, leading Drail carefully towards the point. 'Eloin swapped Bracken's dead fawn for her own at birth. Changed them.'

Drail was staring at both of them now, reaching for Sgorr's meaning. Suddenly terror awoke in his eyes.

'So the one with the oak mark is Brechin's fawn?' he whispered, almost choking. 'And . . .'

Sgorr let him get there on his own.

' . . . And a changeling,' gasped Drail. 'The Prophecy. It's true.'

The lord staggered forward in the grass. He lurched to the side and Sgorr made no effort to help him. He was smiling at Eloin triumphantly.

Over the coming months the news of Rannoch and the Prophecy wrought a dramatic change in Drail. He seemed to age visibly, to sag inwardly. He began to spend all his time by the Home Oak, always surrounded by Draila, muttering to himself and asking any deer he could what they knew of the Prophecy.

Sgorr did nothing to discourage this. Indeed he positively fed Drail's terror. He himself would visit Drail and recite it, nodding gravely and pretending to interpret its meaning. Every day Drail ordered Sgorr to send out more and more

Draila scouting parties, though of course Sgorr did nothing of the kind.

There was one aspect of Sgorr's plan though that misfired: the desired rift between Drail and Eloin. For rather than estranging her from Drail, now the aged stag seemed to want her with him all the time. Drail seemed strangely comforted by her presence, as though the mother of 'the One' would afford him some protection. He would even ask her about the Prophecy and if she believed in it. Eloin neither confirmed nor denied anything. She wanted to feed Drail's terror but at the same time knew that it was dangerous for her calf. She was silent and fearful and Blindweed's murder had reopened the bitter wound in her slowly healing heart.

So the year grew. With the spring showers the herd's antlers began to fall. First a right or left antler would drop, so for three or four suns a stag would be left with just a single branch on his head. Then the second antler dropped too and the stag walked bareheaded through the home valley. It was always at this time of year that Sgorr felt most powerful and became more vicious among the stags.

After just a few suns new antlers began to rise again on the stags' heads, furred with soft, downy velvet. On the royals they grew like stunted twigs, their points rounded at first, and then, as the moons turned, the branches arced and the tines became sharper and sharper as they flowered above them. This was the time when the stags would normally have begun to box playfully, not being able to test the strength in their antlers. But the deer's natural exuberance found no outlet, except in the training camps of the Draila and their endless forced marches. The flowers grew too and the deer began to moult, their coats turning back to a fine, fiery red. The calving began and the herd was blessed with new life, if a blessing you could call it, for many of the hinds hated their Draila mates and feared for their fawns.

As the sun burnt down the stags came out of velvet and their antlers began to peel so that, for several suns, many a stag walked through the valley with bloody tatters of torn velvet hanging like ribbons from their heads. They rubbed their tines on trees and branches and soon the strong new spikes were clean again. All the while, Sgorr seemed to be waiting for something. It was a burning hot day when a stranger appeared in the valley. The stag asked to see Sgorr and Sgorr had obviously been expecting him for the Draila immediately escorted him into his presence.

Narl was sitting down, ruminating thoughtfully by the stream after a tiring morning lecturing to the Drailing, when a Draila brought word that Sgorr had summoned him to the Home Oak. When he arrived he found Sgorr with Drail and Eloin.

'Ah, Narl, good. I wanted you here,' said Sgorr as the stag arrived. 'There is much to do.'

Narl's master had grown in confidence and authority in front of Drail and Narl suddenly thought that Drail looked terribly old and fragile.

'What is it now, Sgorr?' said Drail almost disinterestedly, gazing across the valley.

'Splendid news, Lord. From the north.'

Drail stirred and looked up slowly.

'Well then, tell me. I could do with some good news.'

'Tharn,' said Sgorr, 'the Lord above the Loch. He's been overthrown. He died on the antlers of his own Outriders.'

'Overthrown. But how?'

'By the deer who I have had dealings with. His name is Colquhar.'

'Will he do homage?' asked Drail, suddenly more interested.

'Indeed.' Sgorr nodded, looking away.

'Then where is he?'

Sgorr paused and measured his words.

'He's agreed to meet you, Lord, but not here. He would make the whole journey,' Sgorr went on slyly, 'but he is fearful of leaving his own herd for too long, in case of a revolt. So I took the liberty of arranging a meeting place.'

'Where?' said Drail almost angrily.

'By the gully where the Draila lost Rannoch and the others.'

Sgorr was delighted that the mention of Rannoch made Drail drop his eyes. The lord shook his antlers.

'But that means . . .' said Drail fearfully, looking beyond the hills, 'that means going out *there*.'

'Don't worry, Lord,' said Sgorr, smiling as he came close to Drail. 'Narl and I will make sure you are well protected.'

Drail looked about him helplessly.

'But I can't leave Eloin and the herd,' he said weakly.

'Eloin will come with us, won't you, my dear?' said Sgorr, swinging round to face the hind. 'To look after your lord.'

'But *he* is out there,' said Drail suddenly and his voice was almost pleading, 'somewhere.'

'Yes. But he is still young and can do nothing to harm you. Just think of it. When Colquhar pays you homage, you will truly be Lord of Herds, for then none can oppose you in the Low Lands. All the Herla shall be yours, prophecy or no prophecy.'

Drail looked up meekly at Eloin.

'I suppose you are right,' he muttered. 'But if we are to go we must hurry. And I want your best Draila with me at all times. Do you understand me? At all times.'

'Yes, Lord, of course,' said Sgorr, looking towards Narl. His single eye was glittering furiously.

The party set off the very next morning. Drail, Eloin, Sgorr and Narl were escorted by ten Draila stags that Sgorr had picked especially for the purpose. They travelled as quickly as they could, allowing for their leader's limping gait. Once they left the protection of the home valley Drail became very nervous and Sgorr made a point of mentioning the Prophecy at every turn. So when, after five suns, they reached the wood where Rannoch had first met Crak, Drail was at his nerves' end.

Evening was coming in as they began to rise towards the gully, the gathering twilight casting gloomy shadows through the trees. Drail was especially jumpy now and at every unfamiliar sound, a broken twig or a bird breaking from the undergrowth, the old stag started nervously. All the while Drail wanted to hang back to browse but Sgorr kept insisting they should hurry to meet Colquhar. After a while the deer heard a low, booming grumble. It was the river and now Sgorr pulled up the Draila.

'I think it's best we leave the escort here to protect our backs,' he said quietly, 'while we four go on ahead. You, me, Narl and Eloin.'

Drail looked fearfully at Sgorr but in the state he was in he would have done almost anything Sgorr told him.

'Colquhar is proud,' Sgorr went on, 'and he will not thank you for forcing him to do homage in front of so many stags.'

They pushed on through the trees, leaving the Draila stags on guard behind them. Drail's heart was pounding as they broke the cover of the trees and the great ravine plunged before them towards the craggy river. They were standing on the very spot where Crak had told Rannoch about the bridge and, as Drail stepped towards the ravine, he looked around nervously, expecting to see other stags at any moment. But to his surprise there was no one there. No one at all. Just the bare earth and the thundering chasm.

'Well,' he said as he looked down into the void, his voice wrestling with the sound of water, 'where is he?'

'Colquhar?' Sgorr smiled coldly, stepping up behind Drail as he stood by the drop. 'Colquhar is not coming, Drail.'

'What?' cried Drail, wheeling round. 'What do you mean not coming?'

'Exactly what I say.'

Eloin and Narl looked quizzically at each other.

'But what of his homage?'

'He will do homage,' said Sgorr slowly, 'all in good time. But first, in order to get him to . . . to abandon Tharn, I had to let him believe that he could keep his herd much as it is, with the Outriders still in place. He is probably with them now.'

'With the Outriders still in place?' said Drail. 'Then why have you brought me here? I don't understand.'

'No, Drail, you never have,' said Sgorr. 'But rest assured that one day Colquhar will submit.'

'So when may I expect his homage?'

'Not to you, Drail,' snorted Sgorr contemptuously, 'but to me and to the Sgorrla.'

Drail looked at Sgorr with horror as he began to understand what Sgorr was saying.

'Sgorr!' he cried. 'Traitor . . .'

'Don't think of it as a betrayal,' sneered Sgorr. 'Think of it more as breaking ranks. How could you ever expect a deer like myself to remain loyal to a vain, foolish, superstitious soft-foot like you? You must admit it would be the height of stupidity. To follow a deer who is frightened of a prophecy.'

'But the Prophecy,' whispered Drail. 'You believe in the Prophecy?'

'No, Drail, I have never believed in the Prophecy. Nor in Herne. I thought I could work with you when I found a deer who wanted to drive out Anlach and the spirit of Herne. But that's the difference between you and me. I wanted to drive Herne away because I do not believe in him. I believe that the Herla must serve intelligence and reason. Serve *me* in fact. Across the Great Land. But you would change the old laws because you believe them and fear them. You are a fool, Drail.'

'Swine,' spat Drail furiously. For the first time anger and something of his old courage were rising in him.

'Incidentally,' said Sgorr calmly, 'since you are so interested in the Prophecy, there is more news from the herd above the Loch. Rannoch and the hinds arrived there the winter before last.'

Eloin, who had been listening in horrified amazement, began to shake violently but Drail stood stock-still. His mind was suddenly on fire. The monumental nature of Sgorr's betrayal and the sudden talk of the Prophecy made his head reel, but the image of a fawn's face had just leapt into his mind.

'The mark,' he whispered in a strangled voice. 'The mark.'

'Still a victim of your own fears,' said Sgorr contemptuously.

'I'll go away,' muttered Drail. 'Yes. Go far away and hide myself in the High Land. Hide from His wrath.'

'And getting it wrong to the last.'

Drail looked up. His eyes were misty with confusion but now he saw the hate in Sgorr's eye and with it he spied his own fate.

'Yes, Drail,' cried Sgorr, his words echoing through the wide ravine. 'I am here to free the Herla from lies.'

Sgorr suddenly leapt forward. He gave Drail a violent buffet to his flank and the old deer was hurled backwards. Drail's hoofs scrambled on the edge of the ravine but found no foothold. They touched air, and with one last bellow of confusion, Drail fell into the void, his body and his antlers spinning above the spray, falling past the grey stone, crashing onto the rocks below.

The three deer stood there silently in the thickening dark, looking down on the broken stag as the air howled around their heads. At last Sgorr spoke again, calmly and with a ring of amusement.

'Now that's finished, Narl, we can get to work.'

Narl looked at him in bewilderment. 'You will work for Colquhar's submission?' he muttered.

'Narl,' said Sgorr, smiling, 'you really must learn to be more imaginative, more ambitious.'

'But what is more ambitious than to be Lord of Herds?'

'To be Lord of all the Great Land, of course. To subdue both the Low and the High Land. To bring all the herds together, not in homage, but as one, serving my will. To unite the Herla. To bring even the Clovar under my dominion.'

Sgorr's voice seemed to have grown in power and strength as his words echoed back and forth across the ancient ravine. Narl looked back at him in amazed admiration.

'Then we will see,' cried Sgorr triumphantly, 'when the Great Herd is mine and order is brought to the Herla. When they are taught to serve reason. To break free from their instincts which make them nothing but weaklings.'

Narl feared to speak.

'But go, Narl,' said Sgorr suddenly, coming out of his reverie. 'Tell the Drai . . . No, tell the *Sgorrla* that we are coming. When you get back to the herd you will have much work.'

'In the herd?'

'Yes, Narl. There were those two calves last summer for a start. Then there are many others.'

Narl and Eloin both blinked at Sgorr.

'That's right, Narl, you must get to work removing the last traces of Drail's bloodline. Now, leave me. I want to talk to Eloin.'

Narl nodded and turned away, but Sgorr pulled him up again.

'Narl, there is just one other thing,' he whispered. 'We can also expect visitors. Colquhar is not quite won over to our cause, but he did agree to one concession, in return for my support. He has agreed to hand back our hinds and their calves. We must prepare them a special welcome.'

As Eloin heard this and Narl backed away, she spoke for the first time, her voice shaking with anger and fear.

'You won't harm him, Sgorr,' she hissed, 'or any of them.'

'Is that a threat, my dear?' said Sgorr, pleased that this last piece of news had had exactly the effect he had anticipated.

'Yes, Sgorr, it's a threat,' said Eloin, 'by Herne and by all the strength in my blood.'

Even Sgorr shivered a little at her tone, though the sensation gave him a strange pleasure.

'Well, that is up to you, my dear, isn't it?' he said, 'and how much you do to please me. And it's right you should talk of blood, for soon our bloodline will be flowing through the herd.'

Eloin's bold eyes flashed.

'Is there nothing you won't do, Sgorr? Nothing you fear?'

'Nothing,' answered Sgorr coldly, 'except stupidity.'

'Then it is you that is the fool, Sgorr. And one day you shall learn that. When the Prophecy is fulfilled.'

'Not you as well,' said Sgorr, almost yawning and shaking his head. 'I had expected better from you.'

'Why won't you believe it?' said Eloin. '*On his brow a leaf of oaken, changeling child shall be his fate.*'

'Yes, yes, I know all that,' cried Sgorr irritably, 'and no doubt one day Herne himself will come down, carrying Starbuck in his antlers, to tell us all we've been naughty little Herla.'

'You can mock, Sgorr,' spat Eloin, 'but don't you see? It's all coming true.'

'I admit that parts of it have provided some useful coincidences, very useful indeed. But anyway, it doesn't matter now. Because I *know* the rest of it isn't true.'

Eloin suddenly lifted her head to Sgorr's eye. The certainty in his voice had struck a warning note.

'You know?' she whispered.

'Oh yes. You see there is just one minor thing that I neglected to tell you about Colquhar's news. Rannoch can never do me any harm, fawn mark or no.'

Eloin's voice was faint above the sound of water, her words as strangled as Drail's had been.

'Why not?' she said, trembling.

'Because, my dear,' said Sgorr, gazing out over the fearful abyss, 'Rannoch was torn to shreds by dogs above the loch. He is dead, Eloin, dead.'

9

Escape

Clothed in white samite, mystic, wonderful.
Alfred Lord Tennyson, 'The Coming of Arthur'

'Call yourself an Outrider?' cried Alyth furiously as the stag beside her gave her another buffet with his antlers. 'You're nothing but Draila filth.'

'It's orders, that's all,' answered the stag a little guiltily. 'Anyway they're called the Sgorrla now and I've nothing to do with those scum. Be quiet and keep moving.'

Alyth glared at the stag but it was clear he was in no mood to argue and the hind ran on towards her friends. Shira, Canisp, Fern and Bracken were ahead of her now, flanked by ten Outriders. The hinds were both nervous and tired for they hadn't rested in several suns, and the stags, ashamed of what Colquhar had asked them to do but too proud to admit they were in the wrong, had been foul-tempered ever since the party had set off from the loch. They had taken out their resentment on their charges.

None of the Outriders had been pleased when Colquhar had given the orders to hand the incomers back to Sgorr and there was still much resentment above the loch. Tharn's sudden death had come as a great shock to many of them.

But Colquhar, as the strongest of the Outrider captains, was
not an unworthy successor in the herd.

Colquhar had finally convinced them that the only way
to preserve their independence was to conciliate Sgorr. So
much was happening in the Low Lands with Drail's own
murder at the hands of traitors – as Sgorr had put it out –
and with talk of a Great Herd, that the Outriders were keen
to cling to any hope of maintaining their position. But the
work they were engaged in now still stuck in their throats.

Ahead of this group of deer ran more Outriders and in
the middle of them came three stags and two young hinds.
Although they too were nervous about returning to the home
herd, the sun was shining, there was a strange excitement in
their journey and their youthful spirits could never be
subdued for long. As the young friends travelled, they kept
breaking out in nervous talk.

The twins were walking together now and Bankfoot was
at their side. Willow and Peppa had grown into fine young
does and they looked remarkably alike, although Peppa had
a little splash of blackish fur on her right ear. Bankfoot
had his second head of antlers, which made him very proud
for he was no longer a pricket. As well as the the twin beams
that rose above him, thicker and more curved than in a first
head, he also had two brow tines that pointed out ahead.
He was only just coming out of velvet and because he was
still unused to the strange, itching sensation around the base
of his antlers, he kept shaking his head irritably. Bankfoot
was as fat as ever and the Outriders' refusal to let him stop
and graze just added to his annoyance and discomfort.

In front, Tain and Thistle were deep in conversation. They
also had their second heads and they were growing into
handsome young stags, although Thistle's antlers looked
stronger and larger than Tain's.

'Why are the Outriders in such a hurry?' said Peppa, as they went. 'I'd like to stop for a while.'

'I know,' said Willow. 'I think they just want to get it over with.'

'I don't see what Sgorr w-w-wants with us,' said Bankfoot nervously.

'Nor do I,' agreed Peppa, 'since Rannoch . . .'

'Don't, Peppa,' said Willow immediately, wincing with an almost physical pain. 'Don't remind me.'

There was a sadness in the young hind's eyes as the memory of that day on the hill suddenly flashed into her mind. She missed Rannoch bitterly and the thought of her friend's death at the teeth of those terrifying dogs still haunted her. But what was unbearable was that she had never even seen the fawn's body.

After Rannoch had drawn off the dog, Willow had waited all night in the bracken until the humans had left the scene of the hunt, carrying the carcasses of the dead deer away with them on their horses. Then the fawn had crept out to look for her friend. The memory of the scene still made her sick but there had been no sign of Rannoch; just the blood-soaked grass to whisper of his bitter fate. In a daze she had stumbled around searching for him, until she had seen that young human and fled through the heather.

In spite of the blood and the ferocity of the dogs, some distant hope lingered inside her and, as the seasons passed, Willow had watched and waited, in vain, until hope itself had begun to fester.

'I know W-w-willow,' said Bankfoot gently. 'I m-m-miss him dreadfully too.'

'What does Canisp think about our going back, Bankfoot?' asked Peppa suddenly.

Bankfoot gave her an odd look.

'I d-d-don't know,' answered the young stag. 'I haven't asked her.'

With the seasons and the coming of their antlers the young stags had grown apart from their mothers. The Outriders had pulled up suddenly and Bankfoot looked back at Canisp. Bankfoot was still young enough to be attached to the hind, but he would rather die than show that he relied on her in any way or ever asked her advice.

'I think Bracken's very frightened,' said Peppa. 'After all, she has most to fear from Sgorr.'

'Poor Bracken,' agreed Willow. 'I'm not sure she even realizes what's happening. She's never been the same since Rannoch . . . left.'

Rannoch's loss had broken Bracken's heart. For months the hind had been unable to speak and had drifted alone through the herd looking for her little fawn. At last the realization that he was really gone had woken in her and for a time Bracken seemed to lose her wits. She kept mumbling to herself about another hind and saying that she had betrayed her trust. The others couldn't understand her when she talked like this, but they sensed her terrible pain and confusion.

To Bracken the world had suddenly become empty and meaningless. In her heart Rannoch had replaced her own dead fawn, and she had felt a special responsibility to protect him because of the prophecy that had woven itself round his birth. Although Bracken had never understood it and had always concealed it from the fawn, the strange events of their flight had begun to confirm the mysterious words. But the promise of the Prophecy, the hope of a new life come suddenly to replace her own loss and the dream of the future had all been torn to shreds.

'We'll stop here,' cried an Outrider suddenly. 'Sgorr can't be far away and Larn will be with us soon.'

The two groups drifted towards the trees where Bankfoot was delighted to have a chance to graze while the hinds wandered down to a stream that burbled below them through the grass. The Outriders around them began to feed, but they kept a keen eye on their prisoners as they did so. Alyth, Fern, Shira and Canisp started to drink greedily but Bracken just stood nearby, gazing dully into the waters.

'That's better,' said Canisp when she had drunk her fill. She looked up towards Bankfoot and twitched her large ears.

'Bankfoot,' she called. 'Bankfoot, why don't you come and drink? It's delicious.'

The young stag stopped feeding and looked towards his mother but then he turned away in embarrassment and some of the watching Outriders chuckled to themselves.

'Not in front of his friends, Canisp,' said Alyth quietly. 'If I called to Thistle like that he'd be furious.'

'But it's so strange,' said Canisp, 'not to be able to talk to him whenever I like.'

'It's Herne's way,' said Alyth, 'that's all.'

Canisp found it hard to let go of her only fawn. Of all the hinds, only Alyth had mated again last Anlach, though her calf had miscarried.

'Anyway,' Alyth went on, 'you shouldn't be worrying about such silly things. We've more important things to think about. Like Sgorr.'

'I don't think we've got much to worry about,' shrugged Fern. 'He just wants us back, that's all.'

'I hope you're right,' said Alyth.

'I agree with Fern,' said Shira, looking towards Bracken. 'Now Rannoch's gone he can't have any real reason to wish us harm. That's what Colquhar said. He told me Sgorr was very shaken up by Drail's death and that he's promised to preserve the Outriders above the loch.'

Bracken had heard this but it hardly seemed to register on her staring eyes. She dropped her head and started to graze. A little way away Tain came walking over to Bankfoot.

'Hello, Bankfoot,' he said. 'We haven't had much chance to talk since we left the loch.'

'N-n-no, Tain, we haven't,' said Bankfoot, noticing the worry in Tain's face. 'What's wrong?'

'Thistle doesn't seem to agree,' said Tain, 'but I'm nervous about going back to the home herd. I've heard such stories and you remember the Draila and the Drailing. Colquhar says otherwise, but why should it be any different now Sgorr's in charge?'

'I d-d-don't suppose it will be,' agreed Bankfoot.

'I've been thinking,' said Tain. 'You heard what that Outrider said. Sgorr must be close. Perhaps we should try to make a break for it.'

'Make a b-b-break for it?'

'Yes.'

'And go where? We can't go back to the l-l-loch.'

'No, I suppose not,' said Tain glumly.

'Besides, I d-d-don't think the hinds would come with us. We'd have to leave them.'

Tain stared back at Bankfoot. He'd never really thought of leaving Shira before.

'Even if they did come,' Bankfoot went on, 'there's B-b-bracken to think of. She's so strange and distant. She'd just slow us up.'

'But if we went alone,' said Tain, 'slipped away at night and kept to the trees, we could make for the mountains and . . .'

Tain stopped. He hadn't thought further than flight and now a cloud seemed to cross his mind.

'What do the others think?' said Bankfoot.

'I've only talked to Thistle and he says I'm talking rubbish. You know he was never very pleased to leave the home herd.'

'Well,' said Bankfoot, 'we should talk to Willow.'

That night, well after Larn, while the Outriders kept watch and the older hinds settled down in the grass, the young friends were found huddled together, whispering in the darkness.

'It's nonsense,' Thistle was muttering irritably. 'Sgorr won't do us any harm. Anyway, just let him try.'

'And I'd be sad to leave Mother,' added Peppa.

'But Tain's right,' said Willow gravely. 'We don't know why Sgorr wants us back. From all I've heard he's cruel and wicked.'

'Some say he killed Drail,' whispered Tain.

'Talk some sense,' snorted Thistle, pawing the grass. 'Now Colquhar has thrown us out of the Herd above the loch, we've nowhere to go. Sgorr rules in the Low Lands.'

'W-w-what about the High Land?' stuttered Bankfoot suddenly.

All the friends looked at Bankfoot in amazement. They remembered vaguely that during their flight the hinds had talked of the High Land. But it was still a place shrouded in mystery. A land rich in stories and legends about the Herla and the Lera – some full of hope and wonder, others dark and frightening – woven from rumour and ignorance, for no deer either from the home herd or the loch had ever travelled there. Tain was especially interested in the notion, for his passion for stories had grown and grown and even as a fawn he could remember asking Blindweed about the place.

Consequently, though his knowledge was patchy, he knew a little more of the High Land than the others.

'Why not?' said Tain.

'Because we'd never make it,' said Thistle angrily, 'and there's much more to fear up there than from going back to the home herd.'

'I don't know,' said Willow quietly.

'Well I do,' snorted Thistle, turning away furiously and walking off to graze.

'Don't mind him,' said Bankfoot. 'Thistle's always angry nowadays. He's changed so much since his antlers first came.'

'I know,' agreed Willow, 'and he's always so keen to fight. The way he behaved last season, you'd think he was Lord of the Herd.'

'One day I'm sure he wants to be,' said Peppa.

'What I can't understand,' said Willow, 'is why he isn't more angry about going back to the home herd. Why doesn't he hate them for what they wanted to do to Rannoch? I hate them.'

'M-m-me too,' agreed Bankfoot.

'We should escape for *his* sake if nothing else,' said Willow gravely, 'and tell his story to our fawns.'

The friends looked sadly at one another but now Tain suddenly coughed, for an Outrider was drifting towards them. They immediately dropped their heads and pretended to graze, and the Outrider eyed them suspiciously before returning to the others.

Morning came warm and bright and found the Outriders and their captives still by the stream. The Outriders were restless, for after suns of journeying south they knew that Sgorr must be close at hand and there was nothing they wanted more than to put an end to their shameful mission and return to the loch. They were nervous too, for though

Colquhar had promised them that his pact with Sgorr had
secured the independence of the Herd above the loch, they
knew Sgorr's reputation only too well and there was not one
among them who really trusted him. But Colquhar was Lord
above the Loch and before he had come to a decision about
the incomers he had also sat with the Outriders in council.
Now their orders were clear and, as Outriders, they were
bound to obey.

'Come on, you lot,' cried the Outrider who had chosen
the resting place the night before. 'It's time to get going
again.'

It was midday and the sun was high in the clear blue sky
when the deer came over a hill and began to descend steeply
through the long, sweet grass. They came to a meadow and
the ground was thick with daisies and buttercups that glowed
a brilliant yellow around them. Bankfoot was feeling
strangely cheerful, for the sun was on his back and his antlers
had suddenly stopped itching, when he halted in the grass
and looked up the hill in amazement.

There, in the sunlight, a single stag was watching him. Its
antlers rose high above its proud head and it had a fine,
sleek coat. It was a twelve-pointer but what made Bankfoot
start was the colour of the stag's pelt. Its fur was completely
white. The strange hart did nothing for a while as it watched
them and then, suddenly, it turned and vanished over the
hill. Bankfoot shivered and for some reason he thought of
Rannoch.

They travelled on and it was early afternoon when Tain
suddenly looked up and frowned. Coming across the ground,
moving swiftly towards them, he saw twenty stags. Ahead
of them was a stag with no antlers. They had all stopped
now and the young friends moved together nervously. The
Outriders waited silently around them, watching the Sgorrla

suspiciously. When the deer reached them they pulled up and for a while said nothing as they measured the Outriders' strength.

Then Sgorr spoke. As the young friends looked up into his scarred face with its single eye, the twins and the stags shuddered. This was the first time any of them had come face to face with Sgorr.

'Good,' said Sgorr. 'They're all here.'

The Outriders looked back at him but said nothing. Some of them dropped their heads in shame and Sgorr's eye twinkled.

'You've done a fine thing,' he went on, addressing the Outriders in a soft, caressing voice, 'returning these Herla to their own herd. They are very dear to us.'

'I told you so,' muttered Fern among the hinds. 'He means us no harm.'

'It is good to meet you at last,' said Sgorr, walking slowly towards the young deer. 'You caused us no end of trouble, you know. And all for what? For some silly prophecy. But that's all done with. Now *he's* dead.'

Willow stirred and glared at Sgorr. She suddenly felt a violent hatred burning in the pit of her stomach.

'Tell me, though,' said Sgorr. 'Which one of you is the hind that . . . Which one of you is Rannoch's mother?'

Bracken looked up sadly.

'I am,' she said quietly.

'Bracken.' Sgorr greeted her smoothly, suddenly looking towards Narl who was standing just behind him. 'It's a privilege to meet you. I am just sad that I was not Lord of Herds when you were forced to flee . . . so unnecessarily.'

Bracken blinked back at Sgorr stupidly, hardly understanding what he was saying, but Bankfoot noticed that there was a thin smile flickering across Sgorr's lips.

'Very well,' cried Sgorr suddenly. 'Outriders, you have done your duty and now you can return to Colquhar. Tell him that I am pleased and that I send him my respects. Now we will take charge of the . . . of our friends and escort them in safety back to the home herd.'

The Outrider who had been leading nodded gravely and flicked his antlers to the others. They turned without another word and ran back up the hill.

As they went, Sgorr glared angrily after them.

'Outrider scum,' he whispered. 'Your day will come.'

Tain, who was standing close to Sgorr, overheard this with horror but he was distracted suddenly by a shadow in the grass. Tain looked up and way, way above him he saw a black shape circling in the sky overhead. From here it looked like a raven but Tain realized that it was very far away and must be much bigger; an osprey perhaps or an eagle. It hovered for a moment and then tilted its great wings and flew north once more.

'We should be moving,' cried Sgorr suddenly, and his voice had lost all of its conciliating warmth. 'You there, get going.'

The young friends and their mothers found themselves surrounded by Sgorrla. But as they began their journey south, Sgorr hung back with Narl.

'So you've got them back at last, Lord,' said Narl. 'What now?'

'Nothing for the moment,' answered Sgorr coldly. 'We'll have some fun with them when we get back to the home herd. But not too much. I want Eloin to know what I *could* do to them, that's all. Her desire to protect them will put her just where I want her.'

Narl looked hard at his master and nodded.

'But Narl,' said Sgorr suddenly. 'Bracken. I'll make an

exception for her. Spare me the details, Narl, just make sure that Bracken never makes it back to the herd alive.'

They had been travelling for two suns and everything the young friends had seen of Sgorr and the Sgorrla had made them more and more nervous. But their mothers would not be convinced there was anything really to fear, except perhaps Alyth, for hinds can have a habit of hiding from the truth and they were desperate to convince themselves they were in no danger. Besides, on the first evening with the Sgorrla, something strange had happened. The hinds had been feeding together when one of the Sgorrla guards had drifted up and, looking about nervously at the other Sgorrla, he had flicked his head to Fern.

'Listen,' he whispered, 'I can't talk but I've got a message for you from Eloin. She says that you're not to worry. That you'll have her protection.'

Before Fern could say anything the stag drifted away again.

Alyth's continuing fears might have had more effect on the others if it hadn't been for Thistle, for the young stag had already made up his mind that the best thing they could do was to return without protest and make a life in the herd. He made no secret of it when they stopped to graze or ruminate. He had been sad about Rannoch too but that fawn mark had always made him uncomfortable and he hoped that now they would have a chance to return to a normal life.

But on that second sun something happened that swiftly changed Thistle's mind. He was trailing behind the others and he kept trying to talk to the two Sgorrla next to him about the herd and Sgorr. At first they had ignored him but

Thistle seemed so genuinely enthusiastic that at last they relented.

'You've fine antlers,' Thistle was saying now to the stag to his right. 'I want antlers like that one day.'

The Sgorrla snorted but he was obviously pleased.

'What's it like to be in the Sgorrla?' asked Thistle cheerfully. 'Do you have captains?'

'Commanders,' said the deer to his left.

'Commanders,' mused Thistle dreamily. 'That's fine. I'd like to be a commander. To protect the herd.'

The Sgorrla on his right looked at him oddly.

'To keep them in their place, you mean.'

Thistle raised his eyes.

'Yes, yes of course,' he said with embarrassment, keen not to appear ridiculous in front of the two stags, 'and to fight off predators. Wolves and things.'

'You can't fight wolves,' snorted the Sgorrla. 'That's why Sgorr's bait is so effective.'

'Sgorr's bait?'

'Quiet,' interrupted the stag on their left suddenly. 'If the inner Sgorrla heard you talking like that you'd get a gouging.'

'The inner Sgorrla?' said Thistle. 'Who are they?'

'The inner Sgorrla report directly to Lord Sgorr,' said the Stag, 'and keep an eye on us all to make sure we don't stray, that we uphold Sgorr's laws. We've much to thank them for.'

'I don't see why he shouldn't know about Sgorr's bait,' said the other stag. 'After all, it's what makes us so strong.'

'Tell me,' said Thistle.

'It's simple. When a deer is wounded, or old and sick, we take them into the hills and leave them out for the wolves. Sometimes we have to break their legs to stop them running away.'

Thistle was horrified.

'You give them to the wolves?' he whispered.

'That's right,' said the Sgorrla cheerfully. 'It weeds out the weaklings and keeps the herd strong. It also keeps the wolves satisfied and stops them attacking, so we don't have to worry about protecting the herd. Beautifully simple. But that's what Lord Sgorr's teaching us. To use reason and to think clearly. To stop acting out of mere instinct.'

Thistle was appalled and he suddenly felt frightened. Rather than showing it though he tried to change the subject.

'These commanders,' he said, 'I suppose they're the same as Outrider captains.'

To Thistle's amazement the two stags suddenly pulled up and the one on his right glared at Thistle.

'How dare you talk about *them* in front of us?' he spat. 'Mention them again and I'll give you a gouging.'

'I'm sorry,' said Thistle with surprise. 'I've always thought that Outriders . . .'

It was Larn when the deer stopped once more, the hinds and their calves still in two separate groups and the Sgorrla around them. Narl and Sgorr were set apart when Thistle came up to rejoin the young friends who were talking together. They noticed in the twilight that his face was bruised and there was blood on his lips.

'What happened, Thistle?' said Willow.

'Nothing,' snorted Thistle. 'Those filthy Sgorrla.'

'The Sgorrla did that to you?' gasped Tain.

'Yes, for talking about the Outriders.'

'That does it,' said Tain. 'We should make a break for it. All of us.'

This time Thistle was silent.

'But how?' said Peppa. 'They're constantly on the watch.'

'We'll wait till dark,' said Thistle suddenly and resolutely, 'then try and slip away.'

'And Mother?' said Peppa.

'One of us should go and talk to them – see what Alyth has to say.'

'And go where?' said Peppa.

'North into the High Land, like Bankfoot suggested.'

'I'm with you,' said Willow. 'Did you hear how that . . . that thing talked about Rannoch?'

'M-m-me too,' said Bankfoot. 'How could I live in a herd with no Outriders?'

'Then we're all agreed,' whispered Tain. 'Once we've spoken to the hinds we'll keep a lookout for the best spot. We'll need a signal. That the Sgorrla can't understand.'

'What shall it be?' said Thistle.

'How about *Starbuck*?' said Tain.

'I know,' said Willow. '*Herne watches over you.*'

The friends agreed that when the signal came they should prepare themselves for their immediate escape. It was a pretty thin plan but a plan nonetheless and they were soon desperately nervous, looking all the time for some convenient place to make their getaway.

The only thing that worried them was that among the hinds only Alyth wanted to come with them, though she chose to stay with her friends. The others had all decided to stay with the Sgorrla and risk their luck in the herd. None of them could imagine another journey like the flight that had taken them to the loch. So now, as they travelled, the youngsters began to say a secret farewell, in their thoughts, to their own mothers. Though they would never admit it, even the young stags' hearts were heavy.

It was hardest for Peppa for she was deeply attached to Fern, but Willow consoled her and soon all of them had convinced themselves that it was for the best. They knew that if they all tried to escape and were caught it would probably be the hinds that would suffer the most for it. Besides, the hinds agreed to help their young ones by creating a diversion when the signal came.

It came the very next night. There was no moon in the sky and the cloudy evening was unusually dark. It must have been close to midnight but the deer were still travelling, for Sgorr was growing impatient to be back at the herd. Since Larn, they had been making their way along a ridge that banked very steeply below them towards a large forest. The trees offered lots of cover and all the friends had the same thought. But the drop below them was so steep that there seemed no way down, short of breaking their necks.

They were coming towards the end of the ridge when Willow suddenly cried out. Bankfoot swung round and was horrified to see her lying in the grass. The Sgorrla closed in immediately and Sgorr came running up.

'What's this? What's going on?' he cried angrily.

'I'm sorry,' said Willow. 'I tripped and I think I've sprained my foreleg.'

'We can't let that slow us,' said Sgorr. 'Get up. Immediately.'

'Yes, yes,' muttered Willow, struggling in the grass, but as she did so she cried out again. 'I'm sorry,' she said, sinking back. 'It's very bad. I won't be able to move for a while.'

'Nonsense,' said Sgorr furiously. 'You'll get up now. Or the Sgorrla will show you the true meaning of pain.'

'All right,' said Willow. 'Just a few moments. I'll be better in a while. You can't come to any real harm if *Herne watches over you*.'

Willow had raised her voice loudly and though Sgorr

ignored the remark suddenly all the friends' senses were quivering, their eyes flicking back and forth in the darkness.

'Are you all right?' said Tain, coming up to Willow. 'Let me see.'

Tain waited till Sgorr had drifted slightly away, cursing to himself, then whispered frantically, 'What is it, Willow? We'll never get away with your leg injured.'

'My leg's fine,' said Willow, smiling, 'but just back there I noticed a path and there were sheep slots. There must be a way down to the forest.'

Suddenly the friends heard a shout. It was Alyth.

'Herne be with you always, my little ones,' she cried, and the friends realized that the hinds were running away from them, along the ridge.

'What's going on?' shouted Sgorr furiously.

'The hinds,' cried Narl. 'They're trying to escape.'

In the darkness the Sgorrla were suddenly thrown into confusion.

'After them, fools,' cried Sgorr. 'All of you.'

Sgorr began to run too, for Willow's trickery had dulled his suspicions and he did not realize that it was not the hinds but their calves who were trying to escape.

'Now or never,' cried Willow, suddenly springing to her feet as the Sgorrla raced away. 'Follow me.'

The friends leapt after her in the darkness as she ran back along the ridge and, pausing only for a moment, suddenly plunged down the slope. Peppa came next, followed by Bankfoot, Thistle and then Tain. It was a desperate move, for the path was very steep and in the pitch-blackness they could not see where they were going at all.

They found themselves hurtling down the slope, dislodging stones and clumps of grass, terrified they would crash into each other but unable to control their descent, thrust downwards by their own momentum. Several times, Bankfoot thought he would fall and his own weight carried him faster and faster. But deer are sure-footed creatures and, springing and jumping, swerving left and right to avoid trees and boulders that suddenly loomed in front of them in the darkness, they managed somehow to survive the terrible incline.

At last the path began to ease up and Willow, who was still ahead, was able to slow her descent and gain control once again. Panting and terrified, she came to a halt as the ground flattened out at last and ahead she saw that she was right at the edge of the forest.

'Look out,' cried a voice behind her and Thistle, who had overtaken Peppa, suddenly came running up beside her. He was followed by Peppa and Tain.

'I can't st-st-stop,' shouted Bankfoot from behind, but the young stag, wheezing desperately, did manage to stop just behind them.

'We made it!' cried Peppa.

'Not yet,' said Willow, 'not for a good while yet. Come on, the trees are our best hope now.'

As she said it, Peppa gasped. The friends all heard the noise above them now and they realized that a deer was coming down the slope towards them. Thistle dropped his young antlers, determined that he should not suffer another beating. But as the friends peered helplessly into the night, all their eyes opened in amazement when an exhausted hind suddenly emerged from the blackness.

'Bracken!' cried Willow. 'What are you doing here?'

Bracken didn't answer. Her frightened eyes were just dazed. The poor hind had understood nothing of their plan and when the others had begun their diversion, she had been left standing behind the stags. Instinct and confusion had carried her after them.

'We can't leave her here now,' said Thistle.

'No,' agreed Willow, 'there's nothing for it. She'll have to come with us.'

Bracken still didn't understand, but as the friends turned and vanished into the trees, the hind followed dutifully after them.

On the ridge above them the Sgorrla had caught up with the other hinds. They were surrounded and now they no longer made any attempt to run.

'What do you think you were doing?' cried Sgorr furiously when he reached them.

'Nothing,' answered Alyth coldly. 'Just enjoying the evening.'

There was something in her tone that made Sgorr start.

'Quick!' he shouted to some of the Sgorrla. 'Go back and check on the others.'

When the stags returned just a short while later with the news that the youngsters had vanished, Sgorr nodded his head and almost smiled.

'So,' he said. 'Still playing games. Very well then.'

He rounded on the Sgorrla.

'Follow them,' he cried furiously. 'Hunt them down. Don't rest until you've found them.'

The stags nodded gravely.

'But first,' he said, turning back to Alyth, 'we will deal with you.'

Sgorr smiled coldly at Narl.

'Kill them,' he whispered. 'Kill them all.'

Fern blinked in terror as Narl stepped forward.

'But Lord Sgorr,' he said quietly, 'what about Eloin?'

Sgorr was silent for a while.

'Very well,' he said finally. 'But they must be punished. I tell you what, Narl, we'll keep two of them alive, just for Eloin's benefit. And Narl, I'll give you the choice of which.'

As Eloin stood by the Home Oak in the calm evening, waiting for news of the deer who had fled with Rannoch two years before, she was surprised to see Sgorr returning with just four Sgorrla and two hinds at his side. Her gaze followed them all the way into the home valley and at last she recognized who they were. It was Shira and Canisp. Eloin suddenly remembered the two little fawns who had been Rannoch's dearest friends; Tain and fat little Bankfoot.

10

The Boy

O joy! that in our embers
Is something that doth live.
That nature yet remembers
What was so fugitive!
William Wordsworth, 'Intimations of Immortality'

Now we must go back in time, nearly a year and a half
before Drail met his fate in the ravine, to that terrible day
above the loch. The day that the men and the dogs had come
and Rannoch had risked his life to save his friend.

When Rannoch opened his eyes the little deer had no idea
what had happened to him. He was dimly aware of running,
of a desperate and all-consuming desire to escape. But
beyond that, he knew nothing. Not where he was, not what
he had been doing, not even his own name. His head ached
and he felt dizzy and a little sick. He remembered from
somewhere that he had been on a hill and something about
a river and a dead hind, but everything else was dark, as
dark as the air around him.

'That's it,' he suddenly said to himself. 'I'm dead. I must
be dead.'

Rannoch half expected Starbuck or Herne himself to step
out of the shadows to greet him. But now the deer tried to

move and as he did so he realized that he couldn't be dead
after all, for pain suddenly seared through his back leg with
all the unmistakable force of life. The little deer barked in
agony and swung his head up. Above him, through a kind
of tunnel and suspended high above in the inky night,
Rannoch saw the brilliant wash of the Milky Way glittering
in the faraway heavens. He breathed in deeply and the dusty
air made him choke. The scent was a mixture of dry earth
and dying bracken, leaf mould and moss and, moving
through this complex web of smells, Rannoch recognized the
muddied, slightly salty odour of worms.

Well, if I'm not dead I must be dreaming, thought
Rannoch to himself.

The deer's eyes were growing accustomed to the blackness
and as they did so he began to see earth walls rising around
him. Dimly, Rannoch began to understand that he must be
below ground, though he had no idea how he had got there.
He struggled again but he was unable to get up and laid his
head back down on the earth. When he opened his eyes once
more it was still dark above, but the sky was paling and the
stars were beginning to go out. Rannoch shivered and looked
about him.

What's happened to me? he thought bitterly, and as he
did so he felt a strange tingling in his body. He didn't know
what had brought it on, but as he lay there the weird,
unnerving sensation grew stronger and stronger. Then Rannoch's heart began to beat violently. The deer had heard
something. The sound was a kind of scratching, or a shuf-
fling, and it was coming from the earth wall next to him.

Rannoch, his eyes getting bigger and bigger, tried to move
away from the sound. But, wherever he was, there was little
room to manoeuvre and the pain in his leg was almost too
much to bear. Rannoch was trapped. As the light grew

around him, to his horror, Rannoch saw the earth next to his head begin to crumble. It was very slow at first. Little showers of earth shook from the wall. Rannoch was transfixed and as he watched with an impotent, petrified fascination he realized something was coming through the ground itself and that it was coming straight towards him.

'Oh, Herne,' he gasped.

Suddenly the earth began to crack. A large chunk of soil dropped away and something extraordinary happened. A little pinkish nose popped out through the earth and with it two small clawed feet. The nose seemed to hang in the air, sniffing and probing, and then the feet started to scramble once again and a small, furry head appeared through the side of the wall, followed by a tiny black body.

It was a mole. The animal dropped to the floor and its little beady eyes blinked warily in the gloom.

'Who are you?' said Rannoch nervously.

The creature froze at the sound and began to sniff the air, probing it with his subterranean senses.

'What? Who's there?' he said looking around him and blinking again.

'Me,' said Rannoch.

'Who's you?' answered the startled creature. 'Are you a mole?'

'No,' said Rannoch. 'I'm . . . I'm a deer, a Herla.'

The mole blinked back stupidly as his weak eyes, grown lazy with so much time spent underground, began to make out the form of the deer.

'A deer?' said the mole. 'A talking deer? A talking deer that burrows. It's . . . It's impossible. How do you do it?'

'I . . . I don't quite know,' answered Rannoch weakly, still desperately trying to understand what had happened to him. 'I think I've always been able to.'

'What's your name?' said the mole.

Rannoch paused. His head ached violently.

'I . . . I don't know that either, I'm afraid. I . . . I can't remember. I was running from a dog, I think, and then I woke up here and I'm hurt. My leg hurts me, anyway.'

'You must have fallen,' said the mole, sniffing the air above him and vaguely making out the distant sky, 'from up there.'

'I suppose I must,' said Rannoch.

'And you can't remember anything else?'

'I . . . I remember a fawn, I think. And a loch. But that's about it.'

'How strange,' said the mole, just beginning to make out the details of Rannoch's face. 'In all my days I've never come across anything like it. And underground I've seen – or rather smelt – a lot, I can tell you.'

'Can you help me?' said Rannoch feebly, beginning to feel a little sick again.

'Well, I don't see how,' said the mole. 'You're far too big to get through one of my burrows. I suppose I could burrow upwards myself to see what I can see but, to tell you the truth, I'm a little reluctant to do that. You see,' the mole went on, his voice filling with fear, 'up there I think men have been about. I felt their horses yesterday.'

'Men?' whispered Rannoch. 'What are men?'

'You know,' said the mole. 'People. Humans.'

Rannoch felt dizzy. From somewhere, the image of a bridge flashed into his mind. But try as he might to remember, a dark wall seemed to have come between him and his thoughts.

'I don't understand,' said Rannoch.

'You must know about men,' said the mole. 'All Lera fear them. They are the bringers of violence.'

But as the mole said it he suddenly began to shake. From

above, the two animals heard the whinny of a horse and then the sound of voices. Human voices.

'Herne help us,' cried the mole. 'I must get out of here.'

'Wait, please,' begged Rannoch. 'Please. You can't just leave me.'

But the mole was already scrambling back through the hole.

As Rannoch lay there, the voices drew nearer and nearer. Rannoch felt an unbearable fear bubbling up inside his stomach and he began to shake violently. But although he had understood the mole – and he didn't know why – now he could understand nothing of what the voices were saying. They came to him like the sound of water and they made him tremble.

'It's over here,' said the first voice. 'I saw it drop just before the dog pounced. It must have been one of the old hunting pits Father dug last summer.'

'Aye,' said a second voice.

'It came out of the bracken, Liam.'

'Look, over there,' shouted the second voice suddenly.

As Rannoch looked up helplessly, he saw two figures appear at the edge of the pit above him. He did not know it, but they were boys. One was tall, with jet black hair, while the other, the one called Liam, cannot have been any more than twelve years old and was small for his age. Liam was wearing a pair of deerskin breeches and a rough woollen jerkin, and his legs were strapped with woollen bindings. His long locks fell well over his shoulders and were a very dark red. He had a high forehead and his eyes were a pure emerald green. That was normal for his people but there was something in the boy's look, the brightness of his eyes perhaps or the way they seemed to be listening, that spoke of an unusual sensitivity.

The little deer waited nervously at the bottom of the pit, hardly daring to breathe or stir as the boys peered down at him. Then, suddenly, the one with red hair jumped down beside him. Rannoch felt as though his nerve endings were on fire and, as he scented the boy, the sickness in his stomach became almost overwhelming.

'It's a fawn,' said the boy.

'Is it dead?' said the voice from above.

'Nay,' answered Liam. 'I don't think so.'

Now Rannoch shuddered as he felt a hand on his fur. The boy was stroking him.

'He's very pretty,' said the boy beside him. 'He's got a birthmark on its forehead. It looks a bit like a leaf. But I think the poor bairn's leg is broke.'

Rannoch winced in pain as the boy touched his back leg.

'Aye, it's broke all right.'

'Then there's only one thing to do,' said the voice from above. 'I'll get my knife.'

'What do you mean?' cried Liam, standing up.

Rannoch opened one of his eyes now and saw that the boy was above him.

'We'll have to kill it.'

'Why?'

'To put it out of its pain.'

'Nay,' said Liam sternly, kneeling down again by the deer.

'Then what do you want to do with it? You can't take it home with you.'

'Why not?'

'But it'll never live. It's wild and my father says wild things can't live with us.'

'Mother will know what to do,' said Liam gravely.

'But Liam, how will we get it back?'

'I'll strap him to my horse.'

'Hey!' shouted the boy suddenly from above.

'What is it?' said Liam, but for a while no answer came from his friend.

'Nay, it's gone now,' called his friend at last, reappearing above. 'There was another calf. I think it was watching me. But it ran off into the undergrowth.'

Rannoch had understood none of this, but now he suddenly felt a pair of human arms enfolding him. The pain in his leg came again and he found himself being lifted from the ground.

Herne, oh Herne, he thought to himself as his senses began to swim, and the young deer blacked out.

When Rannoch opened his eyes again the confusion hit him even more powerfully and with it came fear. Rannoch could see nothing of the stars or the sky. Beside him glowed an orange light that warmed his side and around him he saw strange shapes that he didn't understand.

He was lying on something soft that felt like fur and smelt comforting and familiar. Next to him was a large object made of wood with four long, straight-sided branches that rose from the ground to another piece of wood that seemed to have been stretched flat and was lying on its side on top of the branches.

There were other wooden things around it and by Rannoch's head, hanging over the fire, was something that looked like a giant puffball with its top cut off. But its surface wasn't dull like a puffball. Instead, it reflected the orange light and from out of it a steam was rising. Rannoch scented the air and suddenly recognized the smell of wild mushrooms. It made his stomach lurch, for the little deer was desperately hungry.

Suddenly the boy was standing over him again. Rannoch peered into the pure green eyes and as they looked back at him, they seemed to bore into him. Rannoch felt his mind reel and he looked away. Then the voices came again. They seemed to be all around him now. First there was one, then two, then three, and the texture of each sounded different to the deer. One – the boy's – was like a spring. Another, like a deep pool. The third was like a waterfall.

'Liam, get some of the leaves from the table and I'll crush them up with a little milk,' said the waterfall.

'Yes, Mother, but why?'

'I'm going to make a poultice to help the leg mend.'

'How does it do that?'

'Nature will do it, for there is strength in the leaves.'

'What's it called?' asked Liam.

'This is dock leaf and that's called dittany,' said Liam's mother. 'It's a special herb. There's even a legend that links it to deer. It's said that when a stag is shot with an arrow it goes into the forest to find the wild dittany and when it eats it it is cured.'

Rannoch listened to the music of these strange sounds and he felt himself growing drowsy.

'Is it true?' said the boy.

'Nay, Liam, no' for an arrow,' answered his mother. 'But it has power to heal, as many herbs do.'

'Oh,' said Liam, a little disappointedly. 'I like the legend.'

'Well, there are plenty of legends surrounding deer,' came another voice suddenly. It was the pool.

'Tell me, Father,' said Liam.

'Well, Liam, the deer's a Christian image for a start. Many saints wear symbols of them. Saint Aidan and Saint Godric, for example. Saint Kentigern, who some call Mungo, harnessed a stag to a plough and so was able to till the land and feed the people. The deer is even a symbol for Christ, because deer sometimes kill and eat the snake, the child of the serpent that tempted Adam in the garden. Then they have to go down to wash away the poison in a stream, in case they die. So the deer reminds us of the baptism of Christ, when all sins are washed clean. Hubert, the patron saint of hunting, was turned from licentiousness back to the Lord God when he saw a stag in the forest with a golden cross in its antlers.'

Rannoch winced with pain. As the noise hummed around him he could feel a hand on his leg and something being rubbed into the fur. It stung at first, but then Rannoch felt his leg begin to tingle with a deepening warmth that eased the pain.

'But I prefer the old legends,' the boy's father went on, 'about Herne.'

'Herne,' said Liam excitedly.

'Yes. In the north some say Herne talks through the deer and even takes on the deer's shape. When he does not come in the shape of a man.'

'Do you believe in Herne, Father?' asked Liam.

'Herne the Hunter?' said his father gravely. 'Nay, Liam, not really. But I believe he's a way of talking about man and about animals. Like all good stories.'

'Well I believe in Herne,' said Liam, 'and I shall call my calf Herne.'

'If he lives,' said the boy's mother quietly.

'Well, Herne needs rest – all the rest he can get,' said her husband. 'But now I must be gone. There's to be a parley.'

'A parley?' said the boy excitedly.

'Aye, there's news from King Alexander. The Norsemen have been raiding again from the Western Isles. Haakon is all over the north.'

'Will you have to fight them, Father?' asked Liam, suddenly more interested in this talk of fighting than in the deer.

'One day, perhaps,' answered his father, 'if the Great Land is ever to be united or free. Haakon's rule in the Isles must be brought to an end. We must raise the west. There will be war and much bloodshed before the land is healed.'

Rannoch opened his eyes. The voices had drifted away and the little deer found himself alone again. He stirred uncomfortably, but the fire warmed him and his leg felt a little better. Most of all, the weight of fear he had felt when the humans were near him had lifted, though the strange smells in the room still made him sick at heart. He closed his eyes once more.

In the coming weeks, Rannoch felt as though he was drifting through a land of dreams. He was always by the orange light and his head buzzed with the sound of human voices that haunted both his waking hours and his sleep. He couldn't understand anything of their meaning and whenever they were near he felt afraid and he hated the unnatural scent that they carried.

But they brought him milk to drink and berries and grass to eat and with time he grew less afraid of the boy, who would come to him and stroke his head and rub a strange green leaf onto his leg. The boy would sit and watch him intently, which always made Rannoch uncomfortable, for he found that he could never hold his gaze for more than a few moments.

Both awake and asleep, Rannoch struggled to remember what had happened. With time, some of the pictures of his journey began to come back to him. He remembered things fitfully, or all jumbled together like leaves swirling in a storm. He remembered being on a hill with other deer whose names he didn't know but who he felt were friends. He remembered the chase above the loch and hiding in the bracken with a little fawn who he felt especially close to. He remembered a park, and a fawn being carried off by a vixen.

But with these images were mixed others that seemed not to belong to him at all. Images of a deer called Starbuck and a pair of magic antlers. Of talking to a wolf and of feeling a terrible pain in his head. And the one memory that came most clearly to Rannoch was that for some reason he had always been running.

Rannoch had little idea of the length of time he had been with the humans, when one day the boy came to him and lifted him up and carried him outside. The day was bright and a breeze was blowing and Rannoch scented the air delightedly, feeling a sudden strength flowing back into his limbs.

The boy carried the deer over the grass and, as Rannoch looked back, he saw the place where he guessed he must have been kept while the humans fed and tended to him. The walls were made of rough stone, and piled on the top was earth and grass. Smoke was rising from the roof and twisting up into the blue sky.

The boy stopped and Rannoch found himself being lowered to the ground. Rannoch watched him as he walked over to a long wooden fence and, lifting a piece of cord, pulled at it. A part swung away and then the boy began to beckon to the deer. Rannoch eyed him nervously. Then he slowly began to understand that the boy was asking something of him. He was asking him to get up.

Rannoch began to struggle and as he did so he realized that the pain in his leg was now only a dull ache. Suddenly he was on his feet. He tottered and then stepped forward. Rannoch could stand. He ran forward into the field. In the distance he could see a great expanse of hills and sweeping trees and, at that moment, his heart began to soar.

*

It was several months since Rannoch had been rescued from the pit and the little pedicles on his head had grown. The deer could now clearly remember much of what had happened to him, though not his own name and nothing of the Prophecy. He had spent his time in the fenced field, eating and regaining his strength as his leg healed fully. Every day the boy would come down to see him and Rannoch had grown used to his call and would run up to him and even, at times, let him stroke his muzzle or touch the bumps on his head. He felt grateful to the boy and, though he could not understand his words, when they were together the deer sometimes imagined he could tell what the boy was thinking.

There was something else that drew him strangely to the human fawn, for he would often see Liam riding back to his dwelling on a horse, like the creatures he had seen in the gully. The horse never showed any interest in the deer, but where before it had only struck horror in him, as Rannoch got used to the sight, it filled him with wonder that an animal like himself should, so calmly, allow the boy to mount its back and come when he called. Rannoch began to think that the humans must have a very strange power indeed.

But now something happened that caused a deep stirring in Rannoch. He felt it first as an itching in his head. Then, one morning, two antler spikes broke through his pedicles. As the suns passed, they rose straight up above his head; twin tines, furred in velvet. They grew at extraordinary speed and soon Rannoch had his first head. But somehow this made him more and more restless. His frustration at not being able to remember who he was brought the anguish of longing to his heart too. He would run around the field, tossing his head to and fro and stamping the earth. Liam was fascinated by this and every day he came down to watch the deer. In turn, this began to irritate Rannoch and the boy's interest would send him running angrily to the far side of the field. More suns and moons passed and, as summer ripened, Rannoch began to rub his antlers against the fence, pulling off the soft fur that covered them as he did so, so that the tines stood out like birch branches.

'Why can't I remember who I am?' Rannoch would say desperately to himself as he scraped and buffeted with his antlers. There was some memory he was reaching for in particular, that he knew was close at hand, but which frightened him terribly.

Rannoch stayed in the field near the humans' dwelling, wrestling with his thoughts and his troubled memories as summer turned to autumn and the leaves began to fall. Autumn grew and Rannoch felt another unfamiliar sensation overwhelm him. He became more and more restive and he kept thinking of the Herla out there in the wild. Strangely, he could hardly stand to be with the boy now and whenever Liam came down to give him extra feed, Rannoch would ignore his calls.

Rannoch suddenly felt angry at the boy and desperately confused in himself. A deep longing was growing inside him. The deer would stand in the field and bellow and bark and the shaking anger that welled up inside him made him want to hit out. Sometimes, Liam would come and stand watching this for ages on end, and when Rannoch looked into his eyes he recognized something in them; a strange kind of violence that made him even more nervous. Rannoch would run away again but now he thought he must be sick, for he did not understand that the spirit of Anlach was burning in his blood.

Anlach passed and with it Rannoch's restlessness. Winter settled round him; the snows fell thick and fast, and in the neighbouring hills the Lera sought desperately for food and shelter. But in the field the boy brought Rannoch dry straw, bark that tasted of wood smoke, and delicious ferns and conkers that he had gathered from the forest. In the bitter cold, Rannoch took this gratefully and after a while the scent that came with it no longer made him sick.

So at last spring came again and then something else happened that made Rannoch question. It was a rainy spring day and Rannoch had been buffeting at the fence with his head when his right antler suddenly snapped off. Though Rannoch knew that this must be natural, he looked down with surprise at the antler lying there in the grass. Liam was even more startled when he saw it there that evening. The boy bent down and picked it up and his young eyes opened in wonder as he began to examine the strange object. He turned it in his hands, and ran his fingers across the roughish, wood-like surface.

'It's like a branch, Herne,' whispered Liam wonderingly.

Rannoch watched him from a distance and though he didn't understand Liam's words, he noticed that the sound of the boy's voice was changing, the water becoming deeper.

His second antler fell on its own and Rannoch walked bareheaded once more, as he had done as a fawn. As the hot sun came, Rannoch's antlers began to grow again and this time, as well as the spikes, two brow tines sprouted forwards. Although Rannoch couldn't see them and there was no feeling in the antlers except at the base, he sensed that they were growing stronger, and when he scraped the velvet across the fence he found that by twisting his head he could score a line in the wood. It gave him great pleasure to catch the beam of the fence between the tines of his antlers, push against the wood and feel it bend under his weight.

Then one day in high summer, when the sun was blazing down and Rannoch had shed his velvet and was standing at the far end of the fenced field looking out thoughtfully

towards the hills, the deer suddenly heard a strange sound.
It was just below him. As he looked down Rannoch was
amazed to see the grass move, then the earth seemed to swell
and bubble up and a head popped up through the ground.

Rannoch eyed the mole coolly. He hadn't forgotten how
the creature had deserted him.

'At last. At last I've found you,' cried the mole breathlessly.

'What do you want?' said Rannoch coldly.

'I wanted to see if you were all right,' answered the mole,
pulling his whole body through the ground and shaking off
the earth.

Rannoch looked down with little interest.

'You know I've felt terrible ever since I left you,' said the
mole. 'But really, there was nothing I could do. Then I heard
from the moles around here that there was a deer living near
the humans and I wondered if it was you. When they told
me you had a white mark on your forehead, I knew.'

'White mark?' said Rannoch suddenly.

'Yes,' said the mole, 'that looks like a leaf.'

Rannoch felt a violent jolt to his stomach.

'Say that again,' he whispered.

'What?'

'About the mark.'

'You've got a birthmark that looks like a leaf.'

Rannoch suddenly turned and, to the mole's amazement,
he ran straight towards the edge of the field. He stopped at
the fence and stood pawing the ground and staring out at the
hills.

'*On his brow a leaf of oaken,*' whispered Rannoch
fearfully.

In his mind Rannoch was grasping towards something
and it was as though a voice had begun in his head. A voice

from the past that was telling him things from his dreams. A part of Rannoch didn't want to listen, while a part of him yearned to know everything.

Over the next three suns Rannoch's memories grew in strength. First he remembered the flight from the herd, then why he had had to flee. Next came the journey and Bhreac's death. The Prophecy came back slowest of all, for the deer's subconscious had suppressed what he most feared. But it was linked with those deer he had seen in his dreams, who he knew were close to him and who he longed to recall. As their names came back to him – Willow and Bankfoot, Thistle and Tain, Peppa, and his own mother, Bracken – all the associated memories returned too. Rannoch shuddered as those other names returned to haunt him: Blindweed, Drail and Sgorr.

When Rannoch met the mole again, at the far side of the field, he looked very grave.

'I remember now,' said Rannoch, 'what my name is.'

'Well?' said the mole.

'My name is Rannoch.'

'Rannoch.' The mole nodded.

'Yes, and it was because of this mark that we had to flee the home herd.'

'The home herd?'

'That's right. From Drail and Sgorr. It's all because of the Prophecy.'

'Prophecy!' said the astounded mole.

'Yes. There's a prophecy about Herne and the deer.'

The poor mole was so confused by this that he just shook his little head. Rannoch lay down and began to chew the cud thoughtfully. The mole shuffled closer.

'Tell me,' he said quietly, looking up at his twin pointed antlers.

'Tain taught it to me before I left the loch.'

'Go on,' said the mole.

Rannoch looked warily at the mole. But then he began to recite the verses that old Blindweed had recited to the young fawns on the hill.

'When the Lore is bruised and broken,
Shattered like a blasted tree,
Then shall Herne be justly woken,
Born to set the Herla free.

On his brow a leaf of oaken,
Changeling child shall be his fate.
Understanding words strange spoken,
Chased by anger, fear and hate.

He shall flee o'er hill and heather,
And shall go where no deer can,
Knowing secrets dark to Lera,
Till his need shall summon man.

Air and water, earth and fire,
All shall ease his bitter pain,
Till the elements conspire
To restore the Island Chain.

First the High Land grass shall flower,
As he quests through wind and snow,
Then he breaks an ancient power,
And returns to face his woe.

When the lord of lies upbraids him,
Then his wrath shall cloak the sun,
And the Herla's foe shall aid him
To confront the evil one.

Sacrifice shall be his meaning,
He the darkest secret learn,
Truths of beast and man revealing,
Touching on the heart of Herne.

Fawn of moonlight ever after,
So shall all the Herla sing.
For his days shall herald laughter,
Born a healer and a king.'

When Rannoch finished the mole shrugged.

'So, it's you this Prophecy is talking about?'

'Yes,' said Rannoch. 'I mean, no. I mean, parts of it seem to be about me. The fawn mark, anyway. But I've been thinking and thinking about it and it can't be me. It's simple. I'm not a changeling. Bracken is my mother. Besides, there's so much of it that I don't understand . . . that seems impossible . . . about Herne and the Island Chain. No, it's just a story, like the stories about Starbuck.'

'But if it *is* true . . .' said the mole, looking wide-eyed at Rannoch.

'It isn't,' said Rannoch, almost angrily. 'I'm just a deer. Like my friends.'

Rannoch looked wistfully towards the distant hills.

'I wonder how Willow is,' he said quietly.

'*Born a healer and a king*,' muttered the mole, nodding his head gravely.

'Stop it,' said Rannoch.

'I'm sorry,' said the mole, 'but it seems to me there is more to you than meets the eye. Even my eyes.'

Rannoch was silent and sullen now. Although he wouldn't admit it to the mole, he suddenly felt frightened and very alone.

But as summer grew fatter the mole and the deer spent many hours together when the boy wasn't around, discussing the Prophecy and talking of the Great Land. The mole wondered why Rannoch showed no sign of escaping from the field and returning to his friends, for although Rannoch was growing quickly and could easily have jumped the fence, the mole would find him still there, sun after sun.

'Rannoch,' he said one day in early autumn as they sat together in the grass, 'why do you stay here with the humans? Why don't you return to your herd?'

Rannoch shook his head.

'Because I don't know how to find them,' he said sadly, 'and besides . . .'

'Besides?'

'When I was with them I caused them nothing but problems. Perhaps they're better off without me.'

'But you can't stay here. Look, I was talking with my cousin the other day and I explained about this prophecy of yours. He said, why don't you go and ask the seals, on the western shores? My cousin says seals are wise and knowledgeable creatures and know everything about everything. You at least can talk to them.'

'Seals?' said Rannoch.

'Yes,' said the mole. 'They live by the sea.'

'What's the sea?' asked Rannoch.

'Well, I don't really know,' answered the mole. 'But it lies beyond the land and . . . well . . . it's where the seals live.'

Rannoch was quiet again and thoughtful. In truth, he wasn't sure he really wanted to learn anything about the Prophecy at all.

'I must be on my way again,' he said to himself half-heartedly now, 'but perhaps it's better to wait until the spring comes to travel. Then we'll see.'

Anlach came round and Rannoch's blood rose in him once more, turning the four-pointer's feelings to anger and his thoughts to Willow and his friends. Again Rannoch found the boy's company distressing, only less so than the year before. He ran back and forth through the grass and bucked and kicked or rose up to box with the air.

Then suddenly something happened that threw the young stag into utter confusion as he wondered about Herne and the Prophecy. It was nearly the end of Anlach and Rannoch was feeding restlessly, when he suddenly saw the mole coming towards him. The little creature dipped his head as he shuffled up to Rannoch and greeted him warmly. But as Rannoch stood there, listening to the mole, the deer was suddenly appalled. He couldn't understand what the creature was saying to him. Not a word.

Rannoch blinked down in amazement at the mole but, no matter how hard he tried, he could not make sense of the little Lera. As the mole went on talking Rannoch suddenly threw back his antlers and, with a desperate snort, he turned and ran across the field, leaving the startled mole on his own again.

'Herne,' cried Rannoch desperately, 'what's happening to me?'

The incident with the mole deeply unsettled the deer but Rannoch grew even more confused when, at the end of Anlach, the mole came to visit him again and Rannoch found that once more he understood the Lera.

It placed an even greater doubt in the deer's mind about the truth of the Prophecy and his own powers. As winter settled over the human dwelling, it threw Rannoch in on himself, so when the snows fell on his dull brown coat, the deer became sullen and listless and was reluctant to talk to his friend. The mole would watch him and shake his head sadly, but though he made a point of visiting his friend whenever he could, he had his own loved ones to tend to in the threatening winter.

Spring came a second time to the field and the mole was glad to see that with the sunlight and the new flowers, Rannoch was in better spirits. Their friendship blossomed again and he and Rannoch would tell each other stories and talk of the creatures and the forests. But the mole noticed that Rannoch began to talk less and less of Willow and his friends.

Rannoch shed his antlers again and they grew once more. He had his third head. This time the brow tines were larger and the well curved beams forked in two at the tops, like crab's claws. When the mole came to visit him one day, he nodded as he looked at the deer, for the fawn in the pit had now grown into a fine young stag.

Yet as summer arrived, still Rannoch made no move to escape the fenced field or the boy. The mole would tremble as he watched Rannoch take food from Liam's hand and stand letting the boy stroke his fawn mark. Then, one day, as he approached the deer, the mole's expression was very grave, for he had come to talk seriously with his friend.

'Rannoch,' he said, as he shuffled up, 'how are you?'

Rannoch smiled down at him.

'Well, thank you,' answered Rannoch cheerfully. 'The human brought me some delicious berries yesterday.'

The mole nodded.

'Rannoch,' he said quietly, 'I've some news for you. It's about the Herla. The Lera say there is great trouble.'

Rannoch went on chewing the grass.

'They say the Herla are suffering,' the mole continued.

Rannoch didn't answer.

'Aren't you interested, Rannoch?' said the mole quietly.

'Yes,' answered Rannoch, looking up now, 'but I just bring more suffering.'

'But don't you want to know what's happened to your friends? To Willow and Tain and your mother?'

'Of course,' answered Rannoch sadly. 'I think about them all the time.'

'And the Prophecy?'

Rannoch looked at his friend guiltily.

'Rannoch,' said the mole, his voice growing severe, 'can't you see what's happening to you?'

Rannoch stared back at him.

'You've grown tame, Rannoch,' whispered the mole fearfully. 'Tame.'

Rannoch looked at the mole in silence and suddenly a light woke in his eyes. *Tame.* The word came like the warning call of the hind in winter. As a young fawn Rannoch had heard the hinds use it, though he never really knew what it meant. But it had always carried fear in its sound, a fear greater even than the howl of the wolf. Rannoch suddenly remembered his old friend Quaich and the terrible herd in the park.

In the weeks that followed, Liam noticed that something had deeply affected Rannoch and when Anlach arrived he found it impossible to even approach him. Rannoch stamped the ground if he tried to get near and lowered his antlers angrily. The boy would shake his head sadly and call to him, but Rannoch never once answered.

Until one day, at the end of Anlach, when the skies had grown chill with the promise of rain and Larn was close at hand, the boy did something that made Rannoch wonder. He came down to the field and, calling to Rannoch gently, he lifted the rope from the fence post and swung open the gate.

Rannoch stared at him in amazement, not knowing what he meant, but the boy just stood gazing sadly back at him. If Rannoch had come closer he would have seen the tears in his piercing green eyes. Then, very quietly, the boy turned and walked back to his dwelling, without once looking round.

When the mole pushed up his nose through the earth to find his friend the next morning, he saw Rannoch standing by the northern fence gazing up to the hills. To the south, the gate still stood open.

'Are you all right, my friend?' asked the mole.

'Yes,' answered Rannoch, 'but it's time. To be on my way again.'

'To find your herd?' said the mole delightedly.

'Yes.' Rannoch nodded. 'To find my own kind once again. But first I must find the seals and see if they can help me to understand the Prophecy.'

'Yes,' said the mole, 'you have been with the humans for a long while.'

'I want to thank you,' Rannoch said suddenly, 'for telling me I was changing. The humans have a strange power.'

'Yes,' agreed the mole. 'The Lera must guard against it.'

'I shall miss you.'

'And I you.' The mole smiled.

The deer dipped his head to touch the mole's nose.

Then he turned away. Rannoch pawed the ground and then, suddenly, he raced towards the fence. He pushed with his legs and Rannoch's body and head, with his pair of three-pointed antlers, rose into the air and sailed smoothly across. He landed lightly and without once looking back, Rannoch began his quest.

11

To the Sea

Round the cape of a sudden came the sea,
And the sun looked over the mountain's rim:
And straight was a path of gold for him,
And the need of a world of men for me.
Robert Browning, 'Parting at Morning'

Rannoch didn't stop running until he had left the mole and
the boy far behind him. It was a glorious feeling to be free
once more and, as Rannoch went, he began to realize how
much he had missed in the company of the boy. He breathed
in the rich scents around him and marvelled at the beautiful,
twisting shapes of the trees. He listened to the voice of the
wind and stopped to look at every bird that darted by, or to
examine the tracks of the Lera around him. Although he
knew that winter was near and his heart was now filled with
thoughts of the strange Prophecy and of what had become
of his mother and his friends, for a time he simply revelled
in the wonder of running where he willed.

But after a while Rannoch's mood began to change. He
grew lonely and began to miss the mole. He wondered what
on earth the seals could tell him of Herne and the Prophecy,
and whenever he thought of the verses he felt angry and
confused.

Rannoch was travelling west now and he had just crossed a river when he noticed strange tracks in the ground. They were smaller than a deer's and every now and then the ground behind them had been smoothed flat, as if the animal were dragging something behind it. Rannoch sniffed the place and though the scent was very strong, it came from no Lera that he knew. Rannoch decided to follow it.

The trail took him up the bank of the river and then disappeared altogether at a place where a tree trunk had fallen right across the path of the water. Rannoch stopped and looked around, but he could see nothing. He was about to turn away again when he suddenly saw something flash through the water. At first he thought it was a fish but the shining trail it left behind it was so wide that it would have to have been a very big fish indeed.

Rannoch paused, then he heard a dripping sound and suddenly a dark shape slid from the river and darted up the side of the tree trunk. It was on the top of the trunk now, in the middle of the stream, and Rannoch blinked at it in disbelief. It was smaller than a fox, longer and thinner, with sleek brown fur, a long tail and strange little feet. It had a pointed face, with bright, quick eyes.

The animal looked around and then ran down the trunk straight towards Rannoch. When it got to the end it lifted itself on its back legs and rose like a snake. It hovered there in the air, peering at Rannoch, as the deer, who was hardly more than a large antler away, peered back at it in amazement. Then it turned again and, slipping back off the log, it disappeared into the water with hardly a sound.

Rannoch stepped forward.

'Hey there,' cried Rannoch, 'come back.'

For a moment there was no sign of the creature. Then

suddenly its little head popped straight out of the water, just below Rannoch.

'Were you talking to me?' he said.

'Yes,' answered Rannoch.

'How?' said the startled animal, showing his teeth.

'I've always been able to do it.'

The creature disappeared again and then re-emerged on top of the tree trunk. He shook himself in a great spray of droplets and ran up close to Rannoch. Again he lifted himself, so that he nearly touched the deer's nose with his own. Then he made a strange twittering sound and ran round in a circle three times.

'What are you?' he asked, as he came to a stop.

'I'm a Herla,' answered Rannoch, 'a deer. What are you?'

'I'm an otter,' said the otter proudly. 'What do you want?'

'I just wanted to say hello, that's all. My name's Rannoch.'

'Well, hello. Now I can't stand here talking to you. My mate is sick.'

'Sick?' said Rannoch, stepping closer. 'What's wrong?'

'I don't know,' answered the otter sadly, 'but she won't eat.'

'Is there anything I can do?' said Rannoch with concern.

'What could *you* do?' answered the otter disdainfully. 'You may be able to speak my language, but what do you know about otters?'

'Nothing, I suppose,' agreed Rannoch, 'but when we're sick we go into the forest and find berries and bark that make us well again.'

'Yes. Yes, of course,' said the otter, 'but there's nothing here she wants. She says that the only thing she knows to make her well is the grass that grows from the sea. But I can't very well leave her to go and get it, can I?'

'The sea?' said Rannoch, hardly believing his luck.

'Yes. That lies at the end of the land.'

'What is the sea?' said Rannoch.

'The sea is where the rivers go and where the salmon come from. The sea is the greatest thing in the world. Have you really never seen the sea?'

'No.'

'Well, this *is* strange. First I meet a creature that can talk to me. Then I find he has never even seen the sea.'

'I'll go for you if you like,' said Rannoch suddenly. 'To the sea, I mean. I'll get your mate the grass.'

'You?' said the startled otter.

'Yes. If you tell me how to get there.'

'There's nothing to it,' said the otter. 'And the grass grows all over the sea.'

'Well, then,' said Rannoch.

The otter eyed the deer carefully.

'You really mean it?'

'Of course I do,' said Rannoch. 'Just tell me where to go.'

'Go north-west and you'll strike a large loch. It's a sea lake. Follow its southern shores due west. You'll soon hit the sea. The grass grows on its banks.'

Rannoch nodded and he set off, promising to be as quick as he could.

'By the way, my name's Keela,' cried the otter, as he watched him go. 'I'll be waiting for you.'

It took Rannoch three suns to reach the loch Keela had mentioned and as he travelled the landscape became wilder and wilder. He traversed a high mountain and again felt the wind stirring the gorse grass. The contours of the land rose and fell more and more dramatically around him, and at last Rannoch saw it. The loch was huge, much bigger than the lake where Tharn lived, and north from its tip a river ran into the hills. As the otter had told him, Rannoch swung

south along its edge before striking due west. He travelled
for another sun, hardly pausing to sleep, stopping only to
graze a while.

When the next sun was high, Rannoch scented something
on the wind. It came to his nostrils, strange and bitter. The
loch suddenly opened, the land fell away, the trees on the
southern edge came to an end and Rannoch's eyes opened
wide in wonder. Before him was a vast sweep of water that
suddenly swallowed up the lake. The wind tore at it, shaking
its surface into curls of foam, so that it seemed for a moment
to Rannoch that a herd of white deer was running ahead of
him.

It stretched to the north, where Rannoch saw land floating
on its surface and beyond, great mountains rising into the
sky. To the south Rannoch saw yet more land, for he was
looking down the stretch of water that today is known as
the Firth of Lorn and out towards the Island of Mull, but
beyond that there was nothing – just water as far as the deer
could see. Rannoch stood stock-still and felt the wind that
hit him fill his nostrils with spume. He suddenly felt alive
and strong. It seemed as though he were touching the edge
of a great mystery.

'So, this is the sea,' he said to himself as he gazed and
gazed at the moving water. Then he came down the slopes
of the hill and Rannoch felt the ground turn from earth and
grass to a strange, soft powder that his hoofs sank into as
he walked. Rannoch stopped on the edge of the shore,
scented the air for danger and then began to run forward
across the beach.

Gulls were circling high overhead, screeching on the
ragged wind, riding the currents of air or diving suddenly
into the foaming waves. As Rannoch went he noticed strange
coloured rocks on the sand that were cupped or long and

thin, with spirals on their sides. Then he saw that the sand was covered in snails, like the ones that lived on the trees in the forest. But when he turned them over with his nose he found they were empty or full of sand and when he stepped on them they shattered under his hoofs.

Rannoch approached the edge of the water gingerly and saw it foam and fizz and crash against the beach. Many times the deer had seen the wind work on the face of the loch, making it move and spray and flurry, but this mighty loch seemed to be moving on its own, shrugging its shoulders against the land. As Rannoch came nearer, the scent that had hit him so powerfully before came again and he could taste it on his lips.

Then Rannoch began to see brown stems, like weed, thrown up on the beach or washing back and forth on the waves. Some of this was thick and rubbery with long stalks like the stems of giant mushrooms, while some was thinner with no stem at all. Where it had been thrown up high on the sand where the water could no longer reach it, it had dried and it crackled underfoot. The deer sniffed it and it smelt like the wind.

He nibbled at it and it tasted bitter but not altogether unpleasant. Rannoch knew immediately that there was something strong and wholesome in it that he sensed came from the water. But while the stag was standing there he suddenly heard a strange barking sound. He realized that the noise was coming towards him across the waves. It came from a large rock, lapped by the surf. The rock was covered with long grey stones and, as the deer looked on, one of these stones began to move forward and fell into the sea. It popped up again and Rannoch realized that the stone had eyes and whiskers. Rannoch stepped into the surf as the water foamed around his hoofs.

'Are you a seal?' he called above the wind.

The seal's head disappeared under the water again before re-emerging closer by. Rannoch nodded politely to it but the seal said nothing. At first Rannoch thought that it must be frightened of him.

But this was not true, for Rannoch was looking at Rurl. Rurl lived in the sea and had seen and heard of far stranger things than a deer who could talk to him. He had heard the mighty blue whales singing to one another from halfway across the world and knew of the giant turtles that bury their eggs in the sand by moonlight. He had heard stories of the the narwhals jousting in the wastes of the arctic, watched by men in their great carved trees until they stood amazed and thought that unicorns had abandoned the earth and gone to live in the water. He knew of the sea cows that moan as they rock their children in their arms and the plankton that blooms like a million forests in the warm waters of the Gulf Stream. He himself had talked to the lobster and the dolphin, for the things of the sea have always understood one another's song, carried in the waves and the wind and the currents that ride the world.

He knew about the land too, because he was partly of the land and had travelled far up the estuaries and chatted to the salmon returning to spawn and die in the rivers that bore them. They had told him about the valleys, the forests and the mountains, and about the creatures of the land too; the wolf, the bear and even the red deer. They had also told him something about man, with his bright hooks and his great nets that meant death to their kind.

But at this frightened talk of man Rurl had smiled a little inwardly, for he knew more of man than the salmon. He had seen him build his villages on the edge of the sea and cross the waves to settle on the islands that specked his home.

Rurl was an unusually inquisitive seal and he had circled the shores of Scotia from the mull of Arran to the Isle of May. He had basked in the sunlight on the Summer Isle and wrestled the storms around Cape Wrath. He had tasted the waters of the northern sea and lain in the sands off Burghhead Bay. Coming round Rattray Head he had seen one of their crafts dashed into splinters on the rocks and had listened to the men wail in terror as they went to their cold graves. In Lunan Bay he had seen men set out with their nets and had stolen fish from them, while on Bass Rock he had eaten his fill as boys came down to the sands to pluck mussels from the shore in their wicker baskets.

Rurl knew a little too about the crofters' cold lives on the Islands of Lewis and Uist to the west, of their fires and their songs. Of the great carved trees that swept up the mighty Forth in the east to feed the settlements of Edwinburgh, and of the beacon lights that burned on the hills above Inverness. He also knew of the men from the north who came in their long crafts to Shetland, Orkney and the Western Isles. Sometimes they came to load and unload but at other times, when they came the sea would turn red with blood and men would die in the sand.

The seal knew now that more and more of them were journeying out of the cold lands and that something new was happening around the islets and coves where he slept on the slippery rocks or basked in the chill waters. But of this he cared little, for to him all men were the same. They were like whelks or molluscs that would cling to any rock they could find until the storms of life came once more to wash them away.

From the beach Rannoch called to the seal again but still he did not answer. Rurl was indeed a wise creature, but by nature he was also rather disdainful and he only spoke when he felt like it. Rannoch snorted and lowered his head to pick up some of the seaweed in his mouth. He gripped a long strand and shook it. The seal suddenly ducked under the water and shot towards the beach, flapped out of the surf, barking and snorting, and lumbered up the sand, waving his flippers awkwardly. It was such a peculiar sight that Rannoch dropped the seaweed and almost laughed.

'What are you looking at?' said Rurl haughtily. He knew just how foolish he looked on land.

'Nothing,' said Rannoch, trying to hide his amusement. 'I've come to get some of the grass that grows in the sea. It's for Keela, the otter. His mate is sick and I promised—'

'The otter?' snorted the seal. 'What do you want to have to do with him? They're all silly creatures. Anyway, that won't do any good,' he added, looking scornfully at the seaweed on the ground. 'If she eats that it will only make her worse.'

'Oh,' said Rannoch.

'You want the other kind,' continued the seal, pointing his nose to the dry seaweed that Rannoch had tasted before. 'Over there.'

'Thank you. Thank you very much,' said Rannoch.

The seal snorted again and shrugged.

'That's all right,' he answered. 'If you'll go out of your way to help a sick otter, I suppose it's the least I can do.'

'To tell you the truth,' said Rannoch nervously, 'that's not the only reason I'm here.'

The seal eyed him suspiciously.

'You see, I need your help,' said Rannoch quietly.

'My help?'

'Your advice. I was told that seals . . . well . . . that they know everything about everything.'

The seal looked rather pleased.

'And there are things I need to know,' said Rannoch.

'About what?'

'About this mark on my forehead.'

Rannoch stepped forward and dipped his head towards the seal.

'Very pretty,' said Rurl a little coldly, when he had finished examining the fawn mark.

'No, you don't understand,' said Rannoch suddenly, feeling embarrassed. 'There's a prophecy.'

Rurl looked up at Rannoch. Any animal that has had a whale somersaulting over its head and lashing the sea to steam is very difficult to surprise and the seal wasn't in the least bit thrown. But he loved to collect stories and the truth was he had seen so much of the world that he was often bored and a little lonely.

'I think you'd better tell me everything,' said the seal quietly.

So Rannoch began. He told Rurl all about the home herd and fleeing Sgorr and the Draila, at which Rurl nodded, for he too had heard of Sgorr. He told him of how they crossed the bridge and lost Bhreac and how they met the strange deer in the park and came at last to the loch and settled under Tharn's protection. He told of the chase and the snarling dogs too. But it was only when Rannoch got to the part about the boy that Rurl opened his eyes in sheer amazement.

'So you've spent time with man?' he said quietly.

'Yes.' Rannoch nodded.

'Very strange, very strange indeed. Were you frightened of him?'

'Yes and no,' answered Rannoch. 'There were times when . . . when I felt a strange power there, a kind of . . .' Rannoch paused. 'Well, a kind of violence. But at other times, with the human fawn at least, I felt I almost understood him. Not his words, but what he was thinking.'

The seal was quiet for a moment and he looked very serious.

'So I want to know if there's any truth in the Prophecy,' said Rannoch, 'and if it's better for my friends if I never return to them at all. Can you help me?'

'I don't know,' answered the seal, shaking his head gravely. 'You say you're no changeling?'

'No. But the other things. The feeling and the dreams and . . . well, none of the others can understand Lera.'

Rannoch was surprised at himself. This was the first time he had ever tried to convince anyone that there *was* something special about him. At this Rurl looked hard at Rannoch. He coughed and then slapped one of his flippers on the sand.

'Ah now,' he said, 'I was coming to that. Now that does make you sort of different, but it doesn't prove the Prophecy.'

'What do you mean?'

'I mean, how do you think I find out about the world? I've had conversations with dolphins that would make your fur stand on end. I've talked to penguins and kittiwakes. I've chatted to sharks – from the rocks, of course – and I've even had a long talk with an albatross, though I wouldn't recommend it – they've really got very little to say for themselves.'

'But I never learnt it,' said Rannoch.

'You don't need to learn it; all Lera could do it if they wanted to. Or rather if they'd only stop thinking of themselves and being afraid all the time. Listen for a change.'

The seal's tone had grown rather serious.

'There was a time, in the old days, when all the animals conversed as a matter of course. But they lost the knack. Don't ask me why. Most of the sea creatures can still do it but that's the trouble with the land, I suppose. It cuts you off. Splits you up, if you know what I mean.'

Rannoch looked rather relieved.

'But why couldn't I understand the boy?' he asked.

'Ah. No animal can talk to man and no animal should,' Rurl muttered.

'But man is an animal too, isn't he?'

The seal paused. He looked at a loss.

'I suppose so,' he said at last, 'though even my knowledge of the world grows dark when it comes to man.'

Rannoch was disappointed.

'Oh, I know certain things about man,' said the seal. 'I know that man is always fighting and killing. I know too that death is coming to the Great Land because of him.'

'Death,' whispered Rannoch.

'The men from the north are at work again. They are coming across the water in their carved trees. Their king has even been in the west and one day when they come both man and Lera will bleed, for man is the bringer of violence.'

As Rannoch listened he thought of the boy again and how sometimes his eyes had seemed so kindly.

'But look,' said the seal suddenly, 'I'm quite famished with all this talk. I'll fish for a while and then I'll dive for sea grass. It's getting dark, but at least there'll be a moon tonight. Then we can talk again.'

Rannoch nodded and the seal lumbered back down the beach and dived into the waves. The deer noticed how awkward and ungainly he was on the land but when he returned to the water, how swift and graceful. That night a full moon came up. Across the waves the mountains and the islets and the slopes of Mull were swathed in cloud that drifted around the sparse trees or broke on the rocks and hung in mysterious shapes about the mountain backs. The

water shone in the moonlight and shrugged restlessly back
and forth as though unsettled by the moon, so that even the
shrimps began to listen to its plaintive call. Rurl dived for
fish, which he threw up flapping onto the slippery rocks, and
when he was done he brought the deer the very best seaweed
that he could find. Further down the beach he lolloped up
onto some flat stones and Rannoch lay down in the sand
and together they began to talk again in the moonlight.

For three suns Rannoch stayed on the beach with Rurl
and the seal told him something of what he knew about the
land of Scotia. About the huge mountains, always lost in
rain and cloud, which lay to the north and shrugged down
to the very edge of the sea. About the thousand coves that
dotted its splintered shores and the dark subterranean rivers
that some said led far, far underground and up into the vast
land-bound lochs that crossed the country.

He told him also how he had often dived for the sea grass
to make himself well and of the other things in the sea that
could cure a seal. Rannoch showed a special interest in this
and when he asked Rurl if he had learnt it from his mother,
the seal explained that some of it he had, but that other
things he had found out for himself. The secret, he said, was
to trust and listen, for the animals know the things they
need, while scent and colour can tell them many of the
plants' mysteries. As Rannoch listened the sea crashed and
swayed as it had done since the forming of the world.

Rurl also told him about what he knew of the Herla and
what had become of them while Rannoch had been away.
He had heard that Drail was dead, murdered by traitors, it
was said, and that Sgorr now called himself Lord of Herds
and his Sgorrla were moving everywhere. That the Low
Lands were his, though above the loch there were still Outriders proud to call themselves by that name.

When Rurl mentioned the loch, Rannoch looked up with a keen interest.

'My friends,' he said, 'any news of my friends? Willow and Bankfoot and my mother, Bracken.'

Rurl suddenly looked very serious.

'I'm not certain,' answered Rurl, 'but the first night you came I asked a seagull to fly east and try and find out everything he could.'

'And . . .'

'And he met a golden eagle who lived by the loch and knew something of the Herla. She said that last summer, when you were still with the boy, something very strange happened. The hinds and the young deer who she had seen coming out of the snows nearly two years before were suddenly rounded up together. They were driven south by a group of stags and seemed to be travelling against their will.'

'Go on,' said Rannoch gravely.

'The eagle followed them and when they had travelled a long way they were met by a group of stags from the south, led by a hornless deer. They were handed over to them.'

'Sgorr,' gasped Rannoch. 'But that means that Bracken and my friends are in Sgorr's clutches. I know he means them harm. I've got to help them, Rurl.'

'He means you more harm,' said Rurl quietly, 'if he finds out you are still alive.'

'I can't help that,' said Rannoch desperately. 'I must try to save them.'

'Do try to think, Rannoch,' said Rurl, almost angrily. 'What can you possibly do? You are still a young stag. You are alone and have no herd or Outriders to help you. Your path is uncertain and wherever you go you are marked with that leaf on your forehead. Sgorr's spies are everywhere and will kill you at the first opportunity.'

'This mark has caused me nothing but trouble,' said Rannoch bitterly.

He was thoughtful for a while.

'Perhaps I should go back to the loch,' he said at last, 'and ask the Outriders for help.'

'No,' said Rurl, 'they have not yet submitted to Sgorr, but Colquhar has taken the lordship and the eagle says he has a kind of alliance with Sgorr.'

Rannoch fell silent. Though he suddenly felt a biting guilt towards his mother and his friends, which was mixed with a mounting loneliness, he knew that the seal was right. That night he hardly talked to the seal at all as he gazed out sadly across the bitter sea. But the next morning, bright and fresh, when Rannoch had been dozing on the shore, Rurl suddenly flapped, barking, onto the sand. He seemed more cheerful and he was unusually excited.

'I've been talking to the others about you,' he said, 'and how we might help you in your quest.'

'My quest?' said Rannoch.

'To find out if that mark means anything. If there's any truth in the Prophecy.'

'You can tell me, then?' said Rannoch breathlessly.

'No,' answered Rurl, shaking his strange head, 'but there are others who might be able to.'

'Others?'

'Yes. To the north, in the High Land.'

Rannoch's eyes narrowed.

'Who?' he whispered.

'Herla. Like you. There are tales of a strange herd up there. Herne's Herd they call themselves. They are said to have a deep knowledge of Herne and to worship according to the ancient Lore. Perhaps they can tell you more than I can.'

Rannoch stirred.

'But how would I find them?' he asked.

'That I don't know,' said Rurl, 'except that they are said to live in the northern shadows of the Great Mountain.'

'The Great Mountain?'

'Yes. Some even believe that Herne himself lives on the Great Mountain.'

Rannoch shivered.

'So you think I should go up there?' he said rather disconsolately.

'If you really want to find out.'

'But what about my mother and my friends?'

Rurl looked at Rannoch and he suddenly felt bitterly sorry for the deer.

'Whatever you decide, Rannoch, you must be careful. Sgorr will do everything he can to destroy you.'

'Yes,' said Rannoch thoughtfully, 'it seems I'm a danger to everyone now, whatever I do. I'll go north. At least until I find out . . . what I am.'

'But there you must be careful too,' said Rurl gravely, 'for the herd I told you of, there are dark rumours surrounding them, Rannoch.'

'What rumours?'

'Of strange powers,' answered Rurl, 'and some say they have knowledge of man. Your own journey and the words of the Prophecy link you in some way to that creature.'

Rannoch nodded but then Rurl suddenly gave Rannoch a very strange look.

'Rannoch,' he said quietly, 'have you ever thought what the first verse might mean? . . . *Then shall Herne be justly woken . . .*'

Rannoch was silent.

'That you're . . .'

'Don't say it, Rurl,' said Rannoch. 'Don't.'

Rannoch stared at the seal and once again he felt a fear rising inside him. But with it came an anger, at everything that had happened to him. The anger made him feel stronger suddenly and a resolution began to awaken in his mind.

'Rurl, it's time I left you,' he said suddenly. 'Keela will be waiting and I've delayed too long.'

Rurl nodded sadly.

'Take care, Rannoch,' he said, as the deer turned to leave. 'If you ever need me, the other creatures of the sea can carry a message. One day I'll be glad to hear how you fare and if there's any truth in this prophecy of yours.'

As Rannoch picked up the seaweed in his mouth and trotted back up the beach the seal was genuinely sad to see him go. But Rurl was suddenly distracted by the darting silver flurry of a fish and he dived into the waves to hunt. A little girl, a crofter's child who was collecting pebbles nearby, saw Rannoch too. The sight thrilled the child and she ran back to her parents to tell them that a huge red deer with great antlers was eating seaweed on the shore.

Rannoch ran, laying down the seaweed only to graze and drink, heading east up the edge of the loch and not stopping once to rest. When he reached the tree and the river, Keela was looking out for him and the otter turned in circles when he saw him for his mate had grown worse. He took the seaweed gratefully and pulled the dangling, salty stems down into the fresh water, up again across the dry earth, and into the hole in the river bank where his mate was curled asleep.

Keela woke her gently and she began to gnaw at it and, though she blinked and winced a little, she went on chewing with her sharp teeth, for she knew that it was good for her. Rannoch spent that night lying down in the grass by the river, dozing or listening to the wind and the rushing water.

Though it reminded him of the sea, he knew somehow that in its nature it was different.

Rannoch woke early the next day and to his delight he found Keela and his pretty mate both sitting on the tree stump watching him. She was obviously much recovered.

'Thank you,' she said shyly to the deer, 'for helping us.'

'Yes,' said Keela. 'Now what can we do for you?'

'Perhaps we can fish for you?' said his mate.

Rannoch shook his head and smiled.

'No, it's enough to have helped you. But now I should be on my way again. There is one thing, though, I'd like to know, if you can tell me. I'm trying to get to the Great Mountain.'

Keela nodded and described the best route he could, for he and his mate had often visited other otters that lived around its foothills. With that, looking wistfully to the south where he knew his mother and his friends now lay suffering Herne knew what fate, Rannoch turned north on his own.

'Rannoch,' called Keela as the deer went, 'we shall look out for you. Always remember, the otters shall be your friends. But, Rannoch, we thought you'd better know. Be careful. There are Herla about.'

12

Wolf

When the stars threw down their spears,
And water'd heaven with their tears,
Did he smile his work to see?
Did he who made the Lamb make thee?
William Blake, 'The Tyger'

As Rannoch passed the loch where he had turned west towards the sea, the mountains began to rear above him and the deer's mood swiftly sank. As the bens climbed around him, brooding giants hidden in mist, loneliness crept in on him once more. He thought bitterly of his friends. He also felt the threat of Sgorr all around him and the threat of what he was rising to face, of Herne's Herd and the dark rumours surrounding them. But worse than all this was the fear of the mysterious High Land and what he might discover about himself up there in the north.

As he traversed those great slopes he would stop often and look back and scent the breeze. But on Rannoch went, rising higher and higher, instinctively avoiding the valley bottoms and using the dying bracken as cover. Of man or Lera he saw little, for even in the days when men would come to settle in these wild parts, there would be few places to find shelter.

Around him the country became strange and forbidding. Huge forests tore above him. Cliff faces lowered and groaned. Waterfalls spluttered out of the mist and even the most secret of stones were visited by the wind. The young deer felt he was lost in a country of shadows and inwardly he trembled.

He was just descending through a sparse wood, to drink at the burn he had spied below it, when he lifted his nose to the breeze.

The scent was unmistakable. A group of Herla were coming downwind and moving fast. Rannoch's legs began to shake and he felt a terrible apprehension in his stomach. He had not met one of his kind in so long and now, while he yearned to be reunited with his own, he had no way of knowing if these Herla were friend or foe.

Rannoch was wondering what to do, whether to run back up the hill or hide where he was, when the deer appeared below him and stopped to drink at the burn. The stags, six of them, all ten- and twelve-pointers, had obviously been running for a while, for their thick coats were drenched in sweat and steam rose from their backs into the cool air.

'We can't go on like this,' said one of them wearily when he had refreshed himself. Rannoch realized he could hear clearly what they were saying. He was upwind of them and they obviously hadn't seen him, so he kept very still and listened.

'No, but we can't go back without them,' said another. 'You know what Sgorr would do to us.'

Rannoch's senses were instantly on alert.

'It's your fault for losing their tracks in the first place,' said a third, addressing the first.

'It's not my fault,' came the angry response. 'If that herd

of cattle hadn't crossed the stream, their slots would have been as clear as daylight in the mud.'

Deer, thought Rannoch, as he listened. They're hunting for deer.

'Well, what are we going to do?' said another stag.

'Keep looking until we hunt them down. Those are our orders,' said the first.

'But what if they make it into the High Land?'

'Now that's different. You know Sgorr has forbidden any southern Herla to cross into the High Land on pain of death.'

'I've always wondered why.'

'It's not a Sgorrla's job to ask questions but to obey.'

'I know, I know, I was just wondering,' said the stag a little nervously.

'Well, I'm not sad it's so,' said another stag. 'You know the rumours. They say that Herne's Herd eat any deer they capture and because they have learnt their ways from man, their ghosts are forever trapped on the Great Mountain, to haunt the heather and howl like snow demons.'

'Nonsense,' said the stag who had reminded them of the Sgorrla's duty, 'and I'll have no talk of Herne or Herne's Herd, right? What are you thinking of? Talking as if these were the old days, before Sgorr freed us and we began again with Sgorr's Year. You'd pay for that if we were back home.'

'It seems to me we'll pay anyway if they escape into the High Land and we're not allowed to follow them,' said the deer sullenly.

'So they mustn't escape,' said the stag, 'whatever happens. We must take them back with us or not go back at all.'

'Then they'll get it.'

'We've more chance of getting it than they have,' said the stag who had just spoken.

'Why's that?'

'Remember those two deer that came from the north? They say that they're under Eloin's protection and as long as Sgorr wants Eloin, he won't harm them.'

Rannoch stirred. The name had lit a distant light in his memory.

'Then why does he care so much about getting these ones back? We've been searching for well over a year now.'

'You know what Sgorr's like. Hates to be beaten. Besides, they're all still quite young. Not like the ones that came back. Those two were just ageing hinds. Probably too old for retraining anyway. But these. "Give me a Herla before their fourth growth and they're mine for ever," Sgorr always says.'

'But they're not all young 'uns,' said another stag suddenly. 'There's that one with them, the hind. If it wasn't for her being so slow they'd have been long gone seasons ago. I'm sure she's wounded. What's her name?'

'Bracken.'

Rannoch felt a jolt. His mother, alive and obviously close at hand. And who were these youngsters the stags were talking about? Could it really be Willow and Bankfoot and the others? Rannoch suddenly felt hope swelling in his chest.

'We'll never get them if we stand around here all day, chattering like hinds,' said the stag who had talked the most. 'Come on, let's get moving.'

With that the Sgorrla set off. Rannoch stood there above the burn, hardly able to believe what he had heard.

'I must find them,' said Rannoch to himself desperately, turning up the hill, 'and quickly.'

But by the next sun Rannoch had seen no signs at all of other deer. He rested in the pale, cloudy day on the side of a mountain and slept amid the gorse. He had a dream that day like the dreams he remembered having as a fawn. He dreamt of Herne.

The great deer was standing alone in a clearing and the sunlight had turned his red coat to gold. Rannoch could not see his face in the dream and all he was aware of was the god's mighty antlers with their twelve sharp points, fanning like the branches of the trees. In the dream the god began to stamp the ground and a wind started to blow. Darkness came down and as the wind howled it tore at the ground and the branches in the forest began to break and split.

Suddenly the air was filled with a terrible noise like thunder and the trees began to fall, wrenched from the ground so that their roots rose like human fingers, spiders and beetles and a thousand secret things in their clutches. Then the god stood alone on a barren moor. The air was cold and fresh and the landscape stretched as far as the eye could see. The god began to buck his head and run, swift and free, and a voice was saying, 'The forest. The forest is always with you.'

Rannoch woke with a start and looked around. Though the sky was overcast he could sense that Larn was near and he got up and shook himself. The evening was cold and damp and the wind was moaning gently around the mountains.

Rannoch was about to set off again when he felt his legs shaking. He thought at first it was the dream, but then his whole body began to quiver. His nostrils were filled now with a powerful scent that made him sick with fear.

Rannoch twitched and peered about him. Then he heard it. It ran through his body, a noise that took him back to a place far away. A noise that deer know even in their dreams. The low, lonely howl of a wolf.

Rannoch saw them standing, sleek and powerful, on the foothills of the facing mountain. Their silver fur stood out clear against the brown earth. They were scenting the ground but one of them suddenly lifted its head and saw Rannoch. He began to howl and the others lifted their muzzles to his call. They too saw the deer and their howls rose above the wind, their voices filled with hunger. Then suddenly they began to move, down the slopes, across the valley, towards Rannoch. The deer turned and fled.

Though the wolves were far off and Rannoch was fast, fear had him by the throat and he ran blindly up the sides of the mountain, hardly looking where he was going. He could think of nothing but escape. His nostrils were full of the scent of the wolves and terror had come over him like a dark cloud. He could do nothing but give in to his instincts. As he ran he tried desperately to think, to plan, but nothing came except the beating of his heart. He was like the deer in the gully trying to clamber up the walls as the dogs snapped at their heels.

'Think,' he kept saying to himself, as the wolves called behind him and he caught their scent again on the breeze, but poor Rannoch could think of nothing but flight.

At last he began to tire and as he slowed he heard a strange sound above which distracted him and broke the spell. Rannoch had climbed quite high and reached a water-fall, tumbling down the rocks in front of him. The deer suddenly felt calmer and he stopped and looked up. The torrent of water that burst from the rocks above fell a good tree's height down the side of the mountain into a small pool formed by a bowl of jutting rock. There it churned and frothed and sent up sparks of watery light and clouds of cool vapour.

This pool, in turn, spilt down the mountain below him into a larger pool, where it turned into a stream and disappeared off through the rocks. Rannoch was at the edge of the higher pool now and he suddenly realized that his way was barred. But the blinding fear that had gripped him had receded and he could think again.

He was shaking badly and he could feel panic rising in him again, but he fought the feeling. The thoughts came clearly. To turn back now and try and drop down to reach the lower pool might be fatal for he could hear the wolves in the distance, and above him the mountain became very steep and offered no way around the falls.

But ahead, on the far side of the pool, Rannoch noticed a ledge of rock that jutted out over the water. From the look of it it was just wide enough to stand on. From there it was only a short jump to the other side. The ledge was a fair leap but not too hard for a deer, if he didn't slip on the mossy stones.

Rannoch stepped forward and tried to measure the jump. The force of the draught created by the waterfall was very powerful and it made him shake. Rannoch was having second thoughts when he heard a low howl, dangerously close by, that left him no choice. He took a few steps back, ran forward and sprang.

Rannoch felt the wind and water around and below him. There was a rush of noise and he landed on the ledge. But the rock was wetter than he had thought and he missed his footing, slipping sideways, back towards the waterfall. He scrambled desperately as he was engulfed in water and darkness.

Then suddenly the torrent stopped and he was still standing up. Rannoch blinked and looked around amazed as he saw the sheet of water was now in front of him. The deer was behind the waterfall itself. As he had slipped sideways he had passed straight through it.

Rannoch now saw that the ledge he had jumped on was

part of a wider outcrop of rock that led back to a small cave. He shook himself and his eyes became accustomed to the darkness. The air in the cave was cold and from the noise that thundered around him the deer felt that he was in the heart of the torrent itself. But as he looked he realized he could see out through the flashing film of water ahead into the fading daylight. He saw the outline of mountains and the distant trees. Then he began to tremble again as he saw the shape of a wolf. It was standing on the spot where Rannoch had jumped, sniffing the ground, slavering as it tried to pick up the scent it had just lost.

Rannoch hardly dared breathe as he watched the animal through the glassy curtain. He could see its sharp, yellow-green eyes and its white teeth. Its ears were pressed forward and its long muzzle was craning across the pool. It lifted its neck so that Rannoch could see the fur bristling along its throat, and let out a cry that shook through the cave.

As he stood, only a few antlers away from his most dreaded enemy, Rannoch remembered the stories he had heard as a fawn and the silence that always descended on the Herla when the name of the wolf was spoken. Terror seized him once more. Yet from somewhere inside him a voice was telling him that he had to resist this terrible feeling. That now the feeling itself was his enemy as much as the wolf outside the cave.

The deer hovered between these dim, half-formed thoughts and his instinct to flee, to hurl himself out through the water itself. But he didn't move. The other wolves were at the pool now, sniffing and nosing the ground and growling angrily. He strained to listen through the water but he could only hear their snarls of hunger.

He must have stood there listening and watching for a good while as the wolves ran back and forth trying to find their quarry. But they could see no sign of the deer and at last they turned away, back in the direction they had come. They were hungry and irritable, keen to pick up some other prey to feed their bellies.

At last Rannoch stepped towards the water and began to press his antlers through the curtain. But suddenly he froze again. One of the wolves had broken from the pack and now it was back at the pool. This time, instead of trying to pick up Rannoch's scent, it seemed itself to be measuring the distance to the ledge. Suddenly it sprang and landed on the rock to Rannoch's left, but as it did so it slipped too on the damp moss. Not towards the water and the cave but to the right and the edge of the falls. With a desperate yelp, the wolf disappeared over the drop.

Rannoch was too startled to do anything. He backed into the cave and stood there shivering, transfixed by the sound of the water. The darkness came in and a moon rose. Its pale blue light shone on the curtain of water and danced on the edge of the cave as the deer listened to the world outside. No scent came to his keen nostrils and no sound to his straining ears. Glittering shadows shimmered before his frightened eyes and at last he lay down and slept, exhausted by his flight.

When Rannoch opened his eyes again it took him a while to realize where he was. He thought at first he was listening to the sound of the sea. Outside the daylight had come again and Rannoch stepped through the curtain of water onto the ledge and, slipping only a little, sprang onto the grassy slope.

Rannoch shook himself dry and looked about him. The day was overcast again and the sky was already beginning to speck. It was much colder than it had been the sun before and he shivered as he began to make his way down the slope.

But as Rannoch reached a mound above the lower pool he paused again, not knowing what to do. There, stretched motionless on a flat rock below, lay the wolf.

The animal's eyes were closed and there was blood on the stone beside it. But the deer could see from its shallow breathing that the wolf was still alive. Rannoch snorted angrily and flicked his antlers forward. The smell of the animal frightened and sickened him and he turned away. But as he did so he had the same feeling that had come upon him on the escarpment. Somewhere a voice seemed to be saying, 'Listen, Rannoch, listen.'

He turned back and for a time stood watching the stricken creature. Five times Rannoch tried to leave the wolf that day. But every time something called the deer back. He tried to graze, he told himself not to be so foolish, that this Lera had wanted to kill him, that this was his most hated enemy, but Larn found the deer still standing there above the pool.

The wolf had not opened its eyes all day and its tongue lolled from its mouth as it slept. Even from this height Rannoch could see that its belly was injured and, though it stirred now and then, the deer sensed that it was close to death. A wind came up and it started to rain hard. Still the wolf lay there. Night came down and it got colder, and Rannoch stood there, uncertain and afraid. But at last the deer wound down to the side of the water and stepped onto the rock. He approached the wolf desperately slowly, scenting the ground, ready to run at any movement.

Rannoch was finally standing above him. The wolf was shivering badly and its coat was soaked through. The blood on the stone beside it had been washed away by the rain, but now Rannoch could see the wound that cut into its side and suddenly he was reminded of the boy. The wolf's proximity made Rannoch shake, and every muscle in him was trying to revolt. It was as though an unseen force was repelling him. But, at last, the red deer dropped down and laid himself by the wolf's side to give it warmth.

It was another sun before the wolf opened his eyes. He found himself alone on the rock. He tried to lift his head and as he did so he saw the waterfall and the ledge above him and he remembered with anguish what had happened to him. He began to whimper pitifully and struggled to get up.

'Lie still,' said a voice from somewhere above him. 'You'll need to save your strength.'

When he saw the antlers and the deer's young face with a white mark in the centre of its forehead peering down at him, the wolf thought he must be dreaming, or that the fall had knocked out his wits. He blinked and struggled again.

'I said lie still,' said Rannoch quietly.

Now the wolf was certain. A deer was talking to him. Weak as he was, the sight filled the wolf with rage. He began to snarl, curling up his upper lip so that the sharp canines stood out, hard and white. Rannoch watched him warily, but even if the wolf had been strong enough to get up and spring, up there on the mound Rannoch was far out of reach.

'Be still,' called Rannoch again. 'It won't do you any good. You're in no state to chase a stag.'

The wolf opened his jaws furiously again and then, distracted by the realization that he could hardly move, he started to whimper and lick his paws. The creature was in a great deal of pain. At last he looked down to examine the open wound that he could now feel burning his belly.

'What's this?' he cried angrily as he did so. 'What has happened to me?'

On his stomach, where the cut was deepest, the wolf saw that a strange green mixture had been smeared across the

fur. It was made of wet leaves. The wolf struggled in fear
and began to growl again.

'They're only leaves,' said Rannoch softly from above,
looking down on the herb he had found growing in a small
copse beyond the waterfall. 'They'll do you good.'

'You did this?' said the amazed wolf.

'Yes.'

'Poison,' snarled the wolf suddenly, remembering all the
things in the forest that his mother had long ago told him
could kill a wolf. 'You're trying to poison me.'

'If I'd wanted you to die,' said Rannoch coldly, 'I could
have left you to die in your sleep in the rain.'

The wolf eyed Rannoch slyly but seemed a little reassured
by this although, in truth, he was too dazed to believe what
was happening to him.

'If you're hungry,' said Rannoch, 'I've brought you what
I could. There, to your right. Try and eat something.'

The wolf turned his head and saw a small pile of berries
and nuts on the rock. He sniffed them and turned away in
disgust.

'Squirrel food,' he growled. 'What do you take me for?'

'I'm sorry,' said Rannoch, not without amusement, 'it was
all I could find. But try and eat it all the same.'

'Come down here and I'll eat,' snapped the wolf. 'That'll
make me well.'

'Is that a way to talk to a Lera that's trying to help you?'

'Is this a way for a Lera to behave?' growled the wolf.
'To tease me with nuts and berries? For a deer to help the
hunter? It's . . . it's unnatural. It's against the law.'

Rannoch said nothing up there on the rock.

'Why do you do this?' muttered the wolf angrily. 'Leave
me alone. I'd rather die than have this.'

'What harm is there in one Lera helping another?' said Rannoch quietly.

'Harm? What harm? All the harm in the world.'

The wolf began to snarl again and laid down his head sullenly on the rock.

'The berries will help heal you,' said Rannoch. 'You must eat something or you'll die.'

Again the wolf growled.

'Please yourself,' said Rannoch. 'I'm hungry, even if you're not, and I'm going to graze. I'll come and see you at Larn. Perhaps by then you'll have changed your mind.'

Still the wolf said nothing, so Rannoch turned and trotted away. The wolf lay still for a while, brooding on his strange fate. But as the day wore on he grew hungrier and hungrier. At last he peered about him and when he was certain that Rannoch was nowhere near, he turned to the berries and sniffed them again, curling his nose up distastefully.

Very reluctantly, he picked up a few of the berries on his long tongue and swallowed them. They tasted bitter but not too unpleasant and there was moisture in them. In truth, in the hard winters when game had failed or his pack had been lost in the forests without food, even the wolf had turned to such food to save him from death. Now the strange flavour on his tongue made him realize how famished he really was and suddenly he was gulping down the food beside him. When he had finished he looked around him again rather guiltily and laid down his head.

'It's good for me,' he muttered. 'It'll make me strong again and then . . . then we'll see.'

Rannoch got back to the rock before Larn. It had started to drizzle and the deer was in low spirits. But now he smiled to himself as he looked down on the wolf. He was stretched out asleep and beside his head the berries had gone.

Rannoch pressed his soft lips around the new berries he had just collected and began to make his way down the slope.

He approached the rock as cautiously as before, watching the steady rise and fall of the wolf's sleek fur, making certain of the rhythms of sleep. But when he was sure, the deer stepped up beside him and dropped the berries on the ground. In an instant the wolf's eyes were open and, with a snarl that shuddered through his whole body, he swung his muzzle to the right and snapped viciously at Rannoch's leg. Rannoch jumped sideways and swung down with his antlers as the wolf's muzzle closed on the cold air. He had missed.

Now the wolf was struggling on the rock, trying to get up, snapping at the deer, snarling and growling as his pink gums slavered furiously. Rannoch stood there shaking, staring in horror at the animal in front of him. Then, without a word, he turned and ran back up the slope. Above, he stopped and looked down at the creature, then he trotted away into the approaching dark.

But Rannoch didn't go far. He wandered for a while through the gorse and bracken, his face raised to the cold wind, his muzzle spattered with rain. Above him an eagle was circling and he watched it until the faint, high speck vanished into the canopy of night. In the distance the snow-topped mountains were misty and bleak and as the deer listened to the howling echoes of the air he felt angry and alone.

For two suns Rannoch grazed the slopes of the mountain, lost in thought, turning his antlers again and again to the north but never stirring far from the waterfall. Then, at last, when he could think no more, he went back to the falls and looked down.

The wolf's eyes were open and though he saw the deer above him, he hardly stirred. He was too weak. All the berries had gone. The animals said nothing for a while, watching each other warily until, finally, the wolf murmured in a faint, exhausted voice.

'I'm hungry. I must eat or I shall die.'

'And why should you live when you try to kill me?' said Rannoch quietly and without anger.

'It is my nature,' answered the wolf sullenly. 'I can do no more about it than the mountains about the sky. I no more choose to hunt you than the eagle chooses to fall on the vole or the fox to kill the hare. Why should I not, for I must live?'

Rannoch stared at the wolf and after a good while he nodded his antlers.

'Yes, you must live,' he whispered as he backed away.

Rannoch was gone for a short while, but when he came again to the rock and laid the berries beside the wolf, he didn't stir until the deer was clear of his teeth. He stretched out his tired muzzle gratefully and gobbled up the sparse food.

With the coming suns Rannoch brought the wolf more berries and watched him from a distance as he gradually began to recover his strength. At last he was just able to drag himself to the pool and drink long and deep from the icy water. It quenched the burning thirst which the wolf had only been able to hold at bay by lapping at the rainy puddles that had formed on the rock beside his sickbed.

On the next sun the wolf tried to stand up. He managed it for a while, but then his legs gave way and he collapsed again. That evening Rannoch was feeding on the mountain when he saw two hawks fighting high above him and something drop to earth. Rannoch ran up to see what it was and found a dead field mouse on the ground. He picked it up by the tail and carried it down to rock where he threw it to the wolf. Rannoch turned away with disgust as the wolf took the dead Lera in its mouth and bit in to it, tearing the flesh and gnawing on the small bones. But the meal restored him even more and that Larn he stood for longer on the rock.

As night came in and a few stars peeped through the swirling clouds, Rannoch came to see him again.

'How are you feeling?' he asked quietly from above.

The wolf licked his paws and nodded.

'You've saved my life,' he said. 'I'll be well soon.'

'Then it is nearly time for me to be on my way,' said Rannoch.

'Yes, that is well,' said the wolf in a strange voice. 'But tell me. I do not understand. Why have you done this?'

'Because you needed my help,' said Rannoch quietly. 'Because I can and ... and because ... because I want to know.'

'Want to know what?' said the wolf.

'Many things. What I am. What you are. Why you hunt me.'

'Why I hunt you?' said the wolf, smiling. 'Because I want to run with the wind and have a full belly. Because I want to win a mate with sleek, silver fur and listen to my brothers howling their song to the sky. Because I too want to know ...'

'Then tell me something about you,' said Rannoch.

The wolf looked oddly at the deer and then he too nodded. 'Very well.'

So Rannoch came further forward over the ledge and listened to the wolf below the rumbling waterfall. He heard of his brothers who ran in great packs across the high mountains, of their calls and their quarry. He learned of the hard, bitter winters that strangled the earth and made their coats grow thick and coarse. Of how the wolf had nearly died in the foothills to the north when he had been separated from the others and had wandered for days through the snow without scenting a single Lera.

Rannoch trembled as the wolf told him of the chase and what signs they looked for when they went out to feed. Of how the pack would worry their prey and bring it down, then fight and argue over the carcass. Of how, after days of fruitless hunting, to find and catch just one small hare could bring the greatest pleasure.

But Rannoch heard too of the she-wolf and her flashing eyes. Of the song of the storm on the mountain top and the joy of running free at mating time. He heard of the wolf's love of his cubs and how the little ones would gambol and tumble in the snow, until their paws were tired with playing and they would run back home and bury their tiny silver muzzles in their mother's fur. He heard too of the loneliness of the wolf and his bitter cries when the wind told him that he must fight or die.

As he told the deer this he began to growl and his fur bristled, for the wolf was remembering his home and the world that was his own. He grew silent and sullen after a while and eventually stopped talking. So the two Lera were left to listen to the sound of rushing water.

Rannoch set off early the next sun to collect berries for the wolf and when he returned and looked over the edge, he saw him lying with his head on his paws. The deer trotted down to the pool and was approaching the flat rock when the wolf began to growl. The hair was standing up on the back of his neck and suddenly he arched his spine and stood up. Rannoch froze.

'Don't run,' whispered the wolf in a sleek, cold voice. 'It would be more than your life's worth.'

Rannoch dropped the berries and tilted his antlers forward.

'You're well again,' he said.

The wolf nodded and looked at Rannoch slyly.

'I'm glad,' said Rannoch.

'Damn you!' cried the wolf suddenly. 'Why are you glad? Don't you know how dangerous it is for you?'

'I'm glad all the same,' said Rannoch calmly. 'Besides, you won't harm me.'

The wolf looked at him carefully.

'No,' he whispered bitterly, 'I won't harm you.'

'Then perhaps we have learnt something,' whispered Rannoch. 'Both of us.'

'No,' snapped the wolf, 'we have learnt nothing. Except that the world is stranger than we think. Now go quickly, for I may not be able to help myself.'

The wolf was straining forward, the tendons in his legs quivering violently as he looked at the red deer. He was beginning to show his teeth.

Rannoch nodded.

'Very well,' he said softly, 'but I will not forget this time we have spent together.'

'Go now. Hurry!' cried the wolf suddenly.

Rannoch turned and ran back up the hill and when he looked back from the ledge above, the wolf was standing gazing at his broken reflection in the pool.

'Goodbye,' called the deer.

The wolf didn't answer at first but as Rannoch turned to leave, he swung round and called up to the deer.

'Listen to me,' he cried. 'You have saved my life and for that I thank you. So go, and may you run free and may your antlers grow. I will not forget you. No, nor that strange mark on your forehead. But mark me too, do not fool yourself.

For we are enemies, you and I. That is how it is and how it must be. Nothing may change that, for that is the law. So when I run with the pack again and my belly is empty, when my cubs growl for food and the she-wolf demands meat, I will hunt you. You and your kind. Then I will forget this strange meeting. Yes, and be glad to forget it too.'

The wolf was snarling now as he tried to master his feelings. Without another word Rannoch dropped away from the rock and set out across the mountainside. He trotted slowly at first across the steep slope, but then the deer began to run, his head up, his antlers swaying in the breeze. Soon he was hurtling across the heather as the wind scoured the scent of the wolf from his nostrils.

Only when the deer was a long way away did Rannoch stop and look back. The mountainside was empty but as he looked Rannoch heard the wolf's call come to him across the wind. Where once it would have only made him start in fear and run for his life, now the deer heard something else in it. Some new complexity. Rannoch heard both hunger and need. But in this call, in this low angry note that rose to meet the air, Rannoch also heard pain.

The deer turned back and looked out toward the mountains rising above him. The clouds and the mist hung low over the day and their dark edges were heavy with rain. On the deer ran. But as he went something else came with the biting loneliness that descended to greet him. A terrible sadness.

13

Reunited

Mountains divide us, and the waste of seas—
Yet still the blood is strong, the heart is Highland.
John Galt, 'The Lone Shieling'

The weather was changing rapidly now and as Rannoch travelled further north towards the Great Mountain and Herne's Herd, looking all the time for signs of Bracken and the others, great splinters of rock rose around him, stone screes scarred the green and the mountains loomed ever higher through the hanging mist.

Down their slopes ran seemingly endless streams and rivulets as their tops shed the weight of the autumn rains. They turned the valley bottoms into vast bogs that Rannoch slopped and waded through as he went. The rain seemed never to stop, so that when the skies did clear for a while, grumbling with thunder, Rannoch felt as though he had swum through a huge sea that had soaked into his bones. Rannoch swung west, following the contours of the mountain behind him, and after a while he began to catch a now familiar scent on the wind. Again he smelt the breath of the sea.

It was morning when the deer came to another sea loch. The sides of the mountain he was on plunged sheer to the water and all around they rose up again in walls of stone. The cold wind lashed the surface of the lake and through the mist Rannoch saw a strange sight. He knew instantly it was the work of man. It stood on a promontory, its squat granite walls black and forbidding – a castle. As he gazed at it Rannoch was reminded of the men in the gully with their swords and axes.

Rannoch followed the line of the loch now and after a while he saw tracks. He knew immediately they were the slots of red deer. In the soggy ground Rannoch made out the marks of at least five animals and as he examined their size and shape and the distance between the fore and back hoofs, his heart leapt, for he realized that they weren't just stags that had been this way, there were hinds too. He began to scent the air but could smell nothing, so he pressed on excitedly. It wasn't until he had travelled for a good while more that Rannoch saw them in the distance, through the mist. There were six of them, grazing together. Rannoch's heart began to race.

'I'm s-s-soaked through,' said Bankfoot miserably as he stood there in the rain, and the mist swirled around the little group of deer. Bankfoot was a six-pointer and his antlers were growing stronger.

'I know, Bankfoot, it's horrid,' said the hind next to him. Willow had grown into a very fine deer. Her smooth coat was the colour of fire-bracken, while her clear, black eyes glinted like jet.

'Th-th-thistle never stops grumbling,' said Bankfoot, looking towards the young stag who was talking to Tain and Peppa a little way away. They had all grown since their escape over a year before. Peppa looked even more like her sister and both Tain and Thistle had their third heads too, though Thistle's antlers looked stronger than Tain's.

'Yes,' agreed Willow, 'and I'm worried about him. Though he hates the Sgorrla, he seems to hate running from them even more.'

'Yes,' said Bankfoot, but then he added, 'But when Thistle decided on es-es-escaping with us he did throw his whole heart into it. We wouldn't have made it this f-f-far without him. Remember the fight at the burn?'

'I know,' said Willow. 'He's a natural leader.'

'M-m-more than an Outrider,' agreed Bankfoot.

'Not more,' said Willow, 'just different. But it's Bracken I'm most worried about. Her leg's very bad. It's slowing us up terribly.'

They both looked over to the hind. She was standing on her own, grazing half-heartedly across the soggy ground. Her leg had been wounded over two moons before and it still wasn't healing.

'It's n-n-not just that,' said Bankfoot. 'Some days she hardly seems to know what's happening at all. She's never got over Rannoch.'

Both of them still hated to think of that terrible day. The day the riders had come.

Willow gazed out into the mist.

'I still miss him terribly,' she said quietly.

'M-m-me too,' nodded Bankfoot.

'But look at us,' said Willow suddenly, affecting a cheerfulness. 'As gloomy as Herne's Wood. Come on, we've got to keep moving.'

Bankfoot began to move over towards the others. But he suddenly stopped dead. Like all young bucks his sense of smell had grown more and more acute and now he had scented something.

'What is it, Bankfoot?' said Willow when she saw how tense his face was. 'Is there danger?'

'I d-d-don't know. I th-th-think it's another deer.'

'Sgorrla?' whispered Willow, staring fixedly through the mist.

Suddenly a gust of wind cleared the mist away and the two of them saw a young stag running straight towards them. But now Willow, whose eyes were especially sharp, was shaking and shaking uncontrollably.

'W-w-willow,' whispered Bankfoot, 'what is it?'

'It can't be.'

'W-w-what?'

'Bankfoot,' whispered the hind, hardly daring to breathe. 'Look at his forehead.'

Bankfoot strained his young eyes and suddenly he too was trembling.

'It's im-im-impossible,' he stammered.

But as the deer drew closer Willow could now clearly see the white oak leaf on his brow. Then Willow was running towards him, bounding as fast as her legs would carry her.

'Rannoch,' she cried, 'Rannoch, you're alive!'

Of all the strange meetings that Herla can face in the wild, that was possibly the strangest. Rannoch, returned from the dead, surrounded by the little party of deer, themselves at their nerves' end from the strain of their flight. Months of fear and flight, the mystery of Rannoch's disappearance, the strange explanation that he gave of a pit high above the loch and Rannoch's own unbounded joy, all blended together to produce an overwhelming mixture of exhilaration and wonder.

The deer could hardly stop talking, the friends quizzing Rannoch about everything that had happened to him and marvelling at his account of Rurl and the wolf. Rannoch asked each of them in turn about the loch and Tharn, Colquhar and their journey, and they had so many questions that they hardly had time to discuss where exactly they were going. It was approaching Larn when Rannoch reminded them that the Sgorrla were close and that it was better if they talked as they travelled.

So the friends set off again. As they went it was Bankfoot who explained proudly how they had escaped from the Sgorrla and wandered south for moons, driven further and further away from the High Land by the pursuing stags. The going had been desperately slow, for the Sgorrla were hunting everywhere and Bracken found it hard to keep up. So, hiding in copses and caves sometimes for moons on end, they had eventually turned north again.

The most moving meeting of all was between Rannoch and Bracken. When Rannoch went up to her, Bracken looked quizzically into his face and as she stared at the fawn mark only the faintest flicker of recognition came into her sad eyes, mingled with a note of fear.

'Mother, it's me,' Rannoch said gently, and the young stag licked her muzzle and tried to tell her what had happened to him.

Bracken said nothing as she listened and Rannoch knew that she barely understood him. But he examined her wounded leg and fetched some of the special leaves he had used on the wolf and, very gently, rubbed some of the healing tincture into the cut. From then on the hind hung on Rannoch's every word and kept as close to him as she could.

Tain, Bankfoot, Willow and Peppa could hardly contain their joy at Rannoch's reappearance though all of them looked at his fawn mark and wondered what it really meant. Only Thistle was a little colder than the rest, though he tried to hide it. He listened to Rannoch's story carefully and when he gazed at his friend's forehead and six pointed tines, his eyes betrayed a strange wariness. But by the time they had all spent a couple of suns travelling together, it was almost as though they had never been parted.

Larn was well passed and they had all sat down together to rest in the wet grass.

'So you were travelling into the High Land too, Rannoch?' said Willow.

'Yes, I'm looking for a herd, Willow. They call themselves Herne's Herd. They live in the northern shadows of the Great Mountain. Rurl told me they might have some answers. I thought of coming to help you but . . . but first I had to know more.'

'About the Prophecy?' said Willow quietly.

All the friends looked at each other nervously. They were surprised that Willow had mentioned it so openly, but each of them had secretly wanted to ask Rannoch. They had been waiting for a chance to get him on his own. But Willow, knowing more of Rannoch's heart than the others, wanted to bring it out into the open as quickly as possible. Rannoch knew immediately what they were all thinking.

'The Prophecy can't be true, can it, Mother?' he said softly, looking at Bracken. The hind looked back suddenly with a fearful glance but she said nothing and Rannoch went on. 'But maybe parts of it are true, and the seal told me this herd might know something.'

'I've heard of them,' said Tain. 'An Outrider above the loch used to talk about them, but nothing he told me made me want to meet them.'

All the deer looked at Tain.

'What do you mean?' said Thistle.

'Only that there are strange rumours surrounding them,'

said Tain, already getting carried away with his own imagination, 'dark legends. Of ghosts and cannibalism and—'

'Stop it,' said Willow.

'It's all right,' Rannoch whispered in the darkness, 'I've
heard the rumours too. But there's something else. The
Sgorrla I overheard the other day said that Sgorr has forbidden any deer to go into the High Land. Maybe there's
something up there he fears. Something that could help us
fight him.'

'Well, if the l-l-legends are true about this herd,' Bankfoot
interrupted, 'you'll need some g-g-good friends with you, at
any rate.'

Rannoch smiled.

'Thank you, Bankfoot,' he said, 'but I can't expect any of
you to follow me there. Who knows what I'll find. Tell me,
though, what were you all planning to do in the High Land
when you got there?'

'Get away from Sgorr, first off,' said Tain. 'Then, who
knows.'

'Find another herd,' added Willow, 'and join them. That
was Thistle's idea. Then,' she went on, 'rear some fine little
Outriders, far away from the Low Lands.'

Rannoch looked back at Willow. It was only their flight
and the strange adventure they found themselves on that had
stopped her from finding a mate, Rannoch found himself
thinking. But he wasn't sad that she had not already stood
with another.

'B-b-become an Outrider,' added Bankfoot enthusiastically, looking at Peppa, 'and roam the hills, free as the day
and p-p-proud to stand in the heather and guard the herd
from harm.'

'But aren't you frightened, Tain, of what's up there?' asked
Rannoch suddenly.

'Oh, there are other stories about the High Land apart from the ones about Herne's Herd,' answered Tain cheerfully, forgetting all about ghosts and cannibalism. 'Stories that Blindweed used to tell me.'

'Like what?' said Rannoch.

'Well, some say that in the High Land a deer is safe from everything.'

'Go on,' said Rannoch, for the talk of Herne's Herd and the Prophecy had made them all nervous and he was glad of this chance of a distraction.

'That up there the Herla are free from fear and never want for anything, for the High Land has forests as wide as the moon and oaks that reach to the stars. There is no need for a Corps in the High Land because there is no danger to Herla and they may chew and graze all day long in the sunshine and run where they will.'

'N-n-no danger?' whispered Bankfoot. 'No predators?'

'None,' said Tain, 'because Starbuck sealed the High Land from the rest of the world and only the Herla may come there.'

'Tell us, Tain,' said Rannoch.

'All right.'

So as the others settled down around him in the grass, Tain began.

'It was when Starbuck had come off the Great Mountain,' he said, 'and met Herne again. Herne was still angry with him for stealing the antlers and Starbuck knew it, so he was especially respectful when he approached him. He bowed low and begged the lord to help him, for he was still looking for a place where the Herla would be safe from harm. Now as Herne listened coldly to Starbuck he suddenly had an idea. He chuckled to himself, for he had decided to play a trick on the deer.

' "Very well," he said, "I will help you. But first I will set you a test and if you fail it you must never ask me for my help again. You must go into the forest beyond and walk for two suns until you come to the Great Clearing. When you find it you must place something there of your own. And it *must* be of your own. When you do it, that thing will have the power to keep out any Lera that threatens you. But Starbuck, there are two other things. First, you must eat nothing in the forest, nothing at all, and secondly, as you go you must not carry anything in your mouth."

'Now Herne was very pleased with himself, for the conditions he had set meant that Starbuck could carry nothing with him to the clearing. Nothing except the antlers on his head. It was spring and Herne had an idea that Starbuck would wait until he got to the clearing to shed his antlers and so win the magic. But Herne had other ideas. He would send down branches and vines in the forest that would catch on Starbuck's antlers and break them off long before he finished his journey.

'Well, Starbuck listened closely to Herne and the clever deer knew that the god planned to trick him. But he pretended to be very grateful at this chance and said he would do his very best. So Starbuck went to the forest. But instead of making straight for the clearing, he waited at the edge of the trees and began to graze. He munched on leaves and grass, careful not to touch anything within the forest itself. At the next sun Herne came to find him and was surprised to see him still there, eating away.

' "Why have you not set out on your journey?" asked Herne.

'Starbuck now pretended to be very frightened and answered in a faint voice, "Lord, the journey ahead will be long and I must eat nothing in the forest. So I am feeding now, as much as I can."

'Then Starbuck did something that was very clever indeed. While Herne was watching him suspiciously he said, "And Herne, these antlers on my head are very heavy. I fear they may slow me down among the trees, for I may catch them in the branches."

'With that Starbuck went up to one of the trees and began to knock his antlers against the trunk. The antlers were dry and brittle and they' soon snapped off. When he saw this Herne shook his head for he thought that Starbuck must be a very stupid animal after all and, now that there was no chance of the deer succeeding in his quest, Herne turned away and went up to the great stone to sleep in the sunshine.

'But Starbuck had broken off his antlers precisely to put Herne off his guard and when he saw that the god was asleep he turned and ran into the forest as fast as he could. In two days the deer reached the wide clearing. There he stopped and, running round its edge, he began to cough and bring back the grass which he hadn't eaten at all, but kept in his stomach as he ran. He placed the little globes of fodder in a wide circle right round the clearing and then he called to Herne.

' "Lord, Lord, wake up. I have completed my task."

'When Herne saw what Starbuck had done he was furious that it was he who had been tricked. In a rage he decided to kill the deer, but as he was approaching, Starbuck cried, "Lord, remember your promise, for you said that anything I placed in the clearing would protect me from any Lera that threatens me. Now you are a god, Lord, but you are a Lera too, for you have the shape of a Herla."

'At first Herne was even more angry, but as he looked at

Starbuck standing there proudly in the clearing, he suddenly felt compassion for the clever creature and began to laugh.

' "Very well, Starbuck, again you have tricked me and again I must grant your wish. So wherever you place those pellets they will protect you. But Starbuck, I *am* a god and do not like to be tricked, so from now on you and the Herla shall eat like this for ever. For you must hold your food in your stomach and bring it back again when you want to feed." '

'Starbuck did not care much about this for now he had a way of protecting the Herla. So he thanked the god and left the forest and then he began to run, leaping and springing as he did so. He travelled for months on end, right across the High Land until he had circuited it entirely. And as he went he stopped to chew the cud and left pellets of magic grass on the mountain tops. So, at last, the whole country was ringed like the clearing in the wood and no Lera who wanted to harm a deer could pass. That is why the High Land is a magic place and why there the deer are always safe.'

Tain finished on this triumphant note and the deer nodded their appreciation.

'Well told,' said Rannoch, 'and a very beautiful story too.'

'Yes, it is beautiful, isn't it?' agreed Tain thoughtfully. 'If only it were true.'

'You don't think there's any t-t-truth in it, then?' said Bankfoot.

'No, not really,' answered Tain, 'though I believe that what Blindweed said about the High Land had some truth. That there are great forests and plenty of food and cover for a deer. Perhaps there really are less Lera to hunt us.'

'Well, now,' said Rannoch quietly, 'we should get some

sleep, for whatever we find up there, we daren't stay here much longer. It's not safe.'

But with his friends around him once again Rannoch suddenly felt safer than he had done for longer than he cared to remember.

14

The Fearful Glen

For I dipt into the future, far as human eye could see,
Saw the Vision of the world and all the wonder that would be.
Alfred Lord Tennyson, 'Locksley Hall'

It was mid-morning when the friends got on their way and it was much colder than it had been, a frost making the grass spark and glitter. After a time, as they journeyed north-west, they came past the opening to a great glen with sheer cliffs and jagged rock peaks that reared into the skies. This they passed and headed on towards the edge of a sea loch they could now see ahead of them. They reached the sea after a sun and the friends grew quiet as they walked and the mountains and the water overawed them.

Rannoch pulled them up as they came close to the end of the loch. In the distance, spreading out from the edge of the water, they could now see dwellings, smoke furling up from their low rooftops. There were people by the water too and carved trees like the ones Rurl had described.

The others stirred as their scents came to them across the wind, but Rannoch told them not to worry for they were still far away. Rannoch could see, though, that to travel ahead would bring them close to the encampment, so he decided to turn back and strike east through the valley they had passed the sun before, hoping to turn north again as soon as they could. This they did and soon the red deer were entering the glen's wide flanks.

A strange hush fell on the deer as they walked. Never before had they seen country like this. They felt they were entering a world of dreams. The vast walls of the glen rose around them like sleeping giants as the track they were taking along the valley bottom wove left and right through the hills, following the river gurgling through their centre. Ahead loomed three great spurs of rock and the rich, dark green of the valley and the slate black of the mountains seemed to swallow them up. Soon they felt like tiny moving specks lost in an immensity of stone. High above them the cry of birds echoed against the dizzy crags and the mist swayed and broke across the trees.

In the late afternoon they crossed the river and the sun managed to break through the clouds. The deer's spirits rose for the glen had grown eerily beautiful under its gentle light. They came to a small loch but they didn't pause to drink or ruminate in the winter sunshine as they would normally have done, for they all felt an urgency to press on, as though something were chasing them through the mighty valley. The sombre mystery that hung about the place made the deer tremble and start at the slightest sound, so by the time night came down they were at their nerves' end.

'Do you feel it?' whispered Willow to Rannoch breathlessly, as the deer stopped in the twilight.

'Yes,' said Rannoch, 'there's something strange about the place. I don't know what it is yet.'

'Herne's Herd?' said Bankfoot.

'No, I don't think so and I don't sense any immediate danger,' answered Rannoch. 'But it's very odd. Like some feeling far away.'

Bankfoot looked nervously at Rannoch's fawn mark.

The deer went on as silently as before. The darkness turned the crags and the stones into fearful shapes and the air seemed to hold an impossible stillness. With the night it began to rain again and soon the deer were miserable. They stopped and grazed a little, then huddled together in the shadow of the hills. At last Rannoch suggested that they move on, so the deer crept ahead through the darkness as the wind wailed through the valley. They began to imagine that they too were a part of the old tales, of the legends that run with the Herla.

After a while, however, Rannoch started to grow restive again and kept stopping to scent the air or listen to the wind. But it was a good while before they heard a sound that made them all stop in their tracks. It rose, strange and mournful, around the rocks; a plaintive piping like an eerie wind. The young deer crowded together and listened and when it stopped, finally and suddenly, Rannoch nodded.

'I thought so,' he whispered. 'There are humans up ahead.'

'What shall we do, Rannoch?' asked Tain. 'Go back?'

'We could,' said Rannoch, 'or we could wait till the sun comes. But I think it's dangerous to stay here. I'm for going on.'

'M-m-me too,' stammered Bankfoot. 'I d-d-don't want to go back the way we came. It makes me nervous.'

Rannoch asked the others what they felt and it was decided that he should lead them on, but they were preparing to set off when Bracken suddenly spoke. It was the first thing she had said since they had been reunited.

'I don't think I can,' she said hoarsely. 'I think I'll stay here.'

'But you can't, Mother,' said Rannoch.

'Just leave me, I'll be all right. I'll come on in the sunlight.
You wait for me up ahead.'

'No, Mother,' said Rannoch firmly. He could see she was
shaking badly. 'It'll be all right, I know it will.'

But Bracken just shook her head and said desperately,
'Just leave me. Can't you see I don't want to come yet?'

Rannoch looked Bracken tenderly in the eyes and began
to speak very quietly.

'We're all afraid, Mother. But it's far more dangerous to
stay here on your own. Nothing will happen, for if we get
close to the humans they'll be asleep and have no desire to
harm us.'

Bracken shook her head.

'I can't. It's as though everything around me is black.'

'I know. It's as though you were trapped in a gully. But
you can control it. Fight the blackness until you can think
again. That's the secret, Mother. Follow in my tracks and
every time you feel it threatening to overcome you, breathe
and think; think of something special. Anything. Think of
the High Land or Starbuck or Herne, and as long as you can
think, it will be all right.'

Bracken looked at Rannoch pleadingly but at last she
nodded.

'Right. Listen to me, all of you,' said Rannoch. 'I know
something of men, so I'll lead. Stay close and do what I do.
Walk slowly if I do, run if I run. I will lead us round them if
I can and tomorrow we'll be well away from here, munching
heather in the sunlight.'

The young stag nodded resolutely, turned and led them
on.

Above them the sky began to rumble and it started to
rain. The water came down in torrents, great pebbles of wet,
so that the deer were soon dripping and the ground began

to turn to mud as the water splashed and slurried down the sides of the valley. After a while they dimly made out the source of their fear.

The dwellings were grouped loosely across the side of the valley the deer had been travelling along. But, unfortunately, where the encampment hit the side of the mountain the rock buckled inwards and then rose sheer. It was impossible to skirt them to the right. Willow expected Rannoch to stop and lead them across to the slopes on the far side of the glen. But the deer did nothing of the kind. Hardly slowing and not once turning round, Rannoch led them off the slopes and straight down towards the encampment.

As the smell of men hit their nostrils there was not one of the other deer who did not want to turn and run. Each of them felt it. Fear came over them like a fog. But they remembered what Rannoch had said and struggled to keep the feeling at bay, and Rannoch's strange calmness as he walked ahead gave each of them confidence.

The encampment was quite large with squat boulder walls and peat roofs slung low on the stone houses. The dying embers of open fires outside spat and fizzled their last in the rain, but little smoke came from the rooftops and the only sound that the deer heard was the cacophony falling from the sky. A path ran straight up through the main group of dwellings, and though it had turned to pure mud Rannoch began to follow it. The deers' heads hung low as they squelched through the mud behind him, hardly daring to breathe. So the line of Herla crept on in the pouring rain through the very centre of the village.

Bracken, who was in the middle of the group, kept looking back nervously at Willow behind her. Although the hind was herself petrified, she nodded to Bracken calmly and kept going without a sound. A horse whinnied mournfully from somewhere and a dog began to bark, but Rannoch neither ran nor quickened his pace. At last the houses began to disappear and the piled boulders dropped away.

Only then did Rannoch suddenly throw back his antlers and run, straight up the slopes of the glen. The others followed him instantly and soon the deer were racing away from the camp as fast as their legs would carry them.

'Rannoch, you got us through,' cried Willow delightedly.

To her surprise, Rannoch didn't answer her. He just kept on going, straight ahead through the soaking grass. He didn't stop for ages and when he did so he still said nothing, but looked about him desperately. Then he ran up the side of the valley to the very edge of the cliff, where an outcrop of overhanging rock formed a kind of open cave. Here Rannoch stopped at last and the others joined him, glad to get out of the wet.

The friends began to talk excitedly and Bankfoot found some leaves at the back of the cave which the exhausted deer munched on gratefully. Their sense of relief was overpowering. Only Rannoch stayed apart, at the front of the cave, refusing to eat or say anything, looking back across the glen. Willow walked up to him quietly.

'Rannoch,' she said softly, 'Rannoch, what is it? What's wrong?'

Still the deer said nothing.

'Rannoch, please tell me, you're frightening me.'

Now Rannoch started and seemed to come out of a reverie.

'Willow,' he said, his eyes clearing, 'is it you?'

'Yes. What is it, Rannoch? Can I help you?'

'No, I don't think so,' said Rannoch bitterly, 'It's this feeling. I can't get rid of it. Willow, I'm afraid.'

'We were all afraid, Rannoch, but it's gone now. You led

us through. You know, Rannoch, it's right what you said about fighting the feeling and thinking at all costs. There was a point out there when—'

'No, Willow, I'm still afraid. The feeling's still here. It's got something to do with this place.'

'It's a strange place, but I don't think I understand. I'm sorry.'

'I don't really understand either. When we came to the humans I thought at first that we should cross the valley to try to avoid them. But then something took hold of me. I don't know what it was. I wanted to get close to them again, I think. To learn more about them. To see if they were like—' Rannoch stopped. 'Anyway, I was all right at first, walking up through their stones, but as we went something else happened. Something new came over me.'

'What, Rannoch?'

'I was listening very closely for any noise that meant we should run. But as I listened I suddenly thought I could hear the humans, breathing all around me. Then I knew that they were asleep among their stones. But as I concentrated, everything around me suddenly began to grow light and it wasn't raining any more. The path we were on was dry and as I looked up a mist was rolling towards me across the glen. But, Willow,' said Rannoch, trembling violently now, his voice strangled with pain, 'the mist was made of blood. The whole glen was red and as it came down I suddenly felt a terrible pain. It was linked to those sleeping bodies around me. But there was something else. Some feeling that I couldn't quite touch. Like anger. Then suddenly my ears were filled with screams and the air was thick with the smell of death. I looked up and realized we had come to the edge of their stones and I began to run. But the mist was still everywhere.'

'Rannoch,' whispered Willow, 'how horrible. Perhaps something happened here.'

Like humans, Herla believe that places can be haunted by the ghosts of past events.

Rannoch thought for a while.

'I don't know. I can see a little more clearly now but I need to think for a while. Alone, if that's all right.'

Willow nodded and left Rannoch to himself. She went to the back of the cave and lay down next to the others who had no desire to travel any further in the rain and were just grateful to be under cover. Thistle was chewing quietly on a ball of grass and Tain and Bankfoot asked Willow what was wrong with their friend. Willow just shook her head and told them not to worry. After a while the hind closed her eyes and began to doze as the driving rain pounded down on the rocks around them. When the red deer woke, the rain had stopped and it was growing light outside. Rannoch was still standing at the front of the cave.

The others were already stirring, so Willow got up and walked over to Rannoch. She said nothing at first but just gazed out with him into the approaching morning. The soaring valley was now lost in a thick mist that hung heavily in its bottom and made it look strangely peaceful.

'I'm all right,' muttered Rannoch quietly.

'I think we should be on our way,' said Willow kindly.

Rannoch nodded but Willow could see that Rannoch was in no state to lead them. So she went up to the others and whispered something to Bankfoot. He understood immediately.

'C-c-come on, everyone,' Bankfoot cried cheerfully, 'it's t-t-time to go and if you don't mind I w-w-want to lead.'

'You lead?' snorted Thistle. He would have argued if

Willow hadn't silenced him with her eyes and nodded to where Rannoch was standing.

So Bankfoot led the deer out of the cave into the misty dawn. The stones reared up again around them as the light swelled in the glen. Bankfoot, Tain, Thistle, and Peppa were soon running on ahead while Rannoch and Willow hung behind with Bracken trailing after them. As they went Rannoch kept stopping and looking back through the mist.

They travelled on like this for the morning. The mist cleared and the huge glen stood out stark in its vaulting majesty. Towards late afternoon, though, the deer realized they had nearly reached its end so they crossed to its northern slopes and began to climb. This side of the glen was less steep than the other slopes, though still difficult, and after some effort the deer found themselves high above the valley.

Here Rannoch stopped for a long time, gazing down at the immense cavern of grass and stone. Willow and Bracken stood with him but Willow didn't interrupt his thoughts and waited until at last he spoke to her.

'Willow,' he said softly, 'I think I understand now. I know why I wasn't sure about the danger. It's because it has nothing to do with us. Nothing to do with Herla. It's about them. Humans, I mean.'

'What did you see?' asked Willow.

'Death,' said Rannoch quietly. 'I saw death and pain and betrayal.'

Rannoch looked at the hind.

'But it's all right. It's a long, long way away.'

'Then the red mist and the vision?' whispered Willow. 'Something did happen here, then, years ago?'

Rannoch was silent at first and when he spoke he was looking down towards the encampment.

'No, Willow,' he answered softly, 'the thing I saw . . .'

Rannoch was staring hard now and his eyes were glassy. 'The thing I saw is still to come.'

In the valley below, which men call the Valley of Weeping and where one day the human heart of Scotia would bleed with the news of a dark betrayal and a terrible massacre, hardly a blade of grass stirred in the breeze.

With that Rannoch shook his antlers and turned. He led Bracken and Willow up, up and out of the fearful glen.

As they turned north once more, the deer realized that winter was coming in fast and they were rising to meet it, for every sun it grew a little colder. It was about seven suns after leaving the glen that they woke one early morning to find their greying coats covered with a thin, powdery sprinkling of snow.

They had reached a high mountain now which they started to climb. They didn't climb much higher than the edge of the trees, and here they sheltered from the wind that had begun to batter the other side of the mountain. They were also below the snow line, for only two weeks before the tops of the mountain had been draped with the first heavy cloak of winter. To a casual observer they might just have been animals struggling towards the edge of what was destined to be one of the hardest seasons ever seen in Scotia. But an onlooker with a keener eye might have noticed that one, with a coat slightly redder than the rest, would at times hang back and pause as though lost in thought, before shaking his antlers and moving on. But they would need the eyes of an eagle or a sparrowhawk to see the white mark in the centre of the deer's head.

If that onlooker could have changed his shape and travelled with them, for a while he might have learnt something of their hearts and their needs and of what they saw as they looked out at the world. He would have felt the wind change suddenly, turning its breath on the eastward side of the mountain, and a cold grip the air with a new threat that made the deer shiver even under their thick fur. He would have felt the skies above grow so heavy that it seemed as though they could press the mountain flat with the weight of the ice congealing in the heavens.

He would have known too, like the deer, that danger was settling around them. For when the clouds finally opened, instead of the interminable, drenching rains that in autumn and winter turn the edge of the High Land to bog, the brittle air was suddenly sharp with huge snowflakes that piled quickly and thick on the earth, and the deer were soon turned to moving smudges on a sheet of white. Then perhaps he would have wanted the journey to end and to be safe in a warm bed listening as a storyteller, grown huge and sinister in the firelight, painted him pictures of the world.

On they went until the snow stopped and the morning brought them off the slopes down into a valley, its patterns and form lost under the sweeping white. It stretched ahead, flat as a sigh, before rising up again into the arms of a mountain that seemed to climb higher than anything about it. On its tops and flanks the snows were heavy and, high above, the wind lashed across the white.

As the deer looked up they all shivered.

'The Great Mountain,' whispered Tain.

They spent the day on the foothills, wondering what to do next and scraping at the hard ground to get to the sparse nourishment beneath. There wasn't one of them that didn't feel a strange sense of awe and foreboding as they hovered in the shadows of the Great Mountain, for they had come to the edge of the Herla's own myths.

Rannoch had drifted away on his own and was trying to

feed on a clump of dead hawthorn when he suddenly heard
a noise. As he looked up and through the bushes he spied a
face, watching him intently; a pair of huge, nervous eyes in
a smudge of brown. The face suddenly vanished.

'Who's there?' called Rannoch.

The bushes rustled and a deer stepped out into the open.
It was the smallest deer Rannoch had ever seen, though it
had a magnificently bushy winter coat with spiky grey hairs.
The deer was a young stag but with only one small, straight,
pointed antler on its head. Rannoch realized it must be
shedding.

'Hello,' said Rannoch, for he felt not the least sense of
fear at the sight of this Clovar.

The deer blinked back at him and started to shake.

'Don't be frightened,' said Rannoch quietly. 'I won't hurt
you. My name's Rannoch. I'm a red deer. Who are you?'

The deer still looked terrified and said nothing.

'Come, come. It's all right. What's your name?'

'Teek,' said the deer at last, in a tiny, high-pitched voice.

'Well, Teek,' said Rannoch, 'pleased to meet you. What
kind of Herla are you?'

'I'm a roe deer,' piped Teek. 'I live in the next valley.'

'How many of you are there?' asked Rannoch.

Rannoch knew something of the habits of roe deer from
stories Bracken had told him as a fawn, but he had never
met one before.

'About a hundred,' said Teek.

'A hundred?' cried Rannoch, astonished. Roe deer are
usually solitary creatures and never live in large groups.

'That's right, including the hinds and the Outriders.'

'Outriders?'

Rannoch was even more startled.

'Yes,' said Teek, 'I'm an Outrider. One day I hope to be a captain.'

Now Rannoch was amazed. It was strange to associate such a small and obviously timid deer with an Outrider and to imagine this herd living in the shadow of the Great Mountain.

'I didn't think that roe were so sociable,' he said.

'No, not normally,' answered Teek rather sadly, 'but we've started to live in herds to protect each other. Ever since *he* came.'

'*He?*'

'Sgorr. I thought you were one of the Sgorrla. That's why I was so wary.'

'The Sgorrla have been here already?' whispered Rannoch.

'Oh yes,' said Teek, 'they're patrolling everywhere. The length and breadth of the Great Glen.'

'But why should roe deer worry about the Sgorrla?'

'Why? Because of Sgorr's decree. That all the Herla should pay homage to him.'

'All the Herla?' gasped Rannoch. 'The Clovar too?'

'Yes. Red, roe and fallow.'

'But he can't,' said Rannoch.

'It was because of the threat of Sgorr that we formed the herd in the first place and now our lord is thinking of moving us north, into the High Land. Although Sgorr has forbidden any Herla from crossing.'

'I know,' said Rannoch, shaking his head gravely.

'So now we don't know what to do.'

'Go north,' advised Rannoch.

'But we fear to,' said Teek, growing nervous again, 'because . . .'

Teek stopped and his huge eyes blinked fearfully at Rannoch.

'What is it?'

Teek's little voice was barely audible.

'Herne's Herd,' he whispered.

Rannoch started.

'Do you know of them?' he asked urgently. 'Do you know where they are?'

'Beyond the Great Mountain,' said Teek.

'Then they don't live on the mountain itself?'

'No . . . well not from what we've heard. They never go near the Great Mountain, except to die,' said Teek, looking up at the swirling white. 'For them the mountain is sacred. They believe that Herne lives on its top and they can only join Herne in death. Sometimes, when the wind is right, we can hear their souls calling from the mountain top.'

Rannoch shivered and looked up too. He felt a strange stirring in his guts, like a kind of longing.

'Then where do they live?' he asked.

'On a high moor, it's said, beyond the Great Mountain. But not far. Some of our Outriders say they have even seen them. Those that returned.'

'What do you mean those that returned?'

'Most who have dared to venture into the High Land have never returned.'

Both the deer were quiet now and the cold air was full of fear.

'But why are you so interested in Herne's Herd?' asked Teek suddenly.

Rannoch hesitated.

'Just curiosity.' He shrugged. 'We are going north too, into the High Land, to escape from Sgorr. It's best to know what we're facing.'

'You are going north? I shall tell the council that. They'll be pleased that some of the red Herla hate Sgorr too. But now I should really be getting back.'

Teek dipped his head.

'Herne be with you,' he said.

'And with you too.'

As Rannoch ran back to the others, thinking bitterly of Sgorr and what he was doing to the Herla and feeling a swelling guilt rising in him that he was leaving the Low Lands, he kept looking up again and again to the lonely summit of the Great Mountain.

'Are you really up there, Herne?' he whispered as he ran.

But when he reached his friends he had already decided what he was going to do. They were gathered together, discussing the journey and the best route to follow into the High Land.

'We'll have to skirt its flanks,' Thistle was saying. 'It would be far too dangerous in this weather to try and climb it, though in the summer it'd be much quicker.'

'Starbuck climbed it in winter,' said Tain.

'Starbuck is in a story,' said Thistle, 'and we are real Herla.'

'Rannoch,' said Willow as he came up, 'Thistle thinks we should try and skirt the mountain and keep to the foothills to avoid the cold.'

Rannoch nodded.

'Yes,' he said, 'I think that's just the route you should take.'

'What do you mean the route *you* should take,' said Willow.

'I'm going to climb it,' said Rannoch quietly, looking up at the mountain above him.

'B-b-but you can't,' cried Bankfoot.

'I'm going to try.'

'But why?' said Willow.

'Because it'll be quicker if I'm ever to find this strange herd and . . . because I want to know if He really lives up there. Herne.'

The other deer were aghast. What Rannoch was contemplating was terribly dangerous. Besides, all the others had grown up thinking of Herne only as an idea, a legend; a bit like Starbuck only different. Something they believed in, of course, but not as something that was actually real; not real like heather and the Home Oak. But here was Rannoch talking about Herne as though he was something you could see and scent.

'We'll meet up again in the High Land,' said Rannoch, 'when the spring comes and I've found out all I can about Herne's Herd.'

'Well,' said Bankfoot suddenly, 'if that's what you've decided, I'm c-c-coming with you.'

'And me,' added Tain. 'What a story that will make.'

'No,' said Rannoch, 'I've got to do this alone.'

'I'm coming as well,' said Willow suddenly.

'No, Willow.'

'If you think I'm going to abandon you now I've only just found you again,' said Willow, 'you're wrong.'

'Can I come as well?' said Peppa, looking fondly at Bankfoot. The stag almost blushed.

The twins were standing side by side and Rannoch suddenly realized how deeply fond he was of them both.

'We'll all go,' said Willow, 'if that's what you really want to do. Besides, if we try to skirt round, who knows where the Sgorrla are lying in wait for us. One thing's for sure: they won't be up there.'

But Rannoch held his ground.

'Thistle, tell them they're being foolish,' he said, looking suddenly towards his mother. 'There's much less chance of us all crossing it and Mother will never make it.'

Thistle nodded.

'You lead them round,' said Rannoch.

'No,' said Tain, 'Thistle can take Bracken round if he wants, but I'm determined.'

The others agreed. Rannoch tried to argue but they kept insisting and after a while his resistance began to break down. But then something happened that decided it for all of them.

'Look,' Tain suddenly shouted to the others.

'There,' cried Peppa.

In the distance, from both east and west, two groups of red stags were coming straight towards them, bucking their antlers in the snowy air. There must have been over thirty of them.

'Sgorrla,' cried Rannoch bitterly. 'Quickly!'

There was only one possible means of escape and that was straight up.

15

A Vision

I have had a most rare vision. I have had a dream, past the wit
of man to say what dream it was.
William Shakespeare, 'A Midsummer Night's Dream'

The clouds were heavy with snow as they fled up the sides
of the Great Mountain. A wind came up too which blew
hard into their faces and the thought of Herne above them
and the Sgorrla below soon subdued their spirits. Then it
started, great thick snowflakes, and very quickly the deer
could hardly see further than their slots. They sank deeper
and deeper into the cold white and the wind grew stronger
and stronger. They bunched together instinctively but, within
just a little while, the blizzard had become so strong that
they could hardly make any headway at all. The storm,
though, had at least masked them from the pursuing Sgorrla,
and after a while it died a little and they found the going
easier. But as they went they all thought of Herne, waiting
above them in the bitter snows.

After a time they came to a great spur of rock and scraggy
tree above them and they were forced to swing west. In the
blizzard, they didn't know that they were now travelling
along a narrow ridge that dropped dangerously away to their
right and left. The ground was quite steep and the deer

slipped and stumbled, their forelegs sinking into the snow so that they were forced to kick and jump to make any progress at all. The air was bitingly cold and the wind and snow got worse as the deer inched painfully up the mountain. They did not know what a dangerous position they were in, for several times the deer came close to the edge of the spur and it was only luck that stopped one of them slipping and crashing down onto the rocks.

But eventually the mountain flattened out a little. It was here that Rannoch found a place that offered some temporary shelter. It was hardly a cave, but a rock overhang where the wind had actually scooped out the newly fallen snow, creating a kind of snow pit below a lip of stone. There was plenty of room for them all and they nestled together for warmth for a while, shivering in the hollow, their thick winter coats and young antlers flecked with white, the frost rising around their nervous breath.

'It's worse than Herne's winter,' said Tain, as they looked out from the mountain. It had suddenly stopped snowing, though, as quickly as it had started, and now they shivered bitterly for they could see the dangerous path they had just taken. To their horror they saw that at one point they had crossed an outcrop of frozen snow which seemed to have nothing supporting it at all and edged out over a sudden, plunging drop.

As the deer pressed on they now found themselves on the edge of a defile with a clear stretch of firm, open snow banking not too steeply above them, which was crisp and firm under their feet. This they began to climb and after a while a thin sun even managed to pierce the clouds and offered a brittle warmth to the deer.

The sun didn't last. As they reached the top of the defile, the slope above them opened further and rose swiftly. It started to snow again and with the snow came a wind whose breath had been hardened on the mountain top. Worse than this, though, the deer had now reached the ice line where, with height, the fallen powder had compacted and turned hard and glassy. Their feet began to skitter and slip across the solid ground. Lower down the mountain the going had been hard because of the depth of the snow and the deer had sunk into it nearly up to their haunches, but now they found they could hardly get a purchase on the ground at all. Several times they slipped, and at one point Peppa, who had climbed higher than the others, lost her footing and might have been injured if her slide back down the slope had not been blocked by a painful collision with Tain.

It was Willow who had the idea of threading across the ice face and then turning back a little higher up, so that they ended up zigzagging back and forth. In this way the deer managed to climb. But now a new danger confronted them, for traversing the mountain like this brought them to the edge of small ravines and sudden drops with no clear edges in the snow. The deer could not see them until they were right on top of them. Several times Rannoch nearly came to grief, only to see the danger just in time.

The higher they got, the colder it became, and as the day wore on the wind grew more and more fierce. When they were trying to move into its path, as it blew from the east across the mountain, they felt like twigs that could be snapped in two at any moment. But when they traversed back again, they found they were forced forwards too quickly to keep a firm foothold on the ice. Worst of all, night was now coming in. The darkness came suddenly and with the moaning wind and thoughts of Herne and what they would encounter above them swirling through their heads, there wasn't one of them who didn't tremble. Except perhaps poor

Bracken whose leg had got worse and who was so exhausted that she could hardly think at all.

Peppa, who was travelling with her, suddenly called out to her.

'Bracken, Bracken, you're wandering.'

The deer had just started to drift down the slope.

'What?' muttered the hind in a dreamy voice. 'I'm sorry, I'm so sleepy I can hardly keep awake.'

'You must stay awake, Bracken,' cried Peppa.

'I know. But it's so hard. I keep thinking I'm by the loch and it's summer.'

Peppa shivered as a blast of snowy wind whistled round her head.

But just as Bracken had spoken they were interrupted by the terrified bark of a stag up ahead. It was Rannoch. By the time they reached him, the deer was pounding the ice with his hoofs.

'What is it?' cried Peppa.

Bankfoot shook his head at his friend.

'Thistle, what's happened?' shouted Peppa, but now she could see at least part of the cause of Rannoch's distress, for Rannoch had come to the edge of the cliff.

'Willow,' gasped Rannoch.

Peppa looked around her and, to her horror, she realized that her sister had vanished. Just in front of them, where the ground suddenly dropped away into the void, the snow was marked and scuffed where Willow, blind with cold, had slipped and fallen over the edge.

'No,' cried Peppa bitterly.

The friends inched forward and stood staring out stupidly over the drop. They could see very little for the snowflakes swirled and scurried thick before their eyes.

'Willow,' sobbed Rannoch, 'Willow, what have I done?'

Peppa and the others began to shout and call, but they heard and saw nothing from below. They fell silent, numbed by cold and loss. The wind moaned around their heads as though the heavens were feeling the pain and rage that rose in each of the deer's hearts. Willow was gone. But still they stayed where they were until Bracken's eyes began to mist over with pain. It was Tain who came to his senses first, and none too soon.

'Rannoch,' he cried, 'we must keep moving. We'll die if we stay here much longer. Look at Bracken – she can hardly stand up.'

Rannoch said nothing. He was still staring out hopelessly over the drop.

'Rannoch. This is no time to give up, Rannoch. What would Willow have said?'

Rannoch lifted his head and looked longingly at his friend. Then he nodded gravely.

'Yes,' he whispered, 'yes, Tain, you're right. We must get moving. Listen to me, all of you. We've got to keep going, to keep warm. There'll be time to mourn Willow.'

Thistle was the first to move but as Rannoch started to follow the others, Tain stopped him.

'Bracken,' he whispered.

Bracken was still standing there, looking out over the drop. Her whole body was shaking.

'Mother,' cried Rannoch over the wind, 'you've got to come.'

Bracken made no answer.

'Mother, please. There's nothing we can do.'

'What's wrong?' cried Tain.

'She won't move,' said Rannoch desperately.

'Bracken. Can you hear me?' said Tain. 'It's me, Tain.'

Rannoch dropped his muzzle and began to nudge Bracken

in the side. It swung her slightly to the right, but the deer seemed to hear and see nothing. Rannoch's nudges got stronger but they still had no effect in rousing her.

'Mother,' pleaded Rannoch, almost at his wits' end. 'Can you hear me? If you—'

But with that Bracken turned her head slightly.

'Quiet,' she said suddenly, 'listen.'

The two startled stags pricked up their ears to listen, but all they heard was the howling fury of the night. Rannoch shook his head sadly.

'Nothing.'

'Just the wind,' agreed Tain.

'No. Wait,' said Rannoch suddenly. 'What's that?'

The wind had died a little again and as Tain strained to listen he thought he heard a very faint voice. The deer's senses were on full alert now and Peppa had joined them. For a while their hopes fought the wind and faded as the sound they thought they had heard was lost again below the mountain's angry cry. Then suddenly the wind dropped almost completely and the deer were sure. Below them they could hear something calling. It was a hind calling Rannoch's name.

'Willow,' cried Rannoch.

'Rannoch. Rannoch, is that you?' came the voice.

'Willow. Where are you? We can't see you.'

'I'm below you, I think. But I can't see you either.'

'Are you hurt?' cried Rannoch.

'No, Rannoch, just a little bruised. The snow broke my fall. I think I was very lucky, though. There are rocks everywhere. But Rannoch, I've found a cave. We could shelter. It's warm and dry.'

'A cave,' whispered Tain. 'Thank Herne.'

'But Willow,' cried Rannoch, 'how do we reach you?'

'I don't know,' said Willow. 'I've tried running along the mountainside to find a way back up, but it's too dark and the snow is very deep.'

In fact the snow was getting deeper and deeper, for the storm was intensifying. The deer's relief that Willow was alive was soon lessened by the realization that their situation was, if anything, worse than before. For now they were separated from the hind by a good drop and, no matter how hard they tried, they could find no way down. Rannoch sent Thistle and Bankfoot to scout ahead and behind them, but they soon returned to report that the weather was now so bad that to search along the edge of the ridge would be fatal.

Rannoch tried desperately to think of a way out, but nothing came to him. The night wore on and the air began to freeze. High above them the wind, caught in rock fissures and coves, howled mournfully and Rannoch shivered as he thought of what Teek had said about the souls of the dead stags from Herne's Herd haunting the mountain.

Willow began to grow more and more worried for her friends, for at least below them she was protected from the full brunt of the storm. She tried to persuade Rannoch and the others to move on without her, but the deer refused to leave her and before long they were so cold and wet that they couldn't have made it very far anyway. The others lay down and very soon their forms began to disappear under the heaping snow, so that they looked like ghostly statues. Only Rannoch stood, talking less and less frequently to Willow, hoping in vain that some idea would come to him to save them from the mountain.

At last he did something he had never done before.

'Herne,' he whispered. 'Herne, if you're up here, please help us. Save my friends at least.'

But Rannoch's heart grew heavier. The wind and snow

howled and raged and his bones began to ache. He felt the last drops of energy ebbing away from him. Even Willow was defeated. Below her friends, she too lay down and closed her eyes.

It seemed all hope had gone when Rannoch suddenly lifted his head. He had heard a noise above him. It came faintly at first, like a strange creaking. Rannoch's eyes opened in amazement as he caught sight of a black shape moving towards him. Its path was irregular and every now and then it was knocked sideways by the terrible blasts of wind. Then, just as it was overhead, it was suddenly caught in a scurrying loop of air. There was a dreadful screech and the thing fell like a stone. It landed in a snowdrift, not three antlers from where Rannoch was standing. There was a flurry of snow-flakes and then the black shape began to hop up and down as a series of angry sounds, which Rannoch clearly recognized, exploded from its beak.

'Nevermore. Nevermore. Never seen anything like it. Like it.'

'Crak!' cried the amazed deer.

The raven swung round and cocked his head. But he didn't seem at all surprised to see Rannoch.

'Crak, it *is* you. What are you doing here?'

'Well may you ask,' snapped the bird. 'Trying to get home. Get home. Crak, Crak. But this weather's impossible.'

'But it's extraordinary,' cried Rannoch.

'Extraordinary? Extraordinary? Crak, Crak. What's extraordinary is a herd of deer trying to cross the Great Mountain in a blizzard. That's what's extraordinary. Crak, Crak.'

Suddenly from below came Willow's voice.

'Rannoch, what's happening?'

Crak jumped again and shook out his wings.

'Now I've seen it all. Seen it all,' he screeched. 'A talking deer. Stags who try to cross the Great Mountain and now a deer that can fly. Can fly.'

Rannoch explained what had happened and after a while the bird began to calm down a little.

'Well, from the looks of it,' he said, 'you'd better get away from here. Or else. Or else.'

'Yes, Crak. But I'm afraid you were wrong, we can't fly.'

'Nor you can. Nor you can. Crak, Crak. Well, I can. If only just. You mentioned a cave. A cave. Perhaps we can help each other. I was getting rather worried myself up there. Perhaps I can find a way down to your cave and we'll all be safe. Crak, Crak.'

With that the raven flapped his wings and tried to take off. On the first attempt the wind was so strong that Crak was actually upturned by it and ended up back where he'd started with his beak buried in the snowdrift. But on the second go he managed to launch himself out over the edge, just where Willow had fallen, and with a furious cawing, disappeared into the storm.

It seemed ages before Crak returned, flapping frantically and cursing all the time.

'Herne's beak but it's bad,' he cried.

Then he closed an eye, stood on one leg and peered irritably at Rannoch.

'Well?' asked the stag.

'Well,' said Crak, 'it's difficult. But just possible. Along there. Can't see the way from up here. Up here. A thin ledge. Crak, Crak. A little jump and then a careful deer can make it.'

'Saved!' cried Rannoch. 'Crak, you've saved us again.'

'Not yet. Not yet. But you'd better hurry or none of us will see the morning. Nevermore. Nevermore.'

Rannoch nodded and began to rouse the others. Bracken could barely stand, but with help and with Crak hopping along ahead, the deer set off again through the storm. With some difficulty the bird guided them to a ledge that jutted out some way into the night. Thistle had seen it earlier, but what he had been unable to see was that if they made it to its furthest point and jumped a little way to the left, they could reach a lower slope that banked less steeply.

Tain made the jump first, then Thistle and Peppa. Bankfoot slipped a little but he made it too. Rannoch waited behind to help Bracken and when it came to it he was terrified that his mother would fall. But Bracken seemed to raise herself to the challenge and with Crak flapping encouragement, the old hind threw herself out over the edge and landed safely with the others. Finally came Rannoch and soon the party found themselves walking easily downwards. The ground opened out a little and they came to a path. After just a little time, through the bitter wind and snow, they spotted Willow.

She led them straight along the mountainside to the cave mouth. It was a narrow opening with a boulder lip, but inside it was unexpectedly large. It was dry too and comparatively warm. Crak hopped around delightedly while Bracken laid down by the entrance and closed her eyes. But as Rannoch entered the cave mouth he stopped and his ears came up.

'What is it, Rannoch?' asked Willow.

'I don't know,' said Rannoch.

'Man?' whispered Willow.

'Yes. But long, long ago. It's . . . it's like that place on the hill. Do you remember? Only much older. Much, much older.'

And . . . there's something else. Something familiar yet . . .
yet very strange.'

With that there was a cry from Bankfoot.

'Come and l-l-look,' he called.

He was standing at the back of the cave and Rannoch
and the others joined him. Outside the snow had stopped
temporarily and the clouds were suddenly punctured, letting
through a shaft of bright moonlight that reached to the back
wall. As their eyes grew accustomed to the gloom, they saw
what had startled him. On the arching wall of the cave, faint
but unmistakable, were the coloured images of running deer.
The sight hushed the friends. They looked at each other in
the gloom with their huge, startled eyes, but this was quite
beyond their understanding.

'Come on, let's get some sleep,' whispered Rannoch after
a while.

'Quite right. Quite right,' cried Crak.

The deer and the bird settled themselves in the cave. It
was a haunting place and as they listened to the screaming
wind outside and thought of the god who was said to haunt
the mountain and of the images on the wall, some of them
wished they had never set foot in it at all.

A small pool at the back of the cave, fed by the steady
drippings from the roof, had frozen up and when the
draughts of air brushed across it they came to the deer chill
and bitter; but the cave was considerably warmer than the
world without.

Willow had sat down at Rannoch's side and now she laid
her head on his flanks and closed her eyes. Crak, who himself
was quite exhausted, hopped to a corner of the cave and
now he stood quite motionless, his head tucked low into his
great, black wings.

As Rannoch lay there he suddenly felt angry and ashamed.

'I'm sorry, Willow,' he murmured. 'If I'd lost you I don't know what I would have done. I should never have tried to climb the Great Mountain, Herne or no Herne.'

But the young hind was already fast asleep.

The only sound in the cave now was the deer's breathing and the moaning wind. Rannoch's eyes strayed towards those images on the wall and then he looked towards the ice pool. He didn't know why, but he felt as if something in that pool held a message. Rannoch closed his eyes and slept.

In his sleep Rannoch had the sense that he was coming closer to a great mystery. It had something to do with the cave and the mountain, and it lay in the real world around him.

In truth the deer had indeed come to a very mysterious place. For here, thousands of years before, the first men to inhabit the land of Scotia had lived and hunted, eaten and slept and painted their strange pictures on the walls.

But apart from man and his images, there was something else in that cave on the Great Mountain. Rannoch had sensed it when he first entered the place. Something that linked him and his kind to the land and the centuries. In that pool, down through the fissured ice, lay something discarded by time: a fossil. It had been changed into stone by prehistory, just as the cold had changed and hardened the form of the water.

At the pool's bottom lay the fossilized remains of an antler. But it was no antler that Rannoch and the others would have understood. It was the beam of a creature named Megaloceros; a deer that had once stood six feet tall and whose antlers in turn rose six feet in height above its mighty head. It had belonged to the giant of deer, long since vanished from the planet, which, ten thousand years before, had been

driven by the weather from its natural home on the plains
to die up here on the mountain.

Rannoch woke. He had sensed a change in Bracken's
breathing. The deer sounded in great pain and she wheezed
terribly as she struggled for air. But Rannoch didn't wake
her. He knew that the best healer now was rest.

The storm was growing worse and worse. In the valleys
below, crofters and villagers looked up at the slopes of the
Great Mountain and shuddered. They knew that the weather
would bring death to any man or animal caught on its slopes.
Indeed, when it cleared and the snow lay calm again on its
sides, the broken bodies that were hidden under its icy shroud
included both man and beast. High in the foothills a young
man had been caught in the blizzard and now he lay buried,
his once warm body as cold as stone. Bird and animal had
fallen into its clutches too. Sheep and ram were sealed in its
winter tomb; a vixen that had strayed foolishly from her set
lay hardening in the white, and even cattle had strayed too
far into the foothills, never to return to their winter pasture.
They lay trapped in the glistening powders, a mute testament
to life and death.

All night the blizzard raged and the red deer slept fitfully
in the cave. They heard the wind die in the middle of the
next morning. Tain was the first to venture outside. The cave
mouth was now completely blocked with snow and he was
forced to carve through the snow wall with his antlers and
push clear with his head. But when at last he had made an
opening, the sunshine streamed through gloriously. The
others began to help him and soon they were all outside on
the crisp ground, enjoying the winter sunshine and the fresh
air and thanking Herne they were still alive.

With Crak flapping above them, the deer began to thread
their way slowly back along the path towards the spot where

they had descended the night before. Some way beyond it the ground opened again and they found that the way was easier.

It was a strange sight. High on the side of the Great Mountain, moving in single file, seven red deer rising up and up through the winter white. Like the mountaineers in days far ahead who rope themselves together in moving lines, the deer followed carefully in one another's slots, leaping now and then to free their thin legs from the deep powder.

As they went, Tain could hardly contain his excitement.

'Just think of it,' he kept saying. 'The Great Mountain. Only Starbuck crossed it in winter and now I'm doing it. Oh, what a story this will make. I wonder what we'll really find on the top.'

This made the others look at each other nervously. The morning and the bright sunshine had done something to dispel their night terrors, but now the thought of Herne made the mountain suddenly seem terrible and threatening once more.

Willow frowned at Rannoch.

'Do you think He's up there?' she whispered.

Rannoch lifted his antlers. The sky was as blue as a crocus. The snow flashed and sparked in the sunshine and crunched pleasantly under the deer's feet. Now and then gentle gusts of wind would lift its surface around them and whirl the snow into the icy air.

'I don't know,' he said quietly.

It was close to afternoon when the deer neared the summit and found they had to traverse one last steep ridge. But when they finally reached the top, the mountain opened broad and flat in front of them. A southerly wind was blowing and, out of excitement and relief, the deer started to race through the snow. Rannoch looked up to see Crak circling above his head.

'Goodbye. Goodbye,' called the bird. 'You've done it. You've climbed the Great Mountain in winter. That's something to tell them. You've come to the highest place in the Great Land. Sgorr can't touch you now. Perhaps deer really can fly. Crak, Crak.'

'Thank you, my friend,' called Rannoch. 'We couldn't have done it without you.'

But as the bird rose into the air something extraordinary happened. Tain, who was below him, realized that he could understand what the bird was saying too.

'Good luck. You're really in the High Land now,' called Crak.

'But, Crak. Won't you stay a while?' cried Rannoch after him.

'No. No. Crak, Crak. I must get back to my own. But I'll see you again, Rannoch. Farewell. Farewell.'

The raven circled higher and higher until he became a tiny black speck etched against the blue. Then he was gone.

Rannoch ran on, his heart suddenly expectant. The others were ahead of him now and when he came to a halt next to Willow, the deer were silent. Rannoch's heart began to race as he followed their gaze. They could see right across the mountain top. But if they had expected to find Herne they were disappointed. There was no one there at all.

Instead the land of Scotia lay glittering before them, mountains and valleys, swathed in white, floating below like mighty clouds. They could see for miles across the deep blue sky. But what they saw made them question. None of the deer had really known what to expect but after Tain's story each had associated the High Land with Herne and the forest. But now, as they looked north, they did not see mighty forests at all but bleak, treeless hills, rising and falling, and bare moors cut by huge lochs and rivers.

Thistle was the first to speak.

'Well, Tain, Herne's Wood, eh? A place where the deer may be safe? It looks more dangerous than any country I have ever seen. Look how exposed we shall be.'

'That was just a story,' said Tain coldly, but in his heart he was deeply worried too.

'W-w-well, we can't stay here,' said Bankfoot.

He was looking towards the west and the others immediately realized what he meant. Great, heavy snow clouds were billowing before them. The weather was changing again.

'We should get down the other side as quickly as possible,' said Tain.

He looked over to Rannoch and the deer nodded. So, with Tain leading, the stags began to descend. Only Rannoch lingered, with Willow at his side.

'Come on, Rannoch, we should be going,' she said.

'You go, Willow. I want to be alone up here a while. Maybe He'll come if I'm alone. Don't worry, I'll join you soon.'

Willow nodded and set off after the others. There, on the top of the Great Mountain, Rannoch stood alone, and he felt bitterly disappointed. He suddenly let out a bellow.

'Herne,' he cried. 'Where are you, Herne? I'd thought to find you here. Do you really exist except in dreams?'

But nothing returned to the deer except the aching silence of the world.

Rannoch began to move forward and then to run. But as Rannoch ran something overcame him. His eyes were open and yet he didn't see the snow beneath his feet. It was as though he could suddenly see miles ahead of him, out onto the moors across the High Land. He could see herds of wild deer moving freely across them. Then images came to him from his dreams, and though he knew he wasn't asleep, they were as clear as the day.

'The forest. The forest is always with you,' he heard himself crying, and there was triumph in that cry.

As Rannoch ran on in his waking dream his eyes began to mist over and when they cleared he saw a sight that made his head swim.

In front of him, in the snow, stood a mighty deer.

Its body was larger than a full-grown stag, with antlers that arced high above its strange head. But they were not like any antlers of this world. Two tines bore out straight ahead and above the strange palmed bez tines long hoops of bone flowered into brave coronets. The creature's face was covered almost completely in fur, below its muzzle there billowed a mighty white mane, and its hoofs were black. Rannoch stopped and blinked and then his breath failed him as he realized that this was no vision at all, but as real as the mountain and the snow and the cold, cold air.

'Herne,' he gasped. 'Herne. You've come at last.'

16

Birrmagnur

And now the leaves suddenly lose strength.
Philip Larkin

As Rannoch approached the deer god nervously it dropped
its great, shaggy head and let out a low bellow that seemed
to make the whole mountain shake. Rannoch froze.

'Herne,' he whispered again.

But at this the strange apparition pushed forward his
muzzle and seemed to chew the air. His thick, wide lips
began to quiver and, to his horror and then amazement,
Rannoch realized that the god was laughing.

'Why do you call me Hoern?' the creature said suddenly
in an extraordinary, singing voice.

Rannoch stared back in utter bewilderment.

'Because I thought . . . I thought you . . .'

'I see what you thought I was,' chuckled the animal, still
munching the air. 'Most gratifying. But you are wrong. My
name is Birrmagnur. I am flesh and blood, like you, I think.'

'Yes. I can see that now,' said Rannoch, feeling deeply
embarrassed. 'But what are you? I mean, I don't want to be
rude, you look like a deer but . . . but if I may say so, a very
strange deer indeed.'

'I could say the same for you,' answered the animal slowly,

chewing the air again as though ruminating on his thoughts. His expression was still very amused.

'I am rangifer,' he answered quietly. 'A reindeer.'

'A reindeer?' exclaimed Rannoch, almost as amazed as if it *had* been Herne. Rannoch had heard tell of the reindeer in stories, but he had never actually seen one and he had always thought they only existed in fable.

'That is right. Who are you?'

'My name is Rannoch.'

'Well, Rannoch, I am pleased to meet you,' said the reindeer politely.

'And I you. But tell me, what are you doing so high on the Great Mountain?'

'Before you came I was trying to graze'.

'To graze? Up here? But what about the storm?'

'It was bad, but I am used to such weather where I come from.'

'Where you come from?'

'I am from across the northern seas. The reindeer call it Druugroot, or the Land of the Northern Snows.'

'From beyond the seas? But how?' said Rannoch, in even more amazement.

'It is a long story,' answered the reindeer rather sadly, 'but I came with men in their carved trees and now I try to go home.'

'You've spent time with man?' asked Rannoch with surprise.

'Yes,' said the reindeer casually.

'Are you alone?'

'Now I am. I was separated from the others long ago. Seven bulls and twenty females. It's the females I miss the most, but I doubt I shall see their antlers again.'

Rannoch took a step forward and tilted his head.

'Their antlers?'

The reindeer nodded mournfully.

'You mean . . . you mean your hinds have antlers?'

'Yes, of course,' said the reindeer.

'Well, it seems there is a lot I have to learn,' said Rannoch to himself, shaking his head.

But now Birrmagnur turned his own great head to the west and grunted. Across the snow Willow, Tain and the others were coming towards them. They came nervously through the snow, scenting all the time, their eyes as wide as pebbles.

'Don't worry,' called Rannoch, 'there's nothing to be frightened of. His name's Birrmagnur. He's a reindeer.'

Tain looked at Rannoch as though he had just stolen the magic antlers. One by one the others came up to the reindeer and eyed him up and down. They circled him slowly and scented him, then, as was natural, the young stags knocked antlers with him. All the while Birrmagnur tolerated this like an indulgent father and when it was over he chewed the air for a while as the others looked on, hardly knowing what to say.

'Where are you going?' Birrmagnur asked at last.

'North, into the High Land,' said Rannoch. 'I'm looking for a herd that lives near here. Herne's Herd.'

'*We're* looking for them,' interjected Willow.

Birrmagnur stopped chewing and eyed Rannoch with interest.

'Why would you want to find them?' he asked carefully.

'That's a long story too,' answered Rannoch. 'Do you know of them?'

'Oh yes.' The reindeer nodded seriously. 'Any Herla that has travelled in the High Land knows them, for they rule the Herla here. They have always done so.'

'Have you seen them?' asked Rannoch.

'Some of them. But not their home herd. And I don't think I want to.'

'Why not?'

'They are to be feared,' answered Birrmagnur gravely, 'for they have dark ways.'

'Tell me.'

'I only know what the others told me,' said Birrmagnur, 'when they dared to talk about them.'

'The others?'

'Yes, a herd near here, in a valley to the east by the red river. I stayed with them for a while when I first came to the High Land. They call themselves the Slave Herd.'

The deer looked at Birrmagnur in astonishment.

'They serve Herne's Herd,' Birrmagnur went on. 'They collect berries for them and special fungi and in return Herne's Herd permits them to stay by the red river. Every now and then stags from Herne's Herd come and take away their fawns. They never see them again.'

The friends' astonishment was turning to horror.

'What do they want their fawns for?' asked Willow quietly.

'Nobody knows, but there are rumours.'

'But how does the Slave Herd continue if they are taking their fawns?' asked Rannoch.

'They don't take many. Perhaps two or three a year. For there are other Slave Herds right across the High Land.'

'But why don't they fight?' said Thistle suddenly.

'I think they've forgotten how,' answered Birrmagnur. 'Herne's Herd has held sway for so long, since the ancient times and beyond, that they don't really know any other way.'

Rannoch looked out from the Great Mountain. His heart was suddenly very heavy. Somewhere inside himself he had hoped that perhaps in the High Land the Herla might be free from the kind of evil that Sgorr was spreading everywhere. But now it seemed that an even greater darkness was gathering around him.

'Can you tell me where I can find this herd?' he asked.

'No, my friend,' answered the reindeer. 'I know they are not far. Beyond a high moor. But I couldn't lead you there.'

Rannoch looked disappointed.

'But I could lead you back to the Slave Herd,' said Birrmagnur. 'Then, when they come for the fawns, you could follow them. If you are really determined to find them.'

'Would you do that for us?' said Rannoch.

Birrmagnur thought for a while and then he nodded slowly.

'Yes. It will not take long and it would be good to have some company again. But I will only lead you to the edge of their valley, then I will be on my way. I must get to the coast again and I am tired of the Herla in your land. They are all mad.'

So it was agreed and Rannoch and the others, with their new companion the reindeer, began to descend the Great Mountain. As they walked through the snow and the clouds on the mountain top behind them turned black and brooding, Rannoch began to question the reindeer.

It seemed that Birrmagnur had travelled to the Great Land two summers before, inside one of the carved trees that Rurl had told him about. It had been a bitter voyage and several of his number had perished on the way. But when they had reached the land – somewhere towards the west, as far as Rannoch could make out – there had been twenty-seven of the reindeer left alive. They had been herded ashore and placed in a wide stockade where humans had come to stare at them and marvel at their strange antlers and great, shaggy

coats. Then the Norsemen who had first captured Birrmagnur on the icy plains of his northern home, had filled
their carved trees with human food and hollow stumps full
of red water and had sailed away again.

As Birrmagnur talked, Rannoch listened quietly and
thought of his own time with the boy. But he also thought
of what Rurl had said about the men from the north and
their king; about bloodshed coming to the Great Land.

Birrmagnur had been kept in the stockade for a summer
and a winter and when Rannoch asked him how he felt and
what he thought of the humans, the reindeer shrugged his
shoulders and told Rannoch how in his land man and reindeer often lived together. Although Birrmagnur told Rannoch
proudly that he had been born rangifer or free, there were
many of his kind who lived in great herds that were looked
after by men called Lapps, who drove them across the snows
and relied completely on them to live. They took their
milk, and wore their coats and used their antlers for tools.
They even used them to pull wood across the ground which
they would then ride on. As Birrmagnur spoke of this
relationship with man it seemed more natural to Rannoch,
though he recalled the deer park too and shuddered.

Birrmagnur explained how, one day, a storm had come
and broken down part of the wooden fence that had held
them in and the reindeer had escaped. Not all of them, for
some had become too tame. But Birrmagnur had persuaded
the others to join him and together they had set out
towards the north. Soon after they had been attacked by
wolves. Two of their number had been killed and Birrmagnur
had been separated from his friends. He had wandered for
several suns looking for them, but without success, and eventually had started to travel east, avoiding the signs of man
as much as he could and thinking all the time of some way

to get home. He had been alone for two moons before he had come to the Slave Herd and joined them.

Rannoch soon realized he could learn much from the strange deer, for Birrmagnur knew many things. He knew about the sea and the mountains, the rivers and the waterfalls. He knew about winter and summer pastures and the spirit of the storm. But above all he knew about snow. He told Rannoch how in his land they had fifteen different names for snow. He told him how to recognize when it was coming and how long it would last. How to avoid the deep drifts and how best to forage for food. How, in the terrible blizzards that swept the northern lands, the reindeer could survive by scraping out shallow holes and lying down, huddled close together, until the storm passed.

Rannoch was deeply impressed by the reindeer and his admiration turned to wonder when, just a sun after they came off the Great Mountain, one of Birrmagnur's great antlers dropped from his head. The second followed only a sun later and the strange deer looked even more peculiar as he led them towards the Slave Herd. When Rannoch expressed surprise that he was shedding in winter, Birrmagnur just shrugged calmly and explained that reindeer always shed in winter and, indeed, that he was surprised his antlers had fallen so late. Apparently reindeer normally shed just after the rut, at the very beginning of winter, but with no females around the process had been delayed.

In turn, Rannoch began to tell Birrmagnur about all that had happened to them since they had left the home valley all those suns ago. When he came to the mark on his head and the Prophecy, Birrmagnur did not laugh at him as Rannoch had feared he might, but shook his head gravely and looked closely at the oak leaf.

'So that's why you want to know about this herd?' he whispered.

Rannoch nodded.

'Rannoch,' said Birrmagnur suddenly, 'the deer from Herne's Herd are said to have a prophecy too. I don't know exactly what it speaks of, but they are waiting for something and it is connected with the fawns.'

That night something strange happened that unnerved Rannoch. They were sheltering from the snow in the lee of a hill and Rannoch was trying to find what food he could, when he fancied he heard a sound in the darkness above him. He wandered up to where he had heard the noise and though there was no one there, he saw deer slots in the snow. This was the route the friends had travelled, so he couldn't be certain they hadn't made them themselves, but the slots looked larger than their own and here and there the ground was scuffed away as though a deer had been standing there for some time.

Two suns later it had started to snow again when Birrmagnur led them to the bottom of a narrow valley with a river running down the middle of it. The deer now understood why Birrmagnur had called it the red river, for its water was a livid rust colour and when they drank from it it tasted strange and brackish.

'This is where I will leave you,' said Birrmagnur. 'You will find the Slave Herd up there. They are harmless enough, though odd in themselves. They're led by a hind called Liath.'

'A hind?' said Thistle with surprise.

'You will see,' said Birrmagnur. 'Now I must be on my way again.'

Rannoch felt sad and disappointed, but he could hardly protest. Birrmagnur had already done more for them than they had any right to expect. So they took their farewells.

'Goodbye, Rannoch,' said the reindeer as he turned away, 'I hope you find what you're looking for.'

As the deer walked on up the valley they soon began to scent the new herd's musk boundaries and spy their droppings. Almost immediately they saw four deer coming towards them. They were hinds, but when they reached the friends they completely ignored the stags and the leading hind went straight up to Willow.

'Herne's Hope to you,' she said curtly.

Willow hardly knew what to say to this strange greeting.

'Herne's Hope,' repeated the hind gruffly when Willow didn't answer.

'And Herne's Hope to you too,' said Willow coldly.

'Feed well until the Coming,' said the hind. 'Where do you come from?'

Willow had taken an instant dislike to the deer. She felt like turning and giving her a kick with her hoof. Thistle came forward but Rannoch stepped in his way and nodded to Willow.

'From the south,' answered Willow.

'Hmm. That's well,' said the hind. 'For a while we thought your stags were . . .'

She paused.

'But it would have been too soon for another collection,' she went on. 'Where are the other hinds?'

'There are no other hinds,' answered Willow, 'except me, Peppa and Bracken.'

'So you lead the herd?'

Willow looked at Rannoch, who nodded very gently again.

'Yes.'

'Good,' said the hind. 'My name is Liath.'

Willow hardly cared to answer but she decided on tact.

'Mine's Willow. This is Rannoch. He—'

'This is Hoy, Scappa and Aith,' said Liath, interrupting Willow and still ignoring the stags. 'If you come with us we will show you the herd. You are welcome enough, I suppose. At least our stags could do with some help.'

'That's very kind of you, I'm sure' said Willow sharply, holding back her anger, 'but I must ask my friends. Rannoch has been very—'

'Do you lead or not?' snapped Liath. 'Perhaps you have been too long alone. Bring the stags and we will put them with the others.'

Liath and the hinds turned away disdainfully, leaving the amazed party alone again.

'What cheek,' said Willow. 'I'd like to box her muzzle.'

'I think I've seen everything now,' said Tain.

'It's very strange,' agreed Rannoch.

So the party followed, with Willow, Bracken and Peppa taking the lead. The Slave Herd was grazing further up the valley, around the banks of the red river. It looked a safe enough spot and there were good vantage points to spy for predators. But as Rannoch spotted the Outriders topping the hills, he realized that they were all hinds.

The main body of the herd, hinds again, were bunched together by the waterside drinking or grazing or sitting down to ruminate, and as the group approached some looked at the stags coldly or turned their backs on them, while others stared with interest at their antlers. Liath was waiting by an old wallow and she addressed Rannoch for the first time.

'You,' she said. 'You'll find the stags up there. Ask for Haarg. He'll tell you what to do.'

Rannoch's temper was beginning to fray but he decided to bide his time. So, with only a wink to Willow, he led the stags off up the hill.

The main stag party was a long way off. There must have been forty of them and as they approached Bankfoot gasped.

'Rannoch, l-l-look at their heads.'

'They haven't got any antlers,' said Tain.

It was true, or partly true, for though it was far too early in the year for shedding, most of them stood bareheaded – hummels – while others had the beginnings of antlers that that had grown into strange, gnarled shapes.

'W-w-what's the matter with them?' said Bankfoot.

'I don't know,' answered Rannoch, 'but there's some mystery about this place. Come on.'

He ran on up to a stag that was standing on his own.

'I'm looking for a stag called Haarg,' he said.

The deer blinked but said nothing and instead pointed vaguely with his head. Haarg was higher up still, chewing on some old bracken that he had uncovered beneath the snow. He can only have been about six or seven but his eyes looked tired and sad.

'Are you Haarg?' asked Rannoch.

The stag nodded and went on chewing.

'Liath told us to find you. Are you the lord?'

Haarg smiled wearily.

'The hinds rule in the Slave Herd,' he answered simply.

'So it seems,' said Rannoch.

'But why?' interjected Thistle.

'You are not from a Slave Herd?' Haarg said, looking puzzled.

'No.'

'It's always been thus,' answered Haarg. 'We do what we're told and they look after us.'

'Look after *you*?' snorted Thistle with disgust.

'Yes, but mostly we keep separate. Until we're needed for

mating. Then the hinds come and choose some among us. So the herd goes on and we can provide fawns.'

'The hinds choose you?' gasped Thistle. They were all amazed now.

'Yes,' replied Haarg, as though it was the most natural thing in the world.

'And is there no Corps?' said Rannoch. 'No council?'

'The hinds sometimes sit in council when small decisions need to be made. About where next to look for lichen and fungi. But mostly orders come down from *them*.'

'Herne's Herd?' said Rannoch.

'That's right,' answered Haarg and his eyes suddenly became misty with fear.

'Tell me about Herne's Herd.'

'You mean you don't know?' said Haarg with surprise. 'Doesn't every Herla in the High Land know about them?'

'We are not from the High Land,' said Rannoch quietly.

Haarg looked up at Rannoch now. He munched on a limp spray of bracken and then shrugged.

'Their home herd lies to the east, beyond the Standing Stones. That's all I know.'

Rannoch pawed the ground.

'Do you know how to reach them?'

'Of course not. That is forbidden. It would be sacrilege.'

Although Rannoch was desperate to ask many more questions, he thought it best not to rush things. The friends began to scrape in the snow for pasture, while the Slave Herd seemed completely untroubled by their presence.

When Rannoch and the others had left the hinds, Peppa and Willow had found a comfortable spot for Bracken to ruminate and set to work finding out as much about the hinds as they could. They all looked healthy, but they had a cold, strangely arrogant air about them. Several of them had calves and these hinds seemed to enjoy a special position in the herd, for the stags would bring the mothers food, especially the mothers suckling male fawns. When the twins saw the males' heads they were as startled as their friends.

It seemed that in itself the hierarchy among the hinds was not that unusual, though, for Liath had won her pre-eminence by boxing for her place with the others at the beginning of the year, as is normal with hinds in any red deer herd. She was strong and fit and, at six, had already reared three calves. But the twins soon found out that there any resemblance with the home herd before Sgorr or with the herd above the loch ended.

They were up on the hill and had met a hind called Sep. She was ruminating on her own when they came up to her and the old hind seemed less aloof than the others. They had been chatting for a while when Peppa asked her about the hinds guarding the valley.

'The Outers,' said Sep.

Peppa looked keenly at Willow.

'Yes, the Outers,' said Peppa. 'How are they chosen?'

'Only the best hinds get to be Outers,' answered Sep, 'for they have to know how to box and run fast.'

'And no stags are . . . Outers?'

Sep looked surprised.

'Of course not, my dear. Who's ever heard of a stag being an Outer?'

Again Peppa looked at Willow but her sister shook her head.

'You don't think much of the stags, do you?' said Peppa.

Sep munched on thoughtfully. She had browsed a juniper tree earlier and had just tasted the delicious flavour again.

'There's not much to think of. I was quite fond of Teeg,

I suppose, when I made my stand with him and we had a calf.'

Now Peppa's bright eyes opened wide. Willow was listening closely too.

'*Your* stand?'

'Yes. He was a good worker and never said much. I chose him for that, I think. And though his antlers were misshapen he even had a half head. I almost miss him, though it's never good to admit it.'

'Tell me,' said Willow, 'when did you ... when did you make this stand?'

Sep was thoughtful again.

'Oh, it must have been six years ago now.'

'Six years? And you never mated again?'

'No,' said Sep almost sadly.

'But why?' asked Peppa.

'There are plenty of hinds who mate more than once and have fine daughters in the herd or good strong buck workers, but there's always the risk ... well, you know ...'

'No,' said Peppa.

'It's not that I minded having a buck ...'

'But?'

'But that's the chance you take if you do have one. They might be chosen and they're really very sweet when they're calves. You get to miss them.'

Willow looked gravely at her sister.

'You have to be very unlucky, and at least the rest of the herd helps with the feeding,' Sep went on. 'You can get quite fat with all the food they bring you when you're suckling. But in the end all that waiting can be very hard on the nerves.'

'So they only take the male fawns?' asked Willow.

'Of course.'

'And they chose your fawn?' said Peppa quietly.

Sep nodded and though her face had grown a little sad again, there was a strange confusion in her eyes.

'Tell me,' said Willow kindly, 'what happens to them?'

'No one really knows,' answered Sep, and then her face brightened. 'But Liath says they are honoured.'

As Willow and Peppa walked back off the hill towards Bracken, the twins were silent.

It was well past Larn on the next sun and a new moon had come up. Rannoch and the others were grazing when Bankfoot lifted his head. A deer was coming downwind towards them and through the darkness the stags saw Willow. She looked grave and was obviously doing her best to remain concealed.

'I've found you,' she whispered as she came up. 'I had to skirt right round the valley to avoid being seen.'

'What's wrong, Willow?' said Rannoch.

'Nothing. But they don't like the hinds talking to the stags. They say it's unnatural.'

Rannoch nodded and looked strangely towards the red river.

'What have you found out?' he asked.

'Plenty. There must be about ninety deer in the valley. There's no Home Oak but the hinds congregate over there, at a place they call the gathering ground. It's where the stags take all the berries and mushrooms they're made to forage for. It's also where they come when its time for a collection.'

'When they take the fawns?'

Willow nodded gravely.

'And we found out something else,' she said. 'They only take male calves.'

'And Herne's Herd?' asked Rannoch.

'We discovered what little we could. I didn't want to press

it too much in case Liath and the others grew suspicious. For some reason I don't think we should let the hinds know we want to find Herne's Herd.'

'I don't think there's much point asking them where they are anyway,' said Rannoch. 'Haarg says it's forbidden to know. The only thing we can do is wait until they come again and follow them, like Birrmagnur suggested. It'll give us a chance to learn as much as we can about the High Land. Perhaps make some friends too. We may have need of them in the future if we ever want to form our own herd.'

Willow nodded.

'Well, I'd better get back to Peppa and Bracken,' she said. 'Peppa doesn't like it here at all. We'll try and come and see you when we can.'

'Good,' said Rannoch.

'And Rannoch,' said Willow, smiling as she turned to leave, 'try not to work too hard.'

So, as winter settled around them they stayed with the Slave Herd by the red river and though Bracken wasn't much use, Willow and Peppa devoted themselves to winning over some of the hinds, while the others made friends among the stags.

They soon found out how strange the herd really was, for if the hinds were slaves themselves, they treated the stags as worse than slaves. The stags were made to do all the work collecting the crop, and if any of them complained, the hinds would gather together to punish them viciously, kicking them and buffeting them with their heads. But the stags put up no resistance; they were as docile as lambs.

This shocked the friends, especially Thistle, but whenever they asked the stags about it and why they wouldn't fight, they just shrugged it off, saying that it had always been the way and that it was the natural order of things, like Herne's Lore.

Rannoch tried to find out what the berries and fungi were for, but none of the slave stags knew. All they knew was that Herne's Herd used it for some secret purpose, as they had always done, and that they had to gather as much as possible in time for the collection.

It was only very special types of plants that they were looking for. They sought three types of mushroom and fungus; a strange hooded variety with a bright orange cap speckled with white that the humans call fly agaric; a weird yellow-white fungus that looked like rubbery coral and is sometimes called jelly antler fungus; and the most prized of all and the hardest to find – a club-shaped white mushroom that bubbled like spume and was crowned with blood-red beads. Among the plants they sought a livid purple plant with sprays of minute lavender berries and a dark green fur lichen with sprouting fronds that looked like newts' feet.

Every morning, even in the bitterest weather, they would go up to the hills to scrape wearily in the snow and at the end of each tiring day, Larn would find them all trooping back to the gathering ground to deposit their meagre spoils. They worked so hard that they were always exhausted, which partly explained their lack of resistance to the hinds.

Rannoch also tried to find out as much as he could about the High Land. Haarg's knowledge was sketchy because he had never moved away from the red river, but it seemed that there were many such Slave Herds across the north, as far as the great sea to the north-east. But Rannoch also discovered that it wasn't just fear of Herne's Herd that kept the Slave Herds in place; it was also belief. This explained Liath's strange greeting.

They called it Herne's Hope, for although they hated and

feared Herne's Herd, they also believed that they were the keepers of some ancient pact with Herne that would be fulfilled one day, at the time of the Coming, as they called it, when the Great Land would be made whole again. Then the Slave Herds would join Herne's Herd and all the Herla who believed would be taken up to the stars.

This talk had a strangely unnerving effect on Rannoch and as the suns passed he began to have bad dreams like the dreams he had had as a fawn. He had remembered too what Rurl had said to him by the sea, about the meaning of the Prophecy, and every time he thought of Herne's Herd and what he might discover about himself, he shuddered.

One dream came to him clearly one late winter's night. He was standing by a pool in the moonlight and the wind around his head was whispering softly to him.

'Rannoch, you want to know what you are?' it called. 'You want to meet Herne?'

'Yes,' said Rannoch dreamily.

'Then look into the pool, Rannoch.'

In his sleep the deer stepped forward and looked down.

There, in the moonlight, he saw his own face looking back at him.

Rannoch woke with a start and shuddered furiously.

'No,' he whispered, 'it can't be true. It can't.'

Rannoch told his friends nothing of his dreams but he found solace in talking to Haarg about his own strange beliefs. Haarg and Rannoch were talking like this one sun on the hillside. The weather had grown milder and the snows were already beginning to melt. Rannoch had seen less and less of Willow and Peppa and he was helping Haarg with his labours, as he often did now, when Haarg looked nervously about him and asked him about Herne.

'But you believe in Herne, don't you, Rannoch?' he whispered.

Rannoch stopped scraping at the ground.

'Yes, I think so,' he answered, 'though I didn't find him on the Great Mountain.'

Haarg stared at him as though he had just seen a ghost.

'You've been on the Great Mountain?'

Rannoch nodded.

'But if *they* ever found out it would be certain death for you,' said Haarg.

'Then they mustn't find out,' said Rannoch simply.

Haarg was quiet for a while. He looked sad.

'I should like to visit the Great Mountain,' he said quietly, 'before I die.'

'Then why don't you?'

'It is forbidden. I can never leave the red river. That is *their* decree.'

Rannoch felt bitterly angry. He stamped the ground and tossed up his antlers.

'Haarg,' he said, 'have you never thought of escaping?'

Haarg looked out wistfully across the snowy moors.

'How could I?' he muttered. 'I've no antlers and there is much danger out there for a Herla. Besides, Herne's Herd would only track me down.'

'But have you never wanted to be free?'

'We will be freed at the time of the Coming,' answered Haarg flatly, shaking his head, 'when we will go up to roam through the stars.'

'No,' said Rannoch, 'I mean free to be a real Herla in the Great Land. Free to wander the hills and drink from the burn and loch. Free to wallow in the cool mud, to chew the heather and gorse and follow a breath of wind if it takes your fancy.'

Haarg's eyes had grown wide with wonder.

'And never have to collect berries and fungi again?'

'Never.'

'Like the Outriders you told me about?'

'Yes, Haarg, like the Outriders. Though with their freedom is mixed something else; the duty to protect the herd.'

'Then they are slaves like us,' said Haarg.

'No, Haarg, for they choose to be Outriders. And they roam where they will, while guarding the herd too. They answer only to their captains and their service to the herd brings a greater freedom within them, or so Mother says.'

'What's it like to be an Outrider?'

At this Rannoch grew a little embarrassed. He realized that he had been telling Haarg only what had been repeated to him by Bracken.

'I don't really know,' he said. 'My father was one. His name was Brechin. But that's all I know about him. Bracken doesn't really like to talk about him. I think he died long ago.'

But suddenly there was a bark from behind. The two deer turned to see four hinds coming towards them.

'Haarg,' cried one of them furiously, 'why aren't you working?'

Haarg dropped his head and, without a word, began to scrape at the ground again. The hinds drew close and they would have kicked at Haarg if they hadn't seen Rannoch's young antlers and thought better of it.

'Well get on with it,' said the hind as they turned away again. 'You know it's nearly spring and the collection could come at any time.'

As the hinds wandered away, Rannoch stirred in the snow. The collection would bring a chance to find the herd that ruled in the High Land, and perhaps some answers to his quest. Yet even if they did hold some secret knowledge of Herne, somewhere inside himself Rannoch had already begun to hate them and their rule. As he looked at Haarg scraping wearily in the snow he was suddenly determined to help the deer. It was just a question of how.

The first moon of the new year came and the hinds began to grow more aggressive towards each other, testing the pecking order that had grown up between them the year before and boxing with their forelegs. This was the hinds' Anlach. But Liath won out again and the hinds settled down once more. Willow and Peppa stayed aloof from all this, though they could not avoid one or two fights themselves, and they continued to quiz the hinds and make friends as best they could.

Spring ripened in the High Land. The bracken grew thick and lush and on the open moors spine grasses and heather rose to meet the sunlight. The thistle came into flower and grouse and pheasant flashed through the rocky valleys as the eagle and the osprey looked down from their misty crags.

The friends shed their antlers and the hummels looked at them with wonder as spring turned to summer and their antlers rose again. This time they were growing their fourth heads and now their tines looked very impressive indeed. They had all grown bez tines off the central beams and their high, branching tops were sharp and well curved. Bankfoot's antlers were the weakest but Rannoch looked so fine that at a distance he could have passed for a royal. Like Thistle, his body was much heavier and more thickset, his hind haunches had filled out and he walked with a firm, prancing gait.

It was the middle of August and they were all growing impatient for the collection. The hinds had expected it to come much earlier but still they waited and the harvest went on. Rannoch had shed his velvet when Willow found him standing alone by the red river and looking thoughtfully into the water.

'Rannoch,' she called, 'Rannoch. Peppa was talking to Hoy this morning and she says they are expecting the collection any sun now.'

'Yes,' said Rannoch, 'we must be ready to follow them when they come. Peppa, you and Bracken should stay together as much as you can now. We'll do the same. Then we'll be ready to leave when the right moment arrives.'

Willow nodded.

'But, Willow, I want you to be especially watchful for the next few suns.'

'Why?' said Willow.

'Because I'm going away for a short time. You'll be in charge.'

'Going away?'

'Not for long. I've got to do something to help Haarg.'

'But how?' said Willow.

'The stags' antlers,' he said, 'and the structure of the herd. It's not natural as they think it is. I think it's a kind of sickness. They only believe it's natural because they've never known any different. That adds to the power that Herne's Herd has over them. But I think it would be different if they went away from the valley and this river.'

'I don't understand,' said Willow.

'Their antlers,' said Rannoch. 'I think it's the red river that has stunted them. I'm going to follow it upstream.'

'What can I do?' said Willow.

'Look after the others and watch for the collection.'

'Right,' said Willow. 'If there was any trouble I think at least a few of the hinds would be on our side. Not all them like the way the herd is run.'

'Very well, then.'

Rannoch set off that same morning, following the course of the river north-east. It took him through high, wild country and it was the middle of the next morning when he began to grow nervous. He had climbed above the eastern banks of the river and he scented them across the bracken. But the familiar urge to start and run was tempered now by a deeper knowledge of what he was looking at.

The encampment was not large but it was stranger than anything Rannoch had encountered, either with the boy or in the fearful glen. The houses grouped around the river were of peat and stone as usual, but around them loomed strange earth mounds and pits where the hill had been scoured away. In the centre of it all was a great cave mouth and here men were at work, pushing carts piled high with coloured stone down to the river's edge. Others were sifting through the stones and when they had finished they tipped the contents of the carts into the water, so that where the river passed through the encampment its current had turned a deep and livid red.

Rannoch blinked as he tried to understand what he was seeing but, without really knowing why, he realized that it was because of this place that the stags in the narrow valley were sick. Rannoch had come across a mine, giving up copper and minerals to serve the humans and help them build. But it also filled the river with its mineral waste, polluting the life-giving water.

Rannoch watched gravely and turned away.

When he got back to the Slave Herd he went straight to see Haarg. That Larn they could be seen on the hill, talking long and hard together as the stars flickered in the sky. Haarg kept shaking his head while Rannoch pawed the ground, and they both looked down solemnly at the river.

*

When Rannoch told Willow and the others what he had
discovered about the red river they immediately stopped
drinking from it, though they hardly understood what
Rannoch meant. Most of the stags among the Slave Herd
stopped drinking too and there was great tension in the
valley. It was partly because all the deer knew that the collection was close at hand and three young fawns had already
been picked out by the hinds. But it was also because the
stags were beginning to act strangely.

The twins saw it one early afternoon when they were
ruminating on the hillside. They were close to a group of
harvesting stags and one of them had stopped what he was
doing and was gazing out wistfully into the distance. As he
did so three hinds came sauntering by and when they saw
him one of them immediately ran up.

'Get back to work,' she cried angrily.

But the stag did nothing.

'Did you hear what I said?'

Still the stag ignored her and the hind turned her back to
his haunches and, with a scornful dip of her head, she kicked
him. Willow and Peppa fully expected the stag to return to
work, for they had witnessed such a scene any number of
times, but instead the stag let out a bellow and, dropping his
own head, he kicked back. His hoofs hit the hind full on
and she barked with surprise. She was so startled she just
turned and ran back to the others.

'Good for him,' whispered Peppa.

It was eight suns since Rannoch had returned from the
mine and he was standing with the others near the red water.
Willow had joined them and she had told them all about the
incident and other acts of rebellion they had seen in the herd.
The hinds were furious.

'What are the stags going to do?' she was asking now.

'I don't know,' said Rannoch. 'It shook them up. Most of them have stopped drinking.'

'Yes,' said Willow, 'I noticed that. And there've been more and more arguments on the hillsides. The hinds say some of the stags are refusing to harvest.'

'What are the hinds doing about it?' asked Thistle.

'I think they're confused,' said Willow. 'They're too worried about the collection at the moment to do anything much. What do you think will happen, Rannoch?'

'Maybe nothing at all,' he answered. 'There's some real discontent now but they're all too enthralled with Herne's Herd and Herne's Hope to be able to really think for themselves.'

But Rannoch suddenly stopped talking. He was looking across the river and in the gauzy evening light he saw Peppa running straight towards them. She was making no attempt to stay concealed.

'Willow, Rannoch, hurry,' Peppa cried as she reached them. 'They've come.'

Rannoch started.

'When?'

'Just now. Twenty stags arrived at the gathering place. Liath, Hoy and some of the others were waiting. They gathered up the harvest in their mouths and they took the calves with them – Furl, Calla and Ragnur. Then they vanished over the western path. If we hurry we can follow their tracks. I've left Bracken waiting.'

'Then we must be quick,' said Rannoch. 'I'm only sorry we can't do more for Haarg. Come on.'

With Rannoch leading, the friends sped towards Bracken. The hind was deeply bewildered when they got to her but Peppa and Willow took charge of her and the deer rose out

of the valley, following the slots that had churned up the
western earth. But as they crested the hill they pulled up.

In front of them, barring their way, was a wall of hinds.
Over thirty of them. Liath stood at the front and her eyes
were blazing.

'What are you doing?' she cried furiously.

'We are leaving,' said Rannoch.

'I wasn't addressing you,' said Liath.

'Nevertheless, I want—'

'Silence!' shouted Liath. 'A stag must not talk to a hind
like this. Willow, where do you think you are going?'

Willow stepped forward and her eyes were blazing.

'Get out of my way,' she whispered furiously, lifting her
head towards Liath.

'What?'

'I said, get out of my way.'

Liath hesitated. She was not used to being talked to like
this by either stag or hind, but there was something
dangerous in Willow's look that made her pause. Rannoch
came up beside Willow.

'Do as Willow says,' he whispered. 'We are going to—'

'Silence!' cried Liath once more. 'I have never heard such
a thing. It is because of you and your lies that the stags are
restless.'

'They are not lies,' said Rannoch calmly. 'The river is
making your stags sick because of what man puts in it. If
you left this place they would be well again.'

'Left this place?' laughed Liath. 'Are you mad? Abandon
the ancient duty of the Slave Herd?'

'Perhaps Herne's Herd have been telling you lies,' said
Rannoch quietly.

Liath's eyes opened in amazement.

'How dare you speak of them?' she said.

'I don't know, Liath, what they are,' said Rannoch in a more conciliatory tone, 'but I'm going to find out.'

'You're what?'

'We're going to follow them.'

'No,' gasped Liath. 'It's forbidden.'

'Nevertheless.'

But at this Liath began to thump the ground with her back legs and as she did so the other hinds came forward. At the same moment Tain, Thistle and Bankfoot all stepped up beside Rannoch and Willow. The friends stood shoulder to shoulder, dipping their antlers as Willow glared at Liath. Willow looked at the other hinds too, some of whom had talked of leaving the herd. They dropped their eyes at her gaze and, for a moment, they hesitated. But only for a moment, for it was thirty against six, not counting poor Bracken, and hinds when roused can use their teeth and their legs to great effect.

But suddenly Peppa cried out, 'Look, it's Haarg. Haarg's coming.'

It was true. At his side were two of the braver slave stags named Skein and Tannar and Haarg was leading the hummels up the hill towards them.

'What are you doing here, Haarg?' said Liath contemptuously as the stags arrived. 'Get back to your harvest.'

'No, Liath,' answered Haarg, nervous but emboldened by the stags at his back, 'we want to talk. About what Rannoch says of the river and our antlers.'

'It's lies,' said Liath.

'No, it isn't. I saw it with my own eyes five suns ago. Man is putting something into the river.'

'And what if they are? Do you think *they* would let us escape? Have you forgotten our duty? We must be humble until the Coming, for that is Herne's Hope.'

The hinds and the stags were head to head now, measuring each other up.

'Herne's Hope has kept us enslaved for generations,' said Haarg. 'My father believed in it and his father and his father before him. But none of them ever lived to see the Coming. And if it does come, what does it really bring? We will roam the stars, but Liath, have you ever thought what a thing it would be to roam the heather?'

There was a rumble of agreement amongst the stags, while some of the hinds began to bark with disapproval.

'Silence,' shouted one hind.

'Madness,' cried another, jostling a stag.

'No, let Haarg speak,' called a stag above them, and suddenly the air erupted into an explosion of angry cries.

But of this Rannoch, Willow and the others heard nothing more, for in the ensuing fight only one or two of the hinds from the Slave Herd even noticed that they had slipped quietly away.

17

The Dance of the Fawns

Half-recognized kingdom of the dead:
A deeper landscape lit by distant
Flashings from their journey.
Geoffrey Hill, 'The Stone Man'

Rannoch led them on as fast as he could. Although the tracks left by the stags from Herne's Herd were easy to follow in the soft ground, it was soon clear that they were travelling at tremendous speed, and after a time the friends found it harder and harder to keep up. Where the ground was too hard or rocky to leave slots, Rannoch picked up their signs in broken twigs and clumps of hair caught on the heather and bracken, or simply in the lie of the land and the most likely path a deer would follow.

Oddly, every now and then and at regular intervals, the deer came on circles left by the stags' hoofs, where they had clearly stopped to talk and scuffed the ground away. In the centre of these circles they found broken branches or clumps of gorse or some token that seemed to have been placed there as part of a strange rite.

When they had been travelling for four suns, the deer grew increasingly nervous. Rannoch was especially on edge, for as they drew closer to Herne's Herd he was beginning to wonder what he was doing running straight into the antlers of these mysterious Herla. He had little idea what he would say to them when he found them and he was haunted by the thought of what he might discover about himself. Whenever he closed his eyes to sleep now he dreamt of Herne.

One such dream, which came as the dawn began to chase the stars from the sky, had a deep effect on him.

In his dream Rannoch found himself on a barren moor and a wind was blowing around his head. There was a voice in the wind and Rannoch knew that it was Herne.

'What is it you are seeking?' whispered the wind.

Rannoch stirred in his sleep.

'To understand,' Rannoch found himself saying, 'to be free.'

'To you is granted much understanding,' came the voice, 'but you are Lera too. You may not understand all things.'

'Then how can I be free?'

'What is freedom?' laughed the wind.

'Freedom is running with the Herla,' murmured Rannoch. 'Freedom is living as an Outrider.'

'Yes. But what of *them*?' came the voice. 'What of the Herla you have abandoned in the Low Lands?'

The wind grew stronger and, mixed in its cries, Rannoch heard the anguished calls of stricken deer.

'Oh, Herne,' moaned Rannoch, as though in pain, 'will you never leave me be? Will I never be free?'

'Freedom is firstly within,' boomed the howling voice.

'But what must I do?'

'Remember what I told you long ago. You must listen, Rannoch. Listen to what you are and never forget.'

In Rannoch's dream the wind died to a faint echo and all that was left was a whispering sigh on the breeze.

'You cannot escape your destiny,' said the wind, and the voice and the dream were gone.

It was late morning and a summer mist hung lightly across the moor they were travelling over. The ground had begun to rise steeply and the deer felt strangely expectant. They were cresting a ridge when Bankfoot, who was a little way ahead, stopped suddenly.

'L-l-look,' he gasped.

Ahead of the deer, at the highest point of the moor, was a giant stone circle. The vast blocks of granite reared up in front of them through the mist that curled and wisped around their sides. Each block, hewn roughly by long-dead hands from some distant mountain, rose to the height of a young tree and they had been placed at regular intervals in a wide, closed arc. In the very centre of the circle was a stone altar.

'The Standing Stones,' whispered Rannoch.

'But w-w-what made . . .?'

'Man.'

Rannoch was right, for the stone circle had been thrown up in neolithic days by a tribe even older than the Picts who came to inhabit the northern lands of Scotia. They had already stood here, on this barren moor, for over two thousand years and their ancient purpose had long been lost to the wind and rain and the cycles of the moon. For the people who carved the rocks and dragged their massive forms across the High Land, this had once been a holy place; a place to worship not the images of man or even of animals, but the raw, unconscious power of life itself; a kind of anchor to the spinning stars. Great injustices had been committed here and scenes of horror still echoed through the stirring energies of the place. The deer felt it now as Rannoch led them forwards. Their senses quivered with the touch of the unknown and the unknowable.

As Rannoch neared the circle he stopped again. The ground was badly scuffed. Rannoch scented the earth and nodded. The stags had passed by this way, and only very recently.

'Stay c-c-close to me, Peppa,' whispered Bankfoot.

'Rannoch, come and look at this,' called Tain suddenly.

He was standing close to one of the stones. On the ground, in the space left between two of the blocks, Rannoch saw an antler. As he looked, he spied other antlers placed in each of the open doorways, following the full course of the circle.

'What does it mean?' whispered Tain.

Rannoch shook his head, but behind him he could sense that the others were dangerously nervous. Bracken was shaking almost uncontrollably.

'Come on,' he cried, 'we should keep moving.'

As they followed the incline of the moor they saw further signs of Herne's Herd. But the heather rustled in the breeze as they ran and the beauty of the day eased their sense of foreboding. Close to Larn they entered a wide valley with more tree cover than that had seen in a long while. The place was very pretty, thick with wild flowers, and there was a deep stillness about it.

They pressed on up the valley and were climbing the far hill when they heard a frantic fluttering and saw the bracken shiver in front of them. It was a grouse. She had been sleeping inside a knotted bowl of bracken which had tightened itself around her flapping feathers when she had suddenly been woken by the approaching stags.

Rannoch walked slowly up to her.

'Don't worry,' he called, 'we won't harm you. We're looking for the herd nearby.'

The bird flapped again and then settled back, stunned, on the earth. Her tiny, beady eyes looked dazed.

'It's true, then,' said the grouse breathlessly. 'There is a deer that talks, stalking the High Land.'

'How did you hear of it?' asked Rannoch.

'All the birds are talking about it.'

'Can you help us?' said Rannoch. 'Have you seen a herd nearby?'

'Oh yes,' said the grouse, 'but you don't want anything to do with them.'

'Why not?'

'All the Lera around here fear them,' said the bird. 'They have strange ways. Some say they kill their own. Others that they are ghosts of deer long dead.'

'Where are they?' asked Rannoch.

'Just over this hill,' answered the bird. 'But I'm warning you.'

Rannoch thanked the poor, bemused grouse and they wandered on. They stopped again at a clump of stunted trees and were looking down into the next valley when Rannoch spotted them ahead. The scouts were spread out loosely across the higher ground, grazing in the evening. They were surprisingly large. The fawns were set apart from them, in a small group, surrounded by other stags. To the deer's amazement, they realized there were no hinds at all. Herne's Herd was completely male.

'They look pretty ordinary to me,' said Thistle.

'What do we do now?' asked Tain.

'I don't know yet,' said Rannoch. 'Perhaps I should go in on my own and show myself. Then, if they're hostile, you can get away.'

'If you're going in,' said Willow, 'we'll all go in together.'

As she said it something extraordinary happened. One of the stags let out a great, shaking bellow. It was a call that Rannoch and the others were only used to at Anlach and they looked up in amazement. It was followed by another bellow and another as the stags answered. Their antlers began to rise up and down rhythmically and their calls took on a kind of swaying, lilting chant. Then the groups of stags came together in living circles, dipping their heads to each other and pawing the ground.

'The marks we saw,' whispered Tain.

'Let's get away from here,' said Rannoch. 'I've got to think.'

But as they turned to retrace their steps they started in fright.

Fifteen stags had come up behind them and were racing straight towards them, bucking and bellowing as they came. Instinctively, the deer turned to flee along the ridge but now they were in full view of the herd. The air was suddenly rent with angry cries and stags were rushing towards them from all directions. If they had wondered whether the herd would be hostile, now they were left in little doubt.

'Hurry,' cried Rannoch, trying desperately to think of what to do. 'Form a circle.'

The deer drew together in a circle and there they all stood, in the surrounding darkness, waiting for their fate.

The stags took no time at all to reach them and as they approached there was fury in their eyes. The groups came together and swept round and round the friends, stamping their hoofs as they went and rearing up to paw the air, letting out angry bellows like the calls they had heard on the hill.

Quite suddenly, they all came to a stop with the largest of the stags facing Rannoch.

'Get ready,' Rannoch whispered, as the friends stared back at the great antlers.

The lead stag stared angrily at Rannoch and then let out a single bellow that seemed to draw down the day.

But instead of charging, the stag pawed the ground again and stepped forward. Then, quite suddenly, he let out a shout as he lowered his antlers. It was picked up by all the surrounding stags, and in turn they dipped their heads.

'Hail,' cried the leading stag. 'Hail and blessings to Herne. Herne's Hope is fulfilled. The legend has come to pass.'

'I c-c-c-can't get anywhere near him.'

Poor Bankfoot looked at his wits' end. It was two suns after they had met Herne's Herd and Bankfoot was talking nervously to the others.

On that strange evening which still filled them all with amazement, they had been separated immediately from Rannoch. Almost as soon as the stags had finished bowing to Rannoch, the lead stag, whose name was Kaal, had led him away on his own, to a nearby copse of birch trees on the higher slopes, where the friends could see him now, surrounded by a constant guard.

Bankfoot and the others, meanwhile, had been taken down to the bottom of the valley, to a small burn, and told that as long as they didn't stray towards Rannoch or try to escape, they were free to roam at will. The stags had been civil enough, though in their eyes and the language of their antlers there had been a veiled threat.

'They're keeping him under g-g-guard,' Bankfoot went on, 'day and night. A guard of honour, they call it, but I'm not so sure. When Rannoch went with them he whispered to me that he'd try and send word, but I've heard nothing.'

'At least he seems well enough,' said Tain.

'But can they really believe he is Herne?' said Thistle, shaking his head.

'Perhaps he is.'

As Tain said it the friends looked at each other with a mixture of wonder and fear.

'That's what the Prophecy says,' Tain whispered.

'No. I can't believe it,' muttered Bankfoot uncomfortably. 'Not R-r-rannoch, who played with us as calves and used to like jumping l-l-logs. I've always known he was special, but Herne?'

'And he said it himself,' said Willow, 'he's no changeling.'

They looked at Bracken and she said nothing, but deep in her glassy eyes there was a flicker of terror. The others, though, seemed comforted by her presence. Rannoch's mother was the living proof that the Prophecy could not be true.

'Th-th-there's another thing,' said Bankfoot suddenly, dropping his voice. 'That first night they took him off up the mountain somewhere.'

The deer looked at each other fearfully.

'They frighten me,' said Peppa. 'They have such strange ways. Those circles they keep making.'

'Yes, Peppa,' agreed Tain, 'I think they're praying, in their own way.'

'It's not natural,' said Peppa. 'Remember those horrid stones? Who's heard of deer collecting antlers?'

'They're all unnatural, if you ask m-m-me,' said Bankfoot. 'They f-f-frighten me far more than the deer in the park, though their eyes have a similar look. Have you seen how bloodshot they are? There's something g-g-ghostly about them . . . and violent.'

But Willow was looking up the valley and she was no longer listening to her friends.

'It can't be,' she gasped. 'What's he doing here?'

Coming towards them across the grass, at a steady trot, was a deer with a great, shaggy coat and high, hooping antlers. When he reached the startled deer the reindeer looked very grave.

'I'm glad I've found you,' said Birrmagnur, as he lumbered to a halt. 'They've been holding me at the northern end of the valley. When I heard what had happened I realized instantly it was you, but it took all my powers of persuasion to get them to bring me here.'

'But, Birrmagnur, what are you doing here?' said Willow, though she was comforted by his looming presence. 'We never expected to see you again.'

'No, nor I you. But I was captured two suns after I left you with the Slave Herd. They brought me straight here.'

'But why?'

'They wanted to find out all I knew about Rannoch. They saw us coming off the Great Mountain.'

'Saw us?'

'Yes, and followed us for a full sun until they lost us in the snow. Then they picked me up on my way back, though they wouldn't have found it nearly so easy if I'd been in antler,' he added proudly.

'They haven't harmed you?'

'No, though when they first saw us we were lucky they didn't kill us all. It is sacrilege to visit the Great Mountain. But then, of course, they saw Rannoch's fawn mark. They actually thought Hoern himself had come down from the mountain top. The Marked One they call him. For centuries they have prayed for his coming at the Hoern-Meet.'

'The Herne-Meet?' said Tain.

'Yes, when they meet in their circles to pray.'

'So they *are* praying?' said Tain.

'Their whole life is dedicated to Hoern, as far as I can see.'

'And now that He has come at last,' said Willow, 'or so they think, what happens?'

'I don't really know. But I think they are waiting for something else, some happening.'

'I w-w-wish we could just talk to Rannoch,' said Bankfoot.

'We're going to,' said Willow suddenly.

'B-b-but how?'

Willow looked hard at her friends and the reindeer. Her eyes had a steely, determined look.

'I don't know about the Prophecy,' she said slowly, 'but I know about Rannoch. He won't want anything to do with these Herla. Think of how he hated what they were doing in the Slave Herd. No. We've got to make a plan.'

'A plan?' said Tain.

'To rescue him.'

All day they discussed how to get to Rannoch and by nightfall they had a fairly good idea of what they were going to do. But it was a dangerous plan and needed some preparation, so they decided to attempt it in three or four suns' time when the moon was full.

The sun after next Tain was sitting down in the heat, chewing over his thoughts and a particularly rich ball of grass, when Bankfoot ran up to him.

'Tain,' he said under his breath, 'before we try to rescue Rannoch, there's s-s-something I've got to find out and I want you to come with me.'

'I'll help if I can, Bankfoot,' said Tain, 'but what is it?'

'I w-w-want to know where they take Rannoch. We won't involve the others. It might be dangerous.'

Bankfoot got his chance that same evening. As dusk came in and the friends were grazing on the hill, he spotted a group of stags setting off to the east. Rannoch was in the middle of them. Bankfoot hurried over to Tain and together they slipped after them.

They followed at a careful distance. A warm breeze had come up, shaking the heather and whispering through the bracken. Bankfoot and Tain shuddered as they approached the place where the stones stood. As they climbed the hill, high to the north of Scotia, a full moon rose in the sky, and the deer stopped and blinked in awe and disbelief. The ancient stone circle, a tall tree in diameter, was silhouetted against the giant yellow moon which hung like a mighty island in the ghostly sky. They could see everything in its sallow light as the wind grew stronger and stronger. Thirty stags were inside the ring of stone and in the very centre was a form they both recognized instantly. It was Rannoch.

As they crept nearer, hardly daring to breathe, they heard a voice. It was Kaal, the lead stag who had first addressed Rannoch at his capture.

'Lord Herne,' Kaal cried, 'enlighten us. Fulfil the ancient destiny of the Herla.'

Bankfoot was no more than three trees from the circle now and as he caught sight of his friend's face he shuddered. Rannoch's eyes were a livid red, staring with a fury he had never seen before.

Rannoch dipped his head and then let out a great bellow that rose high above the wind.

Then Kaal spoke again.

'Bring the fawns,' he called. 'Let them dance.'

Four of the stags stepped out of the circle and, to Tain and Bankfoot's amazement, a group of fawns appeared at the far end of the stone ring. They walked forward slowly, swaying their heads as they came and when Bankfoot caught sight of their eyes, he saw they had the same frantic look as Rannoch's.

Now the stags in the ring began to bellow and bark in unison and Kaal cried out once more.

'You who are the future, dance for Herne, dance for the Lord of Violence.'

The fawns began to sway around Rannoch in the moonlight, moving in a circle and throwing their heads left and right as they went. The stags' bellows climbed to a kind of pounding, rhythmic chant as the fawns rose on their hind legs or turned around and around and bucked and swayed under the moon.

'Herne,' cried the stags as the fawns danced, 'Herne, Lord of Night.'

The fawns got faster and faster and before Bankfoot and Tain's terrified, staring gaze they seemed to turn to shadows in the ghostly moonlight. Things not of this world. Driven on by some unheard, unearthly music. Spirits or demons. Or both. The dancing rose to a fever pitch and then, suddenly, one of the fawns broke from the ring and stepped up to the stone altar in the very centre of the circle. Bankfoot recognized Ragnur from the Slave Herd.

The dancing fawns swayed on and on around Ragnur and the altar. But suddenly, to Tain and Bankfoot's horror, Kaal broke into the centre and the stag rose up on his haunches. With a single blow he brought his front hoofs down on Ragnur's head. The little fawn fell dead to the earth.

Bankfoot gasped. He was shaking so badly his front hoofs were nearly hammering the ground.

'Sacrifice.' Tain shuddered. 'That's what they're doing up here. They're sacrificing the fawns.'

In front of them Rannoch suddenly reared up too on his back haunches. He bucked his antlers violently to the moon, kicked at the air in a frenzy and then, from the very depths of his soul, he bellowed once more.

'Herne is pleased,' he cried, in a voice his friends hardly recognized. 'Now leave me. It is finished.'

Tain and Bankfoot turned and fled. They didn't stop until they were in sight of Birrmagnur and the others, but as they neared the group, hardly daring to believe what they had seen, Tain whispered desperately.

'Bankfoot?'

'W-w-what is it?' said his friend.

'Can it be true? Can he really be Herne?'

When Bankfoot and Tain told them about the sacrifice, the friends were horrified and Birrmagnur kept shaking his head, but the look in Tain and Bankfoot's eyes left no room for doubt. Only Willow refused to accept it.

'They've done something to him. They've got him under some kind of spell,' she said. 'It's even more important we see him.'

'What shall we do?' said Tain.

'Carry on with our plan,' answered Willow.

'But if he's . . .'

'At least we shall get to talk to him,' said Willow.

At last the others relented. It was set for the next sun's Larn and they agreed to meet just before. They were all desperately nervous but each, apart from Bracken, had their part to play in the plan and concentrating on what they had to do at least helped stop them from succumbing to fear.

'Right,' said Willow as the evening star began to glow in the sky. 'Birrmagnur, you're to lead; Peppa and I will come later when Bankfoot—'

But Willow suddenly stopped talking. Ten stags were coming in their direction.

They dipped their antlers as they approached.

'Herne has summoned you,' said the leading stag gravely. 'All of you are to come.'

Before they had even had a chance to put their plan into action, the friends found themselves being led up the hill towards Rannoch. When Willow caught sight of him standing there in the shadow of the birch trees, next to Kaal and a guard of scouts, she leapt ahead.

'Rannoch,' she cried, 'are you all right? We've been so worried. We couldn't understand why they wouldn't let us see you and—'

'Silence,' cried Rannoch, suddenly pawing the ground.

Willow looked back in amazement.

'Rannoch, it's me, Willow.'

Rannoch's eyes seemed to stare straight through the hind. Bankfoot, Thistle, Tain and Birrmagnur came up and Peppa stood at the back with Bracken, who was trembling violently and kept looking at Rannoch warily. Bankfoot noticed that the ground where Rannoch was standing was strewn with the berries and fungi they had been collecting in the Slave Herd.

'Rannoch, it's good to see you again,' said Birrmagnur calmly.

'You risk your lives,' said Rannoch coldly, 'talking to me thus.'

Now Kaal stepped forward. His eyes were as red as the river.

'You will bow your heads when you address Herne,' he bellowed. 'You are in the presence of a god.'

'Rannoch, p-p-please,' said Bankfoot, 'have you forgotten your friends?'

Rannoch blinked at them as though struggling with some distant memory.

'I remember you from my dreams,' he said at last in an empty voice. 'But I have passed through the kingdom of the dead, to a place none of you may visit. The Prophecy is fulfilled. Do you not see this mark?'

'A fawn mark. Just a fawn mark. That's what you always said,' cried Willow. 'Don't you remember, Rannoch?'

'For too long I have been trying to fool myself,' said Rannoch. 'You know the Prophecy. *Then shall Herne be justly woken.* Well, Herne has woken. Among His own.'

'But Rannoch,' said Willow.

'Enough. Now you must go from this place. Go north. Go south. Only go. You and all those who are not true Hernling.'

Rannoch snorted, as though in disgust, but as he spoke Birrmagnur fancied he saw Rannoch's eyes clear, just for a moment. When Rannoch spoke again, however, as coldly as before, the reindeer realized he must have been mistaken.

'Hurry, I am weary of you,' said Rannoch.

But now Bankfoot stepped forward.

'N-n-no,' he said, 'I can't believe it. After all we have been through. This isn't you, Rannoch. They have done something to you. It wasn't you I saw among those st-st-stones.'

As soon as Bankfoot said it, he knew he had made a grave mistake.

'What's this?' cried Kaal, tossing up his antlers, his eyes flaring. 'He has seen the rite. It is sacrilege.'

Rannoch looked to the stags and for just a moment he seemed to hesitate.

'Take him,' he cried suddenly.

Before Bankfoot could do anything he was surrounded.

'No,' cried Willow.

The hind was frantic now and as one of the guards approaching Bankfoot passed behind her, she let out a vicious kick with her back legs. It caught the stag full in the side and he bellowed in pain. He swung his antlers down, scything at her soft flanks but Willow jumped backwards.

'Run, Bankfoot,' cried Willow. 'Run.'

Bankfoot leapt forward, but as he did so the stags closed. His way was barred. Now Thistle, Tain and Birrmagnur had dropped their heads and all of them were fighting. The air was suddenly shattered with the clatter of jousting antlers. Though Thistle and Tain fought hard, Birrmagnur fared the best for the stags were unused to the reindeer's strange, looping antlers and could not get a purchase on their curved points. Birrmagnur was soon in the centre of the mêlée, scything angrily about him, slashing at the assaulting guards and inflicting heavy damage.

But it was hopeless. As soon as Willow cried out and the fight began, the whole herd had been roused and now they raced to defend their god. In no time at all the friends were completely outnumbered and a wall of stags had stepped between them and Bankfoot. The friends backed off, Tain's face bleeding badly and Thistle pawing at the earth.

'You,' said Rannoch, addressing Willow and the others. 'You fool with your lives. But because you have shared Herne's journey, I will allow you to leave unharmed. Go from here today, for your eyes are not permitted to see what must take place now.'

'Rannoch,' shouted Willow, 'you can't. Not to Bankfoot.'

'Go,' cried Rannoch furiously, 'quickly.'

There was nothing more to be done. The friends were forced back down the hill, leaving Bankfoot to his fate. As the stags drove them from the valley back in the direction of the Slave Herd, Willow, blind with rage and grief, looked back bitterly at her friend.

'Don't worry, Willow,' whispered Birrmagnur next to her. 'When we are out of sight we'll wait till dark and try to rescue him.'

But the reindeer was deeply worried and his eyes showed it.

By the birch trees, Rannoch was standing next to the stags encircling Bankfoot.

'Lord Herne,' said Kaal to Rannoch as he watched Willow and the others leave, 'we must make the sacrifice tonight.'

'Yes,' agreed Rannoch, looking gravely at Bankfoot, 'but make certain the whole herd is at the stones. They must all see how Herne repays unbelievers in blood.'

Bankfoot's hoofs were so heavy he could hardly walk as they led him up the hill to the stone circle. The moon's eerie, mysterious brilliance illuminated the pagan round. Rannoch led the way this time, flanked by his guard and followed by the fawns and the rest of Herne's Herd. Most of the herd hung back from Rannoch as he entered the round and Bankfoot was thrust forward. As he stepped inside the ring of stone, Bankfoot shivered as he saw the dead fawn still lying there on the ground next to the altar.

Kaal now entered the circle with the scouts and they each went up to Rannoch in turn and bowed their antlers, dropping berries and fungi from their mouths.

'Herne,' they cried.

'Herne,' cried all the stags in the herd, now surrounding the stones; and they dipped their antlers. 'Lord Herne.'

'Will you feast?' said Kaal in the circle.

Rannoch shook his head.

Bankfoot was prodded forward roughly and he found himself standing next to the altar. He was flanked by three deer and Kaal. The stags began to sway their antlers, the fawns were led in to dance, the chant swelled. Bankfoot closed his eyes and waited for the blow. The frenzied dancing seemed to go on for ever and by his side Bankfoot could sense Kaal getting ready to strike.

The dancing reached a fever pitch and Bankfoot braced

himself but as it rose to a crescendo, Rannoch let out a terrible bark.

'Enough,' he cried suddenly. 'Enough. Herne demands silence.'

The stags and the fawns stopped moving, transfixed by Rannoch's voice.

'Herne,' cried Kaal nervously, 'what is it? Are you displeased with the sacrifice?'

Rannoch stamped the ground.

'Yes, Kaal, Herne is displeased,' he cried furiously. 'Herne is displeased with the sacrifice. With you. With the herd.'

A sudden terror gripped the deer.

'Why, Lord? Why have we displeased you?'

'Why?' cried Rannoch. 'You ask me why? You who live in superstition and fear. You who believe only in the dark, in death and in violence. You who murder your own fawns and do it in my name. You dare to ask me why?'

The stags both inside and outside the stone circle began to back away.

'Stay where you are,' cried Rannoch angrily, 'until I have taught the Herla a deeper magic than death. Until I have shown you the way of Herne the Healer. You who would sacrifice this young stag in the name of the Lord of Stags, watch and fear me.'

Rannoch stepped forward, past Bankfoot, to where the dead fawn was lying. He dipped his head and very gently brushed his flank with his antler.

'I who have the power to turn nature back,' cried Rannoch, 'I command you to get up.'

The silence was deafening now, but to Bankfoot's amazement the little fawn began to twitch. Its flanks shuddered, its head stirred and suddenly it stood up and shook itself.

The herd gasped and some of the stags dropped to their haunches in fright.

'Now,' cried Rannoch in a voice that shook like thunder, 'because you have so displeased me I command you, all of you, be gone from this place never to return. Herne's Herd is disbanded. The Slave Herds shall be free. Across the High Land the Herla shall roam as they will. Go together and live like Herla, or go separately. But never again take Herne's name in vain. All of you, out of my sight.'

They didn't need to be told twice. The stags began to bellow and, kicking and butting each other, they burst from the stone circle. The stampede had begun. The rest of the herd went scattering across the moor, running for their lives. Only Rannoch, Bankfoot and the fawn were left in the man-made ring. Bankfoot hardly dared stir. He looked at Rannoch and found his legs were pinned to the ground with terror.

'H-h-herne,' he stammered, closing his eyes again, 'Herne. Don't harm me. Now I know it's all true about the Prophecy. I'm sorry I ever doubted it but if you'll—'

But suddenly Bankfoot heard a snort. It rumbled up into a great bellow of laughter.

'Oh, Bankfoot, silly old Bankfoot, don't you recognize your old friend?'

Bankfoot opened his eyes in an amazement, even greater than that he had felt at the sight of Herne.

'That's right, it's me, Rannoch.'

Where just before Bankfoot had been staring at the incarnation of a living god, now he was looking at his old friend again.

'But h-h-how?' gasped Bankfoot. 'The fawn, I saw him die.'

'Not die,' said Rannoch, smiling, 'though he was badly stunned when Kaal caught him with his hoofs. That's why I ordered them all to leave that night. So I could help him. Come on, Ragnur, say hello to Bankfoot.'

The little fawn trotted up quite happily.

'I saw my real chance when I realized the little one wasn't dead. Then I really planned to set the fox among them. I'm only sorry I didn't stop it sooner but with the berries and the ghostly dancing I was caught up too for a while. If Ragnur here hadn't be so intelligent and helpful I don't know what I would have done. Together we formed our plan when they had left, didn't we, Ragnur?'

Ragnur beamed up at Rannoch.

'I fixed Ragnur up as best I could and then told him to stay by the stones and play dead if anyone came, ready for the next time they wanted to hold a sacrifice.'

Bankfoot nodded, though he was still amazed.

'First I wanted to get you all away, though, just in case anything went wrong. I couldn't get a message to you so I had to pretend to order you from the valley, though I'm sorry I had to frighten Willow so badly. But then you nearly spoilt it all,' chuckled Rannoch, 'when you blurted out that you'd seen the rite. As it is, though, I think it helped the effect.'

'So . . . so it was all pretence.'

'No, Bankfoot, not all,' answered Rannoch quietly.

'What do you mean?'

'I mean,' said Rannoch – and something grave entered his voice – 'that there was a time when I nearly believed them. When I wanted to believe them.'

'Your eyes, up there on the hill. They terrified me.'

'Yes. But that was mostly the berries and the fungi the Slave Herds have been collecting. They have the power to bring on waking dreams, Bankfoot. It affected all of them. It was only after the first sacrifice, when you thought they'd killed Ragnur, that I shook off its influence and from then on I had the devil of a time pretending to eat it in front of Kaal and the stags. But there was something else, Bankfoot, that was more than the fungi. In that circle, when the fawns were dancing in the moonlight. For a moment I almost thought I *was* Herne. There was something of Herne there, until . . .'

Rannoch fell silent.

'Until . . .?'

'Until they almost killed Ragnur, of course. Then something woke in me and I threw off the visions.'

'What do you mean?'

'I mean, as I felt the violence of that place, of those stones and the Herla, I remembered a feeling I have had all my life. The feeling I had at the fort and with the wolf. The urge to heal.'

'And Herne?'

Rannoch smiled.

'Theirs is a belief that has thrived here for centuries in the High Land and it's true what Rurl told me – they did have knowledge of man. It comes from the circle. They learnt the rite of sacrifice from watching man among his stones. But I know that if ever the Herla are to live free in the High Land, or anywhere else in the Great Land, then they must never worship Herne like that.'

'So you . . .?'

Rannoch looked carefully at Bankfoot.

'No, Bankfoot,' he said quietly, 'I am not Herne. I am a Herla'

'And the Prophecy?'

Rannoch gazed ahead into the night. A strong breeze was blowing across the High Land into the young deers' muzzles, but Rannoch didn't answer. He suddenly felt much older. He stirred in the darkness and as he did so he fancied he had heard something moving beyond the stones.

'Well, I suppose we should t-t-try and find the others,' said Bankfoot after a while, 'though they'll never believe it.'

'Bankfoot,' said Rannoch quietly, 'I learnt something else too.'

'W-w-what?'

'It's about Sgorr. I know where he's from,' whispered Rannoch. 'This was once his herd.'

Bankfoot looked at Rannoch in astonishment.

'Sgorr's herd?'

'Yes, but there's something else, Bankfoot,' said Rannoch. 'Kaal said it's to do with an island and something Sgorr hid there long ago. He says Sgorr fears its discovery more than anything else.'

'What?'

'I don't know,' said Rannoch. 'It's an even darker secret.'

Part Three

18

The Branding

And the Lord set a mark on Cain.
Genesis 4, 15

'Alive? What do you mean he's alive?'

Narl backed away nervously into the shadows. He had never seen Sgorr so angry. His master was older now and the fur around his muzzle was flecked with grey, which somehow gave a more sinister aspect to the scar across his face.

'It must be him,' said Narl. 'He's grown and has his antlers. But that mark on his forehead is just the same. The oak leaf.'

'But how?' said Sgorr in disbelief.

'The spies weren't sure. But from what they could learn he was hurt and then rescued,' said Narl, his voice dropping away to a frightened whisper, 'by humans.'

'By humans?' whispered Sgorr. For the first time ever Narl noticed something like fear flicker across Sgorr's single eye. But it soon passed.

'Yes, then he escaped into the High Land,' said Narl nervously, 'with his friends. The ones who got away from the Sgorrla.'

'Am I surrounded by incompetents?' cried Sgorr. 'Have

the guards along the Great Glen punished. Kill one guard in each garrison.'

Narl nodded.

'And why did the spies disobey my orders anyway,' said Sgorr angrily, 'and enter the High Land?'

Narl dropped his eyes fearfully.

'They thought it best, Lord,' he answered, 'when they saw that mark.'

'So he's alive,' said Sgorr, looking out into the darkness. 'Well, well. And in the High Land too. At least they'll know what to do with him there.'

Narl looked strangely at Sgorr. He didn't understand what his master meant.

'There's more,' Narl went on slowly, testing Sgorr's responses all the time. 'I don't quite understand it, but the spies spoke of a herd. Herne's Herd they called it.'

Sgorr swung round suddenly and glared at Narl.

'Yes,' he said.

'You know of them, my lord?' said Narl with surprise.

'A little,' said Sgorr, smiling. 'Go on.'

'They ruled in the High Land.'

'Ruled?' said Sgorr. 'What do you mean ruled?'

'Well, that's the part that's unclear. The spies say Rannoch has overthrown this herd.'

'Overthrown Herne's Herd?' cried Sgorr, wheeling round in the night. 'Impossible. Take me to these spies, quickly.'

Narl led Sgorr through the darkness. The air was cold for winter was with them and the ground carried a frost that crunched loudly underfoot. The two spies were waiting fearfully for their leader, surrounded by a contingent of the Sgorrla. It had taken them over a year to get back to the home herd for they had got lost in the north and had wandered hopelessly for suns and moons, half terrified of returning to their master. They were two of the stags Rannoch had overheard by the burn and their breath smoked furiously in the darkness.

'You,' cried Sgorr, as he ran up to one of them and thrust his muzzle straight into the spy's terrified face, 'tell me everything you know of Rannoch and Herne's Herd. Leave nothing out. I warn you, I'll know if you're embellishing it just to please me.'

So the Sgorrla began. He spoke falteringly at first until Sgorr shouted at him and threatened him with the Sgorrla's antlers. So he went on, describing the chase across the Great Mountain and the meeting with Birrmagnur. But when he came to their journey from the Slave Herd Sgorr stopped him.

'And you say he spoke to this grouse?' said Sgorr, glancing at Narl.

'Yes, my Lord, though I couldn't understand what he was saying.'

Sgorr's face was suddenly thoughtful.

'Go on,' he said.

The stag continued, telling all they had seen of Herne's Herd and the Standing Stones. The tale took a good time, as the stag dared leave nothing out.

'So,' said Sgorr when it was over, shaking his head, 'the fools fled? Herne's Herd – who have ruled in the High Land for longer than the Herla can remember.'

The spy nodded nervously and looked to his companions. They all wondered why Sgorr seemed to know about Herne's Herd already. Sgorr looked back at him, his eye pinning the deer to the curtain of night. Then suddenly Sgorr began to shake. His legs shook. His shoulders shook. Even the stumps of bone on his head shook. He was laughing. He threw his head back and let out a great bellow of laughter. The Sgorrla

stared at each other in amazement. They had never heard
Sgorr laugh before, nor had they heard anything quite so
unnerving in all their lives.

'It's really too good,' said Sgorr, as the laughter subsided.
'This Rannoch, I think I should like to meet him, Narl. Yes,
I think I should like to meet him very much. But just before
you left,' Sgorr went on, turning back to the spy, 'you heard
him say he wasn't Herne?'

Again the deer nodded.

'You're certain?'

'It was the last thing I heard him say before we left, my
lord.'

'No, of course not,' muttered Sgorr to himself. 'Of course
not.'

'But my lord,' said the spy Sgorrla suddenly, 'can it be the
Prophecy?'

The deer regretted the question immediately. Sgorr's
mouth opened and his teeth were suddenly buried in the
stag's throat. The spy barked furiously and when Sgorr finally
let go, blood was gushing from his neck.

'You know it is death to talk of the Prophecy,' cried Sgorr.

He suddenly turned and addressed all the watching
Sgorrla.

'All of you,' he cried, 'listen carefully to me. Not a word
of what you have heard tonight must pass your lips. Do
you understand me? Not one single word. As far as you're
concerned, the fawn with the oak mark died all those years
ago by the loch. It will go hard with you if I find that any
of it has leaked out to the herds. Do you understand?'

The spies and the assembled Sgorrla nodded.

'Very well then,' he said, his tone becoming soft and
conciliating as he turned back to the spies. 'You. You've done
very well and I am pleased. You will find an honoured place

in the inner ranks of the Sgorrla. For tonight, get them to take you to the feeding grounds and give you some extra bark and berries. Come, Narl, I want to get back to the harem.'

Sgorr swung round and, much to the relief of the deer, disappeared again into the darkness.

But as he ran his eye was burning brightly.

'Narl,' said Sgorr quietly when they were some distance away. 'I want them disposed of.'

'My lord?'

'Get rid of them, Narl. It's the only way to be sure.'

'The spies, my lord?' said Narl.

'No, Narl, you idiot, not just the spies – all of them. All the stags that were there tonight. But try to do it subtly, Narl. Arrange some accidents. Pick them off one by one.'

Narl was silent now as the two of them ran. Normally he would have had no compunction in carrying out his master's orders but Narl was deeply troubled. One of the deer in the Sgorrla guard was his own brother, Rack. As the two deer neared the thicket where Sgorr had his harem, Narl ventured a question. He knew he was the only deer in the herds who could have got away with it.

'My lord,' he said softly.

'What is it, Narl?'

'The Prophecy,'

'What about it?' said Sgorr irritably, but he seemed strangely distracted.

'Can it be coming true? You heard what the spies said. He can speak to the Lera and is in the High Land now. And do you remember that line of verse? *Then he breaks an ancient power.*'

'It is a surprise, I admit,' said Sgorr coldly, 'to hear he has survived. Nothing more. Think, Narl, what this prophecy says. The skies turning black. A Herla commanding man. It is impossible, Narl. And you heard what he said – that he is not Herne. Of course he is not Herne because Herne does not exist.'

'But he has spent time with man.'

Sgorr was silent now, for somewhere in his own black heart fear was fluttering. Man. Rannoch had knowledge of man. And he had met Herne's Herd. Tricked the darkest of the Herla. Sgorr was truly amazed and with his astonishment came a nagging doubt. Had Rannoch already found out? Found out the reason he had sealed the High Land from the Herla until he was ready to destroy Herne's Herd and take revenge? Found out the one thing the herds must never know – his own dark secret?

'No,' cried Sgorr, his spirit suddenly rallying, 'all we have to fear from Rannoch is the superstition and stupidity of the Herla. That's why the stags who heard tonight must be silenced. I do not believe, Narl, but I know that belief is a very powerful force, whether the object of that belief is true or not. But there's something else that can only work in our favour. The spies said Rannoch was travelling with his mother, which can only mean that he himself does not know that he is Brechin's and Eloin's fawn. Which gives us plenty of time to go to work. To have Rannoch . . . removed.'

As Sgorr's mind began to race, he felt a power returning to him and a growing confidence that quickly dispelled the spectre that had suddenly risen in the north.

'Besides, Narl, my dear friend,' said Sgorr with satisfaction, 'if it is true about Herne's Herd, then, without knowing it, this Rannoch is working for my own purposes.'

'My lord?'

'He has removed the last true obstacle to my own ambition, barring that fool Colquhar. Now there will be nothing to stop us when we take the Great Herd into the High Land.'

'Into the High Land?' said Narl. 'But you sealed it.'

'I sealed it until I was ready to confront the power that has kept the Herla enslaved, ready to conquer all the herds across the Great Land.'

'So you did have knowledge of Herne's Herd?'

'Oh yes,' answered Sgorr gravely, his eye narrowing.

He was thinking back to all those years ago when, as hardly more than a fawn himself, they had driven him out of the High Land. For daring— Sgorr stopped himself. Even he feared to remember what he had done that day on the island.

Morning broke like shattered stone around the wintering deer. The icy sky was as white and bleak as loss itself and even the grass seemed to have been drained of colour. Sgorr's breath hung like a wraith around his lips as he lay there, dreaming fitfully. He trembled and opened his eye.

The dream had already gone but as Sgorr struggled to remember the images that had visited him in his sleep, he shuddered and looked out into the day.

Around him sat his harem, guarded as they always were by an outer ring of Sgorrla to make sure they couldn't escape and to allow Sgorr the freedom – normally unknown to any stag once he has made his stand in the mating season – to roam at will through the herd. A stag will stay on constant guard of his hinds, bellowing at short intervals to warn off rivals, but Sgorr had no interest in such undignified behaviour and besides, he had far too much to do in the herd.

Another year had passed since the spies had first brought news of Rannoch from the north and Sgorr had bided his time, plotting and planning and watching with satisfaction as he brought more and more of the Herla under his sway. At the far edge of the hinds sat Eloin. She was old now, like Sgorr, but his heart stirred at how beautiful she still looked. Since the day of Drail's death Sgorr had kept her by his side, hoping against hope that perhaps, one day, she might grow to love him. She would never mate with him, he knew that, but since he had failed to sire calves himself, that no longer mattered to Sgorr. She was a prize that he would never let go of. Brechin's hind, the boldest and most beautiful of all the does.

He realized of course that it was only his threat of doing harm to Shira and Canisp that held her. For after the news he had given her at the ravine, Eloin hardly cared whether she lived or died and it was only the thought of protecting them that kept her from doing herself some fatal harm.

If only you knew that Rannoch is alive, thought Sgorr now as he looked at her. That might bring back the spark to your eyes. But, Eloin, my dear, you must never know.

He looked out across the plain and as the light came his heart swelled at the sight that met his eye. The awesome lines of Sgorrla ranged across the plain, sitting in neat lines, their sharpened antlers bristling in the morning. Now that the herds were coming together, here in a meeting place nearly fifty miles north of the home valley, their ranks had swollen and swollen. Every sun more were coming in to add to Sgorr's might. There were the hinds too and the Sgorrling, also ranged in rows, quiet, submissive, perfectly obedient to his will. Then, to the east and west, the foreign Herla were gathering. The fallow and roe deer. It had been Sgorr's greatest challenge to get them to submit. But here they were too, also ordered, also obedient, serving the greater size and strength of the red deer.

They were his children now and Sgorr gave a deep sigh
of satisfaction as he got to his feet. At once the Sgorrla
around the hinds got up too and bowed their antlers. Eloin
stirred in the grass and looked bitterly at Sgorr.

'Good morning, my dear.'

The hind ignored him.

'There is much to do this sun, Eloin,' said Sgorr, 'and I
think it would interest you to see it. I am preparing a special
surprise for the foreign Herla. To give them a little taste of
my power.'

'Nothing you do could interest me, Sgorr,' whispered
Eloin coldly.

'Come, come, Eloin, you must try to be more civil,' said
Sgorr. 'Otherwise perhaps I shall ask Shira or Canisp to join
me instead.'

Eloin got to her feet, wearily, obediently. She had heard
the threat a hundred times and now she was simply too tired
to resist. There was nothing left in the poor hind to resist
with.

'Very well, Sgorr,' she said quietly, 'show me your
surprise.'

'I am sure you will like it,' said Sgorr.

He led her along the brow of the hill to where Narl was
waiting. Narl bowed to the lord as they approached.

'Is everything ready?' asked Sgorr.

'Yes, my lord. The inner Sgorrla are prepared. They have
been sharpening their antlers for seven suns.'

'Very well,' said Sgorr, 'let us get on with it.'

Narl nodded, turned and led them forward to the edge of
the hill, where an earth mound gave them a perfect vantage
across the plain and the best position from which to address
the herds.

Narl stepped forward. The Herla below them were

already hushed for they had been told to expect an address and stags had been positioned at intervals along the lines to relay Sgorr's words to the farthest edges of the massed deer.

'Herla,' cried Narl, his voice suddenly echoing across the plain, 'you have been gathered here to listen to the words of the leader. So listen well.'

Now Sgorr stepped forward and as he did so a great rumble went up. It started at the back and swept forward towards Sgorr like a wave rushing to meet the shore as the deer began to stamp and dip their heads.

'SGORR!' came the thunderous cry. 'SGORR!'

The sound crashed over Sgorr and he felt himself swell in stature as the power of their voices moved through him like blood turned into pure energy. He paused, basking in the glory of it all, as the sea subsided and became a ripple of awed whispering.

'Silence,' cried Sgorr suddenly, and the stillness was immediate.

'Herla, you are welcome,' he began, 'all of you. Our mission in the Low Lands is almost complete. The Great Herd is assembling. Since Sgorr's Year began, when poor Drail was so cruelly taken from us by traitors, it has taken many years of blood and sweat to achieve. But now, at last, the herds are coming together in an unbroken forest of glory. Only one small insult remains in the Low Lands and soon that will be broken like a twig under our slots. When that is done we will march out to free the herds right across the Great Land. The Great Trek shall begin.'

Again the shout went up.

'SGORR!' they thundered. 'SGORR!'

Across the plain and in the surrounding hills the Lera looked up and trembled.

'Herla,' cried Sgorr again, and once more the silence

echoed through the steely air. 'Know now that you are free
and nevermore will the name of Herne be spoken in the Great
Land. The deer must use reason to confront his enemies.'

Now another shout went up and it made the very air
shake.

'HERNE IS DEAD! LONG LIVE SGORR! HERNE IS
DEAD! LONG LIVE SGORR!'

Sgorr smiled grimly.

'Herla,' he cried, 'red deer, roe and fallow alike shall walk
in triumph, guided by my will. But before we move north
once more and sweep the land before us, you, the Clovar,
must listen.'

Something new had entered his voice.

'Though you too are Herla and are honoured amongst
us, remember also that your true honour is to know your
place in the great hierarchy of the deer. For first among the
Herla are the red deer and first among the red deer are
the Sgorrla.'

The fallow and roe hardly dared stir in the cold grass. The
roe, as naturally independent creatures, felt the pain of what
was happening most. But a group of fallow deer nearby
began to huddle together nervously. In their midst was a
single red stag who had come with them from their home in
the park. His name was Quaich.

'So this day I have called you here to give you a sign,'
cried Sgorr. 'Henceforth the Sgorrla shall be honoured
highest among the Herla and they shall bear a mark as the
badge of that honour. A mark in blood.'

Sgorr's voice rose to a fever pitch of excitement.

'Sgorrla,' he cried exultantly, 'let the Branding begin.'

Just as Sgorr had pre-arranged amongst the red deer, the
members of the inner Sgorrla stamped and stepped out

among the lines and lines of Sgorrla that criss-crossed the plain. They turned to face their comrades.

The fallow and roe deer watched transfixed as the Sgorrla dropped their heads.

'Sgorrla,' cried the inner Sgorrla, 'do you acknowledge the cult of death?'

'We do,' came the rehearsed response, 'for Sgorr has made it so.'

The inner Sgorrla moved forwards in unison. Suddenly, with their brow tines, two hundred antlers were jabbing at the Sgorrla's foreheads; cutting through fur and flesh, twisting and tearing, gouging till their comrades' brows were torn and bloody. Some of the Sgorrla cried out in agony and were silenced by their comrades as blood began to bead across the plain. Most suffered in silence, proud to show their cold indifference to the pain as true Sgorrla.

Then the bloodied Sgorrla changed places with the inner Sgorrla and, using their antlers to mark their comrades, the process began again, until every single Sgorrla head was marked with a wound that would scab and heal to leave a vivid scar that would forever tell of his place in Sgorr's kingdom.

When it was finished the roe and fallow deer stood petrified and a fearful murmur went up among them. If any had come that day with thoughts of opposing Sgorr's will – and there were still a few – those thoughts had evaporated. It was just as Sgorr had intended.

'There, Rannoch,' murmured Sgorr quietly to himself, 'you threaten me with a fawn mark. Well, if you survive, I shall meet your puny leaf with a thousand glistening scars.'

But there was another reason why this particular branding had been determined. A secret reason that only Sgorr and Narl knew.

The spies that had brought the news of Rannoch's survival the year before had long been silenced, as had the guards that had witnessed it. All except Narl's brother, Rack. Narl had protected him for as long as he thought it safe but Rack had grown careless with his tongue. Now Rack too lay dead on the plain, silenced by the Sgorrla who was branding him. Just as Narl had instructed, the Sgorrla's tine had slipped towards Rack's right eye and pierced to the living brain behind.

'So, my dear,' said Sgorr with satisfaction, 'did you enjoy the little surprise?'

'You're mad, Sgorr,' whispered Eloin.

'No, my dear, I am quite sane. For only sanity and reason could have seen the dawn of this brave day.'

'I hate you, Sgorr. I will hate you till the stars grow cold.'

Sgorr felt a tightening in his gut. He wanted to hurt Eloin then. But he held the urge in check, for his knowledge that her beloved Rannoch was still alive without her even knowing it, without her ever knowing it, gave him a strange power over her.

'Well, my dear,' he said, almost indifferently, 'then we shall have to come up with something even better to please you, won't we?'

Above the loch a single stag was gazing down from the forest at the shining spring waters. The Lord of the Herd was lost in thought and around him the stags stirred restlessly. The Outriders patrolled the edge of the trees constantly now, for they knew that Sgorr was on the move and that if it came to it, flight was probably the best hope they had. They could have left sooner but for some reason they could only guess at, their lord kept them where they were.

The stag shook his head. Colquhar had grown into a

strong and powerful stag. His eyes were unsettled, though. Strangely he was thinking of Tharn and what he had had to do to secure the lordship. Why hadn't he just fought Tharn, he thought to himself bitterly? He could have beaten him in a fair fight. But Sgorr's spies had come to him, whispering of certainty and promising alliances. Promising that the Outriders would be protected in the Low Lands.

'That's why I did it,' Colquhar told himself now, 'to preserve the Outriders.' But he knew that it was only half true. Colquhar was only too aware of the heights, or the depths, of his own ambition.

'Tharn was a fool,' he told himself half-heartedly, tilting his twelve-pointed antlers and trying to summon thoughts to console himself. 'He was obsessed with Herne. Remember his reaction to that fawn?'

Colquhar was a rationalist and he hated weakness. Indeed that was the main thing that attracted him to Sgorr. He didn't believe in Herne but he did believe in the Outriders. He had been one himself and knew the pride of protecting the herd.

'I was the strongest,' said Captain Colquhar quietly, not without some reason. 'I was the best so it was only right that I took over the herd.'

Again a guilty confusion entered his mind. Hadn't that breached the ancient code of the Outriders itself? To serve without thought of personal ambition, to defend and protect. That was the Outriders' code, that was what made them free. But Colquhar had killed Tharn and taken the herd. He had persuaded the others that it was the only way to survive and now there was blood on his antlers, blood that not even the deep, deep waters of the loch could wash clean.

'Take what you want and pay for it later,' said Colquhar to himself. 'I am the Lord above the Loch.'

But instead of his heart swelling with pride, he suddenly felt a terrible remorse.

And what had he done it all for? To watch Sgorr conquer the Low Lands? To see all the Herla forced to come together in subservience? To see fallow and roe deer bound in an unnatural union? It wasn't homage that Sgorr wanted but total dominion, and he would stop at nothing until he'd seen the Outriders driven from the Great Land for ever.

'What a fool I've been,' said Colquhar to himself bitterly, 'to believe that he'd stop at the loch. He'll never stop. Never.'

Colquhar's troubled thoughts were suddenly interrupted by the approach of six Outriders through the trees. They were led by Braan, the stag who had first welcomed Rannoch and his mother to the herd all those years before. Braan, like the others, had been running hard and he looked almost exhausted.

'My lord,' he said, bowing as he came up.

'Braan,' said Colquhar, 'you've been scouting. What news?'

Braan looked grave.

'Bad news, my lord. They're less than two suns from here, though they seem to have stopped for a while.'

'How many?' asked Colquhar.

'It's hard to tell,' answered Braan, shaking his head. 'Over two thousand. We counted fifteen herds, not to mention all the roe. They've been moving steadily north and they're coming in our direction. The devastation is terrible. They've cut a swath through the forests and the browse line stretches as far as the eye can see.'

'Then the time has come,' said Colquhar quietly.

'What shall we do, Lord Colquhar?' asked a young Outrider suddenly. His name was Scal.

'What do you think we should do?' said Colquhar.

'I don't know,' said Scal. 'Go into the High Land, perhaps. We might be safe, and there are the rumours . . .'

'Rumours?' said Colquhar.

'Of a deer with a mark,' whispered Scal. 'They say he's come to free us all. That he rose from the dead and will take the Herla across the sea.'

'What's this?' said Colquhar, looking round at Braan.

The Outrider shrugged.

'There are rumours, it's true, my lord,' he answered. 'There have been for some time. And we met some roe mumbling of it the other day. There is talk again of the Prophecy.'

'The Prophecy?'

'Some say that Rannoch never died. This deer to the north, they say he has an oak leaf on his brow, like the fawn's.'

Colquhar said nothing for a while as he gazed across the loch to the south. He had hated Rannoch and feared that mark, but now this strange news came like a breath of hope from some distant shore, carried on the wind to a land where all hope had gone.

'Shall we take the herd north,' asked Scal quietly, 'and find this Herla?'

Still Colquhar was silent.

'We could make a stand up there.'

'Abandon the forest and the loch?' said Colquhar suddenly. 'Because of rumours of a prophecy? Never.'

'But my lord, they are too strong for us.'

'Scal,' said Colquhar quietly, 'you are an Outrider. That you must never forget. Outriders do not run from danger. They do not flee when they should fight. They do not hide in gullies and hedgerows. They are bound to protect the herd at whatever cost. At the cost of their own lives if necessary. No. We shall make our stand here.'

Colquhar swayed his great antlers. At that moment something of his former glory was restored to him, for he had not been the same since guilt had begun to eat away at him. He was suddenly an Outrider once more.

Scal, Braan and the others exchanged nervous looks, for they knew how hopeless it was to fight Sgorr. But something else was stirring in them too, the honour that was their bloodright. They drew up and dipped their antlers.

'Very well, then,' said Colquhar. 'Be ready at all times and bring me news as soon as you have any.'

They nodded as one and returned to their duties guarding the Herd above the Loch. The last free herd in all of the Low Lands.

The news was a long time in coming, for it was soon clear to the deer that Sgorr was waiting till the herd's antlers shed and grew again.

Colquhar's Outriders shed themselves, but as their antlers rose once more on their proud heads the sight brought little cheer to their hinds and their young calves. They realized what was coming and in their hearts they were trying to resign themselves.

When it came it was not like the storm they were all expecting to break suddenly over them. The waters of the loch were still and the sun was shining brightly when ten stags came sauntering up the valley.

They were Sgorrla and when the Outriders emerged from the trees and surrounded them angrily, they noticed with disgust the deep scars that marked their brows. But although there must have been seventy Outriders around them – for as Colquhar awaited his fate he had appointed more and more to their ranks – the Sgorrla looked back at them disdainfully. They seemed beyond fear, untouchable. They smiled coldly as they were led into Colquhar's presence.

'Lord Colquhar,' said Narl, without bowing, 'Lord Sgorr is waiting with the herd below the loch.'

'Waiting for what?' snorted Colquhar.

'For you to renew your oath of homage to him,' answered Narl.

'Renew my oath,' said Colquhar bitterly, 'and is that all he wants?'

'Why yes,' lied Narl, 'what else? It has been years since you paid him homage.'

'And if I do this thing,' said Colquhar quietly, 'he will leave the Herd above the Loch in peace? He will let the Outriders remain?'

Narl dropped his eyes for an instant.

'Of course,' he answered. 'That is your old pact. Sgorr has united the herds. He needn't worry about you and you needn't worry about him. He admires you, Colquhar, and wants you to continue, in peace and amity.'

Colquhar looked at Braan and he saw that the Outrider was shaking his head.

'So what does Sgorr want me to do?' said Colquhar.

'Come with us. We will take you in honour to Sgorr.'

Colquhar suddenly swung round.

'So, Braan,' he said firmly, 'shall I do this thing? Will you come with me?'

Before Braan could answer Narl interrupted him.

'No, Lord Colquhar,' he said quietly, 'Sgorr wants you to come alone.'

Colquhar looked into Narl's eyes and this time Narl didn't look away. He held his gaze openly and in that knowing, slightly amused look Colquhar saw that his own fate had already been sealed. But Colquhar didn't resist. He was almost glad, now that it had come.

'Very well,' he said quietly. 'I will accompany you.'

'No, Lord,' cried Braan, stepping forward, 'it's a trick.'

'Silence, Braan. Sgorr and I have a pact and I must pay him homage. Then the Outriders will be safe. But Narl,' said Colquhar, 'I want to talk to Braan alone for a while. I will meet you and the Sgorrla by the edge of the loch.'

Narl nodded and led the Sgorrla out of the wood as Colquhar stood there in the clearing next to Captain Braan.

'What are you doing?' said Braan when they were out of earshot.

'Going to meet Sgorr,' answered Colquhar simply.

'But it must be a trick,' cried Braan. 'Why do they want you alone?'

'I am sure it is a trick,' said Colquhar quietly.

'Then . . .'

'Yes, Braan. But I am not afraid to die. Perhaps I can redeem a little of the harm I have done,' said Colquhar sadly.

'No,' said Braan passionately, 'we will fight. The Outriders will fight.'

'No, Braan. I've been a fool. Even till now I thought we could make a stand. My vanity led me to believe that I could win back my own honour by sacrificing the herd. But I cannot. You must get them away, Braan. Take the herd north. Who knows, maybe the rumours about Rannoch are true.'

'But you said that Outriders do not run.'

'But nor do they sacrifice themselves pointlessly. Go north, Braan, and if you can, build a force to defeat Sgorr.'

'While you sacrifice yourself pointlessly?' said Braan.

'Not pointlessly,' answered Colquhar, 'for I plan to win the herd time. And who knows, if I can get near Sgorr . . .'

Without another word Colquhar stepped into the open and ran down towards the loch.

As Narl and the Sgorrla led him away, they looked up at the surrounding trees and even the Sgorrla felt the stirrings of remorse, for the Outriders above the Loch were dipping their antlers in silent tribute.

The Outriders were unaware of the forces that were gathering around them as they did so. As Colquhar journeyed south, silent contingents of Sgorrla were already approaching the loch from the north, east and west. If Colquhar had thought to save the herd he was already too late. His sacrifice was an empty one. Colquhar's Outriders were already surrounded.

It took Narl's party three suns to reach Sgorr and when Colquhar finally came down to meet the herds he trembled at the sight. Sgorr was set apart, on a hill, and though he was encircled by a Sgorrla guard, they had been ordered to stand as far apart from him as they could while still making sure of his safety. As Narl led Colquhar forward they saw in the distance that Sgorr seemed to be talking to something in the grass.

'Well, why don't you answer me?' Sgorr was saying. 'Speak to me, damn you.'

There came a squeal of pain from the ground. Lying on the earth was a ferret. It was snow white and, being an albino, its little eyes stood out pink in its frightened face. They were glassy now and terrified. The ferret's fur was stained with blood.

'Come,' said Sgorr, 'it can't be too difficult. My spies tell me *he* does it all the time. Is it true?'

Sgorr lifted his front hoof and brought it down on the ferret's back leg. It snapped it clean in two and again the ferret squealed and spat in agony. Sgorr's eye blazed furiously as he tried and failed to interpret the strange sounds.

'You're not making any sense at all,' said Sgorr, 'but I'll tell you this. If it's true and the Lera are seeking his help, they'll suffer for it. All of them. Do you understand me?'

The ferret's pink eyes blinked up at the deer, but the animal had understood nothing of what Sgorr had said.

'It isn't true, is it?' Sgorr smiled. 'You can't understand me, or him. It's all lies. Well, no matter. You for one will never understand anything again.'

As Narl and Colquhar passed through the ring of Sgorrla they started as they saw Sgorr rise up on his hind legs and come crashing down on his front hoofs. When they reached him the ferret was lying dead in front of him.

'So you've come, Colquhar,' said Sgorr casually, as he saw the Lord above the Loch approaching him. He began to scrape his slots through the grass, wiping the blood from his hoofs.

'Are you ready then to renew your homage?'

'If need be,' answered Colquhar coldly, looking around him. 'The Outriders send you welcome. In honour of our pact.'

'Ah yes, our pact.' Sgorr smiled. 'Well, I'm afraid that is what I wanted to talk to you about. You see, this pact of ours, I'm rather bored of it. In fact, it's dissolved.'

If Sgorr had expected the news to startle Colquhar he was disappointed, for the stag looked back at him without emotion.

'Do you think I'm such a fool,' said Colquhar quietly, 'to believe that our pact meant anything?'

'Then what are you doing here?' said Sgorr.

Colquhar didn't answer, but as Sgorr looked at him his eye suddenly glittered.

'I see,' he said, 'how noble. You thought to buy them time, didn't you, Colquhar? Time to escape?'

Colquhar dropped his eyes.

'My poor Colquhar,' whispered Sgorr. 'If you think you've helped them, I'm afraid you're mistaken. Even as you left the loch we had them surrounded. So as we speak your Outriders are being destroyed.'

Colquhar looked up and stared at Sgorr in horror but he knew immediately that Sgorr was telling the truth. Colquhar bellowed in fury and, dropping his head, he lunged at the leader. But as he did so Narl thrust himself forward and knocked Colquhar in the side. It was enough to push him off balance and save Sgorr a gouging. In an instant the Sgorrla had surrounded their leader.

'Bravely done, Colquhar,' said Sgorr contemptuously from behind the wall of Sgorrla, 'but you shall pay for that.'

Colquhar recovered himself and raised his head to Sgorr.

'Very well,' he said quietly. 'Then get on with it.'

'Get on with it?'

'You brought me here to kill me, Sgorr,' said Colquhar quietly. 'The sacrifice will have been in vain but I no longer care. I no longer care to live.'

'The sacrifice?' said Sgorr. 'How touching. But you're wrong, Colquhar. I have no intention of killing you. I will have the Sgorrla amuse themselves with you a while for that last impertinence, but apart from that you shall live as a part of the Great Herd.'

'Live?'

'Oh yes. To your eternal shame, to the eternal shame of the Outriders. The last of their kind and the most degraded. Take him away.'

Colquhar bellowed bitterly as the Sgorrla surrounded him

and drove him away. Sgorr stood watching and he gave a
deep bark of satisfaction.

'This is a great day, Narl. A very great day indeed.'

'Yes, Lord.'

'Now, Narl,' said Sgorr, 'is he ready?'

'Yes, Lord, he's waiting nearby.'

'Then bring him to me.'

Narl nodded and ran down the slope. When he returned
there was a young stag with him. Unlike the Sgorrla of which
he too was a part, the stag's forehead was unmarked.

'You have your orders,' said Sgorr as they arrived.

The young stag nodded silently.

'We must put an end to these lies and rumours once and
for all,' said Sgorr, 'so there must be no mistake. No mistake
at all.'

Again the stag nodded and then he turned silently and
ran through the grass. His uncommonly bright eyes carried
a grim purpose. A purpose for which he had been trained
since birth. All his life he had been made ready for this
moment and now he had his orders, and his mission lay to
the north.

19

A Healer

... but it lies
Deep-meadow'd, happy, fair with orchard lawns
And bowery hollows crown'd with summer sea,
Where I will heal me of my grievous wound.
Alfred Lord Tennyson, 'The Passing of Arthur'

A stag was lifting his head to the morning. The four tines
on each of his antlers were covered in velvet and his coat
was a rich red. Around him the moorland grasses quivered
the colour of saffron and the craggy mountains had blushed
a deep, lush purple. Suddenly, from the mass of blue above
him, there came a furious shrieking and a flash of black and
gold shot through the air. Talons glinted in the bright sky
and as the eagle closed on its quarry there came another
shriek and then silence.

The stag looked about him fearfully, scenting the wind
and testing the distances with his large eyes. The deer was
unusually nervous for he was not used to travelling alone
through the High Land. He had grown up in a Slave Herd
and the past week's journey had provided him with a bewil-
dering array of new sensations; some terrifying, others rich
with wonder and delight. But although he would not have

given up a single one of them to feel safer than he did, he was beginning to grow a little lonely.

A new look came into the stag's eyes as he caught a voice on the breeze. He swung his head to the east and the secret whispering of the senses that had already told him what was there was instantly confirmed as he caught sight of another deer coming towards him through the heather. It was a young hind. The stag pawed the ground and though it was not yet Anlach, he felt excitement stirring inside him. He ran towards her.

'Hello there,' he called cheerfully.

The hind stopped but though she too was on her own, there was little in her look that spoke of fear. She nodded her sleek head to the stag.

'Are you alone?' asked the stag.

'Yes,' answered the hind. 'You?'

The stag nodded and as he did so he noticed that her right front leg was matted with blood. The wound was deep.

'You're hurt?' said the stag.

'Yes, I had a fall.'

'I'm sorry,' said the stag in that matter-of-fact way common to Lera, which is as much as to say that a wound is a wound and there's little you can do about it so it's probably best not to dwell on the fact.

'It won't heal,' the hind went on. 'In fact, I think it's getting worse. So I'm going south towards the Great Mountain, to see if He can help.'

The stag looked at her with a new interest.

'He?'

'The Healer, or whatever they call him.'

'The Marked One, you mean,' said the stag gravely. 'I'm going to find him too.'

'Are you wounded?'

'No,' answered the stag, 'but I want to join his herd in the shadow of the mountain. Since the Slave Herds were disbanded many of us have been travelling south to see him and they say he never turns a Herla away.'

The hind nodded.

'Do you think he is the one?' she asked suddenly in a whisper.

'I don't know,' said the stag. 'They say that he denies it. He won't have any of the Herla talk about it. Says his oaken fawn mark is no sign of anything. But there are many who don't believe him. What have you heard?'

The hind shrugged.

'All I really know is that he helps animals. And not just the Herla but all Lera. He can speak their language.'

'Yes, I've heard that too,' said the stag.

'Then he has power,' said the hind gravely.

'But even that he denies is anything very special,' said the stag, shaking his head, 'or so they say. He claims that all Lera can do it if they try.'

'But he can heal?' asked the hind hopefully.

'Oh yes,' answered the stag.

The hind was reassured.

'I tell you what,' said the stag suddenly, 'why don't we travel together? To be honest I've been a little lonely since I left my herd and four eyes are better than two. I heard wolves last night.'

The hind readily agreed and the two new companions set off through the heather. They chatted happily in the warming sunshine as they went and soon they were delighted with the pleasure of one another's company, for the day was uncommonly beautiful and since that dark night when Herne's Herd had fled the Standing Stones, a new spirit of freedom and hope had been stirring in the High Land.

Besides, their hearts were full of expectation for they were both on a strange pilgrimage.

'So, I wanted to know if you can help my chicks,' said the pheasant nervously. 'They say you can.'

She ruffled her feathers and looked up pleadingly at the deer standing above her. The stag was an eight-pointer, and though his two brow tines were slightly misshapen he was uncommonly pleased with the head, especially now he had come out of velvet.

'No, I'm afeared I can't,' answered the stag falteringly, stirring in the grass. 'It's not being me you want. You're seeking out for Rannoch. I saw him last on the west hill.'

The pheasant thanked the deer and flew off to find him. Haarg shook his head as the pheasant took off, for it was a relatively new sensation to be talking to a Lera like this. He wasn't very good at it but he was proud that he was one of the deer who was beginning to master it, though he found it much easier to do when he wasn't in antler.

To be in antler. Haarg marvelled at what had happened since his herd had left the red river and the stags' antlers had come. The herd was cured and the Slave Herds gone, and it was all thanks to Rannoch.

Rannoch and his friends had decided to join them after they had come down from the Standing Stones two years before. They had settled in the valley they now occupied, near the Great Mountain, and, as more and more Herla in the High Land had learnt of the overthrow of Herne's Herd and come down to see the strange newcomer with the fawn mark, their ranks had swollen to over two hundred red deer.

Haarg looked out across the herd now and nodded as he saw the stags away on the hill and below them in the wide bowl of the valley, the hinds grouped loosely together and set well apart. He spotted Liath among them and smiled to himself again. Since the skirmish above the river and the healing of his antlers, Liath treated him with a new respect. Well, perhaps that was only to be credited. He was an Outrider after all.

'An Outrider,' muttered Haarg to himself delightedly, 'an Outrider.'

Haarg stirred with satisfaction as he rolled the strange word around his tongue. In fact he still couldn't understand why Rannoch had refused the title. When they had discussed the future of the herd and Thistle had insisted on naming the Outriders, Rannoch had been strangely disinterested.

As Haarg thought of his friend a confusion entered his mind. Rannoch was nearly seven years old and his head had its full growth. He had the strong build of a royal and by rights he should have led the herd. He was expected to have mated too. But since his meeting with Herne's Herd just the opposite had happened. Rannoch had become very solitary, spending his time tending to the wounds of any Lera that asked. When Anlach had come the year before and even the friends had begun to argue over the hinds, Rannoch had shown no interest at all, but instead had gone away on his own to look for leaves and berries.

As the herd watched Rannoch helping and talking to the Lera and tending to the wounds among the stags and the hinds, they were all grateful for his strange powers and they knew that he was different. Yet it seemed to cause Rannoch himself nothing but pain. All of them knew better than to talk about the Prophecy that he had brought with him out of the Low Lands – except in private, for the habits of belief die hard and many among the Slave Herd still muttered of Herne's Hope.

What does it matter if he believes it or not? thought Haarg

to himself suddenly. We are free, aren't we? Maybe Herne has come already.

Haarg walked over to a single apple tree nearby and looked up at the delicious fruit hanging from its boughs. He stretched upwards with his mouth but couldn't reach, so he tilted his head and struck at an apple with his right antler. The top tine just caught it and the apple fell to the ground where Haarg picked it up in his lips and bit deep into the flesh. There was a satisfying crunch and a bubbling spurt of juice as the deer munched happily on the fruit.

Haarg suddenly caught a scent in the air and he turned to see a stag running towards him.

'Captain Tain,' he called with pleasure, and trotted over to meet him.

'Hello, Haarg,' said Tain cheerfully. 'I've just been over the eastern hills and several more Herla have come in. Anything to report?'

'Not really,' said Haarg. 'I saw Captain Bankfoot this morning and he says everything is well.'

'Good,' said Tain. He was a ten-pointer and he nodded his fine head of antlers. 'The hinds are a little restless, though. They can scent Anlach. The stags too are beginning to argue and they're moving in closer to the hinds.'

'Nothing abnormal, then.'

'No. Except this morning I was talking to a couple of black swans by the burn and they had news from the south,' said Tain.

Since he had first begun to understand Crak back on the Great Mountain, Tain of all the deer, apart from Rannoch of course, had become most skilled at talking to the Lera.

'Bad news?'

'Yes. The Lera there are terrified. They say something

terrible is happening in the Low Lands and it's because of
the Herla. Sgorr is on the move, Haarg.'

'Sgorr,' whispered Haarg, conjuring with the name.
'What's he like, Tain?'

'I was only a very young fawn then,' said Tain, shaking
his head, 'but if half the things they say about him are true,
he must be very terrible.'

'More terrible than Herne's Herd?' asked Haarg nervously.

'Who knows? But his cruelty cries out across the Low
Lands. Those stags who crossed the Great Glen last spring
and managed to avoid the Sgorrla, they were so frightened
they couldn't talk about it for moons. They say he even
tortures the Lera. I've heard some very dark tales.'

'Has Rannoch said anything else about it?' asked Haarg.
Tain paused and shook his head.

'You know how he is,' answered Tain a little sadly. 'I
think he just wants to live as a Herla and forget about Sgorr.
I can't really blame him,' added Tain. 'He's been through so
much.'

'Yes,' agreed Haarg, 'and we all have much to be grateful
to him for.'

The two captains began to graze in the evening and soon
the simple pleasure of munching on fresh grass and feeling the
late summer breeze on their backs had carried away all
unpleasant thoughts of Sgorr and the troubles of the Herla
in the Low Lands. Below them the hinds looked up and felt
comforted by the sight of the Outriders on the hills. Two
hinds were walking together now, talking quietly.

'Can you feel it, Willow?' said Peppa, looking around her
as they walked. 'Anlach's nearly here.'

'Yes,' replied Willow, 'the hinds know it's coming and I
saw two stags fighting yesterday over Selif.'

'It'll be good for the herd to have some new fawns.'

'Yes, Peppa, and good for you to join a harem. Several stags are interested in you, you know, and there's always Bankfoot. You know how he likes you.'

'But what about you, Willow?' said Peppa. 'It's time you thought about mating. We've been here two years now.'

Willow suddenly looked a little sad. Neither Willow nor Peppa had mated, though they were very old to have their first fawns. The herd was settling into a kind of normality but their strange journey had gravely disrupted the natural rhythms of their lives.

'Oh no, I don't think so,' answered Willow quietly.

'But you'll have to eventually. It was all you could do last Anlach to avoid it and you know how keen Thistle is. He'll be even more determined this year.'

'Thistle?' snorted Willow angrily. 'I'll never stand with Thistle. He's changed so much, Peppa. Grown so arrogant.'

'We've all changed, Willow. And I suppose it's only natural. Thistle's a royal now and even Bankfoot fought last year.'

Willow smiled at the thought of her old friend. Though they were nothing compared to Thistle's antlers, Bankfoot had five tines on each of his antler beams.

'A Captain of the Outriders,' she said proudly.

'I do miss him, Willow,' said Peppa suddenly. 'Bankfoot, I mean. I miss all of them. The hinds and the stags have grown so far apart.'

'Yes, but that's natural as well,' said Willow, 'though I miss them too.'

Peppa saw the look in Willow's eye.

'Perhaps he'll fight for you this Anlach,' she said softly.

Willow shook her head.

'No. He's so distant nowadays. Always up in the hills

tending to the Lera. He doesn't seem to care much about the doings of the herd. Why should he be any different this year? And last year it was so upsetting to watch him, Peppa. How he hated it when the stags began to fight for the hinds. I think it caused him a physical pain. He kept telling them to stop it. Saying that we should live in peace and friendship and that we hadn't learnt anything from Herne's Herd. He kept talking about wolves and things. And, you know, I think what happened up there among the Standing Stones deeply affected him, Peppa. Changed him in some way. Thistle is always saying so. He keeps jeering at him.'

'Don't,' said Peppa, 'it's too awful the way Thistle pushes him.'

'Yes,' agreed Willow, 'but in some strange way I think Thistle's disappointed with him. You know how set Thistle is in his ideas and he's determined there should be a Lord of the Herd. He thinks we'll all go to ruin if there isn't.'

'Thistle wants to be the lord himself, that's why. He's always showing off his antlers.'

'Part of him wants to be Lord of the Herd, Peppa, but I think part of him just wants Rannoch to fight for it. He tried to get him to fight again last Anlach, remember, though Rannoch wouldn't have anything to do with it. Just went off into the hills.'

Peppa shook her head again.

'You know,' said Willow in a whisper, 'I even asked him. Rannoch, I mean. I asked him to fight for me. But he wouldn't.'

Above them the evening star was already shining down on the herd. It shone down on the twins and Tain and Haarg on the hill, on Captain Bankfoot who was sitting in the heather enjoying a thick bush of delicious whortleberries and on Captain Thistle who was standing on the southern edge of the valley, ruminating as he gazed out into the distance. It shone down too on an old hind called Bracken who was lost in her own fearful thoughts near the burn, and on a royal stag with a white oak leaf on his brow who was up on the hill talking to a pheasant.

'They'll be fine,' said Rannoch to the pheasant in a gentle voice, 'as long as they get some fresh water to drink. Now I'm sorry, but there are others to tend to.'

'Thank you, Rannoch,' said the mother bird, rising suddenly into the air. 'If we can ever do anything in return—'

Her voice was interrupted by another from behind the stag.

'You never give yourself a rest, Rannoch.'

Rannoch swivelled round and smiled when he saw who it was.

'Birrmagnur,' he said with pleasure, 'it's good to see you.' Rannoch paused.

'But I hope nothing's wrong,' he added. 'You're not wounded, are you?'

'No, my friend,' answered the reindeer, 'though I could do with more of your company. I've hardly seen anything of you in two moons.'

'No,' said Rannoch, 'but there's so much to do. Especially with so many Herla coming from the north.'

'You have a great gift, Rannoch.'

'It's nothing,' answered Rannoch immediately. 'Just berries and leaves and listening to their needs. It doesn't come from me.'

The reindeer lifted his head to the breeze.

'From Hoern?' he said.

'Perhaps. But we all know instinctively what's good for us, Birrmagnur.'

The reindeer nodded. Since he had decided to stay with

the herd for a while he had thought long and hard about
Rannoch and the oak leaf on his head. He was worried
about his friend. Again and again he had heard Rannoch
telling them that the Prophecy was false and that all they
had to do was live as Herla. Yet he himself seemed to find it
so hard to live a normal life.

'You look tired, my friend,' he said quietly.

'I suppose I am. I've had some strange dreams lately.'

'Of Hoern?'

'No, about Sgorr. And a deer on a hill in the moonlight.
They frighten me, Birrmagnur.'

Birrmagnur grunted.

'Some more deer came over the Great Mountain fleeing
from the Sgorrla. The news is very dark.'

'I know,' said Rannoch sadly, 'and it's not just the Herla.
All the Lera are suffering too. Some of the things I've seen!
I wish I could do something to help them, but as long as
Sgorr has sealed the High Land at least we are safe.'

A strange look came into Birrmagnur's eyes.

'You know some of them still mutter about the Prophecy.
They think you will free the Low Lands. They say you should
fight Sgorr.'

'Fighting,' snorted Rannoch suddenly, and the passion in
his eyes surprised even Birrmagnur. 'Fight Sgorr, fight Thistle.
Is that all the Herla can think of?'

'It's probably because the stags are growing more restive
with Anlach coming again.'

'Anlach?' said Rannoch with a faraway look, as though
he was trying to remember something. It was already
growing dark around them.

'Yes, Rannoch. Don't you feel it?'

'Yes, I feel it,' answered Rannoch quietly, 'as much as

Thistle or Tain or any of the others. But I hate it, Birrmagnur.
It reminds me of Herne's Herd.'

'But Rannoch,' said Birrmagnur, 'don't you want to be an
Outrider? Don't you want mates and calves of your own?'

Rannoch looked down sadly over the herd. He was
thinking of Willow and he missed her desperately.

'I don't know, Birrmagnur,' he said, shaking his antlers.
'All I can think is that I don't want to become like them, like
Herne's Herd. They worshipped violence. And you know,
when Anlach comes it seems to do something to me. Sometimes I can't understand the Lera any more.'

'But isn't Anlach natural?'

'Birrmagnur,' said Rannoch suddenly, 'will you come with
me? I want to show you something.'

Rannoch turned and led the reindeer over the brow of the
hill. He ran straight through the long grass to a spot he had
visited many times before. It was a patch of once muddy
ground which had dried out with the summer, and now the
circle of earth was cracked and parched. Birrmagnur pulled
up with distaste. His nostrils were suddenly filled with a foul
scent that made him start in disgust as he looked down.

There, in the centre of the earth, were two skeletons. The
bones had been picked clean and had settled on the ground
opposite each other. Birrmagnur gasped as he saw, in between
the two opposing skulls, two pairs of antlers resting on the
ground. They were still locked together.

'It's Skein and Tannar,' said Rannoch sadly. 'Do you
remember them from the Slave Herd? It happened last year
during the rut. They must have locked antlers and not been
able to free themselves. They starved to death.'

'Hoern's breath,' said the reindeer, shaking his head sadly.

'Herne!' snorted Rannoch. 'Is this really Herne's way,
Birrmagnur? Is this what He asks of us? All this fighting.

There is so much pain and violence in the world. I think that
if Herne exists He must be terribly cruel. Crueller than Sgorr,
crueller even than man.'

The reindeer was silent for a while. He was deeply moved.

'I'm sorry, Rannoch,' he said at last. 'I wish I could help
you.'

The two friends fell silent as they walked back towards
the herd. The evening was bright with a half moon rising
and they were coming down the eastern slopes when they
saw Bankfoot running towards them. He looked frantic.

'Rannoch, Birrmagnur, thank Herne I've found you.
You've got to come quickly.'

'What is it, Bankfoot?' said Birrmagnur.

'H-h-herla,' said Bankfoot in his distress, for the Outrider
had almost lost his stutter and it only came back when he
got very excited. 'All stags. There must be over forty of them
coming up the valley.'

'More High Land incomers?' said Rannoch.

'No, Rannoch. They're from the south.'

'Sgorrla,' gasped Rannoch, and though he had just been
talking to Birrmagnur of his hatred of fighting and violence,
the instincts of the Outrider drove him and his two friends
straight towards them.

When they reached the newcomers they were reassured,
though, for the stags had bunched together in the middle of
the herd and they seemed to be talking calmly enough to the
deer who had gathered round them. Willow and Peppa were
there and Bracken too. Tain was running down from the hill
and Rannoch slowed as he caught sight of Thistle standing
before the newcomers.

'Are you with the Sgorrla?' he heard one of the deer
shouting to the stags.

'No,' answered a voice that sounded caught with pain

and exhaustion. 'We are Outriders. The last of the Outriders in the Low Lands.'

His words echoed round the herd.

As Rannoch came among the stags he saw in the darkness that they had been fighting. Some of them had wounds on their flanks and haunches and others had broken antlers. Their fur was thick with sweat and matted blood.

'It is two moons since they came on us,' the exhausted voice went on, 'Sgorr and his minions. There were hundreds of them. We managed to escape through the trees but they have taken our hinds and fawns. Colquhar is dead. The last vestige of freedom has vanished from the Low Lands.'

Now Rannoch began to recognize some of the stags from the Herd above the Loch and as he drew near the speaker he spotted Braan. Braan was nearly ten now and Rannoch could see from his heavy rump how much he had aged, but his antlers were still strong and he had the same pride about him.

'What can we do?' Rannoch heard Willow saying suddenly.

'Nothing for the moment. Sgorr has united all the herds. There were even roe and fallow deer among them. But we have come to seek your help.'

'Our help?'

'Yes. We are looking for the Marked One, the fawn that came amongst us. They say He never died but came into the High Land to free the Herla here. News of Him has spread across the south. They say He can heal and talk to the Lera. It's the Prophecy.'

The whole herd was listening intently.

'No, Braan,' said Rannoch suddenly, 'it is not the Prophecy.'

'Rannoch,' cried Braan delightedly, 'then you *are* alive.'

The wounded Outriders were looking at the white oak leaf.

'Yes, I'm alive.'

'Then you must help us. We'll rest and then lead the Outriders south.'

'What for?' said Rannoch quietly.

'What do you mean what for? To fight Sgorr, of course.'

'Fighting,' said Rannoch, shaking his head, 'always fighting. How many of you are there, Braan?'

'Forty-eight of us survived the battle.'

'Which with our Outriders – some of whose antlers are still as weak as rotten wood – makes perhaps two hundred stags. How many stags would you say Sgorr has?'

Braan paused. He could see what Rannoch was hinting at.

'I don't know,' he said quietly, hanging his antlers. 'He has brought all the herds together and the roe deer too.'

'Perhaps two or three thousand Herla – or maybe more?'

Braan nodded.

'And about eight or nine hundred stags,' said Rannoch. 'Well trained, used to fighting.'

The Outriders began to murmur discontentedly.

'But that doesn't matter,' cried Braan, suddenly brightening. 'The Prophecy. We'll have Herne on our side. We'll have you.'

The herd around them were beginning to nod excitedly.

'No, Braan,' cried Rannoch, 'you will not have me. Herla are not meant to fight. I was not born to fulfil some silly prophecy. I will stay here with my mother and teach the Herla a different way.'

'But the Outriders?' said Braan.

'You are welcome to stay with us,' said Rannoch simply, 'and we will tend to your wounds.'

'Tend to our wounds?' cried Braan in disgust. 'Hide here like old hinds while Sgorr enslaves the Herla and drives out the spirit of Herne? That's not the Outriders' way.'

'Have you forgotten,' said Rannoch coldly, 'that Colquhar served Sgorr? That when it suited your purpose your brave Outriders handed over Willow and my mother and my friends to the mercy of the Sgorrla? Shira and the others are still with him. If I could help you – and I can't – don't you think they'd be the first to suffer?'

'It lives in our memory, to the undying shame of every Outrider above the Loch,' said Braan bitterly. 'We betrayed you. But we were forced to. Colquhar convinced us that it was the only way that he could preserve the existence of the Outriders in the Low Lands. That is all he really lived for. But although he pretended to serve Sgorr, somewhere his heart was true. And he made a brave death.'

'I am glad to hear it,' said Rannoch with little feeling. 'Did Tharn make a brave death too?'

Braan hung his head again.

'So you won't help us,' he whispered.

'I'm sorry,' said Rannoch, and this time he meant it.

'Then we are lost.'

'No,' cried a voice angrily, 'if Rannoch won't help you, I will.'

Thistle came running through the centre of the stags and his eyes were blazing at Rannoch.

'You?' said Braan, looking up in surprise.

As Thistle drew up he turned his antlers to acknowledge Willow.

'If I can,' he said.

'But will the herd follow you?' asked Braan. 'You are not the lord.'

'Our herd has no lord,' said Thistle with disgust,

addressing all the deer, 'for it seems that it is no longer blood that flows through the veins of our Outriders but pond water.'

'Has no lord?' said Braan. 'But Rannoch—'

'Rannoch does not lead us any more,' said Thistle coldly. 'He prefers being the Lord of the Lera to being a real Herla.'

'Thistle,' said Rannoch quietly, 'you don't know what you are saying. You can't defeat Sgorr. He's too powerful. Would you lead the herd to certain death beyond the Great Mountain?'

'I would lead those who would follow to fight and perhaps die with honour,' cried Thistle, 'like Outriders. You'll come with me, won't you, Haarg? And you, Bankfoot and Tain?'

The two friends looked down in embarrassment.

'And Birrmagnur,' said Thistle, 'you'll help us, won't you?'

The reindeer said nothing.

'If this is your plan,' said Rannoch calmly, 'I oppose it.'

'At last,' cried Thistle, swinging round suddenly towards Rannoch. 'Then you'll fight me, Rannoch. To see who leads the herd? To see if Braan shall have our aid?'

Thistle bellowed. He ran straight up to Rannoch and as they came parallel the two deer seemed to be testing each other for just a moment, locked in an invisible conflict. Their antlers were of the same size and the battle would have been well matched. But Rannoch did nothing.

'So you won't fight me then?' said Thistle at last.

Rannoch hesitated. He was fighting with himself now.

'No, I won't fight you,' he answered quietly, and he turned away.

'But Rannoch,' cried Willow.

Rannoch gave Willow a pained look. He glanced at Bankfoot and Tain and at his frightened mother standing next to the reindeer. The whole herd was hanging on his words now as he stood among his friends and the wounded Outriders.

'Braan, I will be on the hill,' he said quietly, 'if you need me to help those wounds heal.'

But Braan didn't answer. He looked coldly back at the stag. Rannoch paused. He felt hundreds of expectant eyes boring into him, trained on the fawn mark.

'What is it you want of me?' he cried with sudden anguish.

Then Rannoch began to run, through the grass, up the hill.

As he went two Herla were entering the valley and they stopped apprehensively as they saw the herd gathered so closely together in the looming shadows. One was a stag and the other was a hind with a wound on her leg. They did not notice a third stag coming in from the south. His face was young and his eyes unusually bright and, unlike his kind, his forehead was unmarked.

20

The Island

Even the wisest man grows tense
With some sort of violence
Before he can accomplish fate,
Know his work or choose his mate.
W.B. Yeats, 'Under Ben Bulben'

Let this cup pass from me.
Matthew 26, 39

There was nothing that either Thistle or Braan could attempt until the Outriders' wounds were healed. Besides, they really had no idea what they were going to do against the might of Sgorr's Herla. However, in the suns that followed the confrontation with Rannoch, many in the herd began to look on Thistle with a new respect, and although nothing had really been settled, some even began to talk of him as the lord. Many a Larn in the coming days would find him and Braan standing apart from the rest of the herd, discussing the fate of the deer in the Low Lands.

Bankfoot and Tain looked on this with growing distress, for their loyalties had been torn in two. While their first loyalty was to Rannoch, they both felt that they had some duty to help Braan and the Outriders. Neither of them really acknowledged Thistle as Lord of the Herd, but they admired him for his courage and they were both desperately proud of their own positions as Outrider captains.

Birrmagnur found himself in an even more difficult position. He felt deeply for Braan and the others and what he had heard of Sgorr made the reindeer bitterly angry. But he was older and more circumspect than the rest and though he was as bemused as any about the Prophecy, he realized that Rannoch had been right about the impossible odds that faced them if they ventured south. He would argue this point forcefully and ask the deer why they couldn't be happy living in the protection of the Great Mountain, free from Sgorr, or even moving deeper into the High Land.

Of all the friends, though, Willow was the most badly affected. She loved Rannoch deeply but she couldn't fathom what had come over him now, and his denial of Anlach had already gravely disappointed her. She knew he was in pain but this sudden refusal to help the Outriders was the worst of all. As the suns passed Willow kept watching Thistle.

It was not that the whole herd was of one mind about what to do. Many of the hinds and even a sizeable number of the stags agreed with Rannoch and could see no hope of confronting Sgorr. Since the Slave Herds had been dissolved, they had only just begun to grow comfortable with their lives as free Herla, and many could see no reason to endanger that. The herd was split and while the Outriders, new and old, ranged the hills, others would look up to Rannoch talking to the Lera and tending to the sick, and nod to themselves.

There were many to attend to also after the battle above the loch. The Outriders' wounds were deep and many had grown infected. Rannoch set those deer who supported him to collecting leaves and making poultices to help their wounds heal. At first the Outriders resisted, but Rannoch's touch was so gentle and their needs so great, that they grudgingly submitted to his aid and were soon grateful for it. Not one who came from the south died of his wounds.

But now something happened that, for a brief time, subsumed not only thoughts of Sgorr or the Low Lands, but of the Prophecy too. Anlach arrived.

The stags began to fight for the hinds and soon the chill air was echoing with the bellow of rutting deer and the knock and clatter of jousting antlers. Heads were lowered in a conflict more primitive and consuming than any battle against Sgorr. Nature was stirring again in the deer's veins, turning them against one another, testing their strength and challenging them to prove themselves in the greatest battle of all; the battle for survival.

As Rannoch looked out on the rutting stags his heart was deeply troubled as it had been ever since that night among the Standing Stones. For his time with Herne's Herd had indeed had a deep effect on him and he was still wrestling to understand why.

He thought he had found an answer to his quest up there on the hill when he knew for certain that he was not Herne. He thought too that he had found a way of being free and living as a Herla. But as they had settled with the herd and tried to build a life, Rannoch had found that the violence that had so terrified him among Herne's Herd, that he had smelt on the jaws of the wolf and sensed in the fearful glen, dwelt in the heart of the Herla too. In his own heart.

He had sensed it first when he had been with the boy and his antlers had come. And he felt it now as the deer jousted and boxed and fought for the hinds. Somewhere in him, Rannoch too longed to test himself against the other deer, to fight for his own hinds and to make his stand. To fight for

Willow. Yet he was a healer, he knew that now, and he wanted to help things, not to harm them. And what he had told Birrmagnur about his power was true. When Anlach came and the blood rose in him, the ability to heal and to understand the Lera seemed to grow dim and fade.

Many times Rannoch would think of that and of the Prophecy and shake his head. So much of it seemed to be true, so much impossible. But deep inside, Rannoch was glad that his confusion meant that he could ignore those words that Blindweed had first mouthed to the calves. For with the years he had begun to think more and more of one line of the Prophecy that made him tremble: '*Sacrifice shall be his meaning.*'

He was thinking about the words now and all across the herd stags stood bellowing sentinel to the hinds that they had won in the rut when Birrmagnur came walking towards him through the grass. He looked grave.

'I've found you at last,' said the reindeer quietly as he arrived.

'I've been looking for berries and horse chestnuts,' began Rannoch, as cheerfully as he could.

'Rannoch,' interrupted Birrmagnur, 'the others asked me to find you and tell you. They're going away.'

'Who?'

'Thistle and the Outriders. They're going south.'

'They'll be destroyed,' said Rannoch quietly. 'Is that what they really want?'

'Rannoch, I'm going away as well,' said Birrmagnur, dropping his head.

'You, Birrmagnur? You're going with them?'

The reindeer shook his head.

'No, Rannoch, it's time I found my own kind again.'

'But why? Why don't you stay with us?'

Birrmagnur paused and chewed the air.

'What is it?' said Rannoch.

'It is not right, my friend,' said Birrmagnur, 'that Thistle is looked on as Lord of the Herd.'

'I will not fight him.'

'Nor Sgorr?'

'No. The Outriders can do nothing against Sgorr.'

Birrmagnur nodded.

'I'm sorry for you, Rannoch,' he said, gazing at the white oak leaf on Rannoch's brow, 'but there's other news. Willow has submitted to Thistle. She has joined his harem.'

Rannoch looked back at his old friend but he said nothing.

'They have not had time to mate, and now they are going south she will join him. Peppa too.'

'But they can't,' cried Rannoch with horror, 'not Willow and Peppa.'

'That's what they plan to do.'

'Thank you for telling me,' said Rannoch sadly.

'Rannoch,' cried Birrmagnur suddenly, 'you must choose. Choose to help them or not. Or fight Thistle for Willow. But you cannot continue to live like this.'

Rannoch was silent.

'Well,' said Birrmagnur, 'I will come and say goodbye again. First I must make my farewells among the herd.'

As Rannoch watched his friend walking away he felt desperately alone. He looked out across the hills and there in the distance he saw Thistle moving slowly down the slope. In the valley below the Outriders were waiting for him and by his side Rannoch recognized the companion of his youth, Willow.

'We're all here,' Thistle said as he reached the assembled deer. It was a ragged-looking bunch. 'How many are coming, Braan?'

'All forty-eight Outriders from the loch,' answered the stag, 'and with your thirty Herla, that makes about eighty.'

'If Rannoch had been with us we could have trebled that,' said Thistle bitterly. 'Another twenty stags came from the north last week. But the rest of the herd listens to him and they fear Sgorr.'

'It's a pity Haarg won't come,' said Braan. 'He could have added to our numbers too. But he says he can't leave Rannoch, not after everything he's done.'

Willow looked sadly at Thistle as they talked of Rannoch. But she knew now that her duty lay with her friends.

'I wish he would change his mind,' said Braan. 'Even if this prophecy isn't true, to have him with us would lift the Outriders' morale. If the Sgorrla heard of it, maybe we could persuade some of them to desert.'

'Our best plan is to try and get as close to Sgorr as possible,' said Thistle, 'like we discussed. Then if a group of us can infiltrate the herd and kill him . . .'

Braan nodded, though the thought of what lay ahead of them filled none of the deer with any confidence. Thistle saw the look in their eyes and he tried to raise their spirits.

'Captain Tain,' he said firmly, 'Captain Bankfoot. You will take ten Outriders and scout ahead as we travel. We must not be seen. It's vitally important.'

Bankfoot and Tain lifted their antlers.

'But have we time to say goodbye to him?' said Willow.

Thistle looked keenly at Willow.

'Yes,' he said at last, 'but you must hurry, we're leaving before Larn. Winter is almost here and if we don't beat it, we won't be able to cross the Great Mountain until the spring. Who knows what will have happened in the Low Lands by then?'

The friends looked at each other almost guiltily. None of

them could really believe that this was where their journey
with Rannoch was coming to an end.

'Willow,' said Thistle, 'you don't have to come, you know.
None of my other hinds want to. You can stay here with the
herd and be safe.'

Suddenly Willow's eyes blazed.

'Thistle,' she said frostily, 'you called me at Anlach and I
came. You are my lord now. Do you think I fear the danger?'

'And you, Peppa?' said Thistle.

'I'll stay with my sister,' said the hind, though she was
looking at Bankfoot.

When Willow found him, Rannoch was sitting on his own
in the grass, ruminating sadly. Peppa, Bankfoot and Tain
had already said their farewells and Rannoch looked deeply
distressed. Again he had tried to dissuade his friends from
going south, but it had been to no avail.

'Rannoch,' called the hind quietly as she walked up.

Rannoch turned his head immediately.

'Willow.'

'Rannoch, I have come to say—'

'I know,' interrupted Rannoch, getting to his feet. 'I
wish I could say something to—'

'You can't, Rannoch. I have decided. My duty lies with
my friends and . . . with Thistle.'

Rannoch smiled almost bitterly.

'He's a fine stag,' he said.

'He's brave,' said Willow coldly, looking intently at
Rannoch, 'and he has a good heart.'

Rannoch nodded.

'But you have a good heart too, Rannoch,' said Willow
suddenly, 'and you were brave. Once. I would have stood
with you. If . . . if only you . . .'

Rannoch winced, but he didn't answer the hind.

'Why don't you come with us, Rannoch? We'll fight Sgorr together.'

'You can't fight Sgorr like that,' answered Rannoch, 'and I'm tired of fighting.'

'But they need your help,' said Willow.

'The Lera need my help too.'

'The Lera. Are they more important to you than the Herla? And what of the Prophecy?'

'The Prophecy is a lie, Willow. I've told you.'

'I know, you're not a changeling. But can't you see, Rannoch? So many of them believe it. They need to believe it. At least it gives them hope. With you leading us, perhaps we would have a chance.'

'A chance to do what? To destroy our herd?'

'Our *herd*,' said Willow scornfully. 'You call it a herd? When the best Herla in it refuses to lead? When at Anlach he won't even . . .'

Willow caught back the words. Rannoch looked hard into the hind's brave and beautiful eyes and in their glitter he caught a hardness that came close to contempt. But again he said nothing.

'Then I was right,' said Willow at last, shaking her head.

'Right?'

'To accept Thistle. At least he acts like a stag.'

Now it was Rannoch's turn to grow angry.

'Then he can die like a stag too.'

Willow stared back at Rannoch. Her eyes were flaming.

'You're a coward, Rannoch,' she cried furiously, turning on her haunches, 'a coward.'

'Willow,' whispered Rannoch.

But the hind was gone.

As Willow, Thistle and the others left the herd that Larn,

a sudden bellow shook the air and they paused and looked
back at the hill. Rannoch was above them. The six tines on
each of his antlers scything the air, the red deer threw his
head back and let out another bellow that rose in the sky,
bitter and lonely and so full of pain that even the stags
around him, driven by the blinding needs of life, stopped to
listen. Then suddenly Rannoch turned and ran, as fast as he
could, away from the herd and into the rain that had begun
to sheet through the evening.

Rannoch ran through the night and didn't stop until
morning came, bleak and grey and with little welcome. His
thoughts had exhausted him and now he lay down and closed
his eyes, desperately trying to shut out the guilt that was
threatening to overwhelm him. When the dream came,
Rannoch murmured painfully in his sleep.

He was standing on the seashore and looking out towards
an island. He had never been here before but he recognized
the place and as he looked the water suddenly began to glow
and a voice was whispering in its currents.

'Rannoch,' it said, 'Rannoch, you have nearly crossed
over. But before you can fulfil the Prophecy, you must know.
Know the secret. Then you will be certain.'

Rannoch woke and shuddered. The morning had hardly
advanced but the troubled deer got to his feet and ran on. It
was Larn five suns later when Rannoch finally got back to
the herd and saw that only a few stags now patrolled the
hills. He paced restlessly towards the hinds. He was looking
for Bracken.

He found his mother at the bottom of the valley, sitting
on her own in the sodden grass. She looked older than he
remembered and Rannoch suddenly felt desperately sorry for
the poor hind. He had neglected her in the past two years,

while he spent so much time with the Lera and the sick, and he realized that he had not visited her in nearly a season.

'Mother,' he said quietly as he padded up.

'Rannoch,' said Bracken, 'Rannoch, is that you?'

'Yes, Mother, how are you?'

'Well enough,' whispered the hind uncertainly, 'and you, Rannoch?'

'Well enough too,' said Rannoch sadly, 'though Thistle has won Willow. They have gone south to fight Sgorr. I fear for them, Mother.'

Bracken stirred. She recognized the names but in her confused thoughts she could hardly recall who Thistle and Willow were.

'Mother,' Rannoch went on suddenly, 'will you tell me about my father? About Brechin? You've never really talked about him.'

The hind blinked back nervously at Rannoch.

'I want to know about him,' said Rannoch, 'all about him. He was an Outrider, wasn't he? I wish I'd met him, Mother. I wish he was here now. There are so many things I'd ask him. About being an Outrider, about the Herla.'

Rannoch had wandered a little away from Bracken now and his back was turned as he spoke. His voice broke into her thoughts, but suddenly the hind wasn't listening any more. Her dim senses had been roused by something stirring nearby in the trees, twenty branches away. In the corner of her eye she saw a young stag and he was watching Rannoch intently.

'I'm sure he could have advised me,' Rannoch went on as Bracken got to her feet, 'told me whether I should follow them. I can't let them face Sgorr alone.'

But Bracken couldn't hear Rannoch any more. The stag by the trees had dropped his antlers and, without a sound, he was running straight towards Rannoch. The old hind wanted to stamp, to cry out, but she found herself choked, paralysed with fear.

Suddenly Rannoch heard a strangulated bark. He turned just in time as he felt his mother's flanks bump against his own. Beyond her was a stag and Rannoch gasped as he saw its head lowered, its antlers burying themselves in Bracken's side where the hind had put her own body between him and his assailant.

'Mother!' cried Rannoch desperately.

The stag twisted and disengaged its head and Bracken fell forwards. Now there was nothing between the two of them and the stag lunged again. But the element of surprise was gone and in an instant Rannoch dropped his head and met the stag's antlers with his own. They locked and both their bodies shook like trees in a wind.

They disengaged again and Rannoch scythed his head left and right, but his antlers met nothing but thin air. On the ground beside him Bracken was beginning to kick.

'Mother!' gasped Rannoch, and suddenly a fury awoke in him.

He lunged towards the stag. Again they met and now their antlers were caught, the tendons in their legs straining for dominion, their muscles beading with sweat. For ages they pushed backwards and forwards, their heads lifting and falling, until at last Rannoch managed to disengage again and lash out with his tines. This time his trez tines connected and his assailant bellowed at the pain that had opened viciously in his throat. And suddenly the stag was running, running as fast as he could. For he was trained to attack and kill in stealth and was not used to fighting a deer of Rannoch's size except on his own terms. His mission had failed.

But he would never make it back to his master beyond the Great Mountain, for Rannoch's wound had been fatal.

'Mother,' cried Rannoch, running up to the hind who was lying in the grass now, 'Mother, what happened?'

'I don't know,' whispered Bracken, her breath pained and rasping. 'He came from the trees. He must have been sent to harm you.'

'To harm me?' said Rannoch. 'But who?'

'Sgorr,' whispered Bracken. 'Sgorr sent him.'

'Why now?'

'Rannoch, listen to me,' said Bracken suddenly, flexing in pain. 'There is little time and there is something I must tell you.'

Bracken's eyes were suddenly bright as though the shock of the attack had swept years of darkness from her clouded mind.

'What do you mean little time?' said Rannoch.

'I am dying, Rannoch. I can feel it. That stag's antler has pierced my heart.'

'No, Mother,' cried Rannoch, 'I will heal you.'

'No, Rannoch, not even you could do that.'

'But Mother . . .'

'I am not your mother, Rannoch.'

Rannoch stopped. He stared at Bracken in blank amazement.

'Not my moth—'

'No,' whispered Bracken, and as he listened it seemed she was telling him something he had known all along. 'You were changed, Rannoch, at birth.'

'Then who?' gasped Rannoch.

'Eloin. Eloin is your mother. The hind who said goodbye to you all those years ago. She was one of Captain Brechin's hinds. But that night when Drail and Sgorr killed your father on the hill—'

'Killed my father?'

'Yes, Rannoch, and destroyed the Outriders.'

'Sgorr,' whispered Rannoch, his voice trembling. 'And my dreams.'

'Yes. Sgorr was coming to kill you. And when Blindweed saw that mark he was afraid for you. So we switched you with my fawn who died. Changed you round.'

'Then it's true,' cried Rannoch, 'I *am* a changeling.'

'Yes, Rannoch, you are a changeling.'

'Then the Prophecy . . .'

'Oh Rannoch,' gasped Bracken bitterly, 'I'm sorry I didn't tell you sooner. But I wanted to protect you. There's some danger in this prophecy. Do you remember when you used to play as a young fawn and so hated to have the berries smeared across your head? For a long time I thought it couldn't be true but now . . . now . . .'

Bracken stopped talking. She could hardly talk any more. The fur on her flank was soaked in blood. Rannoch gazed at her in silence. He wanted the ground to swallow him up.

'But moth— Bracken, you should have told me,' said Rannoch bitterly.

'I know, Rannoch,' gasped the dying hind, 'but I didn't want anything to harm you. For I've loved you like a mother . . .'

Bracken winced again in agony.

Rannoch stepped forward and very gently he dipped his head towards the hind and licked her on the muzzle.

'I know,' he said tenderly, 'and the most wonderful mother . . .'

'Oh, Rannoch.'

Bracken's back legs were beginning to shake. Rannoch threw back his antlers in agony.

'So, Herne,' he cried angrily, 'you shall have your way. You don't want me to heal at all. You want me to fight.'

'Rannoch, what are you going to do?' asked the hind weakly.

'Do? I am going to follow Thistle and Willow and the Outriders into the Low Lands. I am going to save Eloin and the others, if I can. I am going to kill Sgorr and avenge my father.'

'But Rannoch,' said Bracken, 'what you said about Sgorr and the Herla, it's true. There are too many of them. What can you do?'

'I don't know. Raise the rest of the herd and send word through the High Land. They will come if I call, I'm sure of it. Then, who knows? Die well with the Outriders if need be. Isn't that what it says? *Sacrifice shall be his meaning*. Well, if it comes to that. For what must be must be.'

'Then you will follow them to your own death,' said Bracken sadly.

'Mother,' said Rannoch, 'don't worry about me. Lie still. First of all I must cure you.'

Bracken was staring up at Rannoch. She was growing delirious and she no longer knew what Rannoch was saying.

'Goodbye, Rannoch,' she whispered, 'goodbye. I hope you can forgive me.'

'Bracken,' cried Rannoch, 'wait. Don't leave me.'

But it was over. Bracken was dead.

'Herne,' cried Rannoch furiously, 'what have you done? Why have you done this to me?'

Rannoch bellowed and bellowed again and swung his antlers to and fro. In that moment his heart was consumed with anger, and as he thought of Sgorr and his father and

Willow, he felt the violence of Anlach rise and swell up inside him. But with the terrible anger that now burned in him came something he had never experienced before, a clarity. He suddenly realized that what he was feeling was different to the simple passions that stirred at Anlach or the violence that had been bred at the Stones. For at the thought of Sgorr and what he had done, his heart was filled by a desire not just for revenge, but for justice. Rannoch's course was set.

'Take them south, Haarg,' said Rannoch as they stood on the hilltop, 'as quickly as you can. I've sent word north too.'

Haarg nodded gravely. Around him stood nearly a hundred Outriders.

'But where are you going, Rannoch?' asked Haarg.

'West, Haarg. There's something I must find out before I meet Sgorr.'

'What?'

'It was something they told me when I was with Herne's Herd,' said Rannoch. 'I've never told any one else except Bankfoot. Something Sgorr did, long ago, for he came from that herd and they drove him out for it. Only the stag who witnessed it knew exactly what took place and the secret died with him. It's something Sgorr fears the Herla knowing. It happened on an island out to sea, to the west where man has raised his stones. Kaal told me where it is.'

'And you're going to find out what happened?'

'Yes. For if Sgorr so fears others knowing it, it is a grave weakness in him that can only help me when I finally . . . when I finally test this prophecy.'

Haarg looked keenly at Rannoch.

'Then it's true?'

'Yes, Haarg, it's true. But I still don't know where it will lead. Now you must hurry, my friend, if we are to do any good. You must stop the others reaching Sgorr first.'

As Rannoch ran west towards the sea, Haarg and the Outriders set off from the herd towards the Great Mountain. But as a wind began to blow across the High Land something else was stirring in the heather. There were voices travelling through the undergrowth. A strange whispering in the briers and across the moorland grasses. A call carried through the sky. Rannoch had summoned the Lera.

Rannoch's mind was filled with thoughts of Willow and his friends as he ran, for though he still had no real plan, he was desperate that he should be in time to help them. But something else clouded his mind. The threat of a sacrifice.

No matter, thought Rannoch now. If I must make a sacrifice then I shall and willingly. But first I must know what Sgorr's secret is.

Rannoch looked up at the heavens.

'Herne, you must guide me now,' he cried into the night, 'for I am doing your will, whatever that may be.'

The wind moaned around Rannoch's head but suddenly and strangely he felt less alone. On he ran towards the west.

On the fourth sun Rannoch's heart quickened as he scented the sea. The stones that Kaal had told him of reared in front of him, charred and blackened against the dull grey sky. But Rannoch paused fearfully, for everywhere he saw the signs of destruction. The men's stones had been broken down, the earth was burnt and scarred, and everywhere Rannoch saw human bodies. Their fawns, their hinds and their bucks lay dead on the bleeding earth, their heads broken, the strange shining sticks that Rannoch had seen at the hunt lying useless at their sides. Again Rannoch was reminded of Herne's Herd and the terrible mist in the fearful glen. He shuddered as he walked through the killing ground.

Rannoch walked on and suddenly the ground dropped steeply away, tumbling towards the sea that swept ahead of him. There it was, just as Kaal had described it to him. The island he had told him of lay in the far distance, swathed in cloud, but its three high, wooded peaks were unmistakable. Rannoch's heart sank. It looked so far away and the wind was beginning to lash the water into a fury. Rannoch had little experience of swimming and he remembered Bhreac and her death in the river.

'Sgorr did it,' said Rannoch to himself, 'and so shall I. With Herne's help.'

The deer tipped down the mountainside.

When he came to the shore he paused fearfully again and looked out to the distant island. To swim that far seemed impossible, and the water was growing fiercer and fiercer. Rannoch bellowed and plunged into the sea.

The icy water closed around his fur and filled his muzzle with salt as his head and antlers went under. His eyes began to sting and the stag kicked furiously, scrabbling with his hoofs on the sliding current. Up he bobbed and slowly he began to move forward in the sea, his head just above the water, his antlers licked with spume and spray. From the sky above it started to rain and Rannoch's ears were filled with the clamorous patter of rain on wave.

On he struggled and after a while he had left the land behind him. But the island seemed to grow no closer and further out Rannoch began to feel the tug of current and tide. His fur felt heavy too, like a great coat that dragged him down, for Rannoch had his winter pelt and the sea was making it heavier and heavier. The waves swelled, breaking over his face, and as he swallowed great gulps of salt water he gagged and spat and struggled to breathe.

With time, though, he realized that by waiting for the rise

of the wave and swimming less the water would bear him up and lift his head and antlers above the surface. Yet this made him slower and still the island seemed an impossible distance. Rannoch could feel the strength in his legs beginning to ebb away.

It seemed as though he had been swimming for ever. He felt sick from all the salt water he had swallowed and his eyes were in terrible pain. Rannoch was close to exhaustion and he could hardly hold his head up any more.

'Oh, Herne,' he gasped, 'Herne. Help me.'

Every movement was an agony and Rannoch's head began to swim.

'Herne, what do you really want of me?' gasped the deer. 'Is this the sacrifice foretold by the Prophecy? But if it is, what is it for? What is it all for?'

The deer's head was suddenly engulfed by sea water as a wave broke over him. He kicked and spluttered but there was no strength left in him. Down he went again.

'Herne,' he cried as his head rose to the surface once more and through the salty gauze of water he spied the island still lost in the distance, 'if you don't help me, then what of my friends? What of the Herla? Have you abandoned us?'

But Rannoch was lost. Down he went again and this time he had nothing to fight with. The sea closed over his antlers.

Rannoch felt something brush his side. Then something was underneath him too, bearing him up. Rannoch was lifted, up and out, so that it seemed as if he was riding on the water itself. He found himself thrust forward and suddenly he had the strength to swim again.

'Herne,' cried Rannoch, and as he did so he found he could breathe again.

Suddenly a head broke the surface in front of him. It was a seal.

'Rurl,' gasped Rannoch.

There were other seals with him, swimming by Rannoch's flanks and carrying him through the water.

'What are you doing here?' spluttered Rannoch.

'I could ask the same of you, Rannoch,' barked the seal. 'But now we must get you to the shore.'

So on Rannoch was carried, half swimming, half born up by the lithe bodies, towards the island and Sgorr's dark secret.

As Rannoch saw the sand in front of him and a great rock on the shore, his heart felt strong again and he tossed his antlers in the sea. The seals had dropped away from him now and with one last effort Rannoch kicked at the waves, found his legs touching sand and rose out of the water. As he did so Rurl splashed from the waves too, barking and flapping in the gull-driven day.

Rannoch shook himself furiously and looked down with infinite gratitude at the seal, lying there on the shore.

'Rurl,' he gasped, 'I don't know how to thank you. I thought I was lost.'

'No need to thank me, Rannoch,' said the seal. 'It's good to see you again after all these years. You've grown but that mark is just the same.'

Rannoch nodded.

'Yes,' he said quietly, 'and it means more to me now, I think. Though I still fear where it will lead.'

'The Prophecy?' said the seal.

'Yes, Rurl, I found out that I am a changeling, that—'

'It's all right, Rannoch, I know all about it,' said Rurl.

'You know?'

'Yes and about Herne's Herd.'

'But how?'

'The Lera, Rannoch. The Lera have been watching you

for longer than you think. Anyway, I spoke with an otter two suns ago and he told me about your mother and your plea to the Herla in the High Land. That you are going south again. But first he said you were making for the west coast. That's how I found you. We've been swimming up and down ever since.'

'Thank Herne you did.'

'So you found out what you wanted to know about Herne from Herne's Herd?' asked Rurl.

'Yes and no. At least I know that I am not Herne but that . . . that the Prophecy is true.'

Rurl nodded.

'Many things kept me from believing it. What you said about my power to speak to the Lera for one. You were right, Rurl, Tain can do it now and Haarg; many of the other Herla too.'

Rurl nodded once more.

'But something else is happening,' said Rurl quietly, 'that I hadn't expected from the land. They're all beginning to speak to each other, Rannoch. All the Lera.'

Rannoch looked at the seal and shivered. It was more than just the cold.

'Rannoch, there's one thing none of them could tell me, though,' said the seal, 'about man. Did Herne's Herd . . . did they have . . .?'

'Yes, Rurl,' said Rannoch quietly, 'they knew of man. They knew of man's violence, anyway. Sgorr knows of it too, for he came from Herne's Herd. But he has an even darker secret that is hidden here on this island.'

Rurl had heard rumours of a secret.

'So Sgorr knows about the bringer of violence?' he said gravely.

Rannoch paused thoughtfully.

'Perhaps you're right and men bring violence,' he said at last. 'Yes, yes they do. But there is something else about man . . .'

'They are bringing violence now,' said Rurl.

'What do you mean?'

'For ages now they have been coming from the north in their great carved trees, more than I have ever seen before. And when they reach the land they strike and kill.'

'The stones I saw . . .' said Rannoch. 'That's what happened.'

'Yes. They have been preying on the land right along the west.'

'What is happening?' whispered Rannoch.

'The seals say that their king from the north has landed once more on the islands to the west. That he would be lord there. But there are other men coming across the Great Land to meet him. The Lera whisper that the people of the Great Land want the islands back so that their land will be whole once more. There will be a fight.'

'Rurl,' Rannoch whispered. 'Rurl, the Prophecy. *To restore the Island Chain*. That's what it means.'

The two Lera looked at each other with wonder in their eyes as the wind licked off the sea. As the air howled and moaned it seemed as though Herne was speaking to them. But the sound made Rannoch feel neither strong nor brave.

'Rurl,' he said suddenly, 'I'm afraid.'

'Why, Rannoch?'

'It talks of sacrifice. The Prophecy. I wish . . .'

'What?'

'This burden would pass from me.'

The wind rose and swirled, shaking Rannoch's antlers and sending sand scurrying across the beach, whipping into the animals' eyes. Then it died again and the sound that filled their ears was the sound of the waves on the shore.

Rannoch dropped his head suddenly. He felt ashamed.

'No. That cannot be,' he said quietly. 'My friends are in danger and Sgorr has enslaved the Low Lands, just as Herne's Herd enslaved the High. Wherever it leads, I know I have to face him.'

'If I can help you, Rannoch, I will,' said Rurl quietly.

'You have already helped me, more than I could ever ask,' said the deer. 'But if you will stay with me now, perhaps we may face Sgorr's secret together.'

Rurl readily agreed and Rannoch led him over to the great rock that rose on the shore. Set back from it, where the sand turned to grass, they noticed more human stones. It was a dwelling like the one where Rannoch had been tended to by the boy, but the peat roof and the walls had fallen in and the place looked blackened and burnt. It was a crofter's cottage, but it had not been destroyed by the men from the north as the animals thought. For, years before, the humans that lived here had destroyed it themselves, in heartbreak and fury at the bitter tragedy that had befallen them.

As the seal watched, the deer began to dig with his hoofs, throwing the sand back around the great stone, searching for the thing that Sgorr had buried here. The thing that would give him a clue. It was a while before Rannoch found anything and then, suddenly, he felt something under his slots. It was hard and hollow. He began to dig more furiously in the wet sand until, at last, it was uncovered. The two Lera looked down in horror.

There, in the sand before them, lay Sgorr's terrible secret.

21

The Outriders Return

Ancestral voices prophesying war.
S.T. Coleridge, 'Kubla Khan'

Thistle needn't have been nervous about the coming winter, for it was unusually warm as the band of Outriders descended once more into the Low Lands. A strange haze hung over the land as they came down off the slopes of the Great Mountain, and there was a rare stillness in the air. The sky was cloudless, and though the approaching winter had tilted the warming sun away from the earth's axis, it felt more like summer than November. But it gave the deer little pleasure, for there was fear in their tread as they looked out into the day. They walked in lines of five abreast, a phalanx of tilting antlers. Thistle and Braan walked at the front, silently, their heads held high, matching each other's gait and pausing together to survey the land below them. If they expected to have to fight at any moment, now at least their fear was premature, for there was not a Sgorrla in sight.

Suddenly, from the south-west, a small band of stags came running towards them.

'Captain Bankfoot,' cried Thistle as they ran up, 'what signs?'

'It's odd,' answered Bankfoot, nodding his antlers in

salute, 'but there's no sign at all of the Sgorrla. We picked up a musk boundary a while back, but it was very old.'

'But I thought Sgorr was moving north,' said Braan, shaking his head.

'Have you noticed the stillness?' said Tain suddenly. He had been walking behind Braan.

'Yes, Captain,' answered Thistle, 'I think we all have.'

'It's eerie,' said Tain, 'like a kind of emptiness.'

'I think I know what it is,' said Willow. 'Have you noticed how few Lera there are around?'

Thistle nodded his head gravely.

'Yes, yes I have. It's as though they've all run away. Well, we must keep our eyes peeled and we should try to find some tree cover as soon as possible.'

The Outriders set off once more. Towards Larn they came to a small forest of beach and elm and, glad to get under-cover, they plunged into the gloom. Tain and Bankfoot were walking together now and both of them shared the same confused feelings of fear and excitement as the eighty Out-riders began to thread through the trees. When the friends had settled in the High Land they had both been proud to be styled Captain, but it was only now that they were begin-ning to know what it meant to be real Outriders. To look fear in the face and not shrink from it.

'Tain,' whispered Bankfoot in the twilight, 'is it all right to feel like I'm feeling? I mean, to be a little . . . nervous.'

Tain smiled.

'Of course it is, Captain,' he said. 'I feel the same.'

'Really?'

'Yes, and that's natural. Even Starbuck got frightened at times. Do you remember the story of Herne's hoof?'

Bankfoot nodded.

'It shows that the Herla should value their fear,' said Tain, 'for it keeps us wary and wariness keeps us alive.'

'What do you think Thistle's got in mind?' asked Bankfoot quietly.

'You heard what he said, about getting to Sgorr. But I think that's as far as it goes. I know Braan is determined to rescue their hinds, Herne willing.'

'Herne willing, indeed,' agreed Bankfoot as the two friends walked on.

'Tain,' said Bankfoot after a little while more, 'I wish Rannoch was with us. I feel better somehow when he's around.'

'I know, Bankfoot.' Tain nodded sadly. 'But we're on different journeys now. Rannoch made his choice and I can't blame him.'

'But if the Prophecy were true . . .'

'But it's not. It's just a story like all the stories about Starbuck. So we shall have to face Sgorr without his help and fight him like true Outriders.'

Bankfoot's spine tingled, but suddenly there was a bellow up ahead. One of the Outriders was rearing in the air and kicking his front legs in terror, as if boxing with some imaginary opponent. They both ran forward and saw that the stag was on the edge of a clearing. They gasped as they caught sight of the thing that had startled him.

There, in the darkening circle, strewn across the ground and hanging from the brittle branches, the deer saw Lera. They were all dead. There were stoats and mink, rabbits and field mice, two fox cubs lying on the earth and, hanging skewered on a nearby branch, an otter. The stench of death hung everywhere.

The Outriders trembled as they looked on at that ghastly scene.

'What's happened here?' cried Thistle furiously.

'Sgorr,' whispered Braan.

Amid the choking smell of decay, the deer caught the faint scent of their own kind hanging in the still air and they knew that the Sgorrla had been here.

'It's terrible,' cried Willow. 'What is he doing to the Great Land?'

'That must be why there are so few Lera about.' Bankfoot trembled. 'They're fleeing from Sgorr.'

'Sgorr,' said Thistle bitterly. 'I didn't think even he could sink to this. Well, let him come, for when I meet him he shall pay dearly for this.'

The Outriders pushed on through the trees but a fury was beginning to stir in their hearts.

They rested that night on the edge of the forest and the next morning plunged into a deeply wooded valley that was cut by a series of burns. Strangely for the season, the streams were very low and it was clear to the Outriders that there had been little rain in many suns. A sense of foreboding was growing in their hearts as they travelled with no sign of other Lera about them. Tain was banking the far hill when he stopped and called to the others.

'Quiet,' he hissed, as loudly as he dared.

The Outriders, some of whom had been discussing the scene in the forest, others who had been trying to raise their spirits by talking of the old days, fell silent immediately, as a true Outrider was trained to do. Thistle and Willow were the first to reach Tain, who was gazing down into the next valley. Wider than the one they had just crossed, it was even more heavily wooded on its far slopes and through the middle of it, going south-west, ran an earth track.

'Sgorr?' whispered Thistle, as the other Outriders began to crest the hill too.

Tain shook his antlers.

'No. Listen.'

The deer began to listen intently and soon they caught on the wind the sound that Tain had first heard as he crested the hill. It was coming from the far north-western end of the valley, where the track swung past a wood and out of sight. It rose on the wind like a kind of wild howling that made the air throb. Bankfoot suddenly realized that he had heard it somewhere before.

'The noise we heard in the glen,' he whispered.

Now something was added to the strange sound that put the Outriders instantly on edge. A scent was coming towards them down the valley and they all knew what it was. The Outriders began to back away in the grass.

'Lie down,' ordered Thistle.

They did as they were told and it wasn't long before they saw them. The noise rose even higher and suddenly, from the corner of the trees, they began to appear, marching straight down the track. Some were on foot, moving in columns, and others came on horseback.

'The shining sticks,' gasped Willow, 'like the ones I saw with Rannoch in the gully.'

Most of them did have swords at their sides, while others carried long wooden poles with strange-coloured leaves tied to their tops that fluttered and flapped in the breeze. The deer looked at each other nervously. Soon the valley was filled with their sounds, for there were hundreds and hundreds of them.

'Where are they going?' whispered Peppa.

'I don't know, but something's happening,' answered Willow gravely.

The deer stirred fearfully in the grass as the men came on. But if they were frightened of being seen they needn't have worried, for the humans were far below and their heads and hearts were too full of thoughts of warfare and the enemy that was waiting for them to the west, to give any time for the hunt. The men marched through the valley and the deer watched until the last of them disappeared down the track and their strange sounds were lost on the wind.

The Outriders did not notice that from the far hill, as they watched the humans, a group of stags was watching them too.

They crossed the valley themselves and entered the far trees. Now Captain Bankfoot and Braan took some Outriders to scout ahead, while the others wove on slowly through the forest. It was nearly dark when Willow strayed into a thick clump of undergrowth and started, for something was moving beneath her. Suddenly, a little black-brown head with tiny shining eyes popped up from the dying leaves, and when it saw Willow its eyes blazed with hatred and the creature spat violently before springing away. It dashed forward but as it did so, it caught sight of five Outriders ahead of it. Again it spat and swivelled round.

Its escape was barred both to the left and right by the surrounding Herla and the creature seemed to be in a frenzy of terror. As the Outriders spotted it, it spat again and bared its teeth, and then, in a single bound, it leapt for a nearby tree. It landed on the trunk and, in a flash, shot upwards and along the lower branch.

Tain and Thistle were below it now and they raised their antlers to the little animal.

'You there,' called Tain, 'don't be frightened.'

The creature glared at Tain and hissed.

'Don't be frightened, I said. We don't want to hurt you.'

Once more the creature spat but then it stared at their brows and a little of the anger went out of its eyes.

'You're not marked?' it said suddenly.

'I'm sorry?' answered Tain with surprise.

'Your foreheads. They're not branded like the Sgorrla's.'

Tain blinked. He was thinking of Rannoch.

'No.'

'What do you want?' said the creature.

'Nothing,' answered Tain.

'Deer always want something,' said the creature bitterly. 'Usually to hurt and kill the Lera.'

'We don't want to hurt you,' answered Tain quietly. 'It's other Herla that do that.'

'So you are not with *him*,' whispered the creature. 'Sgorr.'

'No, we are not with Sgorr.'

The little animal seemed to relax considerably. Willow and Peppa had come up now and the rest of the Outriders – those that had come from the loch – were pressing in too, fascinated by the sight of Tain talking to a Lera.

'Who are you?' asked Tain.

'I'm called Sek. I'm a pine marten,' answered the creature. 'I came up here to hide.'

'From Sgorr?'

Sek nodded sadly.

'But who are you if you're not with Sgorr,' he said suddenly, 'and what are you doing here?'

'We're Outriders,' answered Tain. 'We've come to find Sgorr.'

'Find Sgorr?' whispered the creature, sucking in his breath. 'But Lera flee Sgorr. Why would you want to find him?'

'To kill him,' answered Tain simply.

The pine marten cocked his head and his little eyes glinted excitedly.

'Kill him? Then it's true, what the Lera are whispering.'

'What's true?'

'The Prophecy.'

Tain looked at Willow with amazement.

'They say He's coming. To avenge us all. For many suns there has been talk of nothing else in the Low Lands. He's the Lera's only hope.'

Again Tain looked at Willow and both of them felt a quickening in their hearts.

'Do you know where Sgorr is?' asked Tain.

'Oh yes. He's very close. If you . . .'

As the pine marten began to explain, the Outriders from the loch stirred expectantly. They could not understand what the creature was saying, but they could see from Tain's expression that something very important was being discussed.

'What is it, Captain Tain?' one asked eagerly, when the creature had finished.

Tain shook his head gravely and the Outriders pressed in to listen.

'Sgorr. He's just two suns away, to the south, with the Great Herd. They have settled around a small lake. There are over three thousand of them. From the sounds of it Sgorr has the Sgorrla in constant training. He sends them out every day and they practise their viciousness . . .'

Tain's voice had dropped to a whisper. He looked sadly at his friends.

'They practise their viciousness on the Lera. That's what happened in the clearing. The animals round here are terrified. Some even believe that Sgorr wants to exterminate them all.'

The Outriders shuddered.

'Then we must strike quickly,' said Thistle suddenly, 'for all our sakes.'

'It's going to be hard,' said Tain. 'We'll have to get through the Sgorrla for a start. And then it seems he's guarded day and night.'

'But we will have the element of surprise,' said Thistle. 'Sgorr is not expecting anything, least of all an attack right at the heart of his power base. If we can just infiltrate the herd.'

'No,' said Tain suddenly, 'it's not possible. The Sgorrla are all marked. They'll recognize us.'

Thistle looked very grave.

'Well, we'll have to try. Use the cover of night to cloak us. Travel in stealth. Use the instincts of the Outrider to find a way through.'

The others nodded but with that they heard a noise up ahead. Something was approaching fast through the trees. The Outriders readied, but before Thistle could issue any orders, Braan came crashing through the branches. He was followed by the three Outriders who had gone scouting ahead with him and Bankfoot.

'Bankfoot,' he cried as soon as he saw Thistle, 'they've got Bankfoot.'

'Who? Who has?' said Thistle.

'The Sgorrla,' panted Braan. 'They took us by surprise. We'd come to the top of a small hill and Bankfoot told us to wait while he ran down to spy the land, but as soon as he got to the bottom they came from the trees. There must have been twenty of them. There was nothing we could do.'

'Then we must rescue him,' said Tain.

'They're moving fast,' said Braan. 'They'll probably be back with Sgorr before we can catch up with them.'

'But we've got to try.'

'Did they see you, Braan?' asked Thistle suddenly.

'No,' answered Braan, 'we were shielded by a copse.'

'Then they still don't know we're here,' said Thistle gravely.

'Well, they'll know soon enough,' cried Tain, already preparing to set off.

'Wait, Tain,' said Thistle, 'you musn't be so hasty. Our greatest hope now is the element of surprise and they still don't know we're here. But if we go blundering into camp to rescue Bankfoot, it could ruin everything. Think, Tain. The Sgorrla are all marked, as you said.'

Tain paused.

'But we've got to do something. I'll steal in at night.'

'Yes, it's possible,' said Thistle, 'but we must be careful. I wish I'd known about their brands sooner, because there's not one of us who could get into Sgorr's camp easily without being spotted. And as for getting past the Sgorrla . . .'

'Yes, there is.'

Thistle swung round to find Willow standing behind him. Peppa was next to her. He blinked with surprise at the hinds.

'We could go,' said Willow calmly, 'Peppa and me. Their hinds are not marked. We could get into the camp.'

'No, Willow,' said Thistle immediately, 'I won't hear of it.'

'Why not?' said Willow. 'What notice will the Sgorrla take of two hinds moving through three thousand deer? At the least we can find out where they're holding Bankfoot, at best try to rescue him. Besides, somebody needs to find out about Sgorr.'

Again Thistle shook his head.

'No, Willow, I'm not putting you in danger.'

'Then why did you let us come?' snorted Willow. 'To tend to your wounds perhaps, or watch you die? No, Thistle, we came to help you fight Sgorr and though we have no antlers

and may just be hinds, our eyes and ears are as good as
yours and I hope our courage is as great.'

Thistle looked at Willow's fine face and bold eyes and
was silent.

'Besides,' said Willow, 'there's something else I want to
do. If I can get into their camp, I want to try and find Fern.'

Both Tain and Thistle felt a tightening in the gut, for they
had hardly dared think of their mothers.

'But Willow . . .' said Thistle.

'It's settled then,' said the hind. 'Braan, can you show us
where they captured Bankfoot? We'll pick up their tracks
and follow them straight into camp.'

Thistle could see the determination on Willow's face and
he realized it was pointless arguing with the hind.

'Very well, Willow,' he relented at last, 'then listen to me.
If you can get into camp you must do as I say. Find out
where they're keeping Bankfoot and anything you can about
Sgorr, then get away again. We'll need to arrange a meeting
point. Tain, ask Sek if he knows the country round here.'

Tain nodded and turned to the pine marten.

'But Willow,' Thistle went on, 'you must promise me not
to try anything foolish.'

Willow looked back at Thistle and smiled, but the hind
nodded.

'Sek says he knows a good spot where we can wait,' said
Tain. 'He says there's a corrie about a quarter of a sun from
Sgorr. There's plenty of water.'

'Very well,' said Willow, 'we'll meet you there. Sek can
tell us how to find you. Now we must hurry. Braan, show
us where you lost Bankfoot.'

Willow spent a few moments talking to the pine marten
and then, nodding gravely, she took her farewell of Thistle

and Tain. She and Peppa turned with Braan and ran off into the evening.

The Outriders watched them go, tilting their antlers gravely among the trees. They all felt deeply proud of the hinds.

Sgorr lowered his head and took in a great gulp of water through his thin lips, then, looking around the lake at the massed deer stretching around him as far as his eye could see, he sighed with a grim satisfaction.

Rannoch was probably dead by now, he thought, and the Great Herd was ready to go north. The Sgorrla were at the very peak of their training and the Lera's daily suffering kept them in constant trim. He had drawn them all back from the Great Glen to prepare for the trek north and to help with the 'Cleansing'. Sgorr smiled as he thought of the orders he had given to exterminate the Lera in the Low Lands. It took him back to all those years ago, to that day when the wolf had taken his eye.

They'll pay, he thought to himself. They'll all pay. Across the Low Lands and the High.

As Sgorr thought of the High Land, again his mind turned to Rannoch.

'The Healer. Isn't that what they called him?' snorted Sgorr to himself with disgust. 'So, has my assassin done his work or is Rannoch just hiding in the heather?'

Sgorr suddenly felt strangely unnerved. He often thought of Rannoch now and even dreamt of him. Although he told himself there was no truth in the Prophecy, those thoughts always made him nervous. Somewhere deep inside him there was a nagging doubt, some secret voice that kept whispering to the stag of the future. Sgorr kept the voices at bay, but still the doubts came.

He looked up. Narl was coming towards him. When Narl got to the Sgorrla bodyguard he stopped and exchanged a few words with them, then came straight up to his master.

'Lord,' he said.

'The reports?'

'More word of the humans,' answered Narl. 'They are everywhere. They all seem to be travelling west.'

Sgorr nodded.

'When I was a fawn, Narl,' he muttered, 'they always used to tell me that when man is on the move the Herla should beware.'

'What do you think they are doing?'

'Who knows. But they are carrying their shining sticks, so there will be bloodshed. That's what man is best at. That's what I have learnt from him.'

Narl suddenly looked keenly at his master. This was the first time he had ever heard Sgorr talk of man in this way.

'You, Lord?' he whispered. 'You have knowledge of man?'

Normally such an impertinent question would have brought an angry response, but Sgorr was feeling indulgent.

'Yes, Narl. A greater knowledge than that fool of a fawn.'

Narl waited as his master took another drink from the loch.

'But I never knew,' said Narl quietly when Sgorr raised his head again.

'You never needed to know. These things are best kept secret from the Herla.'

Narl stirred. He felt deeply privileged to be allowed into his master's confidence.

'But don't you fear them, Lord? Humans, I mean.'

'Fear is for weaklings, Narl. Haven't I taught you that yet? No, I don't fear man. I admire him. For man is the thinker and has power over the Lera, which he gains with his mind and his reason. Man too is the bringer of violence and violence gives victory, if you know how to use it.'

Now Narl shifted uncomfortably. Though Narl was no stranger to violence, to talk of man in this way sounded like a kind of sacrilege.

'How does man tell us about violence, Sgorr?'

Sgorr noticed the use of his name with irritation, but he let it pass.

'Man shows us how to master and direct it. There is violence in all things, Narl, but most creatures are slaves to it, as Herne's Herd were slaves to their mad belief. But man is no one's slave and so can use his violence as he wills. No, Narl, far from fearing man I would have the Herla be like him.'

Narl looked at his master in amazement and he suddenly felt a shiver run down his spine.

'Be like him?' he gasped.

'Yes, and we have made a start. For soon we will be marching to the High Land and then, let the Lera really beware, when Sgorr is on the move.'

With that there was a pained bellow and both Sgorr and Narl looked out across the lake. In the distance they could see a group of Sgorrling gathered around the water. The deer were shouting and taking turns to run at a Herla. It was a stag.

'Go on, kick the old fool, spike him,' cried one pricket, as another launched himself forward. When he neared the stag, the pricket turned and kicked at him with his back legs. The stag swung round and lashed out with his antlers, but missed the pricket altogether and bellowed in fury and frustration.

'That's how the Sgorrling treat traitors,' sneered the young deer.

'Go on, kick him again,' cried the deer that had spoken first. 'Kick him hard. Make Colquhar suffer.'

A third pricket ran forward to kick the stag and again Colquhar swung round and missed. He lifted his head sadly and barked in pain. But there was little he could do against the Sgorrling. Colquhar couldn't see them; he was blind.

Beyond the stag, across the wide plain, hundreds and hundreds of hinds, kept closely guarded and regimented by the Sgorrla, were grazing in the unnaturally warm day. Normally so many hinds together would have set up a great clamour as they discussed the life of the herd, or their favourite stags, or the journey that was facing them, but now a strange stillness hung over them, as though they were frightened to speak or had lost interest in the world around them.

But amongst them, when the Sgorrla weren't watching, some of the hinds would drift together and, looking about nervously, snatch a few moments of greedy conversation. Five of them had come together now and, pretending all the while to graze, they were whispering to each other. Two of them were from the home herd and three from the loch.

'When are we going north?' whispered one.

'Who knows,' said another. 'When Sgorr decrees it.'

'Then those Sgorrla filth might stop throwing their weight around the herd,' said a third who was from the loch.

'Shhhh,' whispered the first hind, 'you don't know what you're saying.'

The hind looked about her.

'Yes I do. I hate them and Sgorr.'

The others blinked at her fearfully.

'I don't know why you put up with it,' the hind went on.

'But what can we do?' said the first hind. 'Sgorr's power is absolute.'

'But there are many among the stags who have grown to hate him,' said a fourth hind. 'I've heard them talking. When they dare.'

'And it's more than their life's worth. Sgorr had ten of them killed last week. The inner Sgorrla never stop hunting down traitors. No. Nothing can challenge Sgorr now.'

'I put my faith in Him,' said the last hind quietly. She was also from the loch.

'Who?'

'The One in the north.'

The hinds fell silent.

'He will sacrifice himself to free us all,' whispered the hind. 'That is what He was born for.'

'Don't talk like that,' said one of the hinds from the home herd. 'If the Sgorrla overheard you—'

'No,' interrupted the second hind, 'I've heard about him too. Teela was talking about it only the other day. You know Tecla – she stood with Rack last Anlach, before he was killed. The rumours say He's coming to fulfil the Prophecy and free us all, to restore Herne's law. That He was born here amongst us and fled long ago.'

'What's that?' came a voice behind them. The hinds started but when they turned it wasn't Sgorrla they saw but another hind.

They all recognized the old hind for she was famous in the herd, but they were surprised to see her amongst them now. Sgorr kept her at his side perpetually, but in the past suns Sgorr had been busy with thoughts of the march north and Eloin had persuaded him to allow her to wander for a little while every sun, down through the herd. She had just been to see Shira and Canisp, and was walking back when she overheard part of their conversation.

'Nothing,' answered the hind that had been speaking, dropping her eyes guiltily.

'Come, my dear,' said Eloin, 'I know you were saying something.'

The hinds looked uncertainly at one another.

'Please don't tell Sgorr,' said the first hind. 'If you do we wouldn't . . .'

'Don't worry,' said Eloin gently, 'I will tell Sgorr nothing, nothing at all. I promise.'

The hind from the loch, who had first spoken of the Prophecy, looked into Eloin's face. The fur round her muzzle was grey and she seemed terribly tired.

'He's coming,' she said, 'to free us all and fulfil the Prophecy. Herne is coming.'

'Ah,' said Eloin sadly, 'I thought that's what you were saying.'

'Have you heard of it too?' said the hind. 'Do you know of the Prophecy?'

'Oh yes, I know of it.' Eloin smiled.

'But do you think it's true?'

'Go on believing it, my dear, if it gives you hope,' said Eloin quietly, and she turned and walked slowly away.

As she went, Eloin shook her head. Poor things, she thought to herself sadly. If they only knew that Rannoch is dead. But they need something to believe in. It can do them no harm.

As Eloin thought now of Rannoch, she felt that familiar anguish in her heart. With the years, the pain of loss and grieving had hardly grown any fainter. She could still picture Rannoch in her mind's eye. His little face blinking up at her in the night. It was too cruel. Her beautiful fawn, torn to shreds by dogs.

Rannoch was gone and Brechin was gone. Blindweed too.

Only Shira and Canisp remained as a fragile link to her past. She had told them both the truth about Rannoch and the night by the stream. Many times in the past suns she had asked them to recount the story of their journey to the loch and dwelt lovingly on their descriptions of Rannoch as he began to grow. But the stories had always ended in the same way. In the pained silence of the hinds as she asked them about that day in the gully.

Eloin looked out across the lake and spotted Sgorr with Narl. The hatred she felt for him swelled in her stomach as she watched ten Sgorrla rushing towards them. They were escorting a single stag.

'Lord Sgorr,' cried one of the Sgorrla, rushing ahead.

'What is it now?' snapped Sgorr, furious at being interrupted.

'To the north,' panted the stag, 'a sun away. Herla stags.'

Narl looked at his master.

'Well?' said Sgorr.

'They came off the Great Mountain,' said the stag nervously. 'They're Outriders.'

'Outriders? Are you certain?'

'None of their heads were marked like the Sgorrla's.'

'None of them? Are you absolutely positive?' said Sgorr quietly. The stag was surprised by the urgency of Sgorr's question.

'Yes, Lord.'

'You didn't see one among them,' said Sgorr, 'with a white mark on his head, like a leaf?'

'No. I'm sure of it,' said the Sgorrla. 'We watched them for a sun. We'd been shadowing the humans as they travelled west.'

Sgorr nodded to himself. He was pleased.

'How many of them are there?' he asked.

'Eighty and there are two hinds with them. They're coming towards us.'

'Well, well,' said Sgorr, 'eighty Outriders and a couple of hinds come to face a thousand stags. They're certainly brave, I'll give them that.'

'Lord Sgorr,' said the Sgorrla, looking back towards his companions, 'we captured one of them.'

'Bring him,' said Narl immediately.

The Sgorrla called to the others and the stag they had been escorting was pushed forward. His face was badly bruised and there were cuts along his sides.

'*You*,' said the leader as soon as he saw Bankfoot.

Bankfoot glared furiously at Sgorr as the leader eyed his antlers.

'You've grown, I see.'

Bankfoot said nothing.

'So tell me, what are you doing here? Why are there Outriders with you?'

Again Bankfoot was silent.

'Come now, you must want something. Did Rannoch send you?'

Bankfoot's eyes flickered, for he was amazed that Sgorr knew Rannoch was alive. But as soon as he had been captured by the Sgorrla, Bankfoot had determined that silence was his only course of action.

'Still dumb,' snorted Sgorr. 'No matter. Your master is probably dead by now and the Sgorrla will soon loosen your tongue. Take him up to the big sycamore and guard him carefully until I have time to come.'

The Sgorrla moved in around Bankfoot.

'And don't think of trying to escape,' said Sgorr. 'You may have succeeded once but to do so again would cost dearly, as it did those two hinds that day.'

Bankfoot swung his head up.

'What do you mean?' he whispered.

'They paid with their lives,' said Sgorr. 'What were their names, Narl?'

'Alyth . . . Alyth and Fern.'

'Ah yes.'

'You killed them?' gasped Bankfoot, his legs beginning to shake.

'No,' said Sgorr, smiling, 'you killed them. And if you try anything there are always the other two. Shira and Canisp.'

Bankfoot felt the shock of his mother's name like a physical blow.

'Take him away,' cried Sgorr.

'And what shall we do about the others, Lord Sgorr?' said the lead Sgorrla.

'Do?' said Sgorr, as though surprised that he should have to do anything at all.

'Yes, Lord.'

'Let me face them,' cried Narl suddenly stepping forward. 'I'll take some of the Sgorrla. If they're coming from the north they'll have to pass by the corrie to get to us. I can trap them there.'

Sgorr thought for a while.

'Very good,' he said at last. 'Eighty shouldn't be too difficult to handle. Take a hundred and fifty of the Sgorrla and a contingent of the fallow deer as well. It's time they got their antlers wet and we can sacrifice a few of them to soften the Outriders up a bit before you move in for the kill.'

'You heard the lord,' said Narl immediately, addressing the Sgorrla. 'Get them ready and choose some of the fallow. Fifty should do it.'

The Sgorrla nodded and marched Bankfoot off through the grass.

'Well, Narl,' said Sgorr cheerfully when the Sgorrla had gone, 'this is a surprise.'

'Do you think He sent them?' asked Narl.

'While he hides himself up in the north?' said Sgorr. 'It's possible, but I prefer to think that our assassin wasn't trained in vain. Well, we shall find out more when I've had time to question the prisoner. But just in case he tries anything, bring those two hinds to me and double the guard around them and Eloin.'

Narl dipped his antlers.

'If anyone tries to get to them, Narl, to rescue them, you have your orders. Kill them all.'

'Eloin too?' said Narl.

'All of them.'

Again Narl bowed.

'When you have removed the Outriders,' said Sgorr, 'send word and then stay where you are. It's time the Great Herd was on the move – this pasture is quite grazed out. I'll meet you by the corrie. And Narl, be sure to keep one or two of them alive, won't you? I want to question them too.'

'Very good, Lord Sgorr,' said Narl proudly, and he turned and ran to join the Sgorrla.

Sgorr stirred thoughtfully and looked out across the Great Herd. The rows and rows of antlers stood out like a winter wood. Sgorr's heart swelled.

'Herne,' he whispered 'if you weren't just a fairy story I'd call you down from the skies to witness this. Those fools in the High Land worshipped you as the Lord of Violence. But you aren't, are you, Herne? Not even man is the Lord of Violence. I, Sgorr, am the Lord of Violence.'

Again Sgorr's eye ranged across the mighty herd and suddenly he began to laugh.

'Eighty Outriders. Is that all you throw at me, Rannoch?'

He paused and sucked in the warm air. At that moment Sgorr felt quite invincible.

22

The Corrie

I know a trick worth two of that.
William Shakespeare, 'Henry IV, Part One'

The Outriders were moving swiftly now and Thistle kept scanning the terrain restlessly as they ran, looking for the spot Sek had told them about, the place where they had agreed to wait for Willow and Peppa. They were coming off a high mountain, close to late afternoon, and the weather was even warmer than it had been the sun before, so the deer's spirits were cheered a little by thoughts of long, hot summers in the Low Lands.

'It's so hot,' muttered Braan, 'for this time of year.'

Tain, who was walking beside him, looked up at the sun before the glare made him turn away his eyes again.

The Herla had no words to understand what was happening to the sun now. Tain thought of Herne but his comprehension could not carry him to the truth of it. For, hundreds of thousands of miles above them, the sun, which at the dawn of the earth itself had stirred dead matter into life, was blistering and bubbling, spots of fire bursting at its edges, sending out swords of flame miles high to cut the natural rhythm of the seasons. As the deer looked up, it was almost as if the world itself was about to change.

The track the deer were following wound steeply down the mountainside, which was sparsely wooded with sudden outcrops of scrubby trees, interspersed with rocks and great boulders. Lips of stone and rock overhangs provided beetling vantage points over the land beneath. Below them, as they moved south, they could see a wide plain that stretched out from the base of the mountain they were on towards the undulating hills beyond. To the east was a forest and to the west another steep mountain, with a small river at the base of its foothills.

The path they were on tipped suddenly downwards and as the deer got closer to the mountain's base they saw the small lake at its bottom, feeding a stream that snaked away into the distance towards the far river. The water was a deep blue-green and the banks of the lake were strewn with rocks and rubble that time had torn away from the hill and cast about its feet. The lake was set well back, in a kind of natural hollow, and the black mountain walls rose almost sheer around it. The sides of the mountain stretched far away beyond the lake on either side, forming a kind of pass straight ahead of them, no more than two trees across, opening out to the plain beyond.

'The corrie,' whispered Thistle.

As they came to the water, their hoofs skittered on the scree slopes, dislodging slate and rock, and the still air in the corrie began to echo with their sounds. Tain and Braan were the first to drink from the little lake, and they found the water sweet and refreshing. Soon the others were collecting around it too, stirring the surface with their thirsty lips.

But Thistle looked up all the while and shook his head as his eyes ranged nervously around the place.

'Is anything wrong?' asked Tain.

'Yes, Captain,' he answered gravely, 'it gives plenty of

cover and the water's sweet, but if we were ever caught here we wouldn't stand a chance.'

Tain looked keenly at Thistle.

'Perhaps we should go back up the mountain. Height will give us an advantage and plenty of warning. Herne willing.'

'No,' said Thistle, 'this is where we've agreed to meet Willow and this is where we must wait. I only hope they hurry.'

As Thistle was talking to Tain, Willow and Peppa were gazing down in horror at the Great Herd. They had followed the Sgorrla's tracks right to the herd's edge and now the twins paused by a large rock as they wondered what to do. Larn was approaching and Willow decided they should stay where they were until darkness, and then try and steal among the deer. So they both sat down to ruminate quietly, looking out nervously at the rows and rows of grazing stags.

It was well after Larn when they slipped off the hillside. They felt fear welling up in their stomachs as they approached and came among them, but the deer were too preoccupied with thoughts of the Great Trek, and they hardly noticed the twins in the darkness.

'We should get among the hinds,' whispered Willow as they went. 'Try and find out more about Sgorr, if we can, and if any of them have seen Bankfoot.'

Peppa nodded to her sister.

On they went and as they passed the rows of red deer, and the fallow and roe deer too, they felt the unnatural quietness of the place. A group of Sgorrla passed close by, but the twins dropped their heads to graze, and because they had drifted close to a clutch of hinds, it looked as if they were part of the group and the Sgorrla moved off.

They pressed on, and at last, near the lake, they found

themselves in the very centre of the Great Herd, with hinds all around them. Again they pretended to graze in the darkness, but as they did so, they came close to a small band of hinds talking urgently together.

'Prophecy or no prophecy,' one hind was whispering gravely, 'that's what I heard and I believe it.'

Willow began to move closer.

'But he was from our herd,' said another hind, 'and he had an oak leaf on his head.'

'Yes,' said the first hind, 'but he died. Years ago. They say he was torn apart by wolves.'

Willow's ears came up and she looked over to Peppa.

'Then there's no hope,' said another hind.

'There's always hope. Even some of the stags— Hey, you there. What are you doing?'

The hind that had done the most talking had spotted the twins. Willow realized there was nothing for it but to try and bluff it out. She lifted her head and trotted straight over to the hinds. Peppa took her lead and followed her sister as calmly as she could.

'Well, what are you doing there?' asked the hind again.

'Nothing,' answered Willow calmly. 'We were just grazing.'

'Why aren't you with your own?' said the hind. 'You know it's forbidden to wander after Larn.'

'I know,' lied Willow, and then she thought of what the hinds had being saying about hope and the Prophecy. Willow decided to take a risk.

'But it's good to break the Sgorrla's rules now and then, isn't it?' she whispered.

The hind looked at Willow suspiciously.

'Are you sure . . .' she asked coldly, 'that you're not spies?'

Peppa winced but the hind never saw it.

'Spies?' answered Willow calmly. 'If you think I'd spy for Sgorrla scum, then perhaps you and I should take a walk and discuss it properly.'

The hind looked hard at Willow and she didn't like the fire that flickered in her eyes.

'All right,' she said, 'no need to get excited. If you can talk so openly about the Sgorrla then you're free to graze near us.'

Willow nodded.

'Tell me,' she said, 'where does Sgorr rest these days?'

'Still over by the great oak,' said another hind. 'Why?'

'No reason. Except that one day I should like to tell him what I really think of him.'

'And it would be your last day,' said the hind, smiling, 'if you could get anywhere near him.'

'What do you mean?'

'You know they never let anyone through. He's guarded day and night by at least twenty Sgorrla, even when he travels through the herd. They even have a guard around Eloin.'

Willow looked up.

'Eloin?' she said.

'That's right.'

'Poor Eloin,' said Willow. 'They say her only friends are those four hinds that returned from the loch.'

'Two, you mean,' said the hind looking oddly at Willow. 'What's your name? I've never seen you around here before.'

'Er, no . . .' stammered Willow. 'My sister and I . . . we only came in seven suns ago.'

'Then how do you know of Eloin?' asked the hind carefully.

'Oh, the others are always talking of her and her friends.'

The hind looked over at Peppa and when she saw her she looked back at Willow and pawed the ground.

'You're twins,' she said with surprise. 'The spitting image.'

'That's right,' said Willow.

'It's odd I haven't seen you around before. You stand out enough.'

'We like to keep ourselves to ourselves,' said Willow quickly. 'Not all the hinds feel as we do about Sgorr.'

Her words seemed to reassure the hind.

'No, no indeed,' she muttered in the dark, 'and if I were you I wouldn't talk so openly about it. But you'll soon learn.'

'Eloin's friends,' said Willow, ignoring the warning. 'Now what are they called again?'

'Shira and Canisp.'

'That's right,' said Willow casually but feeling a sudden weakness in her legs. 'Shira and Canisp. I'd like to meet them one day.'

'No chance of that.'

'Why not?'

'They always used to keep them separate, under constant guard. Then, this morning when they brought that prisoner in, they put them both with Eloin.'

Both Willow's and Peppa's heads had come up and they were listening intently.

'Of course,' said Willow, 'the prisoner. Where are they keeping him?'

'You do ask a lot of questions,' said the hind, growing suspicious again. 'Over there, by that sycamore.'

'Ah yes,' said Willow, her eyes glinting. 'Well, we'd better be getting back.'

The hind shrugged but as Willow and Peppa set off in the direction of the sycamore, Willow suddenly turned and called to her.

'But he didn't die, you know.'

'Who?' said the startled hind.

'The one with the fawn mark, the one who fled from the herd. He's still alive. I've seen him myself.'

All the little group had heard it and as the twins vanished into the night, the hinds looked at each other in amazement.

'That was close,' whispered Peppa as they ran. 'I thought for a moment we were lost.'

'I know,' said Willow. 'But did you hear?'

'Mother?' said Peppa.

'Yes, and Alyth. What can have happened to them?'

'Perhaps they escaped when we did,' said Peppa. 'Alyth never really wanted to come back.'

'No,' agreed Willow, but her heart was deeply troubled.

As the twins went on through the darkness, a breeze came up and they noticed that a mist was settling around the herd, drifting in wisps across the grass. It grew thicker as they neared a great sycamore tree, set apart from the edge of a wood, and they stopped as they spotted a group of Sgorrla guards through the fog. There were five of them, four ruminating in a semicircle near the tree, and one on his own, patrolling up and down. Nearby a stag was asleep in the grass.

Although they were still a good way off and it was quite dark, Peppa recognized him immediately and winced as she saw the cuts and bruises on his side and face.

'Bankfoot,' she gasped.

'Hush, Peppa, they'll hear us,' said Willow. 'We must try to think of something.'

Peppa looked hard at her sister.

'But Willow, you know what Thistle said. We've found out where they're keeping him and something of Sgorr too. Shouldn't we—'

'We're here now,' said Willow, smiling, 'so it's our duty to try and rescue him.'

Peppa's eyes opened wider but she didn't argue, for she was suddenly desperate for Bankfoot. So, in the darkness, the twins backed into the trees at the edge of the wood by a large clump of bushes and began to whisper together. After a while they had formed a sort of plan. It was a terrible risk and the hinds stared at each other fearfully when they hit on it.

'We'll have to trust to darkness and the fog to work it,' said Willow, dropping her muzzle and scooping up some earth and dried bracken. When she lifted her head again she stepped closer and rubbed her nose across Peppa's ear, obscuring the black fur.

'That's better,' she said when she had finished. 'Now not even Herne could tell us apart. If we get separated, we'll meet by the rock.'

'Right.' Peppa nodded. 'Who'll go first?'

'I will,' said Willow.

'No, sister,' said Peppa suddenly.

Before Willow could argue, Peppa had turned and sprung off towards the Sgorrla. Willow waited nervously for a while and then followed her sister into the fog.

Peppa ran straight ahead through the mist, her muzzle raised and her tail twitching. When she was about a tree away she started to graze as she drifted closer and closer towards the lone guard patrolling, while the other guards talked quietly in the night. The guard didn't see her at first but after a while he heard a sound and looked up, his eyes trying to pierce the deepening mist.

'Who's there?' he said.

Peppa didn't answer.

At first the guard thought he must have been mistaken

but then a gust of wind cleared the fog for an instant and he clearly saw Peppa standing there, staring back at him.

'You there. Hind,' he called gruffly. 'What are you doing here?'

Again Peppa said nothing and waited as the swirling cloud closed around her once more. As soon as the fog came in again she leapt to the right, so when the breeze cleared the spot where she had been standing, she seemed to have vanished. The guard blinked and shook his head, for he was tired and his eyes were sore. But then another gust revealed Peppa again, still standing and watching him, but off to the right.

'Hey, you,' he said. 'You know you're not allowed around here.'

Peppa tilted her head quizzically and then whispered in a strange voice, 'Don't be afraid. I won't hurt you.'

The guard was almost too startled to answer.

'Hurt me?' he said in amazement. 'A hind hurt a Sgorrla guard?'

'Not just any hind,' answered Peppa as gravely as she could.

'What do you mean?' said the guard. 'Who are you? What do you want?'

'Herne sent me,' said Peppa, and just as she did so another bank of fog rolled in around her. This time she jumped to the left and skirted a little way around the guard.

'Stand still,' said the guard angrily. 'You know it is forbidden to mention Herne.'

'Forbidden?' whispered Peppa through the mist. 'Who could forbid it?'

'Lord Sgorr,' said the guard. 'And when I—'

'Peace,' said Peppa. 'Herne has a message for you. He wants you to know—'

'Silence,' said the guard even more furiously. 'What nonsense are you talking?'

'Don't you believe in me?' whispered Peppa. 'In Herne?'

Again the fog closed in on Peppa and she darted round the guard. This time she didn't wait for him to address her before speaking.

'Here I am,' she whispered, 'all around you.'

'Stand still, I say,' snorted the guard, swinging round. 'Stop playing games.'

Peppa's face was clearly visible again and she held the guard's gaze coldly.

'Games?' she answered. 'This is no game. The Sgorrla's cruelty is no game. Why are you torturing me?'

The guard was about to lunge at Peppa when she backed into the fog.

'Hey, come back,' he said, but just as he spoke another voice came through the night, right behind him. When the guard turned he was amazed to see Peppa's face, or what he thought was Peppa's face, still gazing at him through the fog. It was impossible that the hind could have run round him so fast.

'I am still here,' said Willow, imitating Peppa's voice as best she could.

'But . . . how . . .' stammered the guard, as Willow backed into the fog herself and vanished.

'Because Herne is all around you,' said Peppa from behind the guard, 'in the mist, in the trees, in your dreams and worst nightmares.'

Again the guard turned and there was the hind, back in the spot where she had been speaking before. The guard could hardly believe his eyes. He stamped the ground and shook his head. He thought he was dreaming. The fog had once more swathed Peppa in mystery as she whispered through the night.

'Fear me . . .'

' . . . For I come when you least expect it,' Willow went on, reappearing to the left of the guard. He was really shaken by now and kept swinging back and forth as the twins played their game of voices.

'I need some sleep,' muttered the guard to himself, and Willow and Peppa fell silent.

'Hey, Praal, what's up,' said another deer suddenly through the darkness. 'I thought I heard voices.'

It was the guard's commander, who had been ruminating by the Sycamore earlier and had brought another Sgorrla with him to check up on the patrol.

'Nothing, sir,' answered Praal, still bewildered by the twins' trick.

'What do you mean, nothing? You were talking to someone.'

The guard started to stammer.

'There was a hind over there . . . or at least over there . . . but . . .'

'What's wrong with you, Praal?' said the commander angrily. 'Make sense.'

'She said she was Herne,' whispered the guard in a voice that was beginning to tremble, 'and that she was everywhere.'

The commander peered into the fog but could see nothing. Yet something about the night and the eerie cloud unsettled him, for they were all nervous with the coming trek and their own night's work with Bankfoot had filled their hearts with darkness.

'Rubbish,' he barked. 'There's no one out there at all.'

'She came from there,' said the guard, 'but in an instant she was behind me again.'

'Praal, have you lost your wits?' snapped the commander. 'You'll pay for this in the morning.'

'You must not punish him for telling the truth,' came a still, calm voice out of the fog. The commander looked up and now he caught sight of Peppa too.

'Who are you?' he cried as she backed away.

'Herne,' said Willow from the right, emerging from the fog for just a moment.

The commander looked at Praal in amazement.

'Catch her,' he shouted.

'Which way, sir?' said Praal.

'Over here,' cried Peppa.

'No, here,' shouted Willow.

The three stags hesitated, looking left and right, and then they leapt forward, towards the spot where Willow's voice had come from. They plunged into the mist and as they did so they caught sight of the hind's silhouette racing for the trees.

Willow ran as fast as she could and as soon as she entered the forest she ducked into the bushes where the twins had been talking earlier and froze, her breath hovering on the night air. The guards had been too startled by the sudden apparition to be thinking clearly and they ran on blindly in the darkness, blundering straight past Willow as they did so. The hind waited for just a few moments and then crept out and made for the sycamore.

'Peppa, is that you?' she whispered through the fog as she caught sight of a shape in front of her.

'Yes.'

'They're falling for it,' said Willow.

'Thank Herne.'

The mist was thinning again now and the twins could see the two remaining guards by the tree and Bankfoot still

sleeping on the ground. The guards had heard the commotion
and were looking around warily.

'But there's no time,' said Willow. 'The others will give
up soon enough.'

'Then we must hurry,' said Peppa, and she sprang
forward. Willow gasped as her sister ran straight up to the
guard on the right. He swung round as he saw her coming
out of the mist and barked a warning at her but, quick as
lighting, Peppa turned and gave him an angry kick before
springing away again, back into the fog.

The guard paused in astonishment and then looked from
Bankfoot, who was still sleeping, to his comrade.

'Watch him,' he grunted to the other guard and he leapt
after the hind.

The last remaining guard was now close to Bankfoot,
gazing around in confusion as Willow stepped out of the fog
a good way away from where Peppa had vanished.

'What the . . .?' said the guard in amazement.

'Ghosts,' cried Willow, loud enough to wake Bankfoot
from his painful sleep. When he opened his eyes and caught
sight of Willow, Bankfoot was almost as amazed as the
guard, but he lost no time.

'Stand there,' cried the guard to Willow, dropping his
antlers threateningly as she approached.

'You can do nothing to a ghost,' cried Willow as she
walked up to him.

'I'll give you a gouging,' said the guard.

He never noticed Bankfoot behind him. He felt it first in
his back right-hand leg. The brow tine went straight into his
haunch and the guard suddenly bellowed in pain. But as he
swung round, Bankfoot struck again, this time at his hoofs,
and he was knocked clean off balance. As he fell, Willow
turned and lashed out furiously with her hind legs. The blow

struck the Sgorrla straight in the face and he was thrown sideways.

'Come on, Bankfoot,' she cried.

The hind was already running and Bankfoot didn't argue. Tired and injured as he was, he raced after her into the mist. The guard on the ground was too dazed and confused to even know what was happening.

They ran and ran, along the edge of the wood, and now night and the fog came to their rescue for none of the herd spotted them. After a while they rose up the hill and Willow caught sight of the rock where she had agreed to meet Peppa if they got separated.

'We'll wait here, Bankfoot,' she panted as they came to a halt. 'I hope to Herne she got away.'

They weren't long in waiting. They soon heard a deer coming towards them through the darkness. It was Peppa and she was alone.

'Thank Herne,' cried Willow delightedly.

'I had the devil of a time getting rid of that soft-foot,' said Peppa, smiling at Bankfoot.

The sisters stared at each other and suddenly they both burst out laughing.

'If it's that easy,' said Peppa, beaming, 'maybe there's some hope after all.'

'Come on, then,' said Willow when they had calmed down a little. 'We'd better get back to Thistle. They'll be waiting and we've seen enough here. We've even got a little surprise for them,' she added, smiling at Bankfoot. 'I only wish we'd been able to find out about Fern.'

As she said it Peppa saw the look on Bankfoot's face.

'Bankfoot, what is it?' she asked. 'What's wrong?'

Bankfoot dropped his eyes.

'Bankfoot, you know something, don't you?'

Bankfoot gazed helplessly at the twins.

'I'm sorry,' he whispered, 'but they died. Fern and Alyth together, on the v-v-very day of our escape.'

Willow and Peppa stood side by side and lowered their heads. Their joy and exhilaration at rescuing Bankfoot had turned to despair. When Willow raised her eyes to Bankfoot again, they were burning with anger.

'Come then,' she said. 'The quicker we get back to the others, the quicker we'll have our revenge.'

'How far away are they?' said Bankfoot quietly.

'Not too far,' answered Willow. 'They're waiting for us at the corrie.'

'The corrie?' cried Bankfoot in horror. 'But that's where the Sgorrla are going now.'

'Then they know about the others?' gasped Willow.

'Yes, they saw us all on the hill. Before they captured me.'

'How many are there?'

'Over a hundred and fifty. Fallow deer too.'

'Then we can still beat them there,' cried Willow. 'But there's no time to lose.'

As Thistle looked out over the little lake in the sunlight, he pawed the earth restlessly. The night had been fitful and the day's wait even worse, for as Thistle examined the terrain he had grown more and more unhappy with the meeting place. He was frantically worried about Willow too and kept scolding himself for ever having let the twins go.

Thistle suddenly started. Bits of slate and rock were skittering down the side of the mountain. As Thistle and the others looked up they could see nothing above them. But now Tain cried out. Stags were coming straight towards them through the pass.

'Quick,' cried Thistle, but as he said it one of the Outriders bellowed. He was looking up at the mountain again. On the slopes above them antlers were appearing everywhere. Hundreds of them.

'Hurry,' shouted Thistle, his voice reverberating through the corrie. 'Form up.'

They didn't need to be told twice. The eighty stags came together in the stone hollow, their backs to the lake, one group turned to the walls of the mountain, and the other, led by Thistle, facing towards the pass.

'What do we do?' cried Tain frantically.

'Fight,' answered Thistle. 'But let them come to us. If they charge, you and Braan take a corps of Outriders right and left of them. Hit them from the sides.'

Braan and Tain nodded and turned their antlers to face the oncoming stags. They noticed for the first time now that the fifty deer coming towards them were fallow, and the sight of them, so much smaller than themselves, raised their spirits a little. But instead of charging, the fallow deer stopped just beyond the entrance to the corrie. They seemed to be waiting.

A silence had descended and suddenly a stag was calling out from the mountain above them.

'Outriders,' cried the lone Sgorrla, gazing down coldly, 'you are surrounded. There's no escape.'

'What do you want with us?' shouted Thistle angrily.

'Nothing but your servitude,' cried the stag, 'or your lives. But first I want to know if He is among you. The one with the mark.'

'Rannoch,' whispered Tain.

'Who dares ask?' cried Thistle, stamping the ground and bucking his head.

'My name is Narl. But I demand to know in the name of Lord Sgorr.'

'You can tell your master,' cried Thistle contemptuously, 'that He is not with us, but that the Outriders have returned to the Low Lands to free the Herla from Sgorr's tyranny. To restore Herne's law.'

'Herne's law,' snorted Narl. 'There is no Herne. There is only Sgorr.'

Narl suddenly stopped. He had spied something below him.

'So,' he called down the mountainside, 'Braan, you are here too? With some of your traitors, I see. Aren't you a little too old for such foolishness?'

Braan snorted and stamped.

'Come down here, Narl,' he shouted angrily, 'and I will show you how I can fight.'

Narl smiled. He wouldn't have dreamed of doing anything of the kind.

'Braan,' he answered, 'the privilege of age and power is that others can do the fighting for you, if you know how to rule. Tharn never understood that. Outriders never could. Colquhar had more chance of doing so but he chose to follow the dumb instincts of the Herla. Which is why he lives, reviled by the Great Herd and as blind as his own beliefs.'

Braan looked up in amazement and his eyes flashed with anger.

'Lives?' he gasped.

'But enough,' Narl went on. 'It is time.'

Narl suddenly bellowed and dropped his antlers, and on cue some of the Sgorrla on the slopes around him began to descend towards the Outriders. Several of the Outriders ran up to meet them but now there came a bark from the pass. Part of the group of fallow deer were charging towards them too.

Seeing them, Thistle cried, 'Come on.'

Thistle, Tain, Braan and about twenty other Outriders raced forward to meet them. Braan and Tain split left and right as they went and suddenly the corrie was filled with the clatter of antlers and the bark of fighting stags. But the fight stopped again almost as soon at it had started. Tain was rushing into the fray and he had just gouged one deer with his bez tine when he suddenly realized that the fallow deer were fleeing from them, back to the pass.

'After them,' he cried delightedly to the others, and was about to rush after them when Thistle called him back.

'Tain, Captain Tain, come back,' he ordered. 'That's just what they want you to do.'

Tain pulled up and Thistle led them back to the lake where the Outriders were holding off the stags. They were surprised to see how few of the Sgorrla had ventured down the mountain. But it was soon clear why, for now the fallow deer were attacking again. The Sgorrla on the mountainside had no intention of engaging properly but instead were pressurizing the Outriders' flanks, drawing off as many stags as they could from the main body of Outriders, while the fallow deer charged in.

But each time the fallow charged they would fight only briefly and then turn and run back towards the pass. Tain and Braan led Outriders to meet each sally and soon their antlers were red with blood and several of the fallow deer lay dead on the edge of the pass.

'This isn't hard,' cried Tain as he returned from yet another engagement. His leg was bleeding where a palm antler had caught him unawares, but none of the other Outriders were seriously hurt and Tain was delighted that his first real test as an Outrider was proving him worthy. But Thistle looked back at him gravely, for it was the fifth time the fallow deer had struck and Thistle suddenly realized what Narl was doing. He was slowly sapping the Outriders' strength.

Again the fallow deer came on. They seemed to have no thought for their own welfare and soon more and soon more of them lay dying in the grass. Braan had noticed how terrified their eyes looked. But Thistle could see that the Outriders were tiring. Braan and Tain looked quite exhausted with their efforts. It was growing dark in the corrie too, the evening draining the colour from the lake and turning the Outriders to shadows among the broken stones. But still they fought on as the stars pricked through the sky.

'Do you think we can hold them?' cried Braan as he and Thistle met once again by the water.

Thistle pawed the earth.

'The fallow deer are easy enough,' answered Thistle, 'though they've tired us out. That's what Narl wants. When he sends in the Sgorrla, who knows what will happen. Our best bet is to make a run for it. We wouldn't have a chance on the mountain but if we could break through the pass there's a chance for us.'

But as he said it there was a bellow from above them. They looked round and realized that the Sgorrla on the mountainside were disengaging.

There was still enough light to see to the pass and Braan shuddered as he realized that the fallow deer too were drawing back. Then, through the middle of the pass and the bleeding ranks of fallow deer, pushing and shoving them as they came, they saw the Sgorrla. A hundred of them. Advancing in lines and swaying their antlers. They looked strong and fresh. The Outriders tilted their antlers nervously.

'Come on,' cried a stag suddenly. 'Which of the Outriders will be first into battle?'

It was Tain.

'I fight with Captain Tain,' cried Braan, running up to him.

Thistle was with them in an instant.

'We must try and break through the middle,' cried Thistle desperately.

Thistle could see that the Sgorrla had stopped now and were waiting in their neat lines. Forty of them had come ahead of the others and were stamping the ground.

'It looks like they're going to attack in groups, like the fallow,' said Thistle. 'Well, first we must test their strength. We'll split into two. Braan and I will lead one party and Tain another. It doesn't matter which attacks first.'

'I'll go,' said Tain immediately.

'Very well. Test them as the fallow tested us,' said Thistle. 'And Tain. When I call, pull out immediately.'

Tain nodded gravely and with forty Outriders at his back he led them forward. Thistle and Braan watched as their friend approached the pass. When they were a tree's length away the front Sgorrla suddenly leapt towards them and the Outriders charged. Their bucking antlers locked and their bodies crashed together. The two groups became one.

Thistle's heart beat furiously as he caught sight of Tain and then lost sight of him once again in the mêlée. But as he looked on, it was clear that the Sgorrla were far too strong for the exhausted Outriders.

'No,' he cried as he saw an Outrider fall. Then another and another.

'Call them back,' cried Braan.

Thistle rushed forward. The stag began to bellow furiously but if he had even heard him there was little Tain could do, for the Sgorrla were clearly overpowering them.

'We've got to help them,' cried Braan.

'Come on then,' shouted Thistle.

The second group of Outriders rushed forward, but as they did so they heard a great bellow from among the fighting stags and one of them rose up furiously on his back legs.

'Pull out,' cried the deer.

It was Tain.

The others had heard him and the Outriders were disengaging, kicking furiously with their hind legs to get away. The Sgorrla seemed to have no desire to follow and suddenly Tain was running back towards the lake, followed by the Outriders – those that had survived, for only twenty of them returned from the fight.

'It's hopeless,' cried Tain as he ran up. His neck was badly bloodied. 'They're far too strong for us.'

Thistle nodded.

'And they've sharpened their antlers,' panted Tain. 'I've never known anything like it. Did you see the marks on their heads?'

'We'd never make it through the pass,' said Braan. 'What can we do?'

Thistle shook his head.

'We can't make it back up the mountain, that's for sure,' he said quietly.

'Then we're lost,' whispered Tain.

The deer were silent as they stood in the corrie. Their hearts as tired as their poor bodies.

'Very well then,' said Thistle after a while. 'We shall just have to try to make it through the pass. If even one of us survives, perhaps he can still get to Sgorr.'

With that there was a great shudder of barking across the grass. The Sgorrla – all of them now – were advancing, lined again in rows. The Outriders turned to face them, their legs trembling with fear and exhaustion.

But when they were still quite a way away, to the Outriders' surprise, the Sgorrla suddenly stopped.

'What is it?' whispered Braan.

'Listen,' said Tain.

Above them, from the slopes of the corrie, the Outriders now heard the bark of angry deer and the clatter of sparring antlers. They could not see what was happening in the darkness but they suddenly realized that somewhere above them stags were fighting.

'Who?' cried Thistle.

From all sides, rocks and boulders were showering down the slopes of the corrie, a waterfall of stone splashing into the still pool. Then, to the friends' utter amazement, stags began to emerge from the shadows, leaping onto the grass and rushing towards them.

'Narl,' cried Tain furiously.

'No,' shouted Braan, 'look.'

'Willow,' cried Thistle delightedly. 'It's Willow and Peppa.'

'And look who's with them,' said Tain.

The friends' amazement could hardly have been greater, for at the twins' side now came not only Bankfoot but Haarg too. The fear that had gripped the Outriders was instantly transformed as the incoming stags greeted them.

'I don't know how you worked this magic,' cried Thistle as Willow ran up to him, 'but I'm glad—'

'Don't say it,' said Willow. 'We rescued Bankfoot, as you can see, but then we heard you were in danger and were rushing back to warn you when we met Haarg here. You'd better listen to what he has to say.'

'Herne be with you,' panted Haarg. 'I'm sorry we couldn't get through sooner. We weren't sure how many Sgorrla were on the mountain.'

'But I thought . . .' Tain started to say.

'We've been following you for days,' Haarg went on, 'and by the looks of it we've arrived just in time.'

'Yes,' said Thistle. 'How many of you are there?'

'A hundred Outriders.'

'With us that makes about a hundred and sixty. Narl can't have more than that. So maybe we've got a chance. If we can survive the night.'

Haarg peered through the darkness, back towards the pass, and though he could see them only dimly, he realized that the Sgorrla were retreating again.

'Tomorrow we can try and break through,' said Thistle.

'And by then there may be even more of us,' added Haarg.

'More?'

'Yes,' said Willow quietly, 'the Herla are coming from the north.'

'But how . . .?' said Thistle.

'Rannoch.'

'Rannoch,' cried Tain delightedly and Thistle gazed at Willow in wonder. The hind was smiling.

'After you left,' Haarg went on, 'Rannoch raised the herd. Sent word north too. He kept talking about the Prophecy and it all being true.'

'But where is he?' said Thistle.

'Herne only knows. He went west. Told me to catch up with you as quickly as I could and stop you trying to reach Sgorr. He said that I should make you wait until he came.'

Thistle looked very gravely at Willow.

'Well it's too late for that now,' said Thistle quietly.

But the Outriders stirred around him. Though the air was chill in the bowl of night and many of them were badly wounded, talk of Rannoch and the Prophecy, the reappearance of Bankfoot and the twins, not to mention the sudden increase in their numbers, had lifted their spirits beyond measure. Hope was stirring once again.

Suddenly they heard a voice from above them that echoed angrily across the corrie.

'Outriders,' cried Narl in the darkness. 'Outriders, listen to me. To resist is useless. You have new friends now and perhaps you think you can escape. But you can't. If you give up now, I give you my word that none of you will be harmed.'

'Narl,' answered Thistle instantly and angrily, letting his voice range through the blackness, 'save your lies. We are Outriders and will never surrender. But there are enough of us now to fight you and others are on their way.'

'Indeed,' answered Narl coldly, though there was some faint note of uncertainty in his voice. 'But I don't need to fight you, and you will never make it through the pass alive. Meanwhile, Lord Sgorr is bringing the Great Herd north and then what can you do? Die. I can simply hold you trapped here till then.'

'Then do your worst,' shouted Thistle.

But Narl's voice had unsettled the Outriders.

'Very well,' whispered Thistle. 'Until the morning. Then we will see.'

The distant stars shone down from the cold heavens as the Great Herd waited for dawn to break in the Low Lands and for daylight to herald their journey north.

After so many moons here the land was grazed out and the trees browsed to the wood, and they were all expectant and restless. But something else was stirring through their ranks now in the darkness. News had just reached them of the battle at the corrie, together with strange rumours of Herla coming out of the High Land. Some of the Sgorrla even talked of Outriders and others muttered darkly of an old enemy.

A contingent of the inner Sgorrla was moving amongst them, checking up on the foreign herds and making sure that the Sgorrla had their orders for the next day's exodus. It had all been carefully planned and Sgorr had given instructions that they should make for the corrie as fast as they could. But something else had made their commander especially vigilant. In the late hours of darkness Narl and ten Sgorrla had returned to the herd. Narl had been running hard and had asked to be shown into Sgorr's presence.

'What's wrong?' said one of the Sgorrla to the commander as they paced the herd in the darkness.

'Who knows?' answered the stag. 'Something about these Outriders, I bet.'

'Nothing to worry about?'

'No, though it won't please Sgorr. He was angry enough when he heard the prisoner had escaped and he's nervous about the trek.'

'We'd better watch it tonight then. What happened up there?'

'A skirmish. We've got them pinned down though.'

'So there'll be some fighting.'

The commander shrugged.

'A bit of mopping up. I doubt you'll get to see any of it. You'll have to get your kicks somewhere else. Make do with the Cleansing.'

'I suppose so. Though there'll be enough to think of in the coming suns.'

'True enough,' agreed the commander, 'especially with all these humans moving west. Their stands, where they rest and feed by their orange light, are everywhere. We've lost a good number of the stragglers to their shining sticks already.'

'Serves them right for straying,' snorted the Sgorrla. 'That'll teach them the meaning of discipline.'

'It's a bit late for them to learn anything now,' chuckled the commander.

Both the deer laughed. Their party had come to a copse that ran a little way along the edge of a meadow above the lake, where many of the fallow deer had settled. The commander and the Sgorrla were ahead of the others and they pulled up suddenly, the commander gesturing for the others to do the same. He had heard something through the copse, where the trees suddenly thinned out. It was a pair of fallow stags, whispering in the darkness.

'But it was just a silly dream,' one was saying.

'No, I heard him clearly,' said the other.

'But you said you'd been dozing.'

'Yes, but it was just as I was waking up. The voice came through the trees. As clearly as I'm talking to you now.'

'And?'

'And it told me to listen.'

'Didn't you go and see who it was?'

'I didn't care to,' answered the fallow deer. 'Besides, I was half asleep.'

'There you are, then.'

'No, it wasn't in my dream,' insisted the deer. 'It was in the wood.'

'And didn't you ask who was there?' said the deer gravely.

'Of course I did.'

'Well?'

At this the deer's voice dropped to an almost inaudible whisper.

'The voice, it said this: "I am he you have betrayed. And I am you. I am . . ."'

The deer paused.

'Well?' whispered the other deer.

'Herne.'

The listening Sgorrla looked at each other in amazement but the commander shook his head.

'Is that all?'

'No. I went on talking to him. "What do you want of me?" I said. "For you to heal yourself," came the voice. "But how?" I asked. "By listening to Herne's Lore. You are what you are. Sgorr can never change that." '

Again the Sgorrla stirred but still the commander held them back.

' "But what should I do?" I said. "Look for me," came the voice, "for I have come to free the Herla. To fulfil the Prophecy." '

'The Prophecy,' gasped the other deer.

'That's what he said. Do you know the Prophecy?'

'I heard it when I was a young fawn,' answered the fallow deer. 'What else did the voice say?'

'Nothing. After that there was nothing – just the wind in the trees. I called out. "Wait," I cried. "Tell me more." But nothing came back. I ran towards the place I'd heard it . . .'

'Well?'

'Well, this is the really strange thing. The trees were very widely spaced and there was a clearing. But there was no one there at all. No one.'

'But it was dark. Maybe a calf was playing tricks.'

'It was no calf. And in the clearing there were slots.'

Beyond the trees the Sgorrla looked wonderingly at their commander.

'Shall we take them?' whispered the deer who had been addressing him earlier.

'No,' he whispered back, 'we don't want any trouble so

close to the trek. But if there's any fighting to be done tomorrow make sure they are at the front of it.'

So the Sgorrla passed on and the fallow deer were left to discuss the strange visitation.

'What do you think it means?' said the Sgorrla as the commander led them through the night.

'Just foolish talk,' answered the commander. 'I've been hearing such nonsense more and more of late. It must be because of the trek. The deer are nervous.'

The Sgorrla ran on until they came to the top of a wide meadow by a beech forest. The trees here were badly scarred and the branches broken away where the Sgorrla had been sharpening their antlers, for this was a Sgorrla training ground and among the groups spread across the meadow many pairs were locked together now, testing the strength of their antlers even in the dark. They never rested.

The commander moved through them, nodding his head approvingly at the sight of his stags. The Sgorrla were at the peak of fitness but, having been kept in training throughout Anlach, many of them were frustrated and spoiling for a fight.

Well, let's hope there are some of these Outriders left, thought the commander to himself as he walked.

He reached a group of the Sgorrling, and smiled as he saw the prickets trying to sharpen their single antlers too. As he passed by, one of them looked up and nudged the deer next to him.

'Hey,' he whispered excitedly, 'that was a commander.'

'What do you know about it?' said the Sgorrling next to him scornfully.

'I know. I saw him training some of the Sgorrla yesterday.'

'Well, what of it?'

'I'm going to be a commander one day,' said the pricket.

Some of the other Sgorrling looked up at him and smiled.

'You'll never make a commander,' snorted one.

'Oh yes I will, when my antlers have grown. Then I'll show you.'

'No you won't. You'll never even make the Sgorrla. You couldn't fight a brailah.'

The deer lifted his head angrily.

'Say that again,' he snorted, coming forwards in the night.

'I said you couldn't fight a brailah.'

'Do you want a tine in your eye?'

Now the second deer came forward. The two of them stood facing each other, testing the strength of each other's gaze. Since they were only prickets they couldn't lock antlers, but they knew how much damage a single antler could do. Suddenly they dropped their heads and began to spar, clicking and jabbing, trying to find a way through.

'Go on,' cried another pricket excitedly, 'stick him.'

The others began to shout and stamp delightedly.

But suddenly the two Sgorrling pulled away and dropped their heads guiltily. A stag was standing behind them in the darkness.

He must have been six or seven years old and his great antlers rose frighteningly above them. They couldn't see his face very clearly in the blackness but they all thought he was a Sgorrla.

'Why are you fighting?' asked the stag quietly.

The young stags glared at each other.

'He said I'd never make a commander,' said the first sulkily.

'And he won't. You need to be able to really fight and you need strength and courage, don't you? That's why you're in the Sgorrla, isn't it?'

'I?' said the stag, and then he paused. 'Tell me,' he went on softly, 'do you like fighting?'

Again the stags looked at each other, this time with surprise.

'That's what the Sgorrla are for,' said the first. 'That's why the Herla are greater than all the Lera. That's what Sgorr said before he started the Cleansing.'

In the darkness the young deer fancied he caught a furious glint in the stag's eyes.

'And you want to kill things?' said the stag gently.

'Oh yes, when I'm old enough.'

The stag shook his head.

'And do you really think that is Herne's way?' he whispered in the night.

'Who?' said the pricket.

'Herne. When I was a fawn,' the stag said, smiling as he addressed all the youngsters, 'I found many better things to do than fight, you know. We'd play for suns and suns, and listen to the stories of Herne and Starbuck.'

'Play?' said one of the prickets with interest.

'Oh, yes,' said the stag. 'But I suppose Sgorr's changed all that.'

'Hush,' whispered the Sgorrling that had spoken first. 'You must call him Lord Sgorr.'

'I'll do nothing of the kind,' answered the stag.

Now the youngsters looked at each other and there was fear in their eyes.

'I'll tell on you,' said the youngster who had wanted to be a commander. 'I'll tell the inner Sgorrla.'

'Come now,' answered the stag without anger. 'That isn't very brave, is it?'

The deer looked down guiltily.

'But if you really want to tell the Sgorrla, why don't you

say that there is a stag in the herd who thinks that Sgorr is nothing more that a lying soft-foot and the Sgorrla no better than vermin?'

The pricket shuddered.

'Tell them that their days are numbered and that the fawns will one day run free again through the heather and play together as fawns should.'

With that the stag turned and vanished into the night, leaving the stunned Sgorrling looking after him in silence.

A wind had come up and above their heads the clouds were skitting through the sky, breaking up the surface of the heavens and fretting the canopy of stars with ribbons of darkness.

23

Eloin

If I were hanged on the highest hill,
Mother o' mine, O mother o' mine,
I know whose love would follow me still,
Mother o' mine, O mother o' mine.
Rudyard Kipling, 'Mother o' Mine'

On the edge of the Great Herd an old hind was looking up through the veil of night now, gazing at the twinkling specks of light that spattered the sky above her. They had no meaning for her, except in the tales told to her as a fawn, tales of Herne and Starbuck. As her eyes ranged the heavens they came upon two stars that were close together and brighter than the rest and suddenly the hind's heart tightened in anguish.

'Brechin,' she whispered, 'you're up there, aren't you? With my little Rannoch. You're looking after each other.'

Eloin shook her head and looked around. There were Sgorrla all about her, but the guard had been told to stand off in a wide ring, and inside the ring two other hinds were coming towards her. Both were younger than Eloin but their muzzles were beginning to grey with age too. It was Shira and Canisp.

'How are you, my dear?' said Canisp as the two hinds
came up.

Eloin smiled.

'Well enough. But I was thinking about *them*.'

Canisp nodded.

'Poor Eloin,' she said. 'I think about Bankfoot all the
time.'

'And I about Tain,' sighed Shira.

'Look at us,' said Eloin sadly. 'Three old hinds lost in the
world, with nothing but our memories to feed on.'

'At least we're together, my dear,' said Canisp.

'Yes, and at least your fawns are alive and free,' agreed
Eloin.

'But why should Sgorr want to keep us here?' said Shira
suddenly.

Eloin looked strangely at her friend. She had never told
the hinds that the real reason she stayed with Sgorr was to
protect them. But she too wondered why Sgorr had suddenly
doubled the guard over all three of them.

'I heard the Sgorrla talking,' said Shira. 'There's been
fighting nearby. Maybe it's got something to do with that.'

'Fighting?' said Eloin with surprise.

'Yes. It can't be true, but I heard mention of Outriders.'

'Outriders?' gasped Eloin.

'Yes,' said Shira, 'they said there are Outriders in the Low
Lands again.'

'Not for long,' said Eloin angrily. 'Not if Sgorr has anything to do with it.'

'Maybe we shall learn more with the morning. When the
Great Trek begins.'

Eloin sighed.

'The Great Trek,' she said quietly, shaking her grey

muzzle. 'I don't think I shall make it, you know. I am too old and my heart is tired.'

'We shall all make it together,' said Shira.

'Well, if it's really coming,' said Eloin, 'perhaps we should all get some rest.'

The hinds nodded and Eloin wandered away from her friends, nearer to the Sgorrla where there was a small group of trees, elms and a great aged oak. The old hind sat down in the grass and sighed as she looked into the darkness. Canisp's mention of Outriders had affected her deeply and now she was thinking of Brechin again. She could see his fine features in her mind's eye, his great antlers shining in the sunlight. She could almost hear his strong, gentle voice and smell his scent. Eloin closed her eyes. Brechin was gone for ever, murdered that night on the hill. That terrible night when she had given birth to Rannoch, her little fawn whose life she had tried to save, only to have it snatched away by Herne. Eloin suddenly felt desperately old and bitterly alone. The hind began to doze and in the dreams that stole over her thoughts she was troubled.

Eloin suddenly woke. It was still pitch-black and above her the stars had been blanked out by heavy clouds. A breeze was murmuring through the trees and rustling the grass. The old hind stirred. A stag was coming towards her. She could see the outline of his antlers now as he approached through the night. He was walking slowly, but in the darkness she could not tell which one of the Sgorrla guards it was.

'What are you doing here?' she said angrily as the stag drew nearer. 'You know Sgorr does not allow you to approach unless I call.'

The stag stopped but said nothing.

'Well,' Eloin went on, 'answer me. Why are you disturbing my sleep?'

The stag lifted his head.

'Answer me.'

'Mother,' the stag whispered through the darkness.

Eloin looked up in amazement.

'What did you say?'

'Mother,' whispered the stag again.

Eloin's heart trembled.

'Mother, it's me. Rannoch.'

Eloin struggled and tried to get up. But the stag was by her side now, and as Eloin blinked fearfully up at him in the darkness, she felt as if her heart would burst with joy. There on the stag's fine forehead, between his splendid branching antlers, was the white oak leaf.

'But it can't be. You can't . . .'

'It can, Mother,' said Rannoch quietly. 'I am alive and have returned to fulfil the Prophecy.'

Eloin blinked back at him, but as she looked into those eyes and caught his scent, she knew immediately that it was true. Her fawn had come back to her.

'Rannoch, it's really you? My little calf grown into a fine stag?'

'Yes, Mother,' smiled Rannoch, smiling 'and I'm sorry it has been so long. But I never knew.'

Eloin was on her feet now. She stood there, gazing at him, waiting for the dream to end. But it didn't. She closed her eyes and opened them again. But the stag was still standing there in front of her, the white mark as real as her own unbounded happiness.

'But how, Rannoch, how?' she said at last.

'There is no time,' said Rannoch quietly. 'I will explain everything once my work is finished.'

'But what are you doing here?' gasped Eloin, suddenly

fearful and looking around towards the Sgorrla guard. 'It's not safe.'

'I've come to face Sgorr,' said Rannoch quietly, 'and end his tyranny.'

'No, no you mustn't,' cried Eloin. 'We must get you away,'

'The time for flight is long passed,' answered Rannoch quietly. 'I must face Sgorr and I need your help.'

'No,' said Eloin. 'No.'

In that instant she realized that her fawn was in terrible danger and suddenly the part of the Prophecy that had haunted her for so long flashed through her head.

'But Rannoch,' she gasped, 'you mustn't. The Prophecy . . . You mustn't sacrifice yourself.'

'If that is what Herne asks of me, Mother,' said Rannoch simply, 'that is what I must do. I cannot escape my destiny.'

'But Rannoch . . .'

As Eloin looked at him, standing there so boldly in the night, she suddenly fell silent. Now the amazement of seeing her fawn was giving way to a silent awe.

'If Herne wills it,' she murmured.

'We must hurry,' said Rannoch. 'My friends are in dreadful peril. Bankfoot, Tain and Willow are caught in a nearby corrie.'

'Bankfoot and Tain?'

'Yes, and I've got to help them somehow. But first there is something I must do. I want to meet Sgorr, face to face.'

'But why?' said Eloin in a whisper, wondering at how her fawn had grown, and then she paused. 'You've come to kill him?'

Rannoch shook his head.

'No,' he said quietly, 'not yet. If I am to free the Herla from years of lies, then Sgorr's death alone will not suffice.

They must all witness a stronger sign. But first I want Sgorr to know that I am here.'

'But he will have you killed,' said Eloin.

'Not if I get to him alone,' said Rannoch. 'And there you can aid me.'

Eloin nodded.

'But Mother, as soon as you have shown me to him,' said Rannoch gravely, 'you must get safely away from here. That is also why I came to the herd – to help you escape.'

'Shira and Canisp are with me,' said Eloin, looking over to the two hinds who were lying down some way away. They were both asleep. 'They're the only ones left from your flight.'

'Good,' said Rannoch, delighted that the hinds were still alive, 'that is very good. But don't wake them yet. Where is Sgorr?'

Eloin looked out into the night.

'I don't know. Inspecting the herd.'

'You must call him, Mother,' said Rannoch, 'and somehow get the guards away, so I can speak with him alone. Then you must take Shira and Canisp into the hills until it's over.'

Again Eloin looked fearfully at Rannoch.

'Are you certain this is what you want?' she said.

'I have no choice,' answered Rannoch quietly. 'I wanted to live as a free Herla in the High Land, but how could I be free when the Herla are crying out? When the Lera are being killed and the land itself is in pain? The things I have seen, Mother.'

Eloin stared gravely at her fawn. He had grown beyond her comprehension and as she gazed at his fine face, and at the six tines rising proudly on either side of his head and the fawn mark that had begun his journey all those years ago, she marvelled. She nodded and walked nearer to the ring of

Sgorrla. The guards nearest to her were asleep in the grass, completely unaware of the stranger that had crept through their ranks in the night.

'You,' cried Eloin to one of them, 'wake up.'

The Sgorrla stirred immediately and lumbered to his feet, embarrassed at having been caught napping.

'I want to see Lord Sgorr . . .'

Rannoch couldn't hear any more. He had drawn back into the cover of the trees. He watched Eloin as she gave instructions to the guard, and though his thoughts were consumed with the coming battle and of what Herne wanted of him, now he silently blessed the god for having kept her alive long enough for him to see her again. He looked over to Shira and Canisp, asleep in the grass. How they would wonder if they could see Bankfoot and Tain.

Eloin padded back towards Rannoch.

'It's done,' she whispered.

'Good, now go and wake the others and get them ready.'

As the Sgorrla guard raced away to find Sgorr, his master was not inspecting the Great Herd as Eloin had imagined. He had finished consulting with Narl and now he was sleeping near the meadow where the Sgorrla were training. His sudden naps were more and more frequent these days and the Sgorrla were used to standing guard over the old stag as he took his rest. One of them was looking at him now, wondering what his master was thinking as Sgorr stirred uncomfortably on the ground.

Sgorr twitched again. He was dreaming. He knew he was dreaming but it was as clear as if his eye had been open. He was sitting in the grass near the meadow, but the Sgorrla weren't around him. It was night and a great moon hung above him in the sky, lighting the trees and the hard earth. Then suddenly a stag was coming towards him. His head was lowered and one of his antlers was broken and as Sgorr looked on in amazement it seemed to him that the stag's body was glowing, shimmering in the pale blue wash of the distant moon.

'Who are you?' whispered Sgorr fearfully in his sleep. 'What do you want?'

The stag stopped and then raised his head. Sgorr pulled back in horror as he saw his face, scarred and mangled and covered in blood.

'Brechin?' he gasped.

Brechin stood before him in that ghostly light, the Outrider's dead eyes looking coldly down on the deer.

'Brechin, it isn't you,' hissed Sgorr. 'You're dead. We killed you.'

Very slowly the ghostly stag began to shake his head.

'What do you want of me?' said Sgorr, shivering in his sleep. 'What have you come to tell me?'

Still the apparition said nothing.

'Speak to me,' cried Sgorr. 'Speak.'

But with that the captain turned his bloodied head and walked slowly away. The moon seemed to go out suddenly and Sgorr cried out. His body was drenched in sweat. The old stag gasped and opened his eyes.

'Lord Sgorr,' a Sgorrla was saying nervously as he stood over his master. 'Lord Sgorr, are you all right?'

'What?' said Sgorr as he got slowly to his feet and shivered violently. 'Of course I'm all right. It was just a dream.'

Sgorr looked around him fearfully in the darkness.

'Lord Sgorr,' said the Sgorrla quietly, 'one of Eloin's guards is here. She wants to see you.'

'Eloin?' said Sgorr, shivering again and thinking of Brechin.

'Yes, Lord.'

'I've no time to see Eloin. Narl has already taken more Sgorrla to meet these Outriders and morning is not far off.'

'Yes, Lord,' said the Sgorrla, 'but she says she needs you.'

Sgorr stopped and looked at the Sgorrla in amazement.

'Needs me?'

The Sgorrla nodded.

'Eloin says she needs me?'

The Sgorrla was silent.

'Very well, then,' said Sgorr, smiling, 'if my favourite hind needs me, I must go to her.'

Sgorr found Eloin standing on her own near the trees. Shira and Canisp were a way off murmuring to each other, and they looked fearfully at him as he arrived. The Sgorrla guards were standing guiltily around her, trying to look as alert as possible.

'Well, my dear?' said Sgorr sarcastically. 'They say you need me.'

The old hind smiled.

'Sgorr,' she said quietly, 'I am so glad you have come.'

Sgorr looked at her carefully.

'I've been very worried,' Eloin went on. 'I've hardly seen anything at all of you of late.'

'I thought you hated me to be near you,' said Sgorr coldly. Eloin dropped her eyes.

'I know. I know,' she said. 'I did. In the past. But . . .'

'But?'

'I am so lonely, Sgorr.'

A flicker of suspicion crossed Sgorr's eye, but he felt a tightening in his stomach too. To hear Eloin talk so tenderly was something he had never known before and now his heart was wrestling with his instinct.

'Go on,' he said.

'Maybe I've been wrong,' whispered Eloin. 'Maybe I've

misjudged you. I can see now how much you've done for the Herla. How much they admire you.'

Sgorr stirred. The hind's words were so strange and unfamiliar, yet so much what he had always longed for that he felt a sudden pain in his heart.

'I need to talk to you, Sgorr,' Eloin went on, 'as we have never talked before. Then maybe I will understand. I have thought of late that perhaps your cruel— your anger is because of me. Because I couldn't love you.'

For the first time Sgorr's eye looked sad.

'Yes,' he said, 'perhaps I have been angry. Perhaps . . .'

'It must be so hard for you,' said Eloin, 'with so much responsibility for the Herla. Even a lord needs friends.'

'I do get lonely,' said Sgorr quietly.

'There is so much I want to tell you, Sgorr,' said Eloin as passionately as she could.

'Go on, my dear, go on.'

'No, Sgorr, I can't. Not with all these Sgorrla about. Tell them to go away, just for a little while. Then we can talk.'

Sgorr hesitated, but his longing had already overcome his natural suspicion. He suddenly swung round to the stags.

'You,' he cried, 'get out of here. All of you. I will come to you when the morning is with us.'

The startled Sgorrla thought Sgorr was angry with them and, without a word, they did as they were told.

'Canisp, my dear,' called Eloin when they had gone, 'Shira. I want to talk to Sgorr. Will you go too for a while?'

Her eyes were trained on the hinds, and there was a hardness and clarity in them. They knew full well what Eloin wanted them to do.

'So, Eloin,' said Sgorr quietly when the hinds had left as well, 'we're alone at last.'

'Yes.'

'What would you say to me?' whispered Sgorr tenderly.

'Only this,' cried Eloin suddenly. 'I hate you, Sgorr, and I will always hate you.'

Sgorr looked back at her in amazement.

'In your vanity do you really think,' blazed Eloin, 'that I could feel anything for you? You who murdered Brechin and destroyed everything I have ever cared about.'

'Then why?'

'To get you alone. Shira and Canisp are already escaping and now I am going to join them, and I will be free of you for ever.'

Sgorr stood stock-still as Eloin backed away into the darkness. He was too startled to do anything at all.

'But first there is someone else who would talk with you,' called Eloin, and then she was gone, running after her friends.

Sgorr paused. His senses were tingling. And then he heard it, a twig breaking behind him. He swung round to see a stag stepping from the trees. It was still dark, but light was coming now, slowly, filtering through the strangely warm air. His eyes opened wide as he looked at the strong antlers, at the white mark in the centre of the deer's head.

But Sgorr did nothing.

'So,' he said quietly, 'you have come at last?'

'Yes, Sgorr,' answered Rannoch, 'I have come.'

Sgorr nodded. He was thinking hard, but he realized that with the Sgorrla so far away he was desperately vulnerable.

'And you are here to kill me?'

'It is you, Sgorr, who sends assassins,' answered Rannoch coldly.

'Ah yes,' said Sgorr, 'and I should have trained him better. So you're still alive, Rannoch? Well, well, quite the survivor, aren't you? Then let me tell you something. I am pleased to meet you at last.'

'Pleased?' said Rannoch.

'Oh yes,' said Sgorr, 'for I have heard what you have done in the High Land. I have spent a life trying to achieve such a thing. To destroy Herne.'

'You're wrong, Sgorr,' said Rannoch quietly. 'I was born to fulfil Herne's law.'

'Ah,' said Sgorr, 'that mark. Then tell me, why did you overthrow Herne's Herd?'

'Because they did not really believe in Herne,' answered Rannoch. 'They believed only in violence. As you do.'

'You have your mother's eyes,' said Sgorr suddenly. 'She's a fine hind, Rannoch, and clever too. When I think of how she tricked me just now!'

'Then you know she's my mother?'

'I have known for years.'

'So you know it means that I am a changeling.'

'Still the Prophecy,' said Sgorr. 'Do you think you can frighten me with it?'

'Why won't you believe it, Sgorr?'

'Why?' said Sgorr angrily. 'Because it is lies. Like the lies Herne's Herd tried to fool me with.'

'You spread a different kind of lie,' said Rannoch.

'No, I bring the Herla reason and power. I bring them freedom.'

'You bring them violence and death. But I will show you another way, when the Prophecy comes to pass.'

'What?' said Sgorr contemptuously. 'When you blot out the sun and summon our enemies to aid you? When you summon man? You're a fool, Rannoch. No Herla can summon man.'

'They're all around us,' answered Rannoch quietly. 'They are here to restore the Island Chain.'

Sgorr paused. Something in the way Rannoch had said it

made him tremble. It was another link in the Prophecy. But Sgorr shook off the feeling.

'Dreams and nightmares!' he spat. 'Man will never come to your aid.'

'He already has once,' said Rannoch, 'and I have knowledge of man, Sgorr. The Prophecy talks of that too.'

'Knowledge of man?' scoffed Sgorr. 'What knowledge can there be that is greater than mine? All my life I have tried to study man, not as Herne's Herd learnt from him, turning his power to superstition, but learning from the power that is greater than the Lera's. Learning to think.'

'Is that what you learnt on the island?' said Rannoch coldly.

Sgorr swung his head up suddenly.

'So you know?' he gasped.

'Yes, Sgorr, I know.'

Sgorr suddenly felt a terrible weakness enter him.

'How much do you know?' he said.

'I know that you swam to the island as a young deer,' whispered Rannoch. 'I know that you stole a human fawn, Sgorr.'

Rannoch's voice was trembling as he spoke.

'And I know that you killed it,' he said sadly, his voice echoing round the trees.

Sgorr's eye peered back at Rannoch in the coming twilight. He suddenly felt afraid.

'But I do not know why,' whispered Rannoch.

'And you would never understand,' said Sgorr quietly.

'Tell me,' said the stag.

Sgorr peered back at Rannoch and there was fury in his look.

'Very well. I went there to study man and learn from him. For suns I watched the humans in their dwelling. I learnt many things. That's where I got the idea of sharpening the Herla's antlers, from watching them grinding their shining sticks. Many other things too. But then the human hind had a fawn.'

'And you stole it and killed it. Why?'

'Why?' cried Sgorr. 'Because I wanted to be stronger than them. Stronger than Herne. I made a sacrifice to myself. So I should never be afraid of anything again. I wanted the strength of his spirit to enter me and make me invincible.'

Rannoch looked back at the burning fury in Sgorr's eye and he trembled as he realized that the thing he and Rurl had only guessed at on the island was true. They had hardly dared believe it as they had looked down at the little skeleton buried there in the sand, at the gaping skull and the ribs around the upper chest, broken and torn away.

'So you . . .'

'Yes,' spat Sgorr, on the edge of frenzy, 'so I ate its heart.'

Rannoch looked at Sgorr now and he felt almost sorry for him.

'And when the leaders of Herne's Herd discovered it, even they drove you out?'

'I had transgressed the oldest law for they worshipped man as much as Herne. But though I admire man, I will worship nothing. Nothing.'

Sgorr was trembling with rage.

'So that's why you sealed the High Land?'

'Until I could be sure that Herne's Herd was destroyed and my secret safe. The Herla would never understand,' said Sgorr almost sadly, 'why it was . . . why it was necessary.'

'You are evil, Sgorr,' said Rannoch quietly.

'There is no evil,' answered Sgorr furiously.

'You must be destroyed,' said Rannoch, but there was little anger in his voice.

'And you will destroy me?' snorted Sgorr. 'I am old, Rannoch, and you could kill me here and now. But there are those who will step into my place. Narl, and others. The Herla are strong now and the Great Herd is invincible.'

'You're wrong. For the Herla are coming from the north. The Outriders will fight you'

'Outriders? They can do nothing. By tomorrow your friends will have been destroyed. They are trapped now, at the corrie. If you kill me they will still be destroyed and how then will you have served your god? You have failed, Rannoch, failed.'

'Not yet,' said Rannoch, 'and that is what I have come to tell you. I thought perhaps I could reason with you, but now I see that is impossible. Well, Sgorr, know this. I will be there tomorrow and Herne will be at my back.'

Sgorr looked at the stag standing there so defiantly and he suddenly felt a strange admiration for him.

'Then come on,' he said quietly, 'to fulfil your prophecy. For not even you know the end of it. You know what it says, Rannoch? If it is true, then you are the sacrifice. If you come tomorrow, you will die, Rannoch.'

Rannoch stared back at the hornless deer and inside he trembled also, but he snorted and turned away. Light was cracking all around them now.

'Mark me,' he whispered, 'tomorrow I will come again. So look for me, Sgorr, and fear me.'

With that Rannoch was gone.

Sgorr stood there shaking in the grass.

'Very well,' he hissed, 'then, if I have to, I will fight Herne himself.'

Rannoch ran as swiftly as he could away from the herd, towards the corrie. He was thinking now of his friends and of Willow. He would be with them soon. To fight and die with them if necessary. But first he had one more thing to do. He was looking for one of the human stands and for an antler to take with him to the fray, an antler of wood and sap, that burnt with the humans' orange light.

24

The Stand

Be through my lips to unawakened earth
The trumpet of a prophecy! O, Wind,
If Winter comes, can Spring be far behind?
Percy Bysshe Shelley, 'Ode to the West Wind'

'We must rush them now, break through the pass,' said Thistle gravely.

The sun was high in the corrie and the clouds had cleared. The light was glittering off the lake now as the Outriders faced the day. The night had been nerve-racking for them all, but the Sgorrla had not attacked and at least they were rested. All morning they had been discussing what to do and now, as the day wore on, the urgency of their situation was crowding in on them again. They had noticed, though, that the Sgorrla seemed a little distracted and fewer than ever were in the neck of the pass.

'It shouldn't be impossible to get through,' said Tain, 'if we stay close together and run fast. The fighting will be worst in the centre of the pass, though. It's very narrow and the Sgorrla will hit us from the slopes.'

'Willow,' said Thistle, 'I want you and Peppa in the centre of the Outriders.'

'No,' said Willow immediately, 'I can kick and—'

'Please, Willow, you've done enough already. Do as I say.'
The hind looked steadily back at Thistle and then she
nodded.

'Well then,' said Thistle quietly, 'let's get on with it.'

He turned to the Outriders. There were over a hundred
and sixty of them, standing by the water with their antlers
tilting expectantly. Thistle felt that they could face anything.

'Come on,' he cried suddenly, 'let's show the Sgorrla what
we're made of.'

Thistle began to run and Tain and Bankfoot leapt after
him. Then the Outriders were all running, through the corrie,
towards the pass.

'Willow,' cried Thistle as they ran. He was just in front
of her.

'What is it?'

'When you were in the herd, did you you hear anything
of Alyth?'

Bankfoot overheard the question and he looked painfully
at Willow.

'No,' called the hind sadly, 'nothing.'

The Sgorrla in the pass saw them coming but many among
their number had wandered away to graze and others were
still high on the mountainside. They hadn't expected the
Outriders to try and break out quite so suddenly and anyway
they were waiting for reinforcements. They began to rally,
their commanders bellowing orders, but when the Outriders
hit them they had, if not quite the element of surprise, then
the force of an attack on their side.

Soon the narrow pass was alive with fighting deer, as the
Outriders began to battle their way through. They were
making headway already, cutting and jabbing and rising on
their haunches. The Sgorrla came down on them from the

slopes, but the Outriders fought them off as every effort was turned to breaking through the pass.

Willow and Peppa stayed in the middle of the Outriders and they both wished they had antlers. But the hinds were not completely protected from the fighting. At one point a Sgorrla overreached himself on a charge and, pushing past an Outrider, came within an antler's length of Peppa. The hind saw him and lashed out with her back hoof, catching him in the face just as he lowered his head.

'We're going to make it, Willow,' cried Peppa amid the throng, 'we're going to make it.'

Ahead of them the hind could already see the end of the pass.

But a wall of deer rose up in front of them and again the way was barred.

'One last push,' cried Thistle, lunging forwards. He met a large Sgorrla head-on and their antlers locked. Tain and Bankfoot dropped their antlers too and suddenly the way was clear again.

'That's it,' shouted Thistle, but as he did so Willow gasped.

A single Sgorrla was coming at him full tilt, hurtling down the side of the mountain. The stag dipped his head as he ran and literally sprung from the slope, hurling himself at Thistle. Willow ran forward to try and get between them, but the cups of the stag's antlers caught Thistle in the side and the deer stumbled and fell, somersaulting over as he did so. Willow pulled up as soon she saw him fall, as did Bankfoot and Haarg. Around them the Outriders swept on through the pass as Bankfoot fought off the lone Sgorrla. They had already put some distance between themselves and the rest of the pursuing Sgorrla so Willow rushed to Thistle's side.

He lay there motionless on the earth.

'Thistle,' cried Willow, 'Thistle.'

Thistle didn't move.

'Quickly, Thistle, before they're on us again.'

Willow had seen the Sgorrla's antlers strike and she knew that they couldn't have gone in deep enough to do any real harm. But as she looked down at Thistle, she realized with horror what had happened. It wasn't the antler that had done for Thistle, it was the fall. The deer had broken his neck.

'No, Thistle, it can't be,' she gasped.

But the deer didn't stir. Bankfoot came to Willow's side and stared down in amazement at his dead friend.

'I didn't even have time to tell him about Alyth,' whispered Willow bitterly.

'That was one mercy, at least,' said Bankfoot quietly.

But there was no time to mourn.

'Quickly,' cried Haarg behind them. 'They're coming on again.'

Blind with rage, Willow and Bankfoot began to run after Haarg towards the head of the pass, where they could see Tain leading the Outriders out into the plain beyond. Tain had no idea of what had happened and now the captain's heart was thrilling with courage and pride as he raced away. They had made it through.

But as the Outriders cleared the far end of the pass and swept into the plain, the forest curving to their left and a river swerving away to the right with more mountains beyond, the deer were met with a sight that threw them into confusion and despair. Tain pulled up in horror and the band of Outriders did the same. They all came to a halt.

There in front of them, as far as the eye could see, the Outriders were confronted with Sgorrla. Fallow and roe deer too. There must have been a thousand stags, stretching from the forest to the river. An army of antlers. The Great Herd was before them, waiting silently in the day.

Willow, Bankfoot and Haarg reached them too and though their thoughts had been on Thistle, lying dead in the pass, the sight of the Great Herd swept everything else from their minds. The friends and the Outriders looked at each other in despair.

'We could turn back,' cried Braan.

'No, they're coming through the pass,' panted Bankfoot.

'Quickly, make for the trees,' shouted Tain, but as he did so and some of the Outriders swung to the left they saw more antlers emerging into the daylight at every passable point of the forest.

'The river,' said Bankfoot, but on the far side of the water a line of deer were already moving up to block their escape. There, on the wide plain, the hundred and sixty Outriders – so impressive a sight in the home herd or even in the corrie – were dwarfed by the regiments of deer that surrounded them.

'Tain,' cried Peppa desperately. 'Tain, what shall we do?'

'Thistle,' said Tain, suddenly waking from this vision of hopelessness, 'let's try to . . .'

But as he looked round Tain realized that Thistle was missing.

'Thistle, where's Thistle?'

He was looking at Willow and the hind shook her head sadly.

'He never made it through the pass.'

Tain gazed back at her in horror but now the captain's instincts began to rally for he realized that without Thistle the Outriders were leaderless. He turned to scan the plain desperately and almost immediately his eyes settled on a patch of ground to the west, near the forest, that rose a way above the plain; a hillock of rock and heaped earth with a single rowan tree growing in its middle, but wide enough for a good many deer.

'There,' cried Tain, 'we'll make our stand there.'

Braan had seen it too and he was already bellowing to the Outriders as he turned towards it. Like a flock of birds the deer swung after him and again they were running, making for the higher ground. The Sgorrla saw what they were doing and instantly fifty of them broke from the facing wall of deer and rushed forward to try and cut them off. But the mound was closer to the Outriders than to the Great Herd and as the Sgorrla drew near, Braan and Tain had already reached it. The Outriders flowed up its sides after them and as they did so the Sgorrla pulled up and, bucking their antlers angrily, turned back to the main body of the herd.

There the Outriders settled. The four old friends, with Braan and Haarg at their side, gathered round the rowan tree, the other stags all about them. They made a brave sight, but a desperate one too. Silence fell on the plain and the Outriders waited, but the Sgorrla didn't move. The deer across the river made no attempt to cross the water and to the east the Sgorrla stayed in the shadow of the trees. Behind them the pass was sealed again with stags, but they did not advance either. They were all waiting.

Suddenly, as the Outriders looked on at their impenetrable enemy, the ranks of the Sgorrla in front of them began to stir and then parted. Through the middle of them came two deer. From the hillock the friends recognized Narl and at his side was an old stag whose bare head stood out clearly among the waves of antlers.

'Sgorr,' hissed Braan.

Narl and Sgorr had reached the front of the stags and

they began to range up and down the columns of waiting deer, inspecting their antlers and nodding approvingly.

Sgorr smiled inwardly. His night terrors and the shock of meeting Rannoch had passed away with the morning and now his courage swelled as he looked on. The Outriders were so few compared to the Sgorrla, the odds nearly ten to one. Though Sgorr was concerned about the Herla coming from the north, his scouts had seen nothing at all and he knew that they would never reach the Outriders in time. They were doomed.

'He has lost, Narl,' whispered Sgorr delightedly.

Narl nodded. He had been amazed when Sgorr told him of Rannoch's visit, but any fear that had woken in his heart was dispelled by the sheer might of the Great Herd.

'Today we will put an end to the Prophecy,' said Sgorr. 'Before Larn comes we will put an end to Herne once and for all. And if he dares to come we will put an end to Rannoch too.'

Narl smiled.

'Narl, I will watch from those trees,' said Sgorr, nodding casually towards a cluster of birches. 'Bring some Sgorrla to guard me. But first I want to talk to these fools.'

Narl gave the order as Sgorr walked forwards. The distance to the mound was some twenty tall trees, but the plain dipped slightly and in the still air Sgorr's voice carried clearly to the waiting Outriders and across the ranks of the Sgorrla too.

'Outriders,' he cried, 'I had thought to let you live, for Narl tells me you fought well in the corrie. But now I see you, I feel nothing but contempt. You will never see another Larn.'

Sgorr dipped his head and as the Outriders stood there they trembled, for across the grass came a terrible sound.

A violent clicking. The Sgorrla were knocking their antlers together in rhythm.

The dreadful noise carried far through the day, even to the slopes of the surrounding mountains where three old hinds trembled as they watched the tragic scene.

'I'm frightened, Willow,' whispered Peppa as the clicking swelled across the plain.

Willow smiled sadly at her sister.

'If we're to die,' she answered, 'then at least we will die together.'

Peppa lifted her head. Bankfoot and Tain were listening now and the friends drew near and looked at each other silently. Bankfoot gazed at Peppa sadly, for he had never even told the hind what he felt for her. But they had all been through so much together and they knew each other so well, that words now seemed barely necessary.

'You know,' said Bankfoot after a while, smiling as he looked at the splash of black by Peppa's ear, 'I always longed to be an Outrider. And here I am, an Outrider captain. But for what? I'll never even get a chance to guard the herd. It's funny, really.'

'Don't say it, Bankfoot,' said Tain quietly. 'Be proud to be a captain.'

Bankfoot looked at his friend and nodded.

'I am,' he whispered.

'And I'm proud that I've known you,' said Willow, 'all of you.'

'If only Rannoch would come,' said Peppa.

'No, Peppa,' whispered Tain, 'it is better that he's not here. What could he do? If there are more Herla coming from the north they'll never make it through the pass in time. And Rannoch alone, he would just add his carcass to ours. I'm glad he's not here.'

'And at least I know now,' said Willow, 'that he was never a coward. But I wish . . . I wish . . . Our parting was so terrible.'

The friends were silent again and across the plain the clicking subsided.

'They're coming on,' whispered Haarg.

The ranks of the Sgorrla were advancing towards the mound. Not all of them came. Some three hundred. Walking at first. Then trotting. Then breaking into a charge.

'Captain Bankfoot,' said Tain, lifting his antlers.

'Captain Tain,' answered Bankfoot proudly.

'If this is the last story, Bankfoot, then let's make certain it's the best.'

Bankfoot nodded and drew himself up. The Outriders were gathered in concentric rings around the rowan tree, and as the Sgorrla came on, Tain and Bankfoot, Braan and Haarg stepped forward through their ranks, to each side of the stand.

The Sgorrla drew nearer and now the Outriders could see the livid scars on the stags' foreheads and the points of their sharpened antlers. Then they hit, rushing up the sides of the hillock like a tidal wave. Even within the rings of Outriders, Willow and Peppa felt the shock of it. All around the hinds, stags were suddenly fighting, bellowing and lashing out. The little hill dissolved in a frenzy of thrusting haunches. Sgorrla was pitted against Outrider. Antler against antler. The Outriders seemed to rock to and fro, pushed this way and that by the impact from all sides.

The battle raged on, but in the midst of the desperate mêlée neither Peppa nor Willow could be sure how the Outriders were faring. Now and then they would catch sight of Bankfoot or Tain, Braan or Haarg, scything with their heads or rising up on their haunches, rallying the Outriders or rushing to the aid of another stag. They saw deer fall around them but could not tell which side they belonged to. The one thing the hinds were sure of, though, was how hopeless their plight was.

Suddenly, through the Outriders nearest to them, a stag came hurtling straight at Willow.

'Look out,' cried Peppa, and Willow just managed to step aside to avoid his antler thrust. He swung round again and Willow caught the surprise in his eyes to see a hind in the midst of the Outriders. But he dropped his antlers again and lunged.

From the left came Haarg, who had seen the stag break through the Outriders and abandoned his position at the front of the fight. He was just in time. He thrust the Sgorrla aside and brought his trez tines up and under the deer's muzzle, tearing his throat open in a single slash.

But as the Sgorrla fell, Haarg felt himself knocked sideways in turn and a stabbing pain tear into his chest. Another Sgorrla had broken through and was goring him.

'Help him,' cried Willow desperately to the surrounding Outriders. 'Help Haarg.'

Three Outriders came to their aid and the Sgorrla paid the price for his courage. The Outriders were on him.

'Thank Herne,' whispered Willow, for although he was wounded, Haarg was still on his feet. But as the hind turned back to her sister she cried out in agony.

Peppa was lying among the rocks, blood streaming over the ground.

'No, Peppa, not you too,' sobbed Willow, her front legs buckling before her.

Willow's head came down above her sister's and she saw the fatal gash in Peppa's throat that the Sgorrla must have inflicted on her only moments before he had charged Haarg. Peppa's blood was already sinking into the grass.

The hind's eyes were still open but they were beginning to stare.

'No, Peppa, no,' cried Willow bitterly.

Peppa tried to lift her head but it was no good.

'I should never have allowed you to come with us . . .'

'Quiet, Willow,' whispered Peppa, 'look to yourself, for I will soon be with Herne.'

'Peppa!' cried Willow again.

But it was already over. The hind closed her eyes and laid her head on the earth.

Willow staggered to her feet and now she could see that around her the fighting had died down. The Sgorrla were retreating and through the thronged Outriders, who were beginning to regroup on the mound, Tain and Bankfoot were coming towards her.

'We held them,' cried Bankfoot, 'we held them all right. But it was close, when they—' Bankfoot stopped. 'No!' he cried. 'No!'

The three friends stood over Peppa's corpse by the rowan tree, their heads bowed. Around them on the mound the grass was littered with bodies. Along with many Sgorrla, forty Outriders had fallen in the fight. But while that first terrible charge had very nearly overwhelmed the Outriders, across the plain the Great Herd was virtually unaffected and already two other groups of stags, two hundred in each, were advancing again.

'It's finished,' said Tain, shaking his head. 'We'll never survive another attack.'

Bankfoot stamped the ground furiously.

'Th-th-th-then the Sgorrla will die with us to avenge Peppa.'

But now Tain drew Bankfoot aside.

'Bankfoot,' he whispered, looking back towards Willow, 'will you do something for me?'

'Anything, Tain.'

'Will you stay with Willow to the end and give your last to protect her?'

Bankfoot stared at Tain. They both knew that they would all die in the next assault, Willow too, but Bankfoot nodded.

'Gladly,' he said.

The two old friends clicked their antlers and prepared themselves. By the birch trees Sgorr was nodding approvingly as he watched the final assault on the mound. It had been almost too easy. The Sgorrla came on as Tain and Braan and the wounded Haarg ran to the front of the Outriders. Once more the mound was submerged in a sea of fighting. By the rowan tree Bankfoot stood with Willow and they waited quietly together.

The ring of Outriders around them began to weaken and then the Sgorrla broke through. Three of them. This time they came straight for Bankfoot.

'Get behind me, Willow,' cried Bankfoot, 'with your back to the tree.'

The hind did as she was told.

'To me,' cried Bankfoot, rising up on his haunches and pounding the air with his hoofs. 'To me.'

But there was no one to help him.

'Come on then,' he shouted furiously, 'Sgorrla f-f-filth.'

The Sgorrla paused, momentarily held at bay by the fury in Bankfoot's eyes. But then they advanced and lowered their heads. Bankfoot dug in with his back feet and readied. On the first charge only one Sgorrla came at him and Bankfoot held the blow on his antlers. The Sgorrla seemed unnerved but now they all came at him together. Bankfoot knocked aside the first blow with his head, but the second Sgorrla locked his antlers and as he did so the third dipped towards his chest. The brow tine went in and Bankfoot gasped.

'Swine,' he cried.

But now he felt another antler gouge him and suddenly the strength went out of his legs.

'Forgive me, Willow,' he cried as his legs gave way.

Bankfoot's head hit the ground. He looked up to see the three Sgorrla standing above him, dipping their antlers, poised for the kill. Bankfoot turned his head away.

But as he did so, his eyes came in line with the eastern forest. His vision had been impaired by the blow to his head and, as his head began to swim and he finally lost consciousness, he fancied he saw a strange sight. In the distance, through the fighting deer, Bankfoot saw a light glowing through the day and as he closed his eyes he heard, very faintly, a voice.

'The forest, look to the forest.'

At the forefront of the battle, Tain had heard the shout too and suddenly the fighting deer were disengaging, turning in amazement towards the woods. Now, across the ground, came the bark of terrified deer and the Sgorrla on the edge of the trees were running left and right in confusion and terror, out onto the plain. Tain gasped.

The trees. The trees behind the deer. Their branches were glowing. A strange smoke furled up from the dry branches and everywhere a bright orange glow began to fleck through the woods. A furious crackling sound came to Tain's ears. Across the plain the Great Herd was watching in wonder as the Sgorrla nearest to the trees fled.

Whatever was happening Tain knew it could not save the Outriders, but at least the attacking Sgorrla had been distracted and had temporarily lost the advantage.

'Outriders,' cried Tain. 'Outriders, drive them back. It's your only chance.'

The Outriders had heard the call and instantly they were fighting again, a new hope filling their hearts. The sight of the light and their fellow Sgorrla fleeing in terror had discouraged the Sgorrla on the mound, and in their own confusion they found themselves being driven back off the little hill. Their ranks wavered and then, suddenly, they turned and ran.

'Bankfoot,' cried Willow desperately as Tain ran over to her. But Tain was gazing towards the trees. The glow was growing stronger and stronger.

'What is it, Tain? What's going on?' panted Haarg as he reached the rowan.

'I don't know,' whispered Tain fearfully.

Now all the deer on the plain fell silent as they watched the furious sparks leap from the trees. The bark was unusually dry from the lack of rain and the strange warmth, and already the flames were catching and jumping from branch to branch.

The Sgorrla that had been lining the forest had fled back to the main body of the Great Herd, and the attacking Sgorrla had reached it too. Among the stags a frightened whispering went up as they watched the glow eat away at the branches. Only in the centre of the trees was there no orange light and now, from the shadows, stepped a single, twelve-pointed stag.

In his mouth he carried a branch. It was glowing too. As the Herla watched, the stag suddenly reared up on his hind legs and cast the branch into the air in a shower of sparks. He bellowed furiously and brought his hoofs crashing to the earth.

Tain came forward from the rowan tree.

'Rannoch,' he gasped. 'Rannoch has come.'

In the heavens there was a grumble of thunder, for on the edges of the horizon storm clouds were beginning to gather.

All their eyes were trained on Rannoch as he stepped forward. The stag, his antlers cutting through the air, walked slowly, surely, his head held high, towards the birch trees where Sgorr was standing with Narl. When he was about four trees away he bellowed and rose on his haunches again.

Sgorr's heart tightened.

'Sgorr,' cried Rannoch, his voice like thunder, 'I told you I would come. And I am here. I have summoned man's light to avenge my father and the Outriders.'

Now a furious murmur went up among the Sgorrla, for they had heard his words and some had seen the fawn mark on his head.

'Herla,' cried Rannoch again, 'you did not believe in me, or in Herne, but now you will pay the price. For I am the Marked One that you drove from the herd and now I have come to fulfil the Prophecy.'

Many of the assembled deer looked at each other in wonder. Next to Sgorr, Narl stirred fearfully.

'It's true,' whispered Narl. 'It's true.'

Sgorr's eye seared into Narl and then he snorted in disgust and stepped forwards himself. The Sgorrla guards around him were looking nervously at their master, but Sgorr pushed angrily past them.

'Rannoch,' he shouted scornfully across the plain, 'you cannot frighten me with your human trickery or the tricks you used on Herne's Herd. For the orange light must feed on the trees and can do us no harm here. As I told you, I too know the mind of man.'

Again the stags looked nervously to their master, for the sight of the fire in the forest and the smell of burning wood

had terrified them. But Sgorr's confidence and his knowledge
of the orange light seemed to reassure them.

Rannoch stamped the ground.

'Yes, Sgorr, you know something of the mind of man. But
you only know of his violence. So why don't you tell them,
Sgorr, what you did? Why don't you tell them that you killed
a human fawn and ate his heart?'

Some of the deer gasped and looked with horror at their
leader. Sgorr felt a thousand questioning eyes on his back.

'What of it, Rannoch?' he spat. 'That is past. Now we
are here to face each other.'

'Very well then, Sgorr,' cried Rannoch. 'Then come out
to fight me. On your own if you dare. Enough stags have
died already this day and I am loath to kill any more.'

Sgorr smiled coldly.

'How can you harm a thousand stags, Rannoch?' he cried.
'No. You had your chance last night and you should have
taken it. But now you are on your own and you must pay
the price for your belief. You're a pretty sacrifice, Rannoch.
Sgorrla,' shouted Sgorr suddenly, 'take him. Take him now.'

But the Sgorrla held their ground. All of them.

'Obey me,' cried Sgorr furiously, swinging round.

The deer looked back nervously.

'You needn't fear him,' cried Sgorr. 'Look at him. He's
just a stag. Any one of you could take him.'

But still the stags hesitated. It wasn't just fear that held
them now, but the thought of what Sgorr had done.

'You,' cried Sgorr to one of the older Sgorrla. 'You will
obey me.'

The stag dropped his eyes.

'Herne is with him,' he whispered, 'and you . . . you . . .'

'Herne is not with him,' spat Sgorr. 'He's a Lera, nothing
more.'

Sgorr turned to another stag.

'You. I command you.'

The stag shook his head too. He was looking at Rannoch and in his eyes shone the light of devotion. It was Quaich.

But suddenly another stag stepped forward from the ranks of the Sgorrla. It was the Sgorrla commander who had been inspecting the herd the night before.

'I'll face him, Lord Sgorr,' he said.

A Sgorrla stepped up behind him. Then another and another. They nodded to Sgorr and he smiled coldly.

'Very good,' he said. 'You will be rewarded. Now bring me his antlers.'

Suddenly twenty stags were running towards Rannoch. He rose on his haunches for a third time and boxed the air as he bellowed again, and then he turned and ran towards the mound and the Outriders. As the Sgorrla saw him and thought he was fleeing the forest and the terrible light, their fear began to subside and suddenly others were breaking away to join the chase.

'He'll never make it,' whispered Willow desperately as Rannoch raced towards them.

The Outriders were all transfixed as Rannoch made for their ranks, but as they watched him they could see that the Sgorrla were gaining on him. There were nearly thirty at his back and Tain shuddered as they saw another group of Sgorrla coming from the right.

'We've got to help him,' cried Willow.

'What can we do?' gasped Tain. The Sgorrla were nearly on him.

But Tain suddenly stood stock-still. Around him a shadow was spreading across the grass.

'What is it, Willow?' he whispered.

Then they heard it. In the sky. A furious cawing and

flapping. The Outriders looked up and gasped. The sky was turning black. Above them hundreds and hundreds of black shapes were moving through the air. The sound was deafening.

'Ravens,' cried Willow, 'they're ravens. Crak is here.'

'*Then his wrath shall cloak the sun,*' whispered Tain gravely. 'Willow, it *is* the Prophecy.'

As the Sgorrla reached Rannoch they suddenly began to bark in fear and dropped their heads. Others rose up and lashed at the air, boxing the sky and the swarming birds. The black cloud was descending on them. The ravens were pecking at their eyes and flapping at their antlers. The chasing deer came to a stop as Rannoch ran on. He had made it to the Outriders.

The Great Herd watched in horror as their comrades fought off the birds. The Sgorrla were lashing at the air, driven to a frenzy by the pecking.

The Outriders dipped their heads as Rannoch reached the rowan tree and looked aghast at the scene of devastation. Bankfoot's eyes were closed. He lay on the ground next to Peppa. Around them both the ground was covered in blood.

'Then I've come too late,' cried Rannoch bitterly.

'Thank Herne you have come at all,' said Tain. 'Rannoch, it's good to see you again.'

Rannoch looked helplessly at Peppa and Bankfoot. Then he looked around at the Outriders.

'Where is Thistle?' he asked.

Willow shook her head.

'I am sorry,' said Rannoch quietly, 'but I had to make sure my mother was safe.'

'Your mother, Rannoch?' said Willow with surprise. 'Bracken is here too?'

'No, Willow, Bracken is dead. And she was not my mother.'

Tain and Willow gasped.

But suddenly Rannoch stepped further forward. He was looking keenly at Bankfoot. The stag twitched, stirred painfully in the grass and opened his eyes.

'Rannoch,' he whispered dreamily. 'Rannoch, you're here.'

'Stay still, Bankfoot,' said Rannoch, 'there will be time to heal you. If there is time at all.'

'But Herne is with us now,' said Braan. He too was badly wounded.

'Herne may be with us,' said Rannoch gravely, 'but years of wandering have taught me how strange his ways can be. For if Herne is a healer, he is a hunter too, and he may yet demand the ultimate sacrifice.'

The Outriders stirred and above them now another dark shadow passed across the fading sun. The ravens had done their work and now they were returning home – those that would fly again, for many of them had died in the fight.

'Thank you,' whispered Rannoch, 'thank you all. But now we have need of a stronger help than yours. Our only hope is if *they* come in time.'

'They?' said Tain.

Suddenly there was another bellow from the plain and the friends turned. Although they couldn't hear what he was saying now, they knew that Sgorr was once more addressing the Great Herd.

'You see,' cried Sgorr, 'they are just Lera. Nothing more than pecking birds. But we are stags. Sgorrla. Invincible. Look at him and his Outriders. There can't be more than sixty left.'

Sgorr was working himself into a frenzy.

'But we, we are an army. Those marks I put on your heads will protect you and this time I will lead you myself. Although I am old and I have no antlers, I will show you that I am not afraid.'

The Sgorrla watched their lord, and though fear was stirring through their ranks, for years they had been trained to do his bidding and, in the fading light, Sgorr looked strangely magnificent. He turned and began to move towards the mound; Narl followed him. The Great Herd stirred, then they came on, a thousand deer heading towards the Outriders. More Sgorrla were crossing the stream and moving out from the pass too. Their training had won. Now the sky was full of heavy rain clouds, swollen by days of evaporation in the unearthly heat.

On the mound Rannoch lifted his head.

'No time,' he whispered sadly, 'no time,'

Then the stag turned and addressed the Outriders.

'My friends,' he called, 'will you follow me? Will you follow this mark, in the name of Herne?'

The Outriders nodded their antlers and began to bark.

'Very well then,' cried Rannoch, 'let us face our destiny.'

Rannoch turned and with Willow, Tain and Braan at his side, he led the Outriders off the mound to their deaths.

Nearer the Sgorrla came and nearer, but as the friends readied themselves for the terrible impact, Willow suddenly cried out. She could hardly believe her eyes.

'Look,' she barked, 'the pass.'

Through the pass behind them, where the Sgorrla had moved forward, deer were running towards them, fighting as they went, trying to break through to the Outriders.

'It can't be,' shouted Tain.

But they all recognized the deer leading them. It was Birrmagnur. There were other reindeer at his side too, maybe fifteen of them, and behind another hundred or so Herla. Most of the newcomers were red stags but Rannoch's heart thrilled as he saw roe deer among them, and one deer in particular running ahead of them.

'Teek,' cried Rannoch in amazement, 'it's Teek. From the edge of the Great Mountain. This day may have more surprises than I'd thought. Come on.'

The Outriders raced forwards towards Birrmagnur and Teek and before any of the Sgorrla had reached them, they had come together, swelling the depleted ranks of the Outriders once more.

'Birrmagnur,' cried Rannoch, 'I'm glad to see you, my friend.'

'I brought all I could, Rannoch,' cried the reindeer, 'when the Lera told me you were coming to face Sgorr. I found my friends below the Great Mountain.'

Rannoch looked at the band of reindeer. They were an impressive sight.

'There are many others coming,' said Birrmagnur, 'but I fear they won't be here in time.'

The Great Herd was closing in on them from all sides now, charging in fury and bellowing as they came. Although he lifted his nostrils to scent the wind, Rannoch's heart was heavy.

Closer and closer they drew.

'Herne,' whispered Rannoch. 'Help us now, Herne.'

In the sky the clouds had grown black and suddenly there was a rumble of thunder. Lightning flecked off the heavens and it started to rain. But the Sgorrla were on them. The whole plain became a mass of fighting deer. In the centre of them Rannoch lashed back and forth, rising to box or butting left and right. Tain was at his side and Birrmagnur too. The reindeer's strength and bulk proved a mighty force against

the Sgorrla and the friends held them at bay. But around
them the Outriders were already beginning to fall. One after
another. It was hopeless. On they fought, bravely, for the
honour of the Outriders, but their hearts were fired now
only by desperation and as the rain grew heavier it added to
their despair. They could see the light of triumph burning in
the Sgorrla's eyes.

'Goodbye, Rannoch,' called Willow above the mêlée, as
she caught sight of the stag. Rannoch's eyes came level with
the hind's and the look in them now was one of defeat.

'Has this mark brought us to this, Willow?' said Rannoch.
'I am sorry for everything.'

'Don't, Rannoch,' cried Willow. 'At least we will rest
together. For ever.'

But suddenly the fighting Herla heard a sound that froze
all their hearts.

It rose amongst them, a terrible howling. The voice of an
enemy far more terrifying than any Herla that faced them.
Then the real enemy was moving amongst them, snarling
and biting, tearing at the Sgorrla's legs and haunches.

'They've come!' cried Rannoch gravely, but with triumph
in his voice. 'They've come at last!'

Other animals were moving through the deer, hundreds
of them, their shining, silvery fur glistening in the wet. They
growled as they came, slavering and biting, but only at the
stags whose heads were marked. The Outriders they left
alone. They moved like lightning and in their teeth there was
terror. The wolves had come at last.

'He commands the Lera,' cried a petrified Sgorrla. 'Herne
has come to punish us. To punish Sgorr for what he did.'

'Sgorr, Lord Sgorr,' cried Narl in the midst of the fray,
but as he turned to his lord, Narl gasped. Sgorr was surrounded. Three wolves were advancing on him, curling back

their lips to show their teeth and growling furiously. Sgorr was trying to back away but the old stag had nowhere to run. He too showed his teeth but now he looked tired and helpless.

'Come then,' cried Sgorr suddenly and defiantly. 'Come, Herne. For you have hunted me all my life, haven't you?'

The wolves were about to pounce when suddenly Narl came charging straight at them. The stag dipped his antlers to defend his master and as he did so the wolves leapt at him, all three at once. Narl was lost. He felt death in his throat. But he had died with honour, for Narl had won his master time to escape.

'Rannoch, dear Rannoch,' whispered Willow as the rain came down. 'What is happening?'

'The hunter is amongst us,' whispered Rannoch. 'Stay still, Willow, it will be over soon.'

Everywhere the Sgorrla were standing down, but strangely the wolves didn't attack them for their orders had been to kill only the hornless one. Instead they held the Great Herd at bay.

'You've won, Rannoch,' cried Willow. 'Won.'

But Rannoch wasn't listening to the hind. He was looking out into the distance. Near the edge of the pass he saw a stag, a stag with no antlers, slipping away.

'Rannoch,' cried Tain, running up to him, 'Sgorr is escaping.'

'I've seen him,' said Rannoch.

'I'll bring some Outriders.'

'No, Tain,' cried Rannoch, 'I must do this alone.'

Rannoch began to run as fast as he could through the driving rain towards the pass. When he reached it he caught sight of Sgorr again at its far end. Rannoch leapt forward.

But as he came to the centre of the pass, he pulled up. On the ground in front of him lay Thistle.

'My poor friend,' said Rannoch sadly. 'I'm sorry I failed you. You never really liked me, Thistle, I know that, but I hope you forgave me somehow.'

But no answer came from the dead stag.

'Herne,' cried Rannoch bitterly, 'must we die? Must we all die?'

Rannoch suddenly lifted his head in anger and ran on after Sgorr. He came into the corrie and on the mountainside above the water he saw the old stag scrabbling up the slopes.

'Sgorr,' he cried after him, his voice echoing round the stone cauldron. 'Face me, Sgorr.'

But the deer didn't answer. He vanished over the ridge of the mountain. Up Rannoch rose, his hoofs slipping on the wet scree. He came over the ridge above the corrie and again the slopes reared above him. Rannoch couldn't see Sgorr now but he could see the path he had taken in the wet. He began to thread his way up the steep mountainside.

He rose higher and higher and he kept looking up for Sgorr. Showers of rock and stone skittered onto his head and the stag knew that Sgorr was somewhere above him. Rannoch came to a thin ledge where the mountain sloped back suddenly to another overhang above, crowned by a great rock. The drop below the ledge in front of him was some ten trees while ahead the mountain levelled out. Rannoch paused, fearfully, but he could see that Sgorr had come this way. He stepped out onto the ledge.

Suddenly stones and rocks were showering all around him. Rannoch reared up in terror and as he did so he saw Sgorr above him on the overhang, pushing at the huge rock. It was beginning to sway, to tilt back and forth on the small tor of stones that barely held it in place and had, for centuries, kept it from crashing down onto the ledge below.

'Rannoch,' cried Sgorr furiously, 'do you think you can destroy me with your tricks? Well then, join your beloved Herne.'

Rannoch gasped as the rock lurched and he saw the light of hatred burning in Sgorr's eye.

But with that Rannoch heard a strange sound, a hissing through the damp air. He had heard it before, and something shot past Rannoch's eyes. He stood amazed as Sgorr's head was suddenly thrust upwards.

A thin, tapering branch of wood was sticking from Sgorr's neck and blood was already pouring from his throat. Sgorr staggered forward towards the edge of the overhang, away from the rock which had settled back on its precarious perch. He looked down at Rannoch and now the hatred in his eye had turned to confusion and defeat. Then Sgorr fell, his legs flailing in the air, his body crashing onto the ledge next to Rannoch. He was dead.

Rannoch swung round and, on the mountainside opposite, standing in the wet grass in the twilight, the stag saw a young human. He was already putting another of the tapering branches onto the wooden cross he held in his hands and lifting it to his eyes. Rannoch quivered as the boy's scent came to his nostrils. He turned and ran, leaping off the ledge and scrabbling up the grassy slopes. But the human was after him, running as fast as he could.

Rannoch's heart was beating furiously as he tried to gain a purchase on the slopes. It began to rain again and a wind came up, moaning through the gorse, whispering like a voice Rannoch had heard long ago.

'So, Herne,' cried Rannoch bitterly as he climbed, 'the hunter becomes the hunted.'

Rannoch was slowing now, for the ground was getting steeper and steeper, the earth wetter and wetter. His head lurched forward and he stumbled. He could feel the human behind him. Rannoch scrambled on and suddenly the incline slackened and he was on open, flat ground again. But ahead was a sheer rock face. Rannoch was trapped.

The stag turned to face his pursuer in the twilight and he flinched as he saw the human running towards him through the rain. When he was some two oaks away he came to a stop and lifted the crossbow to his eyes once more. The hard point of the bolt glistened with water. Rannoch backed away, his legs shaking and the fur around his throat beginning to bristle. His senses screamed out, as in his mind he tried to escape the trap. He lowered his antlers slightly.

So you do demand sacrifice, Herne? he thought.

But suddenly the human lowered his arms again. He was looking closely at the deer now, staring at the mark on his forehead. He lifted his arms once more and then lowered them again. As the stag looked fearfully into the human's hungry eyes, trying to hold his gaze, Rannoch's mind woke into astonishment.

Those eyes; that piercing green, yet behind it that same searching gentleness, that desperate, questing need to know. The human fawn had grown, but the contours of his face were the same and around them the locks of red hair. It was the boy, grown into a young man; the boy who had saved Rannoch from the pit.

The deer and the boy stared at each other wonderingly in the dripping evening and the wind climbed around them as their nervous breath rose to touch the air. The wind itself seemed to be speaking and saying, 'Herne, Herne is here.'

Then suddenly the boy raised his hand towards the deer, stretching out towards the mark on his head. He lifted his forefinger for a second and then, without a word, he stepped to the side. Rannoch felt a sudden rush of energy as the space opened, and once more the deer was free, running down the mountainside.

Rannoch stopped and looked back up the slope.

But in the coming dark he could see nothing. The boy was gone.

'*Till his need shall summon man,*' said Rannoch and there was wonder in his voice. Then the red stag turned quietly and walked back towards his friends.

As Rannoch came back through the pass and looked out across the plain, he saw that the Great Herd had finally been subdued. To the east the glow in the forest had gone out. The trees spat and sizzled in the downpour, but beneath the bark, where the water could not cool the elements, the fire still glowed on, so that when the trees dried it would suddenly burst out again, here and there, to feed off the still living matter and transform it into light with its furious alchemy, distilling the life force back into carbon.

The wolves were growling angrily in the rain as they faced the frightened Sgorrla, but as Rannoch threaded through their ranks a wondering hush fell on the deer.

Rannoch reached the Outriders and Willow and Tain ran up to him.

'Sgorr?' asked Willow.

'He is gone,' said Rannoch.

Once again the deer's eyes were trained on Rannoch and now he turned to address them.

'Don't fear them,' cried Rannoch suddenly. 'For this night at least, they will not harm you.'

His voice rose above the rain as the Sgorrla looked at him fearfully. But suddenly one of their number stepped forward.

'Herne,' he cried, dipping his antlers. 'Herne.'

'Silence,' shouted Rannoch immediately, subduing the deer with his eyes, 'for although I come in the name of Herne, I am not Herne. I am a Herla. Like you. Like the roe and fallow deer. Yes, even like the Sgorrla.'

The Outriders stirred around him and a fallow deer stepped forward from among the Sgorrla.

'I will follow you,' he said. 'I would have followed you when you came to visit me in the wood last night, if only you had waited.'

Rannoch looked up at the deer and there was puzzlement in his eyes.

'The deer must follow nothing but their instincts,' he said, 'and the laws of Herne.'

The skies grumbled again and the droplets grew harder.

'But now it is finished,' cried Rannoch wearily, the water splashing off his fur. 'The Prophecy is fulfilled. The Herla are free, in the High Land and the Low. Never again will Sgorr's lies infect the herds. We must live as Herla and nothing else. And never again must we kill one another or harm the Lera.'

The Sgorrla looked wonderingly at Rannoch.

'But what shall we do,' cried another of them, 'without a leader? How will the Great Herd survive?'

'The Great Herd shall not survive,' cried Rannoch, 'for it is against Herne's Law. Anlach is restored. All of you must go back to your own herds, or live alone as the roe. Live free and find your own lords. Then one day those marks on your heads will be healed, healed in the birth of your fawns.'

'So we should fight for our lords?'

'At Anlach, yes,' cried Rannoch, 'for all things must fight, for their own strength and survival. That law is older than the Great Mountain.'

But at this the wolves around them began to growl. They were growing restless and suddenly one among their number stepped up towards Rannoch. Even the Outriders pulled back.

'Rannoch,' he snarled, his yellow-green eyes full of hunger, 'we came when you called and we have done your bidding. But it is time for us to go.'

It was the wolf that Rannoch had healed by the waterfall. Rannoch nodded.

'You have done my bidding,' he said, 'and Herne's bidding too.'

The wolf snarled angrily.

'Remember what I told you, Rannoch,' he cried. 'I came because I owed you a debt and because Sgorr's madness had spread even amongst the wolves. But now the debt is paid. What I said is still true, Rannoch. Never again will the wolves help the Herla. Your blessed law, Herne's Law, has returned to the Great Land. So fear us, Rannoch.'

Rannoch looked down into the yellow-green eyes and nodded sadly, but he said nothing.

With that the wolf growled again and, calling to his kind, he turned away. One by one the wolves began to peel off, padding silently through the soaking grass, their eyes glittering furiously in the darkness as they passed through the trembling ranks of the Herla.

'Willow?' said Rannoch quietly when they had gone.

'Yes, Rannoch,' said the hind, stepping up beside him.

'We must tend to Bankfoot and to the sick. For many have fallen this day.'

'Yes, Rannoch.'

'Willow?'

'What is it?' asked the hind.

'I am tired.'

25

Sacrifice

The magnificent cause of being,
The imagination, the one reality
In this imagined world . . .
Wallace Stevens, 'Another Weeping Woman'

For his days shall herald laughter,
Born a healer and a king.
Herla Prophecy

A young hind was grazing across a moor in the late autumn sunshine. Her coat had a special lustre and her eyes were keen and bright. Nearby other deer were moving towards her in a loose group, running ahead of one another or stopping to graze also. The hind stopped feeding and looked up.

Not far from her was a mound of heaped earth where a storm had uprooted a large tree and as the deer reached it they seemed to flow up and over its sides, some of them springing into the air off its flanks. A young buck, just one and a half years old, stopped on the top of the mound and looked down proudly at the others as he swayed his single antlers. But almost as soon as he stopped another buck ran up the side. His antlers had brow tines.

When he arrived the other deer simply moved away, slipping off the edge of the mound, and the new deer was left to survey his temporary kingdom. None of the Herla around him challenged him, for they were either hinds or prickets. But as he stood there a third deer, a stag with fine branching antlers, came out of the trees. He saw him and strolled casually forward. Before the adult had even reached the mound, the deer on its top, hardly looking towards the stag, also gave way and slipped off down the hill, so that the stag was left to stroll up its sides and stand gazing arrogantly ahead. The hind that had been watching smiled inwardly and went on feeding.

Suddenly, from above them, there came a great bellow. A full-grown male stag was stamping and ruffing out his throat sack, as another stag approached him and eyed the group of females that were clustered together behind him. The bellowing deer moved forward a little and the newcomer seemed to change his mind and turned away. But he swung back again and ran straight towards a hind that was set slightly apart from the other group.

The first stag roared and charged at full speed. The other deer swivelled and dropped his head and the stags' antlers met. Both deer were knocked back by the blow and they dug their haunches into the moist ground and struck at one another again, fencing. This time the approaching deer slipped and then turned and ran. The defending deer snorted and followed him a little way down the hill before veering off and returning to his hinds. Now as he scoured the hill his face bore a proud, almost contemptuous look. His name was Quaich. The deer that had just lost the battle pretended not to notice as he started to graze as casually as he could through the heather.

Anlach was almost over, though, and most of the stags in the herd were exhausted. They had shed nearly half their body weight fighting to defend their hinds, but the season in the High Land was mild and the coming winter would take a light toll. Suddenly, from the bottom of the hill, there was a great burst of laughter. Two fawns were running through the grass, leaping and jumping in the autumn sunshine, delighted with their game of tag.

They stopped, panting, and looked up at the other deer. All across the moor the stags that had mated were patrolling their stands. On the top of the hills the Outriders were looking down on them or gazing out into the distance, ever watchful for any sign of a threat to the herd.

'I hate Anlach,' snorted one of the fawns, 'it's so boring.'

'I know,' agreed his friend. 'The Outriders are always too busy to play with us.'

'And the stags never stop fighting.'

'Let's go and listen to the storyteller,' said the second fawn suddenly. 'He's over by the burn.'

Suddenly there was another bellow from above them. They looked up and the fawns felt a thrill as they caught sight of the single stag, looking down on them majestically from the top of the moor. Around him the heather rustled in the breeze and his proud antlers showed him to be a fine twelve-pointer. He looked magnificent in the misty sunlight; a royal; a king among deer. About his throat the thick fur was a deep red-brown and his eyes were bold and defiant. In the centre of his head, although it was beginning to fade and blend back into the colour of the ruddy fur around it, the fawns could still see the white oak leaf.

Rannoch turned and walked slowly back to his hinds. There were twelve of them and all but one were sitting down in the grass. The one that was standing was more striking than the rest and she had huge, bold black eyes. It was the head hind. Rannoch came up to her and as he drew near she turned her head towards him. They held their muzzles together for a moment, breathing in each other's scent, and stirring with a deep and tender satisfaction.

'Rannoch,' said Willow quietly, 'how is the herd?'

'Well.' Rannoch smiled. 'The Outriders have seen nothing.'

'No humans?'

'No,' said Rannoch, gazing out across the mountains. 'They have gone back to their dwellings.'

'Then it's over.'

'Yes. The Lera say that the Great Land is whole once again.'

'It's a part of the Prophecy I don't really understand.'

'No,' said Rannoch, 'but Crak told me that after . . . after the battle, the humans were fighting by the sea. There was a terrible storm but they drove the men from the north away from the shores of the Great Land. They took back the Island Chain.'

'Why were they fighting?'

'Who knows? To be free.'

'Like us,' said Willow, smiling. 'Maybe they are not so different.'

Rannoch looked at Willow but he said nothing for a while.

'You know, Willow,' said Rannoch at last, 'Rurl died at the humans' battle. The otters told me. He had gone to see what was happening and he got too close to their carved trees. They say he was speared. Poor Rurl, he was always so inquisitive.'

'Rannoch,' said Willow, 'there's another part of the Prophecy that I think about often. That I don't understand either.'

Rannoch turned to Willow.

'You mean the sacrifice?' he said quietly.

The hind stirred in the grass and nodded.

'I went to see Birrmagnur just before Anlach,' said Rannoch softly. 'His calf was sick and on the way I met a Lera. It was a stoat. But when I tried to talk to it, Willow, I couldn't understand it.'

The hind looked into Rannoch's eyes. They were suddenly very sad.

'And Willow,' said Rannoch painfully, 'I think I am losing the power to heal. I could do nothing for Eloin when she grew ill.'

Willow was silent. She knew that the hind's death had hurt Rannoch terribly.

'All my life I have wanted to heal things,' said Rannoch, 'and I have tried. But sometimes I think there is a wound in nature that nothing can heal.'

'And it makes you unhappy,' said Willow quietly.

'In the end, Willow, I had to heal myself,' answered Rannoch, 'and you have helped me do that. I am content to live as a Lera.'

Willow looked fondly into Rannoch's eyes.

'This mark on my head is fading too,' Rannoch went on quietly, 'and sometimes when I think back on everything that's happened, I wonder if it was just a dream. Sometimes it's like a mist that comes down. I can't understand the world any more.'

'What do you mean?'

'I mean that I think that is the true sacrifice, Willow. The Herla are free, thank Herne, but my power and my understanding . . . I must give it up. To be a Lera.'

'But you wouldn't rather be like them? Like the humans? That's what Sgorr wanted.'

Rannoch shook his head but again he said nothing.

'The evil comes from them,' said Willow. 'Do you remember what you saw in the glen?'

'No, Willow,' said Rannoch, 'the evil does not come from them. The evil comes from hurt and fear and trying to deny Herne's Law. But the fight is within each of us – it's just the humans can see further. Sometimes I think that must be very terrible for them.'

Willow nodded. She was looking out across the herd now.

'You know, though, Willow,' said Rannoch suddenly, looking down on the herd, 'in a way all life is a sacrifice, for one day I too will be overthrown as Lord of the Herd, so another stronger Herla may take my place to protect the herd.'

'Rannoch,' said Willow quietly, 'I have something to tell you.'

'What?'

'When spring comes there will be another little Outrider in the herd.'

Rannoch threw up his head.

'What?' he gasped delightedly.

'Yes.' Willow nodded. 'I can sense him already. What shall we call him, Rannoch? How about Brechin?'

As they neared the burn the two fawns that had been playing together caught sight of the storyteller standing by the water, a group of yearlings gathered round and listening attentively to the stag.

'He was the only one to defend her,' he was saying as he strolled back and forth proudly, 'then Captain Bankfoot rose up on his haunches and cried, "To me, to me." '

'But we've heard that story,' cried one of the yearlings.

'Oh you have, have you?' said the stag, looking down at him and smiling. 'Then what would you like to hear about?'

'I want to hear about the Outriders,' said another yearling.

'The Outriders?' said Tain. 'And what do you want to know about the Outriders?'

'What's it like to be an Outrider?'

'It's a fine thing,' said Tain. 'The best thing for a stag. Unless, of course, you're a storyteller.'

'You were a captain, weren't you?' said the yearling.

'I still am a captain,' laughed Tain, 'but it's true I'm not much good to the Outriders with this leg.'

The yearlings craned forward excitedly to take a look at the deep scar on Tain's leg.

'You got it in the battle, didn't you? The last battle.'

Tain nodded.

'And Rannoch healed it?'

'That's right. Though I've still got a limp.'

'Bankfoot's got a scar too,' said another fawn. 'He showed it to me the other day. He told me that he wouldn't have made it but for Rannoch.'

'But my mother says that Rannoch doesn't like to heal the Herla any more,' said one of the fawns suddenly.

Tain looked down at the fawn.

'You mustn't say that,' he whispered. 'Rannoch is very busy, that's all.'

'Why?'

'The Lord of the Herd has a hundred and one things to do. Now stop asking so many questions. I thought you wanted a story. What's it to be?'

'Starbuck,' cried all the calves at once.

'But I've told you all the stories about Starbuck,' laughed Tain.

The fawns looked very disappointed.

'I tell you what,' said Tain, 'I'll tell you a special story. Winter will be coming soon and it's a story for the winter. Birrmagnur told it to me.'

'Birrmagnur,' cried the fawns delightedly. All the fawns were fond of the reindeer and they often crossed the moor to visit the small reindeer herd.

'Yes,' said Tain, 'and this one is about Herne, though Birrmagnur calls him Hoern. It's also about Urgin, the bravest and the most famous of all the reindeer.'

'Urgin?' said one of the fawns.

'That's right. There are lots of stories about Urgin. There is the story of Urgin and the first stone, and Urgin and the ford, and the day Urgin stole the magic antlers.'

'Starbuck!' cried a fawn. 'Urgin is Starbuck.'

The sun, which had been hidden behind a cloud for a moment, suddenly blazed down on the deer. Tain lifted his head, and just beyond the burn he caught sight of a holly bush. Its spiky green leaves were already beading with tiny red berries and Tain nodded to himself.

'Yes, sort of,' said Tain, 'but the best of all the stories about him is the story of Urgin and his helper Clausar. Urgin was just as clever and brave as Starbuck but yet again his antics had angered Hoern and so the deer god sent down a terrible winter to punish his kind. It was after the time of suckling and the snow fell so heavily that there was nothing for the calves to eat.

'But Hoern also let it be known that it was because of Urgin that the reindeer were being punished and that none of them were to help or talk to him. So Urgin wandered far and wide through the reindeer herds, and everywhere he went the reindeer turned away from him. His heart was close to breaking, for he knew that it was because of him that the herds were suffering. But what pained him most was to see the young calves starving, for Urgin loved calves above all. He was at his wits' end but, ask as he might, none of the reindeer would help him.

'Then, one day, he had a bold idea. If he could not ask the reindeer for help he decided he would ask the humans. Urgin knew of a man who lived on his own, away from the herds of other men, who had sometimes helped reindeer calves when he found them caught in the snow. The reindeer called him Clausar, which in their language means "the one who loves animals".

'So Urgin ran as fast as he could to the valley where Clausar lived. He approached his dwelling nervously and saw him toiling in the snow. Clausar was very old and tired and he was trying to carry wood to his dwelling to make the orange light to warm his bones. He had made a large pile of wood on a sled and now he was trying to pull it. But old Clausar was too weak and tired to manage. Straight away Urgin ran up to him and turned his back to the sled and told Clausar to put a rope around his neck and tie it to the sled. Urgin knew how to talk to men as he knew how to talk to all the animals.

'Well, Clausar was so startled that he did just as Urgin told him and soon the reindeer was pulling both the wood and Clausar across the snow. When the old man reached his home he was so grateful that he asked Urgin if there was anything he could do for him in return.

'Now Urgin told him of the terrible winter and of how the poor calves had had nothing to eat. Clausar, who was more like a reindeer than a human, was very moved and he showed Urgin the barn where all year he had been storing up wheat. He knew he himself was very close to death and so he offered to give the wheat to the reindeer. But then Clausar suddenly looked sad, for he realized he was too old to get it to them in time.

'At this Urgin stamped and snorted furiously, for he was bitterly angry with Hoern. Then he had another idea. He asked Clausar to pick out five straws of wheat and bind them with another straw and to divide up the whole barn like this, to make sure there was enough for each of the calves. Next he told Clausar to put them on the sled and once again to rope him to it. Then Urgin waited till Hoern and the reindeer and all the calves were asleep.

'When he was sure that no one was watching him, he raced through the snows as fast as he could, dragging Clausar and the parcels of wheat behind him. Wherever he found a calf he stopped and Clausar would leave the wheat by the calf's head, so that when they woke they found they had something delicious to eat.

'Urgin and Clausar worked on and on,' Tain continued enthusiastically, 'but it was hard for the reindeer, pulling the old man on his own, so that when Hoern and the other reindeer awoke, he had only visited a tenth part of the herd.

'When Hoern saw what had happened, he suspected immediately that Urgin had something to do with it and he was very angry. He went to all the male reindeer and asked them what they had seen. Now many of them had woken in the night and spied Urgin but most were too grateful to him to betray him. But ten reindeer told the deer god that it had been Urgin. The god raged and sent more snow and called on Urgin, who was hiding in the forest, to come forth and explain himself.

'At last, fearing the storm would destroy all his good work, Urgin came out of the forest and bowed his antlers to Hoern. As the god watched him the storm died and his anger melted.

' "Urgin you have disobeyed me, but you did it for the calves and so I shall allow you and Clausar to finish your work," he said.

'Urgin was delighted, until he realized that he still had so much to do.

' "Very well," said Hoern, "then as a punishment I shall rope the ten reindeer that betrayed you to Clausar's sled and they shall pull it as swift as the wind. But you, Urgin, shall lead them, as free as the first reindeer."

'This was done and soon all the calves woke in the snow to find the wheat by their side.

'But when the great work was complete Hoern came to Urgin again.

' "Urgin, do not think you can get off so lightly," he said, "for now, every year, you and the reindeer shall draw Clausar's sled and bring gifts to the calves. For though Clausar is old and near death, the spirit of Hoern shall grow in him and the fur on his chin will glisten like snow and he will help you."

'And so it is,' Tain finished grandly, 'that every year, in winter time, the reindeer bring wheat to their sleeping calves. And the calves can hardly contain their excitement, waiting for Urgin and his helper Clausar.'

The fawns looked in wonder at Tain and the storyteller smiled to himself. Above them a single star began to glint in the heavens. Larn had come once more and a light as old or as young as time itself was shining down on the herd. As the darkness came down on the Great Land a moon rose in the sky, blue and brilliant, and in its mysterious light Tain and the fawns went on talking into the evening. The only sounds drifting across the heather were the burn gurgling through the night and their laughter threading through the darkness.

So the years passed and the Herla flourished. In the High Land and the Low they roamed through the gorse and drank from the lochs and the burns. They padded through the forests and drifted across the great moors, but wherever they went, whether among the trees or to the high barren places of the Great Land, they knew that in their antlers the forest was always with them. At Anlach they fought for their mates and to lead their herds but never again did they kill one another, unless nature herself stepped in to sap their strength through their wounds. With time and in the birth of their fawns the terrible marks that Sgorr had inflicted on the Sgorrla's heads vanished from the herds.

The Lera also flourished. They ran free and hunted each other too, and though the strange whispering that had brought them together to fulfil a prophecy faded from the Great Land, in time to come the badger and the mole, the otter and the raven would tell each other stories and say that once all the animals had been able to understand one another, though only the creatures of the sea know the truth of it.

Man flourished also in the Great Land. Man who would fight and kill and kill again. But nevermore did the men from the north come in their tree ships to the Western Isles. For after the battle that was fought on the shores of the sea, the Great Land was talked of as Scotland and the Norsemen's king, whose name was Haakon, sailed away to his home and grew old in his great dwelling, dreaming of the lands he had once ruled and listening to the ancient Norse sagas.

The herd had moved well to the north of the High Land and now a single stag was walking slowly along the slopes of the mountain above them, away from the deer. He was very old, nearly fifteen, and he looked tired. Although there were sixteen points on them, his antlers had long gone back. When he got to a patch of level ground he stopped and sank wearily to the earth. His muzzle was grey and his eyes were misty. Rannoch lifted his antlers towards the horizon. Across the blue, the billowing white clouds rose like mountains before him.

'Herne is up there,' whispered the stag to himself, 'and Starbuck.'

Then Rannoch shook his muzzle.

'Or is that just a story?' he said to himself sadly, his eyes clouding over and his nostrils swamped by the complex scents around him that he could no longer interpret. 'And am I just an animal?'

With the years everything had become so distant to the deer. The mark on his head had completely faded now. Since he had been overthrown as Lord of the Herd and Willow had gone, he felt more and more alone. But Brechin, who was already an old stag himself, was a favourite among the Captains of the Outriders. Peppa, his second calf, had her own fawns and Rannoch's bloodline coursed strongly though the herd. Thistle would surely lead them one day.

Rannoch closed his eyes. A breeze came up, rustling the grass around him, and Rannoch suddenly stirred. He fancied he caught a voice on the wind.

'Who's there?' whispered Rannoch, looking around him.

'Rannoch?'

'Herne,' he whispered, 'is that you?'

'Come then,' the voice seemed to say.

Rannoch's heart was pounding and strangely he suddenly remembered the boy.

'One more journey, then, before it's all over?'

If only he had the strength. If only he was a young stag again.

Then suddenly Rannoch was running, running like the wind. His antlers were strong and proud once more and in his hoofs was thunder.

The red deer was climbing the sky, lifted up on the great slopes of white, free to run with the Herla for ever.

On a mountain high over Scotland, lying still in the heather, lay the body of a single red stag. Rannoch had passed into eternity.

Lu.

The New Rabbit Handbook

Everything about Purchase,
Care, Nutrition, Breeding, and Behavior

With Color Photos by Well-Known Photographers
and Drawings by Michele Earle-Bridges

Consulting Editor: Matthew M. Vriends, PhD

BARRON'S

New • York • London • Toronto • Sydney

All inquiries should be addressed to:
Barron's Educational Series, Inc.
250 Wireless Boulevard
Hauppauge, NY 11788

Library of Congress Catalog Card No. 89-6902

International Standard Book No. 0-8120-4202-6

Library of Congress Cataloging-in-Publication Data

Vriends-Parent, Lucia.
    The new rabbit handbook: everything about purchase, care, nutrition, breeding, and behavior / Lucia Vriends-Parent, with color photographs by well-known photographers and drawings by Michele Earle-Bridges; consulting editor, Matthew M. Vriends.
        p. cm.
    Bibliography: p. 126
    Includes index.
    ISBN 0-8120-4202-6
    1. Rabbits—Handbooks, manuals, etc. I. Vriends, Matthews M., 1937-   . II. Title.
SF453.V75   1989
636'.9322—dc20   89-6902
                                          CIP

PRINTED IN HONG KONG

9012 4900 987654321

About the Author
    Dutch born Lucia E. Vriends-Parent studied biology, psychology, and music in Australia and the United States. An accomplished pianist with preference for Chopin, Beethoven, and Mozart, she is the author or co-author of several books in Dutch and English, among them Barron's Pet Owner's Manual, *Beagles.*

Note of Warning
    This book deals with the keeping and care of rabbits as pets. In working with these animals, you may occasionaly sustain minor scratches or bites. Have such wounds treated by a doctor at once.
    As a result of unhygienic living conditions, rabbits can have mites and other external parasites, some of which can be transmitted to humans or to pet animals, including cats and dogs. Have the infested rabbit treated by a veterinarian at once (see page 62), and go to the doctor youself at the slightest suspicion that you may be harboring one of these pests. When buying a rabbit, be sure to look for the signs of parasite infestation (see page 62).
    Rabbits must be watched very carefully during the necessary and regular exercise period in the house (see page 27). To avoid life-threatening accidents, be particularly careful that your pet does not gnaw on any electrical wires.

Photo Credits
    Gräfe and Unzer: Front Cover; 127 bottom; 128; Back Cover center, above right.
    R. Lauwers: Inside Front Cover; 37 bottom.
    All other photographs are by D.J. Hamer, Jr.

Contents

Contents

Preface

In the last few years, interest in keeping, breeding, and exhibiting fancy rabbits has increased enormously. This may be seen from the growth in the numbers of members of the American Rabbit Breeder's Association (ARBA), which in 1988 had about 35,000 adult and junior members. In addition, there are hundreds of thousands of unaffiliated rabbit fanciers and breeders. From these numbers we can calculate that as many as 12 million rabbits are kept by fanciers in the United States alone! Mr. Bob Bennet, the well-known American rabbit-expert, has said that this is a conservative guess. This, nevertheless, is a lot of rabbits—even for rabbits!

Yet, numerous new rabbit fanciers have found to their dismay that the keeping and breeding of rabbits is not the simple matter they may at first have thought. This is the common conclusion after these novices have lost a number of youngsters—usually through intestinal disorders caused by incorrect feeding, inadequate care, or substandard accommodations. Contrary to the belief of many prospective or new rabbit keepers, rabbits are very sensitive to monotonous diets or to sudden changes in the diet, as well as to foods that are rotten, fermenting, or moldy. Wet grass or green food with a high moisture content given in too great quantities may be readily eaten but will also lead to dietary disturbances; such foods should never be given to juvenile animals. Other fanciers feed their rabbits a staple diet of pellets—and I would be the last to say that there is much wrong with this strategy. The kind of pellets available on the market today are excellent and save the fancier a lot of time and money. However, the same monotonous diet every day is not an ideal situation. For this reason, I say

much about natural supplements in this book. In addition, I discuss acquisition, management, accommodation, and general care. If these factors are all handled properly, the possibility of a disease outbreak is kept to a minimum.

This book is aimed mainly at those who wish to keep rabbits purely for pleasure. It is less oriented toward those considering rabbits primarily for commercial purposes, a subject on which much has already been published. (See Useful Literature and Addresses.)

At this point I would like to acknowledge, with thanks, the work of my friend, Mr. John Coborn (Queensland, Australia), whose help and knowledge have contributed considerably to the end product. I am also grateful to Dr. Alice DeGroot, MS, DVM, who read the manuscript and made invaluable suggestions. I must also thank my husband, the biologist Dr. Matthew M. Vriends, for his enormous contributions, especially in the chapters devoted to feeding and genetics. Finally, I would like to extend my sincere thanks to Michele Earl-Bridges for her fantastic artwork, and especially for the friendship she has extended to my husband and me over the years; it is surely a great honor to number such a talented artist among one's friends.

As always, I am eager to receive any comments or constructive criticism that may arise from anyone's reading the text.

Loveland, Ohio
Spring 1989   Lucia Vriends-Parent

This book is dedicated to Don Reis,
friend and editor, for whom nothing
is too much!

A Brief History

The Rabbit and Its Relatives

Rabbits belong to the order of harelike animals known as the *Lagomorpha*. This word is derived from the Greek words *lagos*, which means hare, and *morphe*, which relates to form or shape. *Lagomorpha* means literally, harelike, or formed like a hare. At one time rabbits were included with the rodents or gnawing mammals in the order *Rodentia*, but in 1945 Simpson argued that rabbits and their relatives had enough unique characteristics to warrant a separate order of their own.

Some wild cousins of the rabbit. Above: the strange looking, little hamsterlike pika. Right: the jackrabbit, a hare with long ears and powerful hind legs. Left: the cottontail, found from southern Canada to South America, and from coast to coast. The rabbit and its relatives are the targets for more human hunters than all big game combined!

Within the order *Lagomorpha* is the family *Leporidae*, which contains both the hares (of the genus *Lepos*) and the rabbits (of the genus *Oryctolagus*). Rabbits are divided into two types, the wild rabbit (*Oryctolagus cuniculus*) and the tame (domestic) rabbit, which has the scientific name *Oryctolagus cuniculus forma domestica*. The Pikas (of the genus *Ochotona*) and the cottontails (of the genus *Sylvilagus*) complete the order *Lagomorpha*. The jack rabbit of the western plains, which have fully furred young, are more properly considered hares.

Early History

Hares and rabbits originated in the Western Hemisphere, and from there they have dispersed to all corners of the earth, including Europe via Asia. However, there are still more species found in North and South America than in other parts of the world.

The first known member of the family *Leporidae* to be found in Europe was *Lepus lacosti* from the upper Pliocene period in France. Rabbitlike mammals also occurred in the Netherlands, Germany, and Great Britain during the late Tertiary period. Toward the end of the Tertiary and the beginning of the Pleistocene, a period of about 1 million years, rabbits became fairly widespread in Europe.

According to the study of available fossil remains, the rabbits that inhabited Great Britain at the beginning of the Pleistocene were most probably smaller than the modern wild rabbits. During the Ice Age, the abnormal climate drove rabbits from their northerly domains to southwestern Europe. The Iberian Peninsula, which consists of Spain and Portugal, became a sort of reserve for wild rabbits. Evidence from old paintings and manuscripts indicates that although the hare was abundant and well-known throughout Europe, the rabbit stayed in Spain until humans took them to other parts of the continent.

The first known written report of rabbits came from the Phoenicians. During their voyages to the Spanish coast they came across animals that in size, body shape, and habits bore a great resemblance to the rock hyrax or dassie (*Hyrax syriacus*) native to their own lands (modern Syria and Lebanon). The hyrax was referred to in the Hebrew texts as *shaphan* (meaning sly or crafty). It is then not surprising that the Phoenicians named the land *i-shaphan-im* after the animals they found there (literally translated this means "coast of the island of rock hyraxes"). This name for the Iberian peninsula was later translated by the Romans into the Latin *Hispania*, the country we today know as Spain.

The Romans

Roman coins from the reign of emperor Hadrian (76–138 A.D.) show a portrait of the emperor on one side and, on the flip side, a portrayal of Minerva next to an olive tree. Between Minerva and the olive tree is a rabbit, perhaps as a personification of Hispania. Minerva, the goddess of divine wisdom,

The Easter Bunny, harbinger of new light and life!

was the symbol of life emerging from death; and the hare was known to be the first field animal to give birth after the midwinter turn of the sun. The legend of the Easter Hare, as the harbinger of new light and life after the desolation of winter, must have a relationship with the foregoing facts.

Apart from the portrayal of the rabbit on the Roman coin, no further illustrations of the animal are known from this period. According to Imhoof-Blumer and Keller, a number of rabbits appear carved or etched onto gemstones. It is not possible to put an exact date to these works; moreover, the depictions are so small that it is not certain that they are in fact rabbits.

In the second century before Christ, rabbits inhabited the island of Corsica. The Greek historian Polybios, who had been held hostage in Rome, gave the rabbit the Greek name *Kyniklos*, which in Latin became *cuniculus*. This means animals that live in a warren or underground system of burrows.

In the first century B.C. the smallest of the three harelike species living in Italy was named *cuniculus* or rabbit. This species, which originated in Spain, was a welcome addition to the Roman *leporarium*, in which captured hares were kept for culinary purposes. A leporarium was a large, walled garden or enclosed area in which, initially, hares were kept. However, the Romans were quick to discover how well the Spanish rabbits acclimatized to life in the enclosures and began to keep these in addition to the hares. The high walls and the thick vegetation of the leporaria gave the animals good protection against predators, including birds of prey.

In such an ideal situation, the rabbits were extremely prolific. They soon increased in numbers and became an important food source for the Romans. However, certain disadvantages of the animals soon came to light. Unlike hares, the burrowing activities of rabbits enabled them to escape under the walls of their enclosures. Being extremely adaptable, they were able to colonize the surrounding countryside and spread further. At that time, the writer Pliny in his *Natural History* reported that feral (wild) rabbits were causing enormous damage.

A few pairs of rabbits that had been released on the island of Majorca multiplied to such great numbers that the land was laid waste. The human inhabitants of the island petitioned Rome, begging the Emperor Augustus for military assistance to clear the plague, or to find them (the people) another place to live.

Rabbits in the Middle Ages

Although wild rabbits had their domestic uses, they were not anything like the domestic animals we know today. For these we have to thank the French monks who, in the early Middle Ages, kept rabbits in large hutches in which the young were born above the ground.

Rabbits were kept as a source of food—both for the monks themselves and for the many travelers who regularly used the monasteries for overnight shelter.

From the beginning of the Middle Ages, monks bred rabbits. Through study and selective breeding the monks produced rabbits of colors differing from those of the wild variety. In the wild, white or spotted rabbits would stand little chance of survival because they would be too conspicuous to predators. In the protective environment of the monasteries, however, these varieties could be used for further breeding and the development of new varieties.

After further generations of breeding the domestic rabbit thus emerged from the wild *Oryctolagus cuniculus*. The monks kept and used these new varieties in much the same manner as wild rabbits. In the year 590, the bishop of the French township of Tours expressed concern that rabbits were being eaten during the fasting periods in many areas. Apparently, rabbits frequently were not even regarded as meat!

Dispersal of Rabbits

The Romans were responsible for the dispersal of rabbits throughout France and other parts of the continent. It is thought that rabbits were introduced into England from France during the Norman invasion of 1066. It seems that the first rabbits reached Germany in 1149. In that year Abbot Wibald of the Benedictine monastery at Corvey on the Weiser River asked his fellow abbot Gerald, of the monastery at St. Peter de Solignac in the French diocese of Berry, to send him two pairs of rabbits. Because Abbot Wibald asked for two pairs of rabbits, not one buck and three does, Professor Dr. H. Nachtsheim believes that Abbot Wibald was not well informed on rabbit breeding!

For a time, it seems rabbits remained scarce in Germany. The famous natural historian Albertus Magnus, Duke of Bollstaedt (1205–1280), never saw rabbits in Germany. The first mention of the rabbit in German literature is in a natural history manuscript published by Konrad von Megenberg in 1349.

Rabbit Plagues

Early explorers took live rabbits aboard their ships, thereby providing themselves with an almost self-sufficient supply of fresh meat. Thus rabbits were spread to various parts of the world. Although some rabbits no doubt accidentally escaped in new lands, many animals were deliberately released. In some of these areas there were hardly any predators, thus allowing the rabbits to multiply unchecked.

Children enjoy having pets! Even more important, keeping pets teaches children to take responsibility for other creatures. Very small children, however, often find it difficult to relate to a rabbit. In these cases, be ready to provide assistance and an occasional explanation.

A Brief History

In 1418, a group of mariners released a doe with youngsters on the island of Porto Santo, near Madeira. The rabbits multiplied at such a pace that they soon laid waste the whole island. The island became totally uninhabitable and the original human colonists had to leave.

Later, a similar but much larger plague of rabbits occurred in Australia. After their introduction to this southern continent in 1859, they soon became feral and adapted to the arid conditions of the new land. Since there were few natural predators, the rabbits soon multiplied to plague proportions, spreading across the land in huge groups and causing enormous damage. Not only did they destroy crops, the hordes of rabbits also consumed valuable natural vegetation necessary for sheep, cattle, and native wildlife. Many farmers, landowners, and gamekeepers still wage an almost fanatical war against the prolific creatures. Although in some parts of the world the rifle and the catching net may be used to control rabbits, a new method had to be found in Australia. This took the form of biologic control. The disease myxomatosis was introduced into the feral populations to control them.

The myxomatosis virus was isolated from a wild, South American rabbit species. The virus was further developed and modified and used to combat the rabbit plagues in Australia. Later, it was used in other countries as well. Although the disease, at first, had an immediate and enormous effect on the rabbit populations, the prolific animals soon developed a certain immunity to the virus. It now appears that rabbits are almost as numerous as ever. In any case, they have survived remarkably well from the many ravages inflicted upon them.

For three weeks the baby rabbits depend completely on their mother's milk. Soon thereafter they start nibbling on their mother's food and continuously increase their intake of it. At about six weeks of age they will be completely weaned.

General Rabbit Breeding

In a painting by Titian from the year 1530, a Madonna is depicted with a white rabbit. Thus we know that, at that time, there were domesticated rabbits with coat colors that are not found in nature. Moreover, in the second half of the sixteenth century, the natural historian J.C. Scaliger reported black, yellow, white, spotted, gray, and brown domesticated rabbits.

The first comprehensive work on the breeding, feeding, and care of rabbits was published by the German scholars C. Stephan and J. Liebhalt in 1579. The authors mention the use of rabbits as meat animals and as pets.

New varieties of rabbits are produced through a combination of a knowledge of genetics and selective breeding. As new varieties are produced, further breeds may be developed from them until shapes and sizes far from the original wild ancestor are produced. At the beginning of the eighteenth century it is believed there were seven distinct rabbit breeds; a century later this had increased to twelve.

The famous Dutch natural historian, Anthony van Leeuwenhoek, wrote that in the "Golden Century" (1601–1700) wild bucks were crossed with tame black-and-white spotted does. Such crossings were initially carried out to produce heavier offspring for meat. However, at that time wild rabbits were supposed to have a more delicate flavor than tame, so rabbits of the wild color were bred. Luckily for the breeders the wild color is dominant, so most of the offspring had the required wild color (see page 84).

Many paintings from the seventeenth and eighteenth centuries show rabbits of the breeds we now know as Netherland dwarfs and Polish. The latter is the oldest known dwarf race. Dwarf varieties, however, have never been documented in nature. We may assume, therefore, that if miniaturization did occur in the wild, the offspring did not survive long enough to propagate themselves.

A Brief History

Fancy Rabbit Breeding

Around the middle of the last century, a number of breeders started to produce new varieties of fancy rabbits just for the love of it. New breeds arose not only from selective breeding, but use was made of the occasional spontaneous genetic mutations— that is, hereditary changes that resulted in new colors or hair types. By selective breeding the mutation could be preserved and further varieties could be produced. Later, the special characteristics of each breed were laid down as "breed standards."

By maintaining the standards, breed characteristics are retained and can be improved. Today, it is the ambition of every enthusiastic rabbit breeder to produce animals of perfect standard so that they may earn the highest qualifications from judges at exhibitions.

Meat Rabbit Breeding

In addition to breeders of fancy rabbits, there are those who still breed the animals for meat and, more recently, pelts. Many breeds were first produced solely for their quality as meat producers and were economically important in the first half of the present century. Indeed, rabbit and poultry breeding went hand in hand, and even today rabbits are included in the category of "poultry" by many wholesalers and retailers of meat products.

In Belgium and France rabbits had been bred as a food source since the sixteenth century. Rabbit breeding really started in Germany with the Franco-Prussian war of 1870, when the Germans noticed that the French placed great importance on their rabbit culture and, indeed, made quite a bit of money out of it. After their return to Germany they began to import French rabbits, which were much larger and more prolific than the few small animals that were found in Germany at the time.

Around the turn of this century, societies dealing with the propagation of rabbits sprang up in many places. Conferences and exhibitions contributed to ever-increasing improvements in breeding techniques. In England, however, more interest was shown in the breeding of fancy rabbit varieties than in breeding for meat, which was generally imported. Millions of slaughtered rabbits were shipped to England from Australia, France, Belgium, and the Netherlands. It was hard for the English to forego rabbit meat; it became their "Sunday joint." For example, the Netherlands started supplying the London market in 1897, and in 1902 half a million guilders worth of slaughtered rabbits were supplied.

In the United States the Ozark region of northern Arkansas and southern Missouri has become the center of commercial rabbit production. More than 34 million pounds of rabbit meat are produced there each year.

Pelt Rabbit Breeding

Commercial rabbit breeding is not only for meat production. Although frowned upon by some, rabbit pelts are a useful and valuable commodity.

A rabbit pelt is most valuable when the animal has fully completed its molt and new fur has just formed. For many, it is difficult to be certain when the fur is at its best, but with a little practice this can soon be learned. The wet hand is stroked over the fur in both directions, and if no loose hairs adhere to the hand, one can be sure that the pelt is fully mature. Another method is to blow into the fur and look for dark spots in the skin. This is usually done near the tail, which is the last part to grow after the molt. A fully molted animal shows no dark spots on the skin.

Young rabbits at about seven months of age usually have a first-class pelt. However, a hard and fast rule cannot be given, unfortunately, as individual animals develop at different rates. During the molting a treat of oil-containing seeds (sunflower seeds, for example) added to the usual food improves the sheen in the fur. These should be given in moderation, however, as too many can cause diarrhea. The stems and leaves of sunflowers are also greedily eaten by rabbits, and these are also a good treat.

Around the end of the last century and the beginning of the present one, various luxury items, such as shoes and handbags, were manufactured from rabbit leather. Items manufactured from the so-called Havana rabbit skins were very popular.

A fair, but not perfect pelt is one that has no dark spots on the back part but a few along the flanks. A perfect pelt is one that has no dark marks whatsoever. An excellent pelt is one that has no dark marks and has a beautiful, thick fur with a handsome sheen. At one time even the worst pelts had some value as the hair was used for the felt industry (in Australia, rabbit fur is still used to make the famous Akubra felt hats).

Wool Rabbit Breeding

In addition to those rabbits produced for meat and for pelts, there are also those kept solely for wool production. Known as Angoras, these rabbits are sometimes said to have originated in the Turkish province of Angora (close to Ankara), but this is incorrect. The Angora rabbit probably got its name from the fact that it has long fur—similar to that of an Angora sheep, Angora goat, or Angora cat. The name is, however, no more than a handle for various long-haired animals. The earliest report regarding Angora rabbits (although the name came much later) was made in 1723 by Gaston Prenier, who reported that English seamen had offered long-haired rabbits for sale in the port of Bordeaux. These animals are said to have come from southern Russia.

Much interest was shown in these rabbits, and shortly after their appearance in France they appeared in England, where they were further bred and improved. The task was to breed the rabbit with long hair without losing its other characteristics.

In contrast to the meat and pelt breeds, Angoras are not bred in great numbers in the United States. The care of the animals requires a great deal of time. Special care and accommodations are required to ensure that the coat does not become matted or strained. Moreover, failure to provide a properly balanced diet soon has an adverse effect on the development of the fur.

The value of the wool depends on its thickness, quality, and length. The more hair present, the more valuable is the rabbit. The length of the wool for both fancy and commercial breeds must be not less than $3^1/_4$ inches (8 cm). An Angora should produce 11 to 17 ounces (300–500 g) of wool per annum, although most thick-wooled animals produce 11 to 14 ounces (300–400 g).

Angora wool is very light; a sweater made from it weighs about a quarter the weight of a similar sweater made from sheep's wool. The insulating or warmth-holding properties of Angora wool are well known.

Selection

Rabbits as Pets

Rabbits are clean and affectionate animals. With proper care and management a single rabbit becomes an excellent house pet. It is neat by nature and washes itself even more frequently than a cat! A healthy rabbit will wash its entire body, including its feet, every day.

You don't have to groom your animal, although a good daily brushing when it is shedding helps to get rid of loose hair. Gently stroking your hand over the rabbit's pelt helps its coat become shiny.

By the way, rabbits lose their first (baby) coat at about four months of age, depending on the breed; thereafter they molt twice a year, in the spring and in the fall.

Considerations Prior to Purchase

Never obtain rabbits on impulse. Before acquiring any animals, give careful consideration to the possible consequences. Do you, for example, have sufficient time and patience to give the animals the care they deserve? Caring for any animal is a serious responsibility. If you have the slightest doubt about your ability to cope with rabbits, start with a single animal; then you will be able to assess the amount of time and patience required for keeping several.

Note: Before considering the purchase of rabbits, check with local authorities. Ordinances in certain areas restrict or even prohibit the keeping of rabbits.

There are various body types among the rabbit varieties. Center: full-arched. Above left: semi-arched. Above right: short compact. Below left: commerical. Below right: Snaky (Himalayan).

Rabbits are excellent pets! The choice of breeds is very much a matter of personal preference. In any case, it is advisable to have a new rabbit checked over by a veterinarian within a day or so of purchase.

How Much Time Will It Take

A rabbit must have a portion of green food every day. In the summer months this means the daily collection of grass and other green foods that are necessary to keep the animal's fur in good condition. As a rabbit grows, its consumption of green food increases.

Collecting green food every day takes up a lot of time, especially in hot, dry periods when the plants grow sparsely. A rabbit keeper with many animals can become a slave to them to ensure that they do not go short. Should you rely on supplies of reject green food from supermarkets and nurseries, you must also be aware that quantities of such supplies can fluctuate. There are times when green food is plentiful and other times when it is difficult to obtain adequate quantities of reject material suitable for rabbits.

In addition to green food, a rabbit must have hay and other foods (pellets, for example) available at all times. In other words, the animal must receive a good, balanced diet to keep it in optimum condition. The somewhat complicated digestive system of the

Selection

domestic rabbit means that it also requires a quantity of roughage (fiber) in the diet for it to make full use of the other nutrients. Hay and straw are important sources of roughage in the diet. Barley or alfalfa straw and dried pea plants are particularly valuable for this purpose.

Obviously, since the production of the bite-sized rabbit pellet, feeding your animal is no longer a tough job. But, also obvious, rabbits need more than pellets alone!

Therefore, before rabbits are purchased, you must ensure that the necessary time for the proper care of the animals is available. If you do not have the time to regularly attend to the animals, say, three times a day, then you must make the decision: rabbits are not for me.

Further time-consuming tasks include the thorough cleaning of hutches every week, and clean straw must therefore be available every week. In summer, a sprinkling of straw may be adequate, but in the winter a thick straw bed is required for protection against the cold.

With inadequate care and feeding, a rabbit loses condition and suffers stress. Disease quickly sets in, sometimes resulting in an incurable or even a dead animal. Therefore, before starting this fascinating hobby, take heed of the old proverb: Look before you leap!

One or Two Pet Rabbits?

• If you have *little time*, get two female rabbits (does) from the same litter; unrelated does get into serious fights.
• Two male rabbits (bucks) won't tolerate each other; they bite and scratch each other, causing serious injuries.
• One doe and one buck become stressed and restless when left alone in separate cages, unless you have neutered the male.

Male or Female?

• When handled correctly, a rabbit, whether buck or doe, becomes very tame and affectionate.

• However, a young male (approximately four months old) should be neutered by a veterinarian to prevent spraying. (A buck marks his territory with urine.)

Sexing Rabbits

A doe reaches sexual maturity in four to eight months, depending upon the size of the breed. A Netherland dwarf, for example, matures in four months, but a Flemish giant or New Zealand white is seven or eight months old before the does are ready for mating.

Sexing young rabbits is very difficult, as the sexual differences are not yet marked. In adults, however, sexing is relatively easy as the buck has a prominent scrotum.

It is advisable for two people to be present for sexing: one to restrain the rabbit, belly upward and hind legs spread apart, so you can see the two sexual openings, the anus and the sexual orifice; the other person to manipulate the genitalia. The latter applies gentle pressure with middle and index finger to either side of the sexual orifice until either the penis of the buck or the vagina of the doe is evident. Also, the female has a much larger aperture (see page 67).

Purchase of Rabbits

After carefully considering all these above points and deciding that you want to go ahead, you are ready to look for your first animal. In principle, you have the choice between a named variety and a "mongrel" (the latter being an animal of mixed parentage and of no particular variety). Unfortunately, many people have the idea that "a rabbit is a rabbit" and buy the first animal they come across. All too often the result is that the animal quickly becomes sick and dies.

The beginner to rabbit keeping, who will have little experience, should buy the rabbits from a reputable pet store or breeder. If you do not know a reputable supplier, then go to the administration of your local rabbit club and inquire; perhaps join the club. There you will get all the necessary information and you may be able to obtain a magazine or newsletter in which pet stores and breeders regularly offer animals of various breeds for sale.

When purchasing a rabbit, never buy one that is too young, but it is wise to observe them when they are still with the mother. You can then see what the mother and the other members of the litter look like. If you are satisfied, you can express your interest and return at a later date to close the deal.

If rabbits or their accommodations do not look good, then do not buy. You can get a good idea of how well animals are kept almost the moment you walk into the premises. If the hutches are dirty and smelly and the surroundings untidy, then you should immediately assume that the rabbits are not well cared for and go elsewhere. Dirty hutches can be a veritable breeding ground for disease organisms, and there is a good chance that your prospective purchases will be infected with disease.

Choice of Specimens

All youngsters in a litter must look good. If there are any inferior animals or runts, then do not buy as there may be a chance that even the good-looking animals in the litter are infected with disease (which may develop symptoms later).

Young rabbits should be lively. They should be well-fed and plump and have a fine sheen to the fur. Should they have rough, dull fur or are too thin or pot bellied, the animals are sick. These are typical symptoms of such diseases as bloat and coccidiosis.

Sometimes the body is misformed. This is a sign of degeneration. Always take a good look at the body shape and the animal's stance. With meat-producing stock, exhibition quality is not so important but you should still ascertain that the animals are well built. You should always aim for good

health and a strong constitution in your animals. Deviations in body build are signs of degeneration that must be avoided. Maximum results can be obtained only from healthy, well-built stock.

Age at Time of Purchase

Rabbits should not be purchased too young. It happens, unfortunately all too often, that youngsters of only four weeks are taken from their mothers. This is really much too young for them to be denied their mother's milk. The result is digestive problems, the danger of coccidiosis, and a high percentage of casualties.

It sometimes happens that the mother rabbit is mated again when her earlier litter is just four weeks old. This is bad practice as the doe will be irrevocably weakened, resulting in a serious decline in the health and condition of the next litter and leading to many casualties. Young rabbits should stay with their mother for at least eight weeks, after which they should be able to survive on rations of solid food without difficulty.

The doe should then be allowed to rest for at least three weeks before being mated again. If young rabbits are purchased in a pet shop, you should inquire from where the animals came and ensure that this person is a reliable breeder. When several rabbits from different sources are displayed for sale in a hutch, there is always the chance that one or two are infected with disease organisms that can be passed on to all the others. Take utmost care when acquiring stock.

Fancy Breeds

Rather than choose a mongrel, you would normally show preference for a known fancy breed. There is no way of ascertaining the ancestry of the former; moreover, its conformation is rarely what

Selection

we may regard as ideal for a rabbit.

Fancy breeds have been bred for many generations, each breeder doing his or her utmost to improve the quality. An advantage of having fancy breeds is that it is much easier to dispose of a litter from a good doe than from a mixed-breed animal.

By raising offspring from a healthy litter, you can experience many years of pleasure. You gain much more from keeping a fancy breed, not only from the breeding angle but from the aesthetic pleasure and satisfaction that such an animal can give.

Should you require an exhibition standard animal, there is less risk if you buy a full-grown fancy rabbit. In such cases it is prudent to visit an exhibition and try to buy an animal there. This is particularly advisable for those who wish to breed fancy rabbits. For the average rabbit keeper, however, it is much nicer to purchase a young animal about eight weeks old and to rear it yourself. For purebred rabbits, expect to pay between $30 for juniors and $50 or even more for seniors.

Rabbits and Other Pets

Rabbits and guinea pigs usually get along fine. Introduce both animals with caution, however. Well-fed cats shouldn't present a problem, either, but again be cautious and give both animals enough time to "sniff each other out"; interfere immediately when anything appears to go wrong.

Dogs often have the habit of barking and jumping at a new pet, but a well-trained dog, under your guidance, will not harm a rabbit. First, introduce the animals while holding the rabbit in your hand and keeping the dog under control on a leash. Once the dog is reliable with a rabbit that is sitting or being held, proceed to place the rabbit on the ground. Reteach the dog, once again under control on leash, to leave the rabbit alone. Finally, allow the rabbit to hop and play in a fenced yard, and once again teach the leashed dog to leave the rabbit alone. Do not try

to take any shortcuts. Each situation must be dealt with separately because the dog perceives each in a totally different light.

Remember always to pay attention to all your different pets to avoid jealousy. Also, always allow the new rabbit to first familiarize itself with its new surroundings, its cage, and, above all, its keepers, before introducing it to other pet animals.

Rabbit and guinea pig meet for the first time; they usually get along fine!

Technical Terms

It is a good idea to learn some of the technical terms that are used regularly in this book as well as in specialist magazines.

Breed or Race: A rabbit breed (sometimes referred to as a race) consists of animals of the same sort, with the same form, colors, and markings,

The Dutch rabbit (yellow, on the left; blue on the right) rarely weighs more than five pounds. The harlequin (below left) originated in France and became famous for its "patchwork-pelt" of four different colors. The Himalayan (below right) is very docile in temperament.

Selection

which pass on similar characteristics to their off-spring. There are wild races and domestic breeds. The former have developed their characteristics through centuries of climatic influences, changes in food supplies, natural selection, and so on. The latter have been more or less developed by human beings through selective breeding and through the exploitation of spontaneous mutations.

Variety: A variety is a member of a breed with minor differences from the norm, such as color or size. For example, the white and black New Zealand rabbits are varieties of the same race or breed.

Original Bloodstock: The original male and female of the same breed that are used to start a line of offspring. Separate lines from separate bloodstocks can show minor differences in form (such as arrangement of neck or tail), color, or pattern. Once a line is started, it should be continued with members of the same family or near relations.

The Sexes: Female rabbits are referred to as does, and males as bucks. Young rabbits are correctly termed kittens or kits, but in most cases today they are simply referred to as young rabbits or juveniles.

Sex Ratios: When writing about rabbits in ar-ticles or record cards, for example, a simple and speedy means of referring to numbers of sexes is as follows. For 1 buck and 2 does, one writes 1.2, for 3 bucks and 7 does, 3.7, and so on. For additional animals of undetermined sex a third figure may be added; for example, 1.2.3 means 1 buck, 2 does, and 3 animals of undetermined sex, and 0.0.3 simply means 3 animals of undetermined sex. The first figure always refers to bucks, the second to does, and the third undetermined.

Abbreviations: When written on show cards, for example, breeds and varieties of rabbits are often abbreviated to simplify matters. These abbreviations differ from language to language, of course, and even from country to country among English-speaking countries. The abbreviations may even vary from club to club. However, the name of the breed is usually initialed in capitals, for example, NZ for New Zealand rabbit or FG for Flemish giant. Colors and patterns are added in lowercase letters when necessary. Thus a black New Zealand rabbit is abbreviated blkNZ, a white, wNZ. In most cases no punctuation marks are used between the letters. If you are a member of a club, you soon learn the appropriate abbreviations.

Above: The Rinelander is a meat rabbit with an extremely silky and dense coat. Below: The spine of the English spot, one of the oldest of the fancy breeds, is marked with a herring-bone pattern; the eyes are encircled with black.

Accommodations for Rabbits

One of the first considerations for keeping rabbits is the provision of good accommodations. Roughly made, untidy hutches are difficult to clean properly and result in a danger to the animals from disease. Moreover, in a poorly constructed hutch the rabbits are exposed to their greatest enemies, damp and drafts.

If a hutch is too small, the animal has difficulty moving about and the hutch quickly becomes fouled. A rabbit hutch can therefore never really be too large, except in its depth, which should not be more than 32 inches (80 cm) to facilitate cleaning.

It is recommended that hutches be kept outside during the summer and somewhere under cover in the winter (a garden shed or garage, for example). However, rabbits can be kept outside all year. They are able to withstand dry cold very well but are extremely sensitive to dampness, drafts, and strong, cold winds. The morning sun is good for the animals, but strong midday sun can cause dangerous overheating. The hutch should therefore be placed facing southeast. The morning sun then shines into

the hutch, and the animals get some protection against the cold northerly and westerly winds and rain from the west and southwest.

Many diseases can be initiated by openings or gaps in the walls of the hutch. The walls must therefore be solid and waterproof and should preferably be made of strong plywood or tongued and grooved boarding. For an outdoor hutch, the roof can be covered with tarred roofing felt or tiles to render it waterproof. The main requirements for indoor hutches are that the animals receive adequate light and fresh air.

General Hints

As already discussed, an outdoor hutch should be placed facing southeast. If the ground is soft, place some bricks or building blocks under the legs of the hutch to prevent its sinking. The hutch should never be placed directly on the ground as rats and mice can nest under it.

The framework of the hutch can be made from 2×4 inch (2.5×5 cm) lumber. These are jointed and

A Morant hutch can easily be carried to and from a sheltered area. When out-of-doors, place the hutch facing southeast. The morning sun then shines into it and the animals get some protection against the cold northerly and westerly winds.

The wrong housing! The rabbits will be exposed to damp and drafts! A permanent hutch should never be placed directly on the ground as rats and mice can nest under it.

screwed together. Take care that the framework is square and that the uprights are vertical.

The floor, walls, and roof can be made from tongued and grooved boarding. The doors can be made from 1 × 2 inch (2.5 × 5 cm) lumber. The wire-covered door frame can be strengthened with metal angle irons.

The right housing. There is a closed and an open compartment, and the entire structure is raised off the ground.

A gap about ¹/₃ inch (1 cm) wide can be left in the floor at the rear of the hutch to allow the urine to run out. The floor must therefore slope slightly; 1 to 1¹/₂ inches (2–3 cm) over 32 inches (80 cm) is adequate. Do not make a greater slope or the animals slip about.

To minimize odor from the urine, a funnel or gutter can be placed behind the hutch to catch the fluid and pass it into a bucket. A layer of waste oil placed in the bucket floats on the surface of the urine and minimizes the smell. In certain locations you might consider the alternative of allowing the urine to run directly into the ground. If the odor becomes bothersome after a while, the area can be thoroughly hosed, or the soil can be turned.

Measurements

There are many ways of building hutches, and the beginner is well advised to look at a fellow rabbit keeper's hutches to pick up some ideas. Discuss your plans with other breeders. Find out what features of their own hutches they are pleased

A rabbit hutch with six compartments. Various models are available commercially.

with, and be sure to ask them what they would not do if they were building anew. Of course you can also build your own design. The minimum sizes for hutches are as follows:

	Width		Depth		Height	
	inches	cm	inches	cm	inches	cm
Large breeds	47	120	31	80	23	60
French lops	39	100	31	80	21	55
Medium breeds	31	80	31	80	21	50
Small breeds	23	60	31	80	19	50
Dwarf breeds	19	50	29	75	19	50

The measurements given are the minimum for the breed indicated, although the rabbit will certainly not complain if you make the hutch bigger!

Accommodations for Rabbits

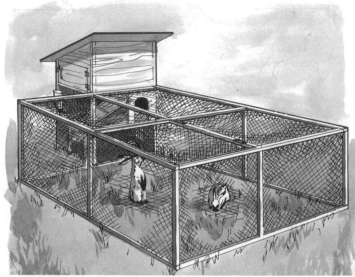

A duplex hutch with open run.

The Rabbit Park or Castle

The winter is traditionally a natural rest period for both the rabbits and their keeper, who uses the time to reflect on the successes and failures of the previous season and begins to plan for the next breeding period. An advantage of this time of the year is that sudden inspirations cannot be carried out too hastily, and one must wait for the new season. The winter gives breeders and fanciers time to carefully consider their plans so that the new season can start with the minimum of upsets.

One of the things that can be considered is how to create a rabbit park. There are two thoughts that come to mind here. Many fanciers think it is just pleasant for their rabbits to have such fine accommodations; others think more about the economics of the rabbits' finding much of their own food.

A consideration that must not be forgotten is that rabbits are by nature burrowing animals, so to prevent escapes the wire netting should extend into the ground all around the enclosure. Depths of 32 inches (80 cm) below the ground surface are frequently recommended, but in practice this is often too little, since rabbits can burrow much deeper. A sure but expensive way of getting around this is to cover the whole area with wire netting just below the surface, placing turf on top of it and allowing plants to grow through it.

Numbers of Animals

The numbers of rabbits kept, of course, depends on the amount of space and the size of the animal. The usual reckoning calls for an average of approximately 16 to 26 square feet (1.5–2.5 m^2) per animal. This works out to quite a bit of land if you want to keep a number of rabbits; not everyone has such an amount available.

A buck may be run with ten to fifteen does; if more than one buck is kept there will be fighting. You must remember that about half the youngsters born in the park will be bucks, and after a time fighting becomes the order of the day. Even the does bite the younger animals. The result is that all the

Accommodations for Rabbits

animals have damaged fur and skin or even more serious injuries, their resistance is reduced, and there is a danger of disease.

Layout

The first task in the construction of a rabbit castle is to site the nest boxes in the enclosure. The boxes are buried in the ground and are closed from above with a removable lid that can be covered with earth. Each box has two or three entrances with sloping pipes leading to about 2 inches (5 cm) above the ground surface. This prevents water from entering during downpours. The spaces around the pipes are filled with earth.

You can of course also place the boxes on the surface of the ground and pile earth up over them to form little hillocks. The rabbits make use of these boxes for shelter almost as soon as they are placed in the enclosure.

The rabbits also soon burrow their own tunnels, at which point you will be unable to inspect some of the nests. Mating then becomes uncontrollable, and the rabbits breed much as they would if totally wild. The end result may be too many rabbits and too many litters produced one after the other. The tough conditions mean that only the stronger animals survive. This has its advantages, but on the other hand weaker animals are more susceptible to disease, which may then affect the whole stock.

The rapid population growth (plus those dead animals below ground) make success almost impossible even in a very large area. In such cases, approximately 100 square feet (10 m^2) should be the minimum amount for each animal.

A good compromise is to build enclosures with concrete floors and walls, in which just a few rabbits are kept. Sand can be used as a floor covering, and trees and shrubs can be planted in tubs to make the rabbit minipark attractive. You should allow approximately 16 square feet (1.5 m^2) per animal in such situations.

Dangers

The possibility of losses from predators is much greater in the rabbit park than if the animals are kept in hutches. Wire netting should be bent outward at the top to discourage cats and other predators from gaining entry.

A collection of rabbits works like a magnet on all the cats in the neighborhood. One day, you see a new litter of rabbits emerge from the nest and gambol about on the ground; the next day the rabbits have decreased in number and soon they have disappeared altogether. Once cats have found a means of entering the enclosure you can be sure that all young rabbits, even those that have been out of the nest for several weeks, gradually disappear without trace.

Dogs can also pose problems for the rabbit fancier as they can even break through the wire netting. The rabbits may also run through holes in the wire to escape. Hawks, owls, and other birds of prey will also take their toll if the enclosure is not protected with overhead screenings.

Your fence should run well below the ground as rabbits are by nature burrowing animals.

Accommodations for Rabbits

Different types of nest boxes. When placed in a rabbit castle the animals use them for shelter almost as soon as they are placed in the enclosure.

Shelters

Adequate shelters should be provided depending on the size of the enclosure and the number of animals. The shelters can be provided with an access door and lockable pop-holes at the bottom of the front, the sides, and the back. The animals can find protection there in bad weather. In addition, the food and water dishes can be placed inside the shelters.

The animals will quickly become accustomed to entering the shelters. Once the rabbits are eating or sleeping inside the shelter it is easy to catch them when necessary by locking the pop-holes. A quantity of fresh hay should be available in the shelters at all times. Green food must be given to supplement that found wild in the enclosure, especially in winter and in periods of drought.

Factors to Consider

Free-range rabbits never become fat; muscles develop well as the animals have unrestricted movement. But, the rabbit park is not ideal for those who want good breeding results. It should be regarded more as a "fun" side of rabbit keeping. Do not expect it to be profitable.

Rabbit Cages for Indoors

A pet rabbit, for example a dwarf rabbit, is best housed indoors in a wire cage with a plastic tray as bottom. Various adequate models, especially designed to house small animals, are available at your

An indoor rabbit cage.

pet store. Choose one that has one or more wide doors on the side of the cage and a removable top, which makes it easier to feed the rabbit and take it out.

For a dwarf rabbit the bottom tray should measure at least 18×28 inches (45×70 cm); the sides should be approximately $5\frac{1}{2}$ inches (14 cm) or more, so the bedding or litter does not fly all over your living room or child's bedroom. It is, in this respect, interesting to know that the U.S. Federal Animal Welfare Act requires that a cage for a large

Accommodations for Rabbits

Keep your eye on your rabbit at all times when it is free in your room or den!

adult rabbit be at least 14 inches (35.5 cm) high, with a floor space of 4 square feet (114 cm²) or more. Minimum requirements for various rabbit weights are as follows:

Up to 4 pounds (1.8 kg)	1½ square feet (45 cm²)
4–8 pounds (1.8–3.6 kg)	3 square feet (92 cm²)
8–12 pounds (3.6–5.4 kg)	4 square feet (114 cm²)
Over 12 pounds (5.4 kg)	5 square feet (153 cm²)

In all cases the minimum height remains 14 inches (35.5 cm).

Each pet shop model comes with a small hay rack. The food and water dishes, however, are usually much too light. I advise heavy, glazed earthenware dishes that won't tip over. Because rabbits should have access to water at all times, I like to introduce an automatic water dispenser. Rabbits get used to it in no time at all. Obviously, a dispenser or earthenware dish should be cleaned on a regular basis.

It is also recommended that an indoor rabbit have the opportunity for taking daily exercises. A run—the so-called Morant or ark hutch (see page 22)—is therefore a necessity. Such a run has an open base (so cover your floor with paper or an old carpet) and can easily be set up. When you want to put your rabbit outside in your yard or on your balcony or terrace, a Morant hutch is the correct solution. Obviously, when taken outside, the Morant hutch can be placed directly on the ground.

The Location of an Indoor Cage

Rabbits are very susceptible to drafts, even when kept as indoor pets. Therefore, never place an indoor cage near a window or door. Because of cold air currents near the floor, it is also advisable to place the rabbit cage on a low table.

Also avoid places near stoves, radiators, and open fireplaces, as well as gloomy corners or next to a radio or television. As far as the latter are concerned please take note of the following: rabbits have sensitive ears and when exposed to ultrahigh frequencies (inaudible to humans) the animal may become lethargic and stressed.

Care and Management

In addition to adequate feeding and housing, other factors are required in the management of rabbits to keep them in prime health. These requirements pertain to not only the animals themselves but also to their accommodations. It should be obvious that one of the most important factors in keeping your animals healthy is the regular cleaning of the hutches and their surroundings. In other words, the animals must be kept in hygienic conditions.

A well-fed rabbit kept in a clean, dry hutch does much better than one kept in a hutch that is seldom cleaned out. The former animal has a greater resistance to disease and is also in better physical and mental condition. Even rabbits can become "nervous wrecks" if afflicted with substandard conditions.

Cleaning the Hutch

Hutches must be cleaned as frequently as possible. Rabbits are creatures of habit and usually deposit all their urine and droppings in a particular corner of the hutch; the rest of their accommodation is kept clean. It is recommended that the hutch be thoroughly cleaned at least once a week with a solution of disinfectant. On other days it is adequate to clean the fouled corners.

If you carry out these tasks at the same time each day and keep to regular feeding times, your rabbit soon becomes accustomed to the routine and greets you with outstretched neck when you arrive. Moreover, a daily routine is much better for the animal; it knows when it can rest undisturbed and learns the times it will have to move, good factors for its mental and physical condition.

When cleaning the hutch, remove the rabbit and put it in a safe place. Never put a nervous animal on a high surface. Should it fall off, it could break a leg or receive internal injuries. A tame rabbit can usually be placed free somewhere near the hutch while you are cleaning it out. It will not run away but is more likely to be curiously interested in what is

going on. Sometimes a curious rabbit will get underfoot to such an extent that you must put it somewhere to keep it out of your way.

Various tools for keeping hutches clean and tidy.

Cleaning implements should include a scraper (a broad-bladed paint spatula is ideal), a hand shovel, a bucket, and a stiff scrubbing brush. The soiled layer is scraped from the floor and then shoveled into the bucket. As has been stated, it is not necessary to scrub the hutch every day, but at least once per week. This should be done with a weak solution of household bleach or with One-Stroke Environ (dilution: half-ounce per gallon of water [15 mL per 3.8 L]). You can then be sure that any germs lurking in the cracks and crevices of the hutch will have been destroyed. The hutch must always be thoroughly dried before the occupants are returned.

If steam cleaners are available for rent in your locality, they are worth your serious consideration. Steam is now usually regarded as the preferred method of cleaning—especially of a hutch in which a rabbit has been seriously ill, or died. Ask at pet shops or hardware stores for necessary equipment.

Care and Management

Floor Litter

The floor of the hutch should be covered with a layer of absorbent material, such as wood shavings, sawdust, or peat. The first is usually the most readily available. The litter acts as an insulating material (especially important in winter) and also quickly soaks up the rabbit's urine. In addition to floor litter, a further layer of clean straw increases the insulation properties.

In the winter hay is a better insulator than straw, but it is much more expensive. If you cannot use hay, try using oat straw, which also has some nutrient value. Barley straw should not be used as the sharp seed husks can sometimes cause injury to the animals' skin. Wheat straw has little nutritive value but is sometimes used for light-colored rabbits as it is not likely to stain the coat (which would lose points in an exhibition).

However, your rabbit will construct a cozy nest with whatever kind of straw or hay you give it. Providing you give it the care and cleanliness it deserves, your rabbit will feel safe and comfortable in its little house.

Composting

The waste material removed from the hutches at cleaning time must be quickly and hygienically disposed of. The quickest method is to burn it; once alight it does not smell bad at all. However, the keen gardener will want to make use of the waste for composting material. Although wood shavings and sawdust rot slowly, rabbit compost is rich in plant nutrients and thus a valuable fertilizer for the garden, even better than farmyard manure!

The compost is best stored in an area enclosed on three sides by a wall. It may be treated with a commercial composting compound so that first class compost is available in a relatively short time. Keepers of large numbers of rabbits can often offset part of their costs by selling the compost.

The area around the hutches must be clean and tidy and free of rubbish and other objects that can provide food and shelter for various vermin. Dry foods should be stored in metal bins to prevent access by rodents. Hay and straw should be stored off the ground on palettes and covered to keep it dry, although good air circulation is required. A good method of storing small quantities of hay and straw is to stuff it in burlap sacks, which are then tied closed and suspended from the ceiling of a shed or other outbuilding.

Hay is an excellent insulator. An old blanket in the winter, however, will be greatly appreicated!

Hutch Damage

When cleaning out the hutch it should always be inspected for damage caused by the weather, by the rabbits themselves, or by rodents that have attempted to enter the hutch. All holes must be immediately patched to keep out drafts and leaks.

Occasionally you come across a rabbit that has the bad habit of gnawing at its hutch, and if nothing is done to prevent this, it will eventually destroy the whole structure. You can help take the animal's mind from its bad habits by providing it regularly with a cabbage stump or twigs to gnaw on. Freshly pruned twigs with a sappy core are the best, but be careful not to include the twigs of poisonous trees or shrubs, such as yew or laburnum.

Care and Management

The most permanent method of "foxing" a persistent gnawer is to cover the vulnerable parts of the hutch with sheet metal, preferably of a sort that is easily bent to shape. Cut the metal to size and mount it on the inner framework of the hutch with screws or flat-headed nails. To prevent possible injury to your rabbit, take care not to leave any sharp edges exposed.

The Importance of Daily Observation

Although a hutch may be clean, roomy, and well lit, you must not forget that a tame rabbit lives permanently in captivity. The rabbit keeper or breeder therefore has a duty to be concerned for the welfare of the animals. This means inspecting them several (at least three) times per day.

When a rabbit hears your footsteps approaching, it will come to the front of the cage to greet you. Its eyes glitter as it follows your movements, and it is as though it is waiting to be handled. Daily contact

Petting, or brushing for that matter, is essential, but do it the right way. Brushing, which should be done at least once a week, gives you an excellent opportunity to examine your pet for signs of disease or injury.

with its keeper is welcomed by a rabbit. It is thus a good idea to visit your animals at the same regular times each day so that they soon begin to expect and enjoy these ritual contacts.

All rabbits should also be regularly handled and petted. Gentle grooming with a soft brush will keep your pets' fur in good condition and help you gain and keep their confidence. Brushing, which should be done at least once a week, also gives you an excellent opportunity to examine each animal carefully for signs of disease or injury.

Such daily inspections of the rabbits while feeding them, brushing them, or cleaning the hutches are important but all too often forgotten. By noticing the smallest thing wrong, such as sudden abnormal behavior, you can often detect a disease in its early stages, when treatment is likely to be more successful and a swift cure can be accomplished. The moment anything odd is noticed, therefore, you should keep a close watch on the animal. Should the situation worsen, it is wise to consult a veterinarian as soon as possible.

Signs of Health and Illness

Your rabbit should always be alert, agile, and full of life. If this is not the case, for example, if your rabbit sits moping in some corner, showing no interest in what is happening around it, this is a sign that all is not well. In such cases you should examine the animal carefully or obtain veterinary advice. During very cold weather your rabbit may sit still with its coat standing out; this is usually no cause for alarm but it is wise to keep it locked in the den and keep a good eye on it for a couple of days to ensure nothing more serious develops. Rabbits are very hardy and can withstand very cold weather, but it is wise to provide them with a good, weatherproof den.

One of your daily tasks is to examine the droppings of your animals; you can easily see any sudden difference in their appearance. The droppings must be firm and round. If they should appear in large, sticky clumps, you must adjust the feeding

Care and Management

A healthy rabbit should always be alert, agile, curious, and full of life.

to prevent further development of diarrhea.

If a rabbit starts sneezing, you must give it a proper examination. Look at the insides of the fore limbs, with which it cleans its nose. If the legs are stained with mucus, you must isolate the animal and consult a veterinarian.

The animal's body must be strong and solid and the bones should never be easily felt through the skin, especially the backbone. The front limbs should be straight and parallel to each other; the rear limbs should sit comfortably below the hindquarters. They should not stick out at the sides or show abnormal angles (which could be a sign of rickets or other abnormalities that you want to avoid at all costs).

The movements of the animal also indicate some important points. Its movements should be supple, lithe, and secure. The ears should move in the direction of each sound, and it should continually twitch its nose.

Special Precautions for Newcomers

The existing stock must not be infected with disease by a newcomer placed with them. New stock should be given a period of quarantine in a separate hutch, as far away from the other rabbits as possible. If the newcomer is still in good health after three weeks, it may then be introduced to the other animals without risk. Fecal samples from newcomers should be examined for coccidiosis at least twice weekly for the first two weeks. The samples must be *absolutely* fresh and must be taken to a veterinarian promptly for microscopic examination. (If necessary, the fresh sample could be placed in a sealed plastic bag and stored in the refrigerator for up to 12 hours prior to transport.)

Caring for the External Organs

Ears

A rabbit is a hearing-oriented animal; that is, a rabbit's hearing is its most important sense. A healthy rabbit must have highly mobile ears that turn in the direction of each new sound. A rabbit's sense of hearing is remarkable—thus the large size of the ears and the ability to move each one indi-

The inside of a rabbit's ear must be inspected regularly and cleaned when necessary. Do not probe inside the ear canal!

Care and Management

vidually. Such a sensitive organ as the rabbit's ear can quickly fall prey to infection, so the inside of the ears must be inspected regularly and cleaned when necessary by wiping gently with a little olive oil or baby oil. Cotton wool or swabs may be used, but never probe inside the auditory canal with the latter. Ear canker is fortunately uncommon, but we must be aware that dust and dirt can easily build up in the long, deep ear opening. This provides an ideal breeding ground for the mites that cause ear canker.

Eyes

"Keep an eye on your rabbit's eyes" at all times. If they are bright and attentive there is no cause for worry. Dull eyes are a sign of poor health or old age; discharging eyes are a certain sign that the rabbit is

Check your rabbit's eyes regularly. Dull eyes are a sign of poor health. Discharging eyes may mean a poor general condition or could indicate a local infection.

sick. In the latter case, it is wise to contact a veterinarian immediately.

Drafts can cause a rabbit's eyes to water. This is easy to see with white or light-colored animals as a reddish stain appears on the nose and cheeks.

Dirt that sometimes accumulates in the corner of

the eyes during sleep can be removed with a piece of damp cotton wool. Do not touch the eyeball, but work around the edges of the eyelids.

In some breeds, particularly some of the larger ones, a condition known as "open-eye" is common. In such cases the lower eyelid hangs down, sometimes almost turning inside out. Such a condition is a genetic defect. Such eyes are easily subject to infection and so should be bathed regularly to remove dirt.

Cataracts or flecks on the pupils of the eyes are sometimes seen in rabbits, particularly in the Dutch and dwarf breeds. Cataracts can reduce the quality of sight. Infections or injuries to the eyes should always receive professional treatment.

Nose

A healthy rabbit's nose should always be dry; one of the most certain signs of disease is a runny nose, which indicates a respiratory infection. If you hold the rabbit's chest against your ear, you may

Grasp the rabbit firmly by the scruff when checking teeth and nose. When you have to check large rabbit breeds, somebody else must restrain the animal.

hear a wheezing or snuffling sound, an indication of lung infection.

Respiratory infections can also be brought about by cold drafts and dampness. The discharge from the rabbit's nose contains disease organisms that can quickly spread to other stock through sneezing, snuffling, or coughing. An infected rabbit attempts to clean its blocked nose with its paws, another sign that it is sick. Such a sick animal must be immediately isolated from the other stock and receive veterinary attention as soon as possible.

Teeth

A rabbit's teeth are very specialized. A pair of chisellike incisors are situated at the front of both the upper and lower jaws. The teeth are kept continually sharp and worn to a convenient length by the action of the upper and lower incisors rubbing continually together during feeding or gnawing activities. The front of the teeth is formed of hard enamel, the back from softer dentine; thus the back wears away more quickly than the front, always ensuring a sharp enamel cutting edge to the teeth.

The thick, "open" roots of the incisors are provided with blood vessels so that nutrients for growth are continually supplied. The chisel edges of the teeth cut off small portions of the food plant. The upper lip is split, allowing more room for biting and gnawing. Behind the upper incisors are two canine teeth, then a space with no teeth at all, and finally the molars, which are used to grind the food finely before it is swallowed. The molars are furnished with grooves and ridges to improve the grinding effect.

The rabbit has strong jaw muscles that enable it to gnaw and chew food for long periods. The ridges on the molars are arranged at right angles to the jawbone. To increase the grinding effect during chewing, the lower jaw is moved backward and forward.

By carefully opening the split lip with thumb and forefinger and at the same time placing a round piece of wood behind the incisors, the rabbit's mouth can be opened so that the teeth can be inspected. (Do not attempt this without a second person to help with restraint of the animal!)

There are rarely any problems with the molars, but sometimes the incisors can grow abnormally. The main cause of this is that the upper and lower incisors may be slightly out of line so that they do not grind together. Also, one of the incisors can break off, allowing the opposing tooth to grow unhindered and causing what is sometimes called "elephant tusk." A rabbit in this condition has difficulty in eating and soon begins to starve. The animal must be taken to a veterinarian, who will clip the teeth to the required length.

Nails

The rabbit's nails or claws also continuously grow. They must be regularly inspected for overgrowth, especially in older animals. If the nails grow too long the rabbit has difficulty moving, and if they are not clipped, the toes themselves can become misformed.

The nails can be clipped with a nail clipper similar to the ones used for dogs and cats.

Care and Management

The nails can be clipped with a nail clipper similar to the type used for cats and dogs. Be careful that you do not cut into the blood vessel; this can be painful to the animal and the nail will bleed copiously. In light-colored animals with light nails, the blood vessel can easily be seen as a red stripe running through the nail, but in animals with darker nails it cannot be detected. Be careful, therefore, not to cut the nails back too far. (To be on the safe side, purchase a styptic pencil or powder at your pet or drug store. Apply this medication promptly to stop the bleeding if ever a nail is accidentally cut too short.)

Feet

The soles of the rabbit's feet should be regularly inspected for signs of injury or accumulations of dirt between the toes (which can be a source of irritation and infection). Should you find matted clumps of soil, try washing them away using applications of warm water and gentle rubbing. If this does not eliminate the problem, you may have to cut the hairs holding the clumps. Work slowly and carefully using a pair of manicure scissors.

An excellent way to pick up a rabbit. A rabbit will feel more comfortable if cradled in the arms, with one hand supporting the animal's weight under its rump.

A good way to hold a large or nervous rabbit. The animal should be restrained firmly by its scruff with one hand, and the other hand used to support the rump/tail area or hold the hind legs.

How to Lift and Hold a Rabbit

At the outset it must be categorically stated that a rabbit must never be picked up by its ears alone. A rabbit must be picked up with both hands, holding it securely but, at the same time, gently. With the left hand, the animal is gripped at the base of the ears and the loose skin at the shoulders; the right hand takes the weight under the tail, and the animal can then be carefully lifted.

Juvenile rabbits are sometimes more difficult to handle as they can be nervous and flighty. Small animals can be grasped gently around the loins with one hand, taking the weight of the body with the other. Once the rabbit has been lifted, it is best to hold it against your chest. The animal thus feels safer and is less likely to struggle. Rabbits should normally be examined on a raised bench or table; in the latter case the furniture can be protected by covering it with a sack or old blanket.

Care and Management

The wrong way to hold a rabbit! The animal may easily fall and injure itself.

The litter box is essential for a pet rabbit that stays indoors. A box for dwarf rabbits needs to have fairly low sides so that they can jump in and out easily.

Can a Rabbit be Housebroken?

Yes, believe it or not, it is indeed possible to housebreak a pet rabbit; however, many animals fail to live up to the fancier's expectations. A definite advantage is that wild and domestic rabbits are in the habit of relieving themselves in one and the same spot; this is an inborn behavior.

Therefore, the best thing to do is to place your new pet rabbit for at least three or four days in a Morant hutch (see page 22) in which you place a cat litter box. Gently place the animal a couple of times per day in the litter box, where it undoubtedly will start sniffing and scratching to its heart's content. We hope it will get the message!

However, generally speaking, rabbits determine their own, definite "toilet spot," which can be behind your couch or in a dark corner of the room.

As soon as you notice that your rabbit is not using the litter box but prefers to relieve itself somewhere in the room, place the litter box at that spot and put some of its droppings in the litter.

Although cat litter is not soft to the touch, many rabbits like it. If the rabbit for one odd reason or another doesn't like cat litter and therefore refuses to use the litter box, a thick layer of hay, with a layer of newspapers underneath it may do the trick.

Patience and especially persistence are the key words to success in housebreaking a pet rabbit!

By the way, the droppings of a healthy rabbit can easily be picked up with a paper napkin or swept up; urine on floor or carpet may be cleaned with soap and water or spray-foam carpet cleaner.

Vacation

It is essential to have knowledgeable friends or acquaintances who can care for your rabbits when you and your family are on vacation. The necessity of membership in a local rabbit club makes itself clear in this case! Neighbors and friends with no knowledge of rabbits cannot be aware of the responsibility of the task. Whoever is to care for your

Care and Management

rabbits while you are away should first visit on several occasions to learn how your operation works. Go through a "dress rehearsal" together.

If you have no club colleague to help, it is possible to enlist the help of an "amateur." Give as much instruction as possible, with a list of things to do each day. Be sure to have an adequate supply of

Traveling/shipping containers designed for cats and small dogs are excellent as rabbit carriers. For traveling with your rabbit by plane, train or bus, request the transportation regulations as well as the size and type container that can be used ahead of your travel date.

Rabbit on a leash. The harness, which is more secure than a collar, should be made of soft leather, fully adjustable to fit snugly. It is best to get the rabbit used to wearing the harness at home first. After a week start to attach the leash and accustom the rabbit to being led. Venture only into quiet areas initially, for example, your garden. Tackle busy areas when the animal accepts the restraint readily.

food (pellets!), hay, and so on; it would be unfair for your friend to have to do the shopping as well!

Give your assistant your vacation address and, in particular, phone numbers at which you can be reached. The telephone number of your veterinarian should also be left with your assistant.

Travel/Transport

Whenever you must transport your rabbit, do so as quickly as possible. Avoid all detours so the

possibility of stress will be cut to a minimum. (This is especially true on the trip home from the pet shop where you purchased your pet.)

The carrier in which you transport the rabbit should be solid, and large enough for the animal to fit in comfortably. The carrier should never be so large that the rabbit might be tempted to jump around in it, for it could hurt itself in the process. There are various proper small dog and cat carriers available at your local pet store; these are excellent

The white and the gray Angora (above left and right) and the brown Angora (below) are well-established colors, but the white remains the most popular color variety. Pet angoras should be clipped at least once a year, preferably in the summer—for obvious reasons!

for transporting your rabbits. Never transport a rabbit in a wire cage. It would jump around and hurt itself. Also, never leave a carrier unattended!

Both the American Rabbit Breeders Associa-tion and the British Rabbit Council have drawn up standard sizes for carriers for each of the rabbit breeds. For more details contact these fine organi-zations (see page 125).

Above left: black-silver. This breed has a black coat with a blue-black undercolor. Above right: blue-silver. This variety first originated in the Netherlands and Germany. Center left: New Zealand, white. This is the most com-mon color variety. Center right: New Zealand, red. The breed, contrary to its name, originated in America! Below left: Satin. Its fur actually has a satin sheen. Below right: White satin. This is one of the more than twenty different color varieties.

Feeding

Principles of Feeding

Feeding your rabbits is a rather simple matter as they will generally try anything you care to offer them. However, this is not to say that they will like all types of small animal foods or that every animal will like the same food.

If you live near a park or woodland, you have undoubtedly seen wild rabbits eating various grasses, weeds, and even tenderly nurtured garden plants! The range of their natural diet runs from lettuce to tulips, and from lilies to beet roots. And they are certainly picky eaters—their special preference is the heart of each plant!

Whether you are feeding gathered or commercial food, the diet for a domestic rabbit should be as varied as possible and high in quality. An ill-fed or underfed rabbit is a pitiful animal. You will also find that an ill-fed rabbit will rarely breed, and if it does is unlikely to raise its litter successfully. A healthy rabbit should be of firm body with a sleek, shiny coat, and sparkling eyes. It is therefore important that domestic rabbits receive a well-balanced diet consisting of the correct ingredients, in the proper proportions.

A balanced diet means that the variety and the quantity of constituents are such that they maintain the rabbit in the best of physical and mental health.

Rabbits require food consisting of edible proteins, carbohydrates, fats, vitamins, minerals, fiber and water in varying quantities, depending on the breed. Provided that these requirements are met the animals will thrive.

The Basis of Health

Rabbits are basically herbivores, or plant eaters, which take vegetable foods in their various forms and, by the process of digestion and metabolism, convert them into valuable materials. Such "food converters" as rabbits are generally not excessively

Good nutrition provides warmth and energy, and supports various physiological and reproductive functions.

demanding. However, there are certain minimum requirements, which form the basis of the health of your animals.

• Feed regularly. A regular feed twice a day is better than three irregular meals! Ideally, feed sometime around seven in the morning and just before dusk.
• The animals must take their food readily; thus do not offer more food until the previous meal has been eaten. Each animal has its individual requirements, and a real rabbit fancier is aware of all the individualities and changes, especially in the feeding patterns.
• Attempt to feed the animals in the most economical way possible. That is, obtain the best foods at the lowest prices.
• Only food in prime condition should be offered, and for reasons of hygiene, hutch and feeding utensils should be kept scrupulously clean.
• Since rabbits are herbivores, their diet can include fruits, roots, sugar beet, and bread, among other items.
• Rabbits are very susceptible to digestive problems. Sudden dramatic changes in feeding patterns must be avoided. If it is necessary to change the

Feeding

feeding pattern, this must be done gradually.

• Green foods that are high in moisture should be offered only in small quantities and *never* to young rabbits.

• In addition to green food, rabbits must have a permanent supply of hay. Always ensure that green food and hay are never moldy. In addition, ensure that green food is not collected from areas where it could be polluted with herbicides, pesticides, vehicle fumes, or droppings of domestic animals.

• Each rabbit should receive a handful of dry food (or concentrated) each day (see page 44).

• Water is the elixir of all life, so rabbits must always have unlimited access to clean, fresh drinking water. With a dry food diet, water is doubly important.

The Rabbit's Digestive System

The feeding habits of the wild rabbit show that it is a converter of raw cellulose. The variety of foods required by a rabbit are therefore similar to those required by ruminants (cud chewers, such as cattle and sheep). These animals are particularly well adapted to make use of the cellulose content of plant material. This is accomplished by the presence of certain bacteria in the digestive tract; without such bacteria the cellulose would be indigestible when it entered the stomach. The bacteria convert much of the material into digestible nutrients.

The digestive organs of a rabbit, however, differ somewhat from those of the ruminants. A particularly well developed cecum is a notable aspect of the rabbit's digestive system. This organ is about 16 inches (40 cm) long. The outside surface reveals numerous folds and grooves. Inside, narrow spiral grooves are arranged about $^1/_4$ inch (5 mm) apart, and the (approximately twenty-five) main folds are about 1 inch (2 cm) from each other. Toward the blind end of the cecum, these folds become fewer and eventually are absent.

The wormlike extension to the cecum, the vermiform appendix, varies from 3 to 4 inches (7–10 cm)

in length and from one-sixth to one-quarter the total length of the total cecum and appendix. It is in the cecum, and also partly in the large intestine, that the bacterial breakdown of plant cellulose takes place in rabbits.

The Rabbit's Diet

Fresh plants are somewhat easier for the rabbit to digest than hay. As long as fresh herbs and vegetables are available, these form the greater part of the rabbit's diet. In addition, dry (or concentrated) foods should also be offered (see page 44).

However, the rabbit's digestive system is not adapted to taking a one-sided diet of green foods high in moisture, such as red and white cabbage, spinach, and lettuce. Such items must be offered in small quantities in addition to the main diet of wild green food. To avoid problems arising from a possible shortage of cellulose material in the diet, good-quality hay should be available all year round.

The hopper can be used to dispense pellets or other dry food on demand.

Feeding

About 3 ounces (75 grams) of hay per animal per day is adequate. In winter, "weed" hay (which is more digestible than grass hay) is recommended. In summer, when the hay is provided as a safety measure, grass or alfalfa hay can be given. (In summer, you should collect a large quantity of "weed" hay for winter feeding.)

Alfalfa can be given either fresh or dried as it is an excellent rabbit food. Red clover is best not given fresh, except in very small quantities with other foods, as it can lead to bloating.

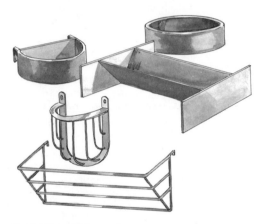

Food dishes and hay racks

Hygiene

No animal likes soiled or wilted food, and rabbits are no exception! Food and water containers should be regularly rinsed, thoroughly scrubbed using soap or detergent and warm water, and then rinsed with cool water. The same procedure applies to the various pieces of equipment that belong in the hutch.

Glass or ceramic water containers or other types of feeders and containers that are cracked or have pieces broken off should be replaced. Cracks are ideal locations for bacteria to gather and sooner or later launch their attack!

It is best to offer hay, greens and roots in a rack. Greens and roots offered on the floor of the hutch or cage quickly become soiled and unpalatable. In either event, the greens and roots must be fresh, and any leftover should be removed toward the end of the day before your rabbits go to sleep.

A clean cotton or burlap sack is ideal for collecting wild fodder. Avoid dragging it along wet ground as it quickly becomes dirty and may soil the collected food. Also, avoid gathering roots, weeds, and twigs from roadsides that are sprayed, used to walk dogs, or border roads carrying heavy traffic. (The toxic level of lead in the herbage is often high and hazardous!)

Quality

As a result of constant research and quality control, the majority of the commercial foods are outstanding. Only the finest foodstuffs—hay, grains, fishmeal, vitamins, minerals, etc., are compressed to manufacture pellets. Seeds are used fresh, when the nutrients are at the highest level. The seeds undergo several cleaning phases before they are processed, and quality control samples are pulled from each batch to document freshness every step of the way. Mixes are processed within days of receiving the order, and all packages are dated when filled.

While the foregoing is generally the case, food for animals should still be judged by the nose and eyes of the experienced caretaker (and naturally, by the animal's response to the food). Food (including pellets!) should smell pleasant, with no traces of dust, as this may cause respiratory difficulties.

Grains, particularly oats, must look plump and glossy; again, watch out for dustiness or mustiness. Feel and smell a sample of the product you are interested in, and talk to an experienced rabbit fancier who can tell you all there is to know about the right rabbit food. Obviously, a reputable dealer or pet show owner/manager will guard his reputation by selling only the best.

Feeding

Quality hay is not easy to obtain and far from cheap! However, alfalfa hay bits, or chews, alfalfa hay, and timothy-hay are frequently available in pet shops year-round, and are usually reasonably priced. Hay can be judged by taking a handful from the center of the bale. If it doesn't smell unpleasant and if there is no dustiness, you can be assured that it is of good quality.

Buy hay with plenty of leaves as it is in the leaves that most of the protein is found. Furthermore, I suggest that you bite some of the hay stems. If they taste sweet and wheaty, all is well! However, if there is a tobacco aroma and a dusty smell, look elsewhere for your pets' food.

Pellets

Pelleted diets are nutritionally complete formulations that can be fed to all ages and breeds. Some breeders believe that pellets are superior to all other foods, since they provide total balanced nutrition in each particle consumed. In fact, most manufacturers state no other type of food need be given to satisfy nutritional requirements, other than water.

If fed on only pellets, however, rabbits—being basically bulk feeders—may grow too fat, especially when housed in small hutches. Therefore, only the correct amount (approximately 3 oz [85 grams] per day for an average size animal), should be offered.

In practice this means a handful of pellets around seven o'clock in the morning, and another handful before dusk. The contents of an average rabbit pellet should be:

		per pound
18%	crude protein	3125 IU vitamin A
3%	crude fat	750 IU vitamin D
14%	crude fiber	3.6 IU vitamin E
8%	ash	0.15 mg selenium
10%	moisture	

There are many excellent brands of rabbit pellets available today. Experiment to find which brand has the greatest appeal to your animal. Judge the quality by the pleasant smell; no traces of mustiness or dust, which could cause respiratory difficulties, should be detected.

Pellets fed in a trough or dish must be finished before you add a new supply, because old pellets render the fresh ones unpalatable!

Green Food

At the first signs of spring in the meadows and hills, the woods and gardens, the first greenery bursts forth, bringing joy into the hearts of rabbit fanciers and their animals. Green shoots that are not available in the winter, fresh grass from the meadows, hills, or woodlands, and various plants including clover and alfalfa all provide an excellent tonic for the animals after the long, hard, boring winter. Also consider the various wild foods discussed in this book (see page 46).

Fanciers who own a piece of land or a large garden find it much easier to collect green food than those who live in the big cities. However, even the

Rabbit eating fresh scat (droppings). This is often proof that various vitamins and minerals are lacking in the animal's daily diet.

latter, with good will and enthusiasm, sees that his or her animals get the best available, even if this means cabbage and other vegetables that are more readily available.

When collecting wild green food, you should avoid areas of pollution from various herbicides and pesticides, vehicle effluent, or dog droppings.

Always ensure that green food is fresh and in first-class condition. It is dangerous for your animals if the food is:

• Partly rotten. Cabbage leaves and potatoes are particularly dangerous, and any rotten parts should be removed before they are given to the animals.
• Fermented. Grass, clover, and alfalfa, laid in a heap in summer, begins to ferment. It is best to collect only enough for a single day's ration. If this is not possible, the food should be spread out to allow the air to reach every part of it. Never use it after three days; otherwise the quality and freshness will have declined. Greens cut during the evening are best.
• Frozen. In winter, frozen cabbage, for example, should not be given to the animals.
• Moldy. Food that is moldy should not be used.

Waste Food

The city fancier obtains most of the animal's green food from kitchen waste, perhaps even from several understanding neighbors, and often from a supermarket willing to dispose of waste material. Leaves and stumps of cabbage of various sorts, pea pods, root peelings, pieces of cucumber, pumpkin, lettuce, spinach, and kohlrabi, rhubarb leaves, beetroot, radish, and even unripe tomatoes: all of these, in a clean and reasonable state, are fine for your rabbits, which will make good use of them. However, be very conservative with the foods that are high in moisture content.

You should be especially careful that green food is not suddenly offered in large amounts. After long periods with little green food the rabbits fall upon it like wolves, and this causes serious intestinal disturbances, including colic and bloat. Always allow your animals to adjust very gradually to new diets.

Other waste materials suitable for your animals include apples and pears and the skins of these and also the skins of potatoes. These can be ground together with stale bread and bran and steamed or boiled to make a mash for autumn and winter rations. It must be noted here that steamed or boiled mash mixtures tend to quickly fatten your animals, but it is good for the manure heap. Mash can also be fed unsteamed or raw. You should ensure that sour mash is not given. On warm days it is best to prepare and give the mash in the evenings. After each meal, the feeding containers should be thoroughly cleaned. Feeding with waste materials should be done with the greatest of care, and never overfeed. Never give the rabbits table waste containing salt or seasonings as these can be a danger to their health. What tastes nice to us will not necessarily provide good nutrition for animals.

Concentrated Food

Under the name concentrated, or dry food, are various grains, such as oats, barley, linseed, soya products, and sunflower seeds. Stale bread is also included in this energy-rich food, which rabbits take greedily. The quantity of dry food to be offered is often exaggerated; you can easily give too much. It is a great source of energy, but if this energy is not used it is quickly converted into fat.

In my own breeding establishment I give each medium-sized animal a daily handful of oats or barley mixed with a little cod-liver oil, which gives an added sheen to the fur. A similar effect can be achieved by giving the animals a small ration of linseed or sunflower seed.

The large breeds I give $1\frac{1}{2}$ ounces (50 g), the medium breeds 1 ounce (30 g), and the small breeds $\frac{5}{8}$ ounce (20 g) of dry food per day in addition to their green food and hay.

The dangers of too much concentrated food in their diet have been elucidated by Dr. Karl Seidel. After examining more than 2000 does that died shortly before giving birth, he found some 1800 with excess body fat. In 90 percent of the dead animals were signs of disease related to a diet too rich in protein and fat!

At times when very large rabbits were popular (Flemish giants, for example), attempts were made to produce rabbits as heavy as possible by feeding rich diets. Such attempts resulted only in infertility, malformation, and internal problems! Luckily, the example of some of the more successful show breeders was followed, and breeders were forced to take a more conservative attitude toward their rabbit breeding. The trend then became, as it should be, more oriented on animals with long, broad bodies, strong legs, and bright eyes, animals that breed and rear their young well.

It should not, however, be concluded that I am totally against concentrated foods. Far from it! I am trying only to warn against the consequences of overfeeding with concentrates. The best means of producing a fine, sleek coat in the animals is to provide small quantities of oil-rich seeds, such as linseed or sunflower seeds. As pure conditioning food you can also give oats, barley, linseed, and sunflower seed. Young rabbits can be given a calcium supplement for the first six or seven months.

Other animals that require concentrated foods are the breeding bucks and the lactating does. Bucks can be given oats or a mixture of oats and barley. Barley is more advantageous for does, especially those with the exhausting task of rearing large litters. Corn should be used with caution. Rabbits are not terribly keen on it, and it is very fattening. It should be used only when animals need to put on weight.

Drinking Water

There is an old belief that rabbits do not require drinking water. Even today, many breeders have their individual ideas about drinking water. One may recommend giving water during the hot summer but not in the winter; another may choose the opposite method; and a third may recommend the

Rabbit drinking from a water bottle. Rabbits should have access to water at all times.

old-fashioned method of giving no water at all.

The question of whether a rabbit requires drinking water is difficult. Of course, all forms of life require water; without it they cannot live. However, the necessary water may be taken directly or indirectly. All foodstuffs contain varying amounts of water, so the amount of water an animal receives depends on what it eats.

So, the animal gets a quantity of water from its food, but is it getting enough? If it is not, then its bodily functions soon suffer unless it gets a supplementary supply of fresh drinking water. In other words, fresh water must be available for emergency use at all times, even if the animals do not appear to be drinking it. There will be a time when they *do* drink it. In practice, rabbits can make very good use of the water content of the food.

The moisture requirement of a rabbit is fairly high. Whether it drinks water depends on the amount of moisture in the food it receives. There is also the possibility that some animals require larger quantities of moisture than others. Therefore, in

Feeding

case of moisture shortage, always ensure that a supply of fresh, clean, not too cold (especially in the winter) drinking water is available.

Collecting Green Food

The rabbit is a natural herbivore. Feeding experiments have shown that many wild green foods have a very high nutritive quality for rabbits. Weeds that stand in the field or garden or "worthless" waste otherwise dispatched to the garbage dump can become valuable items when used as rabbit food. Many green foods are easily digested and contain as much protein as some of the concentrated foods.

The first wild green foods usually appear around the month of April. However, as discussed previously, you should not make a sudden change from a winter to a summer diet; it should be done gradually. Begin with very small quantities of green food, and increase it slowly from day to day. The digestive system must have time to adjust to the new foods. A sudden influx of too much green food can lead to digestive problems, especially bloat, which in serious cases can be fatal.

The green food ration should be as varied as possible. Wild rabbits eat many species of plants in small quantities. Each day, the animals' rations ·should consist of a number of different plant species, thus giving them a choice. Do not force a rabbit to eat an item it does not like. The rabbit knows better than you do what is good for it! Experience has shown that a rabbit does not normally eat poisonous plants unless it is starving, in which case it will probably die.

In this section we discuss only the best known plant species suitable as food for rabbits. Any plant mentioned should be regarded as inedible or even poisonous to rabbits. Therefore collect only those that are mentioned here.

If you have problems identifying the various plants, do not hesitate to obtain the advice of a more experienced rabbit fancier or a nature lover who is familiar with the plants in the area. A good field guide to wild plants and herbs may also come in very useful. Collect young and fresh plants only from a place where they are not likely to be polluted from animals or other sources. (Species marked with an asterisk are not found in North America. They are native to Great Britain, Ireland, and northern Europe.)

Buckwheats

These three species are often difficult to distinguish. Lady's Thumb has obvious dark flecks on the leaves that are barely noticeable in the other two species. All species provide quantities of green food that can be fed with other suitable plants.

Knotted Persicaria (*Polygonum nodosum*)*
  Flowering time: June–October
  Flower: brick-red to whitish
  Height: to 28 inches (70 cm)

Lady's Thumb (*Polygonum persicaria*)
  Flowering time: June into fall
  Flower: pink, rarely white
  Height: to 39 inches (about 1 m)

Pale Smartweed (*Polygonum lapathifolium*)
  Flowering time: July–October
  Flower: reddish to white
  Height: to 60 inches (1.5 m)

Caraway (*Carum carri*)
  Flowering time: May–July
  Flower: white to reddish, in umbels
  Height: to 39 inches (1 m)
Caraway is a widely cultivated garden plant. It may also be found growing wild in clay seams along tracks and ditches, where it is easily spotted from a distance by its conspicuous dark green leaves among the lighter grass. Caraway is a biennial plant. The root can be eaten as a green food, and the young leaves can be eaten as a salad. It is a good animal

food. It is best to use young plants. In older plants the percentage of raw fiber is high (35.9%) and protein is just 10.2% of the dry weight.

Cleaver (*Galium aparine*)
Flowering time: July–August
Height: to 39 inches (about 1 m)
These plants are found in great quantities. They occur in gardens and along hedgerows where they cling to other plants, such as grasses, by means of the numerous hooks situated along the stems. The fresh plant is eagerly eaten by rabbits.

Coltsfoot (*Tussilago farfara*)
Flowering time: February–April (before the leaves)
Flower: yellow
Height: to 8 inches (20 cm)
Coltsfoot is a tenacious weed. The leafless flower stem appears first, followed much later (in April) by the young, felty leaves. These leaves, fresh or dried, form an excellent food for rabbits and are a good prophylactic measure for bloat. The fresh plant is eaten only in small quantities, so it must be given with a mixture of other green foods.

Dried out as hay, it is eagerly devoured. As the leaves are thick, they are best dried on the ground rather than on racks.

Corn Marigold (*Chrysanthemum segetum*)*
Flowering time: June–September
Flower: yellow
Height: to 24 inches (60 cm)
With its beautiful yellow asterlike flowers, the corn marigold gives more the impression of a cultivated plant than a weed.

Corn Spurrey (*Spervula arvensis*)*
Flowering time: June–September
Flower: small and white
Height: 6 to 24 inches (15-60 cm)
This is a weak, weedy annual, often found in sandy districts. Individual plants do not produce much foliage, but as they may be found in large quantities, they are useful for mixing with other green foods.

Dandelion (*Taraxacum officinale*)
Flowering time: April–June and again in September, often year-round
Flower: yellow
Height: to 12 inches (30 cm)
The dandelion is one of the best known early spring flowers. It is an excellent food for rabbits and can be given fresh in unlimited quantities.

You should ensure that collected plants are not stored in a heap or kept too warm; otherwise they begin to ferment. Fermenting plants can cause bloat in the rabbits. Analysis has shown that dandelions are one of the most nutritious food plants for rabbits, being rich in protein and poor in raw fiber. The digestibility percentage is high at an estimated 70 percent.

The dandelion is well known for its curative powers. The bitter, milky sap stimulates the working of all glands, including the milk glands of lactating does. The plant has both laxative and astringent qualities and regulates constipation and diarrhea.

When collecting, cut off the leaves and stalks at ground level; do not remove the root (which, actually, is an extremely difficult thing to do as the dandelion has a long, strong root) as this will grow into a new plant for harvesting later!

Dead-nettles

There are three major kinds of dead nettles suitable as rabbit food:

Henbit or Dead-nettle (*Lamium amplexicaule*)
Flowering time: March–May and sometimes again in September
Flower: purplish red, seldom white; frequently the whole plant is purplish red
Height: to 12 inches (30 cm)

Red Henbit or Spotted Dead-nettle (*Lamium purpurem*)

Flowering time: April–August
Flower: purplish red
Height: to 16 inches (40 cm)

White Dead-nettle (*Lamium album*)*

Flowering time: May–October
Flower: white; sometimes yellowish or pinkish
Height: to 24 inches (60 cm)

These three kinds of henbits or dead-nettles are eagerly eaten by rabbits if given in small quantities with a mixture of other green foods. The protein content is high, 36.9 percent of the dry weight of dead-nettle hay. At least 75 percent of the dry plant is digestible and very useful for lactating does. White dead-nettle is found in large clumps of plants but is somewhat less nutritious than the other kinds.

Dock

In the dock family, we will take two species, bitter dock and green sorrel.

Bitter Dock (*Rumex obtusifolius*)

Flowering time: June–August
Height: to 39 inches (about 1 m)

These are large plants that grow mainly in grassy, shady areas, often in thickets or in the shade of buildings. The lower leaves are fairly broad and blunt, the upper more tapering.

Green Sorrel (*Rumex acetosa*)

Flowering time: May–July
Height: to 30 inches (75 cm)

This plant grows in sheltered sunny spots along ditches and canals. An analysis of the dried material of this plant shows a high protein content and a digestibility of up to 75 percent of the organic content. Common sorrel appears early in the year and provides good green food. It should not be fed daily in too large quantities as it has a high oxalic acid content, which can cause poisoning. Feed it in very small quantities mixed with other green food.

Green sorrel has astringent properties, but it can be mixed with such plants as dandelions. Never use too much. Acid content increases when the flower stems appear, so do not use it then.

Ground Elder (*Aegopodium podagraria*)*

Flowering time: May–September
Flower: white or greenish, in umbels
Height: 24 to 39 inches (60–100 cm)

The ground elder is a very prolific weed that propagates itself from seed or from runners. The shoots form a thick layer, which quickly takes the place of all other plants.

Do not use the plant once the flower shoots have appeared, but it is quite safe to use earlier.

Hogweed (*Heracleum sphondylium*)

Flowering time: July–October
Flower: umbels of white flowerets
Height: to 60 inches (about 1.5 m)

The first leaves of the hogweed appear in early spring. The plant grows on banks and along canals, ditches, and pathways. It is a large perennial with rough, hairy leaves that provides much valuable green food in the early part of the year. Rabbits like to eat this plant very much. It has a high protein content and is very digestible. It is ideal for lactating does.

As no woody fiber forms in the young stems and leaves, it cannot be dried but should be stored in a cool place. For haymaking you must use plants that are neither too young nor too old. It is best given fresh, as green food, mixed with a variety of other plants.

Excellent weeds for rabbits: 1 dandelion, 2 yarrow, 3 shepherd's purse, 4 red henbit, 5 plaintain, 6 oxeye daisy, 7 sorrel, 8 caraway, 9 dock, 10 cleaver, 11 common sow thistle, 12 coltsfoot, 13 silverweed, 14 groundsel, 15 scented mayweed, 16 autumn hawkbit (fall dandelion), 17 knotgrass, 18 redshank, 19 pale smartweed, 20 mugwort.

Feeding

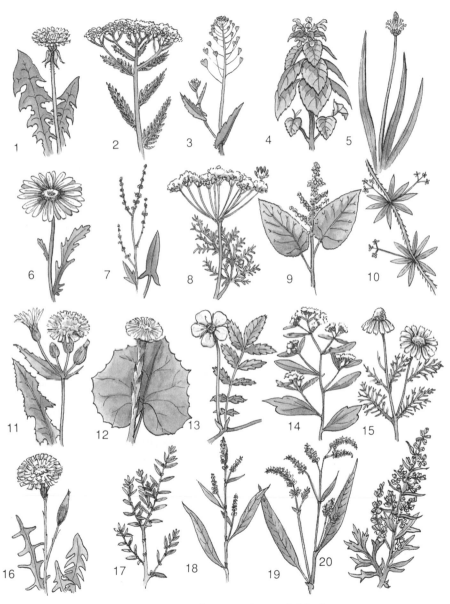

(Weeds/plants for rabbits)

Knotgrass or Prostrate Knotweed (*Polygonum aviculare*)
Flowering time: June–September
Flower: small, pink to white
Height: to 10 inches (25 cm)
This is a common weed found along country paths and tracks, often growing among the grass. Because of its prostrate growth pattern, it is not very conspicuous. However, the plant has ample greenery that is eaten greedily by rabbits.

The Mayweeds*

There are two kinds of mayweeds suitable as rabbit food:

Scented Mayweed (*Matricaria chamomilla*)
Flowering time: May–October
Flower: white
Height: to 20 inches (50 cm); a strongly branching plant

Scentless Mayweed (*Matricaria inodora*)
Flowering time: July–September
Flower: white
Height: to 20 inches (50 cm)
Mayweed can be fed fresh to rabbits in small quantities with other foods. It is best, however, if dried on a rack and mixed with other sorts of hay. The plants should be collected before they are in full bloom; otherwise the stems become too woody.

Mugwort or Bitterweed (*Artemisia tridentata*)
Flowering time: July–September
Flower: small, yellow to purplish brown
Height: to 4 feet (about 1.2 m)
A perennial bushlike weed with inconspicuous flowers. The plants are often very common, growing together in groups along railway embankments, overgrown roadsides, and in thickets. The underside of the leaves is silvery haired.
According to some experts, the plant is worthless as a foodstuff as it is bad tasting to cattle, which leave it alone. Others, however, have a conflicting opinion; they say that rabbits eat large amounts of the fresh plant, and if it is dried on racks, it produces an excellent hay. It is therefore recommended as part of the rabbit's menu.

Oxeye Daisy (*Chrysanthemum leucanthemum*)
Flowering time: August–September
Flower: yellow buttons
Height: to 39 inches (about 1 m)
This is another plant that greens early in the year and is recognized by its leaves, which resemble fern fronds, and its strong, aromatic scent. These plants are eagerly eaten by rabbits in large quantities. An excellent hay can be made from the fully grown plants. For years, this plant has been recognized for its worming properties and its value in relieving digestive disturbances.

Plantain

Three kinds of plantains are suitable for rabbits: the common plantain, the English plantain, and the hoary plantain.

Common Plantain (*Plantago major*)
Flowering time: June–October
Height: to 10 inches (25 cm)

English Plantain (*Plantago lanceolata*)
Flowering time: May–July
Height: to 16 inches (40 cm)

Hoary Plantain (*Plantago media*)
Flowering time: May–August (or September)
Flower: lilac
Height: to 20 inches (50 cm)
Each of these three plantain species is a popular rabbit food. They are as valuable as the dandelion. They do not cause digestive troubles, even when given in large quantities; they regulate the function of the intestines and are generally good for the mucus membranes. They are particularly useful in the rearing diet of young rabbits.

Ragwort (*Senecio vulgaris*)
Flowering time: year-round
Flower: yellow
Height: to 16 inches (40 cm)

The common ragwort is one of the most well-known and abundant of garden weeds, which is often found in enormous quantities. Rabbits are very fond of it as a food. However, it is not very good for conversion into hay.

Red Thistles

There are three kinds of red thistles suitable for inclusion in the rabbit's diet:

Canada Thistle (*Cirsium arvense*)
Flowering time: July–September
Flower: violet-red
Height: to 39 inches (about 1 m)

Marsh Thistle (*Cirsium palustre*)
Flowering time: July–September
Flower: purple
Height: to 78 inches (about 2 m)

Welted Thistle (*Carduus crispus*)
Flowering time: July–September
Flower: violet-red
Height: to 60 inches (about 1.5 meter)

The red-flowering thistles should not be fed to rabbits in fresh condition, other than in small quantities of parts of the young plants. However, as hay, they are eagerly taken. Place in bundles on a rack, but do not stack together when too fresh or mold will set in and the hay will be unusable. Pack loosely together to produce a very fine hay. Do not worry about the sharp spines on the leaves: they certainly won't worry the rabbits! Thistles have a high (23.6 percent of dry weight) protein content.

Shepherd's Purse (*Capsella bursa-pastoris*)
Flowering time: year-round
Flower: white (very small)
Height: 1 to 20 inches (2–50 cm); sometimes to 39 inches (1 m)

This plant is easy to recognize by its little "purses" of seeds. Shepherd's purse is available for most of the year and is often ignored as a wild food; however, it is taken greedily by rabbits. The plants should be collected when young, for when the seed purses appear the rosette-forming leaves will have already started to deteriorate.

Silverweed (*Potentilla anserina*)
Flowering time: May–August
Flower: yellow
Height: 6 inches (15 cm), creeping

This relatively small, creeping plant reproduces from runners and is a meadow weed that is avoided by other animals, such as sheep. In spite of the profusely hairy underside of the leaves, however, silverweed is eagerly eaten by rabbits. By drying it on the ground a good hay can be made from it. Rabbits will eat dried silverweed quite readily as well.

Sow Thistles

The sow thistles are an ideal rabbit food. In contrast to other kinds of thistles, these plants have soft leaves and yellow flowers. All kinds are rich in milky sap. The examples given here are the common sow thistle, the field sow thistle, and the spiny-leaved sow thistle.

Common Sow Thistle (*Sonchus oleraceus*)
Flowering time: June–October
Flower: yellow
Height: to 39 inches (about 1 m)

The lower leaves of this plant are cut in to the rib; the leaves are shiny, usually covered with aphid mildew. The flowers are smaller than dandelions and close during the middle part of the day. Fresh plants contain 9.4 percent dry mass consisting of approximately 20 percent protein and 15.5 percent raw fiber.

Feeding

Field Sow Thistle (*Sonchus arvensis*)

    Flowering time: July–October

    Flower: yellow

    Height: to 60 inches (1.5 m)

The upper leaves are strongly cut in and finish with little "claws" arranged around the stem. The flowers are at least as large as dandelions. The dry material content is 18.36 percent of the fresh plant. The protein content is 13.17 percent. The raw fiber content is low (13.13 percent) and the digestibility is very high (76.8 percent).

Spiny-leaved Sow Thistle (*Sonchus asper*)

    Flowering time: July–September

    Flower: yellow

    Height: to 39 inches (about 1 m)

The leaves of this plant are barely cut in, but the teeth of the leaves are much stiffer and sharper than in the other kinds of sow thistle. The flowers are smaller than those of the dandelion. This species is eagerly eaten by rabbits. The protein analysis of the spiny variety is probably similar to that of the common sow thistle.

Yarrow (*Achilles millefolium*)

    Flowering time: June–October

    Flower: white to reddish

    Height: to 20 inches (50 cm)

The first fine, green fronds of the yarrow appear at the time of the spring dandelions. Rabbits are very fond of the yarrow plant and eat it in great quantities. The plant can also be dried out on racks to produce an excellent hay. Yarrow has a medium protein content and a fairly high content of raw fiber, giving it a nutritive quality similar to alfalfa hay.

The curative properties of yarrow have been known for centuries. Pliny told how the Greek hero Achilles learned of the wonderful properties of the plant from Chiron the herb specialist and with it cured Thelopos, the king of Mysia. The plant is named in Latin *Achillea*, in honor of Achilles.

It is recommended that the rabbit's daily yarrow ration be given partly fresh and partly dried.

Different methods for drying hay.

Haymaking

During the summer months, the feeding of your rabbits should pose few difficulties, especially if you make good use of wild green foods. It is possible for real problems to develop in the winter, however, if you do not prepare yourself by making full use of the summer opportunities. Wild green foods are of great importance, and you can use two methods of preserving them for later use: making hay and ensilage. Ensilage can pose a number of difficulties for the beginner, so it is recommended that he or she stick to making hay, which should pose relatively fewer problems.

The simplest method of making hay is to bind the green plants into bundles and hang them so that they are dried by the wind. They should not hang in full sunlight or the drying process is much too rapid. By drying slowly in a dry, windy but shady spot, the leaves will stay intact on the stems. Another good method is to dry the plants out on racks under cover. The advantages of both of these methods over the normal method of leaving the cut plants on the ground to dry are that they are less reliant on good weather, the drying process is more even, and the hay retains a greater nutritive value.

Not all wild foods are suitable for drying on racks. Plants with thick, heavy leaves, for example, are likely to lie too tightly against each other and prevent satisfactory air circulation. This results in mold forming on the leaves. Young thistles are thus difficult to dry. Full-grown thistles, however, with their prickly, woody stems, can be piled easily and should dry without major problems. Plants with stiff stems are therefore the best for making hay.

The amount and quality of hay produced by particular plants depend on the stage of growth at which they are cut. Young plants have a greater percentage of moisture and of course lose a greater percentage of weight when dried as compared with plants that have already formed woody tissue.

For safety's sake, it is best to refrain from using plants or weeds not mentioned in this book. Many plants are either worthless as food or are poisonous to the animals.

Trees and Shrubs as Food Sources

Tree Leaves

In addition to wild herbaceous plants, we can also supplement our rabbits' ration with the fruits and foliage of trees and shrubs. It is perhaps surprising to learn that the value of such a food source is not widely known. Foliage, especially young foliage, is often rich in protein and can make a welcome change to the monotonous dry rations (see page 43). It can be used fresh but can also be dried out in the form of leaf hay.

Various experiments have shown that the leaves are richest in protein in the spring and the percentage decreases through the summer. A large part of the protein content consists of amino acids. In the same period, the oil content of the leaves increases, and with the resin, pigment materials, and similar factors, has a minimum nutritional value. During the summer, the carbohydrate content of the leaves also increases. Various sugars, such as saccharose,

dextrose, and fructose, form part of these carbohydrates. Various kinds of leaves also produce tannic acid, and this increases during autumn. One should be careful in using leaves at this time; a high tannic acid content affects the taste and digestibility of the leaves.

During the summer, in fresh condition, most leaves produce 30 to 50 percent dry weight. It is thus recommended that leaves are collected when as young as possible. Such foliage makes a good substitute for meadow hay. The young twigs, with leaves, are cut from the tree, leaving any thicker than a quarter-inch (0.5 cm). The best time to cut twigs is in the evening after a warm day so that the carbohydrate content (from the action of the sun) is reasonably high. At nighttime, it is known that carbohydrates are drawn into other parts of the tree.

Foliage Hay

There is some disagreement about the best time to collect foliage for making hay. Some researchers recommend July and August as the best months, as

Chewing fresh twigs is good for teeth and body!

the leaves contain the highest amount of dry weight at that time. As the leaves become older, the percentage of cellulose material, which is of little nutritive value, increases.

The leaves that fall in the autumn are naturally without value as a food. Well-prepared foliage hay, however, has a nutritional value similar to that of good grass hay. The drying of the leaves must be done very carefully; otherwise mold develops and the hay is worthless.

Many experts recommend the leaves from the following trees and shrubs, among others, as good rabbit food: acacia, alder, ash, beech, birch, blackberry, elder, elm, grape, hazel, horse chestnut, maple, mountain-ash, mulberry, poplar, raspberry, and willow. However, the leaves of ash, maple, and elm should not be fed to lactating females as it is said that these impart a bad taste to the milk. The milk becomes bitter and may be refused by the youngsters. The leaves of alder and willow are reported to bring a total end to milk production, so these should certainly not be given to lactating females.

The leaves of cherries are also of great value, and the leaves of apple and pear trees can also be given. The leaves of peaches and plums, however, should not be fed. They contain poisonous substances; for example, cyanide is contained in the leaves and twigs of peach trees.

A sudden change from grass feeding to foliage feeding is, like any sudden change in rabbit feeding, to be avoided.

Selecting Foliage: Tips and Cautions

Acacia: At the end of May and beginning of June, the acacia tree produces shoots and leaves that are very useful as rabbit food. Foliage collected later in the year and also foliage hay from this tree are very valuable foods. In contrast, however, twigs collected in the winter are not very nutritious. The one- and two-year-old twigs are the most useful. The osiers must be cut very finely. They are collected in the late winter and spring before the leaves open and when the nutrients are all in the twig bark.

However, the twigs can still be used after the leaves have opened. The acacia can be cut three times per year without causing damage. One should limit the use to the youngest twigs. The bark from the trunk and the thicker branches produces a poisonous substance that can cause colic attacks in horses. Even small quantities of bark can cause problems for rabbits.

Beech: Young beech foliage is a good food for all rabbits. However, a corklike substance forms as the leaves age, making them difficult to digest. Beech leaves should be used just after they open as they are of little value later.

Tree foliage. Clockwise: acacia, hazel, and willow.

Birch: The leaves of the birch tree age quickly and become indigestible. Young foliage can be used, but in general the birch is of little value as rabbit food.

Above left: The marten is a fur breed. Above right: The Van Beveren rabbit was developed in Belgium at the turn of the century as a meat and pelt producer. Below: The chinchilla has one of the finest coats of all rabbit breeds!

Feeding

Hazel: The foliage of the hazel tree, as already mentioned, is eaten greedily by rabbits. The protein content is not very high, and the amount of raw fiber increases during the summer. The leaves should therefore be collected as early as possible.

Horse Chestnut: Leaves of the horse chestnut should be collected when young as the older foliage becomes hard and indigestible for rabbits.

Lime: The leaves of the lime tree stay tender for a long period. Unfortunately they are often infested with aphids and become unsuitable as food as they soon form a mold that can be damaging to the rabbits. Only leaves free of aphids should be used.

Mountain-ash: The foliage of the mountain-ash is regarded as a valuable animal food in Scandinavian countries. The berries are also eaten eagerly.

Oak: Oak leaves have astringent properties and should be regarded more as a remedy against diarrhea rather than as a food. One should beware of the increase in tannic acid content as the leaves mature, and it is best to stick to young foliage. The American oak has poisonous properties and is best not used as rabbit food.

Poplar: In general, the foliage of the poplar tree is a good food for rabbits. However, the leaves of the black poplar contain a bitter oil and are not eaten very eagerly.

Poisonous Trees and Shrubs

Many trees, shrubs, and plants are poisonous. For example, the following species are poisonous or suspect: rhododendron, azalea, laburnum, wisteria, some clematis species, holly, spindleberry, jimson weed, lords and ladies (cuckoo spit) and purple thorn apple.

Above left: The silver fox is available in several varieties. Each color should be ticked with longer white hairs. Above right: The tan weighs about four pounds. Center left and right, and below left: Vienna white, gray, and blue. Below right: The Alaska is a medium-sized breed which originated in Germany.

Poisonous plants. From left to right: rhododendron, holly, purple thorn-apple, and azalea.

You must therefore be very careful when selecting foliage for feeding to rabbits. Unless the species is recommended in this book as suitable as food (and positively identified), you should best avoid using other plants; it is better to be safe than sorry!

Nuts and Fruits

Having discussed the merits of the foliage of various trees for rabbit food, we now look at the use of various fruits. Acorns, beechnuts, black cherries, chestnuts (wild), hawthorn berries, mountain-ash berries, and privet berries, are all classified as useful foods.

Although the various tree fruits do not have a uniform nutritive value, they form a welcome change for rabbits in their daily food ration. The animals appreciate carefully selected and varied meals each day instead of the same monotonous diet.

Acorns: The fruits of the oak (*Quercus rubra*) and other species, including the American oak. Fruit form: egg-shaped, leathery-shelled nuts.

Feeding

Tree foliage. Clockwise: horse chestnut, beechnut, and black cherry.

Acorns do not contain a large amount of protein (unshelled 4.2 percent, shelled 4.9 percent) but are rich in carbohydrates. It is well known that acorns form a reasonable emergency food for pigs during times of shortages. However, they are less nutritious than chestnuts. Because of the presence of tannic acid and the bitter taste, rabbits often take some time to become accustomed to them. Do not use too many acorns as they can cause constipation. A few acorns are good for lactating females after the birth of the litter.

Beechnuts: The fruit of the beech tree (*Fagus grandifolia*). Fruit form: triangular, leathery shelled nuts.

In times of hardship, beechnuts, with their high fat content (27.4 percent) form a valuable dietary supplement for humans and animals. An excellent oil is produced by pressing the nuts. This oil keeps for years, does not go rancid, and is an excellent cooking oil. The main ingredient of the oil is olein. The fatty acids in the oil are absorbed into the body in an unchanged condition.

The pressed nuts are not wholly without danger, however, as certain poisonous materials may occur in them. The pressed oil contains no poisonous substances; these are situated mainly in the membrane surrounding the kernel.

Poisoning from beechnuts is usually only a danger when large quantities are given to animals. However, some animals are more susceptible than others. Horses, for example, are very susceptible but cows have little trouble with them.

Rabbits eat beechnuts eagerly, and they form a good basic food, but it is perhaps safest not to feed beechnuts to rabbits at all. Acorns and chestnuts are available in greater quantities and pose less danger.

Black Cherry: (*Prunus serotina C.*). Fruit form: a black, juicy stone fruit.

The black cherry tree belongs to the plum family. In the wild, black cherry fruits are shiny black and taste very sour. However, in some years, cultivated varieties produce relatively sweetish fruits. Great numbers of fruits are produced in the autumn, and these fall from the tree and cover the ground with berries. It has been noticed that some free-range rabbits eat them regularly.

As an experiment, four blue Vienna bucks were given unlimited supplies of black cherries over a period of fifteen days. The normal diet was kept up, so that the animals were not forced to eat the berries. Two of the animals ate large quantities of the fruits, but the other two took only small quantities. During the feeding, the animals maintained good condition. The experiment showed that although some rabbits eat the berries more readily than others, they can be used in the feeding ration. They belong as a part of your animals' varied diet.

Chestnuts, Wild: The fruits of the horse chestnut (*Aesculus hippocastanum*) and other chestnut species. Fruit form: spherical, prickly outer case encloses the brown (when ripe) chestnut.

Wild chestnuts are a useful food for rabbits. The dry weight contains 7.5 percent proteins, 3.4 percent fats (oil), and 78.3 percent carbohydrates.

Fresh chestnuts are easily digestible. If dried, this should be done slowly or the taste is altered. It is recommended that the bitter taste be removed as follows: remove the shells, grind the kernels into small pieces, and soak in water for three days, changing the water every few hours. If the animals still do not eat the chestnuts eagerly, you can surmise that the bitterness has not been completely removed and that the nuts require soaking for a further period. Finely ground dried chestnuts should be stored in a dry, well-ventilated spot.

Hawthorne Berries: (*Crataegus monogyna*). Fruit form: round red berries.

Hawthorn is well known as a hedging tree or shrub. The red berries can be collected from hedgerows. It is well known that birds, especially thrushes, are attracted to the berries. Wild rabbits eagerly eat berries dropped by the birds.

It is recommended that the berries be dried in an oven to prevent them from rotting away. They can also be dried slowly in the normal manner.

As with mountain-ash berries, the nutritive value rests with the amount of carbohydrate contained in the fruit skin. A very high raw fiber content results from the inclusion of the pips, which have hardly any nutritive value.

Mountain-ash Berries: (*Pyrus aucupario P. americana*). Fruit form: round, red berries.

The mountain-ash produces large numbers of sour-tasting berries in the early fall. They are highly acidic. They can be used for making a kind of brandy and are also used for making a fairly palatable coffee substitute.

As rabbit food, the berries must first be dried. The trusses are hung on a line in a well-ventilated room, where they are protected from birds.

The feeding value of mountain-ash berries rests mainly with the carbohydrate and sugar content. The protein and fat content is low.

The berries contain small quantities of a poisonous material called parasorbic acid, a pungent-smelling oil. Cyanide can be produced in the pips, but in very small quantities. I have not experienced any great danger from these materials. The berries act as an astringent and are good for curing diarrhea.

Privet Berries: (*Ligustrum vulgare* and *Ligustrum ovalifolium*). Fruit form: black berries.

The privet is well known as a hedging shrub. The somewhat leathery, smooth leaves are regarded by rabbit fanciers as poisonous. Rabbits will not eat the pruned leaves and twigs. This is as good a reason as any not to give them to the animals. Forcing rabbits to eat certain plants can only lead to mishaps.

Air-dried, black privet berries are eaten eagerly by rabbits, however. In colder areas, the number of berries produced is small. If one has access to the berries they can safely be given to rabbits, but only in small quantities.

Rabbit Diseases and Disorders

As with the keeping of all animals in captivity, you should continually be on the lookout for signs of illness. Although many diseases are unlikely to arise if animals are kept in comfortable, hygienic conditions and given a balanced diet, there is always the chance that something may accidentally be introduced. With rabbits, prevention is better than cure, as one who has read the preceding chapters realizes. However, there are certain early signs you can detect that indicate that a rabbit is not 100 percent fit or well.

Dull, lifeless eyes are a sure indication that a rabbit is sick, and if the animal sits moping in a corner with its fur puffed out (at normal temperatures) or grinds its teeth, you can be certain that all is not well. At such times the rabbit's droppings may not be normal and these should be one of the first things you examine when illness is suspected.

An unhealthy rabbit has, among other signs, a dull and rough coat with the skin stretched tightly across the back, glassy staring dull eyes, a watery or slimy discharge from the nose, and a hard and bloated belly.

In any case, you should keep an observant eye for such things at all times so that any problems can be nipped in the bud at an early stage—before it is too late! Some diseases can be quickly diagnosed, and an effective cure can be speedily commenced. Unfortunately, the symptoms of some other diseases are relatively vague, giving the malady a chance to consolidate before you can effectively take action. It is, however, important that rabbit diseases be properly diagnosed to prevent infecting other animals. Dead rabbits should be brought to a veterinarian for post mortem examination. Most areas have state veterinary laboratories for this purpose.

Unfortunately, the scope of this book does not permit a complete summary of all the diseases it is possible for rabbits to become afflicted with. However, I hope to cover the more commonly occurring ailments to enable the reader to recognize them. In any case, it is always wise to consult your veterinarian the moment you suspect something is amiss.

Abscess: An abscess is a localized collection of pus in the tissues of the body, caused, for example, by bacteria and other pathogenic organisms entering the body through a wound. Abscesses can also form in the skin as well as in internal organs, occurring most frequently in the liver and spleen. The majority of bacteria and other organisms are engulfed by the white blood cells, which help to give pus (a mixture of blood cells, bacteria, and other organisms) its light color.

Abscesses are often attributed to bucks fighting and consequently injuring each other. To prevent this you must keep mature bucks separated, especially when housed in small hutches.

Carefully cut away the fur around the infected area, and bathe the abscess in hot water with antiseptic, such as tincture of iodine. When dealing with severe abscesses, consult your veterinarian immediately.

After bathing the abscess, gently squeeze out the pus and then bathe the wound again with an antiseptic solution. (If the gentlest pressure is not effective, do not continue to squeeze!) Repeat this treatment daily until the inflammation begins to recede and the wound starts to heal.

Because of a bad or broken tooth or an infection of the gums, abscesses may occur in the rabbit's mouth. The patient drools at the mouth, and running saliva wets the lower jaw and chest.

The animal is unable to eat, and its general

Rabbit Diseases and Disorders

condition deteriorates rapidly. Consult a veterinarian, although usually there is not much one can do but humanely put the rabbit to sleep.

Bloat: If a rabbit's belly swells dramatically, it is probable that it has bloat. This is caused by a buildup of gases in the intestines and stomach as a result of improper feeding. The food stays too long in the alimentary canal, is only partially digested, and begins to ferment. If the droppings are covered with a slimy coat, there is a good chance that the animal is also suffering from coccidiosis.

The main cause of bloat is a one-sided diet. Young white clover and wet grass in large quantities are commonly suspect. Moldy hay or roots should never be given to rabbits as these can also cause problems. With early detection, the problem can be relieved by an injection from the veterinarian.

Coccidiosis: After snuffles, coccidiosis is the most dangerous disease for domestic rabbits. Many adult rabbits are carriers of this disease, which comes in two forms: hepatic (liver) and intestinal coccidiosis. The latter is much more common. The coccidia form colonies in the intestinal walls and cause a great deal of pain, diarrhea, and wasting. The coccidia multiply first asexually and then sexually.

As the fertilized egg cells are passed out with the infected rabbit's droppings, they can further multiply in moist areas and infect other rabbits. The danger of infection is especially great in the nesting environment, when mother and litter are close together in a small area and the chances of food being infected are much greater. Many breeders use grids in their hutches so that the droppings fall through and pose no danger to the animals. If detected early, coccidiosis may be successfully treated with one of the sulfonimide drugs available through a veterinarian. A creoline or iodine prophylactic may also be used to prevent the disease from obtaining a foothold in the first place. Place 5 mL creoline in a medicine bottle, and fill with water. Mix well and ensure that each animal gets a teaspoonful per day.

This should be done until the young are weaned from the mother.

Tincture of iodine mixed 1 part per thousand in water, can also be used. In both cases, the treatment should begin one week before the birth of the litter. After coccidiosis infections, the hutches should be disinfected with boiling water. To prevent coccidiosis, I give my rabbits a solution of sulfaquinoxaline in their drinking water for one week each month. The same may be used to prevent diarrhea. A weekly dose of Terramycin or Neo-Terramycin also prevents diarrhea. (All of these things are available through your veterinarian.)

Constipation: A rabbit that, in spite of the conscientious care of its owner, takes too much of one type of food or too little of another can become constipated. Constipation means that the waste materials of digestion are not expelled from the body at frequent and regular intervals. Too much dry food and too little green food can, among other things, cause constipation. In a case of constipation, dry food should be temporarily removed from the diet and replaced with extra green food, especially that with a laxative effect. A teaspoonful of mineral oil often helps. In serious cases a little soap solution introduced to the anus by means of a syringe is helpful.

Diarrhea: Diarrhea is not a disease but a clinical sign of some disease process in the body of the patient. Diarrhea simply refers to the voiding of fluid or soft, foul, and sour-smelling feces. It can be caused by inflammation, irritation, or infection of the digestive tract, due to eating food that is too wet, too cold, spoiled, or contaminated with chemicals. Changes in diet from dry to fresh food, damp bedding, and cold and drafts are also often causes of diarrhea, as well as the results of a septicemia (blood poisoning), pressure from a tumor of a gonad or kidney, liver damage, a localized bacterial infection elsewhere causing toxemia, or even a change of environmental conditions or feeding routine.

The patient eats little or nothing, sits hunched up with closed eyes, and becomes listless and uninterested in anything that is going on around it.

Separate the rabbit immediately, and house it in a clean hutch at a distance from the other hutches. Thoroughly clean and disinfect the rabbit's "old" quarters. The bedding in the "sick bay" should be changed at least twice a day. Don't offer fresh greens, only hay (preferably of the second cutting) and some dry bread. Supply camomile tea and some boiled, unsalted rice. A veterinarian should be consulted if the patient suffers longer than two days, as prolonged diarrhea is life-threatening.

Note: When a young rabbit between five and eight weeks of age has diarrhea, there may be a possibility that it is suffering from mucoid enteritis, a fast killer! Often the patient dies in less than twenty-four hours.

The rabbit is listless and squint eyed, has jellylike droppings and a soiled underside, and looks thin, with mucus around the mouth. Because of high fever the rabbit often puts one of its feet in a water dish. When the rabbit is picked up and gently shaken, a splashing sound can be heard within the animal. Consult a veterinarian immediately.

Ear Canker: As with most diseases, ear canker is rare, providing good hygienic measures are the norm. The ears are an ideal hiding place for microscopic mites. These mites burrow into the skin and cause intense irritation. The rabbit holds its head to one side and scratches violently with one of its legs. It also shakes from time to time as if wanting to shake the culprits out.

The symptoms appear in stages: first, red spots and patches, which may also appear around the ear margins. Through scratching, blood spots and infectious ulcers can form, but the conscientious owner does not let it get so far. A pair of forceps and a piece of wadding soaked in a 2 percent solution of hydrogen peroxide is all that is required to clean the ear. Scabs can be loosened and treated with carbolglycerine. If the scabs are hard and difficult to remove, they can first be softened with olive oil. If the treatment is carried out two or three times a week a rapid cure should be accomplished. After a little

time, you can treat the area again as the infection can sometimes be very persistent. (The earmite medication used for cats is also excellent for treating mites in rabbits.) The hutch should be disinfected and all bedding and wadding should be burnt.

Epilepsy: This condition occurs almost exclusively among white, blue-eyed breeds. The characteristic is hereditary and recessive.

The patient shows no outward symptoms until it suddenly lets out a shriek, runs madly around its hutch, and collapses. Sometimes this includes violent shivering motions of the whole body; sometimes the animal just lies stiffly. After a few minutes, the animal relaxes somewhat and may gnash its teeth and salivate at the mouth. During the attack, the pupils will enlarge but slowly return to normal after the attack. The iris stays bluish green for a while before returning to its normal, light blue color.

Eyes, Inflammations of: Used, dirty bedding contains excessive ammonia (from urine) that irritates the rabbit's eyes, which in turn become red and swollen. At first only one eye is affected, in a later stage both eyes become infected. The fur around the eyes and on the cheeks becomes wet and matted.

Other causes for irritation or inflammation of the eyes are drafts, cold, dirt, dust, and injuries due to fights.

Correct the cause immediately, and apply ophthalmic ointment, available from your pet store. Even human eye ointments can be used successfully, as well as a weak aqueous solution of boric acid, which should be applied with a cotton-tipped swab (Q-Tips, etc.).

Note: Be sure there is no corticosteroid in any eye preparation used for injury to the cornea of the eye. Corticosteroids will increase the likelihood of ulceration and possible rupture of the corneal tissue. When in doubt, consult your veterinarian. Eyes are too precious to justify taking any risks!

Fleas: Fleas are external bloodsucking parasites that vary from 1.5–5 mm in length; they are often responsible for transmitting various diseases, for

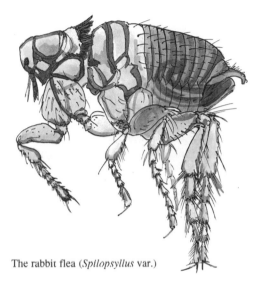

The rabbit flea (*Spilopsyllus* var.)

example, deadly myxomatosis (see page 64).

Dusting with an insecticidal powder especially supplied for this purpose, paying particular attention to the ears, kills all fleas (and other external parasites) present. Remember that scratching and irritation due to the presence of fleas may cause infertility in both sexes! It is obvious that a flea infestation damages the pelts.

It is important to remember that infestation can also occur from domestic pets and other mammals, wild birds, and poultry (fleas are usually versatile in their choice of host).

Cat and kitten flea sprays and powders can be used. Remember that fleas are only on the animal for approximately six to eight hours. The rest of the time they are in the surrounding area. It is equally important, therefore, to attend to the environment of the animal in order to kill the fleas where they live and breed. Anyone with a serious flea problem should consult a professional exterminator company for a concerted program of flea control.

Fractures: When a rabbit favors one of its limbs, remains in a corner, and acts apathetic, it is very possible that the animal suffers from a broken limb. Broken bones are usually the result of dropping the animal from an elevated place or stepping on it accidentally or when it is caught in a closing door. Such accidents can even result in spinal injuries and paralysis.

Hairline fractures heal by themselves; for simple fractures consult a veterinarian; for compound fractures your veterinarian may recommend humane euthanasia.

Heat Stroke: In heat stroke, the body is unable to lower its temperature (normally between 101 and 102°F, [38.3–38.9°C]), which is elevated because of excessive heat and direct sun (during travel, in a hutch without shade, etc.). Panting, which is used to regulate the body temperature, is ineffectual. The rabbit lies at full length, rapidly panting with open nostrils and often foaming at the mouth.

Remove the animal to a cool, shady (not cold and dark!), well-ventilated area where it can move freely. Offer it a dish of water at room temperature and fresh, crisp green food. Cool the animal's head and legs (in that order!) with a cool, damp cloth (see also Salivation, page 64).

Hocks, Sore: This sometimes occurs in the heavier breeds. Smaller breeds, which are more active and have a higher metabolic rate, are rarely affected with this problem. Larger breeds have a much greater pressure on their hind limbs. You should regularly examine the underside of the hocks, which must be covered with hair. Bald patches may eventually turn into open wounds.

Mange: Mange, an uncommon but highly contagious skin disease, is caused by various ectoparasites and characterized by loss of hair and scabby eruptions that fall off into the bedding, contaminating it.

The parasites are similar to those causing ear canker (see page 62), so immediate action on your part is called for. These parasites burrow in the pores of the rabbit's skin, causing intense irritation.

Separate the affected animals as quickly as possible, burn the bedding, and disinfect the hutch

Rabbit Diseases and Disorders

thoroughly. Consult a veterinarian without delay.

The patient must be treated with a topical mange medication, similar to that of ear canker.

Be extremely careful yourself, as mange is also contagious to humans. When the hutches are cleaned scrupulously, however, mange will seldom trouble your rabbitry.

Mastitis: This is inflammation of the teats, which occurs in does that have had their young removed too early. The inflamed teats should be gently massaged with olive oil until the swelling subsides. Mastitis can also occur in any lactating doe and can lead to very serious consequences, including death. Antibiotic treatment may be necessary to save the doe. Kits should be hand fed until the mastitis is under control. See your veterinarian for the cultures and sensitivity tests, which may prove necessary to determine the proper treatment.

Myxomatosis: This "man-made" disease, which has ravaged wild rabbit populations, can be likened to the most frightful of tortures. The disease, which is incurable, is caused by a virus. The disease arrived in France in 1952 after a certain Dr. Armand Delille infected wild rabbits on his estate near Paris as he had problems with the animals. The symptoms of the disease are swelling of the eyes and a puslike discharge followed by blindness and infection of the brain. The ears, nose, and lips swell to hideous proportions, and the animal suffers acute pain. The disease has broken out in collections of

A rabbit suffering from myxomatosis.

tame rabbits, and breeders have been known to lose their complete stock in the course of a week.

Infected animals must be culled as quickly as possible and buried deep in the earth, although, if possible, incineration is even better. Mosquitos and flies are regarded as the principal carriers of the disease, and some species of fleas are also suspected. In some areas where wild rabbits live, breeders have been able to prevent the disease by keeping their animals behind fly screens. Over the years, the seriousness of the disease has somewhat weakened. At one stage, breeders had their stock immunized against the disease, but the immunization caused the animals to develop lumps and lose their vitality although they did not catch the disease.

Although the disease is not at present dangerous to humans, it could eventually become so, as has occurred with other diseases. The hands must be washed well, and in the case of an occurrence of myxomatosis you should not visit other breeders.

Rabbit Syphilis: This disease, more correctly termed spirochetosis, starts with a swelling of the genitalia. The skin cracks and scabs appear that can spread to other parts of the body. This venereal disease is transmitted from animal to animal by direct contact during copulation. This disease, which is caused by a spirochete, cannot affect humans. A good cure is Solu-salvarsan, which is inserted under the skin by a veterinarian. After a week's rest, the animal should be cured. The hutch should be disinfected and all bedding burnt.

Salivation: This condition is fortunately rare and one of which we know little. The victim loses its appetite and mopes, and it has a wet, salivating mouth. At the same time, the forepaws are wet and slimy as a result of the animal wiping its mouth. Sometimes a complete recovery occurs but this should be regarded as sporadic. A fault in the teeth can cause damage to the interior of the mouth. Irresponsible feeding with moldy food or grass that has been stored wet in a heap for too long can be a cause.

Although there is little proof, the disease usually

Rabbit Diseases and Disorders

starts on warm days. Rabbits do not perspire like humans. If the animal is enclosed in a small area, such as in a transport box, and left in the heat of the sun, it loses moisture through its nose and mouth. In a very short time the animal suffers from heat exhaustion. Cooling with water that is not too cold is the solution.

Sex Organs, Inflammation of: Not to be confused with the dangerous rabbit syphilis (spirochetosis), sex organ inflammation often occurs in the fall, especially in smaller breeds. The breeder has decided to breed no more young, as he or she may have bred enough or not have enough room. If the animals are still prepared to breed, the sex organs may swell and become inflamed or even infected. The scabs are removed with lukewarm water, and the area is treated with a little tincture of iodine. Mercury compounds have also been used but you must beware that the animals do not poison themselves by licking the treated spot.

Snuffles: Snuffles is a respiratory disease that manifests itself in copious nasal discharge and labored breathing. A simple cold can be the precursor of snuffles, which is a highly infectious disease and can quickly infect the whole stock. The mucous membranes of the nose swell and become bright red in color. The fluid coming from the nostrils is at first relatively thin but gradually becomes thicker and takes on a yellow color. The patient has obvious discomfort and uses its forepaws as a "handkerchief" to try to relieve the irritation in the nostrils. The infected animal sneezes frequently, and as the disease progresses the lungs become infected, causing the animal to make loud snuffling noises as it breathes. A conscientious fancier, of course, does not allow the disease to reach such a stage and has the animal humanely put to sleep. If the disease is caught in its early stages it may be successfully treated with antibiotics. In some eastern European countries, especially in Russia, attempts are being made to produce rabbits that are immune to the disease.

Teeth, Overgrown: The rabbit possesses two pairs of incisor teeth in the upper jaw and one pair in the lower jaw. These cutting teeth are rootless and continue to grow throughout the animal's life. The front of the incisors has a thick coat of enamel; the back consists of a much softer dentine. During normal gnawing and cutting activities, the back part of the teeth wear out at a much faster rate, ensuring a permanent, chisellike cutting edge at the front. Under normal circumstances the teeth in the upper and lower jaws work against each other, keeping them to a permanent ideal length. Occasionally, however, for one reason or another, the upper and lower teeth do not match and cannot wear correctly. In such cases, the teeth continue to grow until the animal is unable to feed properly. If a tooth breaks off a similar situation may occur. As the teeth are now shaped, they usually continue to grow in this manner.

Above: normal rabbit skull. Below: a skull showing malocclusion ("elephant tusk").

Over the last fifteen years this problem has been seen in dwarf races only once, and even more rarely in other breeds. In a single breed it has been diagnosed as an unpleasant hereditary factor. The clipping and filing of the teeth is only pertinent if the teeth are otherwise growing normally; if not the most humane solution is to have the animal put out of its misery. This can be done in a humane manner by your veterinarian.

Tuberculosis: Tuberculosis no longer occurs in rabbits that receive pasteurized milk.

Tularemia: This rare disease occurs in various rodents and is transmitted to humans, dogs, and rabbits by ticks. The disease was first reported in Tulare County, California; unfortunately there is no treatment as of this writing.

Symptoms in rabbits are ruffled coat, weight loss, sneezing, and an overall weakness; the patient has a light fever (103–104°F; [39.4–40°C]); the normal temperature of a healthy rabbit is between 101 and 102° F (38.3–38.9°C).

When tularemia is suspected, immediately consult a veterinarian, who in turn must report to public health authorities when such a diagnosis is made. Should you or anyone in your family show any symptoms of the disease (fever, weakness, respiratory distress, etc) be sure to contact your own physician at once. When you do so, remember to tell him or her that you keep rabbits.

A Home Emergency Kit

Needle-nosed pliers
Scissors
Tweezers

Cotton-tipped swabs
Adhesive tape ($^1/_2$" width)
Sterile gauze pads
Towels

Heat source (heat lamp or space heater)
Plastic medicine dropper

Hydrogen peroxide (or betadine solution)
Styptic powder

Camomile tea (to wash wounds, irritation of eyes, diarrhea)
Linseed and linseed oil (for constipation)
Peppermint tea (for indigestion, diarrhea)
Sage tea (for swollen or inflamed mucosal lining inside the mouth)

Disinfectant (Lysol, One-StrokeEnviron, Chlorox or a similar liquid laundry bleach)

Telephone number of your veterinarian

Reproduction in Rabbits

The Female Reproductive Organs

The urogenital opening in the doe is known as the vulva; this opens into the vestibule, which runs forward below the rectum. The vestibule continues into the neck of the bladder and then forms a wide tube known as the vagina. The vagina divides to form a pair of convoluted tubes, the uteri. Each uterus becomes very much narrower anteriorly, to form the fallopian tubes (or oviducts). Each of the fallopian tubes opens anteriorly as a wide, funnel-like expansion into the abdominal cavity, each partly covering an ovary. The ovaries are a pair of oval structures about $^3/_4$ inch (2 cm) long situated behind the kidneys. They are constructed from fibrous tissue adequately supplied with blood vessels and contain a number of bodies known as

Procedure for sexing a rabbit. Place the animal on your lap facing away from you, and grasp the scruff firmly. Spread the hind legs and you will see two roundish raised spots: the anal and sexual orifices, respectively (the first being closest to the tail). If you stretch the skin around the sexual orifice a little by pressing down with your middle and index finger, the penis—if the rabbit is a male—will protrude.

follicles. These follicles produce the female egg (ova). Each follicle usually produces a single ovum but occasionally two or more. The smallest follicles lie just under the surface of the ovary and consist of a single ovum surrounded by a layer of epithelial cells (protective tissue).

As the follicles grow, they move toward the center of the ovary. The number of epithelial cells increases and a cavity forms between the outer layer and the cells that directly surround the ovum. This cavity is filled with a protein containing nutritive fluid. The two layers of epithelial cells are joined with strands of connective tissue so that the cells surrounding the ovum are not entirely separated. The innermost layer of epithelial cells is concerned with the transfer of nutrients to the ovum; the outer wall of the follicle consists of fibrous tissue.

At this stage the whole structure is known as a Graafian follicle. The large follicles fill the greater part of the ovary and press so strongly at the walls that the ovary resembles a bunch of grapes.

During the ripening of the ovum, the quantity of nutritive fluid steadily increases until the pressure becomes so great that the follicle wall bursts, liberating the ovum. This process is known as ovulation. The ripening of ova can happen very quickly.

The Corpus Luteum

As soon as the ovum is liberated, the ruptured follicle becomes filled with epithelial cells and surrounded with a network of connective tissue. This is known as the corpus luteum (the yellow body, after the yellow fluid contained in the cells), a temporary endocrine gland that secretes the hormone progesterone. If the ovum is fertilized the corpus luteum enlarges and persists until after the birth of the young; if fertilization does not occur, the corpus luteum remains small and is slowly absorbed, resulting in a period of infertility.

The Uterus

The ovum descends through the fallopian tube, where fertilization occurs, and enters the uterus via

Reproduction in Rabbits

the funnel-like opening at its entrance. The fallopian tube is lined with ciliated epithelial cells that push the ovum toward the uterus. The fertilized egg then develops further into an embryo in the uterus. The wall of the uterus consists of three layers: the outermost layer is a serious membrane, which can be considered a continuation of the lining of the abdominal cavity. Then comes the thick, smooth muscular layer, containing muscles passing lengthwise and then breadthwise and diagonally. Finally, the inner lining of the uterus consists of a mucus membrane provided with numerous glands that secrete a milky fluid. This fluid provides the nutrients necessary to the fertilized ovum in its early stages.

In cattle the uterus consists of a neck (cervix uteri), which runs into the main body (corpus uteri); this splits into a left and a right horn (cornus uteri), each of which runs into a fallopian tube (oviduct). The neck of the uterus forms the connection between the uterus and the vagina, a folded tube that leads to the external sex opening (the vulva). In rabbits, the two uterine horns are totally separated, almost forming two uteri that separately open next to each other into the vagina.

The Male Reproductive Organs

Adult male rabbits have a very prominent scrotum, (the pouch of skin that contains the testicles). The testicles are connected to the penis by the Wolffian duct or vas deferens. Although thin, the Wolffian duct is very muscular. It carries the semen from the testicles to the penis during mating. Semen is formed within tiny coiled tubes enclosed within the testicles. During cold weather, the buck is capable of withdrawing the testicles into the abdomen by muscular contraction.

In male rabbits less than six to eight weeks old, the scrotum is not fully developed. During sexing of a young buck, a minute tubular protrusion will be visible. (Once the male is about two months old this protrusion is easily recognized as the penile sheath.) The penis can be pushed out through the tiny protrusion with both thumbs when pressure is applied on either side. In general, the testicles don't become visible until the buck reaches sexual maturity, which means in approximately two months. At that time the scrotum is clearly visible on either side of the penis.

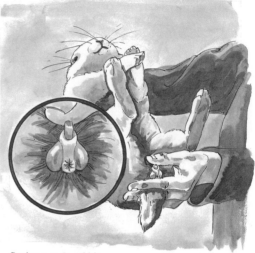

Sexing a male rabbit.

Fertilization

In rabbits there is a more or less unique situation in that the follicles burst and release the ova some ten hours after mating. During mating, the male sex cells or spermatozoa are released in great numbers with a milky seminal fluid and a jellylike substance into the female vagina. The latter substance has the function of forming a plug in the vagina to prevent the semen from running back out. The spermatozoa are furnished with long, paddlelike tails with which they swim through the uterine horns into the fallopian tubes, a process that takes about four hours. The ova, with the remainder of the follicular membrane, form a plug in the funnellike ends of the fallopian tubes. The spermatozoa swim among the ova and fertilize them. Unfertilized ova live for a few hours. If the spermatozoa arrive too late, the ova die. When this occurs, the animal is no longer ripe for fertilization.

After a few hours, the plug loosens and the ova make their way slowly through the fallopian tubes into the uteri, a process that takes about four days.

Development of the Embryos

Fertilization occurs when the head (spermatozoid) of a spermatozoon penetrates the wall of the ovum and the nuclei of the male and female cells fuse to form a zygote, which begins to divide.

During the development of the zygote into an embryo a fertilization membrane forms around it, preventing the entry of further spermatozoa. The membrane gradually binds with the blood vessels of the uterus wall, so that feeding from the uterine fluid is replaced by circulatory feeding directly from the maternal blood. From the ninth day, the outer membrane begins to push into the wall of the uterus, leading to the formation of the fetal placenta. At the same time, a membrane (maternal placenta) forms over the inner walls of the uterus, effectively enclosing the fetus and supplying it with maternal blood. The blood is passed from the uterine walls into the placenta and from there to the fetus via the navel artery, which passes through the navel, bringing nutrients to the new life.

Birth

The formation and development of the placenta are regulated by the corpus luteum. Just before or during the normal birth time (31 to 32 days after mating), the corpus luteum begins to degenerate, the placenta loosens, and the fetus is expelled by muscular contractions in the uterine walls.

By releasing hormones, the corpus luteum hinders the normal function of the uterus, resulting in rhythmic contractions of the muscles. As the corpus luteum degenerates, the uterus resumes its normal functions and birth of the youngsters takes place.

The Breeding Buck

It is important to choose breeding bucks and does in the best of health and first-class condition. Furthermore, they should have a good build and be amply endowed with the points necessary in the standards of the appropriate breed. Only rabbits of such quality produce maximal results.

The breeding buck must be an obvious male and should not have the body build of a doe. The head and body must satisfy the breed standard, and the underfur should be especially thick.

A buck should have a fiery temperament but should not be too aggressive; he should have a certain trust toward his keeper.

It is important that matings be regulated so that the buck is not overworked through too many pairings in too short a period. It is therefore advisable to use a buck for mating over two to three days. Too many pairings in a short period can lead to a decrease in fertility, a weakening effect on the offspring, and a high incidence of juvenile deaths.

A buck is normally sexually mature at an age of four to six months. At this time he is particularly lively. He jumps around in his hutch and strokes his chin restlessly over the straw or food containers. However, it is best not to use a buck for mating until he is at least eight months old, or fully grown.

The Breeding Doe

A doe used for breeding must have a typical female form and meet the standards of the appropri-

Reproduction in Rabbits

ate breed. A further characteristic of a good breeding doe is a broad, well-formed pelvis.

The breeding doe must be in good condition: in other words, not too fat but also not too thin. She must have a good, peaceful character. Restless, nervous, and aggressive animals are not likely to make good mothers, and furthermore, they may pass on these unpleasant traits to their offspring.

A breeding doe must possess at least eight teats (nipples). Animals with fewer than eight teats should not be used for breeding as there is a danger that this property will be instilled in the breed, thus reducing its value. The mother of the buck as well as the mother of the doe must have at least eight teats. Normal teats are small, pinkish protuberances on the belly. Poorly developed teats appear as a mere pimple and are never likely to produce much milk. A doe with poorly developed teats is unlikely to be able to raise her young.

The doe is sexually mature at an age of about six months. A doe should never be mated before she is fully grown as her normal development will be disturbed and she will never reach the required standards.

It is therefore best to mate a doe first at eight to ten months old, never earlier. A doe should always be taken to the buck when she is ready for mating, bearing in mind that a successful mating can occur only when a female is in heat. You can tell when a doe is in heat by her excited behavior; she gathers heaps of bedding and makes a nest from hair plucked from her own body.

Mating

When everything is ready for the mating, the doe is taken to the buck: never the buck to the doe. If a buck is brought to a strange hutch he will be more interested in exploring the new surroundings, inspecting the hutch, and turning over the straw, than in the doe.

If a ripe doe is brought to the buck in his hutch,

however, mating usually occurs very quickly. The mating must be supervised, bearing in mind that you must not only see that the mating is successful, but also be ready to intervene if—as occasionally happens—the doe should attack the buck for one reason or another.

Mating rabbits.

If a buck is ready to mate, he will mount the doe and bite her neck. The penis fills with blood, becomes erect, and protrudes from the sheath. Semen is pushed through the Wolffian duct by strong muscular contractions and forced from the penis into the vagina of the doe. After a successful mating, the male falls off the doe to one side—frequently taking a mouthful of fur with him. Usually his ears are held back, and he often grunts and squeals. The doe, however, is usually quiet and gentle. After the mating is completed, place her in her own hutch, holding her rump up to help retain the semen in her body. A single mating is usually adequate for good fertilization.

Care of the Doe

After mating, the doe is placed into a prepared nursery hutch. Great care should be taken with the

Reproduction in Rabbits

feeding of a doe. If she becomes too fat there is a danger of failure in giving birth. Failures can also occur with animals that become too thin. During the earlier part of the pregnancy there is no need for an extra feed, bearing in mind that the developing young do not require anywhere near the nourishment they require after birth. Ensure, however, that only the best-quality food is given. Green food is essential. Protein-rich dry food is also important. During the last eight days before the birth of the litter, the doe's daily rations should be slightly increased. However, if too much fat-producing food is given in the last week, there is a danger that the young will develop too strongly and cause difficulties during birth.

The rearing of young is an exhausting task for the doe. The young animals grow very quickly. The mother supplies all the nourishment for the young over a period of two months (from the mating), as youngsters feed exclusively on the mother's milk to an age of four weeks. Thereafter, the young begin to feed themselves but they still continue to take the mother's milk. At the age of ten weeks, weaning time, they should all be eating as much solid food as the mother. The best foodstuffs must be reserved for the nursing mother, especially those with a high protein content.

Nursery Hutches

All too often, rabbits are kept in hutches that are much too small and in which the animals can barely move. It is impossible to clean such a small hutch when the doe is nesting; it is then no wonder that breeding fails.

For successful breeding and rearing, a double hutch 32 inches deep, 64 inches long, and 22 inches high (approximately $80 \times 160 \times 55$ cm) is necessary. This is a two-compartment hutch with a removable sliding partition.

The doe is placed in the double hutch fourteen days before she gives birth. The partition is re-moved to make a large hutch from the two smaller ones. A nest box is placed in the end opposite to that in which the droppings are deposited.

A nest box has many advantages, bearing in mind that you should provide conditions as near the natural situation as possible. Rabbits are burrowing animals. The young, especially, appreciate the nest box as a hiding place whenever they are surprised by some new happening.

The doe can also escape from the demanding attentions of the suckling young by jumping on top of the nest box.

A doe is glad to use the nest box for giving birth.

A pregnant rabbit collecting hay for lining her nest.

The birth can take place privately here, and the animal feels secure in the dark surroundings. Moreover, she can build a more compact and cozier nest in the nest box. The newly born young are less likely to be disturbed; they are nice and warm and therefore stay longer in the nest. Nest boxes can be constructed in two different patterns; the first has a lid on top and is used in a hutch that is also serviced from the top. You can then inspect the nest simply by lifting the lid. However, such a nest box is

Reproduction in Rabbits

unsuitable in a normal hutch as you cannot look into it without taking the box out of the hutch. The other type of hutch has a sliding door at the front so that you do not have to remove the doe to inspect the nest.

By using a nest box, it is easy to clean the hutch without disturbing the nest. A little hay and straw can be placed in the nest box, but the doe herself will bring in the required quantity from the hutch and shred it up. Toward the time of birth the doe lines the nest with fur plucked from her own body to make a soft bed for the youngsters. For practical purposes, a nest box has proven its advantages time and time again.

A very young litter in a fur-lined nest. In the wild rabbits are born below ground and a great deal of their life remains concealed from humans.

A female rabbit pulling out hair for her nest.

The Birth

A week before the birth, the hutch should once more be thoroughly cleaned and disinfected. Adequate straw (preferably oat straw) should be placed in the hutch.

After the birth it is recommended that the doe be given some green food or some other tidbits. She eats this greedily, and it gives her some comfort and strength. You should never leave more than eight young with a doe as a rabbit rarely has more than eight teats. It is better to leave six young in the nest and to cull the rest. The remaining youngsters then develop more strongly, making them better breeding animals later and making them less susceptible to disease. The smallest in the litter are culled and brought to a veterinarian.

Young does sometimes have a habit of not making a proper nest and may even throw the youngsters out of the nest box. When this happens, it is possible that you will discover it too late and the young will have already died from the cold. If you can rescue them in time, make a nest from hay, straw, and, if possible, some unspun wool.

Sometimes a doe destroys her nest because she has teat pain. In such cases the doe must be removed

Above: The white rex is also called the ermine rex and is known for its dense coat. Below left: The dalmation rex is white with colored spots. Below right: The Belgian hare is responsible for popularizing the domestic rabbit.

Reproduction in Rabbits

from the hutch so that her teats can be examined. If they are bright red and inflamed, they should be gently massaged with warm oil. The young animals are then positioned at the teats and their suckling should help to relieve the pain. The youngsters are then returned to the nest and the doe is allowed a few hours to herself in another hutch. If she destroys the nest again, you should consult a veterinarian or a more experienced breeder for advice. Such an animal is usually not suitable for further breeding.

After the initial inspection of the nest and the culling of excess young, the nest should be left undisturbed. At the most you should just now and then check that the nest is in order. Take unwanted kits to a veterinarian or to your local humane society. Don't drown or abandon them under any circumstances!

You should keep your hands out of the nest or there is a danger that the young will leave the nest too soon. The young are born with closed eyes, and these open about the tenth day.

In normal circumstances, the young emerge from the nest on the eighteenth or nineteenth day. They then slowly begin to take solid food. At this stage there is a possible risk of digestive disturbances. The feeding of young rabbits therefore requires the greatest of care.

Feeding the Doe

A few days before the expected births of the young, the doe should be given a ration of lukewarm, skimmed milk. This should be continued

Above left: The Dielenaar is a hare-colored Dutch breed. Above right: The Parelfeh was first bred in Germany. Center left: The Thueringer, a German breed, is especially popular in Europe. Center right: The Sallander, a Dutch breed, was developed by D. Kuiper about 15 years ago. Below left: The Huslander is popular only in some European countries. Below right: The Lotharinger is originally from Belgium and France.

A doe and her weaning kits.

while the doe is rearing the litter. The doe must receive sufficient fluids or she will be unable to adequately rear her litter.

The young stay in the nest until they are about three weeks old. If they come out earlier, it is probable that the mother is unable to supply enough milk and the young are forced to search for solid food too soon.

Normally they begin to take solid foods at three weeks of age. This means a major change in the digestive process. When solid food is taken, bacteria play a role in the digestion, which proceeds quite differently from when the diet was solely mother's milk. The stomach and intestines must gradually become accustomed to the new food. The walls of the intestines in freshly weaned animals are extremely sensitive, and the youngsters do not yet have a strong resistance. Incorrect feeding at this stage can have disastrous consequences.

The weaning, in other words, the change from a diet of mother's milk to solid foods, should never take place suddenly or too rapidly. It is absolutely wrong to remove the young from the mother at the age of four weeks. At this age the digestive systems of the young are not yet fully prepared to take a wholly solid diet and disasters are likely to occur in such cases.

Thus, the young must become accustomed to the solid food gradually so that the bacterial flora in the intestines have time to develop. Only when the various kinds of digestive bacteria are present in adequate quantities can the youngsters be expected to take a solid diet without the danger of digestive disturbances.

Solid food for young rabbits must be easily digestible, and you must doubly ensure (even more so than with adult animals) that the food is of the highest quality. Ideally the diet should consist of equal amounts of fresh green food and hay.

Experience has shown that if only grass and green food are given at an early age, there is a high percentage of deaths. From the moment they begin to eat solids until they are about three months old, the animals show a preference for green food and eat too much of it if given the chance. Therefore hay must also be given, not only as normal winter food but also in the summer months. Hay is an important item that must not be missing from the diet.

If you give hay and green food to the doe with young two or three times a day, it is possible that the big portions mean the youngsters eat too much green food and ignore the hay, which is important for the digestive process. It is therefore necessary to feed the animals with small quantities of green food several times a day so that they just have hay to eat between meals. The young, growing rabbits require a great deal of fluid (another reason they are so eager for green food); therefore, mother and family should never be without a constant supply of clean, fresh drinking water.

Care of the Young

It should go without saying that the hutches must be spotlessly clean at all times. The hutches should be double the size of a normal, single rabbit hutch so that they are easier to clean and the young have plenty of room for exercise. Hutches must be kept in a dry, airy spot. Stale air and damp surroundings encourage the growth of disease-causing organisms and are detrimental to the health of your animals.

Despite your taking all precautions, it occasionally happens that a youngster becomes sick. It may sit hunched up in the hutch and refuse to eat. You should not become too alarmed at such an occurrence. The sick animal should be isolated and fed with good hay and appropriate green food (for example, celery) and taken to a veterinarian. In most cases there is not much more you can do. A more serious situation arises if several youngsters show symptoms of disease. These are often digestive disturbances caused by inappropriate feeding or possibly an intestinal infection, such as coccidiosis. Incorrect feeding is usually the cause of a loss of resistance in the animal. The coccidia can then infect the intestinal walls almost without resistance, and the young animals are beyond recovery. To minimize the chances of infection it is essential to provide the animals with the means of maintaining resistance. The doe must receive as varied and natural a diet as possible.

Weak does are themselves more susceptible to coccidiosis and thus pass on the disease organisms to the young. To reduce the possibility of infection, all hutches used should be thoroughly scrubbed and disinfected before the beginning of the breeding season. The disease organisms then have less chance of infecting the doe.

Moreover, you should ensure that the nursery hutch is kept so clean that the young do not have to eat food fouled with droppings. It is recommended that powdered charcoal (Norit) be added to the youngsters' dry food. The binding action of the powder works against the abnormal buildup of gases in the intestines. Too much powder can in fact cause constipation. It is best to use a veterinary preparation for safety's sake.

Reproduction in Rabbits

It is impossible to generalize about the amount of food that should be given to the young. However, this is learned quickly by experience. To get a good idea about whether the diet is adequate, the animals should be weighed at weekly intervals. Young animals should gain approximately $3^1/_2$ to $10^1/_2$ ounces (100–300 g) per week. If this is not the case, the daily ration must be increased so that the youngsters can grow into worthy examples of their breed—animals that do well in exhibition and are excellent for further breeding. This is the main ambition of every breeder.

Rabbit Breeding

Theoretical Background

In this chapter we deal with genetics and heredity—the theoretical background aspects of rabbit breeding. No geneticist or breeder can give infallible rules that guarantee the results of a breeding. However, a knowledge of the basic laws of heredity and the means by which good and bad points are inherited will give you a good idea of what to expect when particular animals are mated together.

An Unknown Monk

Although people have been taming and domesticating wild animals since time immemorial, interest in the genetic aspects of breeding did not develop until the middle of the last century. The greatest step forward in our understanding of genetics occurred in 1900, when the work of the Austrian monk Gregor Mendel (1822–1884) came to light.

Genetics and heredity, when compared with chemistry and natural history, are relatively young sciences. It was only in 1953 that the Nobel Prize winners, James Crick and J.D. Watson, produced their now widely accepted theory on the structure of DNA—the basic genetic material.

Despite these dramatic advances, genetics remains a dynamic young science. What we accept as true today can become obsolete tomorrow, but the secrets unraveled by a little-known monk, which lay undiscovered for nearly a century, are now universally accepted as the basis for our studies of genetics.

The Basics

The body of a rabbit, like that of all other animals, is composed of innumerable tiny living cells. Under high magnification, each of these cells is seen to possess a dark center, or nucleus. The nucleus contains minute, threadlike structures known as chromosomes.

Each species of animal has a specific number of chromosomes in its cells and can be recognized by this fact. Chromosomes are sort of genetic "fingerprints" that enable scientists to recognize a species from a single cell alone. Whatever the breed, a domestic rabbit has forty-four chromosomes, like its wild counterpart. In contrast, a hare has forty-eight, a mouse forty, a human being forty-six, a cow sixty, and so on. The number of chromosomes is always divisible by two, at least in the higher organisms. Should an odd number occur, this is a result of genetic problems. A mule, for example, has sixty-three (the medial number produced as the result of crossing a donkey and a horse, which have sixty-two and sixty-four chromosomes, respectively). When crossings between two different species result in odd numbers of chromosomes, the offspring are invariably sterile. In the human, an extra chromosome in a certain position leads to Down's syndrome. Even numbers of chromosomes are therefore necessary for an animal to function correctly.

By studying the contents of cell nuclei, whatever the shape or size, you can see that the chromosomes occur in pairs of identical size and shape. Such chromosomes are described as homologous pairs. One pair, however, the so-called sex chromosomes, forms an exception to this rule. In human beings, the other forty-four chromosomes, or rather the twenty-two pairs, which are known as diploids (or zygotes), are found in every body cell, with the exception of the ova and the sperm cells. In these sex cells, formed during a reductive division process called meiosis, there are only twenty-two chromosomes, one from each pair. These are known as haploids. Which half of a pair of homologous chromosomes is passed on to a particular sex cell is a matter of chance.

When a male spermatophore fuses with a female ovum, the twenty-two chromosomes in each unite to form twenty-two pairs. In this manner, the correct number of chromosome pairs are made up and passed from generation to generation, but in turn, only half the pairs are passed into the future offspring's sex cells.

Rabbit Breeding

During normal growth, cells divide. In other words, one cell becomes two cells to allow the tissues to enlarge, a process called mitosis. During cell division, each chromosome divides lengthwise. Half of each segment migrates to each of the two developing cells. Thus, the correct number of unaltered pairs of chromosomes will be present in each new cell.

Influence of Genes

A particular part of a particular chromosome, known as a gene, influences one or more specific characteristics in a plant or animal. Genes that influence a given characteristic in different ways are called alleles. The genes for smooth and wrinkled skin in the garden pea, for example, are alleles.

Theoretically, a gene can have any number of alleles, but in reality there can be only two, as there are only two chromosomes on which the gene occurs. If both these chromosomes have the same gene in a given position (locus), the plant or animal is known as homozygous. If each of the pair has different genes, the animal is known as heterozygous for the characteristic influenced by the genes.

An allele that influences a particular observed characteristic in a plant or animal is known as a dominant allele; an allele whose influences are masked by another allele is known as recessive. When a gene contains various alleles, one allele can be dominant to another allele and at the same time can be recessive to a third. For example, this occurs in the color inheritance of agouti (wild-colored) animals.

Although genes in a particular position on a particular chromosome influence a particular characteristic, this can be altered or modified by genes in other positions (loci). In addition we have epistatic genes, for example those that influence the color black, which can suppress the effect of other genes. Insofar as epistatic effects play a role, the normal rules of dominance and recession can be disturbed.

Other Complications

A further complication can arise if the dominant allele does not wholly mask the influence of the recessive allele. For example, crossing a red and a white carnation produces a pink, the color being a mixture of those of the two parents. This is called incomplete dominance. However, since the genes are not combined, further breeding of the pink offspring produces flowers of all three colors.

Incomplete dominance differs from incomplete penetration, in which a dominant allele does not completely affect the appearance of all the plants or animals that carry it. The percentage of animals that reveals the character of the gene is known as the penetration of the allele.

A similar paradoxical situation can occur with recessive alleles. Normally, a recessive characteristic appears only outwardly if the allele is doubly present, that is, if the animal is homozygous to that allele. From time to time, however, the characteristic may appear in heterozygous recessive animals. This can disturb a breeding scheme but is not incompatible with the rules of genetics.

Sex Determination

As we have already discussed, a rabbit has twenty-two pairs of chromosomes. The last pair are the sex chromosomes, and these are different in both sexes. Females have two identical sex chromosomes, and these are usually designated XX. Males have a long chromosome (X) and a shorter one (Y), so that all male animals are designated XY. (This rule applies to most animals except birds and butterflies, in which the opposite applies.)

All female sex cells (the ova) carry only a single chromosome from each chromosome pair. As both female sex chromosomes are X chromosomes, the female sex cell must carry an X. However, a male sex chromosome may carry an X or a Y.

A male produces more or less equal numbers of X- and Y-carrying spermatophores. The sexes of the offspring are therefore determined by whether an X-

Rabbit Breeding

or a *Y*-carrying spermatophore fertilizes the female ova. As this is a matter of chance, it follows that even numbers of male and female offspring should be produced. In most animal species, the *Y*-carrying cells are more agile (thus reaching the ova quicker) or are more acceptable by the ova because a chemical reaction allows them easier entry.

In general, therefore, there are always more male than female embryos. During pregnancy there is a natural selection against male embryos in that more of them die. Nevertheless, there is a higher percentage of male offspring, but natural selection against the so-called stronger sex continues through life so that eventually there are more females than males.

Sex Limitations

Genes for certain characteristics influence male and female animals in different ways. We can illustrate this using the human being. In baldness, the hair of the crown gradually thins, eventually leaving only a border of hair around the edges of the scalp. Baldness, a dominant condition, is symbolized as *B*; nonbaldness, which is recessive, as *b*. The following table shows the outward appearance (phenotype) of the three possible gene combinations in males and females.

Genotype	Phenotype	
	Men	Women
BB	bald	bald
Bb	bald	not bald
bb	not bald	not bald

At first sight it appears that the dominant or recessive qualities change in women, but this is not the case. The way in which a heterozygote shows itself depends on the sex of the person.

Many characteristics of rabbits are determined by the sex in that they show only in one sex or the other or in either sex in totally different ways. These are mostly complex characteristics, such as size,

weight, dimensions of head, and so on.

Unfavorable gene combinations can result in too large does (of the buck type) or too small bucks (of the doe type). Even with identical genes, however, the type can vary depending on the sex of the animal carrying them.

Sex-linked Inheritance

Genes for sex-linked characteristics are located on the *X* or *Y* chromosomes and their outward appearance depends on which sex chromosome. Most of these genes lie on the *X* chromosome, and it is suspected that in such cases the *Y* chromosome is inactive. The classic example of this is the blood disease hemophilia, which animals inherit in a similar way to humans. The allele for the condition is located on the *X* chromosome and is thus carried from mother to son. This causes hemophilia in half the male offspring, who generally die at an early age. Normal sons are not carriers of the allele and cause no problems, but half the daughters are carriers and are responsible for the continuance of the condition in following generations.

Mendel's Laws of Inheritance

When Mendel started his classic work in the monastery, he chose to study the common pea plant and seven of its variable characteristics: height of the plant, seed color, form, and so on. Each of the characteristics occurred in two alternate forms (or alleles); for example, tall and short plants, and brown or white seeds. He discovered that if he crossed true-breeding strains of plants with a single different characteristic and then crossed the offspring, the same sorts would always be produced.

As we have seen, symbols using a capital letter denote dominant alleles. Lower case symbols denote recessive alleles.

The first pair used in a crossing is known as the *P* generation. The offspring in the first generation is

Rabbit Breeding

called *F*1, their offspring *F*2, and so on through the generations.

Monohybrid Crossings

Mendel found three fundamental results to each of the characteristics he studied:

• When plants of true breeding strain but with a single different outward characteristic were crossed together, all the resulting *F*1 generation showed only one of the outward characteristics.
• The characteristics of either sex of the parents did not affect the result.
• When the *F*1 plants were crossed together, the "hidden" characteristic appeared, but only in 25 percent of the offspring.

Although Mendel was unaware at the time, he had coincidentally crossed plants with dominant and recessive alleles. If he had chosen those with polygenic characteristics, in which many more genes are concerned, he would probably not have discovered anything new to science.

In the diagram Mendel's Monohybrid Crossing, the situation as Mendel understood it is illustrated. It is a hypothetical example of dominant blue (*B*) and recessive white (*b*). As the blue parent can pass on only the *B* and the white parent only the *b*, it follows that the whole *F*1 generation can be only *Bb* and thus all of the flowers would be blue (the color of the dominant parent).

If offspring from the *F*1 generation are paired together, three blue and one white characters should be passed on to the *F*2 generation. In reality, however, the proportion is one homozygote blue (*BB*), two heterozygote blue (*Bb*), and one homozygote white (*bb*). Because of the dominance of the *B*, the *BB* and *Bb* present the same appearance (blue). Thus, they are indistinguishable except in the product of their offspring. *BB* produce only blue offspring; *Bb* can produce either blue or white offspring as they are born of parents with one or two *b* alleles.

Mendel's Monohybrid Crossing

*P*1	*BB* (blue)	×	*bb* (white)
*F*1		*Bb* (blue)	
*F*2	*Bb* (blue)	×	*Bb* (blue)

	B	*b*
B	*BB* (blue)	*Bb* (blue)
b	*Bb* (blue)	*bb* (white)

*F*2 ratio	3:1
	(blue) (white)

Great Numbers

The ratios 3:1 or 1:2:1 and others are not necessarily correct when working with small numbers of animals. Mendel used dozens of plants, and the results of the seven studied characteristics produced an average ratio of 2.84:1 to 3.15:1. Although it did not produce an exact 3:1 ratio, it was close enough to this expected result.

As he examined individual plants, the results deviated to as much as 32:1 or 1:1 in place of the expected 3:1. This did not reduce the value of Mendel's work, but it illustrates the role of coincidence in inheritance and it emphasizes the need to think in terms of great numbers when estimating results. This is important to rabbit breeders, who work with litters averaging 6–8 animals and then complain that their expectations do not materialize; these numbers are much too small.

In simple autosomal dominant-recessive situations, as illustrated in the diagram Mendel's Monohybrid Crossing, there are three genotypes (*BB*, *Bb*, and *bb*) and two pheotypes (blue or white)

Rabbit Breeding

possible. There are thus six different pairing possibilities that always produce blue-white combinations. The following table gives the expected results produced from pairings of animals with simple gene series containing a dominant *B* allele and a recessive *b* allele.

Pairing		Parents	Offspring
1.	genotype:	*BB* × *BB*	100% *BB*
	phenotype:	blue blue	all blue
2.	genotype:	*BB* × *Bb*	50% *BB* and 50% *Bb*
	phenotype:	blue blue	all blue
3.	genotype:	*BB* × *bb*	100% *Bb*
	phenotype:	blue white	all blue
4.	genotype:	*Bb* × *Bb*	25% *BB*, 50% *Bb* and 25% *bb*
	phenotype:	blue blue	blue; blue and white
5.	genotype:	*Bb* × *bb*	50% *Bb* and 50% *bb*
	phenotype:	blue white	blue and white
6.	genotype:	*bb* × *bb*	100% *bb*
	phenotype:	white white	all white

In estimating the ratio of the results of a particular pairing, it must be considered that the sex cells have only one allele. A *Bb* animal gives 50 percent *B* gametes (ripe sex cells) and 50 percent *b* gametes; a *BB* animal gives 100 percent *B* gametes. Each gamete from one of the parents has a similar chance of combining with a gamete from the other parent, which in sufficient numbers produces the results expected in the table. The percentages given are therefore only averages of what you would expect from the breeding of sufficient numbers, not necessarily what you would expect in a single litter.

With ten independent pairs of genes in a population, there would be approximately 59,000 possible different genotypes. With twenty pairs of genes this would rise to approximately 3.5 billion. In rabbits there are many more than twenty gene pairs, giving an enormous number of possibilities. It is not difficult to imagine that, with the exception of twins conceived from a single ovum, two animals with precisely the same genotype can never occur. No single animal therefore has a genetic double.

Lethal Factors

Sometimes the expected pattern does not occur, due to serious causes. In mice, for example, there is a yellow hair color that is dominant to the wild (agouti) type color. All yellow mice appear to be heterozygous, as both color varieties occur in the offspring. The ratio is 2:3 yellow and 1:3 agouti in place of the normal 3:1 ratio. The yellow color appears to be dominant, but homozygous mice die in the embryo stage. As we understand, the missing yellow mice are those that have two alleles of the yellow color.

The accuracy of this supposition can be illustrated in that yellow female mice mated to yellow males produce approximately 25 percent dead embryos.

Other fatal (lethal) factors can be caused by recessive homozygous genes, which produce a 3:0 ratio. The action of lethal genes (penetration) is not always 100 percent, and the expected ratio can deviate. For example, some animals may not die in the embryo stage but do not live long after birth. In other cases the animals may be sterile.

Linkage

It has been known for a long time that particular characteristics are closely bound or "linked" with other characteristics—the relationship of blond hair and blue eyes in humans, for example (which does not occur as often as one might think). In other cases the linkage is obvious enough and this can be ascribed to the fact that particular genes lie close to each other on the chromosome. Since the two linked genes are located in the same chromosome, they almost invariably travel together during the meiotic division process. Thus, linked characteristics in general are passed on together.

Crossing Over and Recombination

During meiotic division (reduction division of the sex cells), chromosomes can on occasion mix with each other so that a part of one becomes attached to another. As a rabbit passes on twenty-two chromosomes in its sex cells, some of these can exchange parts. For example, a rabbit can receive a chromosome from its father that is made up of two-thirds from the grandfather on the father's side and one-third from the grandmother on the father's side. This is known as crossing over and recombination.

Crossing over and recombination occurs fairly frequently; in this process, genes that were originally situated on one chromosome can be separated. Crossing over can involve any part of the chromosome, but it is true that the chance is increased when genes are widely separated on the chromosome. Conversely, genes that lie closely together on the chromosome have a greater chance of being passed over together, even in cases when the chromosome on which they reside is involved in the crossing and recombination process.

Certain species of fruit flies (*Drosophilia*) have few chromosomes and are thus popular for genetic research. The position of most of the genes on the chromosomes is known exactly, and the crossing over and recombination process can be precisely estimated. Unfortunately this is not possible with rabbits, and our estimation of the outcome of a mating is often no more than academic wishful thinking. This phenomenon, however, may be an explanation for the unexpected cases in which two simple characteristics that are normally passed on quite readily suddenly disappear.

Phenocopies

Most breeders believe that anything inborn is genetically fixed. This is not necessarily always the case. Inborn means simply "present at birth." A characteristic can be present at birth but may or may not be inherited, just as, for that matter, a characteristic appearing later in life may or may not be inherited. The term *congenital* is useful in this context. Congenital means present at birth, but not carried in the genes. Thus, a condition that was acquired by the offspring while it was in the uterus is deemed congenital—as, for example a disease condition that is present at birth.

If a doe has an accident while carrying a litter, this can lead to (sometimes serious) abnormalities in the development of the fetus. However, the genetic makeup of the fetus is not altered in such cases.

Occasionally, specific environmental factors can be strong enough to change the characteristics of the animals. The effect of a particular gene (or genes) can in such cases be changed or diminished. When this happens, we call the individual a phenocopy.

Anyone who has epilepsy caused by a brain tumor can be compared with someone who has inherited epilepsy, but the former does not pass on the affliction to the next generation. In humans, the thalidomide tragedy is a good example of a phenocopy. Thalidomide was a sedative that, if taken by a woman in a certain stage of pregnancy, caused serious developmental faults in the fetus. In most cases this resulted in a shortening or absence of limbs.

A rare hereditary condition in humans can lead to a similar condition (phocomelia). At the beginning of the 1960s, when the first thalidomide babies were born, it was intially thought that the affliction was genetic. As the number of babies born with such disabilities increased, however, researchers had to look in another direction for the cause. It was then that the connection between the sedative and the tragic consequences was discovered.

Rabbit Breeding

There is another situation in which phenocopying occurs. Take, for example, a dog with inherited floppy ears. The ears can be corrected if treated early enough. The ears may be treated with splints and plasters, for example, so that in most (but not all) cases, they stand pricked up just as if they had been so inherited.

The floppy ears are genetically inherited, however, and the dog will pass such ears on to its progeny, not the ears that have been artificially produced. The dog is a phenocopy, as its floppy ears will be passed on genetically.

Pelt Color

Most mammals are color blind, and therefore, the color patterns and shades of the animal are more important to it than the color itself. In some animals, the color pattern is designed to act as camouflage in its environment, thus making it more difficult for predators to detect it. Other species, which are not necessarily powerful or do not necessarily possess a particularly effective defense mechanism, may show aposematic or warning coloration. In yet another species, the color is designed to show splendor or sexual attraction to a mate.

The wild rabbit has the so-called wild color sometimes referred to as rabbit gray. However, if we examine the individual hairs closely, we see that each one is tricolored; from the skin out it is blue, yellow, and brown, respectively. Some hair endings are black, from which we obtain the typical mixture of brown, black, or gray.

The domestication of rabbits and the following controlled breeding programs have led to a great variety in colors and patterns. All the colors, of course, must be contained in the genetic makeup of the wild ancestors, but they seldom show because of their recessive character. On the rare occasions that conspicuously colored wild rabbits are born, these are usually destroyed by predators before they

have a chance to breed and pass on their characteristics.

With some rabbit breeds, the planners of the breed standards make particular demands with regard to color shades, patterns, and markings. This makes the breeder's task all the more difficult. Insistence on certain colors or patterns means that a considerable number of rabbits of these breeds are not quite up to standard and signify an economic loss.

Normal Hair

With a few exceptions, most mammals have a coat of fur. In most cases, the coat consists of two different layers of pelt, the underpelt and the overpelt. The underpelt consists of a layer of thin downlike hairs, which are usually wavy or frizzy; the overpelt consists of long, thick, and straight hairs, called guard hairs or monotricha.

Most hairs have a central core or medulla, formed from one or more rows of cells containing air channels. The medulla is enclosed by a massive layer, the cortex, which is in turn enclosed by a thin outer membrane, the cuticula. The relative thicknesses of the medulla and cortex vary from mammal to mammal.

Pigment

Although many pigments occur in the hair, the principal pigment in mammals is melanin, of which there are two basic types: eumelanin (brown or black) and pheomelanin (yellow or reddish). The color of the pelt depends on the presence or absence of these melanin types, which are found in the medulla and cortex of the hair. When studying the inheritance of pelt colors, one is really concerned with the genetic factors that affect the pigment granules.

The most frequent means by which the different colors are genetically determined is by the replacement of one type of melanin with the other, but phenotypic changes can also occur due to the influence of other genes that determine the number, shape, and position of the melanin granules.

Melanin is composed of tyrosine, an amino acid that occurs in many foods. A deficiency in tyrosine can lead to malfunctions in the animal's metabolism.

Formation of Color

In 1946, while researching the coat colors of the house mouse, J. Russell discovered that the pigment granules in the hair could be changed in seven different ways. The various color combinations he perceived were caused by the relative changes and the importance of each of these characteristics. The seven aspects were as follows:

1. Color of the pigment granules
2. Shape of the granules
3. Number of granules per medullary cell
4. Number of granules per cortex cell
5. Whether the granules are loosely or thickly grouped.
6. Size of the granules
7. Tendency for the granules to be situated between the medullary cells

Although Russell's work was carried out with house mice, it is probable that corresponding properties of the melanin granules in rabbit hairs give rise to the number of color shades. It is thus obvious that the inheritance of colors is not as simple and clear as it would at first appear to be.

What we perceive as phenotypic is not a simple gene effect but the result of a complicated series of chemical reactions, which are caused not only by the appropriate gene but are also influenced by other genes present in the animal as well as other conditions, such as the age of the animal, the photoperiod, and the environmental temperature.

Rabbit Colors

In practice, the breeder is not as concerned with minor color changes as with other questions, such as whether a particular animal or a particular combination should bring forth offspring with a particular color, pattern, or markings. In this respect it is sufficiently known that whole detailed hypotheses of formulas for the inheritance of colors can be drafted so that the results of pairings can be forecast with considerable accuracy, assuming of course that the breeder takes the trouble to concern himself or herself with the principles.

The following table sets out the genetic symbols for the various coat colors and types. With homozygous (pure-bred) animals, only half the symbols are given. Without going into details, the following is a quick summary of the meanings of the symbols.

A stands for the wild color factor (agouti) and *a* for self colored (all one color); therefore animals with *aa* in the formula are self colored.

B stands for black pigment, and the recessive allele *b* causes the appearance of brown pigment in place of black, or brown-gray in place of rabbit gray.

C is the color factor. This is essential for the formation of melanin. In homozygous animals (*CC*), the color shows completely; the heterozygote condition is usually indistinguishable from *CC*. All animals with *cc* in the formula are, whatever other alleles they may carry, without exception albinos. If an *h* accompanies the *c*, then the animal is partially albino (colored nose, ears, tail, and so on). If an *m* accompanies the *c*, then the animal is marten colored; *ch* with the *c* denotes Himalayan color.

The letter *d* denotes the so-called dilute factor; *D* denotes a dense coloration, which is dominant to *d*, that causes dilution of color. For example, black becomes blue and rabbit gray becomes blue-gray.

The letter *E* is involved with the formation and arrangement of brown and black markings. The letter *E* is responsible for the dark pigment within the whole pelt; *e* is responsible for light red or yellow. In a homozygous condition *ee* forms the yellow color.

It should be obvious that all these alleles are not wholly independent but are influenced by other

Rabbit Breeding

Type of Coat	Gene Symbol	Description
Agouti	A	Agouti pattern
	At	Tan pattern
	a	Self color
Black	B	Black color
	b	Brown color
Dilution	D	Dense color
	d	Dilute color
Color	C	Full color
	cchd	Dark chinchillation
	cchm	Medium chinchillation
	cchl	Light chinchillation
	ch	Himalayan color
	c	Complete albinoism
Extension of black	Ed	Dominant black
	E	Black as found in agouti
	ej	Harlequin pattern
	e	Black as found in yellows and tort
Vienna white	V	Normal color
	v	Blue-eyed white rabbit
English spotting	En	English spotting
	en	No spotting
Dutch pattern	Du	No markings
	du	Dutch markings
	duw	Dutch markings
	dud	Dutch markings
Wide band	W	Normal agouti band of yellow
	w	Yellow band wider than normal
Rex coat	R	Normal coat
	r	Rex coat
	R2	Normal coat
	r2	Rex coat 2 (German short hair)
	R3	Normal coat
	r3	Rex coat 3 (Normandy rex coat)
Angora coat	L	Normal coat
	l	Angora coat or long haired
Satin coat	Sa	Normal coat
	sa	Satin coat
Waved coat	Wa	Normal coat
	wa	Waved coat

alleles or in their turn influence other alleles, which can lead to the appearance of other colors.

For the formulas of the various colors, you can refer to the standards of the various breeds.

Inbreeding

It is generally accepted that inbreeding is the pairing of closely related animals, but what exactly is a "close relationship"? Some breeders use the word *inbreeding* or *incest breeding* for pairings of offspring × parent, or full brother × full sister. Others include such pairings as half-brother × half-sister or grandparent × grandchild. The practice of pairing less closely related animals is generally called line breeding or family breeding.

The proper definition of inbreeding is as follows: the pairing of animals with a closer relationship than the average relationship in the population (breed).

A part of the quantity of genes in a breed is fixed; otherwise it would not form a pure breed. This means that all animals in that breed have a number of genes in twofold; in other words, they are homozygous. Inbreeding with some other breeding systems using purebred animals influences these genes. If genes with alternate alleles circulate in a breed, the first effect is that an inbred animal inherits the same allele from the father and the mother and becomes more homozygous. The more intensive the inbreeding, that is, the closer the relationship of the paired animals, the more homozygous the offspring will be.

Inbreeding and Selection

The breeder has no real control of which alleles from which genes become homozygous as there are two alternatives and each has a similar chance of becoming homozygous. Should one alternative be required, there is an even chance of obtaining the one not required. The breeder hopes, naturally, that

Rabbit Breeding

the required allele is homozygous but must be prepared for disappointment with at least part of the litter.

It is generally accepted that inbred animals are more uniform in characteristics, but this is not necessarily so. If we inbreed animals with the gene structure *Aa*, then we increase the chances of obtaining *AA* offspring as well as *Aa*, thus producing a yield of variable phenotype.

As, in practice, type *aa* is not usually required, the breeder should work with *AA* or *Aa* animals that are not distinguishable from each other. Continuous inbreeding, leaving out the *aa* animals, should eventually lead to a stage at which all offspring are *AA* and the gene is fixed in the breed.

Because the *A* gene becomes fixed in the breed, you notice at this stage a great deal of resemblance between the individual animals produced. However, you should realize that this is not a result of inbreeding alone, but a combination of inbreeding and selection.

Genetic Deviations

It is generally known that frequent inbreeding can lead to genetic defects, and this applies to all animal species. This is the reason that religious and civil authorities forbid the marriage of closely related couples. Some rabbit breeders believe that inbreeding actually causes genetic defects, which is not true.

Many genetic defects are recessive in character and can be passed on only if possessed by both parents. Inbreeding increases the chance of this happening. If the parent animals do not possess genetic defects in the first place, however, they obviously cannot pass them on to their offspring, however intensively we inbreed. Rabbits may have fixed, recessive faults in their makeup that are not necessarily fixed by a gene. Inbreeding not only increases the chance of such faults being passed on but opens the possibility that they will become more serious. Many such characteristics occur more or less regularly, and the genes responsible occur in a number of breeds.

A point about inbreeding is that the chances of bringing such unknown problems to light are increased.

Lethal Defects

What we have discussed here also applies to lethal defects that lead to a variety of misformed animals. It can be stated that all animal species, including humans, carry at least one lethal or semilethal gene; if this combines with another lethal gene from another animal, this leads to another fatal abnormality.

Such births are indeed rare as we do not necessarily pair animals with similar lethal genes and there is also a good chance that the offspring do not inherit the same lethal gene from each parent.

With inbreeding the chances of such lethal factors coming to light are increased, and this has a direct connection with the degree of inbreeding. Imagine, for example, that allele *b*, which is responsible for brown coloration, has a lethal effect and that a group of breeding animals with *bb* genes produces offspring in which 1 percent die at birth or shortly after. It can be estimated that, in this group with 1 percent *bb*, 81% of the animals are *BB* and 18 percent *Bb*.

When a particular group of breeders suddenly decides to follow a regime of sister-brother pairings, the percentage of *bb* offspring in the first produced generation increases to 3.25 percent, the *BB* offspring increase to 82.25 percent, and the *Bb* animals are reduced to 13.5 percent. As *BB* and *Bb* animals are outwardly indistinguishable, the breeders do not notice the quantity of heterozygous animals but are aware of the threefold increase in brown offspring dying at an early age.

Continued inbreeding with *BB* and *Bb* animals will still produce *bb* animals, but in decreasing instances, and eventually only *BB* animals should be produced. I do not suggest that breeders with such a problem should follow a program of inbreeding or even that 1 percent of the animals will be *bb*, but this illustrates what can happen if a program of inbreeding is consistently pursued through several generations.

Inbreeding and Line Breeding: a Comparison

After reading this text, it is possible that the reader will imagine that there is no place for inbreeding as it can lead to all kinds of problems. On the surface, this would indeed seem to be the case, but we must not forget that the fancy rabbit breeder is not necessarily motivated by the ideals of the commercial cattle breeder.

Pig breeders, for example, need to produce a good-quality, uniform product. They are also required to produce as many animals per litter as possible. Fancy rabbit breeders are also interested in uniformity, but they are willing to produce excellent animals at the expense of others. In most cases rabbit breeders do not necessarily expect to make a profit from their hobby. They can, therefore, be more selective to produce the required type of quality animals.

The opportunity of being selective gives rabbit breeders the space for inbreeding, something cattle breeders frown upon.

In the beginning stages of a fixed breed, it is almost essential for inbreeding to be used as it is necessary for the quick development of a specific type. The present situation is somewhat different. Inbreeding plays another or lesser role, but there is always a place for it.

Line breeding is simply a less intensive form of inbreeding, from which the saying: "If you have bad results, blame it on inbreeding. If the results are good, be thankful to line breeding." Whatever results from inbreeding can be accomplished by line breeding to a lesser degree. If intensive inbreeding is successful, then line breeding will be successful to a lesser degree. By the same token, if inbreeding is catastrophic, then so is line breeding, although to a lesser degree.

Know-how

Every breeder has various considerations before beginning, but inbreeding requires deeper consideration of whether it will produce good or bad results. The more you know about your rabbits and their ancestors, the better prepared you are for the results of inbreeding.

Inbreeding is designed to bring two particular genes together, but the breeder has no control over which genes come together. The better the breeding animals (and I use "better" here in its widest sense, to include both body form and character), the better the chances of successful inbreeding.

If, for example, you have a doe with a good head type and she is the granddaughter of a good rabbit with an excellent head and the same type as the doe in question, then it is not unwise to pair her with a relative of the grandfather, provided the chosen buck also has a nice head and a fitting likeness to the grandfather in question. You can also consider pairing her with the grandfather, but before making such a decision you should have good knowledge of the breed in question.

Basic knowledge of the breed's standard and a full basic knowledge of genetic aspects that play a role here are important. In the example just mentioned I discussed only head type, but naturally the good breeder does not work from only a single characteristic.

One must regard the animal as a whole; it is a waste of time to breed an animal with a good head but to neglect the limbs, the coat, and other important points that are not always judged similarly. If you have breeding animals with a good coat and stance, you can in certain cases mix the characteristics.

Continuous Selection

With a program of inbreeding, you must remember not to change direction with each generation. If inbreeding is applied mainly to improve the head type, then it is essential that the best head types be selected from each litter for further breeding.

Rabbit Breeding

There is no point in using another animal because it seems to have better exhibition qualities, other than the head. A program of inbreeding must be carried out with rigorous selection. The more you know your breeding stock, the fewer risks you have to take; in spite of this, however, defects will surface.

The better the breeding animals, the stronger the motive for inbreeding, and every breeder with excellent animals should regularly consider using the system at particular times. This is especially significant when you have an excellent doe or stud buck.

When the animal dies, its genetic influence on every generation is halved and is eventually lost altogether. Intensive inbreeding while the animal is alive helps to bring a strong concentration of its good characteristics into the line, allowing them to be improved upon in later generations. It can certainly help to build the influence of the animal to a higher level after its death, but without inbreeding this is not possible.

Outbreeding

Outbreeding is the pairing of animals that are less related than half the average population to which they belong. In its most extreme form, outcrossing involves the pairing of two different species (for example in the production of mules) or in the pairing of animals from different breeds or races (which is commonly carried out in the breeding of pigs, sheep, cattle, and commercial rabbits). The fancy rabbit breeder must, by definition, breed to purity of race, so that it is pointless to use the more extreme forms of outcrossing.

All outbreedings should be used with the fundamental understanding that useful alleles should be dominant to the less favorable factors. As outbreeding has a tendency to bring out heterozygous animals, the system has a possibility of improving the average quality of animals, but at the same time it has the potential of lowering the value of the breed by negative influence. In other words, it is quite possible that outbreeding may result in some offspring that have lost some of the highly desirable breed characteristics that were present in one of the parents.

With outbreeding, the phenomenon of inbreeding "depression" can be reversed, so that the offspring show the average characteristics of the parents, or even an improvement on the characteristics of one of the parents.

Usually this consists of improvements in general health, in sturdiness, and in size. This phenomenon is known as heterosis or hybrid vigor, and it usually manifests itself most clearly when the differences between the parents are obvious. Thus, heterosis is quite common in fancy rabbits, but it can be minimal or absent if nonrelated animals of the same breed are crossed.

Outcrossing

Outbreeding systems do not necessarily lead to an improvement in the breed as they disturb families or lines that may have just begun to develop nicely. This should result in uniformity, but the progress in particular respects of the race may be difficult to replace.

An outcross is the pairing of unrelated animals in which one or both are from a stud of inbred or line-bred animals. Most breeders who have followed a program of inbreeding have used outcrossings at particular times. Most choose to do this when an unwanted characteristic becomes fixed in a line and an outcrossing is used in the hope of removing it.

Some characteristics can become fixed by inbreeding, as the alleles responsible for the characteristics are duplicated in all the animals. The breeder thus finds that in particular circumstances all animals in the stock show certain undesirable characteristics. Careful selection in a program of inbreeding ensures that such fixed undesirable characteristics are minimized, but unfortunately, they cannot be totally eliminated.

Rabbit Breeding

Timing

The larger the breeding establishment, the longer one can use inbreeding without the necessity of outcrossing, but at a given moment, it will become essential. There are really no hard and fast rules and ideas such as "two generations inbreeding and one generation outcrossing" are laughable generalizations. A capable breeder with numerous good breeding animals can use inbreeding through many generations without experiencing any great problems. However, in actual practice, many breeders tend to resort to outcrossing much earlier than is really necessary.

Outcrossing has no essential value, and breeders with an established line of inbred animals should use it only as a last resort when fixed undesirable characteristics must be worked out of the stock and selection alone does not do the job.

With outcrossing, the breeder must be aware that the inbred animals have many homozygous characteristics (depending on the degree of inbreeding) and that in the offspring of the first generation after an outcrossing most of this homozygosity is lost.

This applies not only to the undesirable characteristics that have emerged, but also to the good points that have been carefully improved by selection. It is thus obvious that an unconsidered outcross can destroy the good work produced from generations of inbreeding.

Application

Let us imagine that a breeder who has applied a regime of inbreeding for some time suddenly realizes that the animals are becoming too small and that their heads are becoming unacceptably small (a common occurrence with inbreeding programs). It is obvious that such defects are caused by genetic rather than environmental influences. In such a case, the breeder has clearly pursued inbreeding too rigorously. His or her only recourse to remedy the siuation is to revervse the breeding strategy. The breeder must introduce corrective factors by outcrossing until the problem is eliminated.

Seen from a genetic angle, the sex of an animal used for the outcrossing is not important, but in practice there is not much point in buying in a doe when a stud buck can be used (perhaps even without the necessity of buying it). Moreover, one or two litters are not sufficient, and although the same buck can be used to service several does, a purchased doe can produce only one litter at a time. The use of a buck in outcrossings therefore works much more effectively.

Ideally, the selected buck must be as near perfect as possible in all respects, but he must be particularly good in size and head structure. It is also desirable to know something of the buck's ancestors, to ascertain that there are no hidden, undesirable characteristics in his line. It would also be a good idea to see the results of the buck's previous litters and to check that the offspring are of sufficient size and have good head dimensions. The buck itself can be a result of outcrossing (within the same breed) or—preferably in the particular case that we are considering—can originate from inbreeding or line breeding in which the animals all show good head form.

It may help if the buck is distantly related to the inbred line, in that the loss of homozygous characteristics is somewhat minimized.

Methods

Once selected, the buck must be paired with various does from the stud. The number of does used depends on the size of the breeding group and the knowledge the breeder has of the breeding stock. In the ideal case, the different does should be mated at around the same time so that the litters are born shortly after each other, giving one an almost instant varied choice of material that can be used to continue the program.

As this is an outcrossing and thus a corrective mating, this should mean that some of the offspring are of better than average quality. Using outcrossing, the aim of the breeder is to produce a limited number of good animals that can be used to advantage in the continuing stud.

As the outcrossing is carried out to improve the size and head form of the stock (in the particular example under consideration), only animals with these improved qualities should be used for further breeding. However, do not lose sight of the fact that all the other points of the offspring's conformation, coat, color, and markings must also be acceptable.

Understanding Rabbits

It is doubtless that the domestication of the rabbit took place in the dim and distant past. However, the development of individual breeds first began in the sixteenth century. Around 1700 there were seven known breeds; today there are about fifty breeds. The wild color of rabbits is dominant over those produced by domestication so that the latter rapidly disappears if tame rabbits are released into the wild.

The ancestor of all domestic rabbits is the wild rabbit. The hare, which at first glance may seem to be a candidate for ancestry, has too many differences for this to be possible. For a start, the skull and the fore limbs are built totally differently. The hare is a free-running species; the rabbit is an inhabitant of burrows. The hare is solitary and even avoids rabbits, which live in gregarious groups. A mating between a rabbit and a hare is impossible.

The hare's pelt color is darker than that of a rabbit. The wild rabbit may be easily tamed, but not the hare. Rabbits have enormous adaptability, as can be seen by the plagues of introduced rabbits that have occurred in the Australian outback. According to Darwin, the rabbits that were released on the island of Santo Porto by the inhabitants in 1418 formed an individual race that at his (Darwin's) time—400 years later—could not successfully breed with normal wild rabbits.

Physical Characteristics

Body Size

The specifications of a wild rabbit are as follows:

Body length: 15 to 17^1/2 inches (38–45 cm)
Tail length: 3^1/2 to 4^1/2 inches (8.5–11 cm)
Forefeet: 1^1/2 to 2 inches (4–5 cm)
Hindfeet: 3^1/2 to 4^1/2 inches (8.5–11 cm)
Ears: 2^1/2 to 3 inches (6.5–7.3 cm)

The weight is usually 2 to 3 pounds (1–1.5 kg) but may occasionally reach up to 6 pounds (3 kg). In the months of January and February, you can distinguish the young from the previous year by their smaller size (and weight). Only during periods of bad weather are adults likely to lose weight.

Color and Shape

The pelt color is brownish gray-yellow. The belly, the inside of the paws, and the underside of the tail are white. If examined closely it can be seen that the guard hairs are ringed with colors and the underhairs are bluish in color. In general, the adults are more intensely and darker colored than the young. Rabbits that live in limestone areas are also darker colored than those that live on lime-poor, sandy ground, the latter being frequently tinted with light gray.

The body build of the wild rabbit is different from that of the hare in relation to differences in their respective ways of life. Living in a burrow, the extremities, such as limbs and ears, are relatively shorter in rabbits. The ears do not reach the point of the snout if pushed forward, nor do they have a black tip as in the hare, although they do have a dark edge. The hind limbs, especially, are shorter than those of the hare, and locomotion is thus different; the rear end is not raised as high.

Bodily Movement

The rabbit is more agile in its movements and is a quick-start sprinter. In the first few yards it is faster than a hare, but it quickly tires and loses to the hare over extended distances. The fastest speed a rabbit can reach in open terrain (sandy heather, for example) is about 24 miles per hour (38 kph) for a short period; a hare can maintain an average of 28 to 32 miles per hour (45–50 kph) for a relatively extended length of time. When danger threatens, a

Knowing the different parts of the body is especially useful when talking with your veterinarian or with an experienced rabbit breeder.

Understanding Rabbits

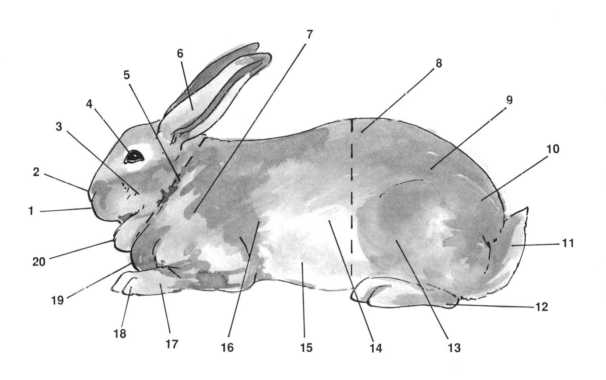

1 mouth	2 nose	3 cheek	4 eye
5 neck	6 ear	7 shoulder	8 loin
9 hip	10 rump	11 tail	12 hock
13 leg	14 flank	15 belly	16 rib
17 foot	18 toe	19 chest	20 dewlap (in females only)

Understanding Rabbits

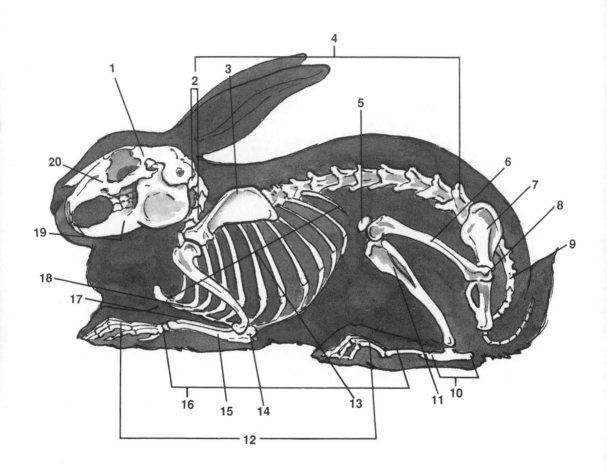

1 skull	2 cervical vertebrae	3 scapula	4 spine
5 patella	6 femur	7 pelvis	8 hip joint
9 caudal vertebrae	10 tarsus	11 tibia	12 phalanges
13 ribs	14 elbow	15 ulna	16 metatarsus
17 radius	18 sternum	19 mandible	20 maxilla

rabbit usually retreats as quickly as possible to its burrow. Should a predator snap at a rabbit's heels, it is just as good as a hare at giving it a kick in the teeth.

The fast locomotion of rabbits is described as "hopping," during which the entire foot leaves the ground. With slower movement, just the toes remain on the ground. The forelimbs are typical of those of a burrower, and the ulna and radius lie next to each other and are of similar strength; in the hare the ulna is narrower and lies behind the radius. The heart and lungs of the burrower are also relatively smaller than those of the free-living hare, which lives a much more fatiguing life.

Teeth

A wild rabbit is a herbivore and feeds exclusively on plant food. This consists mainly of blades of grass and all sorts of wild plants, but also of seeds, fruits, nuts, and bark. Wild rabbits rarely drink; they obtain adequate moisture from their food.

The tooth formula is typical of a herbivore. In the rabbit it is:

$$\frac{2.0.3.3}{1.0.2.3}$$

This means that in each side of the upper jaw there are two incisors, no canines, three premolars, and three molars, and in each half of the lower jaw there are one incisor, no canines, two premolars, and three molars. The incisors are sharp and chisellike, and the enamel on the front grows continuously. The softer dentine at the back is continually worn down, leaving a permanent cutting edge. The premolars and molars have rough surfaces to allow the grinding and chewing of food. As with many herbivores, the canine or tearing teeth have been lost. The upper lip (as in the hare) is split and allows greater mobility during feeding, especially when gnawing at bark.

Senses

The senses of hearing and smell are well developed. The eyes, situated at the sides of the head, give the animal wide angles of sight. The rabbit has long, sensitive whiskers on the sides of its snout, which are useful to a burrower. The nose and the eyes are used extensively in the search for food; the ears are used mainly for the detection of danger. The ears can detect the faintest of rustlings and scrapings as well as louder noises. On hearing suspicious noises, the rabbit sits on its haunches with its ears held high so that it can detect the direction of the possible danger.

Lifestyle of the Wild Rabbit

Wild rabbits live in groups and excavate a labyrinth of burrows that are collectively known as a warren. The rabbits never wander too far from their burrows, always staying close enough to seek refuge if danger threatens. Wild rabbits can cause a great deal of damage, especially in dune areas where their burrowing can destroy dunes and prevent others from being formed. The damage caused

Old World rabbits at waterhole on Wardang Island, South Australia, before myxomatosis was introduced.

Understanding Rabbits

by rabbits is frequently underestimated, probably because rabbits are rarely seen during the day. My husband examined 5 acres of land and discovered that it was home to three times as many rabbits as had been cursorily estimated!

The rabbit is a nocturnal animal, leaving its burrow at dusk to forage. It is a creature of habit, emerging at a particular time each night and feeding in specific areas. In some quiet places it may emerge during the daylight hours. The weather seems to have little influence on their activities; on a beautiful, sunny day not a single rabbit may be about, but often on cold, rainy, or even snowy days many rabbits may be seen going about their business. During the months of January through March, however, the females seem to remain in their burrows.

Rabbits rarely move more than approximately 550 to 650 yards (500–600 m) from their burrows; they are undoubtedly closely dependent on their underground life. A rabbit remains close to its burrow, which provides it with a safe and comfortable resting place.

Rabbits are extremely cautious. As they leave their burrows their pulse rate increases, just like a badger. If danger is detected, they drum their hind feet against the ground to warn their colleagues. This is a social habit that can be compared to the beaver's, which beat their tails on the surface of the water. Like most burrowing animals, rabbits are naturally clean and tidy in their habits. Their familiar droppings are usually repeatedly deposited in a particular spot, and always away from the burrow. The burrow is excavated with the paws. It consists of a living area from which a number of curved exit tunnels radiate. The tunnels are wide at the entrance, becoming narrower. As a family increases in size the warren is enlarged with more chambers and tunnels. Sometimes special escape burrows are constructed, the exits of which are frequently concealed beneath vegetation.

Although rabbits are highly gregarious, pregnant females leave the main warren and excavate a

Fighting male rabbits

nest burrow, often several hundred yards away. The reason for this is that male rabbits, including the father, are aggressive toward the offspring and may even kill them.

The nest burrow is in most cases no longer than 6 feet (2 m) and no deeper than 29$\frac{1}{2}$ inches (75 cm). The burrow appears to be prepared in a single night, and the nest chamber is 8 to 12 inches (20–30 cm) wide. This widened chamber at the bottom of the burrow is lined with dried grass and then with fur plucked by the female from her own belly before the young are born.

After a gestation period of four weeks, the four to ten naked and blind youngsters are born in the nest chamber. The eyes of the helpless babies open after ten days. The mother rabbit cares well for them, visiting them mornings and evenings to suckle them. When the youngsters are still small, the doe carefully closes the entrance to the nest burrow on leaving it, although this is not performed once the young are larger.

The young rabbits grow quickly and stay in the nest for three weeks. The mother stays in the area and keeps watch for danger. At six months the youngsters are ready to reproduce, and they are fully grown in one year.

Young does produce fewer young in a litter than older does (usually three). The first litter is usually born in March, and thereafter a further litter is born every five to six weeks until October. Thus, a healthy female will give birth to a total of about five litters annually. The mating season begins in February or March.

Wild rabbits live for four to eight years.

The offspring of domestic breeds are usually cared for by the mother for a relatively longer period.

Wild rabbits sleep on the bare ground in their burrows, but they may well drag in some straw to use as an insulating layer; tame rabbits will also collect hay or straw and use it to line the floor of their sleeping area.

Rabbits are very clean in their personal hygiene. They are always cleaning their fur. If caught outside in a rain shower, they take advantage of the situation by scrubbing themselves with their paws. Tame rabbits have the same habit.

Rabbits groom themselves very often and very carefully.

Communication

Sounds

Rabbits make vocal and other sounds, some of which are difficult for humans to hear. Some of the sounds are as follows:

• Growling, a short barking growl, which occurs with aggression.
• Low squealing; a very soft noise you can hear only if you are very close. I have mainly heard this when the animals don't want to be petted anymore and are allowed to run free.
• Teeth gnashing; I heard this as rabbits sat on my lap while being petted.
• "Purring" is usually heard when a buck wants to inform a doe that he is ready to mate. The same noise may be made by a male in breeding condition when no does are present. Frequently he collects twigs or pieces of paper, for example, and lays them at your feet.
• Tapping; when a rabbit is afraid it drums it hind feet against the floor; at the same time its pupils become enlarged and it immediately seeks a safe refuge.
• Loud piercing screams—when caught by a predator or a trapper, or when experiencing great pain. (These sounds have been described as "blood curdling.")

Body Language

Various body stances are to be seen in tame rabbits, and it is probable that wild rabbits have the same or similar habits. The more important are as follows:

• A strained, upright stance in which the tail is also stretched. This stance is taken when the animal is preparing to attack, especially if the ears are laid back over the head.
• A strained, sitting stance with laid-back ears is defensive. The animal is ready to use its sharp

foreclaws as weapons against an attacker.

• Rubbing with the underside of the chin on various objects (plants, furnishings, interior of hutch and so on). This is done by male rabbits as a sort of territorial claim to the living area. It is rarely seen in does. (Male rabbits have scent-producing glands on the underside of their chins, enabling them to truly mark their territory. The scent may also be used to mark does.)

• Nudging with the muzzle when the animal desires attention.

• Scratching at the floor with the forepaws is also a sign that attention is required. Once the animal has been picked up and stroked, it will usually stop for the time being.

• If a rabbit likes you it demonstrates this with licking and caressing, which can be compared to "social pelt care." This same type of social behavior is also common between animals kept in pairs or groups.

• Pushing your hand away tells you that the animal has had enough of stroking.

• Sitting up on the haunches helps the animals get a better view of its surroundings, but can also be a sign that it wants to go in or out. A rabbit that sits up by the door of its hutch is indicating that it wants to be let out.

• By lying flat on its stomach with its ears flat over its head and eyes half-closed, a rabbit indicates that it wants to sleep and should thus be left alone. In cold weather, the paws are drawn underneath the body

• Rolling on the back or side while resting indicates that the rabbit is contented.

Above left: The English Lop is known in solid colors (for example selfs, agouti, shaded), and in broken colors, (any color with white.) Above right: The French Lop also comes in solid and broken colors. Below left: The Dutch Lop is an excellent breeder. Below right: The Meissner Lop is a German breed, developed in 1900 by R. Reck.

The Right Foundation Stock

It is very important that anyone beginning a breeding stud of rabbits starts with first-class material: in other words, with purebred pedigree rabbits. A purebred rabbit is an animal that follows certain descriptions, the breed standard. Thus, one also speaks of standard breed rabbits. When such a purebred rabbit has a written record of its ancestry, it is termed a pedigree. When you buy a pedigree animal, therefore, you must ensure that you also get the pedigree papers that give you the names of the parents and further information relating to at least three generations of ancestors on both sides of the family. The information should include the private ear identification numbers, the registration numbers, correct coloration, correct weight, winnings of shows, size of litters, and other information. In short, such information is enormously useful to you as a potential breeder. If the breeder tells you that he or she does not have papers for the animals, it is best to buy elsewhere as these animals are almost certainly without pedigree.

Registration

A pedigreed rabbit is also frequently a registered animal. A rabbit must be purebred and have a pedigree record before it can be registered. To be registered, the rabbit must first be examined by a registrar of the American Rabbit Breeders Association (see page 125 for address of ARBA).

Above: The giant chinchilla was developed by E. Stahl of Missouri by crossing chinchillas with Flemish giants. Below: Flemish giants are excellent pets. The breed which is the largest of all the domestic varieties, needs large hutches and plenty of food!

Tattooing the rabbit's ear with specially designed pliers.

Identification by Tattooing

A serious rabbit fancier identifies every rabbit in the stock with a permanent number tattooed in its left ear. Plier-type tattoo sets are available on the market. I find the best formula for tattooing is the owner's initials, followed by the number of the mother and month and year; for example, LV548, which means L. Vriends, the month (5) May, the number of the mother (4), and the year of birth (8 from 1988). Rabbits should be tattooed after weaning age.

Rabbit Shows

As a member of ARBA you receive the newsletter *Domestic Rabbit*, in which all shows (especially in the spring) are listed. The times and dates are included and also the names and addresses of show secretaries. Your first task is to write to the show secretary and ask to be placed on the mailing list so that you receive the show catalogue as soon as it is available. As soon as the catalogue arrives see if there is an entry form. This should be carefully filled out and returned to the show secretary as soon

Show time! It is the ambition of every enthusiastic rabbit breeder to produce animals of perfect standard so that they may earn the highest qualifications from judges at exhibitions.

as possible with the entry fee (this is normally around $2) for each rabbit entered. Always keep a photocopy of the entry form in case of mistakes over entries or payments, for example.

When the great day of the show arrives, the entered rabbits are placed in all-wire cages of a comfortable size and transported on the rear seat of the car (secured with a safety belt).

To avoid mistakes, it is best not to be too hasty in entering your animals in shows for the first time. Before you enter rabbits it is recommended that you visit a few shows as an observer so that you become accustomed to the procedures; speak to other breeders, and familiarize yourself with the ARBA rules and demands.

When you have accomplished this (and it is not difficult!) you can enter your first animal(s). I recommend that you enter only one, or at most two rabbits for your first shows. Use your best animals, which should be in prime condition.

It goes without saying that the rabbit that you choose to enter should be as close as possible to the standards of the breed you are entering. It is therefore important that you have a copy of the *Standard of Perfection* in your possession; this is also available from the ARBA for a small fee. See Useful Literature and Information (page 125) for the address of ARBA and other information about materials available from this organization.

Rabbit Categories

The ARBA categorizes rabbits before they are registered as follows:

• *Scrub* rabbits are those animals that cannot be identified as to their breed.
• *Grade* rabbits can be identified as to breed but do not have purebred parents.
• *Purebred* rabbits can be traced back along their pedigrees for at least three generations.
• *Registered* rabbits are the true aristocrats as they have pedigrees that stretch much further back. They are registered on the roll of the American Rabbit Breeders Association and can be identified by a tattoo mark in the ear. They carry a registration certificate with tattoo number, date of birth, name of breeder, name of owner if different from that of the breeder, color description, and so on.
• *Full pedigree* rabbits are registered with a district registrar appointed by the ARBA. The registrar tattoos a number on the rabbit's ear and awards a seal (a form of grading). A red seal indicates that both the parents of the rabbit are registered. A red and white seal means that the first and second generations have been registered. A red, white, and

blue seal indicates that the full pedigree has been registered with the ARBA. This seal is attached to the registration certificate and sent to the head office of the association to be stored for reference.

Grand championship certificates are awarded to rabbits that comply with certain regulations regarding their wins at shows. The championship is awarded in a series of legs. The rabbit must complete at least three legs before it can be considered for the supreme award. The legs are as follows:
1. Wins first in a class of not less than five entries owned by not less than three exhibitors.
2. Wins best of breed or best of variety with five rabbits shown in the breed or variety by at least three exhibitors.
3. Wins best opposite sex or best opposite sex of variety, provided there are five or more of the same sex as the winner shown in the breed or variety by at least three exhibitors.
4. Wins best in show.
5. Two legs cannot be honored for the same show on the same rabbit.
6. At least one of the wins must be obtained as an intermediate or a senior, and the awards are to be placed under at least two different ARBA judges.
7. No award can be counted unless it is attained in a regularly sanctioned ARBA show with an ARBA-licensed judge placing the award.
8. The leg for the grand champion must be obtained by the exhibitor from the show secretary where the award was won. Only one grand championship can be conferred on any one particular rabbit.

Glossary of Show Terminology

AA	Any age
AC	Any color
Ad	Adult
AOC	Any other color
AOV	Any other variety
ARBA	American Rabbit Breeders Association
ASS	Adult stock show
AV	Any variety
Blk	Black
B or B	Black or blue
Breeders' class	A class confined to exhibits by the exhibitor
B.R.C.	The governing body of the rabbit fancy in Britain
Brood doe	A doe suitable for breeding
Buck	A male rabbit
CC	Challenge certificate
Challenge class	A class open to all or confined to a whole section—such as fancy breeds, normal fur breeds, rex
Champion	An animal that has won a championship
Doe	A female rabbit
Ear label	A small gummed label that is stuck on the ear of a rabbit at shows and bears its pen number
Guaranteed class	A class in which full prize

The Right Foundation Stock

money is guaranteed regardless of the number of entries secured

Limit class — Usually confined to exhibits that have not won more than three first prizes in open competition

Members' class — A class confined to members of a specified club

Novice exhibit class — Exhibit not to have won a first prize at any show except in members' classes or at table shows

Novice exhibit and exhibitor class — Neither the owner nor the exhibit to have won a first prize at any show except in members' classes or at table shows

Open class — Class open to all except when confined to a breed or breeds or to a specified age group

Pair class — A class for two rabbits of the same variety, matched as closely as possible in size, color, and so on; the sex of the rabbit, unless especially stated in the schedule, is optional

Pen number — The number given to a rabbit at a show, which will appear on the address label sent to the exhibitor, on the show pen, and also in the catalogue and in the judging book

Pen show — Show that provides pens for all exhibits

Ring — The method of marking and recording rabbits

Selling classes — Exhibits to be catalogued for sale

Show (members') — A show confined to members of a specified club

Show (open) — A show open to anyone

Show (penned) — A show at which pens are provided for all exhibits

Show (specialist) — A show confined to a specified variety

Show (table) — A show at which pens are not provided for the exhibits, each after being judged on the table being replaced in its traveling box

Specials — Prizes in cash or kind offered in addition to the ordinary class placings

Specialist club — A society devoted to a particular breed or section, e.g., the Beveren Club, the British Rex Rabbit Society

Specialist judge — A judge recognized by a specialist club as an expert in the variety concerned

Standard — Description of the ideal to be aimed for

Stewards — Officials appointed at

The Right Foundation Stock

Stud buck   An adult buck used for mating

Sweepstake show   A show at which the prize money is not fixed but varies from class to class according to the number of entries received

Team   Three rabbits of the same variety, matched as closely

shows to take charge of the exhibits and assist the judge

as possible in size, color, and so on; the sex, unless specifically stated, is optional

Under 4 mth   A class for rabbits under four months on day of show

Under 5 mth   A class for rabbits under five months on day of show

Youngster   A rabbit under adult age

YSS   Young stock show

The Most Important Breeds

Alaska

The Alaska originated in Germany, when in 1907 the breeder Schmidt from Langensalza and the well-known rabbit judge Max Fischer from Goettingen selectively bred rabbits with the express purpose of producing self colored black animals with a pelt resembling that of the Alaskan fox. After many pairings they were successful. Later, British breeders produced their "Nubians," which were very similar to the continental Alaskas. These were produced by experimenting with, among others, homozygous inherent English spots. A black Van Beveren was introduced in England as "Sitkas." Luckily these needless confusions were soon solved and the breeders of the Alaskas were given credit for their work.

The color of the Alaska is shiny black, the beauty of which is equalled only by that of the tan. Its shape and weight are similar to the Havana. The eyes are dark brown and the toenails are dark. The weight varies between 6 and $8^{1}/_{2}$ pounds (2.7–3.8 kg).

American

The American is a medium size rabbit. It comes in either a blue or white coat. In both cases, the color should be uniform over the entire body.

This medium-sized breed is available in white or blue; the eyes are pink and blue, respectively. The ideal weight of a buck is 10 (4.5 kg) pounds; a doe, 11 pounds (5 kg). The breed is (according to ARBA) rarely seen outside the United States.

American Checkered Giant

Believe it or not, this breed first came from Germany, although its exact origin is somewhat vague. It has been suggested that the breed came about by crossing a Flemish giant (which is quite possibly the case) and a wild, white-colored hare (which is quite impossible!). However it originated, it bears some resemblance to the English spot, with its body carried well off the ground and its chain of spots. The buck weighs 11 pounds (4.5 kg), the doe 12 pounds (5.4 kg) or more. There are two colors, black and blue. The markings (butterfly on nose, eye circles, cheek spots, ears, and spine markings) should be well formed and conspicuous.

The checkered giant, front, came first from Germany, although its exact origin is somewhat vague. The angora has a minimum hair length of $3^{1}/_{4}$ inches (8 cm).

The Most Important Breeds

Angora

Little is definitely known about the origin of this breed. Some writers claim that, like the Ankhara goat and the Angora cat, Angora rabbits originated from the area of Angora in Turkey, but this is doubtful.

The hair length of the modern Angora is a minimum of 3¼ inches (8 cm). There are three kinds of hair; the wool, which consists of fine, silky wavy strands; the somewhat rougher by-hair, which is also wavy and has a fine tip; and the inner hair, which is straight and fine at the root, becoming thicker and then fine at the tip. These three kinds of hair together form the hair structure. The Angora occurs in the colors black, brown, blue, and white (with red or blue eyes).

As soon as the youngsters reach four to five weeks of age, you can begin regular brushing of the fur but they should not be brushed earlier.

The young animals group together for warmth and companionship, resulting in the fur's becoming knotted. Regular brushing is therefore necessary. Later, after they are weaned, it is best to keep each animal in a separate hutch when a good brushing

Angoras are ususally kept in small hutches with a wire floor to protect the droppings from spoiling the coat. The most popular color variety is white.

once a week should suffice. A comb should not be used as much or the wool may be pulled out.

The bottom of an Angora hutch should preferably consist of wire netting with a mesh width of ½ to ¾ inch (1.5–2 cm), so that the droppings fall through into a tray and do not soil the fur.

The wool production requires a rich and varied diet, particularly one with protein-rich dry foods.

Belgian Hare

The Belgian Hare actually resembles the wild hare, both in shape and in size. The breed requires plenty of exercise to keep it in trim.

The origin of the Belgian hare can be credited to England as well as Belgium. In England the breed was produced in 1886 from wild gray-colored meat rabbits that had a lot of dark pigmentation. The hare was not used in the origin of the breed, however much this is falsely declared. In view of its slender and "racy" body form, the breed is a credit to the specialist breeder's art. In 1887, the first Belgian hare club was formed in England, and it was already to be seen in shows the following year. The breed was exported to Germany and then Holland in 1900. Of all the breeds and varieties of rabbits, the Belgian hare is the best known and most typical.

The Most Important Breeds

The Belgian hare can be considered the greyhound of the rabbit world. It has all the attributes of this animal, including colors. The color of the Belgian hare varies from fox to mahogany red over the whole body, which glows fiery red. The belly, sides of the jaw, and the tail are more or less cream to light tan. A narrow, light-colored ring surrounds the hazel-colored eye.

In addition to the original Belgian hare colors, the breed is known with color patterns of the tan rabbit in black.

Van Beveren

This breed originated in Belgium in the province of Beveren west of Antwerp, where it has been bred for many decades. A similar breed, the St. Nicholas blue, came from the same area. St. Nicholas lies on the road from Antwerp to Ghent. The original blue Van Beveren is silvery, light blue, somewhat reminiscent of forget-me-nots. The St. Nicholas blue is darker in tone and was originally bred with a white chest.

The blue Van Beveren was first imported to England in 1915 during World War I, and it soon became very popular. It also rapidly became extremely popular in France and in several other countries. Holland imported its first Van Beverens from Belgium.

The breed standard requires that the body should resemble the shape of a long pear, as it were, cut through its length and the cut side laid flat.

The color of the dense and thick coat must be deep, without silvering. The coat must feel soft and silky to the touch. The Van Beveren is the largest fur breed; its body weight is between 7 and 10 pounds (3.2–4.5 kg). The body is long, broad, and mandolin shaped, with a broad head. The curve from the forehead to the top of the nose is a characteristic of the breed. Another characteristic is the long broad ears, held in the shape of a V.

Van Beverens are frequently spiteful. Consequently, I do not recommend them as pets for families with children.

Blanc de Hotot

This breed was created in France by Madame Eugenie Bernard of Hotot en Auge. This medium-sized white rabbit with brown eyes could be seen in shows from 1912 onward. It was denied that French spots were used in producing the breed, although this breed was also produced through repressed crossing. Thus the colors of the French spot were repressed except for the eyes and a small ring around them. This theory is supported by the fact that in some litters youngsters with eye rings, colored snouts, ear tips, and indications of stripes are produced.

Some years before World War I, Hermann Ziemer from the German town of Husum used a similar method to produce his Husum blue-eyes.

The blanc de Hotot remains popular in France and even has fanciers in parts of Germany.

The animal must be wholly pure, shiny white, without yellow or gray tinging or mixing of hairs of other colors. The color of the iris is silvery, dark brown. Around the eye is a $1/6$ to $1/4$ inch (4 to 7 mm) wide, black eye ring.

The blanc de Hotot belongs to the marked breeds although its body is not marked; it is judged on the intensity of the black eye ring.

Californian

As its name implies, this breed originated in California in 1923 from crossings including chinchillas, Himalayans, and New Zealand whites to produce a quick-growing meat breed. Moreover, the breed has a thick coat to protect it from loss of body heat. The markings of the Himalayan are seen in this breed, although it is not included in the marked breeds.

Many paintings from the seventeenth and eighteenth centuries show rabbits of the breeds we now know as Polish (above left and right) and Netherland dwarfs (below). Polish rabbits come with blue (left) and red eyes. (right.)

The Most Important Breeds

The Californian, which is one of the newer breeds, looks like a very large Himalayan.

The Californian is pure white with Himalayan markings; the snout, ears, legs, and tail are therefore black. The eyes are red.

Chinchilla

In 1913, the French engineer M. J. Dybowski produced this breed using a wild (Garenne) rabbit, a blue Van Beveren, and a Himalayan. In the same year he exhibited the breed in Saint-Maur (Seine), and in the following year in the Paris exhibition. In 1915 they were brought to England by soldiers, and in 1920 they were seen in Germany. The color and fur of the chinchilla is very similar to that of the chinchilla giganta. The first examples reached America in 1919. The popularity of this breed is certainly due to the similarity of its fur to that of the true wild chinchilla (a South American rodent famous for the quality of its pelt). The standard requires fine bones, and an adult can weigh $5^1/2$ to $6^3/4$ pounds (2.5–3.0 kg).

Purebred dwarf rabbits: Above left: blue marten; above right: yellow marten. Below left: Isabel; below right: Rus.

American Chinchilla

There are two types to this breed: the standard type (which is very similar to the preceding breed) and a somewhat larger version that was, in the past, often referred to as the heavyweight chinchilla. One creates these types by selecting and using larger examples of chinchillas. The rounded and full hips and the slight and gradual arch starting at the nape of the neck and finishing at the rump are characteristic. These animals are more meaty than the normal chinchilla.

American Giant Chinchilla

By using American chinchillas and Flemish giants, E. Stahl of Missouri produced this imposing meat breed; the animal's main characteristic is a meaty saddle. Adult bucks weigh about $13^1/2$ pounds (6.1 kg), does about $14^1/2$ pounds (6.5 kg).

Chinchilla Giganta

There are two races of chinchillas, the (small) chinchilla and the giant chinchilla or chinchilla giganta. After World War I the chinchilla giganta was created in England and Germany during the same period. In Germany, the breeders Grueny, Offenbach, and Geyer "chinchillarized" wild rabbits with the use of albinos. In England, Wren, a breeder of Flemish giants, used chinchillas to reach his goal. However, both the chinchilla and the chinchilla giganta are officially recorded as having originated in France.

The pelt is blue at its roots, white in the center, and gray mixed with black at the top. If you blow into the pelt of a good chinchilla a rosette will be observed; this is formed from the dark blue ground color in the center, then the white color forming a ring about half a centimeter thick, and finally a narrower black ring. After this, there are the above-mentioned light gray hairs with black tips of varying lengths.

The pelt color of the chinchilla is classified as gray (wild color); the yellow factor is missing.

The Most Important Breeds

In the past a blue chinchilla was recognized. This originated in England, and owing to its resemblance to the Siberian squirrel, it was sometimes called squirrel chinchilla; however, from a genetic viewpoint, the blue chinchilla was better.

Another variety recognized in the past was the brown chinchilla, which originated in France and Holland. The black of the normal chinchilla was replaced by soft Havana brown. In principle, you can "chinchillarize" all colors. There was even a yellow chinchilla that was, in fact, white with a sort of sooty tinge, especially toward the rear end.

The maximum weight of this breed is about 12 pounds (5.4 kg). A characteristic of the breed is slightly backward sloping ears that are set apart at the top so that, viewed from the front, they form a V shape.

The Chinchilla, which was originally developed as a fur breed, is very docile and makes an excellent pet. The larger version (above) is called the Chinchilla Giganta.

Dutch

In spite of the name, this breed originated in England rather than Holland. However, if the origin is studied in the German, English, or French literature, you will see that it is often referred to as Holland or Belgium. The latter country exported many unrefined examples of the breed to England

The popular Dutch rabbits are by far the most widely kept animals. They make very good pets.

(as meat animals), where they were quickly snapped up by breeders and, in the middle of the last century, refined to the well-known form and labeled "Dutch" rabbits.

This breed has interesting head markings. The head patches circling the eyes must be of similar size on both sides. They must not reach the whiskers. The blaze on the forehead is determined by the shape of the head patches. The division between the white forepart of the body and the colored rear part should form as straight a line as possible and is approximately at the center of the trunk. The white part includes the front legs, extends around the throat, and covers the shoulders. The rear paws should be approximately half-white. The division should be as straight as possible, and each rear foot should be marked similarly.

The Dutch rabbit is to be found in most colors, even in chinchilla. The blue and brown varieties are preferred in darker tones. A three-color variety in black, blue, and brown is also known.

English Lop

It is difficult to say whether the French or the English lop is the oldest breed. Many breeders believe that the English lop originated from the

French lop. In England the animals are bred with ears as long as possible. Originally the animals were considered delicate and were reared only in heated accommodations. However, this led to a weakening of the breed so a new, hardy form was developed that can be easily kept and bred in protected outdoor accommodations.

It is recommended that lops be bred only during the warmer months as it is thought that warmth influences the growth of the ears. Of course, the length and breadth of the ears are also affected by heredity and can therefore, be improved by selective breeding.

In contrast to the French lop, the English lop is more slimly built. The line of the back slopes gently toward the hips. The longer and wider the ears, the more valuable is the animal. The minimum dimensions should be $4^1/2$ inches (12 cm) wide and 23 inches (58 cm) long, measured from ear tip to ear tip and including the width of the head. There is no maximum dimension.

The English lop occurs in all colors including white with red eyes and fawn. Marked lops are also available.

The English lop is one of the oldest breeds. Its ears hang down the sides of the head and touch the floor.

English Spot

The English spot's ancestors include the Flemish giant, English lop, Patagonian, Angora, and Dutch.

As its name implies, this breed originated in England and it is sometimes referred to simply as the "English" rabbit. It was bred from a mixture of Flemish giant, English lop, Patagonian, Angora, Dutch, silver, and Himalayan. If you look at photographs of some of the original animals, you cannot fail to be amazed at how the breed was produced.

In contrast to most medium-sized breeds, the English spot has a distinctive neck that, coupled with its long, slender body, gives it a regal appearance. The markings on the head and body are similar to those of the Lotharinger and the Rheinlander but finer. In contrast to these two similar breeds, the English must have a chain of spots as follows. The chain must run along both sides of the body, and each side must be as similar to the other as possible. It should slope downward toward the hips, where it joins with the flank markings. The chain consists of very small, distinctive spots, each about the size of a green pea. An ideal chain should consist of two symmetrically arranged rows.

These special markings do not make it simple for the breeder but form an enormous challenge.

The ground color of the English spot is pure white, and the spot pattern should be outstanding. The spots may be in any color, including three-colored. The spots themselves, however, should be free of any white hairs or flecks.

Flemish Giant (or Patagonian)

This universally known breed originated in Flanders (Belgium), probably in Ghent and its environs, and before the turn of the century many rabbits were obtained from that city. The animals were originally rather short in body build, with short ears and too fine a bone structure. The enormous weight of the animals (17 and 18 pounds [7.7–8.1 kg] were not unusual) often led them to be misshapen, fat monsters that could barely move themselves about. At the present time, the minimum weight is given as 13 pounds (5.9 kg), but animals of 15 pounds (6.8 kg) or more are not uncommon. The body of a good Flemish giant must be proportionate in length and breadth and it must have a powerful (but not too long) bone structure. A straight back profile running into a wide, rounded rump improves the value of the animal. Viewed from above, the animal has an oblong form in which the shoulders are of similar breadth to the hindquarters. The buck's head should be wide and impressive, with the snout and cheeks in harmony with the width of the skull. The doe should have a somewhat smaller but well-formed head, with a muzzle that is not too narrow. The ears should be thick, strong, and spoon-shaped at the tips. They should stand proudly in the shape of a narrow V. They should have no folds or creases and have a minimum length of 7 inches (17 cm). The white, gray, and steel gray varieties of the Flemish giant may have ears to 8 inches (20 cm) in length.

Although the breed originated in Belgium, German breeders perfected it by increasing its length. American breeders have used such imported animals to advantage and produced some very good strains.

The does have a small dewlap that sits like a swallow's nest on the throat. This dewlap is an unwanted phenomenon that may receive minor or major penalty points in judging. Minor penalty points may be awarded if the chest hair is long and the dewlap not placed directly below the chin. The major penalty points arise from a too large, misshapen, twisted, or double dewlap, coupled with too-long chest hair.

At the present time, does with a small, single dewlap are the most valuable for breeding and exhibiting.

Other than white, the Flemish giant occurs in the following colors: "hare color" (unique), rabbit gray, iron gray, blue gray, chinchilla, and, exceptionally, brown, black, yellow, and orange.

The Flemish giant is the largest of all domestic breeds; it is also one of the most affectionate of pets—if given plenty of attention.

Florida White

This breed was developed chiefly for research. It is a compact, medium-sized animal, weighing between 4 and 6 pounds (1.8–2.7 kg). As its name suggests, it originated in Florida. It is a good meat breed, which was produced using crossings of Dutch and Polish, later with New Zealand white.

The Most Important Breeds

It is a somewhat cobby animal with a compact body and rounded hips and hindquarters. The short ears and the small head give the animal a cute appearance. The short, dense fur is pure white.

French Lop

With its short, wide body, round head, and hanging ears, this breed makes a lasting impression on people who see it for the first time. The breed originated in France, probably from a mutation that was further developed by selective breeding. In 1869, the breed found its way into Germany, where it was further selectively bred and enormously improved. Because of its early sexual maturity and the particularly good, thick pelt, it soon earned popularity as a commercial breed, which was second only to the white Vienna.

French lops first appeared in England at the Crystal Palace Show in 1938.

No single rabbit breed is as impressive as the French lop. Because of the bending of the ears at their roots, a pair of "crowns" is located on the head. The length of the ears measured from tip to tip

The lopears originated in France.

ranges between 15 and 18 inches (38–45 cm), the ideal length being 16 to 17 inches (41–42 cm).

The breed occurs in white (the most popular color), with white or blue eyes, but also in almost all other rabbit colors, including chinchilla. Marked varieties also occur in which the positions of the white marks are not exactly defined. A hooded variety is popular in which the head, snout, ears, and back are colored and the chest and forelegs are white and the belly and hindlegs mainly white. In short, a marked French lop should be as symmetrical as possible.

Individuals of this breed are frequently bad tempered and are somewhat untidy in their hutches. If they hear other rabbits they bang their feet on the hutch floor.

Harlequin

The Harlequin is a difficult variety to breed. Its fur consists of four distinct colors arranged in a patchwork.

This breed also originated in France, where it is still popular today. It was developed from semiwild and Dutch rabbits that were kept in large, fenced enclosures. Old pictures of harlequins show them to resemble badly marked Dutch rabbits. The breed

The Most Important Breeds

was first exhibited in Paris in 1887.

The harlequin is a good fancy breed, which with its strictly prescribed color and pattern standards gives enormous possibilities for the breeder. Because of its distinctive color patterns it is often named "the clown of the rabbits." The ears and head, chest, and forelegs are intense, alternate black and reddish yellow; the body has yellow and black bands, giving the impression of a patchwork quilt. Each ear is colored differently, and each side of the head has the opposite color. The body is covered with obvious banding, and the forelegs each have a different color, reversed on the hind legs. The eyes are dark brown.

A good harlequin is difficult to breed; it requires much skill and dedication to produce well-marked individuals.

Havana

The Havana originated from a mutation, but documentation on the original ancestry has been lost in the mists of time. However, the Havana color was one that was previously unknown. Many animals show a brown tinge that, if viewed in a particular angle of light, gives a reddish glow. The breed first appeared in 1898, bred by a farmer called Honders at Ingen in the Province of Utrecht, the Netherlands. Thus the breed was first given the name "Ingense Vuurogen" (Ingen fire eyes).

Rabbit judge G. Jacobs, with the help of many breeders, crossed the new breed with Himalayans and fixed the new factor. At this time they were renamed Havana rabbits. A similar race originated in France and was first shown to the public at the Paris exhibition in 1902. In the following years, the breed found its way to exhibitions in Germany, Switzerland, and England.

The ground color is glossy, dark brown, similar to that of dark chocolate, and should be uniform from nose to tail. The underside is somewhat duller. A leaning to black or blue is a fault. The pelt must be free of any gray flecking. The deeper the brown color reaches into the pelt, the more valuable the animal. The color of the hair roots is pure blue. Two similar rabbits may be judged on the color of the hair roots. This root color must never interfere with the uniformity of the outer color but may contribute to the depth of color. The eyes are dark brown but glow ruby red under a certain light.

Himalayan

In spite of its name, this breed originated in England. Most of the earlier authors wrote that the breed originated from small silvers and was an albino form of this breed. Professor Dr. Hans Nachtsheim has proven that, genetically, the two breeds have little in common and that the Himalayan originated as the result of a mutation in England in the middle of the last century.

A. D. Bartlett first described the breed in 1857. The Himalayan type is very distinctive. In contrast to the tan and the Dutch, it has a very long, slender body, with a handsome, supple rounding of the hindquarters. The bone structure is relatively long and fine. The body type nicely sets off the glossy black of the extremities.

The medium-size Havana has a rich chocolate coat with a reddish sheen.

The Most Important Breeds

The medium-size Himalayan is very hardy and docile. It is thought that this breed originated in China.

The muzzle marking (or mask) must cover the whole of the muzzle, including the underside of the cheeks. The ears should be deep black and sharply distinct at their base. The fore and hind limbs are also deep black. The black color must cover at least three-quarters of the forelimbs and must come to about 1 inch (2.5 cm) above the heel in the hind limbs. The tail is also pure black. The black may be replaced by blue, brown, lilac, and chocolate. The eyes are red.

Lotharinger

This large breed has the body of a Flemish giant; and the pelt-design resembles the Rhinelander or Thueringer, both of which are medium-sized rabbit breeds (see pages 121 and 123).

The ground color of the Lotharinger (Germany) is white with a full black butterfly marking on the nostrils. The eyes are encircled with a broad black, somewhat ragged ring. Just below the eye, on either side of the head, there is also a small black spot. The ears, approximately 6½ inches (16 cm) in length, are black, and so is the entire length of the neck and spine. Along the haunches and flanks are 5 to 8

rounded spots. Adult rabbits weigh approximately 11 pounds (5 kg).

Marten

This breed originated at roughly the same time in Germany, England, and France. Breeding experiments with chinchillas, Himalayans, and albinos were also being conducted in America and other countries. The marten color is somewhere between that of the agouti (wild color), chinchilla, Himalayan, and albino. Martens do not breed true. The

The medium-size Marten sable is a fur variety. The fur is soft and silky in texture, but also thick and dense, and approximately 1 to 1½ inches long.

offspring split 25 percent for dark marten color, 25 percent albinos, and 50 percent standard marten color. Only dark marten × albino produces 100 percent standard marten color.

Shortly after World War I, the breeder Emil Thomsen in Stellingen, Germany, created his "marten colored Stellinger rabbits." Chinchillas and albinos were always incorporated. The color of the upper part of the head, the ears, the upper and outer sides of the limbs, and the upper side of the tail was dark sepia brown. The deeper the brown color stretches toward the roots of the individual hairs, the more valuable is the animal. This rich, dark, sepia color extends from the forehead and along the back to the tip of the tail and lightens gradually into the cheeks, flanks, and thighs, without flecks or stripes. The width of the deep sepia color on the back is recommended as $3^1/2$ to 4 inches (8–10 cm). The chest, lower shoulders, flanks, thighs, and belly are light sepia-colored. The marten color may be classified as medium or dark. In addition to these varieties of sepia brown, a blue marten was bred in Beieren; its very fine color is reminiscent of Copenhagen porcelain.

The well-known German rabbit judge and author Friedrich Joppich created the yellow marten, which owing to its similarity to the blue-eyed cat breed was also named "Siamese." The yellow marten has been known only since May 1, 1940.

Also around the time of World War II, another variety appeared: the marten rabbit with white tan markings. This was called the Silber Marderkaninchen (silver marten) in German and marten sable in England. In America it is also called the silver marten. It is, in fact, a faulty breed as it has nothing to do with the silver factor. The color is very similar to the standard marten as described here, but the color divisions at the nose, cheeks, eye rims, the insides of the ears, the neck (triangle), belly, and the underside of the tail are white. The chest, shoulders, flanks, hindquarters, and limbs are dotted with long, protruding white-tipped guard hairs.

Netherlands Dwarf

These rabbits originated in the Netherlands, where they became known May 1, 1940. The breeders J. Meijering and C. W. Calcar, among others, had a great deal to do with the breeding and popularization of the race. The best weight is about 2 pounds (.9 kg).

The Netherlands dwarf has a short, compact body and a very short neck, a so-called neckless type! The breed has neat, round contours and plump hindquarters. The legs are straight, thin, and fine.

The head is spherical, with a wide forehead, a strongly curved snoutline, and well-developed cheeks. A poorly developed head (sometimes

The Netherlands Dwarf is the smallest of all rabbits. It comes in almost every color or combination of colors and is a very popular pet.

Dwarf rabbits, like this Siamese sable, are very active. They all require a great deal of exercise.

called mousehead) leads to penalties in exhibition. The eyes are large and stand out from the head.

There is no breed with as many color combinations, and each fancier must decide what choice to make.

Netherlands Dwarf Lop

This breed was created by the Dutch breeder A. de Cock, who took some twelve years to develop it. It first became known in the Netherlands in January 1964. The Netherland dwarf lop must be a miniature version of the French lop. The ear length, measured from tip to tip and including the width of the skull, is 9 to 11 inches (22–27 cm), ideally 10 inches (22.5 cm).

This breed occurs in all known colors, including the sepia and blue marten variants, marked and white. The eyes may be red or blue.

New Zealand Black

This popular breed and the two following breeds, perhaps surprisingly, originated in the United States. The New Zealand black is bred for its excellent meat and also for its high-quality pelt. The fur is pure, uniform black, without rusty or brown tinge. The toenails are dark blue.

New Zealand Red

This breed originated in California, where it has been bred for many decades in many commercial rabbit farms. In addition to robust, wild rabbits, Belgian hares were used in the creation of the breed. The basic color of the New Zealand red is, from nose tip to tail, a warm, beautiful, reddish color, of a fine quality hard to find in other breeds. The color must be free of black, brown, or white patches or ticking.

New Zealand White

Another breed said to have been created in the United States and used extensively for meat and pelt

production is the New Zealand white. Sometimes called the commercial white rabbit, this breed has a massive build and is of medium length, and the fore and hindquarters are of similar breadth. This is a contented, docile breed that makes a good pet.

The haunches and back are well developed, plump, and muscular. The neck is short and powerful. The legs are short but adapted to the body. The head is well developed, with a broad forehead and muzzle. The ear length varies from $4^{1}/_{2}$ to $5^{1}/_{2}$ inches (11–13 cm). The ears are strikingly fleshy and bluntly rounded at the tips. A small dewlap in the does of this breed is tolerated at exhibitions.

Palomino

This American utility breed was created by Mark Youngs of Washington. The breed is very popular and comes in two colors, lynx and golden. A good golden variety has a beautiful, glossy coat, and the undercoat is white to creamy. Moreover, a good animal has evenly dispensed light-gold guard hairs. The lynx variety is bright orange, with a white undercoat. Lynx rabbits that possess an evenly ticked lilac coat have the highest regard at exhibi-

The Palomino rabbit is an American breed. There are only two color varieties: golden and lynx.

tions. The registration weight for bucks is 8 to 10 pounds (3.6–4.5 kg), and for does the weight is 9 to 11 pounds (4.1–5 kg).

Polish

This breed originated in England. Seventeen Polish rabbits were exhibited in a class in Hull as early as 1884, which was won by a breeder who built his stud with wild rabbits. Other breeders used albinos and small silvers, but the resulting animals were too large. The first English breeder of Polish rabbits, John Meynell, from Darlington, used Dutch, among others. He was the individual most responsible for the development and promotion of the breed.

The English Polish is said to have had a brilliant pelt with unblemished fur, a distinctive head and body, ears about 3 inches (7 cm) in length, and a weight of around 3 pounds (1.4 kg).

At the end of the last century, the breed was exported from England to Germany, where it eventually became tremendously popular in the 1920s. We can thank the German breeders for the unique, beautiful, and interesting type of the modern Polish. The Dutch breeder E.B. Notenboom of Rotterdam further improved the Polish, especially the ear form and structure.

The red-eyed white Polish originated in England. The blue-eyed white Polish originated in Germany. The Polish also occurs with rex hair.

Rex

The short-haired rex rabbit originated in France, where, in 1919, Abbot Amedee Gillet found a young rabbit with hardly any fur in a mixed-breed nest. This occurred on the farm of Desire Caillon of Luche-Pringe. A similar phenomenon occurred in the next litter. He saw immediately that this was a mutation that could probably be exploited. A pairing of brother to sister resulted in young with a fluffy coat, due to a strong shortening of the guard hairs.

In 1924, Abbot Gillet showed a collection of these rabbits at the international exhibition in Paris and they caused a sensation. For the first few years thereafter the animals were bred and sold at an

The English Polish rabbit is called the Britannia petite in the United States.

The hair of the rex stands almost at right angles to the animal's skin.

alarming rate. A pair would fetch two, three or even five thousand francs, and the purchasers were able to make handsome profits. Unfortunately, this almost hysterical business did not respect the importance of type, health, and vitality.

It was Professor E. Kohler of Thumenau in the Alsace who had the distinction of being the first to breed colored rex rabbits, and he was very successful. In 1925, the castor and color rex rabbits arrived in Germany, and from there in great numbers (and fabulous prices) to England. At that time an argument arose in Germany between those who preferred the fluffy type of fur and those who stood by a stronger and fuller fur with longer guard hairs.

After much research, Professor Dr. Hans Nachtsheim ascertained that the rex factor was pathological (caused by disease) and that crossing back normal-haired varieties would regenerate normal-haired animals.

Wholly independent of the Gillet rex factor, a breeder of Himalayans, Mme. Delagoutte from the French Department of Eure, discovered a rex factor with a totally different genetic character. After World War I a similar "German" rex factor was developed by the breeder Koop with the assistance of rabbit judge Friedrich Joppich in the German city of Luebeck.

In any case, it is peculiar that brother-sister matings of each of these independently produced rex lines (Gillet, Delagoutte, Koop, and Joppich) result in normal-haired offspring.

Over the course of the years dubious breeders went into the rex business to make a quick buck. Much money has been wasted on this breed in the past, but today one must agree that the breed is healthy and vital.

The hair of a rex stands almost at right angles to the skin and has a length of about $^3/_5$ inch (15–18 mm). The very fine and straight guard hairs are drastically shortened to the same length as the underhairs, giving the animal the appearance of having been shorn. The rex is acceptable in all known colors, including all marten varieties, white (with red or blue eyes), chinchilla, and lynx. Moreover, there is the Swiss dalmatian marked, the soot marked, castor, and opal.

The Rex has a short, soft coat which was developed as a valuable pelt breed in the early part of this century.

Rhinelander

The Rhinelander was developed from various crossings of marked animals from Belgium and France and further crossings with Flemish giants in Germany (Rhineland and Saxony), where they were improved. The markings on the head are known as the butterfly smut, the cheek spots, and the eye rings. The ears have the same color as the other marks. The rest of the head is white, and much value is placed on a sharp separation between the colors. The body markings consist of a herringbone pattern; an approximately $1^1/_2$ inch (3cm) wide, unbroken stripe runs from the neck, along the back to the tail tip. The flank markings consist of a minimum of three (preferably 5 to 8) separate, round patches, situated toward the hindquarters. The Rhinelander is white, with all colors acceptable for the markings as long as they are distinct. A three-colored variety in white, black, and blue is also available.

The Most Important Breeds

Satin

The satin is a breed that lives up to its name. The fur has a glossy, silken sheen that actually resembles that of a fine satin garment. This is due to a mutation in which the layer of guard hairs has been weakened. The stiffness of the hair has been lost, giving it a silky appearance and feel. The breed originated in the United States.

The satin is a medium, longish but compact animal. The fur is of normal length but of a very thin, fragile, and almost transparent structure. The length of the guard hairs is at least $1^1/2$ inches (3 cm). The sheen in the hairs should be visible to the roots when the fur is blown into. The satin is known in Californian, brown, blue, chocolate copper, black, red, chinchilla and, of course, ivory and all of the marten colors. The colors of the satin should be more intense and brilliant than in those rabbits with normal hair.

Silver Fox

In England, first-class silver fox rabbits were bred in great numbers, and the softness and length of the fur was improved by crossings with Angoras. A characteristic of the English silver fox is the long, shimmering, full coat. In the United States and in Germany the breed has dedicated followers who are not put off by the difficulty of breeding true color patterns.

The fur is very thick and has a length of 1 to $1^1/2$ inches (3–4 cm). If ruffled forward, the fur falls back very slowly into its normal position rather than springing back into place as with most other breeds. This is due to the rich underwool. This phenomenon, coupled with the length of the fur, constitute the most important distinguishing characteristic of the breed.

The color pattern of the silver fox is very similar to that of the tan. The breed is recognized in the colors black, brown, blue, medium sepia marten, dark sepia marten, medium blue marten, dark blue marten.

Silvers

There are two major varieties of silvers, the large silvers and the small silvers. The small silver originated in England. Many authors regard the small silver as one of the oldest breeds and say it originated in India or even Siam before it was brought to England.

In contrast, others see the small silver as a mutation that suddenly appeared from one or more silver factors in wild or semiwild rabbits that were kept in early English parks for the purpose of hunting. The observant nature lover will know that, apart from white (albinism) and black (melanism), silver wild rabbits also sometimes occur. In any event, silvers were probably being bred in England as early as 1631.

The black-silver, formerly known as the gray-silver, was the first. According to C.A. House and Allen Watson, in their book *Rabbits and All About Them*, the first breeder of brown-silvers was a Mr. G. Johnson, who crossed black-silvers with Belgian hares.

The yellow-silvers came from France to England, where they were later bred to a deeper color. The blue-silvers are a product of the Continent and the best lines originated in the Netherlands and Germany.

The large silver originated in France, although it is normally regarded as a German breed. It was a much respected and popular breed in the Champagne district of France. In 1911–1912, the German breeder G. Stein of Detmold created a new breed called Germania silver by crossings with small silvers and larger rabbits, producing a light and medium black-silver.

The French large silvers were bred exclusively in the lighter tones, and this was followed in England and Germany. At the same time, however, the German breeder Friedrich Nagel of Neudietendorf was creating medium and dark blue-silvers with the help of Viennas. In Germany, the French large silvers were recognized in light colors and the German large silvers were recognized in medium

The Most Important Breeds

and dark shades. At the same time black animals were officially known as commercial breeds. The arguments about recognizing the Germania and German large silvers started before World War I and continued until 1927, when all sorts of large silvers were classed as a single group.

In the silver rabbits, the pelt changes color at approximately six weeks of age. This process, in which a large number of new hairs with pigment-free silvery-white tips appears, is known as the silvering. The differences between light, medium, and dark silvers are dependent on the intensity of the silvering. The silvers are recognized in the colors fawn, black, brown, blue, and yellow.

Tan

This breed originated in England. The tan mutation was first found among semiwild rabbits in the 1880s at Culland Hall near Brailsford (Derbyshire), where the Reverend Cox used them for breeding. The originals, known as the Brailsford type, were small and nervous, but not so those later bred by Mr. Purnell and known as the Cheltenham type, which

The blue tan, produced by Mr. A. Atkinson of Huddersfield (England), became an instant success.

were larger, more docile, and better colored. Later, the two types were mixed and these formed the basis of the modern tan breed, which is now found throughout the world.

The breed standards dictate that tans are two-colored, namely, black, lilac, blue, or chocolate and the tan color, which is a rusty reddish brown. The tan pattern appears as a ring around the eye about $1/4$ inch (5 mm) in width and also around the nostrils, where it should be narrow, sharply bordered, and fiery colored. The tan-colored throat runs into a narrow, sharply bordered band into the neck. There is a small tan triangle at the front of the base of the ears. The fiery tan color of the chest passes down between the forelimbs, which are tan colored on the insides and back, and down onto the belly. Each toe has a tan-colored fleck. The rear limbs are tan colored on the inside and half the outside. The soles of the feet are nearly white.

Thueringer

This breed originated in Germany, where the breeder David Gaertner from Waltershausen in Thueringen produced it accidentally when experimenting with Flemish giants, silvers, and Himalayans. Later he registered it as a breed. We know that the color is easy to produce, and it was already common in English lops and Dutch for a long time. It was formerly named "Chamois," and rightly so as it surely resembled this animal.

The color must be free of any blue-black or blue shadows, and it can be best described as a light reddish-yellow. There should be no white or black hairs, but the hair tips have a dark pigment known as the "veil." The blue-black to black veil stretches from the snout over the cheeks, ears, chest, shoulders, flanks, hindquarters, tail, limbs, and belly. It must not go higher than the eyes. The stronger and darker the veil, the more valuable is the animal. It should be free of breaks, which often occur on the chest, shoulders, and thighs. The eyes are dark brown.

The Most Important Breeds

Viennese

This middle-sized breed has blue eyes and a steel-blue pelt. It originated in Austria, where it was developed by Constantin Schultz in 1893, using the Flemish giant as one of the parents. The first blue Viennese weighed more than 13 pounds (6 kg). As soon as the breed became somewhat smaller and stronger in color, the animal's popularity grew rapidly.

The body of today's breed is long, and substantially broad in the shoulders and hindquarters. Adult rabbits should weigh approximately 8.8 pounds (4 kg). The breed has a thick coat. The hairy ears should be at least 5 inches (13 cm) in length.

In 1907 the first white Viennese appeared, also with blue eyes. It was created by Wilhelm Muckle, a railroad officer, who used light colored Dutch and Blue Viennese rabbits. Today various colors exist, for example: wild color (gray), various blues, black, and brown. Viennese rabbits are extremely popular in Europe, especially in Germany, Austria and the Netherlands.

Useful Literature and Addresses

Information and Periodicals

The American Rabbit Breeders Association (ARBA)
1925 South Main, Box 426
Bloomington, IL 81701

The ARBA publishes a magazine devoted to the fancy: *Domestic Rabbits*. It contains much useful information on old and new breeds, supplies of stock, and equipment, as well as news about the shows that are held regularly in most parts of the country. An annual subscription is modestly priced, and there are reduced fees for children, senior citizens, and family groups.

Another monthly magazine is: *Rabbits*.
Countryside Publications, Ltd.
312 Portland Road, Highway 19 East
Waterloo, WI 53594

All serious rabbit fanciers in the United Kingdom should subscribe to the biweekly magazine *Fur and Feather*, the official magazine of the British Rabbit Council (BRC).

Fur and Feather
British Rabbit Council
Purfoy House
7 Kirkgate
Newark
Nottingham, England

Membership in the BRC is also essential for the English rabbit enthusiast, as this is the governing body of the fancy. The annual subscription fee is small, and there are reduced rates for children, family groups, pensioners, and so on. The official series of rabbit rings supplied by the Council to members helps them maintain records of their stock.

Useful Literature and Addresses

Books

The American Rabbit Breeders Association, *Official Guide to Raising Better Rabbits*, Bloomington, Illinios.

————, *Standard of Perfection: Standard Bred Rabbits and Cavies*, Bloomington, Illinios.

Arrington, L. R., and Kathleen Kelley, *Domestic Rabbit Biology and Production*, University Presses of Florida, Gainesville, Florida.

Bennett, Bob, *Raising Rabbits the Modern Way*, Garden Way, Pownal, Vermont, 1988.

Downing, Elisabeth, *Keeping Rabbits*, Pelham Books, London, 1979.

Fritzsche, Helga, *Rabbits*, Barron's, Hauppauge, New York, 1983.

Harkness, John and Joseph Wagner, *The Biology and Medicine of Rabbits and Rodents*, Lea & Febiger, Philadelphia , Pennsylvania, 1988.

National Research Council, *Nutrient Requirements of Rabbits*, 2nd edition, National Academy Press, Washington , D.C., 1977.

Sandford, J. C. *The Domestic Rabbit*, Collins, London, 1986.

Wegler, Monika, *Dwarf Rabbits*, Barron's, Hauppauge, New York, 1986.

Purebred dwarf rabbits: Above left: tan; above right: black. Center left: gray; center right: Gouwenaar. Below left: blue-gray. Below right: Harlequin (or Japanese) dwarf rabbits are as difficult to breed as their normal-sized family-members.

Overleaf: Above: Siamese or yellow dwarf rabbits have horn-colored claws and dark brown eyes. The disproportionately large head and the "cobby" body are characteristic of a purebred dwarf. Bottom: a handsome mixed breed dwarf rabbit.

Index

Numbers in *Italic type* indicate color plates. *C1* indicates front cover; *C2*, inside front cover; *C3*, inside back cover; and *C4*, back cover.

Index

Index

Index

Index